CW00801607

MAIGRET

GEORGES
SIMENON

MAIGRET

HAMISH HAMILTON · LONDON

HAMISH HAMILTON LTD
Published by the Penguin Group
Penguin Books Ltd, 27 Wrights Lane, London W8 5TZ, England
Penguin Books USA Inc., 375 Hudson Street, New York, New York 100014, USA
Penguin Books Australia Ltd, Ringwood, Victoria, Australia
Penguin Books Canada Ltd, 10 Alcorn Avenue, Toronto, Ontario, Canada M4V 3B2
Penguin Books (NZ) Ltd, 182 Wairau Road, Auckland 10, New Zealand

Penguin Books Ltd, Registered Offices: Harmondsworth, Middlesex, England

Maigret Goes Home (trans. Robert Baldick)
First published in France under the title *L'Affaire Saint-Fiacre* 1931
This translation first published in Great Britain by Penguin Books 1967

Maigret and the Burglar's Wife (trans. J. Maclaren-Ross)
First published in France under the title *Maigret et la Grande Perche* 1953
This translation first published in Great Britain by Hamish Hamilton Ltd 1955

Maigret Goes to School (trans. Daphne Woodward)
First published in France under the title *Maigret à l'École* 1954
This translation first published in Great Britain by Hamish Hamilton Ltd 1957

Maigret Sets a Trap (trans. Daphne Woodward)
First published in France under the title *Maigret Tend un Piège* 1955
This translation first published in Great Britain by Hamish Hamilton Ltd 1965

The Patience of Maigret (trans. Alastair Hamilton)
First published in France under the title *La Patience de Maigret* 1965
This translation first published in Great Britain by Hamish Hamilton Ltd 1966

Maigret and the Madwoman (trans. Eileen Ellenbogen)
First published in France under the title *La Folle de Maigret* 1970
This translation first published in Great Britain by Hamish Hamilton Ltd 1972

Published in one volume by Hamish Hamilton as ***Maigret*** 1983
10 9 8 7 6 4 3 2 1

Typeset by The Design Team, Ascot, Berks
Printed in Great Britain by Clays Ltd, St. Ives plc

A CIP catalogue record for this book is available from the British Library

ISBN 0–241–13227–4

CONTENTS

MAIGRET
Goes Home

CHAPTER ONE

The Little Girl with the Squint

A timid scratching at the door; the sound of an object being put on the floor; a furtive voice:

'It's half past five! The first bell for Mass has just been rung…'

Maigret raised himself on his elbows, making the mattress creak, and while he was looking in astonishment at the skylight cut in the sloping roof, the voice went on:

'Are you taking communion?'

By now Chief-Inspector Maigret was out of bed, standing barefoot on the icy door. He walked towards the door, which was closed with a piece of string wound round a couple of nails. There was the sound of footsteps hurrying away, and when he got out into the corridor he was just in time to catch sight of the figure of a woman in a spencer and a white petticoat.

Then he picked up the jug of hot water which Marie Tatin had brought him, closed his door, and looked for a piece of mirror in front of which he could shave.

The candle had only a few minutes of life left. Outside the skylight it was still night a cold night in early winter. A few dead leaves were clinging to the branches of the poplars in the market place.

Maigret could stand up only in the middle of the attic, because of the double slope of the roof. He was cold. A thin draught of air, the source of which be had been unable to trace, had chilled the back of his neck.

But it was precisely this quality of coldness which disturbed him, by plunging him into an atmosphere which he thought he had forgotten.

The first bell for Mass... The bells ringing out over the sleeping village... When he was a boy, Maigret did not usually get up so early... He would wait for the second bell, at a quarter to six, because in those days he did not need to shave ... Did he so much as wash his face?

Nobody brought him any hot water... Sometimes the water was frozen in the jug... Soon afterwards his shoes would be clattering along the hardened road...

Now, while he was getting dressed, he could hear Marie Tatin coming and going in the main room of the inn, rattling the grate of the stove, moving crockery about, and turning the handle of the coffee-mill.

He put on his jacket, his overcoat. Before going out, he took out of his wallet a piece of paper with an official slip pinned to it bearing the words:

Municipal Police of Moulins
Communicated for information and possible action to Police Headquarters in Paris.

Then a sheet of squared paper... Laborious handwriting:

This is to tell you that a crime will be committed in the church at Saint-Fiacre during the first Mass on All Soul's Day.

*

The sheet of paper had lain around for several days in the offices of the Quai des Orfèvres. Maigret had noticed it by accident, and had asked in surprise:

'Is that Saint-Fiacre near Matignon?'

'Probably, seeing that it was sent to us by Moulins.'

And Maigret had put the piece of paper in his pocket. Saint-Fiacre. Matignon. Moulins. Words which were more familiar to him than any others.

He had been born at Saint-Fiacre, where his father had been the steward of the château for thirty years. The last time he had gone there had in fact been after the death of his father, who had been buried in the little graveyard behind the church.

A crime will be committed... during the first Mass...

Maigret had arrived the day before. He had taken a room at the only inn in the village: Marie Tatin's. She had not recognized him, but he had recognized her because of her eyes. The little girl with the squint, as they used to call her. A puny little girl who had become an even skinnier old maid, squinting more and more, and endlessly bustling about the bar-room, the kitchen and the yard where she kept rabbits and hens.

The chief-inspector went downstairs. The ground-floor rooms were lit by oil-lamps. A table was laid in one corner. Coarse grey bread. A smell of coffee with chicory, and boiling milk.

'You're wrong not to take communion on a day like today. Especially seeing that you're taking the trouble to go to the first Mass... Heavens! That's the second bell ringing already!'

The voice of the bells was faint. Footsteps could be heard on the road. Marie Tatin fled into her kitchen to put on her black dress, her cotton gloves, and her little hat which her bun prevented from staying on straight.

'I'll leave you to finish your breakfast ... You'll lock the door, won't you?'

'No, wait! I'm ready...'

She was embarrassed to be walking along with a man. A man who came from Paris! She trotted along, a small bent figure, in the cold morning air. Some dead leaves were fluttering about on the ground. The crisp sound they made showed that there had been a frost during the night.

There were other shadowy figures converging on the dimly shining doorway of the church. The bells were still ringing. There were some lights in the windows of the low-built houses: people dressing in a hurry for the first Mass.

And Maigret rediscovered the impressions of his childhood: the cold, the eyes smarting, the tips of the fingers frozen, a lingering taste of coffee in the mouth. Then, on going into the church, a wave of warm air, of soft light; the smell of the tapers and the incense...

'Excuse me, will you?... I've got my own prayer-stool,' she said.

And Maigret recognized the black chair with the red velvet armrest of old Madame Tatin, the mother of the little girl with the squint.

The rope which the bell-ringer had just let go of was still quivering at the far end of the church. The sacristan was lighting the last tapers. How many were there in that ghostly gathering of half-asleep people? Fifteen at the most. There were only three men: the sacristan, the bell-ringer, and Maigret.

...a crime will be committed...

At Moulins the police had treated the matter as a bad joke and had not worried about it. In Paris, they had been surprised to see the chief-inspector set off.

Maigret heard some noises behind the door on the right of the altar, and he could guess second by second what was happening: the sacristy, the choirboy arriving late, the priest putting on his chasuble without a word, joining his hands together, and walking towards the nave, followed by the boy stumbling along in his cassock...

The boy was red-haired. He shook his bell. The murmur of the liturgical prayer began.

...during the first Mass...

Maigret had looked at all the shadowy figures one by one. Five old women, three of whom had a prayer-stool reserved for their own use. A fat farmer's wife. Some younger peasant-women and one child...

The sound of a car outside. The creak of a door. Some light footsteps, and a lady in mourning walking the whole length of the church.

In the chancel there was a row of stalls reserved for people from the château, hard stalls in old, polished wood.

And it was there that the woman took her seat, noiselessly, followed by the peasant-women's eyes.

Requiem aeternam dona eis, Domine...

Maigret could perhaps still have recited the responses to the priest. He smiled at the thought that in the past he had preferred the Requiem Masses to the others, because the prayers were shorter. He could remember Masses which had been celebrated in sixteen minutes...

But already he had eyes only for the occupant of the Gothic stall. He could barely make out her profile. He hesitated to identify her as the Comtesse de Saint-Fiacre.

Dies irae, dies illa...

It was she, all right! But when he had last seen her she was twenty-five or twenty-six. She was a tall, slim, melancholy woman whom he used to catch sight of from a distance in the park.

And now she must be well into the sixties... She was praying fervently... She had an emaciated face, and long delicate hands which were clasping a missal...

Maigret had remained in the last row of straw-bottomed chairs, those which cost five centimes at High Mass, but were free at Low Masses.

...a crime will be committed...

He stood up with the others at the first Gospel. Details attracted his attention on all sides and memories forced themselves upon him. For example, he suddenly thought:

'On All Souls' Day the same priest celebrates three Masses...'

In his time, he used to breakfast at the priest's house, between the second and third Masses. A hard-boiled egg and some goat's cheese...

It was the Moulins police who were right. There couldn't be a crime!

The sacristan had taken his seat at the end of the stalls,

four places beyond the countess. The bell-ringer had walked away with a heavy tread, like a theatrical producer who has no desire to watch his own production.

There were no men left but Maigret and the priest, a young priest with the passionate gaze of a mystic. He didn't hurry like the old priest the chief-inspector had known. He didn't mumble half the verses.

The stained-glass windows were turning pale. Outside, day was breaking. A cow was lowing on a farm.

And soon everybody was bending double for the Elevation. The choirboy's bell tinkled shrilly.

Maigret was the only one who did not take communion. All the women walked towards the altar rail, their hands folded, their faces expressionless. Hosts so pale that they seemed unreal passed for a moment through the priest's hands.

The Mass continued. The countess's face was buried in her hands.

Pater Noster...
Et ne nos inducas in tentationem...

The old woman's fingers parted, revealed a tormented face, opened the missal.

Another four minutes... The prayers. The last Gospel. And then everybody would go out. And there wouldn't have been a crime.

For the warning stated clearly: *the first Mass...*

The proof that it was over was that the sacristan was standing up, was going into the sacristy...

The Comtesse de Saint-Fiacre's head was buried in her hands once more. She was not moving. Most of the other old women were just as rigid.

Ite, missa est... The Mass is over...

Only then did Maigret feel how anxious he had been. He had scarcely realized. He heaved an involuntary sigh. He waited impatiently for the last Gospel, thinking that he was going to breathe the fresh air outside, see people moving about, hear them talking about this and that...

The old women woke up all together. Feet shuffled about on the cold flag-stones of the church. One peasant-woman made for the door, then another. The sacristan appeared with a candle extinguisher and a thin wisp of blue smoke took the place of each flame.

Day had broken. Grey light was entering the nave at the same time as draughts of air.

Three people were left... Two... A chair moved... Only the countess remained and Maigret's nerves went taut with impatience...

The sacristan, who had finished his task, looked at Madame de Saint-Fiacre. A puzzled expression passed across his face. At the same moment the chief-inspector stepped forward.

There were two of them standing close to her, surprised at her immobility, trying to see the face which was hidden by the joined hands.

Suddenly alarmed, Maigret touched the shoulder. And the body tipped over, as if it had been balanced on a knife's edge, rolled on to the floor, and lay motionless.

The Comtesse de Saint-Fiacre was dead.

*

The body had been taken into the sacristy where it had been laid on three chairs placed side by side. The sacristan had run out to fetch the village doctor.

As a result, Maigret forgot how unusual his presence was. He took several minutes to understand the suspicious inquiry in the priest's burning eyes.

'Who are you?' the latter finally asked. 'How is it that...'

'Chief-Inspector Maigret, from Police Headquarters.'

He looked the priest in the eyes. He was a man of thirty-five, with features which were regular but so solemn that they recalled the fierce faith of the monks of old.

He was profoundly disturbed. A somewhat unsteadier voice murmured:

'You don't mean that...?'

They had not dared to undress the countess. They had

vainly held a mirror to her lips. They had listened for her heart which was no longer beating.

'I can't see any wound,' was Maigret's only reply.

And he looked around him at this unchangeable scene in which not a single detail had altered in thirty years. The altar-cruets were in the same place, and the chasuble prepared for the following Mass, and the choirboy's cassock and surplice.

The dirty light entering through a Gothic window was thinning out the rays of an oil-lamp.

It was hot and cold at the same time. The priest was assailed by terrible thoughts.

Maigret did not understand the full drama of the situation at first. But memories of his childhood went on rising to the surface like air bubbles.

...A church in which a crime has been committed must be newly consecrated by the bishop...

How could there have been a crime? Nobody had heard a shot. Nobody had approached the countess. During the whole Mass, Maigret had scarcely taken his eyes off her.

And there was no sign of bloodshed, no visible wound.

'The second Mass is at seven o'clock, isn't it?'

It was a relief to hear the heavy tread of the doctor, a red-faced fellow who was impressed by the atmosphere and looked in turn at the chief-inspector and the priest.

'Dead?' he asked.

All the same, he for his part did not hesitate to unbutton the countess's bodice, while the priest turned his head away. Heavy footsteps in the church. Then the bell which the ringer had set in motion. The first bell for the seven o'clock Mass.

'I can only suppose that heart failure... I wasn't the countess's regular doctor. She preferred to be attended by a colleague in Moulins... But I've been called two or three times to the château... She had a very weak heart...'

The sacristy was tiny. The three men and the corpse could only just fit inside. Two choirboys arrived, for the seven o'clock Mass was a High Mass.

'Her car must be outside,' said Maigret. 'We must arrange for her to be taken home...'

He could still feel the priest's anguished gaze weighing on him... Had he guessed something? The fact remained that while the sacristan, with the chauffeur's help, was carrying the body to the car, he came over to the chief-inspector.

'You're sure that... I've another two Masses to say... It's All Souls' Day... My parishioners are...'

Seeing that the countess had died of heart failure, wasn't Maigret entitled to reassure the priest?

'You heard what the doctor said...'

'All the same, you came here today, to this particular Mass...'

Maigret made an effort not to get flustered.

'Just a coincidence, Monsieur le Curé... My father is buried in your graveyard...'

And he hurried out to the car, an old model, whose chauffeur was turning the starting-handle. The doctor did not know what to do. There were a few people on the square who could not make out what was happening.

'Come with us ...'

But the corpse took up all the room inside. Maigret and the doctor squeezed inside next to the back seat.

'You look surprised at what I told you,' murmured the doctor, who had not yet completely recovered his composure. 'If you knew the situation, you might understand... The countess...'

He fell silent, glancing at the liveried chauffeur who was driving his car with an absent-minded expression. They crossed the sloping square, which was bordered on the one hand by the church built on the hillside, and on the other by the Notre-Dame pond which, that particular morning, was a poisonous grey colour.

Marie Tatin's inn was on the right, the first house in the village. On the left was an avenue of oaks, and, right in the distance, the dark mass of the château.

A uniform sky, as cold as an ice-rink.

'You know, this is going to create some complications...

That's why the priest looked so upset.'

Doctor Bouchardon was a peasant, and the son of peasants. He was wearing a brown shooting-outfit and high rubber boots.

'I was off duck-shooting in the ponds...'

'You don't go to Mass?'

The doctor winked.

'Mind you, that didn't stop me being on good terms with the old priest... But this one...'

They were driving into the park. Now they could make out the details of the château, the ground-floor windows covered by their shutters, and the two corner towers, the only old parts of the building.

When the car drew up near the steps, Maigret looked down through the latticed windows at ground level and caught a glimpse of the steam-filled kitchens, and a fat woman busy plucking partridges.

The chauffeur did not know what to do, and did not dare to open the car doors.

'Monsieur Jean won't be up yet...'

'Call somebody... anybody... There are some other servants in the house, aren't there?'

Maigret's nostrils were moist. It was really cold. He remained standing in the courtyard with the doctor, who started filling a pipe.

'Who is Monsieur Jean?'

Bouchardon shrugged his shoulders and gave a queer smile.

'You'll see.'

'But who is he?'

'A young man... A charming young man...'

'A relative?'

'If you like... In his own way... Oh, I might as well tell you straight away... He's the countess's lover... Officially, he's her secretary...'

Maigret looked the doctor in the eyes, remembering that he had been at school with him. But nobody recognized him. He was forty-two. He had put on weight.

As for the château, he knew it as well as anybody else. Especially the out-buildings. He only had to take a few steps to see the steward's house, where he had been born.

Perhaps it was these memories which were disturbing him so much. Especially the memory of the Comtesse de Saint-Fiacre as he had known her: a young woman who, for the country boy he had been, had personified all that was feminine, graceful and noble.

And now she was dead. They had bundled her like an inanimate object into the car, and they had had to bend her legs. They had not even buttoned up her bodice and some white underwear was poking out of the mourning dress.

...a crime will be committed...

But the doctor maintained that she had died of heart failure. What supernatural power had been able to foresee that? And why call in the police?

People were running about inside the château. Doors were opening and shutting. A butler who was only half-dressed opened the main door a little way, hesitating to come out. A man appeared behind him, in pyjamas, his hair tousled, his eyes tired.

'What is it?' he called out.

'The pimp,' the cynical doctor growled in Maigret's ear.

The cook had been told too. She was looking silently out of her basement window. Dormer windows were opening at the top of the house, in the servant's rooms.

'Well, why doesn't somebody carry the countess to her room?' Maigret thundered indignantly.

All this struck him as sacrilegious, because it did not tally with his childhood memories. It made him feel not merely morally but physically sick.

...a crime will be committed...

The second bell for Mass was ringing. People must be hurrying. There were farmers who came a long way, in light carts. And they had brought flowers to place on the tombs in the graveyard.

Jean did not dare to approach. The butler, who had

opened the car door, stood there utterly crushed, without moving a muscle.

'Madame la Comtesse... Madame la...' he stammered.

'Well?... Are you going to leave her there?... Eh?..'

Why the devil was the doctor smiling sarcastically? Maigret used his authority.

'Come on now! Two men... You' (he pointed to the chauffeur) 'and you' (he pointed to the butler) 'carry her up to her room...'

While they were reaching into the car, a bell rang in the hall.

'The telephone ... That's peculiar at this hour,' growled Bouchardon.

Jean did not dare to go and answer it. He seemed to be in a daze. It was Maigret who rushed to unhook the receiver.

'Hullo... Yes, the château...'

A voice which seemed very close said:

'Will you ask my mother to come to the telephone? She must be back from Mass by now...'

'Who's that speaking?'

'The Comte de Saint-Fiacre... In any case, that's none of your business... Let me speak to my mother...'

'Just a minute ... Will you tell me where you're speaking from?'

'From Moulins... But dammit all, I tell you...'

'It would be best if you came over here,' was all that Maigret said before he hung up.

And he had to press against the wall to let the body which the two servants were carrying pass by.

CHAPTER TWO

The Missal

'Are you coming in?' asked the doctor as soon as the dead woman had been laid on her bed. 'I need somebody to help me to undress her.'

'We'll find a chambermaid,' said Maigret.

And, sure enough, Jean went up to the next floor and came down a little later with a woman of about thirty who cast frightened glances around her.

'Clear off!' the chief-inspector growled at the servants, who asked for nothing better.

He held Jean back by the sleeve, looked him up and down, and led him into a window recess.

'What terms are you on with the countess's son?'

'But... I...'

The young man was thin, and his striped pyjamas, which were of questionable cleanliness, added nothing to his prestige. His eyes avoided Maigret's. He had a nervous habit of pulling at his fingers as if he wanted to lengthen them.

'Wait!' the chief-inspector broke in. 'We're going to speak plainly, to save time.'

Behind the heavy oak door of the bedroom they could hear footsteps coming and going, the creaking of the bedsprings, and orders being given in an undertone to the chambermaid by Doctor Bouchardon. The dead woman was being undressed.

'What exactly is your position at the château? How long have you been here?'

'Four years...'

'You knew the Comtesse de Saint-Fiacre?'

'I... That is to say, I was introduced to her by common friends... My parents had just been ruined by the crash of a little bank in Lyons... I came here as a confidential secretary, to look after the countess's personal affairs...'

'I beg your pardon. What were you doing before?'

'I travelled... I wrote some art criticism...'

Maigret did not smile. In any case, the atmosphere did not lend itself to irony.

The château was huge. From the outside it was fairly impressive. But the interior looked as seedy as the young man's pyjamas. Dust everywhere, old things without any beauty, a host of useless objects. The curtains were faded.

And on the walls, there were paler patches which showed that pieces of furniture had been removed. The best pieces, obviously. Those which had some value.

'You became the countess's lover...'

'Everybody is free to love whoever...'

'Idiot!' growled Maigret turning his back on the other.

As if things were not obvious in themselves. You only had to look at Jean. You only had to breathe the atmosphere of the château for a few moments, and catch the servants' glances.

'Did you know that her son was coming?'

'No... What can that matter to me?'

And his eyes still avoided Maigret's. With his right hand he tugged at the fingers of his left.

'I'd like to get dressed... It's cold... But why are the police bothering about...?'

'Yes, go and get dressed.'

And Maigret pushed open the bedroom door, avoiding looking towards the bed, on which the dead woman was completely naked.

The bedroom resembled the rest of the house. It was too big, too cold, still cluttered up with old ornaments. Trying to lean on the marble mantelpiece. Maigret noticed that it was broken.

'Have you found anything?' the chief-inspector asked

Bouchardon... 'Just a moment... Will you please leave us alone, Mademoiselle?'

And he closed the door behind the chambermaid, went and pressed his forehead against the window, and let his gaze wander over the park which was carpeted with leaves and grey mist.

'I can only confirm what I told you earlier. Death was due to sudden heart failure.'

'Brought on by...?'

A vague gesture from the doctor, who threw a blanket over the corpse, joined Maigret at the window, and lit his pipe.

'Perhaps a shock... Perhaps the cold... Was it cold in the church?'

'Far from it. You didn't find any sign of a wound, of course?'

'No.'

'Not even the barely perceptible trace of a prick?'

'I thought of that... No, nothing at all... And the countess hasn't imbibed any poison... So you see it would be difficult to maintain...'

Maigret was frowning. On the left, under the trees, he could see the red roof of the steward's house, where he had been born.

'In a few words... What is life at the château like?' he asked in an undertone.

'You know as much about that as I do... One of those women who are models of good behaviour up to the age of forty or forty-five... It was then that the count died, and the son went to Paris to continue his studies...'

'And here?'

'Secretaries came along, who stayed for longer or shorter periods... You've seen the latest...'

'The fortune?'

'The château is mortgaged... Three out of four farms have been sold... Every now and then an antique dealer comes to collect some piece which is still worth something...'

'And the son?'

'I can't say I know him very well... They say he's quite a lad...'

'Thank you.'

Maigret was going to leave the room. Bouchardon followed him.

'Between ourselves. I'd like to know how you happened to be in the church just this very morning...'

'Yes, it's strange...'

'I've a feeling that I've seen you before somewhere...'

'That's possible...'

And Maigret hurried along the corridor. His head felt a little empty, because he had not slept long enough. Perhaps he had caught cold too at Marie Tatin's inn. He caught sight of Jean going downstairs, dressed in a grey suit but still wearing slippers. At the same moment a car without a silencer drove into the château courtyard.

It was a little sports car, painted bright yellow, long, narrow, and uncomfortable. A man in a leather coat burst into the hall the next moment pulling off his helmet and shouting:

'Hullo!... Anybody there? ... Is everybody still asleep here?'

But then he caught sight of Maigret, whom he looked at inquisitively.

'What is it?'

'Shh...I must have a word with you...'

Next to the chief-inspector, Jean was pale, uneasy. As he passed, the Comte de Saint-Fiacre gave him a gentle punch on the shoulder and said jokingly:

'Still here, you little rotter?'

He did not seem to bear him any malice. Just to despise him profoundly.

'There's nothing wrong, is there?'

'Your mother died this morning, in the church.'

*

Maurice de Saint-Fiacre was thirty years old, the same age as Jean. They were of the same height, but the count was broad-shouldered and a little fat. Everything about him, especially dressed as he was in his leather coat, breathed life and gaiety. His bright eyes were gay and mocking.

It needed Maigret's words to make him frown.

'What's that you said?'

'Come this way.'

'Well, I'm damned... And I was...'

'You were...?'

'Nothing... Where is she?'

He was dazed, dumbfounded. In the bedroom he raised the blanket just far enough to see the dead woman's face. There was no explosion of grief. No tears. No dramatic gestures. Just three murmured words.

'Poor old girl!'

Jean had thought fit to come as far as the door, and the other, catching sight of him, snapped at him:

'You get out!'

He was getting agitated. He paced up and down the room and bumped into the doctor.

'What did she die of, Bouchardon?'

'Heart failure, Monsieur Maurice... But the chief-inspector may know more about that than I do...'

The young man swung round to face Maigret.

'You're from the police?... What...?'

'Could we have a few minutes' conversation?... I'd like to take a little walk up the road... You're staying here, aren't you, Doctor?'

'The fact is I was going shooting...'

'Well, you can go shooting another day.'

Maurice de Saint-Fiacre accompanied Maigret, gazing thoughtfully at the ground in front of him. When they reached the main drive of the château, the seven o'clock Mass had just finished and the parishioners, in greater numbers than at the first Mass, were coming out and forming groups on the square. A few people were already going into the graveyard, and only their heads showed above the wall.

As the sky grew lighter, the cold became sharper, probably on account of the north wind, which was sweeping the dead leaves from one side of the square to the other, making them spin around like birds over the Notre-Dame pond.

Maigret filled his pipe. Wasn't that his chief reason for

taking his companion outside? Yet the doctor had smoked even in the dead woman's room, and Maigret was in the habit of smoking anywhere.

But not in the château! That was a place apart, which throughout his youth had represented all that was most inaccessible.

'Today the count called me into his library to work with him,' his father used to say, with a hint of pride in his voice.

And the boy that Maigret had been at that age used to gaze respectfully, from a distance, at the baby-carriage being pushed around the park by a nursemaid. The baby in it was Maurice de Saint-Fiacre...

'Does anybody stand to benefit from your mother's death?'

'I don't understand... The doctor has just said...'

He was uneasy. His gestures were jerky. He snatched the piece of paper which Maigret held out to him and which foretold the crime.

'What does this mean?... Bouchardon spoke of heart failure and...'

'Heart failure which somebody foresaw a fortnight in advance!'

Some peasants were looking at them from a distance. The two men aproached the church, walking slowly, following the train of their thoughts.

'What were you coming to the château for this morning?'

'That's just what I was thinking,' said the young man. 'You asked me just now... Well, yes... There is somebody who stood to benefit from my mother's death... Me!'

He was not joking. His forehead was furrowed. He greeted by name a man who went by on a bicycle.

'Seeing that you're from the police, you must have understood the situation already... Besides, that fellow Bouchardon is sure to have talked... My mother was a poor girl... My father died... I went away... Left on her own, I can well believe that her mind became slightly unhinged... First of all she spent all of her time at church... Then...'

'The young secretaries...'

'I don't think it was what you think and what Bouchardon would like to suggest... Nothing immoral... Just a longing for affection... The urge to look after somebody... The fact that those young fellows took advantage of that to go further... Mind you, that didn't prevent her from remaining very pious... She must have had some terrible attacks of conscience, torn as she was between her faith and that... that...'

'You were saying that you stood to benefit?'

'You know that there isn't very much of our fortune left... And people like that gentleman you've seen have hearty appetites... Let's say that in another three or four years there'd have been nothing left at all...'

He was bare-headed. He ran his fingers through his hair. Then, looking Maigret in the eyes, he added after a pause:

'All that remains for me to tell you is that I was coming here today to ask my mother for forty thousand francs... And I need those forty thousand francs to cover a cheque which would otherwise bounce... You see how everything ties up...'

He broke a twig off a hedge they were passing. He seemed to be making a violent effort to prevent himself from being overwhelmed by what had happened.

'And to think that I've brought Marie Vassilief with me!'

'Marie Vassilief?'

'My mistress... I've left her in her bed at Moulins... She's quite capable of hiring a car and driving over here... That puts the lid on it, doesn't it?'

They were only just putting out the lamp in Marie Tatin's inn, where a few men were drinking rum. The bus for Moulins was about to leave, half empty.

'She didn't deserve that!' said Maurice's thoughtful voice.

'Who?'

'Mother.'

And at that moment there was something childlike about him, in spite of his height and slight paunchiness. Perhaps he was at last on the verge of tears.

The two men walked up and down near the church, covering the same ground over and over again, sometimes facing the pond, sometimes with their backs to it.

'Look, Chief-Inspector... Nobody could have killed her, after all... Or else I don't understand...'

Maigret was thinking about that, and so hard that he forgot about his companion. He was recalling every little detail of the first Mass...

The countess in her pew... Nobody had gone near her... She had taken communion... Next she had knelt down with her face in her hands... Then she had opened her missal... A little later, her face was in her hands again...

'Excuse me for a moment...'

Maigret went up the steps and entered the church, where the sacristan was already preparing the altar for High Mass. The bell-ringer, a rough peasant wearing heavy hobnailed boots, was straightening the chairs.

The chief-inspector walked straight up to the stalls, bent down, and called the sacristan, who turned round.

'Who picked up the missal?'

'What missal?'

'The countess's... It was left here...'

'You think so?'

'Come here,' Maigret said to the bell-ringer. 'You haven't seen the missal which was in this seat, have you?'

'Me?'

Either he was an idiot or he was putting it on. Maigret was on edge. He caught sight of Maurice de Saint-Fiacre who was standing at the far end of the nave.

'Who has been near this pew?'

'The doctor's wife occupied this stall at the seven o'clock Mass...'

'I thought that the doctor wasn't a believer?'

'He may not be. But his wife...'

'Well, you'll tell the whole village that there'll be a big reward for whoever brings me the missal.'

'At the château?'

'No, at Marie Tatin's.'

Outside, Maurice de Saint-Fiacre was walking beside him again.

'I can't make head or tail of this missal business.'

'Heart failure, wasn't it?... That may have been brought

on by a severe shock... And it happened shortly after communion, in other words after the countess had opened her missal... Supposing that in that missal...'

But the young man shook his head with an expression of discouragement.

'I can't imagine any piece of news capable of shocking my mother to that extent... Besides, it would be... so horrible...'

He was breathing hard. He stared gloomily at the château.

'Let's go and have a drink.'

He did not make for the château but for the inn, where his entry created a certain embarrassment. The four peasants who were drinking there suddenly felt as if they were no longer at home. They greeted the count with a respect mingled with fear.

Marie Tatin ran out of the kitchen, wiping her hands on her apron. She stammered:

'Monsieur Maurice... I'm still all upset by the news... Our poor countess...'

She at least was crying. She probably wept buckets every time anybody died in the village.

'You were at the Mass too, weren't you?' she said, calling Maigret to witness. 'When I think that none of us noticed anything! It was here that I heard...'

It is always embarrassing in such circumstances to show less grief than people who ought to be indifferent. Maurice listened to these expressions of sympathy while trying to hide his impatience, and, to keep himself in countenance, he went and took a bottle of rum from the shelf and filled a couple of glasses. His shoulders were shaken by a shudder while he drained his glass at one draught, and he said to Maigret:

'I think I caught cold coming here this morning...'

'Everybody here has a cold, Monsieur Maurice...'

And to Maigret she said:

'You ought to take care too. I heard you coughing last night...'

The peasants went off. The stove was red hot.

'A day like today!' said Marie Tatin.

And because of her squint it was impossible to say whether she was looking at Maigret or the count.

'Won't you have something to eat? I was so upset when I heard... that I didn't even think of changing my dress ...'

She had simply tied an apron over the black dress she had put on only to go to Mass. Her hat had been left on a table.

Maurice de Saint-Fiacre drank a second glas of rum, and looked at Maigret as if to ask him what he was to do.

'Come along!' said the chief-inspector.

'Do you want to have lunch here? I've killed a chicken and...'

But the two men were already outside. In front of the church there were four or five carts whose horses were tied to the trees. Heads could be seen moving over the low wall of the graveyard. And in the courtyard of the château, the yellow car was the only patch of bright colour.

'Is the cheque crossed?' asked Maigret.

'Yes. But it will be presented tomorrow.'

'Do you do much work?'

A pause. The sound of their footsteps on the hardened road. The rustle of dead leaves carried along by the wind. The horses snorting.

'I'm exactly what people mean by a good-for-nothing. I've done a bit of everything... Look... The forty thousand... I wanted to start a film company... Before that I was a partner in a wireless business...'

A dull explosion, on the right, beyond the Notre-Dame pond. They caught sight of a sportsman striding towards the animal which he had killed and which his dog was worrying at.

'That's Gautier, the steward,' said Maurice. 'He must have gone out shooting before...'

Then, all of a sudden, he lost his self-control, stamped his foot, pulled a face, and nearly let out a sob.

'Poor old girl!' he muttered with his lips drawn back. 'It's ... it's so disgusting... And that little rotter Jean who...'

As if by magic, they suddenly saw the latter pacing up and down the courtyard of the château, side by side with the doctor, and obviously talking excitedly, for he was gesticulating with his thin arms.

In the wind, every now and then, they could catch the scent of chrysanthemums.

CHAPTER THREE

The Choirboy

There was no sunshine to deform the pictures, no mist either to blur the contours. Everything stood out with cruel clarity: the tree-trunks, the dead branches, the pebbles, and above all the black clothes of the people who had come to the graveyard. The whites, on the other hand, tombstones or starched shirt-fronts or old women's bonnets, took on an unreal, deceptive value: whites which were too white and seemed out of place.

Without the dry north wind which cut your cheeks, you might have thought that you were under a rather dusty glass cloche.

'I'll see you again later…'

Maigret left the Comte de Saint-Fiacre outside the gate of the graveyard. An old woman, sitting on a little bench she had brought with her, was trying to sell some oranges and chocolate.

The oranges were big and ripe and frozen… They set the teeth on edge and rasped the throat, but, when he was ten years old, Maigret used to eat them greedily all the same, because they were oranges.

He turned up the velvet collar of his overcoat. He did not look at anybody. He knew that he had to turn left and that the grave he was looking for was the third after the cypresses.

All around, flowers had been placed on the graves. The day before, women had washed some of the tombstones with soap and water. The railings had been repainted.

Here lies Evariste Maigret...

'Excuse me! No smoking...'

The chief-inspector scarcely realized that he was being spoken to. Finally he stared at the bell-ringer, who was also the graveyard keeper, and thrust his lighted pipe into his pocket.

He could not manage to think about one thing at a time. Memories flooded in on him, memories of his father, of a friend who had been drowned in the Notre-Dame pond, and the child of the château in his handsome baby-carriage...

People looked at him. He looked at them. He had already seen those faces. But then, that man who had a child in his arms, for example, and was accompanied by a pregnant woman, had been a kid of four or five...

Maigret had no flowers. The tombstone was dirty. He walked out of the graveyard in a bad temper, making a whole group turn round as he muttered:

'The first thing we must do is to find the missal!'

He did not feel like returning to the château. Something there distressed him, made him indignant even.

Admittedly he had no illusions about humanity. But he was furious that his childhood memories should have been sullied. The countess above all, whom he had always seen as a noble, beautiful person like a picture-book heroine...

And now she turned out to be a crazy old woman who kept a succession of gigolos.

Not even that. It wasn't frank and open. The notorious Jean pretended to be her secretary. He was not handsome, and not very young either.

And the poor old woman, as her son said, was torn between the château and the church.

And the last Comte de Saint-Fiacre was going to be arrested for signing a bad cheque.

*

Somebody was walking in front of Maigret with his gun on his shoulder, and the chief-inspector suddenly realized that he was making towards the steward's house. He thought he could recognize the figure he had seen from a distance in the fields.

A few feet separated the two men when they reached the yard where some hens were nestling against a wall, sheltering from the wind with their feathers quivering.

'Hey!'

The man with the gun turned round.

'You're the Saint-Fiacres steward, aren't you?'

'And who are you?'

'Chief-Inspector Maigret from Police Headquarters.'

'Maigret?'

The steward was struck by the name, but could not manage to place it.

'You've heard the news?'

'I've just been told... I was out shooting... What are the police...?'

He was a short, sturdy, grey-haired man with a skin furrowed with fine, deep wrinkles, and eyes which looked as if they were lying in ambush behind thick brows.

'They told me that her heart...'

'Where are you going?'

'Well, I can't go into the château with my boots caked with mud and my gun...'

A rabbit's head was hanging from the game bag. Maigret looked at the house towards which they were walking.

'Well, well! They've changed the kitchen...'

A suspicious gaze was fixed on him.

'A good fifteen years ago,' growled the steward.

'What's your name?'

'Gautier... Is it true that Monsieur le Comte arrived without...'

All this was hesitant, reticent. And Gautier did not ask Maigret to come in. He pushed open the door.

The chief-inspector walked in all the same and turned right towards the dining-room, which smelt of biscuits and old brandy.

'Come in here for a moment, Monsieur Gautier... They

don't need you over there... And I've a few questions to ask you...'

'Hurry up!' said a woman's voice in the kitchen. 'They say it's awful...'

Maigret felt the oak table with the corners decorated with carved lions. It was the same table as in his time. It had been sold to the new steward when his father had died.

'You'll have something to drink, won't you?'

Gautier took a bottle out of the sideboard, perhaps to save time.

'What do you think of that Monsieur Jean?... Now I come to think of it, what's his surname?'

'Métayer... Quite a good Bourges family...'

'Did he cost the countess a lot?'

Gautier filled the glasses with brandy but maintained a stubborn silence.

'What had he got to do at the château? As steward, I suppose you look after everything...'

'Everything!'

'Well?'

'He didn't do anything... A few personal letters... In the beginning he claimed to be able to make money for Madame la Comtesse, thanks to his financial knowledge... He bought some shares which dropped in value in a few months... He maintained that he'd win everything back thanks to a new photographic proccess one of his friends had invented... That cost Madame la Comtesse about a hundred thousand francs, and the friend disappeared... Finally the latest thing was some business of printing negatives... I don't know anything about it... Something like photogravure, or heliogravure, but cheaper...'

'Jean Métayer was very busy, in fact...'

'He bustled about a lot for nothing... He wrote some articles for the *Journal de Moulins* and they were forced to accept them because of Madame la Comtesse... It was there that he tried out his negatives and the editor didn't dare throw him out... Good health!'

Suddenly anxious, he asked:

'Nothing happened between him and Monsieur le Comte?'

'Nothing at all.'

'I suppose it's just a coincidence you being here... There's no reason why you should be, seeing it was a case of heart disease...'

The trouble was that it was impossible to meet the steward's eyes. He wiped his moustache and went into the next room.

'Will you excuse me while I change?... I was going to go to High Mass and now...'

'I'll see you later,' said Maigret as he left.

And he had no sooner shut the door than he heard the woman who had remained invisible ask:

'Who was that?'

They had laid paving-stones in the yard where he used to play marbles on the beaten earth.

*

The square was full of groups of people in their Sunday best, and organ music was coming from the church. The children, in their new clothes, did not dare to play. And everywhere handkerchiefs were being brought out of pockets, and red noses were being blown noisily.

Snatches of conversation reached Maigret's ears:

'He's a policeman from Paris...'

'They say he's come about the cow that died last week at Mathieu's...'

A young man all dressed up in a navy-blue suit with a red flower in his button-hole, his face well scrubbed, his hair shining with brilliantine, ventured to say to the chief-inspector:

'They're waiting for you at Tatin's about the lad who stole...'

And he nudged his companions, holding back a laugh which burst out all the same while he turned his head away.

He was telling the truth. At Marie Tatin's the atmosphere was now warmer and thicker. Pipes and pipes of tobacco had been smoked. A family of peasants, at one table, were eating food they had brought from the farm, and drinking large bowls of coffee. The father was cutting a dried sausage with his pocket-knife.

The young men were drinking lemonade, and the old men brandy. And Marie Tatin kept trotting around without stopping.

In one corner a woman stood up when the chief-inspector came in, and took a step towards him, worried, hesitant, moist-lipped. She had one hand on the shoulder of a little boy whose red hair Maigret recognized.

'Are you the chief-inspector?'

Everybody looked in her direction.

'First of all, Chief-Inspector, I want to tell you our family has always been honest… We're poor all the same… You understand?… When I saw that Ernest…'

The boy, very pale-faced, stared straight ahead, without showing the slightest emotion.

'Was it you who took the missal?' asked Maigret, bending down.

No reply. A wild, piercing look.

'Answer the chief-inspector…'

But the lad did not open his mouth. It happened in a flash. The mother gave him a slap which left a red mark on his left cheek. The boy's head shook for a moment. The eyes became a little more moist, the lips trembled, but he did not budge.

'Are you going to answer, curse of my life?'

And to Maigret she said:

'There's today's kids for you!… He's been crying for months to get me to buy him a missal. A thick one like Monsieur le Curé's! Have you ever heard the like?… So, when I hear about Madame la Comtesse's missal. I thought straight away… Besides, I was surprised to see him come home between the second Mass and the third, because usually he eats at the presbytery… I went up to his room and I found this under the mattress…'

Once again the mother's hand descended on the boy's cheek. He made no attempt to ward off the blow.

'When I was his age, I couldn't even read. But I'd never have had enough wickedness in me to steal a book…'

There was a respectful silence in the inn. Maigret had

the missal in his hands.

'Thank you, Madame...'

He was in a hurry to examine it. He made as if to walk to the far end of the room.

'Chief-Inspector...'

The woman was calling him back. She looked embarrassed.

'They told me there was a reward... It isn't because Ernest...'

Maigret handed her twenty francs which she put carefully away in her bag. After which she pulled her son towards the door, grumbling:

'As for you, you jail-bird, you just wait...'

Maigret's eyes met the boy's. It was a matter of only a few seconds. All the same, they both understood that they were friends.

Perhaps because Maigret, in his childhood, had longed for — without ever possessing one — a gilt-edged missal with not only the Ordinary of the Mass, but all the liturgical texts in two columns, in Latin and French.

*

'What time will you be coming back to lunch?'

'I don't know.'

Maigret nearly went up to his room to examine the missal, but the memory of the countless draughts which the roof let in made him choose the main road.

It was while walking slowly towards the château that he opened the book, whose binding was embossed with the Saint-Fiacre coat of arms. Or rather he did not open it. The missal opened itself at a page where a piece of paper had been inserted between two leaves.

Page 221. *Prayers After Communion.*

What was there was a piece of newspaper cut out anyhow which immediately struck the eye as most peculiar, as if it had been badly printed.

Paris, 1 November. A dramatic suicide took place this morning in a flat in the Rue de Miromesnil which had been occupied for several years by Comte de Saint-Fiacre and his mistress, a Russian woman called Marie S...

After telling his mistress that he was ashamed of the scandalous conduct of a certain member of his family, the count fired a bullet into his head and died a few minutes later without recovering consciousness.

We understand that a distressing family drama lies behind this incident and that the person mentioned above is none other than the dead man's mother.

A goose wandering on to the road stretched out towards Maigret a beak wide open in fury. The bells were in full peal and the congregation was shuffling slowly out of the little church, from which smells of incense and extinguished tapers were escaping.

Maigret had thrust the bulky missal into his overcoat pocket, where it made a bulge. He had stopped to examine the fateful scrap of paper.

The murder weapon! A newspaper cutting two inches by three!

The Comtesse de Saint-Fiacre went to the first Mass, and knelt down in the stall which for two centuries had been reserved for members of her family.

And here was the weapon! Maigret turned the piece of paper over and over. There was something peculiar about it. Among other things he noticed the alignment of the type and felt sure that the printing had not been done on a rotary press, as in the case of a real newspaper.

This was just a proof, pulled by hand. That was obvious from the fact that the other side of the piece of paper bore exactly the same text.

The murderer had not taken the trouble to produce a finished piece of work, or else he had not had enough time. Besides, would the countess be likely to think of turning the piece of paper over? Wouldn't she have died first from shock, indignation, shame and fear?

The expression on Maigret's face was terrifying, because he had never before encountered a crime which was so cowardly and so clever at the same time.

And the murderer had had the nerve to warn the police!

Supposing that the missal had not been found...

Yes, that was it! The missal was not intended to be found! For then it was impossible to talk about a crime, or to accuse anybody. The countess had died from heart failure.

He turned back suddenly. He arrived at Marie Tatin's when everybody was talking about him and the missal.

'You know where little Ernest lives?'

'The third house after the grocer's, in the High Street...'

He hurried round there. It was a small single-story house. There were photographs of the father and mother on the wall, on either side of the sideboard. The woman who had already changed out of her Sunday best was in the kitchen, which smelt of roast beef.

'Isn't your son here?'

'He's changing. There's no point in him getting his best clothes dirty... You saw what a scolding I gave him!... A child who has nothing but good examples in front of him and...'

She opened the door and shouted:

'Come here, you bad lot!'

He caught sight of the boy in his underpants, trying to hide.

'Let him get dressed,' said Maigret. 'I'll talk to him later...'

The woman went on preparing the lunch. Her husband was presumably at Marie Tatin's, having his apéritif.

At last the door opened and Ernest came in with a sly look on his face, wearing his weekday suit, the trousers of which were too long.

'You want him to go out with you?' exclaimed the woman. 'But in that case... Ernest... Go and put your best suit on quick...'

'It isn't worth it, Madame... Come along, lad...'

The street was empty. All the life of the district was concentrated in the square, in the graveyard, and at Marie Tatin's.

'Tomorrow I'm going to give you an even thicker missal, with the first letter of every word in red...'

The boy was dumbfounded. So the chief-inspector knew

that there were missals with red letters, like the one on the altar?

'Only, you're going to tell me frankly where you found this one. I shan't scold you...'

It was strange to see the old peasant mistrust awakening in the boy. He said nothing. He was already on the defensive.

'Was it on the prayer-stool that you found it?'

Silence. There were freckles on his cheeks and the bridge of his nose. His thick lips were trying to keep still.

'Don't you understand that I'm your friend?'

'Yes... You gave Ma twenty francs...'

'Well, what of it?'

The child took his revenge.

'When we got back home Ma told me she'd only slapped me for show, and she gave me fifty centimes...'

The boy knew what he was doing all right. What was going on inside that head of his which was too big for his thin body?

'And what about the sacristan?'

'He didn't say any anything to me...'

'Who took the missal from the prayer-stool?'

'I don't know...'

'Where did you find it?'

'Under my surplice, in the sacristy... I was supposed to go and have breakfast in the presbytery. I'd forgotten my handkerchief... When I moved my surplice, I felt something hard...'

'Was the sacristan there?'

'He was in the church, putting out the candles... You know, a missal with red letters costs an awful lot...'

In other words, somebody had taken the missal from the prayerstool and had hidden it for the time being in the sacristy, under the choirboy's surplice, obviously with the intention of coming back for it later.

'Did you open it?'

'I didn't have time... I wanted my boiled egg... Because on Sunday...'

'I know...'

And Ernest wondered how this man from the town

could possibly know that on Sunday he had an egg and some bread and jam at the presbytery.

'You can go…'

'Is it true that I'll have…?'

'A missal, yes… Tomorrow… Goodbye, lad…'

Maigret held out his hand and after a moment's hesitation the boy gave him his.

'I know you're just joking,' he said, however, as he went off.

A crime in three stages: somebody had set the article, or had it set, with a linotype, which could only be found in a newspaper building or a big printing-house.

Somebody had slipped the piece of paper into the missal, after choosing the page.

And somebody had collected the missal and hidden it temporarily under the surplice in the sacristy.

Perhaps the same man had done everything. Perhaps each operation had been carried out by a different person. Or perhaps the same person had been responsible for two of the three operations.

As he was passing in front of the church. Maigret saw the priest coming out and walking towards him. He waited for him under the poplars, near the woman selling oranges and chocolate.

'I'm going to the château,' he said as he joined the chief-inspector. 'That's the first time I've celebrated Mass without even knowing what I was doing… The idea that a crime…'

'It was a crime all right,' said Maigret laconically.

They walked along in silence. Without saying a word, the chief-inspector held out the scrap of paper to his companion, who read it and handed it back.

And they walked another hundred yards without speaking.

'One evil leads to another… But she was a poor creature…'

They both had to hold on to their hats because of the wind, which was increasing in violence.

'I wasn't strict enough,' the priest added in a gloomy voice.

'You?'

'Every day she would come back to me... She was ready to return to the ways of the Lord... But every day, over there...'

There was a bitter note in his voice.

'I refused to go there and yet it was my duty...'

They nearly stopped, because two men were walking along the main drive of the château and they were bound to meet them. They recognized the doctor, with his little brown beard, and beside him, the tall thin figure of Jean Métayer who was still talking excitedly. The yellow car was in the courtyard. Maigret guessed that Métayer did not dare go back to the château as long as the Comte de Saint-Fiacre was there.

There was an ambiguous light over the village. The situation was ambiguous too, with all these vague comings and goings.

'Come along!' said Maigret.

The doctor must have said the same thing to the secretary, whom he brought along with him. When he was near enough he said:

'Good morning, Monsieur le Curé! You know, I'm in a position to reassure you... Sinner though I am. I can imagine your distress at the idea that a crime may have been committed in your church... Well, no... Science is categorical... *Our* countess died from heart failure...'

Maigret had gone up to Jean Métayer.

'I'd like to ask you a question...'

He could feel that the young man was on edge, panting with fear.

'When did you last go to the *Journal de Moulins*?'

'I... Wait a minute...'

He was about to speak. But his suspicions were aroused. He darted a distrustful look at the chief-inspector.

'Why do you ask me that?'

'It doesn't matter.'

'Am I obliged to reply?'

'You are free to say nothing.'

Perhaps not exactly the face of a degenerate, but an anxious, tormented face. And a quite exceptional nervousness, capable of interesting Doctor Bouchardon, who was talking to the priest.

'I know that I'm the one who's going to suffer!... But I'm not going to take it lying down...'

'Of course you're not going to take it lying down...'

'First I want to see a lawyer... I'm entitled to that... Besides, by what right are you...?'

'Just a minute! Have you ever studied law?'

'For two years.'

He was trying to regain his composure, to smile.

'Nobody has laid a charge, and nobody has been caught in *flagrante delicto*... So you've no right to...'

'Very good! Ten out of ten!'

'The doctor says...'

'And I maintain that the countess was killed by the dirtiest swine imaginable. Read this!'

And Maigret held out the printed piece of paper to him. Stiffening suddenly, Jean Métayer looked at him as if he were going to spit in his face.

'A... You said a...? I won't stand for...'

The chief-inspector, gently putting his hand on his shoulder, said:

'But my poor boy, I haven't said anything yet, *to you*. Where's the count? Read that all the same. You can give it back to me later...'

A gleam of triumph shone in Métayer's eyes.

'The count is discussing cheques with the steward... You'll find them in the library...'

The priest and the doctor were walking in front and Maigret heard the doctor's voice saying:

'Certainly not, Monsieur le Curé. It's human! Terribly human! If only you'd studied a little physiology instead of poring over the writings of Saint Augustine...'

And the gravel crunched under the feet of the four men who slowly climbed the steps, which the cold had made whiter and harder than ever.

CHAPTER FOUR

Marie Vassilief

Maigret could not be everywhere. The château was huge. That was why he had only a vague idea of the morning's events.

It was the time when, on Sundays and holidays, the peasants put off the moment of going home, savouring the pleasure of being in a well-dressed group in ths village square or else in a café. Some were already drunk. Others were talking in loud voices. And the children in their stiff clothes were looking admiringly at their daddies.

Inside the château, Jean Métayer, looking rather yellow in the face, had gone upstairs, all alone, to the first floor, where he could be heard walking up and down one room.

'If you'll come with me,' the doctor said to the priest.

And he lured him away in the direction of the dead woman's bedroom.

On the ground floor, a wide corridor ran the entire length of the building, lined by a row of doors. Maigret could hear a hum of voices. He had been told that the Comte de Saint-Fiacre and the steward were in the library.

He decided to go in there, opened the wrong door, and found himself in the drawing-room. The communicating-door leading into the library was open. In a gilt-edged mirror he caught sight of the reflection of the young man sitting on one corner of the desk, looking utterly depressed, and that of the steward solidly planted on his stocky legs.

'You ought to have known that there was no point in insisting,' Gautier was saying. 'Especially for forty thousand francs!'

'Who answered the telephone when I called?'

'Monsieur Jean, of course.'

'So that he didn't even pass on the message to my mother?'

Maigret coughed and walked into the library.

'What telephone call are you talking about?'

Maurice de Saint-Fiacre answered without any embarrassment:

'The one I made the day before yesterday to the château. As I've already told you, I needed some money. I wanted to ask my mother for the required sum. But it was that... that Monsieur Jean, as they call him here, who answered the telephone...'

'And he told you that there was nothing doing? You came here all the same...'

The steward was watching the two men. Maurice had left the desk on which he had been perched.

'In any case, I didn't bring Gautier here to talk about that,' he said irritably. 'I haven't concealed the situation from you, Chief-Inspector. Tomorrow a charge will be laid against me. It's obvious that with my mother dead, I'm the only natural heir. I therefore asked Gautier to get me forty thousand francs for tomorrow morning... Well, it seems that that's impossible...'

'Quite impossible!' repeated the steward.

'Apparently nothing can be done without the permission of the lawyer, who won't gather the interested parties together until after the funeral. And Gautier adds that, quite apart from that, it would be difficult to raise a loan of forty thousand francs on the property which remains...'

He started walking up and down.

'It's clear, isn't it? All cut and dried! I may even be prevented from attending the funeral... But now I come to think of it... One more question... You spoke of a crime... Is it...?'

'No charge has been laid, and probably no charge will be laid,' said Maigret. 'So the case won't come up before the courts...'

'Leave us alone, Gautier.'

As soon as the steward had reluctantly left the room, he went on:

'A crime, really?'

'A crime which doesn't concern the police.'

'Explain yourself... I'm beginning to...'

But just then they heard a woman's voice in the hall, accompanied by the deeper voice of the steward. Maurice frowned and made for the door, which he pulled open with an abrupt gesture.

'Marie! What the...?'

'Maurice! Why won't they let me in?... It's insufferable! I've been waiting for an hour at the hotel...'

She spoke with a pronounced foreign accent. It was Marie Vassilief, who had arrived from Moulins in an old taxi which they could see in the courtyard.

She was tall and very beautiful, with hair which was perhaps artificially fair. Seeing that Maigret was looking at her closely, she started talking volubly in English and Maurice answered her in the same language.

She asked him if he had any money. He replied that there was no longer any question of that, that his mother was dead, and that she must go back to Paris, where he would join her soon.

At this she asked with a laugh:

'What shall I use for money? I haven't even enough to pay for the taxi!'

Maurice de Saint-Fiacre began to panic. His mistress's shrill voice rang through the château and lent a scandalous quality to the scene.

The steward was still in the corridor.

'If you stay here, I'm staying with you!' declared Marie Vassilief.

Maigret told Gautier:

'Pay the taxi-driver and send him away.'

The confusion was growing. Not a material, reparable confusion, but a moral confusion which seemed to be contagious. Gautier himself was losing his composure.

'I must have a word with you, Chief-Inspector,' the young man said.

'Not now.'

And he gestured towards the aggressively elegant woman who was walking around the library and drawing-room as if she were compiling an inventory.

'Who is this silly portrait of, Maurice?' she exclaimed with a laugh.

There were footsteps on the stairs. Maigret saw Métayer go past, wearing a loose-fitting overcoat and carrying a travelling-bag. Métayer must have guessed that he would not be allowed to leave, for he stopped outside the library door and waited.

'Where are you going?'

'To the inn... It's more fitting that I should...'

To get rid of his mistress, Maurice de Saint-Fiacre took her off towards the right wing of the château. The two went on talking in English.

'Is it true that it would be impossible to raise a loan of forty thousand francs on the château?' Maigret asked the steward.

'It would be difficult.'

'Well, do it all the same, by tomorrow morning at the latest.'

The chief-inspector was reluctant to go out. At the last moment he decided to go up to the first floor and there a surprise was waiting for him. While downstairs everybody was bustling about aimlessly, order had been restored in the Comtesse de Saint-Fiacre's bedroom.

It was no longer the ambiguous, sordid atmosphere of that morning. It was no longer even the same body. The dead woman, clothed in a white nightdress, was stretched out on her four-poster bed in a peaceful, dignified attitude, with her hands folded on a crucifix.

Already there were lighted tapers, some holy water, and a sprig of boxwood in a bowl.

Bouchardon looked at Maigret as he came in and seemed to be saying:

'Well, what do you think about it? Nice work, isn't it?'

The priest was praying, moving his lips silently. He remained alone with the dead woman while the other two went off.

The groups in the square had thinned out in front of the church. Through the curtains in the house windows, families could be seen sitting at lunch.

For a few seconds, the sun tried to penetrate the layer of clouds, but only the next moment the sky turned grey again and the trees trembled more than ever.

Jean Métayer was installed in the corner near the window and he was eating automatically while looking at the empty road. Maigret had taken his seat at the other end of the inn room. Between the two of them there was a family from a neighbouring village who had arrived in a lorry. They had brought their own food and Marie Tatin was serving them with drinks.

The poor Tatin woman was distraught. She could no longer make head or tail of what was happening. Usually she only let an attic room from time to time to a workman who came to carry out repairs at the château or on a farm.

And now, besides Maigret, she had a new guest: the countess's secretary.

She did not dare to ask any questions. All morning she had heard frightening stories told by her customers. Among other things she had heard mention of the police...

'I'm very much afraid the chicken is overcooked,' she said as she served Maigret.

The tone of voice was the same in which she would have said, for example:

'I'm afraid of everything! I don't know what's happening! Mother of God, protect me!'

The chief-inspector gazed at her tenderly. She had always had this same timid, sickly look.

'Do you remember, Marie, the...'

She opened her eyes wide. She was already beginning a defensive movement.

'...the business of the frogs?'

'But... Who...?'

'Your mother had sent you to pick mushrooms in the meadow behind the Notre-Dame pond... There were three little boys playing over there... They took advantage of a moment when you were thinking of something else to replace the mushrooms in the basket with frogs... And all the way home you were frightened because things were moving about...'

For a few moments she had been looking at him closely and she ended up by stammering:

'Maigret?'

'Careful! Monsieur Jean has finished his chicken and is waiting for the next course.'

And now Marie Tatin had changed. She was even more agitated than before, but with moments of confidence.

How funny life was! Years and years without the slightest incident, without anything happening to relieve the daily monotony. And then, all of a sudden, incomprehensible events, dramatic happenings, things such as you did not even read about in the papers!

Now and then, while waiting on Jean Métayer and the peasants, she darted a conspiratorial glance at Maigret. When he had finished, she said shyly:

'You'll have a glass of brandy, won't you?'

'You used to say *tu* in the old days, Marie!'

She laughed. No, she did not dare to any more.

'But *you* haven't had any lunch!'

'Yes, I have! I never stop eating in the kitchen... A mouthful now... A mouthful later...'

A motor-cycle went by along the road. Maigret caught a glimpse of a young man who looked smarter than most of the inhabitants of Saint-Fiacre.

'Who's that?'

'Didn't you see him this morning? It's Emile Gautier, the steward's son.'

'Where is he going?'

'Probably to Moulins... He's practically a townsman. He works in a bank...'

People could be seen coming out of their houses, walking along the road, or making for the graveyard.

Curiously enough, Maigret was sleepy. He felt harassed, as if he had made an exceptional effort. And this was not because he had got up at half past five in the morning, nor because he had caught cold.

It was rather the atmosphere which was crushing him. He felt personally affected by the drama, disgusted by it.

Yes, disgusted. That was the word for it. He had never imagined that he would find his native village in these circumstances. Down to his father's grave, on which the tombstone had turned black, and where somebody had forbidden him to smoke! Opposite him, Jean Métayer was putting on a show. He knew that he was being watched. He was trying to keep calm while he was eating, and even to put on a vaguely contemptuous smile.

'A glass of brandy?' Marie Tatin asked him too.

'No, thank you. I never touch spirits.'

He was well-bred. He made a point of displaying his good manners at every opportunity. At the inn, he ate with the same affected gestures as at the château.

When he had finished his lunch, he asked:

'Have you a telephone?'

'No, but there's a call-box over the way...'

He crossed the road, and went on to the grocer's shop run by the sacristan, where the call-box was installed. He must have asked for a long-distance call, for Maigret saw him waiting a long time in the shop, smoking one cigarette after another.

When he returned, the peasants had left the inn. Marie Tatin was washing the glasses in readiness for Vespers which would bring more customers.

'To whom have you just telephoned? Remember that I can find out by asking the operator...'

'To my father in Bourges.'

His voice was curt, aggressive.

'I asked him to send me a lawyer straight away.'

He made Maigret think of a ridiculous little mongrel which bares its teeth before anyone even makes as if to touch it.

'You seem very sure of being bothered?'

'I must ask you not to speak to me again until my lawyer gets here. You can believe me when I say I'm sorry there's only one inn in this village.'

Did he hear the word the chief-inspector muttered as he walked away?

'Cretin!... Dirty little cretin!'

And Marie Tatin, without knowing why, felt frightened of remaining alone with him.

*

The day was to continue to the very end to be marked by confusion and indecision, probably because nobody felt qualified to take command of events.

Maigret, wrapped up in his heavy overcoat, roamed around the village. At one time he was seen in the square in front of the church, at another in the vicinity of the château, where the windows lit up one after another.

For night was falling fast. The church was brightly lit, vibrating with the sound of the organ. The bell-ringer locked the graveyard gate.

And groups of people who were scarcely visible in the darkness consulted one another. They did not know whether or not to call at the château to pay their respects to the dead woman. Two men went off to see, and were received by the butler, who did not know what to do either. There was no tray ready for the visiting cards of callers. The servant went to look for Maurice de Saint-Fiacre to ask his opinion, but the Russian woman replied that he had gone out for a breath of air.

She for her part was lying on her bed, fully dressed, and smoking cigarettes with cardboard tips.

So the butler shrugged his shoulders and let the two callers in.

This was taken as a signal. After Vespers, there were consultations.

'Yes, I tell you! Old Martin and young Bonnet have already been!'

Everybody went in a procession. The château was poorly lit. The peasants walked along the corridor, silhouetted in turn against each window. They pulled their children along by the hand, shaking them to stop them from making any noise. The stairs... The first floor corridor... And finally the bedroom where these people had never set foot before.

There was nobody there but the countess's chambermaid, who watched the invasion in alarm. The peasants made the sign of the cross with a sprig of boxwood dipped in the holy water. The bolder spirits murmured in an undertone:

'You'd think she was asleep!'

And others echoed them:

'She didn't suffer...'

Then their footsteps sounded on the disjointed floor. The stairs creaked. There were murmurs of:

'Hush!... Hold the banisters tight...'

The cook, in her basement kitchen, could see only the legs of the people passing by.

Maurice de Saint-Fiacre came back while the house was still full of people. He looked at the peasants in wide-eyed surprise. The callers wondered if they ought to speak to him. But he just muttered at them and went into Marie Vassilief's bedroom where he could be heard talking in English.

Maigret, for his part, was in the church. The sacristan, holding the candle-extinguisher, was going from taper to taper. The priest was taking off his vestments in the sacristy.

On both left and right were the confessionals with their little green curtains intended to conceal the penitents. Maigret remembered the time when his face had not reached high enough to be hidden by the curtain.

Behind him, the bell-ringer, who had not seen him, was bolting the main door.

The chief-inspector suddenly crossed the nave and went into the sacristy where the priest was surprised to see him appear unexpectedly.

'Excuse me, Monsieur le Curé... Before anything else. I would like to ask you a question...'

In front of him, the priest's regular features wore a solemn expression, but it seemed to Maigret that his eyes were shining feverishly.

'This morning, something strange occurred here. The countess's missal, which was on her prayer-stool, suddenly disappeared and was later found hidden under the choirboy's surplice, in this very room...'

Silence. The sound of the sacristan's footsteps on the carpet in the church. The heavier footsteps of the bell-ringer who was leaving through a side door.

'Only four people could have done that... Please forgive me... The choirboy, the sacristan, the bell-ringer...'

'And I!'

The voice was calm. The priest's face was lit on only one side by the flickering flame of a candle. From a censer a thin wisp of blue smoke was spiralling up towards the ceiling.

'It was…?'

'It was I who took the missal and put it here, until such time…'

The ciborium, the altar-cruets, and the sanctus bell were in their places as in the days when little Maigret had been a choirboy.

'Did you know what was inside the missal?'

'No.'

'In that case…'

'I must ask you not to put any more questions to me, Monsieur Maigret. I am under the seal of the confessional…'

By an involuntary association of ideas, the chief-inspector remembered his catechism. He also remembered the scene he had pictured when the old Curé had told the story of a priest in the Middle Ages who had allowed his tongue to be torn out rather than break the seal of the confessional. He saw it again in every detail in his mind's eye, after thirty-five years.

'You know who the murderer is,' he murmured all the same.

'God knows who he is… Excuse me… I have to go and see a sick person…'

They went out through the presbytery garden. A little gate separated it from the road. Over there, some people who had come from the château were standing about in groups, a little way off, and discussing what had happened.

'You don't think, Monsieur le Curé, that it's your place to…'

But they bumped into the doctor, who muttered under his breath:

'I say, Curé, don't you think the place is turning into something of a bawdy-house?… Somebody ought to try to clean it up, if only to safeguard the peasants' morals!… Oh, so you're here, too, Chief-Inspector! Well, you've done some good work, I must say… At the moment, half the village is accusing the young count of… Especially since that woman arrived!… The steward is going to see the farmers to collect the forty thousand francs which, so it seems, are needed to…'

'Oh, go to blazes!'

Maigret walked away. He felt sick at heart. And now he was being accused of being the cause of all this trouble. What blunder had he committed? Indeed, what had he done? He would have given anything to see the situation develop in a dignified atmosphere.

He strode along towards the inn which was half full.

He caught only one phrase:

'They say that if he can't find the money, he'll go to prison…'

Marie Tatin was the picture of misery. She came and went, a brisk little figure, trotting along like an old woman, although she was not more than forty.

'Is the lemonade for you?… Who ordered two beers?'

In his corner, Jean Métayer was writing, raising his head now and then to listen to the conversations.

Maigret went over to him. He could not read the cramped handwriting, but he saw that the paragraphs were clearly divided, with only a few corrections, and each one preceded by a number.

1…

2…

3…

The secretary was preparing his defence, while waiting for his lawyer to arrive…

A few feet away, a woman was saying:

'There weren't any clean sheets and they had to go and borrow some from the steward's wife.'

Pale, with drawn features, but a determined look in his eyes, Jean Métayer wrote down:

4…

CHAPTER FIVE

The Second Day

Maigret slept that restless yet voluptuous sleep which you experience only in a cold country bedroom which smells of the cowshed, winter apples and hay. Draughts were blowing all around him. And the sheets were icy, except in the one spot, a soft, cosy hollow, which he had warmed with his body. So that, rolled up in a ball, he avoided making the slightest movement.

Several times, he had heard Jean Métayer's dry cough in the next room. Then came the furtive footsteps of Marie Tatin getting up.

He stayed in bed a few minutes longer. When he had lighted the candle, he had not the courage to wash with the icy water in the jug, and he put off that operation until later, going down in his slippers, without a collar.

Downstairs, Marie Tatin was pouring paraffin on the fire, which was refusing to take. She had her hair in curlers and she blushed as she saw the chief-inspector come in.

'It isn't seven o'clock yet... The coffee isn't ready...'

Maigret had a slight worry. Half an hour earlier, when he had been half asleep, he had thought he heard a car driving past. Now, Saint-Fiacre is not on the main road. Almost the only traffic is the bus which goes through the village once a day.

'The bus hasn't gone, has it, Marie?'

'Never before half past eight! And more often than not, nine o'clock...'

'Is that the bell for Mass ringing already?'

'Yes... It's at seven o'clock in the winter, and six o'clock in summer... If you want to warm yourself...'

She pointed to the fire which was finally burning up.

'You really can't bring yourself to call me *tu*?'

Maigret could have bitten his tongue off as he saw a coquettish smile appear on the poor woman's face.

'The coffee will be ready in five minutes...'

It would not be light before eight o'clock. The cold was even sharper than the day before. With his coat collar turned up, and his hat pulled down over his eyes, Maigret walked slowly towards the bright patch of the church.

It was no longer a Holy Day. There were no more than three women in the nave. And the Mass had something scamped and furtive about it. The priest went too quickly from one corner of the altar to another. He turned round too quickly too, with his arms outstretched to mumble: *Dominus vobiscum*!

The choirboy, who was having some difficulty in following him, said: *Amen* at the wrong time.

Was the panic going to set in again? He could hear the murmur of the liturgical prayers and now and then a gasp from the priest as he got his breath back between two words.

Ite missa est...

Had this particular Mass lasted as much as twelve minutes? The three women stood up. The priest was reciting the last Gospel. A car drew up in front of the church and soon hesitant footsteps could be heard outside.

Maigret had remained at the back of the nave, standing right against the door. Consequently, when the door opened, the new arrival found himself literally face to face with the chief-inspector.

It was Maurice de Saint-Fiacre. He was so surprised that he nearly beat a retreat, murmuring:

'I beg your pardon... I...'

But he took a step forward, and made an effort to regain his composure.

'Is Mass over?'

His nerves were obviously on edge. There were rings

under his eyes as if he had not slept a wink all night. And by opening the door, he had brought the cold air in with him.

'Have you come from Moulins?'

The two men were talking with forced politeness while the priest was reciting the prayer after the Gospel and the women were shutting their missals and picking up their handbags and umbrellas.

'How did you know? Yes… I…'

'Shall we go out?'

The priest and the choirboy had gone into the sacristy and the sacristan was putting out the two tapers which had been sufficient for the Low Mass.

Outside, the sky was a little lighter along the horizon. The white walls of the nearest houses stood out in the half-light. The yellow car was there, between the trees in the square.

Saint-Fiacre's embarrassment was obvious. He looked at Maigret in some surprise, astonished perhaps at seeing him unshaven, without a collar under his coat.

'You got up early!' murmured the chief-inspector.

'The first train, which is an express, leaves Moulins at three minutes past seven…'

'I don't understand… You didn't take the train, seeing that…'

'You're forgetting Marie Vassilief…'

It was all so simple. And so natural. The presence of Maurice's mistress could only be an embarrassment at the château. So he had driven her to Moulins, put her on the train for Paris, and on his way back had dropped into the lighted church.

But Maigret was not satisfied. He was trying to follow the anxious glances of the count, who seemed to be waiting for somebody or to be afraid of something.

'She doesn't look an easy person to deal with!' hinted the chief-inspector.

'She's known better days. So she's very sensitive… The idea that I might want to hide our liaison…'

'Which has been going on for how long?'

'Just under a year… Marie doesn't care about money…

There have been difficult times...'

His gaze had at last settled on one point. Maigret followed it and caught sight of the priest who had just come out of the church behind him. He had the impression that the two gazes met and that the priest was as embarrassed as the Comte de Saint-Fiacre.

The chief-inspector was going to call to him. But already, with clumsy haste, the priest called out a rather curt greeting to the two men and went into the presbytery as if he were running away.

'He doesn't look like a country priest...'

Maurice made no reply. Through the lighted window they could see the priest sitting down to his breakfast, and the housekeeper bringing him a steaming coffee-pot.

Some little boys with satchels on their backs were beginning to make their way to school. The surface of the Notre-Dame pond was turning the colour of a mirror.

'What arrangements have you made for...' began Maigret.

And the other broke in far too quickly:

'For what?'

'For the funeral... Did anybody watch the body last night?'

'No. The idea was mooted for a moment. Gautier said that it wasn't done any more...'

They heard the roar of a two-stroke engine in the courtyard of the château. A few moments later a motorcycle went by on the road, heading for Moulins. Maigret recognized Gautier's son, whom he had seen the day before. He was wearing a fawn raincoat and a check cap.

Maurice de Saint-Fiacre did not know what attitude to adopt. He did not dare to get back into his car. And he had nothing to say to the chief-inspector.

'Has Gautier found the forty thousand francs?'

'No... Yes... I mean...'

Maigret looked at him inquisitively, surprised to see him so flustered.

'Has he found them, or hasn't he? I got the impression yesterday that he was raising difficulties about it. Because in spite of everything, in spite of all the mortgages and debts, you'll get much more than that amount...'

No, Maurice still made no reply. He looked panic-stricken, for no apparent reason. And the next thing he said had no connexion with the previous conversation.

'Tell me frankly, Chief-Inspector... Do you suspect me?'

'Suspect you of what?'

'You know perfectly well... I've got to know...'

'I've no more reason to suspect you than anybody else,' Maigret replied evasively.

His companion leapt upon this statement.

'Thank you... Well, that's what you must tell people... You understand?... Otherwise, my position is impossible...'

'What's the bank at which your cheque is going to be presented?'

'The Comptoir d'Escompte...'

A woman was making for the wash-house, pushing a wheelbarrow containing two laundry baskets. The priest, in his presbytery, was walking up and down, reading his breviary, but the chief-inspector had the impression that he kept darting anxious glances at the two men.

'I'll join you at the château.'

'Now?'

'In a little while...'

It was clear that Maurice de Saint-Fiacre did not relish the idea at all. He got into his car like a condemned man. And through the presbytery window the chief-inspector could see the priest watching him drive away.

Maigret wanted to go and put on a collar at the very least. Just as he arrived in front of the inn, Jean Métayer came out of the grocer's. He had simply put a coat on over his pyjamas. He looked at the chief-inspector with a triumphant expression.

'A telephone call?'

The young man retorted acidly:

'My lawyer's arriving at ten to nine.'

He was sure of himself. He sent back some boiled eggs which were under-done, and drummed his fingers on the table.

From the window of his bedroom, where he had gone to

get dressed, Maigret could see the courtyard of the château, the sports car, and Maurice de Saint-Fiacre, who did not seem to know what to do. Perhaps he was going to return to the village on foot?

The chief-inspector made haste. A few moments later he for his part was walking towards the château. And the two men met less than a hundred yards from the church.

'Where were you going?' asked Maigret.

'Nowhere. I don't know...'

'Perhaps to say your prayers in the church?'

These few words were enough to make his companion turn pale, as if they had a mysterious, terrible meaning.

Maurice de Saint-Fiacre was not made for dramatic events. At first sight he was a tall, strapping fellow, a magnificently healthy sportsman. If you looked more closely, you could see signs of his noble birth. Under the muscles, which were overladen with fat, there was hardly any energy. He had probably just had a sleepless night, and it seemed to have taken all the strength out of him.

'Have you had announcements of the death printed?'

'No.'

'But what about the family... the local gentry...?'

The young man lost his temper.

'They wouldn't come! You must know that! Before, yes! When my father was alive... During the shooting season, there were up to thirty guests at a time at the château for weeks on end...'

Maigret knew that as well as anybody else, for when there was a shoot, unknown to his parents, he had often put on the white smock of a beater.

'Since then...'

And Maurice made a gesture which signified:

'Things have gone from bad to worse...'

The whole of Berry must have talked about the crazy old woman spoiling the last years of her life with her so-called secretaries. And the farms being sold one after another. And the son making a fool of himself in Paris.

'Do you think the funeral can be held tomorrow?... You understand... The sooner this situation comes to an end the better...'

A cart full of manure went slowly by and its big wheels looked as if they were grinding the pebbles on the road. Dawn had broken, a greyer dawn than the day before, but with less wind. From a distance Maigret saw Gautier crossing the courtyard and coming towards him.

Then a strange thing happened.

'Will you excuse me?' the chief-inspector said to his companion, going off in the direction of the château.

He had scarcely gone a hundred yards when he turned round. Maurice de Saint-Fiacre was standing on the doorstep of the presbytery. He must have rung the door-bell. And when he saw that he had been caught out, he walked away quickly without waiting for a reply.

He did not know where to go. His whole bearing showed that he was terribly ill at ease. The chief-inspector reached the steward, who had seen him coming towards him and was waiting for him with an arrogant air.

'What do you want?'

'Just a piece of information. Have you found the forty thousand francs the count needs?'

'No. And I defy anybody to find them round here! Everybody knows just how much his signature is worth.'

'So?'

'So he'll have to manage as best he can. It's none of my business.'

Saint-Fiacre was retracing his steps. Maigret could tell he was longing to take a certain course of action and that for some reason or other that was impossible. Making up his mind, he came towards the château and stopped near the two men.

'Gautier! Come to the library for your instructions.' He turned to go.

'I'll see you later on, Chief-Inspector,' he added with an effort.

*

When Maigret passed the presbytery, he had a distinct impression of being watched through the curtains. But he could not be sure, for now that the sun had risen, the light inside had been put out.

There was a taxi standing outside Marie Tatin's. Inside the inn, a man of about fifty, immaculately dressed in striped trousers and a black, silk-edged jacket, was sitting at a table with Jean Métayer.

When the chief-inspector came in, he jumped to his feet and rushed forward with outstretched hand.

'I understand that you are an officer from Police Headquarters… Allow me to introduce myself… Maître Tallier of the Bourges bar… Will you have a drink with us?'

Jean Métayer had stood up, but his attitude showed that he did not approve of his lawyer's cordiality.

'Innkeeper!… Come and take our orders, please …'

In a conciliatory voice he asked:

'What will you have?… In this cold weather what do you say to grogs all round?… Three grogs, my good woman…'

His good woman was poor Marie Tatin, who was unaccustomed to these ways.

'I hope, Chief-Inspector, that you'll forgive my client… If I have understood him rightly he has shown a certain mistrust of you… But don't forget that he's a young man of good family who has nothing on his conscience, and who was revolted by the suspicion he felt all round him… The bad temper he displayed yesterday, if I may say so, is the best proof of his complete innocence…'

With Maître Tallier there was no need to open your mouth. He took everything upon himself, questions and replies, accompanying his words with suave gestures.

'Of course, I don't know all the details… If I have understood correctly, the Comtesse de Saint-Fiacre died yesterday, during the first Mass, from heart failure… Later, I gather, a piece of paper was found in her missal which suggests that her death was due to a violent shock… Did the victim's son — who by a coincidence happened to be in the vicinity — lay a charge?… No!… In any case, I don't think that a charge would be accepted… The criminal operation — if it took place — was not sufficiently clear-cut to justify the opening of an official inquiry…

'We are in agreement, are we not?… No charge, so no legal action…

'Not that that prevents me from understanding the unofficial inquiries you are carrying out on your own…

'It isn't enough for my client not to be prosecuted. He must be cleared of all suspicion…

'Let me make myself clear… What, after all, was his position at the château?… That of an adopted son… The countess, left on her own, parted from a son who caused her nothing but trouble, was comforted by her secretary's devotion and upright character…

'My client isn't an idler… He didn't just lead a carefree life as he could have done at the château… He worked… He looked for investments… He even took an interest in recent inventions…

'Did he stand to benefit in any way from the death of his benefactress?… Need I say any more?… I think not…

'And that, Chief-Inspector, is what I want to help you to establish…

'I must add that there are a few indispensable measures that I shall have to take in conjunction with the solicitor… Jean Métayer is a trusting soul… He never imagined that anything of this sort could happen…

'His belongings are at the château, mixed up with those of the late countess.

'Now other persons have arrived there who probably intend to lay their hands on…'

'A few pairs of pyjamas, and some old slippers!' growled Maigret, getting up.

'I beg your pardon?'

During the whole of this conversation Jean Métayer had been taking notes in a little notebook. It was he who calmed down his lawyer, who stood up in his turn.

'Leave it! I realized the very first minute that I had an enemy in the chief-inspector. And since then I have found that he belonged indirectly to the château, where he was born at the time when his father was the Saint-Fiacres' steward. I warned you, Maître… It was you who insisted…'

It was ten o'clock. Maigret calculated that Marie Vassilief's train must have arrived half an hour earlier at the Gare de Lyon.

'Excuse me,' he said. 'I'll see you later.'

'But...'

He in his turn went into the grocer's over the way, making the bell ring as he entered. He had to wait for a quarter of an hour to get through to Paris.

'Is it true that you're the old steward's son?'

Maigret was more tired than after ten normal cases. He felt utterly exhausted, both morally and physically.

'You're through to Paris...'

'Hullo... The Comptoir d'Escompte?... This is Police Headquarters... Some information... Was a cheque signed Saint-Fiacre presented this morning?... What's that?... It was presented at nine o'clock and there were no funds to meet it?... Hullo?... Don't cut us off, Mademoiselle... You asked the bearer to present it again?... Excellent!... Ah, that's what I wanted to know... A young woman, wasn't it?... A quarter of an hour ago?... And she paid in the forty thousand francs?... Thank you... Yes, of course. Pay up... No, no, there's nothing wrong... Seeing that the money has been paid in...'

And Maigret came out of the call-box heaving a weary sigh.

During the night, Maurice de Saint-Fiacre had found the forty thousand francs and he had sent his mistress to Paris to pay them into the bank.

Just as the chief-inspector was leaving the grocer's he caught sight of the priest coming out of the presbytery, with his breviary in his hand, and making for the château.

He quickened his pace, and almost ran to reach the door at the same time as the priest.

He missed him by less than a minute. When he reached the courtyard, the door was closing on the Curé. And when he rang the bell, he heard footsteps at the far end of the corridor, going in the direction of the library.

CHAPTER SIX

The Two Camps

'I'll see if Monsieur le Comte can...'

But the chief-inspector did not give the butler time to finish his sentence. He went into the corridor and made for the library while the butler gave a sigh of resignation. It was no longer even possible to keep up appearances! People came and went as if they were in a shop. Things had come to a pretty pass...

Maigret paused before opening the library door, but it was in vain, for he could not hear anything. Indeed, that was what made his entrance rather impressive.

He knocked, thinking that the priest might be somewhere else. But a voice, very firm and very clear in the silence of the room, replied immediately:

'Come in!'

Maigret pushed open the door, stopping accidentally on a heating vent. Standing in front of him, leaning lightly against the Gothic table, the Comte de Saint-Fiacre was looking at him.

Beside him, staring at the carpet, the priest remained absolutely still, as if the slightest movement would have driven him away.

What were the two of them doing there, neither speaking nor moving? It would have been less embarrassing to interrupt a pathetic scene than to break into a silence so profound that the human voice seemed to trace concentric circles in it, like a pebble in a pool of water.

Once again, Maigret felt conscious of Saint-Fiacre's weariness. As for the priest, he looked stunned, and his fingers were twitching on his breviary.

'Excuse me for disturbing you...'

His words sounded sarcastic and yet he did not mean them to be. But was it possible to disturb people who were as inert as inanimate objects?

'I have some news from the bank...'

The count's gaze rested on the priest and that gaze was hard, almost furious.

The whole scene was to continue in the same vein. It was as if the characters were chess players thinking with their foreheads in their hands, remaining silent for several minutes before moving a pawn, and then returning to immobility.

But it was not thought which was immobilizing them like that. Maigret was convinced that it was fear of making a false move, a clumsy manoeuvre. Between the two of them there was a misunderstanding. And each one was reluctant to move his pawn, ready to take it back.

'I came to get instructions for the funeral,' the priest felt it necessary to say.

That was not true. A pawn had been badly placed. So badly placed that the Comte de Saint-Fiacre smiled.

'I guessed that you would telephone to the bank,' he said. 'And I am going to tell you why I decided to take that step. It was to get rid of Marie Vassilief, who did not want to leave the château... I persuaded her that it was absolutely essential...'

In the priest's eyes, now, Maigret could read anguish and disapproval.

'The poor wretch!' he must have been thinking. 'He has let himself be caught. He has fallen into the trap. He is done for...'

Silence. The scraping of a match and the puffs of smoke which the chief-inspector blew out one after another as he asked:

'Gautier found the money?'

A very short pause.

'No, Chief-Inspector... I'm going to tell you...'

It was not on Saint-Fiacre's face that the drama was being enacted: it was on the priest's. He was pale. His lips had a bitter twist to them. He was making an effort not to intervene.

'Listen, Monsieur...'

He could not stand it any longer.

'Would you mind interrupting this conversation until we've had a talk together?'

The same smile as before on Maurice's lips. It was cold in the huge room where the finest books in the library were missing. A fire had been laid in the hearth. It just needed a match.

'Have you a lighter or...'

And while he was bending over the hearth, the priest darted a miserable, beseeching look at Maigret.

'No,' said the count, returning towards the two men. 'I'm going to clear up the situation in a few words. For some reason which I don't know, Monsieur le Curé, who is full of good will, is convinced that it was I who... why should I be afraid of words?... who killed my mother!... For it was definitely a crime, wasn't it, even if it doesn't quite fall within the jurisdiction of the law...'

The priest was no longer moving, maintaining that trembling immobility of the animal which feels some danger approaching and cannot face it.

'Monsieur le Curé must have been very devoted to my mother... He probably wished to avoid the château being involved in a scandal... Last night he sent the sacristan to me with forty thousand francs in cash as well as a little note...'

Without any possible doubt, the expression in the priest's eyes was saying:

'Fool! You are done for!'

'Here is the note,' Saint-Fiacre went on.

Maigret read in an undertone:

'Be careful. I am praying for you.'

*

Whew! It was like the effect of a gust of fresh air. Straight away, Maurice de Saint-Fiacre ceased to feel rooted to the spot, condemned to immobility. He also lost that gravity which was contrary to his nature.

He started walking up and down, speaking in a lighter voice.

'That, Chief-Inspector, is why you saw me prowling round the church and the presbytery this morning... I accepted the forty thousand francs, which must obviously be regarded as a loan, first of all, as I have told you, to get my mistress out of the way — excuse me, Monsieur le Curé — and then because it would have been extremely unpleasant to have been arrested at this moment... But we are all remaining standing as if... Do sit down, please...'

He went over to the door, opened it and listened to a noise on the floor above.

'The procession is starting again!' he murmured. 'I think we'll have to telephone to Moulins to have a mortuary chapel installed...' Then he went straight on:

'I suppose you understand it now? Once I had accepted the money, it remained for me to swear to Monsieur le Curé that I was not guilty. It was difficult for me to do that in front of you, Chief-Inspector, without making you even more suspicious... That's all!... This morning, as if you could read my thoughts, you didn't leave me alone for a moment, in the vicinity of the church... Then Monsieur le Curé came here, I don't yet know why, for when you came in he was hesitating to speak...'

His eyes clouded over. To shake off the bitterness which was assailing him, he laughed, a painful laugh.

'It's simple, isn't it? A man who has led a gay life and signed bad cheques... Old Gautier is avoiding me!... He too must be convinced that...'

Suddenly he looked at the priest in astonishment.

'Well, Monsieur le Curé... What's the matter?'

The priest, sure enough, looked gloomy. His gaze avoided the young man, and also tried to avoid Maigret's eyes.

Maurice de Saint-Fiacre understood, and exclaimed even more bitterly:

'There you are! You still don't believe me... And it's the very man who wants to help me who is convinced of my guilt...'

He went and opened the door once again, and, forgetting the presence of the dead woman in the house, called out:

'Albert!... Albert!... Look sharp, man!... Bring us something to drink...'

The butler came in, and went over to a cupboard from which he took a decanter of whisky and some glasses. Nobody said anything. They watched him. Maurice de Saint-Fiacre observed with a peculiar smile:

'In my time, there was no whisky in the château.'

'It was Monsieur Jean...'

'Ah!'

He took a long drink, and then went and locked the door behind the butler.

'There are lots of things like that which have changed,' he muttered to himself.

But he did not take his eyes off the priest, and the latter, feeling increasingly ill at ease, stammered:

'Please excuse me... I must go to my catechism class...'

'Just a moment... You are still convinced of my guilt. Monsieur le Curé... No, don't deny it... Priests are no good at lying... Only there are a few points I would like to clear up... Because you don't know me... You weren't at Saint-Fiacre in my time... You've only heard people talking about me... There are no material clues... The chief-inspector, who was there when it happened, knows something about it...'

'I beg you...' stammered the priest.

'No!... You won't have anything to drink?... Good health, Chief-Inspector...'

His gaze was sombre. He pursued his train of thought with fierce intensity.

'There are lots of people you could suspect... But it's I whom you suspect, and I alone... And I keep wondering why... That's what prevented me from sleeping last night... I thought of all the possible reasons and now I think I know... What did my mother tell you?'

This time the priest went white.

'I don't know anything,' he stammered.

'Come now, Monsieur le Curé... You have helped me, I

agree… You have let me have those forty thousand francs which will grant me a breathing-space and allow me to give my mother a decent burial… I thank you with all my heart… Only, at the same time, you regard me with suspicion… You pray for me… That's either too much or not enough…'

The voice began to take on a tone of anger and menace.

'First of all I thought of having this talk with you outside Monsieur Maigret's presence… Well, now I'm glad that he is here… The more I think about it, the more I detect something odd going on…'

'Monsieur le Comte, I implore you not to torture me any more…'

'And I for my part, Monsieur le Curé, warn you that you won't leave this room until you have told me the truth!'

He was a changed man. He was at the end of his tether. And, like all weak and gentle people, he had turned unduly fierce.

His voice must have been audible in the dead woman's room, which was just above the library.

'You were on good terms with my mother… I suppose that Jean Métayer was one of your parishioners too… Which of the two said something?… My mother, wasn't it?'

Maigret remembered the words he had heard the day before:

'The seal of the confessional…'

He understood the priest's torment, his anguish, his martyred expression under the avalanche of Saint-Fiacre's words.

'What did she say to you?… I knew her, you know!… I was present, so to speak, at the beginning of the decline… All of us here know what life is like…'

He looked around him with unspoken anger.

'There was a time,' he said, 'when people held their breath when they came into this room, because my father, *the master*, was working here. There was no whisky in the cupboards… But the shelves were loaded with books as the cells of a beehive are saturated with honey…'

Maigret remembered that too.

'The count is working...'

And those words were enough to keep farmers waiting for two hours in the anteroom.

'The count called me into the library...'

And Maigret's father was impressed by this summons because for him it was an important event.

'He didn't waste logs, but managed with a paraffin stove which he put close to him, to help out the central heating,' said Maurice de Saint-Fiacre.

And, speaking to the distraught priest, he went on:

'You never saw that... You only saw the château in its decline... My mother who had lost her husband... My mother whose only son was making a fool of himself in Paris and never came here except to ask for money... And then there were the secretaries...'

His pupils were so bright that Maigret expected to see tears begin to flow.

'What did she say to you?... She was afraid of seeing me arrive, wasn't she?... She knew that there would be some new debts to pay off, that something else would have to be sold to save me once again...'

'You ought to calm down the priest said in a dull voice.

'Not before knowing... whether you suspected me without knowing me, right from the start...'

Maigret intervened.

'Monsieur le Curé had hidden the missal', he said slowly.

He for his part had already understood. He was holding out a helping hand to Saint-Fiacre. He could imagine the countess, torn between sin and remorse... Wasn't she afraid of being punished?... Wasn't she a little ashamed in front of her son?

She was a sick woman, easily worried. And it was quite possible that under the seal of the confessional she had said one day:

'I'm afraid of my son...'

For she must have been afraid. The money which went to Jean Métayer and his like was Saint-Fiacre money which rightly belonged to Maurice. Wouldn't he call her to account for it one day? Wouldn't...

Maigret was conscious that these ideas were beginning

to occur to the young man, though as yet in a confused form. He was helping to clarify them.

'Monsieur le Curé cannot say anything if the countess spoke under the seal of the confessional…'

That was clear. Maurice de Saint-Fiacre cut the conversation short.

'Forgive me, Monsieur le Curé… I was forgetting your catechism class… Please don't hold it against me if…'

He turned the key in the lock and opened the door.

'Thank you… As soon as… as soon as possible, I will return the forty thousand francs to you… For I imagine that they don't belong to you…'

'I asked Madame Ruinard, the widow of the former solicitor, for them…'

'Thank you… Good-bye…'

He nearly slammed the door shut, but he restrained himself, looked Maigret in the eyes and snarled:

'What a filthy business!'

'He wanted to…'

'He wanted to save me, I know!… He tried to avoid a scandal, to stick the pieces of the château de Saint-Fiacre back together again as best he could… It isn't that…'

And he poured out some whisky.

'I'm thinking of that poor woman… Look, you have seen Marie Vassilief… And all the other women of Paris… They don't have attacks of conscience… But my mother!… And remember that what she was looking for above all else, with that fellow Métayer, was a chance to give her affection… Then she would rush off to the confessional… She must have regarded herself as a monster… From that to fearing my vengeance… Ha! Ha!…'

That laughter of his was terrifying to hear.

'Can you see me, an indignant son, attacking my mother for… And that priest didn't understand!… He sees life in terms of the Scriptures… While my mother was alive, he must have tried to save her from herself… Once she was dead, he thought it his duty to save me… But at this moment I'm willing to bet that he's convinced it was I who…'

He looked the chief-inspector in the eyes and asked:

'And what about you?'

And as Maigret made no reply he went on:

'For there has been a crime… A crime which only the filthiest swine imaginable could have committed… The dirty little coward!… Is it true that the law can do nothing against him?… I heard something to that effect this morning… But I'm going to tell you something, Chief-Inspector, and you can take it down and use it against me… When I find that little swine, well, well, he'll have to deal with me, and me alone… And I won't need a revolver! No, no weapon at all… Nothing but these two hands…'

The whisky was obviously making him more excited. He noticed that, for he passed his hand over his forehead, looked at himself in the mirror, and pulled a mocking face at himself.

'The fact remains, if it hadn't been for the priest. I'd be in prison even before the funeral! I wasn't very nice to him… And the wife of the former solicitor, who has paid my debts… Who is she?… I can't remember…'

'The lady who always dresses in white… The house which has a gate with gilded spikes, on the road to Matignon…'

Maurice de Saint-Fiacre began to calm down. His outburst had been only a flash in the pan. He began to pour out a drink for himself, hesitated, and swallowed the contents of his glass at one draught, with a grimace of disgust.

'Can you hear that?'

'What?'

'The local people filing past upstairs… I ought to be there, in deep mourning, red-eyed, shaking their hands with a heart-broken air… Once outside, they start talking…'

He added suspiciously:

'Now I come to think of it, if, as you say, the Law is not concerned with the case, why are you staying here?'

'Something new might turn up…'

'And if I found the culprit, would you prevent me from…'

The clenched fingers were more eloquent than any speech.

'I must leave you,' said Maigret. 'I have to go and have a look at the other camp...'

'The other camp?'

'The one at the inn. Jean Métayer and his lawyer, who arrived this morning...'

'He's called in a lawyer?'

'He's a thoughtful fellow... This morning the two sides were lined up like this: at the château, you and the priest; at the inn, the young man and his adviser...'

'You think he could have been capable...?'

'May I help myself?'

And Maigret drank a glass of whisky, wiped his lips, and filled a last pipe before leaving.

'I suppose you don't know how to use a linotype?' A shrug of the shoulders.

'I don't know how to use anything... That's the trouble...'

'You won't, under any circumstances, leave the village without informing me, will you?'

A grave, deep look. And a grave, deep voice:

'I give you my word.'

*

Maigret went out. He was about to go down the outside steps when a man appeared beside him before he could see where he had come from.

'Excuse me, Chief-Inspector... Could you spare me a few minutes?... I've been told...'

'What?'

'That you practically belong to the house... Your father was in my job... Would you do me the honour of having a drink with me at home?'

And the grey-bearded steward led his companion across the yards. Everything was ready in his house. A bottle of brandy whose label proclaimed its great age. Biscuits. A smell of cabbages and bacon was coming from the kitchen.

'From what I've heard, you knew the château in very different circumstances... When I arrived here the decline was beginning... There was a young man from Paris who... This is some brandy from the days of the late count... No sugar, I suppose?'

Maigret stared at the table with the carved lions which had brass rings in their mouths. And once again he felt physically and morally tired. In the old days, he had only been allowed to come into this room if he was wearing slippers, on account of the polished floor.

'I'm in a rather difficult position... And it's you I'd like to ask for advice... We are poor people... You know that a steward's job doesn't make a man rich...

'Some Saturdays when there wasn't any money in the safe, I paid the farmers myself...

'At other times, I advanced money to buy cattle the tenant farmers wanted...'

'In other words, the countess owed you money!'

'Madame la Comtesse knew nothing about business... Money was disappearing all over the place... It was only for indispensable things that it wasn't available...'

'And it was you...'

'Your father would have done the same, wouldn't he? There are times when you mustn't let the local people see that the coffers are empty... I drew on my savings...'

'How much?'

'Another glass?... I haven't counted... At least seventy thousand... And now again for the funeral, it's I who...'

A picture imposed itself on Maigret's mind:

His father's little office near the stables, at five o'clock on Saturday. All the people employed at the château, from the linen maids to the farm labourers, were waiting outside. And old Maigret, installed behind the desk covered with green percale, was arranging coins in little heaps. Each peasant passed by in turn, and signed his name or made a cross on the register...

'Now I don't know how I'm going to get it back... For people like us, it's...'

'Yes, I understand... You've had the mantelpiece changed?'

'Yes, the old one was in wood... Marble looks better...'

'Much better!' grunted Maigret.

'You understand, don't you? All the creditors are going

to descend on the château... The count will have to sell up... And with the mortgages...'

The armchair in which Maigret was sitting was new, like the mantelpiece, and must have come from a Paris furniture shop. There was a gramophone on the sideboard.

'If I hadn't a son. I wouldn't mind, but Emile has his career to think about... I don't want to rush matters...'

A girl walked along the corridor.

'You have a daughter too?'

'No. That's a local girl who comes in to do the heavy work.'

'Well, we'll talk about this another time, Monsieur Gautier. Excuse me. I've still a lot of things to do...'

'Another glass?'

'No, thank you... You said about seventy-five thousand, didn't you?'

And he went off, his hands in his pockets, threaded his way through the flocks of geese, and walked along by the Notre-Dame pond where the water had stopped lapping... The church clock struck noon.

At Marie Tatin's, Jean Métayer and the lawyer were eating. They were having sardines, fillets of herring, and sausage, as *hors d'œuvre*. On the next table, there were the glasses which had contained their apéritifs.

The two men were in high spirits. They greeted Maigret with sarcastic glances. They winked at each other. The lawyer's briefcase was closed once more.

'I hope at least you've found some truffles for the chicken?' said Maître Tallier.

Poor Marie Tatin! She had found a tiny tin of truffles at the grocer's, but she could not manage to open it and she did not dare to admit this.

'Yes, I've found some, Monsieur.'

'Then hurry up! The air here makes a man terribly hungry...'

It was Maigret who went to the kitchen and, with his penknife, cut open the tin while the woman with the squint stammered in an undertone:

'I don't know what to say... I...'

'Shut up, Marie!' he growled.

One camp... Two camps... Three camps?

He felt a need to make a joke in order to forget the realities of the situation.

'By the way, the priest asked me to bring you three hundred days' indulgence. To count against your sins!'

And Marie Tatin, who did not understand the joke, gazed at her burly companion with a mixture of fear and affectionate respect.

CHAPTER SEVEN

Meetings at Moulins

Maigret had telephoned to Moulins to order a taxi. He was surprised at first to see one arrive barely ten minutes after his telephone call, but as he was making for the door, the lawyer, who was just finishing his coffee, intervened.

'Excuse me! That's ours... But if you want a lift...'

'No, thank you...'

Jean Métayer and the lawyer left first in a big car which still bore the coat of arms of its former owner. A quarter of an hour later, Maigret went off in his turn, and on the way, while he was chatting with the driver, he looked at the countryside.

The scenery was monotonous: two rows of poplars along the road, and ploughed fields stretching away as far as the eye could sse, with here and there a rectangular thicket or the blue-green eye of a pond.

The houses were for the most part just cottages. And that was understandable, since there were no small landowners.

Nothing but big estates, one of which, that of the Duc de T—, contained three villages.

The Saint-Fiacre estate had covered five thousand acres, before the successive sales.

The only means of transport was an old Paris bus which had been bought by a peasant and which covered the distance between Moulins and Saint-Fiacre once a day.

'This is real country for you!' said the taxi-driver. 'It's all right now. But in the depths of winter...'

They drove down the high street of Moulins with the hands of the clock of Saint-Pierre standing at half past two. Maigret asked the driver to stop in front of the Comptoir d'Escompte and paid the fare. Just as he was turning away from the taxi to make for the bank, a woman came out of the building holding a little boy by the hand.

The chief-inspector hurriedly looked into a shop-window so as not to be noticed. The woman was a peasant woman in her Sunday best, her hat balancing on her hair, her waist constricted by a corset. She was walking along in a dignified manner, trailing the little boy behind her, without taking any more notice of him than she would of a parcel.

It was Ernest, the red-haired boy who served Mass at Saint-Fiacre.

The street was crowded. Ernest would have liked to stop at each window, but he was towed along in the wake of the black skirt. However, his mother bent down to say something to him. And, as if it had been decided in advance, she went into a toy shop with him.

Maigret did not dare to get too close. All the same, he gathered what was happening from the whistle blasts which soon started coming from the shop. Every imaginable whistle was tried in turn, and finally the choirboy must have decided on a boy-scout whistle with two notes.

When he came out, he was wearing it on a string around his neck, but his mother pulled him along, preventing him from blowing it in the street.

*

A bank like any other in a small country town. A long oak counter. Five clerks bent over desks. Maigret made for the section of the counter marked *Current Accounts*, and one of the clerks stood up to serve him.

Maigret wanted to inquire about the exact state of the Saint-Fiacres' fortune, and above all about any deposits or withdrawals in the last few weeks, or even the last few days, which might provide him with a clue.

But for a moment he said nothing, simply looking at the young man, who maintained a respectful attitude, without showing any sign of impatience.

'Emile Gautier, I suppose?'

He had seen him go past twice on a motorcycle but he had been unable to distinguish his features. What had revealed the bank clerk's identity to him was a striking resemblance to the steward of the château.

Not so much a resemblance of details as a resemblance of race. The same peasant origins: clear-cut features and big bones.

The same degree of evolution, more or less, revealed by a skin which was rather better cared-for than that of the farm workers, by intelligent eyes, and by a self-assurance which was that of an 'educated man'.

But Emile was not yet a townsman. His hair, although covered with brilliantine, remained rebellious, and stood up in a spike on the top of his head. His cheeks were pink, with that well-scrubbed look of country yokels on Sunday morning.

'That is correct.'

He was not at all flustered. Maigret was already sure that he was a model employee, in whom his manager had complete trust, and who would soon obtain promotion.

A black suit, made to measure, but by a local tailor, in a serge which would never wear out. His father wore a celluloid collar. He for his part wore a soft collar, but his tie was ready-tied.

'Do you know me?'

'No. I suppose that you are the police officer…'

'And I would like some information about the state of the Saint-Fiacre account.'

'That's a simple matter. I am in charge of that account as well as all the others.'

He was polite, well-mannered. At school, he must have been the teachers' favourite.

'Pass me the Saint-Fiacre account,' he said to a girl clerk sitting behind him.

And he let his gaze wander over a big sheet of yellow paper.

'Is it a summary that you want, the amount of the balance, or some general information?'

At least he was precise!

'Is the account in a healthy state?'

'Come this way, will you?... Somebody might hear us here...'

They went off to the far end of the room, although still separated by the oak counter.

'My father must have told you that the countess was very unmethodical... Time and again, I had to stop cheques which could not be met... Mind you, she didn't know that... She used to make out cheques without worrying about the state of her account... So that when I telephoned her to tell her, she would get into a panic... This morning again, three cheques were presented and I am obliged to return them... I have instructions to pay nothing out until...'

'The family is completely ruined?'

'Not really... Three farms out of five have been sold... The other two are mortgaged, like the château... The countess owned a block of flats in Paris, and that used to bring in a small income... But then, all of a sudden, she would throw everything off balance... I've always done the best I could... I've had bills delayed two or three times... My father...'

'Has advanced money, I know.'

'That's all I can tell you... At the moment, the credit balance stands at exactly seven hundred and seventy five francs... Mind you, last years land tax hasn't been paid, and the inspector issued a first warning last week...'

'Is Jean Métayer aware of all this?'

'Yes. Indeed, more than just aware of it.'

'What do you mean?'

'Nothing.'

'You don't think he's living in the clouds?'

But Emile Gautier discreetly avoided making any reply.

'Is that all you want to know?'

'Are there any other inhabitants of Saint-Fiacre who have an account at this branch?'

'No.'

'And nobody has been here today to transact any business? To cash a cheque, for example?'

'Nobody.'

'And you have been here all the time?'

'I haven't moved from this counter.'

He was in no way discomposed. He remained a good employee answering the questions of a government official with due courtesy.

'Would you like to see the manager? Not that he could tell you any more than I can…'

*

The lamps were lighting up. The high street was almost as crowded as in a big city, and there were long lines of cars in front of the cafés.

A procession went by: two camels and a young elephant carrying advertisements for a circus installed in the Place de la Victoire.

In the grocer's shop, Maigret caught sight of the red-haired boy's mother, who was still holding her son by the hand and who was buying tins of food.

A little farther on, he nearly bumped into Métayer and his lawyer, who were walking along with a self-important air, talking together. The lawyer was saying:

'…they are obliged to freeze it…'

They did not see the chief-inspector and they continued on their way towards the Comptoir d'Escompte.

People are bound to run into each other a dozen times in an afternoon in a town where all the activity is concentrated in a street five hundred yards long.

Maigret made his way to the *Journal de Moulins* building. The offices were at the front: a concrete façade and modern plateglass windows with a lavish display of press photographs and the latest news written out in blue pencil on long strips of paper.

'Manchuria. The Havas Agency reports that…'

But to reach the printing house, Maigret had to go down a dark cul-de-sac, guided by the din of the rotary press. In a dismal workshop some men in overalls were working at the tall stone-topped tables. In a glass cage at the far end there were the two linotypes with their machine-gun rattle.

'The foreman, please...'

He literally had to yell, on account of the thunder of the machines. The smell of ink took him by the throat. A short man in blue overalls who was arranging lines of type in a forme cupped his hand round his ear.

'Are you the foreman?'

'The stone hand.'

Maigret took out of his wallet the piece of paper which had killed the Comtesse de Saint-Fiacre. The man settled his steel-rimmed spectacles on his nose and looked at it obviously wondering what it was all about.

'Was this printed here?'

'What?'

Some people went past carrying piles of newspapers.

'I asked you whether this was printed here.'

'Come with me!'

It was better in the yard. It was cold there, but at least they could talk in more or less normal voices.

'What were you asking me?'

'Do you recognize this type?'

'It's Cheltenham nine point...'

'From here?'

'Nearly all linotypes are fitted with Cheltenham.'

'Are there any other linotypes at Moulins?'

'Not at Moulins... But at Nevers, Bourges, Châteauroux, Autun, and...'

'Do you notice anything special about this piece of paper?'

'It's only a proof... Whoever did it wanted to make it look like a newspaper cutting, didn't they?... Somebody once asked me to do the same thing, for a joke...'

'Ah!'

'At least fifteen years ago... In the days when we still set the newspaper by hand...'

'And the paper doesn't tell you anything?'

'Nearly all provincial newspapers have the same supplier. It's German paper... Will you excuse me?... I've got to lock the forme ... It's for the Nièvre edition...'

'Do you know Jean Métayer?'

The man shrugged his shoulders.

'What do you think of him?'

'If you take his word for it, he knows the business better than we do. He's a bit cracked... We let him mess about in the workshop because of the countess, who's a friend of the boss...'

'Does he know how to work a linotype?'

'Hmm!... He says so...'

'Well, would he be capable of setting this news item?'

'With a good two hours in front of him... And starting the same line over and over again...'

'Has he sat down at a linotype recently?'

'How do I know? He comes and goes all the time, bothering us with his photos... Excuse me... The train won't wait... And I haven't locked my forme...'

There was no point in persisting. Maigret nearly went back into the workshop, but the frantic activity inside discouraged him. Every minute counted for these people. Everybody was running around. The porters elbowed him aside as they dashed towards the gate.

All the same, he managed to button-hole an apprentice who was rolling a cigarette.

'What do you do with the lines of metal when they've been used?'

'We melt them down.'

'How often?'

'Every other day... Look, the metal pot is over there in the corner... Mind out!... It's hot...'

Maigret went out a little weary, perhaps a little discouraged. Darkness had fallen. The roadway was bright, brighter than usual, because of the cold. In front of a tailor's shop, a salesman who was stamping his feet and had a cold in the head was accosting the passers-by.

'A winter overcoat?... Fine English cloth from two hundred francs... Come inside! There's no obligation to buy...'

A little farther on, outside the Café de Paris where billiard balls could be heard colliding, Maigret saw the

Comte de Saint-Fiacre's yellow car.

He went in, looked around for the man, and, failing to see him, sat down on a bench. It was the smart café of the town. On the platform, three musicians were tuning their instruments and setting out the number of the next piece with the help of three pieces of cardboard each of which bore a figure.

There was some noise coming from the call-box.

'A beer,' Maigret told the waiter.

'Light or dark?'

But the chief-inspector was trying to hear the voice in the call-box. He failed to do so. Saint-Fiacre came out and the cashier asked him:

'How many calls?'

'Three.'

'To Paris, weren't they?... Three times eight is twenty-four...'

The count caught sight of Maigret, walked over to him quite naturally, and sat down beside him.

'You didn't tell me you were coming to Moulins... I'd have driven you over in my car... It's true it's an open car and in this weather...'

'Did you telephone Marie Vassilief?'

'No. I don't see why I should hide the truth from you... A beer for me too, waiter... Or rather no! Something hot... A grog... I telephoned a certain Monsieur Wolf... If you don't know him, others are bound to, at the Quai des Orfèvres... He's a money-lender... I've had recourse to him a few times... I've just been trying to...'

Maigret looked at him inquisitively.

'You asked him for some money?'

'At any rate of interest he liked! He refused, incidentally... Don't look at me like that! I dropped into the bank this afternoon...'

'At what time?'

'About three o'clock... That young man and his lawyer were just coming out...'

'You tried to withdraw some money?'

'I tried, yes! Now don't imagine that I want to arouse your pity! There are some people who get embarrassed by anything to do with money. I don't... Well, after sending the forty thousand to Paris and buying Marie Vassilief's ticket, I'm left with about three hundred francs in hand. I arrived here without expecting anything like this to happen... I've nothing but the clothes I'm wearing now... In Paris I owe a few thousand francs to the owner of my flat, and she won't send down any of my things...'

As he spoke he watched the balls rolling across the green cloth of the billiard-table. The players were humble youths of the town who cast envious glances now and then at the count's elegant suit.

'That's all! I would at least have liked to be in mourning for the funeral. There isn't a tailor round here who would give me credit for a couple of days. At the bank I was told that my mother's account was frozen and that in any case the credit balance amounted to just over seven hundred francs... And do you know who gave me that agreeable information?'

'Your steward's son.'

'Right!'

He drank a mouthful of scalding grog and fell silent still looking at the billiard-table. The orchestra struck up a Viennese waltz which was given a curious accompaniment by the sound of the balls.

It was hot. The light in the café was rather dim, in spite of the electric lamps. It was a typical provincial café, with only one concession to modern times, a notice advertising: *Cocktails 6 francs*.

Maigret puffed slowly at his pipe. He too gazed at the billiard-table, which was crudely lit by lamps with green cardboard shades. Now and then the door opened and after a few seconds a gust of ice air would reach him.

'Let's go and sit at the back...'

It was the voice of the lawyer from Bourges. He passed in front of the table where the two men were sitting, followed by Jean Métayer who was wearing white woollen gloves. But both of them were looking straight ahead. They did not see the first pair until they had sat down.

The two tables were practically facing each other. There was a slight flush in Métayer's cheeks, and his voice trembled as he gave his order:

'A chocolate.'

Saint-Fiacre commented jokingly in an undertone:

'That's right, darling!'

A woman sat down at an equal distance from the two tables, gave a friendly smile to the waiter, and murmured:

'The usual!'

He brought her a cherry brandy. She powdered her face and touched up her lipstick, fluttering her eyelids and wondering whether to direct her gaze towards one table or the other.

Was it burly, easy-going Maigret whom she ought to attack? Or was it the more elegant lawyer, who was already looking her up and down with a little smile?

'Well, there it is! I'll have to lead the mourners in grey!' murmured the Comte de Saint-Fiacre. 'After all, I can't very well borrow a black suit from the butler or put on one of my late father's tailcoats!'

Apart from the lawyer, who was interested by the woman, everybody was looking at the nearest billiard table.

There were three tables in all. Two were occupied. There were a few cheers just as the musicians were finishing their number. And straight away, the sounds of glasses and saucers could be heard again.

'Three ports!'

The door kept opening and shutting. The cold air came in, and was gradually absorbed by the prevailing warmth.

The lamps over the third billiard-table lit up at a gesture from the cashier, who had the electric switches behind her.

'Thirty points!'

And speaking to the waiter, the same voice added:

'A quarter of Vichy... No! A strawberry Vittel...'

It was Emile Gautier, who was carefully coating the tip of his cue with blue chalk. Then he put the marker at zero. His companion was the assistant manager of the bank, a man ten years older, with a waxed moustache.

It was only at the third stroke — which he muffed — that the young man caught sight of Maigret. He greeted him, looking a little embarrassed. After that, he was so absorbed in the game that he no longer had the time to see anybody at all.

'Of course, if you're not afraid of the cold, I can give you a lift in my car,' said Maurice de Saint-Fiacre. 'May I offer you a drink? One apéritif more or less won't ruin me, you know...'

'Waiter!' Jean Métayer called out. 'Get me Bourges seventeen on the telephone!'

His father's number! A little later, he shut himself up in the call-box.

Maigret went on smoking. He had ordered another beer. And the woman, possibly because he was the fattest, of the four men, had finally chosen him. Every time he turned in her direction, she smiled at him as if they were old acquaintances.

She could not have known that he was thinking about 'the old girl', as the son himself called her, who was laid out on the first floor of the château back at Saint-Fiacre, with the peasants filing in front of her and nudging one another in the ribs.

But it was not in those circumstances that he was picturing her. He was seeing her at a time when there were no cars yet in front of the Café de Paris and nobody drank cocktails there.

In the park of the château, a tall lithe thorough-bred, like the heroine of a popular novel, beside the baby-carriage being pushed along by the nursemaid...

Maigret was just a youngster whose hair, like that of Emile Gautier and the red-haired choirboy, insisted on standing up in a spike on the top of his head.

Wasn't he jealous of the count that morning when the couple left for Aix-les-Bains in a motor-car (one of the first he had seen) full of furs and scent? The face behind the veil was invisible. The count was wearing huge goggles. It was all like an heroic elopement. And the nanny held the baby's hand and waved it in farewell...

Now they were sprinkling the old woman with holy water and the bedroom smelt of candles.

Emile Gautier circled round the billiard-table, played a fancy shot and counted solemnly in an undertone:

'Seven...'

He bent down again. He pulled off another shot. The assistant manager with the waxed moustache said in a sour voice:

'Magnificent!'

Two men eyed each other across the green cloth: Jean Métayer, to whom the smiling lawyer was talking incessantly, and the Comte de Saint-Fiacre, who stopped the waiter with an elegant gesture.

'The same again!'

Maigret, for his part, was thinking now of a boy-scout whistle. A splendid bronze whistle with two notes, such as he had never possessed himself.

CHAPTER EIGHT

The Invitation to Dinner

'Another telephone call!' sighed Maigret as he saw Métayer stand up once more.

He followed him with his eyes, noting that he did not go into either the call-box or the toilets. Moreover, the plump lawyer was now sitting on the very edge of his chair like somebody who is wondering whether to get up. He was looking at the Comte de Saint-Fiacre. You might almost have thought that he was about to venture a smile.

Was it Maigret who was in the way? In any case, this scene reminded the chief-inspector of certain incidents in his youth: three or four friends in a café together, and two women at the other end of the room. The discussions, the hesitations, the waiter you called to entrust him with a note...

The lawyer was in the same state of nerves. And the woman sitting two tables away from Maigret misinterpreted it and thought that it was she who was responsible. She smiled, opened her handbag, and powdered her face.

'I'll be back in a moment,' the chief-inspector said to his companion.

He crossed the room in the direction Métayer had taken, and saw a door he had not noticed before which led into a wide corridor with a red carpet. At the far end there was a counter with a big book on it, a telephone switchboard and a girl receptionist. Métayer was there talking to the latter. He left her just as Maigret came forward.

'Thank you, Mademoiselle... You say it's in the first street on the left?'

He made no attempt to hide from the chief-inspector. He did not seem to be embarrassed by his presence. On the contrary! And there was a gleam of joy in his eyes.

'I didn't know that this was a hotel,' Maigret said to the girl.

'You're staying somewhere else, then?... That's a pity... Because this is really the best hotel in Moulins...'

'Haven't you had the Comte de Saint-Fiacre staying here?'

She nearly burst out laughing. Then she became serious all of a sudden.

'What's he done?' she asked with a certain anxiety. 'That's the second time in five minutes that...'

'Where did you send the previous inquirer?'

'He wanted to know whether the Comte de Saint-Fiacre went out during Saturday night... I couldn't tell him, because the night porter hasn't arrived yet... Then the gentleman asked if we had a garage and he's gone over there...'

So all that Maigret had to do was follow Métayer!

'And the garage is on the first street on the left,' he said, a little annoyed in spite of everything.

'That's right. It's open all night.'

Jean Métayer had certainly lost no time for when Maigret reached the street in question, he was coming out of the garage, whistling to himself. The attendant was eating a snack in one corner.

'It's for the same thing that gentleman has just asked you about... The yellow car... Did anybody come and take it out during Saturday night?'

There was already a ten-franc note on the table. Maigret put down another.

'Yes, about midnight.'

'And it was brought back?'

'About three o'clock in the morning...'

'Was it dirty?'

'Not really... The weather's been dry lately, you know.'

'There were two people, weren't there? A man and a woman...'

'No! A man by himself.'

'Short and thin?'

'Not a bit of it! A big healthy fellow.'

Obviously the Comte de Saint-Fiacre...

*

When Maigret went back into the café, the orchestra was playing again, and the first thing he noticed was that there was nobody left in the corner where Métayer and his companion had been sitting.

True, a few seconds later he spotted the lawyer sitting in his own seat, next to the Comte de Saint-Fiacre. At the sight of the chief-inspector he got up from the bench.

'Excuse me. No, do sit down here again, please...'

He did not go away, however, but sat down on the chair opposite. He was very nervous, with flushed cheeks, like a man in a hurry to be done with a difficult task. His eyes seemed to be searching for Jean Métayer who was nowhere to be seen.

'I want you to understand, Chief-Inspector... I wouldn't have taken the liberty of going to the château... That goes without saying... But since we have been brought together by chance on neutral territory, if I may say so...'

And he gave a forced smile. After every sentence, he gave the impression of bowing to the other two men and thanking them for their approval.

'In a situation as painful as this, there is no point in complicating matters further, as I told my client, by being unduly sensitive... Monsieur Jean Métayer understands this perfectly well... And when you arrived, Chief-Inspector, I was saying to the Comte de Saint-Fiacre that we asked for nothing better than to come to an understanding...'

Maigret growled:

'Well, I'll be damned!'

And he thought to himself:

'You, my good fellow, will be lucky if in the next five minutes you don't get the hand of the gentleman you're talking to so suavely right across your face...'

The billiard-players went on circling round the tables. As for the woman, she stood up, leaving her handbag on the table, and went off towards the back of the room.

'There's another who's making a big mistake. She's just had a bright idea. Perhaps Métayer left the room so that he could speak to her outside without being seen?... So off she goes to look for him...'

Maigret was right. With one hand on her hip, the woman was walking up and down, looking for the young man.

The lawyer was still talking.

'There are some very complicated interests involved and we for our part are ready...'

'To do what?' Saint-Fiacre broke in.

'But... to...'

He forgot it was not his glass which was in front of him, and he drank out of Maigret's to keep himself in countenance.

'I know that perhaps this isn't the best place... Or the best moment... But remember that we know better than anybody else the financial situation of...'

'My mother! Go on...'

'My client, with a tact which does him honour, decided to move into the inn...'

The poor devil of a lawyer! His words, now that Maurice de Saint-Fiacre was gazing fixedly at him, were coming from his throat one by one, as if they needed to be dragged out.

'You do understand, don't you, Chief-Inspector?... We know that there's a will in the solicitor's keeping... Don't worry! Monsieur le Comte's rights are respected... But Jean Métayer is a beneficiary all the same... The financial situation is rather complicated... My client is the only one who knows all about it...'

Maigret admired Saint-Fiacre, who was managing to maintain an almost angelic composure. There was even a faint smile on his lips.

'Yes! He was a model secretary!' he said without any apparent irony.

'You must remember that he comes from a very good

family and has had an excellent upbringing. I know his parents... His father...'

'Let's get back to the fortune, shall we?'

It was too good to be true. The lawyer could scarcely believe his ears.

'Will you allow me to offer you both drinks?... Waiter!... The same again, gentlemen?... As for me, I'll have a lemon Raphaël...'

Two tables away, the woman had returned glumly to her seat, for she had failed to find Métayer and had resigned herself to tackling the billiard-players.

'I was saying that my client is prepared to help you... There are certain persons whom he distrusts... He'll tell you himself that some rather shady operations have been carried out by people not over-burdened with scruples... Anyway...'

This was the hardest part... In spite of everything, the lawyer had to swallow hard before going on...

'You've found the château coffers empty... But it's essential for your late lamented mother...'

'Your late lamented mother!' Maigret repeated admiringly.

'Your late lamented mother,' the lawyer continued without batting an eyelid... 'What was I saying?... Oh, yes! That the funeral should be worthy of the Saint-Fiacres... Pending the time when matters can be arranged in everybody's best interests, my client will see to it that...'

'In other words, he will advance the money necessary for the funeral... Is that what you mean?'

Maigret did not dare to look at the count. He fixed his gaze on Emile Gautier who was making another break and waited tensely for the explosion which was about to take place beside him.

But no! Saint-Fiacre had stood up. He was speaking to a new arrival.

'Do sit down at our table, Monsieur.'

It was Métayer who had just come in and to whom the lawyer had doubtless explained by signs that everything was going well.

'A lemon Raphaël too?... Waiter!'

Applause broke out in the room, because the orchestral item was over. Once the noise had died down, the situation was more embarrassing than before, for voices sounded louder. There was now only the click of the ivory balls to break the silence.

'I told Monsieur le Comte, who understands perfectly...'

'Who is the Raphaël for?'

'You came from Saint-Fiacre, didn't you, gentlemen?... In that case, my car is at your disposal to take you back... You'll find it rather a tight fit... I'm already giving a lift to the chief-inspector... How much, waiter?... No, please!... It's my round...'

But the lawyer stood up and was pressing a hundred franc note into the hand of the waiter, who asked:

'The lot?'

'Yes, yes!'

And the count said with his most gracious smile:

'It's really too charming of you.'

Emile Gautier, who watched the four of them go off, making way for each other at the door, was so surprised that he forgot to go on with his break.

The lawyer found himself in front, next to the count, who was driving. Behind, there was only just enough room for Jean Métayer beside Maigret.

It was cold. The headlamps were not bright enough. The car had no silencer, and this made conversation impossible.

Did Maurice de Saint-Fiacre usually drive at this speed? Or was he taking his little revenge? The fact remains that he covered the fifteen miles from Moulins to the château in less than a quarter of an hour, taking the bends on the brake, speeding through the darkness, and once only narrowly missing a cart which was in the middle of the road and which forced him to drive up on the bank.

Their faces were cut by the wind. Maigret had to grip the collar of his overcoat in both hands. They drove through the village without slowing down. It was as much as they could do to catch a glimpse of the light in the inn and then the church spire.

A sudden stop, which threw the occupants of the car

against one another. They were at the foot of the steps. The servants could be seen eating in the basement kitchen. Somebody was roaring with laughter.

'Will you allow me, gentlemen, to invite you to dinner?...'

Métayer and the lawyer looked at each other in hesitation. The count pushed them inside with a friendly tap on the shoulder.

'Come along now... It's my turn, isn't it?'

And in the hall be added:

'Unfortunately it won't be very gay...'

Maigret would have liked to have a few words with him in private, but the other did not give him time and opened the door of the smoking-room.

'Will you excuse me for a few moments?... Have an apéritif while you're waiting... I've some orders to give... you know where the bottles are, don't you, Monsieur Métayer?... Is there anything drinkable left?...'

He pressed an electric bell-push. The butler was a long time coming, and arrived with his mouth full and his napkin in his hand.

Saint-Fiacre snatched it from him with a swift gesture.

'Send for the steward... Then get me the presbytery and the doctor's house on the telephone.'

And to the others he said:

'Will you excuse me?'

The telephone was in the hall, which, like the rest of the château, was poorly lit. Since there was no electricity at Saint-Fiacre, the château had to provide its own current and the generator was too weak. The bulbs, instead of giving off a white light, revealed reddish filaments, as in certain trams when they come to a halt.

The hall was full of great patches of dark shadow in which it was almost impossible to make out any objects.

'Hullo... Yes, I insist... Thank you, Doctor...'

The lawyer and Maigret were uneasy. But as yet they did not dare to admit their uneasiness to each other. It was Jean Métayer who broke the silence, to ask the chief-inspector:

'What can I offer you?... I don't think there's any port

left... But there's some whisky...'

All the ground-floor rooms were in a row, separated by wide open doors. The dining-room first. Then the drawing-room. Then the smoking-room where the three men were waiting. And finally the library where the young man went to get the drinks.

'Hullo... Yes... Can I count on you?... See you soon...'

The count made some more calls, then walked along the corridor running alongside all the rooms, and went upstairs, where his footsteps stopped in the dead woman's bedroom.

Other, heavier footsteps, in the hall. A knock on the door, which opened straight away. It was the steward.

'You wanted to see me?'

But then he noticed that the count was not there, looked in astonishment at the three people in the room, and beat a retreat, questioning the butler as he arrived outside.

'Soda?' asked Jean Métayer.

And the lawyer, full of good will, began with a little cough:

'We both of us have queer professions, Chief-Inspector... Have you been in the police force a long time?... I've been at the bar for nearly fifteen years... So you can imagine that I've been mixed up in the most astonishing cases... Good health!... Here's to you, Monsieur Métayer... I'm glad for your sake about the turn events are taking...'

The count could be heard in the corridor saying:

'Well, you must find some! Telephone your son, who is playing billiards in the Café de Paris at Moulins... He'll bring along what's necessary.'

The door opened. The count came in.

'You've found something to drink?... Aren't there any cigars here?'

And he looked inquiringly at Métayer.

'Cigarettes... I only smoke...'

The young man did not finish what he was saying, but turned his head away in embarrassment.

'I'll bring you some.'

'Gentlemen, I hope you'll excuse the very modest meal

that you're going to eat. We are a long way from the town and...'

'Come,' said the lawyer, on whom the whisky was beginning to take effect. 'I'm sure it will be excellent... Is that a portrait of a relative of yours?'

He pointed to a portrait on the wall of the drawing-room, of a man dressed in a stiff frock coat, his neck imprisoned in a starched collar.

'That is my father.'

'Yes, you take after him.'

The servant showed in Doctor Bouchardon who looked around him distrustfully, as if he suspected a drama of some sort. But Saint-Fiacre received him gaily.

'Come in, Doctor... I presume you know Jean Métayer... His lawyer... A charming man, as you'll see... As for the chief-inspector...'

The two men shook hands and a few moments later the doctor growled in Maigret's ear:

'What have you cooked up here?'

'I haven't... It's him!'

To keep himself in countenance, the lawyer kept going to the little table where he had put his glass, and he did not realize that he was drinking more than usual.

'This old château is an absolute gem... And what a setting for a film!... That's what I was saying only the other day to the Public Prosecutor at Bourges, who loathes the cinema... As long as they go on shooting films in settings which...'

He was talking excitedly, and constantly trying to buttonhole somebody.

As for the count, he had gone over to Métayer and was showing a disturbing affability towards him.

'The saddest thing here is the long winter evenings, isn't it?... *In my time,* I remember that my father too was in the habit of inviting the doctor and the priest... They weren't the same ones as now... But the doctor was already a sceptic and the conversation always ended up by turning to philosophical subjects... And talk of the devil...'

It was the priest, with rings under his eyes, and an embarrassed expression, who did not know what to say and was standing hesitantly in the doorway.

'Excuse me for being late, but...'

Through the open doors they could see two servants laying the table in the dining-room.

'Do offer Monsieur le Curé something to drink...'

'It was to Métayer that the count was speaking. Maigret noticed that he himself was not drinking, but the lawyer, for his part, was well on the way to being drunk. He was explaining to the chief-inspector:

'A little diplomacy, that's all! Or, if you like, knowledge of human nature... They're about the same age, and both from good families... Can you think of any reasons why they should have failed to hit it off?... Aren't their interests related?... The curious thing...' He laughed. He took another drink of whisky.

'...is that it happened accidentally in a café... There's a lot to be said for those good old provincial cafés where you feel as though you were at home...'

They had heard the sound of a motor outside. A little later the count went into the dining-room, where the steward was, and they caught a few words:

'Both of you, yes!... If you like!... That's an order!'

The telephone rang. The count had rejoined his guests. The butler came into the smoking-room.

'The undertaker... He wants to know when he can bring the coffin...'

'Whenever he likes.'

'Very well, Monsieur le Comte.'

And the latter said almost gaily:

'Shall we go into dinner?... I've had the last bottles in the cellar brought up... After you, Monsieur le Curé... We're a little short of feminine company, but...'

Maigret tried to hold him back by his sleeve. The other looked him in the eyes with a hint of impatience, then disengaged himself abruptly and went into the dining-room.

'I've invited Monsieur Gautier, our steward, and his son, a young man with a promising future, to share our meal...'

Maigret looked at the bank clerk's hair, and, in spite of

his uneasiness, he could not help smiling. The hair was wet. Before coming to the château, the young man had checked his parting, washed his face and hands, and changed his tie.

'Let's sit down, gentlemen.'

And the chief-inspector could have sworn that a sob rose in Saint-Fiacre's throat. It went unnoticed because the doctor involuntarily distracted everyone's attention by seizing a dusty bottle and murmuring:

'So you still have some Hospice de Beaune 1896?... I thought that the last bottles had been bought by the Restaurant Larue and that...'

The rest was drowned by the sound of the chairs being moved. The priest, his hands folded on the table-cloth, his head bent, his lips moving, said grace.

Maigret surprised Saint-Fiacre's gaze fixed intently on him.

CHAPTER NINE

A Scene from Scott

The dining-room was the part of the château which had lost the least of its character, thanks to the carved panelling which lined the walls up to the ceiling. Moreover, the room was high rather than large, and this made it not only solemn but gloomy, for guests had the impression of eating at the bottom of a well.

On each panel there were two electric lamps, imitation candles which even had artificial beads of wax.

In the middle of the table, there was a real candle holder with seven branches and seven real candles.

The Comte de Saint-Fiacre and Maigret were sitting face to face, but could only see each other if they strained their necks to look over the flames.

On the count's right, the priest. On his left, Doctor Bouchardon. Chance had placed Jean Métayer at one side of the table, the lawyer at the other side. And next to the chief-inspector there was the steward on one hand, Emile Gautier on the other.

The butler occasionally advanced into the light to serve the guests, but as soon as he took two paces back he was lost in the shadows, and nothing could be seen of him but his white-gloved hands.

'Wouldn't you think we were in one of Walter Scott's novels?'

It was the count who was speaking, in a casual voice. And yet Maigret pricked up his ears, for he sensed an underlying meaning, guessed something was going to begin.

They were only at the *hors d'œuvre*. On the table, all mixed up, there were a score of bottles of red and white wine, clarets and burgundies, and each person helped himself.

'There's only one detail that jars,' Maurice de Saint-Fiacre went on. 'In Walter Scott, the poor old girl upstairs would suddenly start screaming...'

For a few seconds, everybody stopped eating and they felt something like a draught of icy air pass by.

'Incidentally, Gautier, has she been left alone?'

The steward swallowed hurriedly, and stammered:

'She... Yes... There's nobody in Madame la Comtesse's room...'

'It can't be very cheerful.'

At that moment a foot pressed hard against Maigret's, but the chief-inspector could not guess whose it was. The table was a round one. Each person could reach the centre. And Maigret's uncertainty was due to continue, for during the evening the little kicks would follow one another with increasing frequency.

'Has she received many callers today?'

It was embarrassing to hear him talking like that of his mother, as if she were alive, and the chief-inspector noticed that Jean Métayer was so upset that he stopped eating and gazed in front of him with eyes which looked more and more haggard.

'Nearly all the local farmers,' replied the steward's deep voice.

Whenever the butler noticed a hand reaching out towards a bottle he would step forward noiselessly. His black arm, with a white glove at the end of it, would appear. The liquid would flow. And all this was done so silently and skilfully that the lawyer, who was already more than a little drunk, admiringly set the operation going three or four times.

He followed in fascination that arm, which did not even brush against his shoulder. In the end he could not contain himself any longer.

'Marvellous! Butler, you're a wizard, and if I could afford a château, I'd take you into my service...'

'Well, the château will be up for sale soon, and going cheap...'

This time Maigret frowned as he looked at Saint-Fiacre who had spoken in a strange voice which was casual yet a little theatrical. In spite of everything, there was something irritating about these remarks. Were his nerves finally getting on edge? Was this a sinister form of humour?

'Chicken in half-mourning,' he announced as the butler brought in a dish of chicken served with truffles.

And the count went straight on, in the same lighthearted voice:

'The murderer is going to eat some chicken in half-mourning, like the rest of us!'

The butler's arm slipped backwards and forwards between the guests. The steward's voice said in a tone of comic horror:

'Oh, Monsieur le Comte...'

'Why yes! What is so extraordinary about that? The murderer is here, that's certain! But don't let that take away your appetite, Monsieur le Curé! The corpse is in the house too, and that isn't preventing us from eating... A little wine, Albert, for Monsieur le Curé!'

The foot brushed against Maigret's ankle again. The chief-inspector dropped his napkin and bent down to look under the table, but too late. When he straightened up again, the count, without stopping eating his chicken was saying:

'I mentioned Walter Scott just now because of the atmosphere in this room, but also and above all because of the murderer... After all, this is a funeral wake... The funeral takes place tomorrow morning and in all probability we shall stay together until then... It must at least be said to Monsieur Métayer's credit that he has filled the spirits cupboard with some excellent whisky...'

Maigret tried to remember how much Saint-Fiacre had drunk. Less in any case than the lawyer, who exclaimed:

'Yes, excellent! There's no doubt about that! But then my client is the grandson of some vine-growers...

'As I was saying... But what was I saying?... Oh, yes!... Fill up Monsieur le Curé's glass, Albert...

'As I was saying, since the murderer's here, the others find themselves, so to speak, cast in the role of justicers... And that is what makes our dinner party resemble something out of Walter Scott...

'Though you must remember that the murderer in question isn't really in any danger. Isn't that so, Chief-Inspector?... It isn't a crime to slip a piece of paper into a missal...

'While we are on the subject, Doctor... When did my mother's last attack take place?'

The doctor wiped his mouth, and looked around him with a disgruntled expression.

'Three months ago, when you wired from Berlin that you were ill in a hotel room and that...'

'I wanted some cash! That's it!'

'I observed at that time that the next violent shock would be fatal.'

'So that... Let's see... Who knew that?... Jean Métayer, of course... I myself, obviously... Old Gautier, who is almost one of the family... And finally you and Monsieur le Curé...'

He drank a whole glass of Pouilly and pulled a face.

'This is just to explain to you that logically speaking we can nearly all be considered as suspects... If the idea amuses you...'

It was as if he were deliberately choosing the most shocking words he could find.

'If the idea amuses you, we can go on to examine the case of each person separately... Let us begin with Monsieur le Curé... Had he anything to gain by killing my mother?... You are going to see that the answer is not as simple as it may appear... I leave the question of money on one side...'

The priest was choking with indignation and hesitating whether to leave the table.

'Monsieur le Curé had nothing to hope for in that respect... But he is a mystic, an apostle, almost a saint... He has an odd parishioner whose conduct is a source of scandal... Sometimes she rushes to church like the most fervent of the faithful, but at other times she brings down scandal on Saint-Fiacre... No, don't make that face, Métayer... We're all men here... We are, if you like, engaged in advanced psychology...

'Monsieut le Curé has such a fierce faith that it might push him to extreme measures. Remember the times when sinners were burnt to purify them... My mother is at Mass... She has just taken communion... She is in a state of grace... But very soon, she is going to fall back into her sinful ways and be a source of scandal once more...

'Whereas if she dies a holy death, there in her pew...'

'But...' began the priest, who had big tears in his eyes and who was holding on to the table to keep calm.

'Don't take offence, Monsieur le Curé... We are simply talking psychology. I want to show you that the most austere people can be suspected of the worst outrages... If we go on now to the doctor, I'm in a more difficult position... He isn't a saint... And, fortunately for him he isn't even a *savant*... For if he were, he might have put the piece of paper in the missal as an experiment to test the resistance of a weak heart...'

The sound of forks had slowed down to such an extent that it had nearly dropped to nothing. And the guests' eyes were fixed, uneasy, even haggard. Only the butler was unmoved, and went on filling the glasses in silence, with the regularity of a metronome.

'You look gloomy, gentlemen... Is it really not possible for us, as intelligent people, to broach certain subjects?

'Serve the next course, Albert... So we put the doctor on one side, seeing that we cannot regard him as a *savant* or a researcher... He is saved by his mediocrity...'

He gave a little laugh and turned to old Gautier.

'Your turn now... A more complicated case... There are two possibilities... First, you are the model steward, the upright man who devotes his life to his masters and the château where he was born and bred... You weren't born and bred here, but that doesn't matter... In this case, your position isn't clear. The Saint-Fiacres have only one male heir... And the family fortune is rapidly disappearing bit by bit under the nose of that heir... The countess is behaving like a lunatic... Isn't it time to save what's left?

'Now that's as noble as anything in Walter Scott, and your case resembles that of Monsieur le Curé...

'But there's the opposite hypothesis to be considered too! You are a scoundrel and for years you've been taking advantage of your masters' weakness... When a mortgage is raised, it's you who take it up... Now don't lose your temper, Gautier... The Curé didn't lose his, did he?... And I haven't finished yet...

'You are practically the real owner of the château...'

'Monsieur le Comte!'

'Don't you know how to play the game? Because I tell you we are playing a game! We are playing, if you like, at all being chief-inspectors like your neighbour... The time has come when the countess has her back to the wall, everything will have to be sold, and she will find out that it's you who have profited from the situation... Wouldn't it be better for the countess to die conveniently, something which would also save her from making the acquaintance of poverty?'

'And, turning towards the butler, a shadow in the shadows, a demon with two chalk-white hands, he said:

'Albert!... Go and fetch my father's revolver... That is, of course, if it's still here...'

He poured out some wine for himself and for his two neighbours, then passed the bottle to Maigret.

'Will you do the serving on your side?... Whew! We've almost got half-way through our little game... But let's wait for Albert... Monsieur Métayer... You aren't drinking...'

They heard a strangled 'No, thank you.'

'How about you, Maître?'

The latter, his mouth full, his tongue coated, replied:

'No, thank you! No, thank you! I've everything I need... I say , you'd make a wonderful Advocate General, you know...'

He was the only one there to laugh, to eat with indecent gusto, and to drink glass after glass, sometimes of burgundy, sometimes of claret, without even noticing the difference.

They heard the tinny bell of the church clock strike ten. Albert handed a heavy revolver to the count and the latter checked that it was loaded.

'Perfect!... I'll put it here, in the middle of the table... You will notice, gentlemen, that as this is a round table, it is at an equal distance from each person... We have examined three cases... Now we are going to examine three more... But first of all, will you allow me to make a prophecy?... Well, to remain in the Walter Scott tradition, I foretell that before midnight my mother's murderer will be dead!'

Maigret darted a sharp glance at him across the table, and saw a pair of eyes which were shining brightly, as if Saint-Fiacre were drunk. At the same moment a foot touched his again.

'And now I'll go on... But do eat your salad... I come now to your neighbour, Chief-Inspector, on your left, that is to say Emile Gautier... A serious, hard-working young fellow, who, as they say at school speech-days, has made his way by sheer merit and hard work...

'Could he have killed my mother?

'One hypothesis: he worked hand in glove with his father, for his father...

'He goes every day to Moulins... He knows the financial situation of the family better than anybody else... He has every opportunity of seeing a printer or a linotype operator...

'Let's go on... Second hypothesis... You'll forgive me for calling you, Métayer, if you don't know already, that you had a rival... Emile Gautier is no beauty... All the same, he preceded you in the position which you occupied with such tact...

'That was a few years ago... Did he begin to entertain certain hopes?... Had he succeeded, since then, in stirring my mother's tender heart once more?

'The fact remains that he was her official protégé, and that he was entitled to conceive all sorts of ambitions...

'You came... You conquered...

'Why not kill the countess and at the same time throw suspicion on you?...'

Maigret's toes stirred uncomfortably in his shoes. All this was horrible, sacrilegious! Saint-Fiacre was talking as excitedly as a drunkard. And the others were wondering whether they could stick it out to the end, whether they should stay and endure this scene or get up and go.

'You can see that we are faced with a complete mystery… Mind you, the countess herself, up there, if she could speak, would be unable to give us the solution to the problem. The murderer is the only person who knows about his crime… Eat up, Emile Gautier… Above all, don't let this upset you like your father, who seems to be on the verge of fainting…

'Albert!… There must be a few bottles of wine left in the bin somewhere…

'Your turn now, young man!'

And he turned with a smile to face Métayer, who jumped to his feet.

'Monsieur, my lawyer…'

'Sit down, dammit! And don't make us think that at your age you can't take a joke…'

Maigret was watching him while he was saying this and he noticed that the count's forehead was covered with big beads of sweat.

'None of us is trying to make himself out to be better than he is, is he? Good! I see that you are beginning to understand. Take some fruit. It's excellent for the digestion…'

It was unbearably hot and Maigret wondered who had switched off the electric lamps, leaving only the candles on the table burning.

'Your case is so simple that it's positively uninteresting… You were playing a not very amusing part, which nobody is willing to play for very long… Still, you were in my mother's will… That will risked being changed at any moment… A sudden death and it would be all over! You would be free! You would harvest the fruits of your… of your sacrifice… And, dammit all, you would be able to marry some young girl whom you must have waiting for you back home…'

'I beg your pardon!' the lawyer protested, so comically

that Maigret could not help smiling.

'Shut your trap! Drink up!'

Saint-Fiacre was categorical! He was drunk, there could no longer be any shadow of a doubt about that! He was displaying that eloquence peculiar to drunkards, a mixture of brutality and subtlety, of facile eloquence and blurred speech.

'I'm the only one left!'

He called Albert.

'Look, old chap, go upstairs... It must be so dismal for my mother, staying all alone...'

Maigret saw the butler glance inquiringly at old Gautier, who gave a little nod.

'Just a moment! Bring us a few bottles first... The whisky too... Nobody objects to a little informality, I imagine...'

He looked at his watch.

'Ten past eleven... I've been talking such a lot that I haven't heard your church clock, Monsieur le Curé...'

And, as the butler moved the revolver slightly while putting the whisky decanters on the table, the count said:

'Careful, Albert!... It must remain at an equal distance from each of us...'

He waited until the door was closed.

'There!' he said. 'I'm the only one left! I won't be telling you anything new when I say I've never done anything worthwhile. Except perhaps in my father's lifetime... But seeing that he died when I was only seventeen...

'I'm on the rocks... Everybody knows that... The popular weeklies make no secret of the fact...

'I sign dud cheques... I try my mother for a touch as often as I can... I invent the illness in Berlin to get a few thousand francs...

'You will notice that that was the missal trick on a smaller scale...

'Now, what's happening?... The money which is due to come to me some day is being spent by little swines like Métayer... Excuse me, old fellow... This is still transcendental psychology...

'Soon there'll be nothing left... I telephone to my mother, at a time when a dud cheque is just about to land me in prison... She refuses to pay... There are witnesses who can testify to that...

'Besides, if this goes on, there'll be nothing left of the family fortune in a few weeks...

'Two hypotheses, as in the case of Emile Gautier. The first...'

Never in his whole career had Maigret felt so uncomfortable. And it was probably the first time he had had the definite impression of being incapable of dealing with the situation. Events were leaving him behind. Now and then he thought he understood, and the next moment a phrase of Saint-Fiacre's would call everything in question again.

And all the time there was that insistent foot pressing against his.

'Let's change the subject!' suggested the lawyer, who was now completely drunk.

'Gentlemen,' began the priest.

'I beg your pardon! You must bear with me until midnight at least! I was saying that the first hypothesis...

'Damn! Now you've made me lose the thread of my ideas...'

And, as if to help him find it again, he poured himself a full glass of whisky.

'I know that my mother is very tender-hearted. I slip the piece of paper into her missal, in order to frighten her and thus soften her up, with the intention of coming back the next day to ask her for the necessary sum, in the hope of finding her more sympathetic...

'But there's the second hypothesis! Why shouldn't I too want to kill her?

'Not all the Saint-Fiacre fortune has gone. There's a little money left. And in my position a little money, however little, may make all the difference.

'I am vaguely aware that Métayer is mentioned in the will. But a murderer can't inherit...

'Isn't he the man everyone will suspect of the crime? He who spends part of his time in a printing-house at Moulins? He who, living in the château, can slip the piece of paper into the missal whenever he likes?

'Didn't I arrive at Moulins on Saturday afternoon? And

didn't I wait there with my mistress, for the result of this operation?'

He stood up, his glass in his hand.

'Your good health, gentlemen... You look gloomy... The whole of my mother's poor life, these last few years, was gloomy... Isn't that so, Monsieur le Curé?... It's only fair that her last night should be accompanied by a little gaiety...'

He looked the chief-inspector in the eyes.

'Your good health, Monsieur Maigret!'

He was making fun of somebody, but of whom? Of himself? Of everybody else?

Maigret felt that he was confronted by a force against which there was nothing to be done. Certain individuals, at a given moment in their lives, have an hour of fulfilment like this, an hour during which they are, as it were, situated above the rest of mankind and above themselves.

Such is the case of the gambler who, at Monte Carlo, wins all the time, whatever he does. Such is the case of the hitherto unknown member of the Opposition who, with a speech he makes, brings down the government, and is the first to be surprised, since all that he wanted was a few lines in the parliamentary reports.

Maurice de Saint-Fiacre was living this hour. There was a strength in him which he himself had never guessed at before, and the others could do nothing but bow their heads.

But wasn't it drink which was carrying him away like that?

'Let's go back to the starting-point of our conversation, gentlemen, seeing that it isn't midnight yet... I have said that my mother's murderer was here among us... I have proved that he could be myself or any one of you, except perhaps the chief-inspector and the doctor.

'I'm not even sure of that...

'And I have prophesied his death...

'Will you allow me to play the hypothesis game once again? He knows that the Law is powerless against him. But he also knows that there are, or rather will be, a few persons, six at least, who know about his crime...

'There again, we are faced with several solutions...

'The first is the most romantic, the most consistent with the spirit of Walter Scott...

'But here I must open a fresh parenthesis... What is the distinguishing feature of this crime?... It is that there are at least five individuals who were revolving around the countess... Five individuals who stood to benefit by her death, and each of whom may have envisaged the means of bringing about that death...

'Only one dared... Only one killed...

'Well, gentlemen, I can easily imagine that individual taking advantage of this dinner-party to revenge himself on the others... He is done for!... Why not blow us all up?'

And Maurice de Saint-Fiacre, with a disarming smile, looked at each guest in turn.

'Isn't it fascinating? The old dining-room of the old château, the candles, the table loaded with bottles... Then, at midnight, death... You will note that at the same time all possibilities of scandal would be averted... Tomorrow, people would find us and be completely baffled...They would talk of an accident or of an anarchist plot...'

The lawyer stirred on his chair and glanced anxiously around him, into the darkness which began less than a yard from the table.

'If I may venture to recall that I am a doctor,' growled Bouchardon, 'I would recommend a cup of strong black coffee for everybody...'

'And I,' the priest said slowly, 'would remind you that there is a dead person in the house...'

Saint-Fiacre hesitated for a moment. A foot brushed against Maigret's ankle, and he bent down quickly, but once again too late.

'I asked you to give me until midnight... I have only examined the first hypothesis... There is another... The murderer, hunted down, panic-stricken, blows out his brains... *But I don't think he will do that...*'

'For God's sake let's go into the smoking-room!' yelped the lawyer, standing up and hanging on to the back of his chair to avoid falling.

'Finally, there is a third hypothesis... Somebody who

cares for the honour of the family comes to the murderer's help... Wait a moment... The question is more complicated than that... Mustn't a scandal be avoided at all costs?... Mustn't the culprit be *helped* to commit suicide?

'The revolver is there, gentlemen, at an equal distance from every hand... It is ten to twelve... I repeat that at midnight the murderer will be dead...'

And this time he spoke so emphatically that nobody said a word. Everyone held his breath.

'The victim is up there, watched over by a servant... The murderer is here, surrounded by seven people...'

Saint-Fiacre drained his glass at one draught and the anonymous foot went on brushing against Maigret's foot.

'Six minutes to twelve... Isn't this just like Walter Scott? I trust the murderer is beginning to shake in his shoes...'

He was drunk, but he went on drinking.

'Five people at least with reason to rob an old woman deprived of her husband and starved of love... Only one who dared... It will be a bomb or a revolver, gentlemen... A bomb which will blow us all up, or a revolver which will kill only the culprit... Four minutes to twelve...'

And he added in a curt voice:

'Don't forget that nobody knows!'

He seized the bottle of whisky and served everybody, beginning with Maigret's glass and finishing with Emile Gautier's.

He did not fill up his own... Hadn't he drunk enough? One candle went out. The others were on the point of following suit.

'I said midnight... Three minutes to twelve...'

He was talking like an auctioneer.

'Three minutes to twelve... Two minutes... The murderer is going to die... You can begin saying your prayer, Monsieur le Curé... As for you, doctor, I trust you've brought your bag with you?... Two minutes to twelve... One and a half minutes...'

And all the time that insistent foot against Maigret's foot. He did not dare to bend down again for fear of missing something else.

'I'm off!' exclaimed the lawyer getting up.

All eyes turned towards him. He was standing up, gripping the back of his chair. He hesitated about venturing on the three dangerous steps which would take him to the door. He hiccoughed.

And at the same moment a shot rang out. There was one second, perhaps two, of general immobility.

A second candle went out, and at the same time Maurice de Saint-Fiacre swayed, hit the back of his Gothic chair with his shoulders, leaned to the left, tried to regain his balance, but slumped to the floor in an inert mass, with his head on the priest's arm.

CHAPTER TEN

The Funeral Wake

The scene which followed was confusion. Something was happening everywhere, and afterwards nobody could have described anything but the small part of the events which he had seen himself.

Only five candles were left to light the whole dining-room. Huge areas remained in darkness; and, as they moved about, people walked in and out of them as if they were the wings of a theatre.

The man who had fired was one of Maigret's neighbours: Emile Gautier. And the shot had scarcely rung out before he held his two wrists out towards the chief-inspector in a rather theatrical gesture.

Maigret was standing. Gautier got up. His father too. And the three of them formed a group on one side of the table while another group gathered round the victim.

The Comte de Saint-Fiacre was still lying with his forehead against the priest's arm. The doctor had bent down and then looked around him with a grim expression.

'Is he dead?' asked the plump lawyer.

No reply. It was as if, in that group, the action was being played out limply by bad actors.

There was only Jean Métayer who belonged to neither group. He had remained by his chair, trembling and uneasy, and he did not know where to look.

During the minutes preceding his action, Emile Gautier must have decided what attitude to adopt, for he had scarcely put the weapon back on the table before he literally made a declaration, looking Maigret in the eyes.

'He said what was going to happen himself, didn't he?... The murderer had to die... And since he was too cowardly to do justice to himself...'

His self-assurance was extraordinary.

'I did what I considered to be my duty...'

Could the others, on the other side of the table, hear? There were some footsteps in the corridor. It was the servants. And the doctor went to the door to prevent them from coming in. Maigret did not hear what he said to them to get rid of them.

'I saw Saint-Fiacre prowling round the château on the night of the crime... That was how I understood...'

The whole scene was badly organized. And Gautier was hamming terribly when he declared:

'The judges will say whether...'

The doctor's voice could be heard asking:

'You're sure that it was Saint-Fiacre who killed his mother?'

'Positive! Would I have done what I have done if...'

'You saw him prowling round the château on the night before the crime?'

'I saw him as clearly as I can see you now. He had left his car just outside the village...'

'You've no other proof?'

'Yes, I have! This afternoon the choirboy came to see me at the bank with his mother... It was his mother who made him talk... Shortly after the crime, the count asked the boy to give him the missal and promised him some money...

Maigret's patience was nearly exhausted, for he had the impression of being left out of the play.

Yes, a play! Why was the doctor smiling into his beard? And why was the priest gently pushing Saint-Fiacre's head away?

A play, moreover, which was to continue on a note of farce and drama combined.

'For the Comte de Saint-Fiacre was standing up like a man who had just had a nap. The expression in his eyes was hard, and there was an ironic but threatening crease at the corner of his mouth.

'Come here and say that again!' he said.

The cry which rang out was blood-curdling. Emile Gautier was screaming with fear and hanging on to Maigret's arm as if to ask him for protection. But the chief-inspector drew back, leaving the field clear to the two men.

There was somebody who did not understand: Jean Métayer. And he was almost as frightened as the bank clerk. To cap everything, the candle-holder fell over and the tablecloth started smouldering, giving off a smell of burning.

It was the lawyer who prevented the fire from taking hold, by emptying a bottle of wine over it.

'Come here!'

It was an order. And the tone in which it was given was such that they all knew that there was no disobeying it.

Maigret had seized the revolver. A single glance had shown him that it was loaded with blanks.

The rest he could guess. Maurice de Saint-Fiacre letting his head fall against the priest's arm... A few whispered words asking for the illusion of his death to be preserved for a moment...

Now he was no longer the same man. He seemed taller, sturdier. He did not take his eyes off young Gautier, and it was the steward who suddenly ran towards a window, opened it and shouted to his son:

'This way!'

It was not a bad plan. The confusion and excitement were so great that at that moment Gautier had a good chance of making his escape.

Did the little lawyer do it on purpose? Probably not. Or else it was drunkenness which invested him with a sort of heroism. As the fugitive was making for the window, he stretched out one leg and Gautier fell head-long.

He did not get up by himself. A hand had seized him by the collar, was lifting him up and putting him on his feet. And he screamed again as he saw that it was Saint-Fiacre who was forcing him to stay upright.

'Don't move!... Somebody shut the window...'

And he slammed his fist for the first time into his

companion's face, which turned crimson. He did it coldly.

'Now talk!... Tell us all about it...'

Nobody intervened. Nobody even thought of doing so, they were so convinced that only one man had the right to raise his voice.

There was only old Gautier to growl in Maigret's ear:

'Are you going to let him do as he likes?'

Yes, he was! Maurice de Saint-Fiacre was in command of the situation, and he was adequate to his task.

'You saw me on the night in question, that's true enough...'

Then he said to the others:

'Do you know where?... On the steps... I was going in... He was coming out... I was planning to take some of the family jewels to sell them... We found ourselves face to face in the dark... It was freezing... And this little swine told me that he had just come from... Have you guessed? Yes, from my mother's bedroom!'

In a lower voice he added casually:

'I abandoned my plan. I went back to Moulins.'

Jean Métayer had opened his eyes wide. The lawyer was stroking his chin, to keep himself in countenance, and kept glancing towards his glass which he did not dare to go and get.

'That wasn't proof enough... For there were two of them in the house and Gautier could have been telling the truth... As I explained just now, he was the first to take advantage of an old woman's unhappiness... Métayer only came along later... Perhaps Métayer, conscious that his position was threatened, had tried to take his revenge... I tried to find out... Both of them were on their guard... It was as if they were defying me to do anything...

'That's true, isn't it, Gautier?... I was the gentleman with the dud cheques who prowled round the château at night, and who wouldn't dare to make any accusations, for fear of getting arrested himself...'

And in another tone of voice he went on:

'Forgive me, Monsieur le Curé, and you too, Doctor, for inflicting all this filth on you... But as we've already been told, real justice, the justice of the courts, is powerless here... That's so, isn't it, Monsieur Maigret?... Did you understand, at least when I was kicking you under the table just now?'

He was walking up and down, passing from the light into the shadows and from the shadows into the light. He gave the impression of a man holding himself back and only managing to remain calm at the cost of a tremendous effort. Sometimes he went close enough to Gautier to touch him.

'What a temptation to pick up the revolver and fire! Yes, I had said myself that the culprit would die at midnight and you, you became the defender of the honour of the Saint-Fiacres.'

This time his fist struck so hard, right in the middle of the face, that the bank clerk's nose began bleeding profusely.

Emile Gautier had the eyes of a dying animal. He reeled under the blow and looked as if he was on the point of weeping with pain, fear, and panic.

The lawyer tried to intervene, but Saint-Fiacre pushed him away.

'*You* keep out of this!'

And that *you* emphasized the enormous distance which separated them. Maurice de Saint-Fiacre dominated the company.

'Excuse me, gentlemen, but I have another little formality to see to.'

He opened the door wide and turned towards Gautier. 'Come along!'

The other stood rooted to the ground. The corridor was in darkness. He did not want to go out there with his adversary.

It did not take long. Saint-Fiacre went up to him and hit him again, so hard that he was knocked headlong into the hall.

'Up there!'

And he pointed to the staircase leading to the first floor.

'Chief-Inspector! I warn you that...' panted the steward.

The priest had turned his head away. He was suffering. But he had not the strength to intervene. Everybody was at the end of his tether and Métayer poured himself a drink, not caring what it was, he was so parched.

'Where are they going?' asked the lawyer.

They could hear them walking along the corridor, whose flagstones rang with the sound of their footsteps. And they could hear Gautier panting for breath.

'You knew everything,' Maigret said slowly, in a very low voice, to the steward. 'You were working hand in glove, you and your son! You already had the farms, the mortgages... But Jean Métayer remained a risk... So you decided to kill the countess, and at the same time get rid of the gigolo who would fall under suspicion...'

A cry of pain. The doctor went into the corridor to see what was happening.

'It's nothing,' he said. 'The little swine doesn't want to go upstairs and he's being helped along.'

'This is a scandal!... It's a crime!... What is he going to do?' cried old Gautier, rushing out of the room.

Maigret and the doctor followed him. They arrived at the foot of the staircase just as the other two, upstairs, reached the door of the dead woman's bedroom.

And they heard Saint-Fiacre's voice:

'In you go!'

'I can't... I...'

'In you go!'

A dull thud. Another blow.

Old Gautier ran up the stairs, followed by Maigret and Bouchardon. All three arrived at the top just as the door was closing.

At first they could hear nothing behind the heavy oak door. The steward held his breath, grimacing in the dark.

A thin ray of light under the door.

'On your knees!'

A pause. A hoarse gasp.

'Quicker than that!... On your knees!... And now beg her forgiveness!'

A fresh silence which was very prolonged. A cry of pain. This time it was not a punch which the murderer had received but a kick full in the face.

'For... forgive me...'

'Is that all?... Is that all you can find to say?... Remember that it was she who paid for your studies...

'Forgive me!'

'Remember that three days ago she was alive.'

'Forgive me!'

'Remember, you dirty little swine, that you once wormed your way into her bed...'

'Forgive me!... Forgive me!'

'You can do better than that!... Come, now!... Tell her you are a filthy louse... Repeat after me...'

'I am...'

'On your knees, I said!... Do you need a carpet?'

'Don't!... I...'

'Beg her forgiveness...'

And suddenly these exchanges, which were separated by long silences, were followed by a series of loud noises. Saint-Fiacre had lost his self-control. There were a number of thuds on the floor.

Maigret opened the door a little way. Maurice de Saint-Fiacre was holding Gautier by the neck and banging his head on the ground.

When he saw the chief-inspector, he let go, wiped his forehead, and straightened up.

'I've finished,' he said, breathing fast.

He caught sight of the steward and frowned.

'Don't you feel the need to beg her forgiveness too?'

And the old man was so frightened that he threw himself on his knees.

All that they could see of the dead woman, in the dim light from a couple of tapers, was the nose which seemed enormous and the folded hands which were holding a rosary.

'Get out!'

The count pushed Emile Gautier out of the room and shut the door. And the group started going downstairs.

Emile Gautier was bleeding. He could not find his handkerchief. The doctor passed him his.

For the bank clerk was a horrible sight: a battered, blood-stained face, with the nose nothing but a tumour and the upper lip split open...

And yet the ugliest, the most horrifying thing about his appearance was the eyes with their shifty expression...

Maurice de Saint-Fiacre, very upright, like the master of a house who knows what he has to do, strode along the long ground-floor corridor and opened the door, letting in a gust of icy air.

'Get out!' he growled, turning toward the father and son.

But, just as Emile was going out, he caught hold of him with an instinctive gesture.

Maigret was certain that he heard a sob in the count's throat. He started hitting the bank clerk again, convulsively, and crying:

'You swine!... You swine!'

It was enough for the chief-inspector just to touch him on the shoulder. Saint-Fiacre regained his composure, literally threw the body down the steps, and shut the door.

But not before they had heard the old man's voice again:

'Emile... Where are you?'

*

The priest was praying, with his elbows on the sideboard. In one corner Métayer and his lawyer were sitting motionless, their eyes fixed on the door.

Maurice de Saint-Fiacre came in, his head held high.

'Gentlemen,' he began.

But he could not go on. His voice was choked by emotion. He was at the end of his tether.

He shook hands with the doctor and Maigret as much as to say they could now go. Then, turning towards Métayer and his companion, he waited.

Those two did not seem to understand. Or else they were paralysed with fear.

To show them the way, a gesture was required followed by a snap of the fingers.

That was all.

Or was it? The lawyer started looking for his hat, and Saint-Fiacre groaned:

'Quicker than that!'

Maigret heard a murmur of voices behind a door, and he guessed that it was the servants who were there, trying to puzzle out what was happening in the château.

He put on his heavy overcoat. He felt the need to shake hands once more with Saint-Fiacre.

The door was open. Outside, it was a bright cold night, without a single cloud. The poplars stood out against a moonlit sky. Foosteps rang out somewhere, a long way away. And there were lights in the windows of the steward's house.

'No, you stay, Monsieur le Curé...'

And in the echoing corridor Maurice de Saint-Fiacre's voice added:

'Now, if you are not too tired, we are going to watch over my mother...'

CHAPTER ELEVEN

The Whistle

'You mustn't be cross with me, Monsieur Maigret, for looking after you so badly... But what with the funeral...'

Poor Marie Tatin was bustling around, getting whole crates of beer and lemonade ready.

'Especially seeing that those who live a long way off will drop in here for a bite...'

The fields were white with frost and the grass crackled underfoot. Every quarter of an hour the passing-bell of the little church tolled.

The hearse had arrived at dawn and the undertaker's men were waiting at the inn, in a half circle round the stove.

'I'm surprised the steward isn't at home,' Marie Tatin had told them. 'He's probably at the château with Monsieur Maurice...'

Already a few peasants could be seen, who had put on their Sunday clothes.

Maigret was finishing his breakfast when, through the window, he saw the choirboy arrive, holding his mother's hand. But the woman did not accompany him as far as the inn. She stopped at the corner on the road, where she thought she was out of sight, and pushed her son forward, as if to give him the necessary impetus to reach Marie Tatin's inn.

When Ernest came in, he was very self-assured. As self-assured as a boy who, at his school speech-day, recites a fable he has been rehearsing for three months.

'Is the chief-inspector here?'

At the very moment he was asking Marie Tatin this question, he caught sight of Maigret and came towards him, with both hands in his pockets, and one of them toying with something.

'I've come to...'

'Show me your whistle.'

Ernest promptly took a step back, turned his eyes away, thought for a moment, and murmured:

'What whistle?'

'The one you've got in your pocket... Have you been wanting a boy-scout whistle for a long time?'

The boy took it automatically from his pocket and put it on the table.

'And now tell me your little story.'

A suspicious glance, followed by an imperceptible shrug of the shoulders. For Ernest was already cunning. The expression in his eyes said clearly:

'I don't care! I've got the whistle! I'm going to say what I was told to say...'

And he recited:

'It's about the missal... I didn't tell you everything the other day, because I was scared of you... But Ma wants me to tell the truth... Somebody came and asked me for the missal, just before High Mass...'

All the same, he was red in the face, and he snatched the whistle back as if hs were afraid of having it confiscated because of his lies.

'And who came and asked you for it?'

'Monsieur Métayer... The secretary at the château...'

'Come and sit next to me... Would you like a grenadine?'

'Yes... With fizzy water...'

'Bring us a grenadine with soda water, Marie... And you, are you pleased with your whistle?... Blow it for me...'

The undertaker's men turned round as they heard the whistle.

'Your mother bought it for you yesterday afternoon, didn't she?'

'How do you know?'

'How much did they give her yesterday at the bank?'

The boy looked him in the eyes. He was no longer red in the face but pale. He glanced towards the door, as if to see how far he was from it.

'Drink your grenadine... It was Emile Gautier who saw you... He taught you what to say...'

'Yes!'

'He told you to accuse Jean Métayer?'

'Yes.'

And, after a pause for thought:

'What are you going to do to me?'

Maigret forgot to reply. He was thinking. He was thinking that his part in this case had been limited to finding the last link, a tiny link which completed the chain.

It was Jean Métayer all right whom Gautier had wanted to have accused. But the previous evening had upset his plans. He had realized that the man he had to fear was not the secretary, but the Comte de Saint-Fiacre.

If all had gone well, he would have been obliged to go to see the red-haired boy again before long, to teach him a new lesson:

'You must say that it was Monsieur le Comte who asked you for the missal...'

And now the boy repeated:

'What are you going to do to me?'

Maigret did not have time to reply. The lawyer came down the stairs, entered the main room of the inn, and approached Maigret his hand outstretched, with a hint of hesitation.

'Did you sleep well, Chief-Inspector?... Excuse me... I would like to ask your advice, on behalf of my Client... I've such a terrible headache...'

He sat down, or rather slumped on the bench.

'The funeral is at ten o'clock, isn't it?'

He looked at the undertaker's men, then at the people passing along the road, waiting for the funeral to begin.

'Between ourselves, do you think that Métayer's duty is to... Don't misunderstand me... We understand the situation and it's precisely out of a sense of delicacy that...'

'Can I go now, Monsieur?'

Maigret did not hear. He was talking to the lawyer.

'Haven't you understood yet?'

'I mean if one examines...'

'Let me give you a piece of advice: don't examine anything at all!'

'In your opinion it would be better to leave without...?'

Too late! Ernest, who had recovered his whistle, had opened the door and taken to his heels.

'From the legal point of view, we are in an excellent position...'

'Yes, excellent!'

'Isn't it?... That's what I was saying to...'

'Did he sleep well?'

'He didn't even undress... He's a very highly-strung, very sensitive fellow, like many young men of good family and...'

But the undertaker's men were pricking up their ears, standing up, paying for their drinks. Maigret stood up too, took his overcoat with the velvet collar from the coatstand, and wiped his bowler hat with his sleeve.

'The two of you have a chance to slip away during...'

'During the funeral?... In that case, I must telephone for a taxi.'

'That's it...'

*

The priest in his surplice. Ernest and two other choir-boys in their black cassocks. The cross which a priest from a nearby village was carrying, walking fast because of the cold. And the liturgical chants which they were intoning as they hurried along the road.

The peasants were grouped at the foot of the steps. Nothing could be seen inside. Finally the door opened and the coffin appeared, carried by four men.

Behind, a tall silhouette. Maurice de Saint-Fiacre red-eyed, very erect.

He was not in black. He was the only person not wearing mourning.

And yet, when, from the top of the steps, he let his gaze wander over the crowd, there was, as it were, a feeling of embarrassment.

He came out of the château with no one beside him. And he followed the coffin alone...

From where he was, Maigret could see the steward's house which had been his own home, and whose doors and windows were closed.

The shutters of the château were closed too. Only in the kitchen some servants had their noses pressed against the window-panes.

The sound of sacred chants almost drowned by the crunch of footsteps on the gravel.

The bells in full peal.

Two pairs of eyes met; the count's and Maigret's.

Was the chief-inspector mistaken? It seemed to him that Maurice de Saint-Fiacre's lips were touched by the ghost of a smile. Not the smile of the sceptical Parisian, the penniless prodigal.

A serene, confident smile...

During the Mass, everybody heard the high-pitched hum of a taxi. A little swine was making his escape in the company of a lawyer with a hangover.

MAIGRET and the Burglar's Wife

CHAPTER ONE

The appointment-slip, duly filled in, and handed to Maigret by the office porter, bore the following text:

Ernestine Micou, alias 'Lofty' (now Jussiaume), who, when you arrested her seventeen years ago in the Rue de la Lune, stripped herself naked to take the mike out of you, requests the favour of an interview on a matter of most urgent and important business.

Maigret glanced quickly, out of the corner of his eye, at old Joseph, to see whether he'd read the message, but the white-haired 'boy' didn't move a muscle. He was probably the only one in the whole of Police Headquarters that morning who wasn't in shirt-sleeves, and for the first time in so many years the chief-inspector wondered by what official vagary this almost venerable man was compelled to wear a heavy chain with a huge seal round his neck.

It was the sort of day when one's apt to indulge in pointless speculation. The heat-wave may have been to blame. Perhaps the holiday spirit also prevented one from taking things very seriously. The windows were wide open and the muted roar of Paris throbbed in the room where, before Joseph came in, Maigret had been engaged in following the flight of a wasp that was going round in circles and bumping against the ceiling at invariably the same spot. At least half the plain-clothes section was at the seaside or in the country. Lucas went about wearing a straw hat which, on him, assumed the aspect of a native grass hat or a lampshade. The Chief himself had left the day before, as he did year after year, for the Pyrenees.

'Drunk?' Maigret asked the porter.

'Don't think so, sir.'

For a certain type of woman, having taken a drop too much, often feels impelled to make disclosures to the police.

'Jumpy?'

'She asked me if it'd take long, and I said I didn't even know if you'd see her. She sat herself down in a corner of the waiting-room and started to read the paper.'

Maigret couldn't recall the names Micou or Jussiaume, or even the nickname Lofty, but he retained a vivid memory of the Rue de la Lune, on a day as hot as this, when the asphalt feels elastic under one's tread and fills Paris with a smell of tar.

It was down by the Porte Saint-Denis, a little street of shady hotels and small sweetshops. He wasn't a chief-inspector in those days. The women wore low-waisted frocks and had shingled hair. To find out about this girl, he'd had to go into two or three of the neighbouring bars, and it so happened he'd been drinking Pernod. He could almost conjure up the smell of it, just as he could conjure up the smell of armpits and feet pervading the small hotel. The room was on the third or fourth floor. Mistaking the door, he'd first of all found himself face to face with a negro who, sitting on his bed, was playing the accordion; one of the band in a *bal musette*, probably. Quite unperturbed, the negro had indicated the room next door with a jerk of his chin.

'Come in!'

A husky voice. The voice of one who drank or smoked too much. And, standing by a window that gave onto the courtyard, a tall girl in a sky-blue wrap, cooking herself a chop on a spirit lamp.

She was as tall as Maigret, maybe taller. She'd looked him up and down without emotion; she'd said straight away:

'You're a copper?'

He'd found a pocket-book and the bank-notes on top of the wardrobe and she hadn't batted an eyelid.

'It was my girl friend who did the job.'

'What girl friend?'

'Don't know her name. Lulu, they call her.'

'Where is she?'

'Find out. That's your business.'

'Get dressed and come with me.'

It was only a case of petty theft, but Headquarters took a rather serious view of it, not so much because of the sum involved, though this was a pretty large one, as because it concerned a big cattle-dealer from the Charentes, who had already started to stir up his local Deputy.

'It'd take more than you to stop me eating my chop!'

The tiny room contained only one chair. He'd remained standing while the girl ate, taking her time; he might not have been there for all the attention she paid to him.

She must have been rising twenty at the time. She was pale, with colourless eyes, a long bony face. He could see her now, picking her teeth with a matchstick, then pouring boiling water into the coffee-pot.

'I asked you to get dressed.'

He was hot. The smell of the hotel turned his stomach. Had she sensed that he was not at his ease?

Calmly she'd taken off her wrap, her shift and pants, and, stark naked, had gone and lain down on the unmade bed, lighting a cigarette.

'I'm waiting!' he'd told her impatiently, looking away with an effort.

'So am I.'

'I've a warrant for your arrest.'

'Well, arrest me then!'

'Get dressed and come along.'

'I'm all right like this.'

The whole thing was ludicrous. She was cool, quite passive, a little glint of irony showing in her colourless eyes.

'You say I'm under arrest. *I* don't mind. But you needn't ask me to give you a hand as well. I'm in my own place. It's hot, and I've a right to take my clothes off. Now, if you insist on my coming along with you just as I am, I'm not complaining.'

At least a dozen times he'd told her:

'Get your things on!'

And, perhaps because of her pallid flesh, perhaps because of the surrounding squalor, it seemed to him that he'd never seen a woman so naked as that. To no avail he'd thrown her clothes on the bed, had threatened her, then tried persuasiveness.

In the end he'd gone down and fetched two policemen, and the scene had become farcical. They'd had to wrap the girl forcibly in a blanket and carry her, like a packing-case, down the narrow staircase, while all the doors opened as they went by.

He'd never seen her since. He'd never heard her mentioned.

'Send her in!' he sighed.

He knew her at once. She didn't seem to have changed. He recognized her long pale face, the washed-out eyes, the big over-made-up mouth that looked like a raw wound. He recognized also, in her glance, the quiet irony of those who've seen so much that nothing's any longer important in their eyes.

She was simply dressed, with a light green straw hat, and she'd put on gloves.

'Still got it in for me?'

He drew on his pipe without answering.

'Can I have a seat? I heard you'd been promoted and in fact that's why I never ran into you again. Is it all right if I smoke?'

She took a cigarette from her bag and lit up.

'I want to tell you right away, with no hard feelings, that I was telling the truth that time. I got a year inside that I didn't deserve. There was a girl called Lulu all right, whom you didn't take the trouble to find. The two of us were together when we ran across that fat steamer. He picked us both up, but when he'd taken a good look at me, he told me to buzz off because he couldn't stand 'em skinny. I was outside in the passage when Lulu slipped me the pocket-book an hour after so's I could ditch it.'

'What became of her?'

'Five years ago she'd a little restaurant down South. I just wanted to show you everyone sometimes makes mistakes.'

'Is that why you came?'

'No. I wanted to talk to you about Alfred. If he knew I was here, he'd take me for a proper mug. I could've gone to Sergeant Boissier, who knows all about him.'

'Who's Alfred?'

'My husband. Lawfully wedded, too, before the mayor *and* the vicar, because he still goes to church. Sergeant Boissier pinched him two or three times, and one of those times he got Alfred five years in Fresnes.'

Her voice was almost harsh.

'The name Jussiaume doesn't mean much to you, perhaps, but when I tell you what they call him, you'll know who he is right away. There's been a lot about him in the papers. He's Sad Freddie.'

'Safe-breaking?'

'Yes.'

'You've had a row?'

'No. It's not what you'd think I've come for. I'm not that sort. So you see who Fred is now?'

Maigret had never set eyes on him, or, rather, only in the corridors, when the cracksman was waiting to be interrogated by Boissier. He called to mind vaguely a puny little man with anxious eyes, whose clothes seemed too big for his scrawny body.

'Of course, we don't look at him the same way,' she said. 'Poor blighter. There's more to him than you think. I've lived with him close on twelve years; I'm only starting to get to know him.'

'Where is he?'

'I'm coming to that, don't worry. I don't know where he is, but he's got in a proper jam without its being any of his fault, and that's why I'm here. Only you've simply got to trust me, and I know that's asking a lot.'

He was watching her with interest, because she spoke with appealing simplicity. She wasn't putting on airs, wasn't trying to impress him. If she took some time in coming to the point, it was because what she had to tell was genuinely complicated.

There was still a barrier between them, nevertheless, and it was this barrier that she was trying hard to break down, so that he wouldn't get a wrong idea of things.

About Sad Freddie, with whom he'd never had any personal dealings, Maigret knew little more than he'd heard at Headquarters. The man was a sort of celebrity, and the newspapers had tried their best to boost him into a romantic figure.

He'd been employed for years by the firm of Planchart, the safemakers, and had become one of their most skilled workers. He was, even at that time, a sad, retiring youth, in poor health, throwing epileptic fits periodically.

Boissier would probably be able to tell Maigret how he had come to give up his job at Planchart's.

Whatever the cause, he had turned from installing safes to cracking them.

'When you first met him, had he still got a steady job?'

'Not likely. It wasn't me that sent him off the straight and narrow, in case that's what you've got in mind. He was doing odd jobs, sometimes he'd hire himself out to a locksmith, but it wasn't long before I saw what he was really up to.'

'You don't think you'd do better to see Boissier?'

'Housebreaking's his line, isn't it? But you deal with murder.'

'Has Alfred killed anybody?'

'Look, Chief-Inspector, I think we'll get along faster if you just let me talk. Alfred may be anything you'd like to call him, but he wouldn't murder for all the money in the world. May seem soppy to say so about a bloke like him, but he's sensitive, see? Why, he'd pipe his eye for the least little thing. I ought to know. Anyone else would say he was soft. But maybe it's because he's like that, that I fell in love with him.'

And she looked at him quietly. She'd uttered the word 'love' without particular emphasis, but with a sort of pride all the same.

'If one knew what was going on in his head, one wouldn't half get a surprise. Not that it matters. Far's you're concerned, he's just a thief. He got himself pinched once and did five years inside. I never missed going to see him a single visiting-day, and all that time I'd go back on my old beat, at the risk of getting in trouble, not having a proper card and those being the days when you still had to have one.

'He always hopes he'll pull off a big job and then we can go and live in the country. He's always dreamed of it ever since he was a nipper.'

'Where do you live?'

'On the Quai de Jemmapes, just opposite the Saint-Martin Lock. Know where I mean? We've two rooms above a café painted green, and it's very handy because of the 'phone.'

'Is Alfred there now?'

'No. I already told you I don't know where he is, and believe me I don't. He did a job, not last night, but the night before.'

'And he's cleared out?'

'Hang on, will you, Inspector! You'll see later on that everything I tell you's got its point. You know people that take tickets in the National Sweep at every draw, don't you? There are some of them that go without eating to buy them, because they reckon in a day or two they'll be in the money at last. Well, that's the way it is with Alfred. There're dozens of safes in Paris that he put in himself, and that he knows like the back of his hand. Usually, when you buy a safe, it's to put money or jewels away in.'

'He hopes to strike lucky one day?'

'You got it.'

She shrugged, as though speaking of a child's harmless craze. Then she added:

'He's just unlucky. Most times it's title-deeds it's impossible to sell or else business contracts he gets hold of. Only once there was real big dough, that he could've lived on quietly for the rest of his days, and that time Boissier pinched him.'

'Were you with him? Do you keep the look-out?'

'No. He never liked me to. At the start, he used to tell me where he was going to be on the job, and I'd fix it so I was nearby. When he spotted that, he gave up telling me anything.'

'For fear you'd get pulled in?'

'Maybe. Or it may have been because he's superstitious. See, even when we're living together, he's all alone really, and sometimes he doesn't say a word for two whole days. When I see him go out at night on his bicycle, I know what's up.'

Maigret remembered this characteristic. Some of the newspapers had dubbed Alfred Jussiaume the burglar-on-a-bike.

'That's another of his notions. He reckons that nobody, at night, is going to notice a man on a bike, specially if he's got a bag of tools slung over his shoulder. They'd take him for a bloke on his way to work. I'm talking to you like I would to a friend, see?'

Maigret wondered again why she had really come to his office and, as she took out another cigarette, he held a lighted match for her.

'We're Thursday today. On Tuessday night Alfred went out on a job.'

'Did he tell you so?'

'He'd been going out for several nights at the same time, and that's always a sign. Before breaking into a house or an office, he sometimes spends a week on the watch to get to know the people's habits.'

'And to make sure there'll be no one about?'

'No. That doesn't signify to him. I even think he'd rather work where there was somebody than in an empty house. He's a bloke that can get about without making a sound. Why, hundreds of times he's slipped into bed beside me at night and I never so much as knew he'd come home.'

'D'you know where he worked that night before last?'

'All I know, it was at Neuilly. And then I only found it out by chance. The day before, when I came in, he told me the police had asked to see his papers, and must've taken him for a dirty old man because they stopped him in the Bois de Boulogne, just by the place where women go and tidy up.

' "Where was it?" I asked him.

' "Behind the Zoo. I was coming back from Neuilly."

'Then, night before last, he took his bag of tools, and I knew he'd gone to work.'

'He hadn't been drinking?'

'Never touches a drop, doesn't smoke. He'd never be able to take it. He lives in terror of his fits, and he's that ashamed when it happens in the middle of the street, with masses of people who crowd round and feel sorry for him. He said to me before he set out:

' "I reckon this time we're really going down to live in the country." '

Maigret had begun to take notes which he was surrounding automatically with arabesques.

'What time did he leave the Quai de Jemmapes?'

'About eleven, like on the other nights.'

'Then he must have got to Neuilly round about midnight.'

'Maybe. He never rode fast, but then, at that time, there'd be no traffic.'

'When did you see him again?'

'I haven't seen him again.'

'So you think something may have happened to him?'

'He rang me up.'

'When?'

'Five in the morning. I wasn't asleep. I was worried. If he's always scared he'll have a fit in the street, I'm always scared it might happen while he's working, you see? I heard the 'phone ringing downstairs in the café. Our room's right up above. The owners didn't get up. I guessed it was for me, and I went down. I knew right away from his voice there'd been a hitch. He spoke very low.

' "That you?"

' "Yes!"

' "Are you alone?"

' "Yes. Where are you?"

' "In a little café up by the Gare du Nord. Look, Tine," (he always calls me Tine), "I've simply got to make myself scarce for a bit."

' "Somebody see you?"

' "It's not that. I don't know. A bloke saw me, yes, but I'm not sure it was a policeman."

' "Got any money?"

' "No. It happened before I'd finished."

' "What happened?"

' "I was busy on the lock when my torch lit up a face in the corner of the room. I thought somebody'd come in silently and was watching me. Then I saw the eyes were dead." '

She watched Maigret.

'I'm sure he wasn't lying. If he'd killed anyone, he'd have told me. And I'm not going telling you any stories. I could tell he was near fainting at the other end. He's so scared of death....'

'Who was it?'

'I don't know. He didn't make it very clear. He was going to hang up the whole time. He was scared someone'd hear him. He told me he was taking a train in a quarter of an hour....'

'To Belgium?'

'Probably, as he was near the Gare du Nord. I looked up a timetable. There's a train at five forty-five.'

'You've no more idea what café he was 'phoning from?'

'I went on a scout round the district yesterday and asked some questions, but no good. They must've taken me for a jealous wife, and they weren't giving anything away.'

'So all he really told you was that there was a dead body in the room where he was working?'

'I got him to tell me a bit more. He said it was a woman, that her chest was all covered in blood, and that she was holding a telephone receiver in her hand.'

'Is that all?'

'No. Just as he was going to do a bunk — and I can imagine the state he was in! — a car drew up in front of the gate....'

'You're sure he said the gate?'

'Yes. A wrought-iron gate. I remember it struck me particularly. Somebody got out and came towards the door. As the man went into the passage, Alfred got out of the house by the window.'

'And his tools?'

'He left them behind. He'd cut out a window-pane to get in. That I'm sure of, because he always does. I believe he'd do it even if the door was open, he's sort of faddy that way, or maybe superstitious.'

'So nobody saw him?'

'Yes. As he was going through the garden....'

'He mentioned a garden as well?'

'I didn't make it up. As I say, just when he was going through the garden someone looked out of the window and shone a torch on him; maybe Alfred's own, which he hadn't taken with him. He jumped on his bike, went off without looking round, rode down as far as the Seine, I don't know exactly where, and threw the bike in, for fear they'd recognize him by it. He didn't dare come back home. He got to the Gare du Nord on foot and 'phoned me, begging me not to say a word. I pleaded with him not to clear off. I tried to reason with him. He finished up promising to write me *poste restante* saying where he'd be so I could go and join him.'

'He hasn't written yet?'

'There hasn't been time for a letter to get here. I went to the post office this morning. I've had twenty-four hours to think things over. I bought all the papers, thinking they'd surely say something about a murdered woman.'

Maigret picked up the telephone and called the police-station at Neuilly.

'Hello! Headquarters here. Any murder to report during the last twenty-four hours?'

'One moment, sir. I'll put you through to the desk. I'm only the duty constable.'

Maigret persisted for some time.

'No corpse found on the roads? No night calls? No bodies fished up from the Seine?'

'Absolutely nothing, Monsieur Maigret.'

'Nobody reported a shot?'

'Nobody.'

Lofty waited patiently, like someone making a social call, both hands clasped upon her bag.

'You realize why I came to you?'

'I think so.'

'First, I reckoned the police had maybe seen Alfred, and, in that case, his bike alone would have given him away. Then there were the tools he left behind. Now he's bolted over the frontier, no one'll ever believe his story. And he's no safer in Belgium or Holland than in Paris. I'd sooner see him in jail for attempted burglary, even if it meant five years all over again, than see him had up for murder.'

'The trouble,' Maigret retorted, 'is that there's no body.'

'You think he made it up or that I'm making it up?'

He didn't answer.

'It'll be easy for you to find the house he was working in that night. Maybe I shouldn't tell you this, but I'm sure you'll think of it yourself. The safe's bound to be one of those he put in at some time. Planchart's must keep a list of their customers. There can't be that many in Neuilly who bought a safe at least seventeen years back.'

'Apart from you, did Alfred have any girl-friends?'

'Ah! I guessed that was coming. I'm not jealous and, even if I was, I wouldn't come to you with a pack of lies to get my own back, if that's what you've got in mind. He hasn't a girl-friend because he doesn't want one, poor blighter. If he wanted to I'm the one who'd fix him up with as much as he liked.'

'Why?'

'Because life's not so much cop for him, as it is.'

'Have you any money?'

'No.'

'What are you going to do?'

'I'll get by, you know that all right. I only came here because I want it proved that Freddie didn't kill anyone.'

'If he wrote to you, would you show me his letter?'

'You'll read it before I do. Now that you know he's going to write me *post restante*, you'll have every post office in Paris watched. You forget that I know the racket.'

She had risen to her feet, very tall; she looked him over as he sat at his desk, from top to toe.

'If all the tales they tell about you are true, there's an even chance that you'll believe me.'

'Why?'

'Because otherwise you'd be a mug. And you're not one. Are you going to ring Planchart's?'

'Yes.'

'You'll keep me posted?'

He looked at her without replying, and realized that he couldn't restrain himself from smiling good-humouredly.

'Please yourself then,' she sighed. 'I could help you; you may know an awful lot, but there're things people like us understand better than you do.'

Her 'us' obviously stood for a whole world, the one that Lofty lived in, the world on the other side of the barrier.

'If Sergeant Boissier's not on holiday, I'm sure he'll bear me out in what I told you about Alfred.'

'He's not on leave. He's going tomorrow.'

She opened her bag, took from it a bit of paper.

'I'll leave you the 'phone number of the café underneath where we live. If by some fluke you need to come and see me, don't be scared that I'll start undressing. Nowadays, if it's left to me, I keep my clothes on!'

There was a touch of bitterness in her tone, but not much. A second later she was poking fun at herself:

'Much better for all concerned!'

It wasn't until he closed the door behind her that Maigret realized he had shaken, quite as a matter of course, the hand she'd held out to him. The wasp still buzzed in circles at ceiling level, as though seeking a way out, without thinking of the wide open windows. Madame Maigret had announced in the morning that she'd be coming round to the flower market and had asked him, if he were free about noon, to go and meet her there. It was noon now. He paused irresolute, leant out of the window from which he could see the splashes of vivid colour beyond the embankment of the quay.

Then he picked up the telephone with a sigh.

'Ask Boissier to drop in and see me.'

Seventeen years had slipped by since the absurd incident in the Rue de la Lune, and Maigret was now an important official in charge of the Homicide Branch. A funny notion came into his head, an almost childish craving. He picked up the telephone once more.

'The *Brasserie Dauphine*, please.'

As the door opened to admit Boissier, he was saying:

'Send me up a Pernod, will you?'

And, looking at the sergeant, who had large half-moons of sweat on his shirt underneath the arms, he changed it to:

'Make it two! Two Pernods, thank you.'

The blue-black moustache of Boissier, who came from Provence, twitched with pleasure, and he went over to sit on the window-sill, mopping his forehead.

CHAPTER TWO

After swallowing a mouthful of Pernod, Maigret had to come to the point:

'Tell me, Boissier, old man, what d'you know about Alfred Jussiaume?'

'Sad Freddie?'

'Yes.'

And immediately the sergeant's brow had darkened, he'd shot Maigret a worried glance, had asked in a voice no longer the same, forgetting to take a sip of his favourite drink:

'Has he done a job?'

It was always like this with the sergeant, Maigret knew. He also knew why and, by using the utmost tact, had become the only chief-inspector to find favour in Boissier's eyes.

The latter, by rights, ought to have been one himself, and would have been a long time ago, had an absolute inability to spell and the handwriting of a first-form schoolboy not prevented his passing the simplest examinations.

For once, however, the administrative staff had not made a bloomer. They had appointed at the head of his branch Chief-Inspector Peuchet, an old has-been, always half-asleep and, save for drawing up the reports, it was Boissier who got through all the work and governed his colleagues.

That department wasn't concerned with homicide, as Maigret's was. It wasn't concerned with amateurs either, shop-assistants who run off one fine day with the till, or any tripe of that sort.

The customers Boissier and his men dealt with were professional thieves of every kind, from the jewel robbers who put up at the big hotels in the Champs-Elysées, to the bank-smashers and hustlers, who hid out mostly, like Jussiaume, in seedy neighbourhoods.

Because of this, they had an outlook quite different from that of the Special Division. In Boissier's line, they were all craftsmen, on both sides. The battle was a battle between experts. It wasn't so much a question of psychology, as of knowing, from A to Z, the little quirks and eccentricities of everyone.

It was not unusual to see the sergeant sitting quietly outside a café with a cat-burglar, and Maigret, for one, would have found it hard to hold a conversation of this sort with a murderer:

'Here, Julot, it's a long time since you did a job of work.'

'That's right, Sergeant.'

'When was the last time I pulled you in?'

'Must be going on six months, now.'

'Funds getting low, eh? I'll bet you're cooking something up.'

The idea that Sad Freddie might have done a bust without his knowledge put Boissier's back up.

'I don't know if he's really been on the job lately, but Lofty has just left my office.'

That was enough to reassure the sergeant.

'She doesn't know a thing,' he stated. 'Alfred's not the type to go blabbing his business to a woman, not even his own wife.'

The picture of Jussiaume that Boissier now set himself to draw was not unlike that previously outlined by Ernestine, even though he, the sergeant, tended rather to emphasize the professional angle.

'I get browned off with pinching a bloke like that and sending him to the nick. Last time, when they dished him out five years, I damn nearly gave his lawyer a piece of my mind for not knowing how to go about his job. He's wanting, that lawyer is!'

It was hard to define precisely what Boissier meant by 'wanting', but the point was plain enough.

'There's not another in Paris like Alfred for breaking into a house full of people without a sound and going to work there without even waking the cat. Technically, he's an artist. What's more, he doesn't need anyone to tip him off, keep a look-out and all that palaver. He works on his own, without ever getting jumpy. He doesn't drink, doesn't talk, doesn't go acting tough round the bars. With his talents he ought to have enough dough to choke himself with. He knows just where to find hundreds of safes that he put in himself, and exactly how they work, and you'd think he'd only have to go and help himself. Instead, every time he has a go, he comes a cropper or else gets a spell inside.'

Perhaps Boissier only spoke thus because he saw a parallel between Sad Freddie's career and his own, except that he himself enjoyed a constitution that could withstand any number of *apéritifs* imbibed on café terraces and nights spent standing to in all kinds of weather.

'The joke is that, if they put him away for ten years or twenty years, he'd start all over again directly he came out, even supposing he was seventy and on crutches by then. He's got it into his head that he only needs one lucky break, just one, and that he's earned it by this time.'

'He's had a nasty knock,' Maigret explained. 'It seems that he was just getting a safe open, somewhere at Neuilly, when he spotted a dead body in the room.'

'What'd I tell you? That could only happen to him. Then he cleared off? What'd he do with the bike?'

'In the Seine.'

'He's in Belgium?'

'I dare say.'

'I'll ring through to Brussels, unless you don't want him picked up?'

'I want him picked up most decidedly.'

'D'you know where this took place?'

'I know that it was at Neuilly, and that the house has a

garden with a wrought-iron gate in front.'

'That'll be easy. Be back right away.'

Maigret had the grace to order, in his absence, two more Pernods from the *Brasserie Dauphine*. It brought back to him not only a whiff of the Rue de la Lune period, but a whiff of the South of France, particularly of a little dive in Cannes, where he'd once been on a case and, all of a sudden, the whole business was lifted out of the general rut, took on almost the aspect of a holiday task.

He hadn't definitely promised Madame Maigret to meet her in the flower market, and she knew that she ought never to wait for him. Boissier returned with a file, from which he produced, first of all, the official photographs of Alfred Jussiaume.

'That's what he looks like!'

An ascetic face, really, rather than that of a guttersnipe. The skin was stretched tight across the bones, the nostrils were long and pinched, and the stare had an almost mystical intensity. Even in these harshly lit photographs, full face and side view, collarless, with a protruding Adam's apple, the man's immense loneliness made itself felt, and his sadness that was still in no way aggressive.

Born to be fair game, it had been natural for him to be hunted.

'Would you like me to read you his record?'

'It's not necessary today. I'd rather go over the file with an open mind. What I'd like to have is the list.'

Boissier was pleased by this last sentence. Maigret knew that he would be, as he said it, for he intended it as a tribute to the sergeant.

'You knew I'd have it?'

'I was certain you would.'

For, in point of fact, Boissier really did know his job. The list in question was that, drawn from the books of Messrs. Planchart, of the safes installed in Alfred Jussiaume's time.

'Wait till I look up Neuilly. You're sure it's at Neuilly?'

'I've Ernestine's word for it.'

'You know, she wasn't really so dumb to come and look you up. But why you?'

'Because I arrested her, sixteen or seventeen years ago,

and because she played me quite a dirty trick.'

This didn't surprise Boissier, it was all in the game. They both knew where they stood. From the glasses, the pale-coloured Pernod could already be smelt all over the office, inciting the wasp to a kind of frenzy.

'A bank... it's certainly not that..... Freddie never took to banks, because he's windy of the burglar-alarms.... A petrol company that's been out of business for ten years.... A scent manufacturer... he went bankrupt a year ago.'

Boissier's finger came to a stop finally on a name, on an address.

'Guillaume Serre, dentist, 43b, Rue de la Ferme, Neuilly. You know it? It's just past the Zoo, a street parallel with the Boulevard Richard-Wallace.'

'I know.'

They looked at each other for a moment.

'Busy?' asked Maigret.

And in so doing he was again pandering deliberately to Boissier's self-esteem.

'I was classifying some files. I'm off to Brittany tomorrow.'

'Shall we go?'

'I'll get my coat and hat. Shall I 'phone Brussels first?'

'Yes. And Holland as well.'

'Right you are.'

They went there by bus, standing on the outside platform. Then, in the Rue de la Ferme, quiet and countrified, they found a little café-restaurant where there were four tables on the terrace between green potted plants, and sat down there for lunch.

There were only three bricklayers in white smocks inside, drinking red wine with their meal. Flies circled round Maigret and Boissier. Farther along, on the other side of the road, they could see a black wrought-iron gate that should correspond with No. 43b.

They weren't in any hurry. If there'd really been a dead body in the house, the murderer had had over twenty-four hours in which to get rid of it.

A waitress in a black dress and a white apron looked after them, but the proprietor came over to greet them.

'Nice weather, gentlemen.'

'Nice weather. Would you, by any chance, know of a dentist anywhere about here?'

A sidelong nod.

'There's one opposite, over there, but I don't know what he's like. My missus prefers to go to one in the Boulevard Sebastopol. This one'd be expensive, I'd say. He hasn't all that many patients.'

'D'you know him?'

'A wee bit.'

The proprietor paused, looked them over for a while, particularly Boissier.

'You'd be police-officers, eh?'

Maigret thought it better to say yes.

'Has he done anything?'

'We're just making a few enquiries. What does he look like?'

'Taller and bigger than you and me,' he said, looking this time at the chief-inspector. 'I weigh fifteen stone ten, and he must go all of sixteen.'

'How old?'

'Fifty? Round about, anyway. Not too well turned out, which is odd, him being a dentist. Seedy looking, like what old bachelors get.'

'He isn't married?'

'Wait a bit.... Matter of fact, if I remember rightly, he did get married, it'd be about two years ago.... There's an old woman living in the house, too — his mother, I suppose — who does the shopping every morning....'

'No maid?'

'Only a charwoman. Mind you, I wouldn't be sure. I only know him because he comes in here now and then for a foxy drink.'

'Foxy?'

'In a manner of speaking. People like him don't come to places like this, as a rule. And when he does, he always takes a quick look round at his house, as if to make sure he can't be seen. And he looks sheepish, coming up to the counter.

' "Glass of red wine!" he'll say.

'Never takes anything else. I know right away not to put the bottle back on the shelf, because he's bound to have another. He drinks 'em at a gulp, wipes his mouth, and he's got the change all ready in his hand.'

'Does he ever get drunk?'

'Never. Just the two glasses. As he goes out, I see him slip a cachou or a clove into his mouth, so that his breath won't smell of wine.'

'What's his mother like?'

'A little old woman, very dried up, dressed in black, who never passes the time of day with anybody and doesn't look easy to get on with.'

'His wife?'

'I've scarcely seen her except when they go by in the car, but I've heard tell she's a foreigner. She's tall and stout like him, with a high colour.'

'D'you think they're away on holiday?'

'Let's see. I believe I still served him with his two glasses of red two or three days ago.'

'Two or three?'

'Wait a bit. It was the evening when the plumber came to mend the beer-pump. I'll go and ask my wife, to make sure I'm not talking through my hat.'

It was two days previously, in other words Tuesday, a few hours before Alfred Jussiaume discovered a dead woman's body in the house.

'Can you remember the time?'

'He comes, as a rule, about half-past six.'

'On foot?'

'Yes. They've got an old car, but that's the time of day he takes his constitutional. You can't tell me what this is all about?'

'It's not about anything at all. A check-up.'

The man didn't believe them, you could see it plainly in his eyes.

'You'll be back?'

And, turning to the chief-inspector: 'You're not Monsieur Maigret, by any chance?'

'Did someone say so?'

'One of the bricklayers thought he recognized you. If

you are, my wife'd be very happy to meet you in the flesh.'

'We'll be back,' he promised.

They'd had a jolly good meal, and they'd drunk the Calvados which the proprietor, who came from Falaise, had offered them. Now they were walking together down the pavement on the shady side of the street. Maigret was taking little puffs at his pipe. Boissier had lit a cigarette, and two fingers of his right hand were stained brown with nicotine, coloured like a meerschaum pipe.

One might have been fifty miles outside Paris, in almost any small town. There were more private houses than buildings with flats, and some were big middle-class family mansions about a century or two old.

There was only the one gate in the street, a black wrought-iron gate beyond which a lawn was spread like a green carpet in the sunshine. On the brass plate was the legend:

GUILLAUME SERRE
Dental Surgeon

And, in smaller letters:

From 2 to 5 p.m.
By appointment only

The sun struck full on the façade of the house, warming its yellowish stone, and, except for two of the windows, the shutters were closed. Boissier could sense that Maigret was undecided.

'Are you going in?'

'What have we got to lose?'

Before crossing over, he cast a quick glance up and down the street and suddenly frowned. Boissier looked in the direction towards which Maigret was gazing so steadily.

'Lofty!' he exclaimed.

She'd just come from the Boulevard Richard-Wallace, and was wearing the same green hat as earlier that morning. Catching sight of Maigret and the sergeant, she paused for a moment, then made straight for them.

'Surprised to see me?'

'You've got hold of the address?'

'I 'phoned your office about half an hour ago. I wanted to tell you that I'd found the list. I knew it must be somewhere about. I've seen Alfred looking at it, and putting in crosses here and there. When I came out of your office this morning I thought of a place where Alfred might have hidden it.'

'Where?'

'Do I have to tell you?'

'It might be as well.'

'I'd rather not. Not right away.'

'What else did you find?'

'How d'you know I found anything else?'

'You'd no money this morning and you came here by cab.'

'You're right. There was some money.'

'A lot?'

'More than I'd have expected.'

'Where's the list?'

'I burnt it.'

'Why?'

'Because of the crosses. They might have marked the places where Alfred worked and, whatever else, I'm not going to give you evidence against him.'

She glanced at the house.

'You going in?'

Maigret nodded.

'D'you mind if I wait for you outside the café?'

She hadn't said a word to Boissier who, for his part, was staring at her rather sternly.

'Please yourself,' Maigret told her.

And, followed by the sergeant, he crossed from the shade into the sunlight, while the tall figure of Ernestine moved off towards the café terrace.

It was ten past two. Unless the dentist had gone on holiday, he ought, according to the brass plate, to be waiting for patients in his surgery. There was an electric bell-push on the right of the gateway. Maigret pressed it and the gate swung open automatically. They crossed the small garden and found another bell-push by the front door, which was not mechanically operated. After the peal of the bell inside, there was a long silence. The two men listened, both of them aware that someone was lurking on the other side of the panel, and looked at each other. At last a chain was unhooked, the bolt withdrawn, a thin crack showed round the lintel of the door.

'Have you an appointment?'

'We'd like to speak to Monsieur Serre.'

'He only sees people by appointment.'

The crack did not widen. They could dimly make out, behind it, a silhouette, the thin face of an old woman.

'According to the brass plate...'

'The plate is twenty-five years old.'

'Would you tell your son that Chief-Inspector Maigret wishes to see him?'

The door remained for a moment longer without moving, then opened; it revealed a wide hallway with a black-and-white tessellated floor which resembled that of a convent corridor, and the old lady who stood back to let them enter would not have looked out of place dressed as a nun.

'You must excuse me, Chief-Inspector, but my son doesn't really care to receive casual patients.'

The woman was far from unpresentable. She'd an innate elegance and dignity which were remarkable. She was attempting to efface by her smile any bad impression that she might have created.

'Do please come in. I'm afraid that I'll have to ask you to wait a moment or two. For some years, my son has been accustomed, especially in summer, to take a siesta, and he's still lying down. If you'd care to come this way.....'

She opened, on the left, a pair of polished oaken doors, and Maigret was reminded more than ever of a convent or, better still, a rich parsonage. Even the soft, insidious smell reminded him of something; he didn't know what, he tried to remember. The drawing-room that she showed them into was lit only by daylight seeping through the slots of the shutters, and to enter it from outside was like stepping into a cool bath.

The noises of the town, one felt, could never penetrate this far, and it was as if the house and everything in it had remained unchanged for more than a century, that the tapestried chairs, the occasional tables, the piano and the chinaware had always stood in the same place. Even the enlarged photographs on the walls, in black wooden frames, which looked like photographs from the time of Nadar. The man strapped into a collar of the last century, above the chimney-piece, wore bushy side-whiskers and, on the opposite wall, a woman of about forty, her hair parted in the middle, looked like the Empress Eugénie.

The old lady, who might almost have stepped herself out of one of those frames, hovered at their side, motioned them to seats, folded her hands like a Sister of Mercy.

'I don't wish to seem inquisitive, Chief-Inspector. My son has no secrets from me. We've never lived apart, although he's now past his fiftieth year. I haven't the slightest idea of your business or of what brings you here, and, before going to disturb him, I would like to know...'

She left the sentence unfinished, glancing from one to the other with a gracious smile.

'Your son is married, I believe?'

'He's been married twice.'

'Is his second wife at home?'

A shade of melancholy clouded her eyes, and Boissier began to cross and uncross his legs; this was not the sort of place he felt at home in.

'She's no longer with us, Chief-Inspector.'

She moved softly to close the door, and returning, sat down in the corner of a sofa, keeping her back very straight, as young girls are taught to hold themselves in convent schools.

'I hope she hasn't done anything silly?' she asked in a low voice.

Then, as Maigret remained silent, she gave a sigh, resigned herself to begin once more:

'If it's anything to do with her, I was right to question you before disturbing my son. It is about her that you've come, isn't it?'

Did Maigret make a vague sign of assent? He was not

aware of doing so. He was too intrigued by the atmosphere of this house, and even more by this woman, behind whose meekness he could sense an indomitable strength of will.

Everything about her was in good taste: her clothes, her bearing and her voice. One might have expected to meet her in some château or, better still, in one of those enormous country houses that are like museums of a bygone age.

'After he became a widower, fifteen years ago, the thought of remarrying didn't enter my son's head for a long time.'

'He did remarry, two years ago, if I'm not mistaken?'

She showed no surprise at finding him so well-informed.

'He did, indeed. Two and a half years ago exactly. He married one of his patients, a woman also of a certain age. She was then forty-seven. Of Dutch origin, she lived alone in Paris. I won't live for ever, Chief-Inspector. As you see me now, I am seventy-eight.'

'You don't look it.'

'I know. My mother lived to the age of ninety-two, and my grandmother was killed in an accident at ninety-eight.'

'And your father?'

'He died young.'

She spoke as though this were of no importance, or rather as if men in general were doomed to die young.

'I almost encouraged Guillaume to marry again, by saying that thus he would not be left to live alone.'

'The marriage was unhappy?'

'I wouldn't say that. Not to begin with. I think that the trouble arose mainly from her being a foreigner. There are all sorts of little things that one cannot get used to. I don't quite know how to explain. Oh yes. Food, for instance! A preference for this or that dish! Perhaps, too, when she married my son she imagined him to be wealthier than he actually is.'

'She'd no income of her own?'

'A certain competence. She was not badly off, but, with the rising cost of living...'

'When did she die?'

The old woman's eyes opened wide.

'Die?'

'I'm sorry. I thought she was dead. You yourself speak of her in the past tense.'

She smiled.

'That's true. But not for the reason you imagine. She isn't dead; only for us it's as though she were, she's gone away.'

'After a quarrel?'

'Guillaume is not the kind of man who quarrels.'

'With you?'

'I am too old to quarrel now, Chief-Inspector. I've seen too much. I know life too well, and I let everybody...'

'When did she leave the house?'

'Two days ago.'

'Did she tell you she was going?'

'My son and I knew that she would go in the end.'

'She had talked to you about it?'

'Often.'

'Did she give you any reasons?'

She did not reply at once, seemed to be pondering.

'Do you want me to tell you frankly what I think? If I hesitate, it's because I fear you may laugh at me. I don't like to discuss such things in front of men, but I suppose that a police officer is rather like a doctor or a priest.'

'You are a Roman Catholic, Madame Serre?'

'Yes. My daughter-in-law was a Protestant. That made no difference. You see, she was at the awkward age for a woman. We all, more or less, have to go through a few years during which we are not our normal selves. We get upset over trifles. We are apt to see things out of perspective.'

'I understand. That's what it was?'

'That and other things, probably. In the end, she dreamed only of her native Holland, spent all day writing to friends that she had kept up with over there.'

'Did your son ever go to Holland with her?'

'Never.'

'So she left on Tuesday?'

'She went on the nine-forty from the Gare du Nord.'

'The night-train?'

'Yes. She had spent the whole day packing.'

'Your son went with her to the station?'

'No.'

'Did she take a taxi?'

'She went to fetch one from the corner of the Boulevard Richard-Wallace.'

'She hasn't got in touch with you since?'

'No. I don't suppose she feels it necessary to write to us.'

'Was there any question of a divorce?'

'I've told you that we are Catholics. Moreover, my son has no wish to get married again. I still do not understand why the police have seen fit to call upon us.'

'I would like to ask you, Madame, exactly what happened here on Tuesday night. One moment. You haven't a maid, have you?'

'No, Chief-Inspector. Eugénie, our charwoman, comes every day from nine till five.'

'Is she here today?'

'You have come on her day off. She'll come in again tomorrow.'

'She lives in the neighbourhood?'

'She lives at Puteaux, on the other side of the Seine. Above an ironmonger's shop, directly opposite the bridge.'

'I suppose she helped your daughter-in-law to pack?'

'She brought the cases downstairs.'

'How many cases?'

'One trunk and two leather suit-cases precisely. Then there was a jewel-box and a dressing-case.'

'Eugénie left at five as usual?'

'She did, indeed. Please forgive me if I seem disconcerted, but this is the first time I've ever been cross-questioned like this and I must confess...'

'Did your son go out that evening?'

'What time of evening do you mean?'

'Let's say before dinner.'

'He went out for his usual stroll.'

'I suppose he went to have an *apéritif?*'

'He doesn't drink.'

'Never?'

'Nothing except a glass of wine and water at meal-times. Still less those horrible things called *apéritifs*.'

It seemed then that Boissier, who was sitting on his best behaviour in his arm-chair, sniffed the smell of aniseed which still clung to his moustache.

'We sat down to table as soon as he came in. He always takes the same stroll. It became a habit with him in the days when we had a dog that had to be exercised at set times and, I declare, it's become second nature to him.'

'You haven't a dog nowadays?'

'Not for four years. Not since Bibi died.'

'Or a cat?'

'My daughter-in-law loathed cats. You see! I spoke of her again in the past tense, and it' s because we really do think of her as belonging to the past.'

'The three of you had dinner together?'

'Maria came down just as I was bringing in the soup.'

'There was no quarrelling?'

'None. Nobody spoke during the meal. I could tell that Guillaume, after all, was a little upset. At first sight, he seems cold, but really he's a terribly sensitive boy. When one has lived on terms of intimacy with someone for over two years....'

Maigret and Boissier had not heard a thing. But she, the old lady, was sharp of hearing. She bent her head as though she were listening. It was a mistake, for Maigret understood, rose to his feet, and went and opened the door. A man, undoubtedly taller, broader and heavier than the chief-inspector, stood there, slightly shamefaced, for he had plainly been eavesdropping for some time.

His mother had told the truth when she claimed that he'd been taking a siesta. His sparse hair, ruffled, clung to his forehead and he'd pulled on trousers over his white shirt, with his collar still unbuttoned. He wore carpet slippers on his feet.

'Won't you come in, Monsieur Serre?' asked Maigret.

'I beg you pardon. I heard voices. I thought...'

He spoke deliberately, turning his heavy, brooding stare

upon each of them in turn.

'These gentlemen are police officers,' his mother explained, rising to her feet.

He didn't ask for any explanation, stared at them again, buttoned up his shirt.

'Madame Serre was telling us that your wife left the day before yesterday.'

This time he turned round to face the old lady, his brows together. His big frame was flaccid, like his face, but, unlike many fat men, he did not give an impression of agility. His complexion was very pale and sallow, tufts of dark hair sprouted from his nostrils, from his ears, and he had enormously bushy eyebrows.

'What exactly do these gentlemen want?' he asked, carefully spacing out the syllables.

'I don't know.'

And even Maigret felt at a loss. Boissier wondered how the chief inspector was going to get out of the situation. These weren't the sort of people who could be put through the third degree.

'Actually, Monsieur Serre, the question of your wife merely cropped up in the course of conversation. Your mother told us that you were lying down, and we had a little talk while we were waiting for you. We're here, my colleague and myself' — the term 'colleague' gave Boissier so much pleasure! — 'simply because we've reason to believe that you have been the victim of an attempted burglary.'

Serre was not the sort of man who is unable to look others in the face. Far from it, he stared at Maigret as though attempting to read his innermost thoughts.

'What gave you that idea?'

'Sometimes we come into possession of confidential information.'

'You are speaking, I suppose, of police informers?'

'Let's put it like that.'

'I'm sorry, gentlemen.'

'Your house hasn't been burgled?'

'If it had been, I would have lost no time in lodging a complaint myself with the local police.'

He wasn't trying to be civil. Not once had he shown even the vestige of a smile.

'You are, however, the owner of a safe?'

'I believe that I'd be within my rights in refusing to answer you. I don't mind telling you, however, that I have got one.'

His mother was attempting to make signs to him, advising him, probably, not to be so ill-tempered.

He realized this and remained obdurate.

'If I'm not mistaken, it's a safe installed by Messrs. Planchart about eighteen years ago.'

He remained unperturbed. He continued to stand, whilst Maigret and Boissier sat in semi-darkness, and Maigret saw that he had the same heavy jowl as the man in the portrait, the same eyebrows. The chief inspector wondered whimsically what he'd look like with side-whiskers.

'I don't remember when I had it put in, nor is that anybody's business but mine.'

'I noticed, as we came in, that the front door is secured by a chain and a safety-lock.'

'So are lots of front doors.'

'You sleep on the first landing, your mother and yourself?'

Serre deliberately made no reply.

'Your study and surgery are on the ground floor?'

From a gesture on the part of the old lady, Maigret understood that these rooms led out of the drawing-room.

'Would you mind if I took a look round?'

He paused, opened his mouth, and Maigret felt certain it was to say no. His mother sensed this, too, for she intervened.

'Why not comply with these gentlemen's request? They will see for themselves that there has been no burglary.'

The man shugged his shoulders, his expression as stubborn, as sullen, as ever, and he refrained from following them into the neighbouring rooms.

Madame Serre showed them first into a study as peaceful and old-fashioned as the drawing-room. Behind a black-leather-bottomed chair, stood a big safe, painted dark green, of a rather obsolete type. Boissier went up to it, smoothed the steel with a professional touch.

'You see that everything is in order,' said the old woman. 'You mustn't mind my son being in a bad temper, but...'

She stopped as she saw the latter, framed in the doorway, fixing them with the same morose stare.

Then, waving a hand towards the bound volumes which filled the shelves, she went on, with a strained sprightliness:

'Don't be surprised to see mostly books on law. They're part of my husband's library, who was a solicitor.'

She opened one last door. And here the furnishings were more commonplace; it might have been any dental surgery, with a mechanical chair and the usual instruments. Up to half the height of the window, the panes were frosted.

On their way back through the study Boissier crossed to one of the windows, again felt with his fingers on it, then gave Maigret a significant nod.

'Has this window-pane been put in recently?' asked the latter in his turn.

It was the old woman who answered immediately:

'Four days ago. The window was open during the big thunderstorm which I'm sure you remember.'

'Did you call in the glazier?'

'No.'

'Who replaced the pane?'

'My son. He likes doing odd jobs. He always sees to any of our little household repairs.'

At which Guillaume Serre said with a touch of irritation:

'These gentlemen have no right to pester us, Mamma. Don't answer any more questions.'

She turned so that her back was towards him, and smiled at Maigret in a way that meant plainly:

'Don't mind him. I did warn you.'

She showed them to the front door, while her son remained standing in the centre of the drawing-room, and leaned forward to whisper:

'If you have anything to say to me, come and call when

he isn't here.'

They were outside in the sunlight again, which made the clothes cling immediately to their skin. Once outside the gate — its faint creak was reminiscent of a convent gate — they caught sight, on the opposite pavement, of Ernestine's green hat as she sat at a table outside the café-restaurant.

Maigret halted. They could have turned left and avoided her. If they joined her, it would look almost as though they had to give her an account of themselves.

Perhaps out of a sense of decency, the chief-inspector growled: 'Shall we go and have one?'

With an enquiring expression, she watched them come towards her.

CHAPTER THREE

'What did you do today?' asked Madame Maigret, as they sat down to eat in front of the open window.

In the houses opposite also people could be seen eating, and, on every side, the same bright splashes of shirts showed where the men had taken off their jackets. Some of them, who'd finished dinner, were leaning on their elbows out of the window. Wireless music could be heard playing, babies crying, raised voices. A few concierges had brought their chairs out in front of their doorsteps.

'Nothing out of the way,' replied Maigret. 'A Dutch-woman who may have been murdered, but who's probably still alive somewhere.'

It was too early to talk about it. On the whole, he'd behaved slackly. They'd sat about for a long time outside the little café in the Rue de la Ferme, Boissier, Ernestine and himself, and of the three it was Ernestine who'd been the most worked up.

She took umbrage:

'He made out it wasn't true?'

The proprietor had brought them pints of beer.

'Actually he didn't say anything. It was his mother who did the talking. On his own, he'd have thrown us out.'

'He says there wasn't a corpse in the study?'

She'd obviously found out from the café owner about the residents in the house with the wrought-iron gate.

'Then why didn't he tell the police that somebody'd tried

to burgle the place?'

'According to him no one tried to burgle him.'

Of course she knew all about Sad Freddie's little ways.

'Wasn't there a pane missing in one of the windows?'

Boissier looked at Maigret as if advising him to say nothing, but the chief-inspector took no notice.

'A pane has been mended recently; it appears that it got broken four or five days ago, on the night of the storm.'

'He's lying.'

'Somebody's lying, certainly.'

'You think it's me?'

'I didn't say so. It might be Alfred.'

'Why should he have told me all that story on the 'phone?'

'Perhaps he didn't,' interposed Boissier, watching her narrowly.

'And what should I have made it up for? Is that what you think, too, Monsieur Maigret?'

'I don't think anything.'

He was smiling vaguely. He felt comfortable, almost blissful. The beer was cool, and in the shade it smelt almost like the country, perhaps because the Bois de Boulogne was close by.

A lazy afternoon. They'd drunk two pints apiece. Then, so as not to leave the girl stranded so far from the centre of Paris, they gave her a lift in their taxi and dropped her at the Châtelet.

'Ring me up directly you get a letter.'

He felt she was disappointed in him, that she'd imagined him otherwise. She must be telling herself that he'd got old, had become like the rest of them, and couldn't be much bothered with her case.

'D'you want me to put back my leave?' Boissier had suggested.

'I suppose your wife's done all the packing?'

'The bags are at the station already. We were due to go on the six o'clock train tomorrow morning.'

'With your daughter?'

'Naturally.'

'Off you go.'

'Won't you be needing me?'

'You've trusted me with the file.'

Once alone in his office, he nearly dozed off in his chair. The wasp was no longer there. The sun had moved round to the other side of the quay. Lucas had been off duty since noon. He called Janvier, who had been the first to take his leave, in June, because of a wedding in some branch of his family.

'Sit down. I've got a job for you. You've made out your report?'

'I've just this minute finished it.'

'Right! Take a note of this. First you've got to look up, at the Town Hall in Neuilly, the maiden name of a Dutchwoman who, two and a half years ago, married a man called Guillaume Serre, residing at 43b Rue de la Ferme.'

'Easy.'

'I dare say. She must have been living in Paris for some time. You must try to find out where, what she did, what relatives she had, how much money, etc....'

'Right you are, Chief.'

'She's supposed to have left the house in the Rue de la Ferme on Tuesday, between eight and nine in the evening, and to have taken the night-train to Holland. She went to fetch a taxi herself from the corner of the Boulevard Richard-Wallace to take her luggage.'

Janvier was writing words in columns on a page of his note-book.

'That all?'

'No. Get some help to save time. I want the people in the neighbourhood, tradesmen and so on, questioned about the Serres.'

'How many are there?'

'Mother and son. The mother's nearly eighty and the son's a dentist. Try to locate the taxi. Also make enquiries from the staff at the station — and on the train.'

'Can I have transport?'

'You can.'

And that was about all he'd done that afternoon. He'd asked to be put through to the Belgian police, who had Sad Freddie's description but had not yet found him. He also had a long conversation with the passport inspector on the frontier, at Jeumont. The latter had himself gone over the train which Alfred was thought to have taken, and didn't remember any passenger resembling the expert safe-cracker.

That meant nothing. He just had to wait. Maigret signed a few papers on behalf of the Chief, went to have a drink at the *Brasserie Dauphine* together with a colleague in the Records Office, and then back home by bus.

'What shall we do?' asked Madame Maigret, when the table had been cleared.

'Let's go for a stroll.'

Which meant that they'd amble along as far as the main boulevards to finish up sitting at a café terrace. The sun had set. The air was becoming cooler, though gusts of warm air still seemed to rise up from the paving-stones. The bay-windows of the *brasserie* were open, and a depleted orchestra played inside. Most of the customers sat there without speaking, like them, at their tables, watching the passers-by, and their faces melted more and more into the dusk. Then the electric-light made them look quite different.

Like the other couples, they turned back towards home, Madame Maigret's hand crooked in her husband's arm.

After that it was another day, as clear and sunny as the one before.

Instead of going straight to Headquarters, Maigret made a detour by the Quai de Jemmapes, identified the green-painted café, near the Saint-Martin Lock, with the sign 'Snacks served at all hours', and went in to lean against the counter.

'A white wine.'

Then he put the question. The Auvergnat who served him answered unhesitatingly:

'I don't know at what time exactly, but someone rang up. It was already daylight. My wife and I didn't get up, because, at that time, it couldn't have been for us. Ernestine went down. I heard her talking a long time.'

That was one thing at least she had not lied about.

'What time did Alfred go out, the night before?'

'Eleven, maybe? Maybe earlier. What I do remember is that he took his bike.'

A door led straight from the café into the passageway, from which a staircase mounted to the floors above. The wall of the staircase was whitewashed, as in the country. One could hear the racket made by a crane unloading gravel from a barge a little farther on.

Maigret knocked at a door, which half-opened; Ernestine appeared in her underclothes and merely said:

'It's you!'

Then she went at once to fetch her dressing-gown from the unmade bed, and slipped it on.

Did Maigret smile in memory of the Ernestine-that-used-to-be?

'You know, it's really a kindness,' she said frankly. 'I'm not a pretty sight these days.'

'The window was open. There was a blood-red geranium. The bedspread was red, too. A door stood open into a little kitchen, out of which came a good smell of coffee.

He didn't quite know what he'd come for.

'There was nothing at the *poste restante* yesterday evening?'

She answered, worried:

'Nothing.'

'You don't think it odd that he hasn't written?'

'Perhaps he's just being canny. He must be surprised to see nothing in the papers. He probably thinks I'm being watched. I was just going to the post office.'

An old trunk lay in a corner.

'Those are his belongings?'

'His and mine. Between the two of us, we don't own much.'

Then, with an understanding look:

'Like to make a search? Of course! I know. It's your duty. You'll find a few tools, because he's got a spare set, also two old suits, some dresses and a bit of linen.'

As she spoke, she was turning out the contents of the trunk onto the floor, opening the drawers of a dressing-table.

'I've been thinking it over. I've grasped what you were

getting at yesterday. Of course somebody must have been lying. Either it's those people, the mother and her son, or it's Alfred, or it's me. You've no reason to believe any of us in particular.'

'Has Alfred no relatives in the country?'

'He's got no relatives anywhere now. He only knew his mother, and she's been dead twenty years.'

'You've never been anywhere together outside Paris?'

'Never farther than Corbeil.'

He couldn't be hiding out at Corbeil. It was too near. Maigret was beginning to think that he hadn't gone to Belgium either.

'There's no place he used to talk about, that he'd have liked to visit one day?'

'He always said the country, no special part. That summed it all up, to him.'

'Were you born in the country yourself?'

'Near Nevers, in a village called Saint-Martin-des-Prés.'

She took from a drawer a postcard that showed the village church, standing opposite a pond which served to water cattle.

'Did you show him this?'

She understood. Girls like Ernestine soon understand.

'I'd be surprised to find him there. He really was near the Gare du Nord when he 'phoned me.'

'How d'you know?'

'I found the bar, yesterday evening. It's in the Rue de Maubeuge, near a leather-goods shop. It's called the *Bar du Levant*. The owner remembers him because he was the first customer that day. He'd just lit the percolator when Alfred got there. Wouldn't you like a cup of coffee?'

He didn't like to refuse, but he'd just drunk white wine.

'No offence.'

He had some difficulty finding a taxi in those parts, eventually was driven to the *Bar du Levant*.

'A thin little chap, sad-looking, with eyes all red as if he'd been crying,' they told him.

Unquestionably Alfred Jussiaume, who often had red-rimmed eyes.

'He talked a long time at the 'phone, drank two coffees

without sugar and went off towards the station, looking round him as if he was scared of being followed. Has he done anything wrong?'

It was ten o'clock when Maigret at last climbed the staircase at Headquarters, where dust-motes still floated like a mist in the sunlight. Contrary to his usual custom, he didn't glance in through the glass partition of the waiting-room, and went past into the Duty Room, which was almost empty.

'Janvier not in yet?'

'He came about eight and went out again. He left a note on your desk.'

The note said:

The woman is called Maria Van Aerts. She is fifty-one and comes from Sneeck, in Friesland, Holland. I'm going to Neuilly, where she lived in a boarding-house, Rue de Longchamp. Haven't found the taxi yet. Vacher's looking after the station.

Joseph, the office-boy, opened the door.

'I didn't see you come in, Monsieur Maigret. A lady's been waiting for you half an hour.'

He held out an appointment-slip, on which old Madame Serre had inscribed her name in small, sharp handwriting.

'Shall I show her in?'

Maigret put on his jacket that he'd just taken off, went to open the window, filled his pipe and sat down.

'Yes, show her in.'

He wondered what she would seem like outside the framework of her home, but, to his surprise, she didn't look out of place at all. She wasn't dressed in black, as on the day before; she wore a frock with a white ground, on which dark patterns were traced. Her hat was not ludicrous. She moved forward with assurance.

'You were more or less expecting me to call, weren't you, Chief-Inspector?'

He had not been expecting it and refrained from telling her so.

'Do sit down, Madame.'

'Thank you.'

'The smoke doesn't worry you?'

'My son smokes cigars all day long. I was so upset yesterday at the way he received you! I tried to make signs to you not to persist, because I know him.'

She showed no nervousness, chose her words carefully, aimed at Maigret now and then a sort of conspiratorial smile.

'I think it is I who brought him up badly. You see, I had but the one child and, when my husband died, he was only seventeen years old. I spoilt him. Guillaume was the only man in the house. If you have any children...'

Maigret looked at her to try to sum up her background and did not succeed. Something made him ask:

'Were you born in Paris?'

'In the house that you came to yesterday.'

It was a coincidence to find in one case two people born in Paris. Almost invariably, the people he dealt with were more or less directly connected with the provinces.

'And your husband?'

'His father, before him, used to be a solicitor in the Rue de Tocqueville, seventeenth *arrondissement*.'

That made three! To end up in the atmosphere, so absolutely provincial, of the house in the Rue de la Ferme!

'My son and myself have almost always lived alone together, and I suppose that is what has made him a little unsociable.'

'I understood that he'd been married before.'

'He was. His wife didn't live long.'

'How many years after their marriage did she die?'

She opened her mouth; he guessed that a sudden thought made her pause. He even had the impression of seeing a slight flush mount to her cheeks.

'Two years,' she said at last. 'That's curious, is it not? It only struck me just now. He lived for two years with Maria, as well.'

'Who was his first wife?'

'A person of very good family, Jeanne Devoisin, whom we met one summer at Dieppe, at the time when we used to go there every year.'

'Was she younger than he?'

'Let me see. He was thirty-two. She was more or less the same age. She was a widow.'

'Had she any children?'

'No. I don't think she had any relatives, except a sister living in Indo-China.'

'What did she die of?'

'A heart attack. She had a weak heart and spent most of her time under the care of doctors.'

She smiled again:

'I haven't told you yet why I am here. I nearly telephoned to you yesterday, when my son went out for his evening stroll, then I thought it would be more polite to come and call on you. I wish to apologize for Guillaume's attitude towards you and to say that his ill-humour was not directed at you personally. He has such a fierce temperament.'

'So I saw.'

'At the very idea that you could suspect him of dishonest action.... He was like that even as a small boy....'

'He lied to me?'

'I beg your pardon?'

The old lady's face expressed genuine surprise.

'Why should he have lied to you? I don't understand. You didn't really ask any questions. It's precisely to answer any which you should wish to put to me that I have come here. We have nothing to hide. I've no idea of the circumstances that have led you to bother about us. It must be some misunderstanding, or some neighbour's spitefulness.'

'When was the window-pane broken?'

'I told you or my son told you, I can't remember now: during the thunderstorm last week. I was on the first floor and I hadn't had time to shut all the windows when I heard a crash of glass.'

'Was it in broad daylight?'

'It must have been six o'clock in the evening.'

'Which means the charwoman, Eugénie, was no longer there?'

'She leaves us at five. I think I explained that to you also. I haven't told my son that I was coming to see you. I thought that you might like, perhaps, to visit the house, and it would be easier when he's not there.'

'You mean during his late afternoon stroll?'

'Yes. You do understand that there's nothing to hide in our home, and that, if it weren't for Guillaume's nature, everything would have been cleared up yesterday.'

'You realize, Madame Serre, that you came here of your own free will?'

'Yes, of course.'

'And that it's you who want me to question you?'

She nodded her head in confirmation.

'We'll go over your movements again, then, from the last meal that you, your son and your daughter-in-law took together. Your daughter-in-law's luggage was ready. In which part of the house was it?'

'In the corridor.'

'Who brought it down?'

'Eugénie brought down the suit-cases, and my son took charge of the trunk, too heavy for her.'

'Is it a very big trunk?'

'What they call a cabin-trunk. Before her marriage, Maria travelled a lot. She has lived in Italy and Egypt.'

'What did you have to eat?'

The question seemed both to amuse and surprise her.

'Let me see! As it's I who do the cooking, I should be able to remember. Vegetable soup, to start with. We always have vegetable soup, so good for the health. Then I did grilled mackerel and potato purée.'

'And the sweet?'

'A chocolate custard. Yes. My son has always adored chocolate custard.'

'No argument broke out at table? What time did the meal end?'

'About half-past seven. I put the dishes in the kitchen sink and went upstairs.'

'So you weren't present at the departure of your daughter-in-law.'

'I wasn't very anxious to be. Moments such as those are painful, and I prefer to avoid emotion. I said *au revoir* to her downstairs, in the drawing-room. I've nothing against her.

Everybody's as they are made and...'

'Where was your son during that time?'

'In his study, I think.'

'You've no idea whether he had a last conversation with his wife?'

'It's unlikely. She'd gone upstairs again. I heard her in her room, getting ready.'

'Your house is very solidly built, like most old houses. I suppose that, from the first floor, it's hard to hear sounds coming from downstairs?'

'Not for me,' she answered, pursing her lips.

'What d'you mean?'

'That I have keen hearing. Not even a floorboard can creak without my hearing it.'

'Who went to fetch the taxi?'

'Maria. I told you so yesterday.'

'Did she stay out long?'

'Fairly long. There's no rank nearby, and one has to wait for a taxi to come cruising by.'

'Did you go to the window?'

She hesitated imperceptibly.

'Yes.'

'Who carried the trunk as far as the taxi?'

'The driver.'

'You don't know what company the cab belonged to?'

'How would I know that?'

'What colour was it?'

'Reddish-brown, with a coat-of-arms on the door.'

'Can you remember the driver?'

'Not very well. I think he was small and rather fat.'

'How was your daughter-in-law dressed?'

'She wore a mauve frock.'

'No coat?'

'She had it over her arm.'

'Was your son still in the study?'

'Yes.'

'What happened then? Did you go down?'

'No.'

'You didn't go to see your son?'

'It was he who came up.'

'Immediately?'

'Not long after the taxi drove away.'

'Was he upset?'

'He was as you have seen him. He's of a rather gloomy nature. I explained to you that he's really a highly sensitive man, likely to be affected by the smallest happenings.'

'Did he know that his wife was not coming back?'

'He suspected it.'

'She told him so?'

'Not exactly. She just hinted. She talked of the necessity to change her ideas, to see her own country again. Once over there, you understand....'

'What did you do then?'

'I dressed my hair for the night.'

'Your son was in your room?'

'Yes.'

'He didn't leave the house?'

'No. Why?'

'Where does he garage his car?'

'A hundred yards away, where some old stables have been turned into private garages. Guillaume has hired one of them.'

'So he can take his car out and put it back without being seen?'

'Why should he want to hide?'

'Did he go downstairs again?'

'I have no idea. I think so. I go to bed early, and he usually reads until eleven o'clock or midnight.'

'In the study?'

'Or in his room.'

'His room is near yours?'

'Next door. There's a bathroom in between us.'

'Did you hear him go to bed?'

'Certainly.'

'At what time?'

'I didn't put on the light.'

'You didn't hear any noise later?'

'None.'

'I suppose that you're the first down in the morning?'

'In summer I come down at half-past six.'

'Did you go round all the rooms?'

'I went first into the kitchen to put some water on to boil, then I opened the windows, because that's the time when the air is still cool.'

'You went into the study then?'

'Probably.'

'You don't remember doing so?'

'I almost certainly did.'

'The broken pane was already repaired?'

'I suppose so ... yes ...'

'Did you notice any disorder in the room?'

'None, except for some cigar ends, as always, in the ashtrays, and perhaps a book or two lying around. I don't know what all this means, Monsieur Maigret. As you see, I answer your questions frankly. I came especially to do so.'

'Because you were worried?'

'No. Because I was ashamed of the way Guillaume treated you. And also because I sense something mysterious behind your visit. Women aren't like men. In my husband's time, for instance, if there were a noise in the house at night, he never moved from his bed, and it was I who went to look. You understand? It's probably the same with your own wife. Really, it's in a way for the same reason that I'm here. You talked about burglary. You seemed preoccupied with the question of Maria.'

'You haven't had any news of her?'

'I don't expect to receive any. You're hiding certain facts and that makes me curious. It's the same with sounds in the night. I hold that mysteries don't exist, that one only has to look at thing squarely for them to become perfectly simple.'

She was watching him, sure of herself, and Maigret had a slight feeling that she looked upon him as a child, as another Guillaume. She seemed to be saying:

'Tell me everything that's worrying you. Don't be frightened. You'll see that it'll all come right.'

He, too, looked her straight in the face.

'A man broke into your house that night.'

The old woman's eyes were incredulous, with a tinge of pity, as though he'd still believed in werewolves.

'What for?'

'To burgle the safe.'

'Did he do it?'

'He got into the house by cutting out a pane of glass to open the window.'

'The pane that was already broken in the thunderstorm? No doubt he put it back afterwards.'

She still refused to take what he was saying seriously.

'What did he take away?'

'He took nothing away, because at a certain moment his electric torch lit up something that he hadn't expected to find in the room.'

She was smiling.

'What sort of thing?'

'The dead body of a middle-aged woman, which may have been that of your daughter-in-law.'

'He told you that?'

He looked at the white-gloved hands that didn't tremble.

'Why don't you ask this man to come and repeat his accusations to me?'

'He's not in Paris.'

'Can't you make him come here?'

Maigret preferred to make no reply. He wasn't too pleased with himself. He was beginning to wonder if he too was not falling under the influence of this woman who had the comforting serenity of a Mother Superior.

She didn't get up, didn't fidget, didn't show indignation either.

'I have no idea what it's all about and I won't ask you. Perhaps you have some good reason for believing in this man. He's a burglar, isn't he? Whilst I am merely an old woman of seventy-eight who never did anyone any harm.'

'Allow me, now that I know where we are, to invite you cordially to come to our house. I will open every door for you, I will show you anything you may wish to see. And my son, once he's acquainted with the facts, will not fail, in his turn, to answer your questions.

'When will you come, Monsieur Maigret?'

Now she had risen to her feet still perfectly at ease, and

there was nothing aggressive in her manner, just a slight touch of bitterness.

'Probably this afternoon. I don't know yet. Has your son used the car, these last few days?'

'You can ask him, if you like.'

'Is he at home now?'

'It's possible. He was there when I went out.'

'Eugénie as well?'

'She is certainly there.'

'Thank you.'

He showed her to the door. Just as they reached it, she turned round.

'I'd like to ask a favour,' she said gently. 'When I've gone, try for a moment to put yourself in my place, forgetting that you have spent your life in dealing with crime. Imagine that it's you who are suddenly being asked the questions you put to me, you who are being suspected of killing in cold blood.'

That was all. She only added:

'Until this afternoon, Monsieur Maigret.'

Once the door was closed, he stood for a full minute without moving by the doorway. Then he went to look out of the window, soon caught sight of the old lady walking with quick short steps, in full sunshine, towards the Pont Saint-Michel.

He picked up the telephone.

'Get me the police-station at Neuilly.'

He didn't ask to be put through to the station officer, but to a sergeant whom he knew.

'Vanneau? Maigret here. I'm well, thanks. Listen. It's a bit tricky. Jump in a car and get round to 43b, Rue de la Ferme.'

'The dentist place? Janvier, who came here yesterday evening, spoke to me about him. Something to do with a Dutchwoman, isn't it?'

'Never mind. Time's getting on. The chap's not easy to handle, and I can't ask for a warrant just now. You've got to act quickly, before his mother gets there.'

'Is she far away?'

'At the Pont Saint-Michel. I suppose she's going to take a

cab.'

'What shall I do with the man?'

'Bring him in, on some excuse. Tell him whatever you like, that you need him as a witness....'

'And then?'

'I'll be there. Just the time it takes to get downstairs and jump in a car.'

'Suppose the dentist's not at home?'

'You keep watch and grab him before he gets inside.'

'Bit irregular, eh?'

'Quite.'

As Vanneau was going to ring off, he added:

'Take somebody with you and put him to watch the stables that they've turned into garages in the same street. One of the garages is hired by the dentist.'

'Right you are.'

A moment later Maigret was hurrying down the stairs and climbing into one of the police-cars parked in the courtyard. As the car turned round towards the Pont Neuf, he thought he caught sight of Ernestine's green hat. He wasn't sure of it and preferred not to lose time. To tell the truth, he'd given way to a sudden fit of resentment against Lofty.

Once they'd crossed the Pont Neuf, he felt remorseful, but it was too late.

Couldn't be helped! She'd wait for him.

CHAPTER FOUR

The police-station was on the ground floor of the Town Hall, an ugly square building that stood in the middle of a waste land, with sparse trees around and a dirty flag dangling. Maigret could have gone straight from outside into the Duty Rooms; so as not to come face to face with Guillaume Serre, he took a roundabout way through the draughty corridors, where he soon got lost.

Here too the slackness of summer held sway. Doors and windows were open, documents fluttered on tables in the empty rooms, while clerks in shirt-sleeves exchanged seaside gossip and an occasional tax-payer wandered disconsolately about in search of an endorsement or a signature.

Maigret finally managed to light upon a policeman who knew him by sight.

'Sergeant Vanneau?'

'Second on the left, third door along the passage.'

'Would you go and fetch him for me? There should be someone with him. Don't say my name out loud.'

A few moments later Vanneau joined him.

'Is he there?'

'Yes'

'How did it go off?'

'Middling. I'd taken good care to bring along a police summons. I rang. A servant answered and I asked to see her master. I had to wait about a bit in the passage. Then the bloke came down, and I handed him the paper. He read it, looked at me without saying anything.

' "If you'd like to come with me, I've a car outside."

'He shrugged his shoulders, took a Panama hat down from the hallstand, shoved it on his head, and followed me out.

'Now he's sitting on a chair. He still hasn't uttered a word.'

A minute or two later, Maigret went into Vanneau's office, found Serre there smoking a very black cigar. The chief-inspector took up a seat in the sergeant's chair.

'I'm sorry to have troubled you, Monsieur Serre, but I'd like you to answer a few questions.'

As on the day before, the huge dentist surveyed him broodingly, and he had no trace of cordiality in his gloomy stare. Maigret, all of sudden, realized what the man reminded him of: the sort of sultan that one used to see pictures of at one time. He had the girth, the manifest weight; in all probability the strength, too. For, despite his fat, he gave the impression of being very strong. He had also the disdainful calm of those pashas that are depicted on cigarette packets.

Instead of making some sign of agreement, uttering a polite commonplace or even voicing a protest, Serre took a buff-coloured form from his pocket, cast his eye over it.

'I've been summoned here by the Police Superintendent of Neuilly,' he said. 'I look forward to hearing what this superintendent requires from me.'

'Am I to understand you refuse to answer my questions?'

'Emphatically.'

Maigret paused. He'd seen all sorts, the mutinous, the pig-headed, the wilful, the wily, but none had ever answered him back with such unruffled determination.

'I suppose it's no good arguing?'

'Not in my opinion.'

'Or trying to point out that your attitude doesn't show you in a good light?'

This time the other merely sighed.

'Very well. Wait. The superintendent will see you now.'

Maigret went in search of the latter, who did not at once understand what was expected of him, and only grudgingly agreed to play his part. His quarters were more comfortable, almost sumptuous in comparison with the rest of the offices, and there was a marble clock on the mantelpiece.

'Show Monsieur Serre in!' he told the man on duty.

He motioned him to a chair with a red velvet seat.

'Do sit down, Monsieur Serre. It's just a matter of a routine check-up, and I won't waste your time.'

The superintendent consulted a form which had just been brought to him.

'You are, I believe, the owner of a motor-vehicle registered under the number RS 8822 L?'

The dentist confirmed this with a nod. Maigret had gone over to sit on the window-sill and was watching him very thoughtfully.

'The vehicle in question is still in your possession?'

Another nod of assent.

'When was the last time you used it?'

'I believe I've the right to know the reason for this interrogation.'

The superintendent shifted in his chair. He didn't at all like the task which Maigret had entrusted to him.

'Just suppose that your car had been involved in an accident....'

'Has it been?'

'Suppose the number had been notified to us as that of a car which had knocked somebody down?'

'When?'

The police officer threw Maigret a reproachful look.

'Tuesday evening.'

'Where?'

'Near the Seine.'

'My car didn't leave the garage on Tuesday evening.'

'Somebody might have used it without your knowledge.'

'I doubt it. The garage is locked up.'

'You're prepared to swear that you didn't use the car on Tuesday evening, or later during the night?'

'Where are the witnesses to the accident?'

Once again the superintendent looked anxiously to Maigret for support. The latter, realizing that this was leading nowhere, motioned to him not to take it any further.

'I've no further questions, Monsieur Serre. Thank you.'

The dentist rose, seemed for a moment to fill the room with his bulk, put on his Panama hat and left the room, after turning to stare fixedly at Maigret.

'I did what I could. As you saw.'

'I saw.'

'Did you get any lead out of it?'

'Perhaps.'

'That's a man who'll make trouble for us. He's a stickler for his rights.'

'I know.'

It seemed almost as if Maigret was unconsciously imitating the dentist. He had the same sombre, heavy expression. He, in turn, made for the door.

'What's he supposed to have done, Maigret?'

'I don't know yet. It may be that he's killed his wife.'

He went to thank Vanneau, and found himself outside once more, where the police-car awaited him. Before climbing in, he had a drink at the bar on the corner and catching sight of himself in the mirror, wondered what he'd look like wearing a panama hat. Then he smiled wryly at the thought that it was, in a way, a case of two heavy-weights engaged in a fight.

He said to the driver:

'Go round by the Rue de la Ferme.'

Not far from 43b, they caught sight of Serre walking along the pavement with long, rather indolent strides. As some fat men do, he straddled slightly. He was still smoking his long cigar. As he passed the garage he couldn't have failed to notice the plain-clothes man who was keeping a look-out there and had no means of taking cover.

Maigret was reluctant to stop the car at the house with the black wrought-iron gate. What good would it do? They probably wouldn't let him in.

Ernestine was waiting for him in the glass-panelled anteroom at Headquarters. He showed her into his office.

'Any news?' she asked him.

'Not a thing.'

He was in a bad temper. She didn't know that he rather liked feeling bad-tempered at the beginning of a difficult case.

'I had a card this morning. I brought it to you.'

She handed him a coloured postcard depicting the Town Hall at Le Havre. There was no inscription, no signature, nothing save Lofty's address, c/o *poste restante*.

'Alfred?'

'It's his handwriting.'

'He didn't go over to Belgium?'

'Doesn't look like it. He must have fought shy of the frontier.'

'D'you think he might try to get away by sea?'

'It isn't likely. He's never set foot on a boat. I'm going to ask you something, Monsieur Maigret, but you've got to give me a straight answer. Suppose he was to come back to Paris, what'd happen to him?'

'You want to know if he'd be detained?'

'Yes.'

'For attempted burglary?'

'Yes.'

'Nobody could detain him, because he wasn't caught red-handed, and, for another thing, Guillaume Serre hasn't laid a complaint, even denies that anybody broke into his house.'

'So they'd let him alone?'

'Unless he was lying and something quite different happened.'

'Can I promise him that?'

'Yes.'

'In that case, I'll put a notice in the Personal Column. He always takes the same paper, because of the crossword.'

She looked at him hard for a moment.

'You don't seem too sure about things.'

'What things?'

'The case. Yourself. I don't know. Did you see the

dentist again?'

'Half an hour ago.'

'What did he say?'

'Nothing.'

She'd nothing more to say either and used the telephone ringing as an excuse to take her leave.

'What is it?' Maigret growled into the mouthpiece.

'It's me, Chief. Could I see you in your room?'

A few seconds later Janvier came into the office briskly, obviously very pleased with himself.

'I've got plenty of leads. Shall I give 'em to you right away? You got a bit of time to spare?'

His enthusiasm was a little damped by the behaviour of Maigret, who'd just taken off his coat and was loosening his tie to set his thick neck free.

'First, I went to the boarding-house I told you about. It's a bit like the hotels on the left bank, with potted palms in the hall and old ladies sitting around in cane chairs. There aren't many guest much under fifty. Most of 'em are foreigners. English women, Swiss and Americans, who go to museums and write endless letters.'

'Well?'

Maigret knew the kind of thing. It wasn't worth going on about.

'Maria Van Aerts lived there for a year. They remember her, because she made herself popular in the place. She seems to 've been very gay and laughed a lot, shaking her great big bosom. She used to stuff herself with pastries, went to all the lectures at the Sorbonne.'

'That all?' said Maigret, meaning that he couldn't see what Janvier was so excited about.

'Nearly every day she used to write letters of eight to ten pages.'

The chief-inspector shrugged his shoulders, then examined the sergeant with more interest in his eye. He had caught on.

'Always to the same woman, a school friend who lives in Amsterdam and whose name I got hold of. This friend came to see her once. They shared a room for three weeks. I've an idea that even when married Maria Serre kept on writing. The friend's called Gertrude Oosting, she's the wife of a brewer. It shouldn't be hard to find out her address.'

'Ring through to Amsterdam.'

'Will you be wanting the letters?'

'The recent ones, if possible.'

'That's what I thought. Brussels still hasn't any news of Sad Freddie.'

'He's in Le Havre.'

'Shall I 'phone Le Havre?'

'I'll do it myself. Who's free next door?'

'Torrence came back to duty this morning.'

'Send him to me.'

Another heavy-weight, who wouldn't pass unnoticed on the pavement of an empty street.

'You go and stick yourself down in Neuilly, Rue de la Ferme, facing 43b, a house with a garden and an iron gate in front. Don't bother to take cover. Far from it. If you see a chap come out, bigger and taller than you, follow him so that he can see you.'

'Anything else?'

'Arrange to be relieved part of the night. There's a man from Neuilly on duty a bit farther on, opposite the garage.'

'What if the bloke goes off by car?'

'Take one of ours and park it along the kerb.'

He hadn't the energy to go home for lunch. It was hotter than the day before. There was thunder in the air. Most men were walking about with their jackets over their arms, and urchins were swimming in the Seine.

He went to have a bite at the *Brasserie Dauphine,* first having drunk, as if as a challenge, a couple of Pernods. Then he went to see Moers of the Technical Branch, under the overheated roof of the Palais de Justice.

'Let's say about eleven in the evening. Bring the things you need. Take someone with you.'

'Yes, Chief.'

He'd sent out a call to the police at Le Havre. Had Sad Freddie taken a train at the Gare du Nord after all, to Lille, for instance; or, having telephoned Ernestine, had he made a dash straight away for the Gare Saint-Lazare?

He must have gone to ground in some cheap lodging, or be wandering from bar to bar, drinking baby bottles of Vichy water, unless he was trying to stow away on board some ship. Was it as hot in Le Havre as it was in Paris?

They still hadn't found the taxi that was supposed to have picked up Maria Serre and her luggage. The staff at the Gare du Nord had no recollection of her.

Opening the paper, about three o'clock, Maigret read Ernestine's message in the Personal Column:

Alfred. Return Paris. No danger.
All arranged. Tine.

At half-past four he found himself still in his chair, the newspaper on his knee. He hadn't turned the page. He'd gone to sleep, and his mouth felt sticky, his back cricked.

None of the squad cars were in the courtyard and he had to take a taxi from the end of the quay.

'Rue de la Ferme, in Neuilly. I'll show you where to stop.'

He nearly dozed off again. It was five to five when he stopped the cab opposite the already familiar café. There was no one at the tables outside. Farther on the burly shape of Torrence could be seen, pacing up and down in the shade. He paid the driver, sat down with a sigh of relief.

'What can I get you, Monsieur Maigret?'

Beer, of course! He had such a thirst he could have swallowed five or six pints at a gulp.

'He hasn't been in again?'

'The dentist? No. I saw his mother, this morning, going down towards the Boulevard Richard-Wallace.'

The wrought-iron gate creaked. A wiry little woman started to walk along the opposite pavement and Maigret settled for his drink, caught her up just as she reached the edge of the Bois de Boulogne.

'Madame Eugénie?'

'What d'you want?'

The Neuilly household wasn't conspicuous for its affability.

'A little chat with you.'

'I've no time to chat. There's all the housework to do when I get home.'

'I'm a police officer.'

'That makes no odds.'

'I'd like to ask you a few questions.'

'Do I have to answer?'

'It would certainly be better to.'

'I don't like policemen.'

'You're not obliged to. D'you like your employers?'

'They stink.'

'Old Madame Serre as well?'

'She's a bitch.'

They were standing by a bus stop. Maigret raised his arm to stop a cruising taxi.

'I'm going to take you home.'

'I don't care all that much for being seen with a copper, but I suppose it's worth it.'

She climbed into the cab with dignity.

'What have you got against them?'

'What about you? Why are you sticking your nose into their business?'

'Young Madame Serre has gone away?'

'Young?' she said ironically.

'Let's say the daughter-in-law.'

'She's gone, yes. Good riddance.'

'Was she a bitch, too?'

'No.'

'You didn't like her?'

'She was always digging into the larder, and when it came to lunchtime, I couldn't find half what I'd got ready.'

'When did she go?'

'Tuesday.'

They were crossing the Pont de Puteaux. Eugénie tapped on the glass.

'Here we are,' she said. 'D'you need me any more?'

'Could I come up with you for a moment?'

They were on a crowded square, and the charwoman made towards an alleyway, to the right of a shop, began to climb a staircase that smelt of slops.

'If only you could tell them to leave my son alone.'

'Tell whom?'

'The other coppers. The ones from hereabouts. They never stop making trouble for him.'

'What does he do?'

'He works.'

'Doing what?'

'How should I know? Can't be helped if the housework isn't done for you. I can't clean up after others all day long and do my own as well.'

She went to open the window, for a strong, stuffy smell hung about, but it wasn't untidy and, except for a bed in one corner, the sort of drawing-cum-dining-room was almost dainty.

'What's all the to-do?' she asked, taking off her hat.

'Maria Serre can't be found.'

'Course not, as she's in Holland.'

'They can't find her in Holland either.'

'Why do they want to find her?'

'We've reason to believe that she's been murdered.'

A tiny spark kindled in Eugénie's brown eyes.

'Why don't you arrest them?'

'We haven't any proof yet.'

'And you're counting on me to get you some?'

She put some water to heat on the gas, came over to Maigret again.

'What happened on Tuesday?'

'She spent all day packing.'

'Wait a moment. She'd been married two and a half years, hadn't she? I suppose she had a good many things of her own.'

'She'd at least thirty dresses and as many pairs of shoes.'

'Was she smart?'

'She never threw anything out. Some of the dresses dated back ten years. She didn't wear them, but she wouldn't have given them away for all the money in the world.'

'Mean?'

'Aren't all rich people mean?'

'I was told that all she took with her was a trunk and two suitcases.'

'That's right. The rest went a week before.'

'You mean she sent other trunks away?'

'Trunks, packing-cases, cardboard boxes. A removal van came to fetch the lot, Thursday or Friday last.'

'Did you look at the labels?'

'I don't remember the exact address, but the stuff was booked for Amsterdam.'

'Did your employer know?'

'Of course he did.'

'So her departure had been decided on for some time?'

'Since her last attack. After each attack she'd talk of going back to her own country.'

'What kind of attacks?'

'Heart, so she said.'

'She'd a weak heart?'

'Seems like it.'

'Did a doctor come and see her?'

'Doctor Dubuc.'

'Did she take any medicine?'

'After each meal. They all did. The other two still do and they've each a little bottle of pills or drops beside their plate.'

'What's wrong with Guillaume Serre?'

'I don't know.'

'And his mother?'

'Rich people always have something wrong with them.'

'Did they get on well?'

'Sometimes they didn't speak to each other for weeks.'

'Maria Serre wrote a lot of letters?'

'Nearly from morning till night.'

'Did you ever happen to take them to the post?'

'Often. They were always to the same person, a woman with a funny name who lives in Amsterdam.'

'Are the Serres well off?'

'I reckon so.'

'What about Maria?'

'Sure. Otherwise he wouldn't have married her.'

'Did you work for them when they got married?'

'No.'

'You don't know who did the housework at that time?'

'They're always changing their daily help. It's my last

week now. Soon as anybody begins to know the form, they pack in.'

'Why?'

'How would you like to see the lumps of sugar counted in the sugar-bowl and have a half-rotten apple picked out for your sweet?'

'Old Madame Serre?'

'Yes. Just because at her age she works all day, which is her own funeral, she's onto you like a shot if you're unlucky enough to be caught sitting down for a moment.'

'Does she tell you off?'

'She's never told me off. I'd like to see her! It's far worse. She's only too polite, she looks at you in a down-hearted sort of way as if it made her sad to see you.'

'Did anything strike you when you came to work on Wednesday morning?'

'No.'

'You didn't notice if a window had been broken during the night, or whether there was fresh putty round one of the panes?'

She nodded.

'You've got the wrong day.'

'Which day was it?'

'Two or three days before, when we had that big thunderstorm.'

'You're sure of that?'

'Certain. I even had to polish the floor of the study because the rain had come into the room.'

'Who put in the pane?'

'Monsieur Guillaume.'

'He went to buy it himself?'

'Yes. He brought back the putty. It was about ten o'clock in the morning. He had to go to the ironmonger's in the Rue de Longchamp. They never have a workman in if they can do without one, and Monsieur Guillaume unstops all the drains himself.'

'You're certain about the date?'

'Absolutely.'

'Thank you very much.'

Maigret had no further business there. There was really

nothing more for him to do at the Rue de la Ferme either. Unless, of course, Eugénie was merely repeating a piece that she'd been taught to say and, in that case, she was a better liar than most.

'You don't think they've killed her?'

He didn't answer, went on towards the door.

'Because of the window-pane?'

There was a slight hesitation in her tone.

'Does the window have to be broken on the day you said?'

'Why? Do you want to see them go to jail?'

'Nothing I'd like better. But now that I've told the truth....'

She regretted it. For two pins she'd have gone back on her statement.

'You could always go and ask at the ironmonger's where he bought the glass and the putty.'

'Thank you for the tip.'

He stood for a moment in front of the shop outside, which happened in fact to be an ironmonger's. But it wasn't the right one. He waited for a taxi.

'Rue de la Ferme.'

There was no point in leaving Torrence and the plain-clothes man from Neuilly to kick their heels on the pavement any longer. The recollection of Ernestine playing her little joke in the Rue de la Lune came back to him, and he didn't find it at all funny, began to think about her. For it was she who'd started him off on this business. He'd been a fool to rush into it. Only this morning, in the police superintendant's office, he'd made a proper ass of himself.

His pipe tasted foul. He crossed and uncrossed his legs. The partition was open between himself and the driver.

'Go round by the Rue de Longchamp. If the ironmonger's is still open, stop there for a moment.'

It was a toss-up. This would be his last throw. If the ironmonger's was closed, he wouldn't bother to come back, Ernestine and Sad Freddie notwithstanding. Anyway, what proof was there that Alfred had ever really broken into the house in the Rue de la Ferme?

He'd gone off on his bike from the Quai de Jemmapes,

agreed, and at daybreak he'd telephoned his wife. But nobody knew what they'd said to each other.

'It's open!'

Of course, the ironmonger's, where the hardware department could be seen inside. A tall youth in a grey smock came to meet Maigret between the galvanized tin pails and the brooms.

'Do you sell sheet glass?'

'Yes, sir.'

'And putty?'

'Certainly. Have you brought the measurements?'

'It's not for myself. Do you know Monsieur Serre?'

'The dentist? Yes, sir.'

'Is he a customer of yours?'

'He's got an account here.'

'Have you seen him recently?'

'*I* haven't, because I only got back from my holiday day before yesterday. He might have come in while I was away. I can easily tell you by looking up the book.'

The salesman didn't ask the reason why, but dived into the semi-darkness of the shop, opened a ledger that lay on a tall, raised desk.

'He bought a sheet of window-glass last week.'

'Could you tell me which day?'

'Friday.'

The thunderstorm had occurred on Thursday night. Eugénie had been right, and old Madame Serre as well!

'He bought half a pound of putty, too.'

'Thank you.'

It hung by a thread, by an unthinking gesture on the part of the young man in the grey smock who wouldn't be long in shutting up shop. He was turning over the entries in the ledger, more or less for form's sake. He said:

'He came back again this week.'

'What!'

'Wednesday. He bought a pane of the same size, forty-two by sixty-five, and another half-pound of putty.'

'You're sure?'

'I can even tell you that he was in early, because it's the first sale made that day.'

'What time d'you open?'

An important point since, according to Eugénie, who started work at nine, all the window-panes had been in good repair on Wednesday morning.

'Well, we get in at nine, but the boss comes down at eight to open the shop.'

'Thanks, old chap. You're a bright lad.'

The bright lad must have wondered for some time afterwards why this man, who had looked so depressed when he came in, now seemed to be in such high spirits.

'I suppose there's no danger of anyone destroying the pages in this ledger?'

'Why would anybody do that?'

'Why, indeed! All the same, I advise you to keep a look out. I'll send someone round tomorrow morning to photostat them.'

He took a card from his pocket, handed it to the young man, who read with astonishment:

Chief-Divisional-Inspector Maigret
Central Police Headquarters
Paris.

'Where to now?' asked the driver.

'Pull up for a moment in the Rue de la Ferme. You'll see a little café on your left....'

This deserved a pint of beer. He nearly called Torrence and the plain-clothes man to have one with him, but finally merely asked the driver in.

'What'll you have?'

'Mine's a white wine and Vichy.'

The street was gilded by the sun. They could hear the breeze rustling through the big trees in the Bois de Boulogne.

There was a black wrought-iron gate farther up the road, a square of greensward, a house as serene and well-ordered as a convent.

Somewhere in this house there lived an old woman like a Mother Superior and a sort of sultan with whom Maigret had a score to settle.

It was good to be alive.

CHAPTER FIVE

The rest of the day went as follows. First of all, Maigret drank two pints of beer with the taxi-driver, who had only the one white wine and Vichy water himself. By that time it was beginning to get cooler and, as he climbed back into the cab, he'd the notion of driving round to the boarding-house that Maria Van Aerts had stayed in for a year.

There was nothing in particular for him to do there. He was simply following his habit of nosing round people's homes in order to understand them better.

The walls were cream-coloured. Everything was creamy, luscious, as in a dairy, and the proprietress with her floury face looked like a cake with too much icing on it.

'What a lovely person, Monsieur Maigret! And what a wonderful companion she must have made for her husband! She wanted to get married so much.'

'You mean she was looking for a husband?'

'Don't all young girls dream of a bridegroom?'

'She was about forty-eight when she lived here, if I'm not mistaken?'

'But she was still so young at heart! Anything could make her laugh. Would you believe it, she loved to play practical jokes on her fellow-guests. Near the Madeleine, there's a shop I'd never noticed before I found out about it through her, that sells all sorts of joke-novelties, mechanical mice, spoons that melt in the coffee, gadgets that you slide under the table-cloth to lift someone's plate up all of a sudden while they're eating, glasses that you can't drink from, and I don't know what all! Well, she was one of its best customers! A very cultured woman, all the same, who'd been to every museum in Europe and used to spend whole days at the Louvre.'

'Did she introduce you to her prospective husband?'

'No. She was secretive by nature. Perhaps she didn't like to bring him here, for fear that some of the others might be envious. He was a man of very imposing presence, who looked like a diplomat, I believe.'

'Aha!'

'He's a dentist, she told me, but only sees a few patients, by appointment. He belongs to a very rich family.'

'And Mademoiselle Van Aerts herself?'

'Her father left her a good deal of money.'

'Tell me, was she mean?'

'Oh, you've heard about that? She was certainly thrifty. For instance, when she had to go into town, she'd wait until one of the other guests was going too so that they could share the taxi. Every week she'd argue over her bill.'

'Do you know how she came to meet Monsieur Serre?'

'I don't think it was through the matrimonial advertisement.'

'She put an advertisement in the papers?'

'Not in earnest. She didn't believe in it. More for fun really. I don't remember the exact wording, but she said that a distinguished lady, foreign, wealthy, wished to meet gentleman of similar circumstances, with a view to marriage. She had hundreds of replies. She used to make dates with the suitors at the Louvre, sometimes in one gallery, sometimes in another, and they had to carry a certain book in their hand, or wear a buttonhole.'

There were other women like her, from England, Sweden or America, sitting in the wicker arm-chairs of the lounge, from which the smooth hum of the electric fans could be heard.

'I hope she hasn't come to any harm?'

It was about seven o'clock when Maigret got out of the taxi at the Quai des Orfèvres. From the shady side of the street he'd caught sight of Janvier coming along, with a preoccupied expression, a parcel under his arm, and he'd waited to climb the stairs with him.

'How's things, Janvier, my boy?'

'All right, Chief.'

'What have you got there?'

'My dinner.'

Janvier didn't grumble, but he had a martyred look.

'Why don't you go home?'

'Because of that woman Gertrude, blast her.'

The offices were almost empty, swept by draughts, for a breeze had just got up and all the windows in the building were still open.

'I managed to track down Gertrude Oosting in Amsterdam. Or rather, I got her maid on the 'phone. I had to dig up a chap waiting for an identity-card in the Aliens Section, who was willing to interpret, because the maid doesn't speak a word of French, and then call her back.

'As luck would have it, the good lady Oosting had gone out with her husband at four in the afternoon. There's some open-air concert on today, over there, with a fancy-dress parade, and after that the Oostings are having dinner with friends, the maid doesn't know where. She's no idea when they'll be back either, and she'd been told to put the children to bed.

'And, talking of children...'

'What?'

'Nothing, Chief.'

'Come on, out with it!'

'Doesn't matter. Only that the wife's a bit disappointed. It's our eldest boy's birthday. She'd got a special little dinner ready. Never mind.'

'Did you find out from the maid if Gertrude Oosting can speak French?'

'She can.'

'Go on home.'

'What?'

'I told you to go home. Leave me those sandwiches and I'll stay on here.'

'Madame Maigret won't like that.'

Janvier needed a bit of pressure, but finally went rushing

off to catch his train to the suburbs.

Maigret had eaten alone in his office, had gone down for a chat with Moers in the laboratory afterwards. Moers had not left until after nine, when darkness had completely fallen.

'Sure you know what to do?'

'Yes, Chief.'

He took a photographer with him, and masses of equipment. It wasn't strictly legal, but, ever since Guillaume Serre had bought two window-panes and not one, that no longer mattered.

'Get me Amsterdam, please....'

At the other end the maid gabbled something and he understood her to mean that Madame Oosting still hadn't come in.

Then he called up his wife.

'You wouldn't mind coming down to have a drink at the *Brasserie Dauphine*? I've probably got another hour or so to fill in here. Take a cab.'

It wasn't a bad evening. The two of them were as comfortable as outside a café on the main boulevards, except that their view was blocked by the tall pale flight of steps leading to the Palais de Justice.

They ought to have got to work now, in the Rue de la Ferme. Maigret had given them instructions to wait until the Serres had gone to bed. Torrence was to mount guard in front of the house to prevent the others from being taken unawares while they broke into the garage, which couldn't be overlooked from the house, and gave the car a thorough overhaul. Moers and the photographer would take care of that. Everything would be gone into: fingerprints, samples of dust for analysis, the whole works.

'You look pleased with yourself.'

'I can't complain.'

He wasn't prepared to admit that, a few hours earlier, he was far from being in such a good mood, and now he began to have short drinks, while Madame Maigret stuck to barley-water.

He left her twice to go back and call Amsterdam from the office. Not until half-past eleven did he hear a voice which was not the maid's and which answered him in French:

'I can't hear you very well.'

'I said, I'm calling from Paris.'

'Oh! Paris!'

She'd a strong accent, which nevertheless was not unattractive.

'Police Headquarters.'

'Police?'

'Yes. I'm telephoning with reference to your friend Maria. You know Maria Serre, whose maiden name was Van Aerts, don't you?'

'Where is she?'

'I don't know. That's just what I'm asking you. She often wrote to you?'

'Yes, often. I was supposed to meet her at the station, Wednesday morning.'

'Did you go to meet her?'

'Yes.'

'Did she come?'

'No.'

'Had she wired or telephoned you that she couldn't keep the appointment?'

'No. I'm worried.'

'Your friend has disappeared.'

'What do you mean?'

'What did she tell you in her letters?'

'Lots of things.'

She began to speak in her own language to someone, probably her husband, who was evidently standing beside her.

'Do you suppose Maria is dead?'

'It could be. Did she ever write to you that she was unhappy?'

'She was distressed.'

'Why?'

'She didn't like the old lady.'

'Her mother-in-law?'

'Yes.'

'What about her husband?'

'It appears that he wasn't a man, but just an overgrown

schoolboy who was terrified of his mother.'

'How long ago did she write you that?'

'Almost as soon as she got married. A few weeks after.'

'She already talked about leaving him?'

'Not then. After about a year or so.'

'And recently?'

'She'd made up her mind. She asked me to find her a flat in Amsterdam, near ours.'

'Did you find one for her?'

'Yes. And a maid.'

'So it was all arranged?'

'Yes. I was at the station.'

'Have you any objection to sending me copies of your friend's letters? Did you keep them?'

'I have kept all the letters, but it would be hard work to copy them, as they are very long. I can send you the ones that matter. You're sure something's happened to her?'

'I'm convinced of it.'

'Somebody's killed her?'

'Possibly.'

'Her husband?'

'I don't know. Listen, Madame Oosting, you could do me a great favour. Has your husband got a car?'

'Of course.'

'It would be kind of you to drive to Central Police Headquarters, which is open all night. Tell the duty officer that you were expecting your friend Maria. Show him her last letter. Then tell him you're very worried and that you'd like the matter gone into.'

'Should I mention your name?'

'It doesn't matter either way. What you must do is to insist upon an investigation.'

'I will do so.'

'Thank you. Don't forget the letters that you promised to send me.'

He rang Amsterdam again almost at once, asking this time for the number of Central Police Headquarters.

'In a few minutes, a Madame Oosting will be coming to see you about the disappearance of her friend, Madame Serre, *née* Van Aerts.'

'Did she disappear in Holland?'

'No, in Paris. In order to take action, I need an official complaint. Directly you've taken down her statement, I'd like you to send me a wire asking us to make enquiries.'

This took a bit of time. The duty officer at the other end couldn't understand how Maigret, in Paris, could have known that Madame Oosting was coming along.

'I'll tell you that later. All I must have is your wire. Send it priority. I should get it in less than half an hour.'

He went back to join Madame Maigret, who'd begun to get bored sitting about outside the *brasserie*.

'Have you done?'

'Not yet. I'll have one drink and then we'll be off.'

'Home?'

'To the office.'

That always impressed her. She'd only rarely been within the walls of Headquarters, and didn't know how to behave there.

'You look as if you were having fun. One'd think you were playing a joke on somebody.'

'I am in a way.'

'On whom?'

'A fellow who looks like a sultan, a diplomat and a schoolboy.'

'I don't understand.'

'Naturally not!'

He wasn't often in such high spirits. How many Calvados had he drunk? Four? Five? This time, before going back to the office, he swallowed a pint and took his wife's arm before crossing the couple of hundred yards of the quay to reach Police Headquarters.

'I only ask one thing: don't start telling me again that everything's covered in dust and that the offices need a good clean-out!'

On the telephone:

'Any telegrams come through for me?'

'Nothing, Chief-Inspector.'

Ten minutes later the whole squad, with the exception of Torrence, was back from the Rue de la Ferme.

'Did it go off all right? No hitches?'

'No hitches. Nobody disturbed us. Torrence insisted we should wait until the lights had all gone out in the house, and Guillaume Serre hung about for a long time before going to bed.'

'The car?'

Vacher, who'd nothing more to do, asked if he could go home. Moers and the photographer stayed behind. Madame Maigret, sitting on a chair as if paying a visit, assumed the abstracted expression of one who is not listening.

'We went over every bit of the car, which doesn't seem to have been taken out for two or three days. The petrol tank's about half-full. There are no signs of a struggle inside. In the boot, I found two or three more or less recent scratches.'

'As if a large heavy piece of luggage had been stowed in it?'

'That could be.'

'A trunk, for instance?'

'A trunk or a packing-case.'

'Were there any blood-stains inside?'

'No. Nor any loose hairs either. I thought of that. We took a flashlight along, and there's a power point in the garage. Emile is going to make enlargements of the photos.'

'I'm getting onto it right now,' the photographer said. 'If you could wait just twenty minutes....'

'I'll wait. Did it look to you, Moers, as if the car had been cleaned lately?'

'Not on the outside. It hadn't been washed down by a garage. But it looked as if the inside had been carefully brushed. They must have even taken up the mat to be beaten, because I'd a job to find any dust in it. All the same, I've got several specimens for laboratory tests.'

'Was there a brush in the garage?'

'No. I looked. They must have taken it away.'

'So, except for the scratches...'

'Nothing out of the way. Can I go now?'

They were left alone, Madame Maigret and he, in the office.

'Aren't you sleepy?'

She said no. She'd her own special way of looking at the surroundings in which her husband had spent most of his life, of which she knew so little.

'Is it always like this?'

'What?'

'A case. When you don't come home.'

She must have thought it was easy, quiet work, more like a kind of game.

'Just depends.'

'Has there been a murder?'

'More than likely.'

'D'you know who did it?'

She turned her head away as he smiled at her. Then she asked:

'Does he know that you suspect him?'

He nodded.

'D'you suppose he's asleep?'

She added after a moment, with a slight shiver:

'It must be awful.'

'I don't suppose it was fun for the poor woman either.'

'I know. But probably that was quicker, don't you think?'

'Maybe.'

The telegram from the Dutch police came through on the 'phone, with a confirmatory copy promised for the next morning.

'Now then! We can go home.'

'I thought you were waiting for the photographs.'

He smiled once more. Really, she'd have liked to find out. She didn't feel now like going back to bed.

'They won't tell us anything.'

'Don't you think so?'

'I'm sure of it. Moers' laboratory tests won't either.'

'Why not? Because the murderer was too careful?'

He did not reply, put out the light and led his wife into the passage, where the cleaners were already at work.

'That you, Monsieur Maigret?'

He looked at the alarm clock, which said half-past eight. His wife had let him sleep on. He recognized

Ernestine's voice.

'Did I wake you up?'

He preferred not to admit it.

'I'm at the post office. There's another card for me.'

'From Le Havre?'

'From Rouen. He doesn't say anything, still hasn't answered my advertisement. Nothing except my address at the *poste restante*, same as yesterday.'

There was a pause. Then she asked:

'You heard anything?'

'Yes.'

'What?'

'Something to do with window-panes.'

'Good?'

'Just depends for whom.'

'For us?'

'It may do Alfred and you some good.'

'You don't still think I've been telling lies?'

'Not at the moment.'

At Headquarters he picked Janvier to go with him, and the latter took the wheel of the little black police car.

'Rue de la Ferme.'

With the telegram in his pocket, he made the car stop outside the wrought-iron gate, through which the two of them passed looking their most official. Maigret rang. A window curtain moved on the first floor, where the shutters were not yet closed. It was Eugénie, in down-at-heel slippers, who came to the door, wiping her wet hands on her apron.

'Good morning, Eugénie. Monsieur Serre is at home and I'd like a word with him.'

Somebody leant over the banisters. The old woman's voice said:

'Show the gentlemen into the drawing-room, Eugénie.'

It was the first time that Janvier had been in the house, and he was impressed. They heard footsteps coming and going overhead. Then the door opened abruptly and the huge bulk of Guillaume Serre almost filled the entrance.

He was as self-possessed as on the day before, stared at them with the same calm insolence.

'Have you a warrant?' he asked, his lip twitching slightly.

Maigret deliberately took some time taking his wallet from his pocket, opening it, finding a document which he handed over politely.

'Here you are, Monsieur Serre.'

The man wasn't prepared for this. He read through the form, took it over to the window to decipher the signature, while Maigret was saying:

'As you see, it's a search warrant. Enquiries are being instituted into the disappearance of Madame Maria Serre, *née* Van Aerts, on a complaint lodged by Madame Gertrude Oosting, of Amsterdam.'

The old lady had entered on these last words.

'What is it, Guillaume?'

'Nothing, Mamma,' he told her in a curiously gentle voice. 'These gentlemen, I believe, would like to search the house. Go up to your room.'

She wavered, looked at Maigret as if to ask his advice.

'You'll keep your temper, Guillaume?'

'Of course, Mamma. Please leave us, I beg of you.'

Things weren't going exactly as Maigret had foreseen, and the chief-inspector frowned.

'I expect,' he said, when the old lady had reluctantly moved away, 'you'll want to consult your lawyer? I'll probably have a few questions to ask you later on.'

'I don't need a lawyer. Now that you have a warrant, I cannot object to your presence here. That's that.'

The shutters on the ground floor were closed. Until now they'd been in semi-darkness. Serre walked towards the nearest window.

'No doubt you'd prefer more light upon the scene?'

He spoke in a flat voice and if any expression at all could be read into his tone, it was a degree of contempt.

'Do your duty, gentlemen.'

It came almost as a shock to see the drawing-room in full daylight. Serre went into his study next door, where he also opened the shutters, then into the surgery.

'When you wish to go up to the first floor, please let me know.'

Janvier was glancing in bewilderment at his Chief. The latter wasn't quite so buoyant as he'd been that morning or the night before. He seemed to be worried.

'May I use your telephone, Monsieur Serre?' he asked with the same cold courtesy the other had shown him.

'You have every right to.'

He dialled the number of Headquarters. Moers had made a verbal report that morning which, as the chief-inspector had expected, was more or less negative. The particles of dust had been analysed with no result. Or rather, almost none. Moers had only managed to scrape up, from the front of the car, by the driving-seat, a minute quantity of powdered brick.

'Give me the laboratory. That you, Moers? Can you come along to the Rue de la Ferme with your men and equipment?'

He was watching Serre who, engaged in lighting a long black cigar, didn't bat an eyelid.

'All the lot, eh? No, there's no body. I'll be here.'

Then turning to Janvier:

'You can get started.'

'On this room?'

'On any one you like.'

Guillaume Serre followed them up step by step and watched what they were doing without a murmur. He wore no tie and had slipped on a black alpaca jacket over his white shirt.

While Janvier was searching the drawers of the desk, Maigret himself was going through the dentist's private files and making entries in his large note-book.

Really, it had begun to border on farce. He'd have been hard put to it to say precisely what he was looking for. What it amounted to in the end was seeing whether, at any given moment, in any particular part of the house, Serre would show any sign of uneasiness.

When they had searched the drawing-room, for instance, he'd not moved a muscle, standing rigid and full of dignity, with his back to the brown marble chimney-piece.

Now, he was watching Maigret as if wondering what the

latter could be searching for in his files, but it seemed to be more out of curiosity than fear.

'You certainly have very few patients, Monsieur Serre.'

He made no reply and shrugged his shoulders.

'I notice that there are far more women patients than men.'

The other's expression seemed to say, 'So what?'

'I also see that you first met Maria Van Aerts in your professional capacity.'

He found entries for five visits, spaced over two months, with details of the treatment given.

'Were you aware that she was wealthy?'

A further shrug.

'Do you know Doctor Dubuc?'

He nodded.

'He was your wife's doctor, unless I'm mistaken. Did you recommend him to her?'

Wonders never cease! He was talking at last!

'Doctor Dubuc was treating Maria Van Aerts before she became my wife.'

'You knew, when you married her, that she had heart trouble?'

'She told me about it.'

'Was it serious?'

'Dubuc will tell you if he considers it his duty.'

'Your first wife had a weak heart, too, hadn't she?'

'You'll find her death certificate in the files.'

Janvier was more ill at ease than anyone. He greeted with relief the arrival of the technical experts, who would start a bit of life in the house. As the car drew up in front of the gate, Maigret went to open the door himself, said to Moers under his breath:

'The whole show. Go over the house with a toothcomb.'

And Moers, who'd understood and spotted the bulky form of Guillaume Serre, muttered:

'You reckon that'll shake him?'

'It might end up by shaking someone.'

A few moments later, one might have thought that auctioneers had taken over the house and were preparing to put it up for public sale. The men from the Technical

Branch left no corner untouched, taking down the pictures and the photographs, pushing back the piano and the armchairs to look underneath the carpets, piling up cupboard drawers, spreading out documents.

Once they caught sight of the face of Madame Serre who, having taken one glance through the doorway, had withdrawn with a look of distress. Then Eugénie came in grumbling:

'You'll put everything back where it was, I hope?'

She carried on even more when her kitchen was put through it and even the cupboards where she stored her brooms.

'If only you'd tell me what it is you're looking for.'

They weren't looking for anything in particular. Perhaps, when it came to the point, even Maigret wasn't looking for anything at all. All the time he was watching the man who followed in their tracks and never lost his poise for a second.

Why had Maria written to her friend that Serre was really nothing more than an overgrown schoolboy?

While his men continued to work, Maigret unhooked the telephone and got Dr. Dubuc on the line.

'You won't be going out for a while? Can I come and see you? No, it won't take long. Thanks, I'll tell the maid.'

Dubuc had five patients in his waiting-room and promised the chief-inspector to let him in by the back door. It was a stone's throw away, along the wharf. Maigret went there on foot, passed the ironmonger's, where the young assistant of the day before hailed him.

'Aren't you going to photograph the ledger?'

'Presently.'

Dubuc was a man of about fifty, with a ginger beard and glasses.

'You attended Madame Serre, didn't you, Doctor?'

'Young Madame Serre. Or rather, the younger of the two.'

'You never attended anyone else in the house?'

'Let me see. Yes! A charwoman who'd cut her hand, two or three years ago.'

'Was Maria Serre really ill?'

'She needed treatment, yes.'

'Heart?'

'An enlarged heart. Moreover, she ate too much, complained of dizziness.'

'Did she often call you in?'

'About once a month. Other times she came to see me.'

'Did you prescribe any medicine for her?'

'A sedative, in tablet form. Nothing toxic.'

'You don't think she could have had a heart attack?'

'Most unlikely. In ten or fifteen years, perhaps....'

'Did she do anything to get her weight down?'

'Every four or five months she'd decide to go on a diet, but her resolution never lasted for more than a few days.'

'You've met her husband?'

'Occasionally.'

'What did you think of him?'

'In what way? Professionally? One of my woman patients went to him for treatment and told me that he was very skilful and very gentle.'

'As a man?'

'I thought he seemed of retiring disposition. What is all this about?'

'His wife has disappeared.'

'Ah!'

Dubuc didn't give a damn, to tell the truth, and he merely sketched a vague gesture.

'These things happen, don't they? He was wrong to put the police on to find her, because she'll never forgive him.'

Maigret didn't argue the point. On his way back, he made a detour so as to pass the garage, which was no longer under observation. The house opposite had been divided into flats. The concierge was outside on the step, polishing the brass knob of the front door.

'Does your window look out on the street?'

'What's that got to do with you?'

'I'm a police officer. I wanted to find out whether you knew the person who keeps his car in the garage opposite, the first one on the right.'

'That's the dentist.'

'You see him now and again?'

'I see him when he comes to fetch his car.'

'Have you seen him this week?'

'Here! That reminds me — what was all that messing about in his garage yesterday night? Was it burglars? I said to my husband...'

'It wasn't burglars.'

'Was it you?'

'Never mind. Have you seen him take his car out this week?'

'I believe I did.'

'You don't remember which day? Or what time?'

'It was one night, pretty late. Hang on, I'd got up out of bed. Don't look at me like that. It'll come back to me.'

She seemed to be doing some mental arithmetic.

'I'd just got up out of bed, because my husband had toothache, and I'd given him an aspirin. If he was here he'd tell you straight away what day it was. I noticed Monsieur Serre's car coming out of the garage, and I remember saying what a coincidence.'

'Because your husband had toothache?'

'Yes. And there was a dentist opposite the house at that very moment. It was after midnight. Mademoiselle Germaine had come in. Right, then it was Tuesday, because she only goes out on Tuesday nights, to play cards round at some friends.'

'The car was coming out? It wasn't going in?'

'It was coming out.'

'Which way did it go?'

'Towards the Seine.'

'You didn't hear it stop a little farther on, for instance at Monsieur Serre's house?'

'I didn't take any more notice of it. I'd bare feet and the floor was cold, because we sleep with the window half-open. What's he done?'

What could Maigret have answered? He thanked her and moved away, crossed the little garden and rang. Eugénie opened the door, giving him a black, reproachful look.

'The gentlemen are upstairs,' she told him curtly.

They'd finished with the ground floor. From upstairs

noisy footsteps could be heard, the rumble of furniture being dragged across the floorboards.

Maigret went up, found old Madame Serre sitting on a chair in the middle of the landing.

'I no longer know where to go,' she said. 'It's like moving house. What can they be looking for, Monsieur Maigret?'

Guillaume Serre, standing in the centre of a room flooded with sunlight, was lighting a fresh cigar.

'My goodness, why did we let her go!' sighed the old lady. 'If I'd only known....'

She did not state precisely what she would have done had she foreseen the worries that her daughter-in-law's disappearance would bring down upon her.

CHAPTER SIX

It was twenty to four when Maigret made up his mind, twenty-five past four when the questioning began. But the fateful, almost dramatic moment was that when the decision was taken.

Maigret's behaviour had come as a surprise to those working with him in the house at the Rue de la Ferme. Ever since the morning, there'd been something unusual about the way in which the chief-inspector was directing operations. It wasn't the first search of this sort in which they'd taken part, but the more this one proceeded, the more it took on a different nature from any other. It was difficult to define. Janvier, because he knew his Chief better than the others, was the first to feel the change.

When he set them to work, there had been a slight, almost fierce flicker of glee in Maigret's eyes; he had loosed them on the house rather as he might have loosed a pack of hounds on a fresh scent, urging them on, not by his voice but by his whole attitude.

Had it become a personal issue between himself and Guillaume Serre? Or more precisely: would events have taken the same course, would Maigret have made the same decision, at the same moment, had the man from the Rue de la Ferme not been heavier than he, physically and morally?

He had seemed, from the start, impatient to get to grips with him.

At other times, one might have attributed different motives to him, wondered if he didn't take a more or less malicious pleasure in turning the house upside-down.

They had seldom been given the chance of working in a home like this, where everything was peaceful and serene, harmonious in a muted minor key, where even the most outdated objects were in no way ludicrous, and where, after hours of exhaustive searching, they hadn't come across even one questionable detail.

When he had made his pronouncement, at twenty to four, they still hadn't found anything. The search party was feeling a certain amount of discomfort, expecting the Chief to withdraw with apologies.

What was it that decided Maigret? Did he know himself? Janvier went so far as to suspect him of having drunk too many *aperitifs* when, about one o'clock, he'd gone to have a bite on the terrace of the café opposite. On his return, it was true, a smell of Pernod could be detected on his breath.

Eugénie hadn't laid the table for her employers. Several times she'd come up to whisper, now in the ear of Madame Serre, now in that of the dentist. At one moment, they'd caught sight of the mother eating, standing up, in the kitchen, as one might during a household removal, and not long after that, Guillaume having refused to come down, the charwoman took him up a sandwich and a cup of coffee.

They were working in the attic by then. This was the most personal part of the house, more personal than the bedrooms and the linen cupboards.

It was enormous, lit by dormer-windows that shed two large luminous rectangles upon the dingy floorboards. Janvier had opened two leather gun-cases, and a ballistics man had examined the weapons.

'These belong to you?'

'They belonged to my father-in-law. I have never done any shooting.'

An hour earlier, in Guillaume's room, they'd found a revolver, which had been examined, and which Maigret had placed on the pile of objects to be taken away for a subsequent check-up.

There was a bit of everything in that pile, including the dentist's professional records and, from an escritoire in the old lady's room, the death certificates of her husband and her first daughter-in-law.

There was also a suit of clothing on which Janvier had noticed a slight tear in the sleeve, and which Guillaume Serre claimed not to have worn for ten days.

They stumbled about among old trunks, packing-cases, pieces of broken-down furniture which had been taken up to the attic because they were no more use. In a corner stood a child's high chair of an old-fashioned type, with coloured knobs on either side of the tray, and also a rocking-horse, minus tail and mane.

They didn't stop working at lunch-time. The men took it in turns to knock off for a bite, and Moers was satisfied with a sandwich brought to him by the photographer.

Towards 2 p.m., they 'phoned through to Maigret, from the office, to tell him that a pretty heavy envelope had just come by air from Holland. He had them open it. Inside were Maria's letters, written in Dutch.

'Get hold of a translator and put him to work.'

'Here?'

'Yes. He's not to leave Headquarters until I come.'

Guillaume Serre's attitude had not altered. He followed them about, didn't miss a single action or gesture on their part, but not even once did he seem agitated.

He had a special way of staring at Maigret, and one could see that, for him, the others didn't count. It was indeed a match between the two. The plain-clothes men were merely lay figures. Even the police force didn't count. This was a more personal combat. And in the dentist's eyes one could see an indefinable expression that might have been one of reproach or of contempt.

In any case, he didn't allow this large-scale operation to intimidate him. He raised no more objections, submitted to this invasion of his home and privacy with lofty resignation, in which not the slightest trace of anxiety was perceptible.

Was he a weakling? A tough customer? The two theories

were equally plausible. His torso was that of a wrestler, his behaviour that of a self-assured man, and yet, nevertheless, Maria's description of him as an overgrown schoolboy did not appear incongruous. His skin was pale, sickly-looking. In a drawer, they'd found a mass of doctor's prescriptions, pinned together in separate sheafs, some of them dating from twenty years back; the family's medical history could have been reconstructed with the help of these prescriptions, some of which were yellow with age. There was also, in the upstairs bathroom, a small white-painted cabinet containing phials of patent medicine, boxes of pills both new and old.

In this house nothing was ever thrown away, not even old brooms, which were stacked in a corner of the attic beside down-at-heel cracked leather shoes that would never be any use again.

Each time they left a room to launch an attack upon the next, Janvier gave his Chief a look which meant:

'Another wash-out!'

For Janvier still expected to make some discovery. Did Maigret, on the other hand, rely on their finding nothing? He didn't seem surprised, watched them go ahead, puffing lazily at his pipe, sometimes forgetting, for a whole quarter of an hour, to glance round at the dentist.

They realized his decision by implication, and that made it strike them even more forcibly.

Everybody was coming down from the attic, where Guillaume Serre had closed the dormer windows. His mother had just come out of her room to watch them go. They were standing on the landing, in an uneasy group.

Maigret had turned to Serre and said, as if it were the most natural thing in the world:

'Would you mind putting on a tie and a pair of shoes?'

Throughout the day, so far, the man had been wearing slippers.

Serre had grasped his meaning, had stared at him, undoubtedly surprised, but managing not to let it show. His mother had opened her mouth to speak, either to protest or to demand an explanation and Guillaume had clasped her arm, led her back into her room.

Janvier had asked under his breath:

'You arresting him?'

Maigret had made no reply. He didn't know. To tell the truth, he'd only just made up his mind, on the spur of the moment, here, on the landing.

'Come in, Monsieur Serre. Will you take a seat?'

The clock on the mantelpiece said four twenty-five. It was a Saturday. Maigret had only realized that from the bustle in the streets, as they crossed the city in a car.

The chief-inspector closed the door. The windows were open, and papers on the desk fluttered under the weights that prevented them from blowing away.

'I asked you to sit down.'

He himself went into the wall cupboard to hang up his hat and coat there and to rinse his hands under the enamel fountain.

For the next ten minutes he didn't say a word to the dentist, being too busy signing the things that were waiting on his desk. He rang for Joseph, gave him the file; then, slowly and deliberately, he filled the half-dozen pipes set out in front of him.

It was seldom that anyone in Serre's position could stand it for long without asking questions, losing his nerve, crossing and uncrossing his legs.

At last there was a knock at the door. It was the photographer who'd worked with them all day and been sent on a mission by Maigret. He handed the chief-inspector the still damp print of a document.

'Thank you, Dambois. Stay back there. Don't leave without letting me know.'

He waited until the door closed again, lit one of the pipes:

'Would you bring your chair nearer, Monsieur Serre?'

They were now facing each other, separated by the width of the desk, across which Maigret held out the document in his hand.

He added no comment. The dentist took the print, brought a pair of spectacles out of his pocket, examined it carefully and put it down on the table.

'I'm waiting.'

'I've nothing to say.'

The photograph was that of a page from the iron-monger's ledger, the one recording the sale of the second sheet of glass and the second half-pound of putty.

'You realize what that implies?'

'Am I to understand that I'm charged?'

Maigret hesitated.

'No,' he decided. 'Officially, you're summoned as a witness. If you wish, however, I am ready to charge you, more exactly to ask the Director of Prosecutions to indict you, which would entitle you to have legal advice.'

'I've already told you that I don't want a lawyer.'

These were only the preliminary moves. Two heavy-weights were sizing each other up, taking each other's measure, feeling their way, in the office which had become a sort of ring, and silence reigned in the Duty Room, where Janvier had just put his colleagues in the picture.

'I reckon we're in for a long session!' he told them.

'Think the Chief'll go the limit?'

'He's got that look on his face.'

They all knew what that meant, and Janvier was the first to ring up his wife and tell her not to be surprised if he didn't come home that night.

'Have you a weak heart, Monsieur Serre?'

'An enlarged heart, like yourself, in all probability.'

'Your father died of heart trouble when you were seventeen, didn't he?'

'Seventeen and a half.'

'Your first wife died of heart trouble. Your second wife also had heart trouble.'

'According to statistics, about thirty per cent of people die of heart failure.'

'Your life's insured, Monsieur Serre?'

'Since I was a child.'

'Of course, I saw the policy earlier on. If I remember rightly, your mother is not insured.'

'That's correct.'

'Your father was?'

'I believe so.'

'And your first wife?'

'I saw you take the documents away.'

'Your second wife, as well?'

'It's quite a usual procedure.'

'What is less usual is to keep a sum of several million francs, in gold and currency, in a safe.'

'D'you think so?'

'Can you tell me why you keep this money at home, where it can bring no interest?'

'I imagine that thousands of people, nowadays, do the same. You forget the financial bills that have resulted several times in a panic, the excessive rate of taxation and the constant devaluations....'

'I understand. You admit that your intention was to conceal your capital and defraud the Treasury?'

Serre was silent.

'Did your wife — I mean your second wife, Maria — know that this money was shut up in your safe?'

'She did.'

'You told her about it?'

'Her own money was in there as well a few days ago.'

He took his time before answering, weighed his words, let them fall one by one while keeping his eyes fixed gravely on the chief-inspector.

'I didn't find any marriage-contract among your papers. Am I to conclude that you were married under the joint-possession laws?'

'That is correct.'

'Isn't that odd, considering your ages?'

'I have already given you the reason. A contract would have obliged us to draw up a balance-sheet of our respective goods.'

'The joint-possession, however, had no existence in actual fact?'

'We each continued to retain control of our own affairs.'

And didn't all this seem quite natural?

'Was your wife wealthy?'

'She is wealthy.'

'As wealthy as you are, or wealthier?'

'About the same.'

'Does she have the whole of her money in France?'

'Only part of it. From her father, she inherited shares in a cheese factory in Holland.'

'In what form did she keep her other assets?'

'Mainly in gold.'

'Even before she met you?'

'I see what you're getting at. Nevertheless, I will tell you the truth. It was I who advised her to sell out her securities and to buy gold.'

'This gold was kept, with yours, in your safe?'

'It used to be.'

'Until when?'

'Tuesday. At the beginning of the afternoon, when she'd nearly finished packing, she came downstairs and I gave her what belonged to her.'

'Then this sum, when she left, was in one of the two suit-cases or in the trunk?'

'I suppose so.'

'She didn't go out before dinner?'

'I didn't hear her go out.'

'So, to your knowledge, she didn't go out?'

He nodded in confirmation.

'Did she telephone at all?'

'The only telephone in the house is in my study and she did not make use of it.'

'How am I to know, Monsieur Serre, that the money which I found in the safe is *yours alone*, and not yours *and* your wife's?'

Without emotion, still maintaining an expression of weariness or disdain, the dentist took from his pocket a green note-book which he handed to the chief-inspector. Its pages were covered with tiny figures. Those on the left-hand side were headed with the initial O; those on the right with the initial M.

'What does O stand for?'

'Ours. I mean my mother and myself. We've always shared everything, without making any distinction between what is hers and what is mine.'

'The M, I suppose, stands for Maria?'

'You are right.'

'I see a certain figure that occurs at regular intervals.'

'Her share of the household expenses.'

'Every month she paid you the cost of her bed and board?'

'If you like. Actually, she didn't pay me any money, because it was in the safe, but her account was debited with the amount.'

Maigret leafed through the note-book for a few minutes without speaking, got up and went into the room next door where, like schoolboys, the plain-clothes men immediately pretended to be busy.

He gave instructions to Janvier in a low voice, hesitated as to whether he should have beer sent up for himself, swallowed, as if automatically, the dregs of a glass which stood on Vacher's desk.

When he returned, Serre, who had not moved from his chair, had just lit one of his long cigars and murmured not without insolence:

'D'you mind?'

Maigret was loth to say yes, shrugged his shoulders.

'You've thought about this second window-pane, Monsieur Serre?'

'I haven't bothered to do so.'

'You're wrong. It'd be much better if you could find some reasonable explanation.'

'I'm not looking for one....'

'D'you continue to maintain that you have only once replaced the pane in your study window?'

'The day after the thunderstorm.'

'Would you like us to have the weather-bureau confirm that there was no thunderstorm at Neuilly on Tuesday night?'

'It's pointless. Unless it would give you any satisfaction. I'm speaking of last week's thunderstorm.'

'The day after, you went to the ironmonger's in the Rue de Longchamp and you bought a sheet of glass and some putty.'

'I have told you that already.'

'You are prepared to swear that you haven't been back to the shop since then?'

And he pushed across the desk the photograph of the ledger entry.

'Why, in your opinion, should they have troubled to enter these purchases of glass and putty twice in their book?'

'I've no idea.'

'Why should the shopkeeper state that you came in on Wednesday, about eight o'clock in the morning?'

'That's his business.'

'When did you last use your car?'

'Last Sunday.'

'Where did you go?'

'We took a drive for two or three hours, my mother and I, as is our custom every Sunday.'

'In which direction?'

'Towards the forest of Fontainebleau.'

'Did your wife go with you?'

'No. She wasn't feeling well.'

'You'd decided to separate?'

'There was no question of a separation. She was tired, run down. She didn't always get on with my mother. By mutual agreement we decided that she should go back to her own country for a few weeks or a few months.'

'She took her money with her, all the same?'

'Yes.'

'Why?'

'Because there was a possibility that she wouldn't come back. We're no longer children. We're able to look at life calmly. It is a sort of experiment that we are making.'

'Tell me, Monsieur Serre, there are two frontiers to cross before you reach Amsterdam, aren't there? The French customs, on the way out, are fairly strict about the currency regulations. Wasn't your wife afraid that her gold would be discovered and impounded?'

'Am I obliged to answer?'

'I think it's in your own interests.'

'Even if I risk proceedings?'

'They'd probably be less serious than a charge of murder.'

'Very well. One of my wife's suitcases was provided

with a false bottom.'

'Specially for this trip?'

'No.'

'She'd already had occasion to use it?'

'Several times.'

'To cross the frontier?'

'The Belgian frontier and, once, the Swiss frontier. You're aware, I'm sure, that until recently it was easier and less expensive to procure gold in Belgium and especially in Switzerland.'

'You admit your complicity in these transfers of capital?'

'I do.'

Maigret got up, went back into the Duty Room.

'Mind coming here a moment, Janvier?'

Then, to Serre:

'My assistant will take down this part of our interview. Please repeat to him word for word what you've just told me. See that he signs his statement, Janvier.'

He went out, got Vacher to show him the office that had been asigned to the translator. He was a little man with glasses who was typing his translation straight onto the machine and pausing from time to time to consult the dictionary that he'd brought with him.

There were at least forty letters, most of them comprising several sheets.

'Where have you begun?'

'At the beginning. I'm onto the third letter. All three are dated about two and a half years ago. In the first one, the lady tells her friend that she's getting married, that her future husband is a distinguished man, of imposing appearance, belonging to the highest French professional class, and that his mother looks like I can't remember which painting in the Louvre. I can tell you the name of the painter.'

He turned over the pages.

'A Clouet. Painting is mentioned all the time in these letters. When she's saying what the weather's like, she cites Monet or Renoir.'

'I'd like you to begin at the end, from now on.'

'As you wish. You realize that if I spend all night at it, I won't have finished by tomorrow morning?'

'That's why I'm asking you to begin at the end. What's the date of the last letter?'

'Last Sunday.'

'Can you read it to me quickly?'

'I can give you some idea of it. Wait a moment.

'Gertrude darling,

'Paris has never been so resplendent as this morning, and I very nearly went with G. and his mother to the forest of Fontainebleau, which must be adorned with all the glories of a Corot or a Courbet....'

'Is there a lot about the glories?'

'Shall I skip?'

'Please.'

The translator ran his eyes down a page and moved his lips silently as if in prayer.

'Here you are:

'I wonder what effect returning once again to our Holland and its pastel shades will have upon me and now that the time comes near, I feel I'm being cowardly.

'After all that I've written to you about my life here, about G. and my mother-in-law, you must be wondering what has happened to me and why I am no longer happy.

'It's perhaps because of the dream I had last night, which has spoilt my day. Do you recall the little picture that hangs in The Hague museum and made us blush? It isn't signed. It's attributed to a painter of the Florentine School whose name I have forgotten, and depicts a faun carrying away over his shoulder a completely naked woman who is resisting. You remember?

'The faun, in my dream, had G.'s face, and his expression was so fierce that I awoke trembling and bathed in perspiration.

'Not with fear, that was the strangest thing. My memory is confused. There was some fear, certainly, but also another emotion. I'll try to explain it to you on Wednesday, when we'll at last be able to chat as we did so much when you came over on your last trip.

'I'm to leave on Tuesday night, it's settled. There's no doubt about it. So there are only two more days to wait. I've heaps of things to do during that time. It'll pass quickly. Nevertheless, it seems to me still far away, almost unreal.

'Sometimes I have the feeling, especially after that dream, that something will happen to prevent my departure.

'Don't worry. My decision is final. I shall follow your advice. I cannot stand this life here for much longer. But...'

'You in here, Chief?'

It was Janvier, with sheets of paper in his hand.

'It's done. He's waiting for you.'

Maigret took the papers, left the translator to his task, crossed the Duty Room deep in thought.

Nobody, at that time, could have foretold how long the questioning would take. Guillaume Serre looked up at the chief-inspector, took a pen of his own accord from the desk.

'I suppose I have to sign?'

'Yes, here. Have you read it through?'

'I've read it. Might I trouble you for a glass of water?'

'You wouldn't prefer red wine?'

The dentist looked at him, gave the faintest of smiles, inscrutable, heavy with irony and bitterness.

'That, too?' he said disdainfully.

'That, too, Monsieur Serre. You're so afraid of your mother that you are reduced to drink in hiding.'

'Is that a question? I've got to answer?'

'If you wish to.'

'Allow me to inform you then that my mother's father was a drunkard, that her two brothers, who are now dead, were drunkards as well, and that her sister ended her days in a lunatic asylum. My mother has lived in fear of seeing me take to drink in my turn, for she refuses to believe that this tendency is not hereditary. When I was a student, she awaited my return with anxiety, and would even sometimes keep a watch on the cafés in the Boulevard Saint-Michel where I was sitting with my friends. There have never been any spirits in the house and though there's wine in the cellar, she's kept the habit of carrying the key on her.'

'She allows you a glass of wine and water at every meal, doesn't she?'

'I know that she called to see you and spoke to you.'

'Did she tell you what she said to me?'

'Yes.'

'Are you very fond of your mother, Monsieur Serre?'

The two of us have almost always lived together.'

'Rather like a married couple?'

He coloured slightly.

'I don't know what you mean.'

'Is your mother jealous?'

'I beg your pardon?'

'I'm asking you whether, as often happens with a widow and an only son, your mother shows signs of jealousy towards the people you know. Have you many friends?'

'Has this any connection with the alleged disappearance of my wife?'

'I didn't find in the house a single letter from a friend, or even one of those group photographs that one sees in most homes.'

He didn't speak.

'Nor is there any photograph of your first wife.'

Still silence.

'Another thing that struck me, Monsieur Serre. The portrait hanging over the mantelpiece is surely of your maternal grandfather?'

'Yes.'

'The one who drank?'

A sign of assent.

'In a drawer I came across a certain number of pictures of yourself as a child and as a young man, also pictures of women and men who must have been your grandmother, your aunt and your uncles. Always on your mother's side. Doesn't it seem surprising to you that there isn't a single portrait of your father or of his family?'

'It hadn't struck me.'

'Were they destroyed after your father's death?'

'My mother could answer that question better than I.'

'You don't remember if they were destroyed?'

'I was quite young.'

'You were seventeen. What memory have you of your father, Monsieur Serre?'

'Is this part of your interrogation?'

'Neither my questions nor your answers, as you see, are

being recorded. Your father was a solicitor?'

'Yes.'

'Did he take personal charge of his practice?'

'Not often. His chief clerk did most of the work.'

'Did he lead a very social life? Or was he exclusively devoted to the family circle?'

'He went about a great deal.'

'He had mistresses?'

'I couldn't tell you.'

'Did he die in his bed?'

'On the stairs, going up to his room.'

'Were you at home?'

'I'd gone out. When I came back, he'd been dead for nearly two hours.'

'Who attended him?'

'Doctor Dutilleux.'

'Is he still alive?'

'He died at least ten years ago.'

'Were you there when your first wife died?'

He drew his heavy brows together, staring at Maigret fixedly, and his lower lip was thrust out in a kind of disgust.

'Answer me, please.'

'I was in the house.'

'What part of the house?'

'In my study.'

'What time was it?'

'About nine p.m.'

'Did your wife keep to her room?'

'She'd gone up early. She didn't feel very well.'

'Had she felt ill for some time?'

'I don't remember.'

'Was your mother with her?'

'She was upstairs as well.'

'With her?'

'I've no idea.'

'Was it your mother who called you?'

'I think so.'

'When you got to the room, your wife was dead?'

'No.'

'Did she die a long time afterwards?'

'Fifteen or twenty minutes later. The doctor was ringing the doorbell.'

'Which doctor?'

'Dutilleux.'

'He was your family doctor?'

'He attended me when I was a child.'

'A friend of your father's?'

'Of my mother.'

'Did he have children?'

'Two or three.'

'You've lost sight of them?'

'I never knew them personally.'

'Why didn't you inform the police that somebody had tried to break open your safe?'

'I had nothing to inform the police.'

'What did you do with the tools?'

'What tools?'

'The ones the burglar left in the room when he made his getaway.'

'I saw neither tools nor burglar.'

'You didn't make use of your car on Tuesday night or early Wednesday morning?'

'I did not.'

'You were unaware that somebody used it?'

'I've had no reason, since then, to go into the garage.'

'When you garaged your car, last Sunday, were there scratches on the boot and the right mudguard?'

'I didn't notice anything.'

'Did you get out of the car, you and your mother?'

He didn't answer for a moment.

'I asked you a question.'

'I'm trying to remember.'

'It shouldn't be so difficult. You were driving along the road to Fontainebleau. Did you set foot to the ground?'

'Yes. We went for a walk in the country.'

'You mean on a country road?'

'A little path running between the fields on the right-hand side of the road.'

'Could you find this path again?'

'I think so.'

'Was it tarred?'

'I don't believe it was. No. That seems unlikely.'

'Where is your wife, Monsieur Serre?'

And the chief-inspector rose, not expecting any answer.

'Because we've got to find her, haven't we?'

CHAPTER SEVEN

About five o'clock, already, Maigret had got up for a moment to open the communicating door between his office and the Duty Room and had winked at Janvier. A little later he'd got up again to go and shut the window, despite the heat, because of the noise from outside.

At ten to six he passed through the Duty Room, his jacket over his arm.

'All yours!' he told Janvier.

The latter and his colleagues had grasped the situation a long while ago. From the moment when, at the Rue de la Ferme, the chief-inspector had ordered Serre to come along, Janvier was pretty sure that he wouldn't get away from Headquarters very easily. What surprised him was that the Chief had made his decision so abruptly, without waiting to have all the evidence in his hands.

'She's in the waiting-room,' he said under his breath.

'Who?'

'The mother.'

Maigret stationed Marlieux, a young plain-clothes man, who knew shorthand, behind the door.

'Same questions?' asked Janvier.

'The same. And any others that come into your head.'

The idea was to wear down the dentist. The others could take it in turns, go out for a cup of coffee or a pint, make contact with the outside world again, while he would stay as long as need be in the same office, in the same chair.

Maigret began by calling in on the translator, who'd decided to take off his jacket and tie.

'What's she say?'

'I've translated the last four letters. There's a passage in the last but one that might interest you.

'I've made up my mind, Gertrude dear, I am still wondering how it came about. Yet I had no dreams last night, or if I had, I have forgotten them.'

'Does she say much about her dreams?'

'Yes. They're always coming into it. And she interprets them.'

'Go on.'

'You've often asked me what has gone wrong and I answered that you were imagining things and that I was happy. The truth is that I was trying to persuade myself of it.

'Honestly, I've done all I could, for two and a half years, to try and believe that this house was my home and that G. was my husband.

'In my heart, you see, I knew that it wasn't true, that I'd always been a stranger here, more of a stranger than I was in the boarding-house you know, where we two spent so many happy hours.

'How did I suddenly come to see things as they really are?

'Do you remember, when we were little girls? We used to play at comparing everything we saw — people, streets, animals — with the pictures in our photograph albums. We wanted life to be like them. Then, later on, when we began to visit the museums, it was paintings that we used for comparison.

'I did the same here, but I did it on purpose, without believing in it, and this morning I suddenly saw the house as it really is, I saw my mother-in-law, I saw G. with a fresh vision, without illusions.

'I hadn't had any for some time — I mean illusions. You've got to understand me. I no longer had any, but I stubbornly refused to admit it.

'Now that's over. I made up my mind to leave on the spot. I haven't told anyone yet. The old lady hasn't any inkling. She still behaves the same towards me, meek and smiling, so long as I do everything she wants.

'She's the most selfish woman I have ever known.

'Those words are underlined,' the translator remarked. 'Shall I go on?

'*As for G., I wonder whether it won't be a relief for him to see me go. He knows that from the beginning we had nothing in common. I could never get used to the feel of his skin, to his smell. Do you understand now why we've never shared the same room, which surprised you so much at the start?*

'*After two and a half years, it's exactly as though I'd just met him in the street or in the underground, and I have the same feeling of recoil whenever he comes to my room. Luckily it doesn't happen often.*

'*I even think, between ourselves, that he only comes because he believes it gives me pleasure, or because he feels it's his duty.*

'*Perhaps it's his mother who tells him to? It's possible. Don't laugh. I don't know how it is with your own husband, but G. has the crestfallen look of a schoolboy who's just been given a hundred lines. Can you see what I mean?*

'*I've often wondered if he was the same with his first wife. It's probable. He would be the same, I expect, with anyone. These people, you see, I mean the mother and son, live in a world of their own and have no need of anybody else.*

'*It seems astonishing that the old lady once had a husbnd of her own. They never speak about him at home. Besides themselves, there's nobody in the world except the people whose pictures are on the walls, people who are dead, but whom they talk about as if they were more alive than all the living.*

'*I can't stand it any longer, Gertrude. I'll talk to G. presently. I'll tell him that I feel the need to breathe the air of my own country, and he'll understand. What I'm wondering is, how he'll pluck up the courage to tell his mother....*'

'Is there much more?' asked Maigret.

'Seven pages.'

'Go on translating. I'll be back.'

At the door he turned round:

'When you're hungry or thirsty, ring down to the *Brasserie Dauphine*. Get them to send up anything you want.'

'Thank you.'

From the corridor he saw, in the glass-panelled waiting-room, old Madame Serre sitting on one of the green velvet chairs. She was bolt upright, her hands folded in her lap. When she caught sight of Maigret, she made as if to get up, but he passed on without stopping and went down the stairs.

The examination had barely begun and yet it already came as a surprise to see life still going on outside, in broad sunlight, people walking to and fro, taxis, buses with men reading the evening paper on the platform on their way home.

'Rue Gay-Lussac!' he told the driver. 'I'll tell you where to stop.'

The tall trees in the Luxembourg Gardens swayed in the breeze, and all the chairs were taken; there were a lot of bright dresses; some children were still playing along the paths.

'Is Maître Orin at home?' he asked the concierge.

'He hasn't been out for over a month, poor man.'

Maigret had suddenly remembered him. He was probably the oldest solicitor in Paris. The chief-inspector had no idea of his age, but he'd always known him as an old man, a semi-invalid, which didn't stop him from always having a smiling face and talking about women with a wicked twinkle in his eye.

He lived, together with a housekeeper almost as old as himself, in a bachelor flat cluttered up with books and prints, which he collected, and most of the prints dealt with bawdy subjects.

Orin was seated in an arm-chair in front of the open window, his knees covered by a rug, despite the weather.

'Well, m'lad? What a pleasant surprise! I'd begun to think everyone had forgotten me or thought that I'd been laid to rest in Père-Lachaise long ago. What's the trouble this time?'

He didn't try to deceive himself, and Maigret coloured slightly, since it was true that he'd seldom called on the lawyer for other than selfish reasons.

'I wondered just now if, by any chance, you would have known a man called Serre who, if I'm not mistaken, died thirty-two or thirty-three years ago.'

'Alain Serre?'

'He was a solicitor.'

'That'd be Alain.'

'What sort of man was he?'

'I suppose I'm not allowed to ask what it's all about?'

'About his son.'

'I never saw the boy. I knew there was a son, but I never met him. You see, Maigret, Alain and I belonged to a gay set, whose life didn't revolve round the family hearth. We were to be found mostly at the club or behind the scenes at variety shows, and we knew all the chorus girls by their Christian names.'

He added, with a ribald grin:

'If you see what I mean!'

'You didn't know his wife?'

'I must have been introduced to her. Didn't she live somewhere in Neuilly? For several years Alain went out of circulation. He wasn't the only one it happened to. There were even a few who looked down on us, once they got married. I didn't expect to see him again. And then, a long time afterwards...'

'About how long?'

'I don't know. Some years. Let me see. The club had already moved from the Faubourg Saint-Honoré to the Avenue Hoche. Ten years? Twelve years? Anyway, he came back to us. He behaved oddly at first, as if he thought we bore him a grudge for dropping us.'

'Then?'

'Nothing. He went the pace redoubled. Let's see. He went about for a long time with a little singer with a big mouth they used to call... We had a nickname for her.... Something smutty.... I can't call it to mind.'

'Did he drink?'

'Not more than anyone else. Two or three bottles of champagne occasionally....'

'What became of him?'

'What becomes of us all in the end. He died.'

'That's all?'

'If you want to know the sequel, m'lad, you'll have to ask aloft. It's St. Peter's business and not mine. What misdeed has his son committed?'

'I don't know yet. His wife has disappeared.'

'A gay dog?'

'No. Quite the reverse.'

'Juliette! Bring us something to drink.'

Maigret had to stay another quarter of an hour with the old man who insisted on trying to find, among his prints, a sketch of the singer.

'I wouldn't swear that it's a good likeness. A very talented chap did it, one night when the whole gang of us were up in his studio.'

The girl was naked and walking on her hands, and her face could not be seen by reason of the fact that her hair was sweeping the floor.

'Come and see me again, Maigret my boy. If you'd had time to share my humble meal....'

A bottle of wine was warming in a corner of the room and a pleasant smell of cooking filled the flat.

The police at Rouen hadn't been able to pick up Sad Freddie any more than those at Le Havre. Perhaps the expert safe-breaker was no longer in that town. Was he on his way back to Paris? Had he read Ernestine's message?

Maigret had sent a plain-clothes man on a mission along the river-bank.

'Where shall I start from?'

'As far upstream as you can.'

He'd also telephoned his wife that he wouldn't be back to dinner.

'D'you think I'll see you tonight?'

'Probably not.'

He wasn't hoping for too much. He, too, knew that he'd assumed a big responsibility by rushing matters and taking Guillaume Serre down to Headquarters before he had the slightest proof.

Now it was too late. He could no longer let him go.

He felt drowsy, glum. He sat down on the terrace of the *Brasserie Dauphine*, but, after reading right through the bill of fare, he ended by ordering a sandwich and a glass of beer, for he wasn't hungry.

He went slowly up the staircase at Headquarters. The

lights had just come on, although it was still daylight. As his head reached the first-floor level, he glanced automatically at the waiting-room, and the first thing that caught his eye was a green hat that had begun to get on his nerves.

Ernestine was there, sitting opposite Madame Serre, with her hands in her lap like the old lady, and the same air of patience and resignation. She saw him straight away, and deliberately assumed a fixed stare, giving a slight shake of the head.

He understood that she was asking him not to recognize her. Immediately after, she began talking to the old lady as though the ice had been broken some time before.

He shrugged his shoulders, pushed open the door of the Duty Room. The shorthand writer was at work, a pad of paper on his knee. The weary voice of Janvier could be heard, punctuated by his footsteps as he paced up and down the room next door.

'According to you, Monsieur Serre, your wife fetched a taxi on the corner of the Boulevard Richard-Wallace. How long was she away?'

Before relieving him, he climbed up to Moers' attic, where the latter was busy filing documents.

'Tell me, my boy, apart from the brick dust, there were no traces of anything else in the car?'

'The car had been cleaned out very thoroughly.'

'You're sure?'

'It's only by chance that I found a little powdered brick in a fold of the mat, under the driver's seat.'

'Suppose the car hadn't been cleaned and that the driver had got out on a country road.'

'A tarred road?'

'No. Suppose, I'm saying, that he got out, also the person with him, that they'd both gone for a walk on the path and then climbed back into the car.'

'And that it hadn't been cleaned afterwards?'

'Yes.'

'There'd be marks left. Maybe not many. But I'd have found them.'

'That's all I wanted to know. Don't leave yet.'

'Right you are. By the way, I found two hairs in the room of the woman who's disappeared. She was a natural blonde, but gave herself henna rinses. I can tell you what face-powder she used, too.'

The chief-inspector went downstairs again, this time went into his office, thowing off his jacket. He smoked a pipe in there all afternoon. Janvier had smoked cigarettes, and Serre cigars. The air was blue with smoke that drifted in a haze up near the light.

'Aren't you thirsty, Monsieur Serre?'

'The sergeant gave me a glass of water.'

Janvier went out.

'You wouldn't prefer a glass of beer? Or wine?'

Still the same air of bearing Maigret a personal grudge for these little snares.

'Thank you all the same.'

'A sandwich?'

'D'you expect to keep me here much longer?'

'I don't know. Probably. It'll depend on you.'

He went to the door, called out to the plain-clothes men:

'Could one of you fetch me a road-map of the Fontainebleau district?'

He was taking his time. All this was just talk, it was merely scratching the surface.

'When you go for a meal, get them to send up some sandwiches and beer, Janvier.'

'Right you are, Chief.'

The road-map was brought to him.

'Show me the spot where you pulled up on Sunday.'

Serre searched for a moment, took a pencil from the desk, marked a cross wherc the main road met a country lane.

'If there's a farm with a red roof on the left, it'll be this lane here.'

'How long did you go on walking?'

'About a quarter of an hour.'

'Were you wearing the same shoes as today?'

He pondered, looked at his shoes, nodded.

'You're sure about that?'

'Certain.'

His shoes had rubber heels, on which concentric circles were stamped around the maker's name.

'Don't you think, Monsieur Serre, that it'd be simpler and less tiring for you to spill the beans? When did you kill your wife?'

'I didn't kill her.'

Maigret sighed, went to give fresh instructions next door. Couldn't be helped! It'll probably take hours more. The dentist's complexion was already slightly muddier than in the morning, and dark circles had begun to show beneath his eyes.

'Why did you marry her?'

'My mother advised me to.'

'For what motive?'

'For fear I'd be left to live alone one day. She thinks that I'm still a child and that I need someone to look after me.'

'And to stop you from drinking?'

Silence.

'I don't suppose that your marriage with Maria Van Aerts was a love match?'

'We were both nearing our fifties.'

'When did you start to quarrel?'

'We never quarrelled.'

'What did you do with your evenings, Monsieur Serre?'

'I?'

'You.'

'I mostly read, in my study.'

'And your wife?'

'Writing, in her room. She used to go to bed early.'

'Did your father lose much money?'

'I don't understand.'

'Have you ever heard that your father used to lead what they called in those days a fast life?'

'He went about a great deal.'

'Did he spend large sums?'

'I believe so.'

'Your mother made scenes?'

'We're not the sort of people who make scenes.'

'How much did your first marriage bring you in?'

'We don't speak the same language.'

'You and your first wife were married under the joint-possession law?'

'Correct.'

'And she had money. So you must have inherited.'

'Is that unusual?'

'So long as your second wife's body isn't found, you can't inherit from her.'

'Why shouldn't she be found alive?'

'You believe that, Serre?'

'I didn't kill her.'

'Why did you take your car out on Tuesday night?'

'I didn't take it out.'

'The concierge in the house opposite saw you. It was round about midnight.'

'You forget that there are three garages, three former stables, whose doors are adjacent. It was at night, you say so yourself. She may have got them confused.'

'The ironmonger, he couldn't have mistaken someone else for you, in broad daylight, when you went in to buy putty and another window-pane.'

'My word's as good as his.'

'Providing you didn't kill your wife. What did you do with the trunk and the suitcases?'

'That's the third time I've been asked that question. You've forgotten to mention the tools this time.'

'Where were you on Tuesday about midnight?'

'In bed.'

'Are you a light sleeper, Monsieur Serre?'

'No. My mother is.'

'Neither of you heard anything?'

'I seem to remember telling you that already.'

'And on Wednesday morning you found the house as usual?'

'I suppose that, since an enquiry has been opened, you've the right to question me. You've decided, haven't you, to put me through an endurance test? Your detective has already asked me all these questions. Now it's starting all over again. I can see that it's going to go on all night. To save time, I'll tell you once and for all that I didn't kill my wife. I also inform you that I will not answer any questions which have already been put to me. Is my mother here?'

'What makes you think that she is?'

'Does it seem peculiar to you?'

'She's sitting in the waiting-room.'

'D'you mean to let her spend the night there?'

'I shall make no attempt to prevent her. She's quite free.'

This time Guillaume Serre looked at him with hatred.

'I wouldn't like to have your job.'

'I wouldn't like to be in your shoes.'

They stared at each other in silence, each determined not to lower his gaze.

'You killed your wife, Serre. As you probably killed the first one.'

The other didn't move a muscle.

'You'll confess to it.'

A contemptuous smile curled the dentist's lips, and he threw himself back in his chair and crossed his legs.

Next door the waiter from the *Brasserie Dauphine* could be heard putting down plates and glasses on a desk.

'I wouldn't mind something to eat.'

'Perhaps you'd like to take off your coat?'

'No.'

He started to eat a sandwich slowly, while Maigret went to fill a glass with water from the fountain in the wall cupboard.

It was eight o'clock in the evening.

They could see the windows darkening gradually, the view dissolving into specks of light that seemed as far away as the stars.

Maigret had to send out for tobacco. At eleven o'clock, the dentist was smoking his last cigar and the air had got more and more thick. Twice the chief-inspector had gone out for a stroll through the building and had seen the two women in the waiting-room. The second time they'd drawn their chairs closer together and were gossiping together as if they'd known each other for years.

'When did you clean your car?'

'It was last cleaned a fortnight ago, in a garage at Neuilly, at the same time as they changed the oil.'

'It hasn't been cleaned again since Sunday?'

'No.'

'You see, Monsieur Serre, we've just performed a decisive experiment. One of my men who, like yourself, is wearing rubber heels, drove out to the crossing which you marked on the Fontainebleau road. As you stated that you did on Sunday with your mother, he got out of the car and went for a walk along the country lane. It hasn't a tarred surface. He got back in the car and returned here.

'The experts from our technical branch, who're supposed to know their job then examined the mats in the car.

'Here is the dust and gravel that they gathered up.'

He pushed a small paper bag across the desk.

Serre made no move to take it.

'We'd have found the same thing on the mat in your car.'

'That proves I killed my wife?'

'It proves that your car has been cleaned since Sunday.'

'Couldn't someone have got into my garage?'

'It's unlikely.'

'Didn't your men get in?'

'What are you insinuating?'

'Nothing, Chief-Inspector. I'm not accusing anyone — I'm merely pointing out to you that this operation was undertaken without witnesses, therefore without legal warranty.'

'Wouldn't you like to speak to your mother?'

'You'd love to know what I'd have to say to her? Nothing, Monsieur Maigret. I've nothing to say to her, and she has nothing to say to me.'

A thought suddenly crossed his mind.

'Has she had anything to eat?'

'I've no idea. I can only repeat that she's a free agent.'

'She won't leave as long as I'm here.'

'She may be in for a long stay.'

Serre lowered his eyes and his manner changed. After a long hesitation, he muttered, as if slightly ashamed:

'I suppose it would be asking too much to have a sandwich sent in to her?'

'That was done a long time ago.'

'Did she eat it?'

'Yes'

'How is she?'

'She talks all the time.'

'To whom?'

'To a certain person who happens also to be in the waiting-room. A girl who used to be on the streets.'

And again there was a gleam of hate in the dentist's eyes.

'You arranged that deliberately, didn't you?'

'Not at all.'

'My mother has nothing to tell.'

'All the better for you.'

They passed the next quarter of an hour in silence, then Maigret plodded into the next-door room, glummer than ever, motioned to Janvier who was dozing in a corner.

'Same routine, Chief?'

'Anything you like.'

The stenographer was worn out. The translator still worked on in his cubbyhole.

'Go and fetch Ernestine, the one with the green hat, and bring her to Lucas's office.'

When Lofty came in, she didn't look pleased.

'You oughtn't to have interrupted us. She'll start suspecting something.'

Perhaps because it was late at night. Maigret spoke to her more familiarly than usual, without noticing it.

'What've you been filling her up with?'

'How I didn't know why I'd been made to come here, how my husband's been missing two days and I had no news, how much I hate the police and the tricks they're always trying on.

' "They're just keeping me waiting here to try and shake me!" I told her. "They reckon they can get away with anything." '

'What did she say?'

'She asked me if I'd been here before. I said yes, I'd been put through it for a whole night, a year ago, because my husband had had a scrap in a café and they wanted to make out he'd knifed somebody. To start off with, she looked at me like she was sort of disgusted. Then, bit by bit, she began to ask me questions.'

'What about?'

'Mostly about you. I told her eveything bad I could think up. I took good care to add that you always managed to make people talk, however tough you had to get with 'em.'

'What!'

'I know what I'm doing. I told her about the time when you kept somebody stark naked in your office for twenty-four hours, in midwinter, taking care the window was left wide open.'

'There's been no such thing.'

'It shook her. She's less sure of herself than she was when I got here. She spends all her time listening.

' "Does he beat people?" she asked me.

' "It's been known."

'Would you like me to go back to her?'

'If you want to.'

'Only I'd like to be taken back to the waiting-room by one of the men, and have him be rough with me.'

'Still no news of Alfred.'

'You haven't had any either?'

Maigret had her taken back in the way that she'd asked for and the plain-clothes man returned grinning wryly.

'What happened?'

'Nothing much. When I passed byt he old girl, she put up her arm as if she thought I was going to hit her. I'd hardly got out of the room when Lofty burst out crying.'

Madame Maigret rang up to find out if her husband had eaten anything.

'Shall I wait for you?'

'Certainly not.'

He had a headache. He was disgruntled with himself, with everybody else. Perhaps he was a bit uneasy as well. He wondered what would happen if they suddenly received a telephone call from Maria Van Aerts announcing that she'd changed her plans and had quietly settled down in some town or other.

He drank a pint already gone tepid, told them to send up some more before the *brasserie* closed and went back into his office, where Janvier had opened the window. The clamour of the city had subsided. Now and then a taxi crossed the Pont Saint-Michel.

He sat down, his shoulders drooping. Janvier went out. After a long pause, he said musingly:

'Your mother's got it into her head that I'm torturing you.'

He was surprised to see the other raise his head sharply, and for the first time he saw his face look anxious.

'What have they been telling her?'

'I don't know. It's probably the girl who's in there with her. These people like to make up stories so's to seem more interesting.'

'Could I see her?'

'Who?'

'My mother.'

Maigret pretended to hesitate, to weigh up the pros and cons, finally shook his head.

'No,' he said decisively. 'I think I'll question her myself. And I'm wondering if I shouldn't have Eugénie brought down, too.'

'My mother doesn't know anything.'

'Do you?'

'I don't either.'

'Then there's no reason why I shouldn't question her as I've questioned you.'

'Haven't you any pity, Inspector?'

'For whom?'

'An old woman.'

'Maria would have liked to become an old woman, too.'

He walked up and down the office, his hands behind his back, but what he was waiting for didn't come.

'Your turn, Janvier! I'm going to have a crack at the mother.'

Actually he didn't know yet whether he would do so or not. Janvier said later that he'd never known the Chief so tired and so surly as on that night.

It was one in the morning. Everybody at Headquarters had lost confidence, and chagrined glances were exchanged behind the chief-inspector's back.

CHAPTER EIGHT

Maigret was emerging from the Duty Room on his way to look in on the translator when one of the cleaners, who, half an hour before, had invaded the building, came up to tell him:

'There's a lady asking to speak to you.'

'Where?'

'It's one of the two who were in the waiting-room. Seems she's not feeling well. She came into the office I was sweeping out, white in the face like she'd come over queer, and asked me straight off to fetch you.'

'The old lady?' Maigret asked, frowning.

'No, the girl.'

Most of the doors that gave onto the corridor were open. In an office two doors away, the chief-inspector caught sight of Ernestine holding one hand to her breast, and strode quickly forward, scowling his lips framing a question.

'Shut the door,' she whispered when he was within earshot.

And directly he'd done so:

'Phew! I couldn't stick it any longer and that's the truth, but I'm not sick. I put on an act so's to get away from her for a bit. Not that I'm feeling any too bright, either. You wouldn't have a stiff drink about the place?'

He had to go back to his office to get the bottle of brandy that he always kept in the cupboard. Not having any smaller glasses, he poured the spirit into a tumbler and she swallowed it at a gulp, with a shudder.

'I don't know how you manage to take the son. The mother's got me right down. In the finish, I reckoned I'd go crackers.'

'Did she talk?'

'She's wider than me. That's just what I wanted to tell you. To start off I made sure she'd swallowed all the bull I was stuffing her up with.

'Then, I don't know how it happened, she started to pop in a question here and there, all innocent-like. I've been third-degree'd before now and I reckoned I could hold my own.

'With her, I didn't have an earthly.'

'Did you tell her what you were?'

'Not right out. That woman's very, very clever, Monsieur Maigret. How could she have guessed I'd been on the beat? Tell me, does it still show? Then she says to me:

' "You're no stranger to these kind of people, are you?"

'It was your mob she was referring to.

'In the end, she's asking me what it's like in jail, and I'm telling her.

'If you'd told me, when I sat down there in front of her, that I'd give the game away, I'd have refused to credit it.'

'Did you tell her about Alfred?'

'In a way. Without saying exactly what his racket is. She thinks he's a kite-man. She's not all that interested. For three-quarters of an hour now, at least, she's been asking me about life in jail: what time you get up? what you have to eat, what the wardresses act like.... I thought you'd be interested to know and I made out I'd come over queer; I got up saying I was going to ask for a drink, that it wasn't human leaving women to hang about all night....

'Mind if I have another drop?'

She really was worn out. The brandy brought the colour back into her cheeks.

'Her son won't talk?'

'Not yet. Has she said anything about him?'

'She harks to every sound, gets jumpy every time a door opens. Something else she asked me. She wanted to know if I'd met anybody who'd got guillotined. Now I feel better, I'll go back to her. I'll be on my guard this time, don't worry.'

She took the opportunity to put on some powder, looked at the bottle without venturing to ask for a third drink.

'What's the time?'

'Three o'clock.'

'I don't know how she sticks it. She doesn't look tired, and she's sitting up as straight as at the start of the evening.'

Maigret let her out, took a breath of air at a window opening on to the courtyard and swallowed a mouthful of brandy out of the bottle. As he crossed the office where the translator was working, the latter showed him a passage that he'd underlined in one of the letters.

'This dates back a year and a half,' he said.

Maria had written to her friend:

Yesterday I had a good laugh. G. came to my room, not for what you might think, but to talk to me about a scheme I'd proposed the day before to go and spend a couple of days in Nice.

They're terrified of travelling, these people. Only once in their lives have they ever been out of France. Their one trip abroad goes back to the time when the father was still alive and they all went over to London together. Incidentally, it appears that they were all seasick and had to call in the ship's doctor.

But that's nothing to do with the case.

Whenever I say something that doesn't suit them, they don't answer straight away. The just stop talking, and, as the saying goes, one can hear a pin drop.

Then, later on or next day, G. comes up to my room, looking distressed, beats about the bush, finally confesses what's worrying him. Briefly, it would seem that my notion of going to Nice for the Carnival was ludicrous, almost indecent. He made no bones about telling me that his mother had been shocked by it and pleaded with me to give up the idea.

Well, it so happened that the drawer of my bedside-table was open. He glanced into it by accident and I saw him turn pale.

'What's that?' he stammered, pointing at the little automatic

with a mother-of-pearl butt that I bought during my trip to Egypt.

Do you remember? I wrote to you about it at the time. People had told me that a woman on her own was never safe in places like that.

I don't know why I'd put it in that drawer. I replied coolly:

'It's a pistol.'

'Is it loaded?'

'I don't remember.'

I picked it up. I looked in the magazine. There were no bullets in it.

'Have you any ammunition?'

'There must be some somewhere.'

Half an hour later, my mother-in-law came up on some excuse, for she never enters my room without giving a reason. She also beat about the bush for a while, then explained to me that it was most unseemly for a woman to carry fire-arms.

'But it's more like a toy,' I retorted. 'I keep it as a souvenir, because the handle's pretty and my initials are engraved on it. I don't think it could harm anybody much, either.'

She gave in, finally. But not before I'd had to give her the box of ammunition that was in the bottom of the drawer.

The funny part is that, no sooner had she gone, that I found in one of my handbags another ammunition-clip that I'd forgotten about. I didn't tell her....

Maigret, who was holding the brandy bottle in his hand, poured some out for the translator, then he went to give some to the typist and the plain-clothes man who, to try to keep awake, was doodling on his blotter.

When he went back into his office, which Janvier vacated automatically, the bell had gone for another round.

'I've been thinking, Serre. I'm beginning to believe that you haven't been lying as much as I supposed.'

He'd dropped the 'Monsieur', as if so many hours alone together had brought a sort of familiarity. The dentist merely regarded him mistrustfully.

'Maria wasn't meant to disappear any more than your

first wife. Her disappearance wasn't to your advantage. She'd packed her bags, announced her departure for Holland. She really intended to take the night-train.

'I don't know if she was supposed to die in the house or not until she got outside. What d'you say to that?'

Guillaume Serre made no reply, but his expression betrayed much more concern.

'If you like it better, she was meant to die a natural death, by which I mean a death that would *pass as natural*.

'This didn't take place, since, if it had, you'd have had no motive for disposing of her body or her luggage.

'There's another thing that doesn't add up. You'd said good-bye to each other. She'd no reason then to go back into your study. Yet her dead body was lying there at a certain time that night.

'I'm not asking you to answer me, but to follow my reasoning. I've only just found out that your wife owned a pistol.

'I'm ready to believe that you shot her in self-defence. After that you got in a panic. You left the body where it had fallen, while you went to get your car out of the garage. It was then, round about midnight, that the concierge saw you.

'What I'm trying to find out, is what changed both your plans and hers. You were in your study, weren't you?'

'I don't remember.'

'That's what you stated.'

'Possibly.'

'I'm convinced that your mother, however, was not in her room, but with you.'

'She was in her room.'

'So you remember that?'

'Yes.'

'Then you remember, also, that you were in your study? Your wife hadn't gone out to fetch a taxi yet. If she'd brought a cab back that night, we'd have found the driver. In other words, it was before leaving the house that she changed her mind and went to your study. Why?'

'I've no idea.'

'You admit that she came to see you?'

'No.'

'You're being unwise, Serre. There are very few instances, in criminal records, when a dead body hasn't been found sooner or later. We shall find hers. And I'm certain, now, that a post-mortem will reveal that she was killed by one or several bullet wounds. What I'm wondering is whether it was a shot fired by your gun or a shot fired by hers.

'The seriousness of your case will depend on that. If the bullet came from her pistol, the conclusion will be drawn that, for one reason or another, she took it into her head to go and settle some score with you and threaten you.

'Money perhaps, Serre?'

He shrugged his shoulders.

'You leaped at her, disarmed her and squeezed the trigger without meaning to. Another theory could be that she threatened your mother and not you. A woman's more likely to feel hatred for another woman than for a man.

'A final possibility, again, is that your own revolver was not in your room, where you put it soon after, but in the drawer of your desk.

'Maria comes in. She's armed. She threatens you. You pull the drawer open and shoot first.

'In either case, you're in no danger of execution. There can be no question of premeditation, since it's quite normal to keep a pistol in the desk of one's study.

'You can even plead self-defence.

'What remains to be explained is why your wife, on the point of leaving, should suddenly have rushed in to see you with a gun in her hand.'

He threw himself back and slowly filled a pipe, without taking his eyes off the other.

'What d'you say to that?'

'This can go on for ever,' said Serre in a tone of disgust.

'You still refuse to talk?'

'I'm answering your questions obediently.'

'You haven't told me why you shot her.'

'I didn't shoot her.'

'Then your mother did?'

'My mother didn't shoot her either. She was up in her

room.'

'While you were quarrelling with your wife?'

'There was no quarrel.'

'Pity.'

'I'm so sorry.'

'You see, Serre, I've done my best to discover any reason your wife may have had for settling with you and threatening you.'

'She didn't threaten me.'

'Don't be too positive about it, because you may regret your claims later on. It's you who will plead with me or with the jury to believe that your life or your mother's was in danger.'

Serre smiled sardonically. He was tired, slumped in upon himself, his shoulders slightly hunched about his neck, but he hadn't lost any of his self-possession. His beard showed blue through the skin on his cheeks. The sky, beyond the window-panes, was already not quite so dark and the air in the room was becoming cooler.

It was Maigret who felt the cold first and went over to close the window.

'It wasn't to your advantage to have a corpse on your hands. *I mean a corpse that nobody could be allowed to see.* D'you follow me?'

'No.'

'When your first wife died, it was in such a manner that you were able to call in Doctor Dutilleux to make out the death certificate.

'That's how Maria was supposed to die, from apparently natural causes. She had a weak heart too. What had worked once could work again.

'But something went wrong.

'D'you see, now, what I'm getting at?'

'I didn't kill her.'

'And you didn't dispose of her body, together with her luggage and the burglar's tools?'

'There wasn't any burglar.'

'I'll probably confront you with him in a few hours.'

'You've found him?'

His tone was slightly uneasy, all the same.

'We were able to find his fingerprints in your study. You were careful to wipe over the furniture, but there's always some piece that gets forgotten. He happens to be an old offender, an expert in his way, well-known here, Alfred Jussiaume — "Sad Freddie", they call him. He told his wife what he'd seen. She is now out there in the waiting-room with your mother. As for Jussiaume, he's in Rouen and has no further reason to remain in hiding.

'We already have the concierge who saw you take your car out of the garage. We've also got the ironmonger who sold you a second sheet of glass at eight o'clock on Wednesday morning.

'The technical branch will prove that your car has been cleaned since that date.

'That makes quite a lot of evidence, doesn't it?

'When we have found the body and the luggage, my job will be over.

'Then, perhaps, you'll decide to explain why, instead of a, shall we say, lawful corpse, you found yourself landed with a body that you had to dispose of at once.

'There was some hitch.

'What was it, Serre?'

The man pulled a handkerchief out of his pocket, wiped his lips and forehead, but didn't open his mouth to reply.

'It's half-past three. I'm beginning to get fed up. Are you still determined not to talk?'

'I've nothing to say.'

'Very good,' said Maigret, getting up. 'I don't like having to bully an old woman. But I see that I am forced to question your mother.'

He expected a protest, at any rate some display of feeling. The dentist didn't bat an eyelid, and it seemed to Maigret that he even showed a kind of relief, that his nerves relaxed.

'You take over, Janvier. I'll get busy on the mother.'

It really was his intention; he was unable to put it into practice immediately, for Vacher had just appeared, in great excitement, a parcel in his hand.

'I've got it, Chief! Took me some time, but I think this is it.'

He undid the parcel wrapped in an old newspaper, revealing broken bits of brick, some reddish dust.

'Where?'

'On the Quai de Billancourt, opposite the Ile Seguin. If I'd started down-stream instead of starting up-stream, I'd have been here hours ago. I've been all over the wharves where they unload. Billancourt was the only place where a barge unloaded bricks lately.'

'When?'

'Last Monday. She sailed away about noon on Tuesday. The bricks are still there and kids must have been playing around, broken a fair amount of them. There's a red dust covering a good bit of the quay. Shall I take it up to Moers?'

'I'll go myself.'

As he went through the waiting-room, he looked at the two women sitting there in silence. It seemed, from their attitudes, as if there was now a chill between them.

Maigret entered the laboratory, where he felt he'd earned a cup of coffee, which Moers had just made.

'Have you got the sample of brick dust? Like to compare them?'

The colour was the same, the pattern seemed identical. Moers used magnifying slides and an electric projector.

'Does it add up?'

'Very likely. Comes from the same district, anyhow. It'll take me about thirty minutes or an hour to do the analysis.'

It was too late to have the Seine dragged. Nor would the river patrol be able to send a diver down until sunrise. Then, if they found Maria's body, or only the luggage and the tool-box, the circle would be closed.

'Hello! River Patrol? Maigret here.'

He still seemed to be in a bad temper.

'I'd like you to drag the Seine as soon as possible, Quai de Billancourt, at the place where a cargo of bricks was unloaded rccently.'

'In an hour from now it'll be dawn.'

What stopped him from waiting? No jury would ask for further proof to find Guillaume Serre guilty even if he persisted in his denials. Without heeding the typist, who was staring at him, Maigret took a long pull at the bottle, wiped his mouth, went out into the passage and threw open purposefully the door of the waiting-room.

Ernestine thought he'd come for her and sprang quickly to her feet. Madame Serre, however, did not move.

It was the latter to whom Maigret spoke.

'D'you mind coming a moment?'

There was a large choice of empty offices. He pushed open a door at random, closed the window.

'Please take a seat.'

And he began to circle round the room, glancing at the old lady sourly from time to time.

'I don't much like to break bad news,' he growled at last. 'Especially to someone your age. Have you ever been ill, Madame Serre?'

'Except when we were seasick, crossing the Channel, I've never had to call in the doctor.'

'So, naturally, you don't suffer from heart trouble?'

'No.'

'Your son does, however?'

'He's always had an enlarged heart.'

'He killed his wife!' he shot out point-blank, raising his head and staring her in the face.

'Did he tell you so himself?'

He hated to use the old trick of a false confession.

'He still denies it, but that won't help. We've got proof.'

'That he's a murderer?'

'That he shot Maria, in his study.'

She had not moved. Her features had stiffened slightly; one had the impression that she'd stopped breathing, but she showed no other sign of emotion.

'What proof have you?'

'We've found the spot where his wife's body was thrown into the river, together with her luggage and the burglar's tools.'

'Ah!'

That was all she said. She was waiting, her hand stiffly folded on her dark dress.

'Your son refuses to plead self-defence. That's a mistake, because I'm convinced that, when his wife entered the study, she was armed and meant to do him harm.'

'Why?'

'That's what I'm asking you.'

'I've no idea.'

'Where were you?'

'In my room, as I told you.'

'You didn't hear anything?'

'Nothing. Only the door closing. Then the sound of a motor engine, in the street.'

'The taxi?'

'I thought it must be a taxi, since my daughter-in-law had said she was going to fetch one.'

'You're not sure? It might have been a private car?'

'I didn't see it.'

'Then it might easily have been your son's car?'

'He swore to me that he didn't go out.'

'You realize the discrepancy between what you're saying now and the statements that you made to me when you called here of your own accord?'

'No.'

'You stated positively that your daughter-in-law went away in a taxi.'

'I still think that she did.'

'But you're no longer certain about it. Are you so certain now that there was no attempted burglary?'

'I saw no sign of any.'

'What time did you come downstairs on Wednesday morning?'

'About half-past six.'

'Did you go into the study?'

'Not immediately. I got the coffee ready.'

'You didn't go and open the shutters?'

'Yes, I believe so.'

'Before your son came down?'

'Probably.'

'You wouldn't swear to it?'

'Put yourself in my place, Monsieur Maigret. For two days I've hardly known where I am. I've been asked all sorts of questions. I've been sitting in your waiting-room for I don't know how many hours. I'm tired. I'm doing my best to hold out.'

'Why did you come here tonight?'

'Isn't it natural for a mother to follow her son in such circumstances? I've always lived with him. He might be in need of me.'

'Would you follow him to prison?'

'I don't understand. I can't believe that...'

'Let me put it another way: if I made out a charge against your son, would you be willing to share the responsibility for what he did?'

'But since he hasn't done anything!'

'Are you sure of that?'

'Why should he have killed his wife?'

'You avoid giving me a straight answer. Are you convinced that he didn't kill her?'

'So far as I can tell.'

'Is there any chance that he did so?'

'He had no motive for it.'

'But he did!' he said harshly, staring her in the face.

She sat as if in suspended animation. She breathed: 'Ah!'

Then she opened her bag to take out her handkerchief. Her eyes were dry. She wasn't crying. She merely dabbed at her lips with the handkerchief.

'Might I have a glass of water?'

He had to hunt around for a moment, since he didn't know the office as well as his own.

'As soon as the Director of Prosecutions arrives at the Palais de Justice, your son will be indicted. I can tell you now that he hadn't the slightest chance of getting away with it.'

'You mean that he...'

'He'll go to the guillotine.'

She didn't faint, but sat rigid on her chair, staring blankly ahead.

'His first wife's body will be exhumed. I dare say you know that traces of certain poisons can be found in a skeleton.'

'Why should he have killed them both? It isn't possible. It isn't true, Chief-Inspector. I don't know why you're telling me this, but I refuse to believe you. Let me speak to him. Allow me to talk to him in private and I'll find out the truth.'

'Were you in your room the whole of Tuesday evening?'

'Yes.'

'You didn't go downstairs at all?'

'No. Why should I have gone down, when that woman was leaving us at last?'

Maigret went over for a while to cool his forehead against the window-pane, then walked into the office next door, grabbed the bottle and drank from it the equivalent of three or four singles.

When he came back, he had assumed the heavy gait of Guillaume Serre and his obstinate glare.

CHAPTER NINE

He was sitting in a chair that wasn't his, both elbows on the table, his biggest pipe in his mouth, his eyes fixed upon the old lady whom he'd likened to a Mother Superior.

'Your son, Madame Serre, didn't kill either his first or his second wife,' he said, spacing out the words.

She frowned in surprise, but didn't look any the happier.

'Nor did he kill his father,' he added.

'What do you...?'

'Hush!... If you don't mind, we'll settle this as quickly as possible. We'll not bother about proof for the time being. That'll come in due course.

'We won't argue about your husband's case, either. What I'm almost certain of is that your first daughter-in-law was poisoned. I'll go further. I'm convinced that it wasn't done by arsenic or any of the strong poisons that are usually used.

'By the way, Madame Serre, I might tell you that, in nine cases out of ten, poison is a woman's weapon.

'Your first daughter-in-law, like the second, suffered from heart trouble. So did your husband.

'Certain drugs, which wouldn't seriously affect people in good health, can be fatal to cardiac cases. I wonder if Maria didn't provide us with the key to the problem in one of her letters to her friend. She speaks of a trip to England which you once took with your husband, and emphasizes that you were all so badly seasick that you had to be seen by the ship's doctor.

'What would be prescribed in such a case?'

'I've no idea.'

'That's very unlikely. They usually give you atropine in some form or other. Now, a fairly strong dose of atropine can be fatal to a person with a weak heart.'

'You mean that my husband...'

'We'll go into that another time, even if it's impossible to prove anything. Your husband, during his later days, was leading a disorderly life and throwing his money away. You've always been afraid of poverty, Madame Serre.'

'Not for myself. For my son. Which doesn't mean that I would have...'

'Later on, your son got married. Another woman came to live in your house, a woman who, overnight, bore your name and had as much right there as you.'

She compressed her lips.

'This woman, who also had a weak heart, was rich, richer than your son, richer than all the Serres put together.'

'You believe that I poisoned her, having first poisoned my husband?'

'Yes.'

She gave a little strained laugh.

'Doubtless I also poisoned my second daughter-in-law?'

'She was going away, discouraged, after having tried in vain to live in a house where she was treated like a stranger. Very likely she was taking her money with her. By coincidence, she had heart trouble too.

'You see, I wondered from the start why her body disappeared. If she'd simply been poisoned, you only had to call in a doctor who, given Maria's state of health, would have diagnosed a heart attack. Perhaps the attack itself was intended to come on later, in the taxi, at the station or on the train.'

'You seem very sure of yourself, Monsieur Maigret.'

'I know that something happened which obliged your son to shoot down his wife. Let's suppose that Maria, just as she was going to fetch a taxi or, more likely, as she was on the point of telephoning for one, felt certain symptoms coming on.

'She knew you both, having lived with you for two and a half years. She was a widely read woman, in all sorts of subjects, and it wouldn't surprise me if she had acquired some medical knowledge.

'Realizing that she'd been poisoned, she went into your husband's study while you were in there with him.'

'Why do you say that I was in there?'

'Because, unfortunately for her, she laid the blame on you. If you'd been in your room, she'd have gone upstairs.

'I don't know if she threatened you with her pistol or if she merely reached for the telephone to call the police....

'There was only one way out for you: to shoot her down.'

'And, according to you, it was I who...'

'No. I've already told you that it's more likely to have been your son who fired, or, if you'd rather, finished your work for you.'

The drab light of dawn blended with the electric lamps. The lines in their faces were etched more deeply. The telephone bell rang.

'That you, Chief? I've done the test. It's ten to one the brick dust we found in the car came from Billancourt.'

'You can go home to bed, my boy. Your job's through.'

He got up once again, circled the room.

'Your son, Madame Serre, is determined to shoulder all the blame. I don't see any way of stopping him. If he's been able to keep his mouth shut all this time, he's capable of keeping it shut for good. Unless...'

'Unless...?'

'I don't know. I was thinking aloud. Two years ago I'd a man as tough as he is in my office and after fifteen hours we still hadn't got a word out of him.'

He threw open the window abruptly, in a kind of rage.

'It took twenty-seven and a half hours to break his nerve.'

'Did he confess?'

'He spilled everything in one long stream, as if it were a

relief to get rid of it.'

'I didn't poison anybody.'

'The answer doesn't lie with you.'

'But with my son?'

'Yes. He's convinced that you only did it for his sake, partly out of fear that he'd be left penniless, partly out of jealousy.'

He had to restrain himself from raising his hand to her, despite her age, for the old woman's thin lips had just twitched in an involuntary smile.

'Which is a lie!' he said flatly.

Then, coming closer to her, his eyes on hers, his breath on the woman's face, he rapped out:

'It's not for his sake that you're afraid of poverty, it's for your own! It's not for his sake that you murdered, and if you came here tonight, it's because you were afraid he might talk.'

She tried to shrink away, threw herself back in her chair, for Maigret's face was thrust into hers, hard, menacing.

'Never mind if he does go to prison, or even if he's executed, so long as you can be sure of staying in the clear. You believe that you've still many years to live, in your house, counting your money....'

She was frightened. Her mouth opened as if to call for help. Suddenly, with a violent, unexpected jerk, Maigret wrenched from her withered hands the bag that she was clinging to.

She gave a cry, shot forward to retrieve it.

'Sit down.'

He undid the silver clasp. Right at the bottom, beneath the gloves, the note-case, the handkerchief and the powder-compact, he found a folded paper which contained two white tablets.

A hush like that in a church or a cavern enclosed them. Maigret let his body relax, sat down, pressed a bell-push.

When the door opened, he said slowly, without a glance at the plain-clothes man who'd appeared:

'Tell Janvier to lay off him.'

And, as the detective still stood there, in amazement:

'It's all over. She's confessed.'

'I haven't confessed to anything.'

He waited until the door closed again.

'It comes to the same thing. I could have carried on the experiment to the end, let you have the private talk with your son that you wanted.

'Don't you think that you've caused enough deaths already for one old woman?'

'You mean that I would have...'

He was toying with the tablets.

'You'd have given him his medicine, or rather what he would have thought was his medicine, and there'd have been no danger of his ever talking again.'

The corners of the roof-tops had begun to be crested with sunlight. The telephone rang again.

'Chief-Inspector Maigret? River Patrol here. We're at Billancourt. The diver's just gone down for the first time and he's found a pretty heavy trunk.'

'The rest'll turn up as well!' he said indifferently.

An exhausted and astonished Janvier was framed in the doorway.

'They told me....'

'Take her down to the cells. The man, too, as an accessory. I'll see the prosecutor directly he comes in.'

He'd no longer any business with either the mother or the son.

'You can go off to bed,' he told the translator.

'It's over?'

'For today.'

The dentist was no longer there when he entered his office, but the ash-tray was full of very black cigar-butts. He sat down in his chair and was about to doze off, when he remembered Lofty.

He found her in the waiting-room, where she'd gone to sleep, shook her by the shoulder and, instinctively, she put her green hat straight.

'That's the lot. Off you go now.'

'Has he confessed?'

'It was her.'

'What! It was the old girl who...'

'Later!' he murmured.

Then, turning round, since he was assailed by a twinge of remorse:

'And thanks! When Alfred comes back, advise him to...'

But what was the good? Nothing would cure the Sad Man of his mania for burgling the safes that he had once put in, or wean him from his belief that each would be the last and that this time he was really going to live in the country.

On account of her age, old Madame Serre was not executed and left the Court with the complacent air of one who is at last going to set the women's prison in order.

When her son came out of Fresnes jail, after two years, he made straight for the house in the Rue de la Ferme and, that very evening, took the same stroll round the neighbourhood that he'd been accustomed to take in the days when he had a dog to exercise.

He continued to go and drink red wine in the little café and, before entering, to look uneasily up and down the street.

Shadow Rock Farm,
Lakeville, Conn.
May 8, 1951

MAIGRET
Goes to School

CHAPTER ONE

There are certain images which one registers unconsciously, with the precision of a camera, and later, recalling them to memory, racks one's brain to discover where this took place.

Maigret had ceased to realize, after so many years, that each time he arrived, always slightly out of breath, at the top of the steep, dusty staircase at Police Headquarters, he would make a brief pause and glance automatically towards the glass cage which served as a waiting-room and was known to some of his colleagues as 'the aquarium', to others as 'Purgatory'. Perhaps they all did this and it had become a kind of professional reflex.

Even on mornings like this, when bright, pale sunlight, gay as lilies-of-the-valley, was shimmering down on Paris and casting a glow on the pink chimney-pots above the roofs, a lamp was kept burning all day in 'Purgatory', which had no window and whose only light came from the immense corridor.

Sometimes one saw, seated in the armchairs or on the green velvet chairs, various seedy-looking characters, old-timers picked up by some inspector during the night and now waiting to be questioned, or else stool-pigeons, or witnesses who had received their summons the day before and now raised melancholy heads whenever anyone went by.

For some mysterious reason, this had been chosen as the

place to hang the two black frames, with their gold fillets, which held the photographs of policemen killed while on duty.

There were other people who passed through Purgatory, men and women belonging to what is called 'good society'; and they would remain standing at first, as though about to be sent for at any moment — as though they were just here for an unimportant visit. After a longish time they would be seen to move over to a chair on which they would finally sit down, and it was not unusual to find them still there three hours later, shrunk into themselves, mournful-eyed, having lost all sense of their social precedence.

On this particular morning there was only one man in Purgatory, and Maigret noticed that he belonged to the type commonly known as 'rat-faced'. He was on the thin side. His bare, receding forehead was crowned by a fluff of reddish hair. His eyes were doubtless blue or violet, and the forward thrust of his nose was all the more apparent in contrast to his receding chin.

Everywhere, from schooldays onward, we meet people of this kind, and there is, heaven knows why, a tendency not to take them seriously.

Maigret felt he paid so little attention to the man that if, as he opened the door of his own office, he had been asked who was in the waiting-room, he might have been unable to reply. It was five minutes to nine. The window was wide open and a light, goldish-blue haze was drifting up from the Seine. For the first time this year he had put on his thinner overcoat, but the air was still cool; you wanted to drink it in like some light, white wine, and it made the skin on your face feel taut.

Taking off his hat, he glanced at the visiting-card which lay in full view on his blotter. It bore, in pale ink, the words *'Joseph Gastin, schoolmaster'*. And in the right-hand corner, in small letters which he had to bend forward to read, *'Saint-André-sur-Mer'*.

He did not connect this card with the rat-faced man, only wondered where he had heard of Saint-André-sur-Mer. The bell rang in the corridor as a summons to the daily report. He removed his overcoat, picked up the file he had prepared the day before, and set off, as he had done for so many years, to the Chief's office. On the way he met other chief-inspectors, and their eyes all reflected the mood he had noticed in the passers-by in the street.

'This time it's really spring!'

'Seems like it.'

'Going to be a wonderful day.'

Sunshine was pouring in through the big windows of the Chief's office, as though through the windows of a country church, and pigeons were cooing on the stone ledge outside.

Each man, as he came in, rubbed his hands and made the same remark:

'This is spring.'

They were all over forty-five years old; the matters they were about to discuss were serious, in some cases ghastly, but all the same they were as happy as children because of the sudden mildness of the air, and above all because of the light that was flooding down on the city and transforming every street-corner, the house-fronts, the roofs, the cars crossing the Pont St. Michel, into pictures that one would have liked to hang on the wall.

'Have you seen the assistant manager of the bank in the Rue de Rivoli, Maigret?'

'I have an appointment with him in half an hour.'

An unimportant affair. This was an almost empty week. The assistant manager of the branch office of a bank in the Rue de Rivoli, just near the central markets, suspected one of his clerks of dishonesty.

He filled his pipe and looked out of a window while his colleague from General Information was discussing another matter — some business about a Senator's daughter who had got herself into an awkward situation.

Back in his own office, he found Lucas waiting, with his hat already on, to go to the Rue de Rivoli with him.

'Shall we walk?'

It was quite near. Maigret didn't give another thought to the visiting-card. Going past Purgatory, he saw the rat-faced man again, and two or three other 'clients', one of whom was a night-club proprietor whom he recognized and who was there because of the Senator's daughter.

They walked to the Pont Neuf, the pair of them, Maigret with long strides, and the short-legged Lucas obliged to take many more steps in order to keep up with him. They couldn't have said, afterwards, what they had talked about. Perhaps they had merely been looking around them. In the Rue de Rivoli there was a strong smell of vegetables and fruit, and lorries were removing loads of crates and baskets.

They went into the bank, listened to the assistant manager's explanations, walked round the premises, casting sidelong glances at the suspected clerk.

For lack of proofs, they decided to set a trap for him. They discussed the details, then said good-bye. Maigret and Lucas left and found it so warm outside that they carried their overcoats instead of putting them on again, which gave them a kind of holiday feeling.

In the Place Dauphine, they stopped with one accord.

'Shall we have a quick one?'

It was too early for an *apéritif*, but they both felt that the taste of *pernod* would make a wonderful accompaniment to the spring atmosphere, and in they went to the Brasserie Dauphine.

'Two *pernods*, quickly!'

'D'you happen to know Saint-André-sur-Mer?'

'Isn't it somewhere in the Charentes?'

This reminded Maigret of the beach at Fourras, in the sunshine, the oysters he had eaten at about this time, half past ten in the morning, on the terrace of a little *bistro*, washing them down with a bottle of the local white wine, at the bottom of which lay a few grains of sand.

'Think that clerk is a swindler?'

'His boss seems positive about it.'

'He looked a poor devil to me.'

'We shall know in a couple of days.'

They strolled along the Quai des Orfèvres, went up the big staircase, and once again Maigret paused. Rat-face was still there, leaning forward, his long, bony hands clasped on his knees. He looked up at Maigret with what the chief-inspector felt to be a reproachful expression.

In his office he found the visiting-card lying where he had left it, and rang for the office-boy.

'Is he still here?'

'Ever since eight o'clock. He was here before me. He insists on speaking to you personally.'

Any number of people, most of them mad or half-crazy, used to ask to speak personally to the Chief or to Maigret, whose names they had come to know from the newspapers. They would refuse to be fobbed off with an Inspector, and some would wait all day and come back next morning, standing up hopefully whenever the chief-inspector went by, only to sit down and wait again.

'Bring him in.'

He sat down, filled two or three pipes, signed to the man, when he was shown in, to sit down opposite him. Picking up the visiting-card, he asked:

'Is this yours?'

Looking more closely, he realized that the man had probably had no sleep, for he was grey-faced, with red eyelids and unnaturally bright eyes. His hands were folded, as they had been in the waiting-room, with the fingers clenched so tightly that the joints cracked.

Instead of answering the question, he muttered, with an anxious yet resigned glance at the chief-inspector:

'You know about it?'

'About what?'

The man looked surprised, confused, disappointed perhaps.

'I thought it was already known. I left Saint-André yesterday evening and a journalist had arrived by then. I took the night train. I've come straight here.'

'Why?'

He seemed to be intelligent, but was obviously very upset and didn't know where to begin his story. Maigret awed him. He had doubtless known him by repute for a long time and, like a lot of people, looked upon him as someone endowed with almost divine powers.

At a distance he had thought it would be easy. But now he was confronted by a man in flesh and blood, smoking his pipe with short puffs and watching him with wide-open, almost expressionless eyes.

Was that how he had imagined him? Wasn't he beginning to be sorry he had come?

'They must be thinking I've run away,' he said nervously, with a bitter smile. 'If I were guilty, as they feel sure I am, and if I'd meant to run away, I shouldn't be here now, should I?'

'I can't very well answer that question till I know more about it,' murmured Maigret. 'What are you accused of?'

'Of killing Léonie Birard.'

'Who's accusing you?'

'The whole village, more or less openly. The local police chief didn't dare to arrest me. He admitted frankly that he hadn't sufficient evidence, but he asked me not to go away.'

'All the same you went?

'Yes.'

'Why?'

The visitor, too tense to remain seated for long, sprang to his feet, stuttering:

'Do you mind?'

He didn't know where to stand or what to do with himself.

'I sometimes even forget what's going on.'

He pulled a grubby handkerchief from his pocket, mopped his forehead. The handkerchief probably still smelt of the train, and of his sweat.

'Have you had breakfast?'

'No. I was in a hurry to get here. Above all, I didn't want to be arrested before that, you understand.'

How could Maigret have understood!

'Why, exactly, have you come to see me?'

'Because I have confidence in you. I know that if you will, you can find out the truth.'

'When did this lady... what did you you say her name was?'

'Léonie Birard. She used to be our postmistress.'

'When did she die?'

'She was killed on Tuesday morning. The day before

yesterday. Soon after ten o'clock in the morning.'

'And you are being accused of the crime?'

'You were born in thc country, I saw that in a magazine. You spent most of your childhood there. So you must know the sort of thing that happens in a small village. The population of Saint-André; is only three hundred and twenty.'

'Just a minute. This crime was committed in the Charentes?'

'Yes. About nine miles north-west of La Rochelle, not far from the Aiguillon headland. You know it?'

'A little. But it so happens that I belong to Police Headquarters in Paris and have no authority in the Charentes.'

'I thought of that.'

'Well, then...'

The man was wearing his best suit, which was threadbare; his shirt had a frayed collar. Standing in the middle of the room he had his head lowered, and was staring at the carpet.

'Of course...' he sighed.

'What do you mean?'

'I was wrong. I don't know, now. It seemed quite natural at the time?'

'What did!'

'Coming to put myself under your protection.'

'Under my protection?' repeated Maigret in surprise.

Gastin ventured to glance at him, with the air of a man wondering how he stands.

'Down there, even if they don't arrest me, something unpleasant may happen to me.'

'They don't like you?'

'No.'

'Why not?'

'In the first place, because I'm the schoolmaster and the sectetary of the *mairie*.'

'I don't understand.'

'It's a long time since you lived in the country. They've all got money. They're farmers or else *bouchoteurs*. You know the *bouchots?*'

'The mussel-beds, along the coast?'

'Yes. We're right in the *bouchot* oyster district. Everybody owns at least part of one. It's very profitable. They're rich. Nearly everyone has a car or a small van. But do you know how many of them pay income-tax?'

'Very few, I dare say.'

'Not one! In our village, the doctor and I are the only tax-payers. Naturally, they call me an idler. They imagine it's they who pay my salary. When I complain because the children don't come to school, they tell me to mind my own business. And when I told my pupils to touch their caps to me in the street, they asked me who I thought I was.'

'Tell me about the Léonie Birard business.'

'You mean it?'

With the return of hope, his expression had become firmer. He made himself sit down, tried to speak calmly, though he could not prevent his voice from trembling with ill-controlled emotion.

'You'd need to know the lay-out of the village. It's difficult to explain at this distance. As in almost all villages, the school is just behind the *mairie*. I live there too, on the other side of the courtyard, and I have a scrap of kitchen-garden. On Tuesday, the day before yesterday, the weather was just about what it is today, a real spring day, and it was a neap tide.'

'Is that important?'

'At the neap tide, that is to say during the period when the ebb and flow of the tides is slight, nobody goes out for mussels or oysters. You understand?'

'Yes.'

'Beyond the school playground there are gardens and the backs of several houses, including Léonie Birard's.'

'What sort of age was she?'

'Sixty-six. Being the secretary of the *mairie*, I know everyone's exact age.'

'Of course.'

'She retired eight years ago and became practically crippled. She never goes out any more, and hobbles round the house with a stick. She's a nasty woman.'

'In what way nasty?'

'She hates everbody.'

'Why?'

'I don't know. She's never married. She had a niece who lived with her a long time and who's married to Julien, the ironmonger, who is also the village policeman.'

On another day Maigret might have found these stories boring. That morning, what with the sun shining in through his window and bringing a spring-like warmth with it, and his pipe which had an unaccustomed taste, he was listening with a vague smile to words that reminded him of another village, which had also had its dramatic incidents between the postmistress, the schoolmaster and the village policeman.

'The two women aren't on speaking terms any longer, because Léonie didn't want her niece to get married. She's not on speaking terms with Dr. Bresselles, either; she said he'd tried to poison her with his drugs.'

'Did he try to poison her?'

'Of course not! That's just to show you the kind of woman she is, or rather was. When she was postmistress she used to listen in on telephone calls, read postcards, so that she knew everyone's secrets. She found no difficulty in working up bad feeling between people. Most quarrels in families or between neighbours were started by her.'

'So she wasn't popular?'

'She certainly wasn't.'

'Well, then...'

Maigret's manner suggested that this simplified everything, that the death of a woman who was universally hated could bring nothing but delight to everyone.

'But I'm not popular either.'

'Because of what you told me?'

'Because of that and all the rest. I'm not a local man. I was born in Paris, in the Rue Caulaincourt in the 18th *arrondissement* and my wife comes from Rue Lamarck.'

'Does your wife live at Saint-André with you?'

'We live together, with our son, who's thirteen years old.'

'Does he go to your school?'

'There's no other for him to go to.'

'Do the other boys hold it against him, that he's the teacher's son?'

Maigret remembered about that, too. He remembered it from his own boyhood. The tenant-farmers' sons had held it against him that his father was the estate manager, to whom their fathers had to submit accounts.

'I don't favour him, I assure you. In fact I rather suspect he purposely works less well than he could.'

He had gradually calmed down. His eyes had lost their frightened expression. This was no lunatic, inventing a story to make himself interesting.

'Léonie Birard had developed a special dislike of me.'

'For no reason?'

'She used to say I stirred up the children against her. But that was quite untrue, inspector. On the contrary, I always tried to make them behave politely. She was very fat, huge in fact. It seems she wore a wig. And she had a hairy face, a definite moustache and black bristles on her chin. That's enough to set the children off, don't you see? Added to which, she would get into a rage at the slightest thing, for instance, if she saw some child peering in at her window and putting its tongue out. She'd get up from her armchair and shake her stick threateningly. That amused them. One of thier favourite games was to go and make old mother Birard angry.'

Hadn't there been an old woman like that in his own village? In his day it was old mother Tatin, who kept the draper's shop, and the children used to tease her cat.

'I'm afraid I'm boring you with these details, but they have a certain importance. There were some more serious incidents, such as when some boys broke glass panes at her house, and when they threw filth in at the windows. She complained to the police any number of times. The constable called on me, asked me who'd done it.'

'Did you tell him?'

'I said they were all more or less mixed up in it, and that if only she'd stop trying to play at scarecrow by brandishing her stick, they'd probably calm down.'

'What happened on Tuesday?'

'Early in the afternoon, about half past one, Maria, a Polish woman with five children, who works as a char, went to Mère Birard's house, as she did every day. The windows were open, and from the school I heard her shrieks, the words she started to rattle off in her own language, as she does whenever she's upset. Her full name is Maria Smelker, and she came to the village when she was sixteen, as a farm servant; she's never been married. Her children have various fathers. It's said that at least two of them belong to the deputy mayor. He hates me too, but that's another story. I'll tell you later about that.'

'So on Tuesday, about half past one, Maria cried for help?'

'Yes. I didn't leave the classroom, because I heard other people hurrying towards the old woman's house. After a short time I saw the doctor's little car go by.'

'You didn't go to have a look?'

'No. Some people are blaming me for that now, saying that the reason why I didn't move was because I knew what they'd found.'

'You couldn't leave the class, I suppose?'

'I could have done. I sometimes do, for a moment, to sign documents in the office at the *Mairie*. Besides, I could have called my wife.'

'Is she a teacher?'

'She used to be.'

'In the country?'

'No. We were both teaching at Courbevoie, where we stayed for seven years. When I asked to be moved to the country, she handed in her resignation.'

'Why did you leave Courbevoie?'

'Because of my wife's health.'

The subject embarrassed him. He was answering less frankly.

'So, you didn't call your wife, as you sometimes do, and you stayed with your pupils.'

'Yes.'

'What happened next?'

'For more than an hour there was a great to-do. The village is usually very quiet. Noises can be heard a long way off. The hammering at Marchandon's smithy stopped. People were calling out to one another across the garden hedges. You know how it is when anything like that happens. So that the pupils shouldn't get excited, I went and closed the windows.'

'From the school windows you can see into Léonie Birard's house?'

'From one of the windows, yes.'

'What did you see?'

'To begin with, the village policeman; that surprised me, as he wasn't on speaking terms with his wife's aunt. And then Théo, the deputy mayor, who must have been half drunk, as he usually is after ten o'clock in the morning. I saw the doctor, too, other neighbours, the whole lot bustling about in one room and looking down at the floor. Later on, the police lieutenant arrived from La Rochelle with two of his men. But I didn't know that until he knocked on the classroom door, and by that time he'd already put questions to a number of people.'

'He accused you of killing Léonie Birard?'

Gastin threw the chief-inspector a reproachful glance, as if to say:

'You know quite well it doesn't happen like that.'

And in rather flat tones, he explained:

'I noticed at once that he was looking strangely at me. The first thing he asked was:

' "Do you own a rifle, Gastin?"

'I said I didn't, but that Jean-Paul, my son, had one. That's another complicated story. You know what it's like with children, I expect. One morning one of them arrives at school with some marbles, and by next day all the boys are playing marbles, their pockets are bulging with them. Another day someone produces a kite, and kites are in fashion for weeks.

'Well, last autumn, someone or other brought a .22 rifle, and began shooting at sparrows with it. Within a month we had half a dozen guns of the same type. My boy wanted one for Christmas. I saw no reason to refuse....'

Even the gun stirred memories in Maigret; the only

difference was that his, in the old days, had been an air-gun and fired pellets that did no more than ruffle the birds' feathers.

'I told the police lieutenant that so far as I knew, the gun was in Jean-Paul's room. He sent one of his men to find out. I ought to have asked the boy. It didn't occur to me. As it happened, the gun wasn't there: he'd left it in the hut in the kitchen garden, where I keep the wheelbarrow and the tools.'

'Léonie Birard was killed with a .22 rifle?'

'That's the most extraordinary thing. And it isn't all. The police lieutenant then asked me whether I'd left the classroom during that morning, and unfortunately I said no.'

'You had left?'

'For about ten minutes, soon after the morning break. When you're asked a question like that, you answer without thinking. Break finishes at ten o'clock. A little later — five minutes, perhaps — Piedbœuf, from Gros-Chêne farm, came to ask me to sign a paper he needed in order to draw his pension — he was disabled in the war. I usually have the *mairie* stamp in the classroom. That morning I hadn't got it, and I took the farmer along to the office. The children seemed quiet. As my wife isn't well, I went across the yard afterwards, to see if she needed anything.'

'Your wife has bad health?'

'It's chiefly nerves. In all, I may have been away for ten or fifteen minutes, more like ten than fifteen.'

'You didn't hear anything?'

'I remember Marchandon was shoeing a horse, because I heard the hammer clanging on the anvil and there was a smell of singed horn in the air. The forge is next to the church, nearly opposite the school.'

'That's the time when Léonie Birard's supposed to have been killed?'

'Yes. They think someone must have shot her from one of the gardens, or from a window, when she was in her kitchen, at the back of the house.'

'She was killed by a .22 bullet?'

'That's the strangest thing of all. A bullet like that, fired from some way off, ought not to have done her much harm. But the fact is that it went into her head through the left eye and flattened against the skull.'

'Are you a good shot?'

'People think so, because they saw me at target-practice with my son during the winter. It happened three or four times, perhaps. Apart from that I've never touched a rifle, except on a fair-ground.'

'Didn't the Lieutenant believe you?'

'He didn't definitely accuse me, but he seemed surprised that I hadn't admitted leaving the classroom. Afterwards, when I wasn't there, he questioned the children. He didn't tell me what the interrogation led to. He went back to La Rochelle. Next day — yesterday, that is — he came and settled down in my office at the *mairie*, with Théo, the deputy mayor, beside him.'

'Where were you then?'

'I was taking school. Out of thirty-two pupils, only eight had turned up. They sent for me twice to ask me the same questions, and the second time they made me sign my statement. They questioned my wife too. They asked her how long I'd stayed with her. They interrogated my son about the rifle.'

'But you weren't arrested.'

'I wasn't arrested yesterday. I feel sure I would have been today if I'd stayed at Saint-Andre. Just after dark, stones were thrown at our house. It upset my wife a lot.'

'You went off by yourself, leaving her there alone with your son?'

'Yes. I don't think they'll dare do anything to them. Whereas if they arrest me, they'll give me no chance to defend myself. Once I'm shut up I shan't be able to communicate with the outside world. No one will believe me. They'll do whatever they like with me.'

Again his forehead was damp with sweat and his linked fingers so tightly clenched that the blood could not circulate.

'Perhaps I was wrong? I thought that if I told you all about it, you would perhaps come and find out the truth. I'm not offering you money. I know that isn't what interests you. I swear to you, Inspector, that I didn't kill Léonie Birard.'

Maigret extended a hesitant hand towards the telephone, finally lifted the receiver.

'What's the name of your constabulary lieutenant?'

'Daniélou.'

'Hallo! Get me the constabulary at La Rochelle. If Lieutenant Daniélou isn't there, see if you can find him at the *mairie* at Saint-André-sur-Mer. Put him through to me in Lucas' office.'

He rang off, lit a pipe, and went over to stand facing the window. He was pretending to take no further notice of the schoolmaster, who had opened his mouth two or three times to thank him, but had not found the words.

The brilliant yellow glow in the air was gradually gaining over the blue, and the house-fronts across the Seine were changing to a creamy hue; the sun was reflected in an attic window somewhere at a distance.

'Was it you who asked for Saint-André-sur-Mer, Chief?'

'Yes, Lucas. Stay here a minute.'

He went into the next-door office.

'Lieutenant Daniélou? This is Maigret, of Police Headquarters in Paris. I hear you're looking for someone?'

At the other end of the line, the constabulary officer was astounded.

'How did you know that already?'

'It's the schoolmaster?'

'Yes. I was a fool not to keep an eye on him. It never occurred to me that he'd try to give me the slip. He took the train to Paris last night, and...'

'You're bringing a charge against him?'

'A very serious one. And I have at least one damaging piece of evidence, acquired this morning.'

'Who from?'

'One of his pupils.'

'He saw something?'

'Yes.'

'What?'

'He saw the schoolmaster coming out of his tool-shed on Tuesday morning, about twenty past ten. And it was at a quarter past ten that the deputy mayor heard a shot.'

'Have you asked the examining magistrate for an arrest warrant?'

'I was just off to La Rochelle to do it when you rang up. How did you know about it? Have the newspapers...?'

'I haven't seen the newspapers. Joseph Gastin is in my office.'

There was a silence, then the lieutenant let out an: 'Ah!'

Whereupon he would doubtless have liked to ask a question. But he didn't do so. Maigret, for his part, was rather at a loss what to say. He had not made up his mind. If the sun had not been shining so brightly that morning, if the chief-inspector hadn't, a little time ago, suddenly remembered Fourras, the oysters and the white wine, if he hadn't been over ten months without a chance of a holiday, even for three days, if...

'Hallo? Are you still there?'

'Yes. What do you intend to do with him?'

'Bring him back to you.'

'Yourself?'

The tone was not enthusiastic, and the chief-inspector smiled.

'You may be sure I shall not dream of interfering in any way in your investigation.'

'You don't think he's...'

'I don't know. Perhaps he's guilty. Perhaps he isn't. Anyhow, I'm bringing him back to you.'

'Thank you. I'll be at the station.'

Back in his own office, he found Lucas gazing curiously at the schoolmaster.

'Wait another minute. I must have a word with the Chief.'

His work would allow him to take a few days off. When he came back, he asked Gastin:

'Is there an inn at Saint-André?'

'Yes, the *Bon Coin*, run by Louis Paumelle. The food's good, but the rooms don't have running water.'

'Are you going away, Chief?'

'Get my wife on the phone for me.'

All this was so unexpected that poor Gastin was

dumbfounded, not yet daring to feel delighted.

'What did he say to you?'

'He'll probably arrest you the moment we get out of the train.'

'But... you're coming with me...?'

Maigret nodded and took the telephone receiver which Lucas was holding out to him.

'That you, dear? Would you pack me a small suitcase, just underclothes and toilet things?... Yes.... Yes.... I don't know.... Three or four days, perhaps....'

He added gleefully:

'I'm going to the seaside, in the Charentes. Right among the oysters and mussels. Meantime, I'll be lunching at a restaurant. See you presently....'

He felt as though he were playing a joke on someone, like the small boys who had teased old Léonie Birard so much and for so long.

'Come along and have a bite with me,' he said finally to the schoolmaster, who got up and followed him as though in a dream.

CHAPTER TWO

At Poitiers, while the train was in the station, the lights went up all at once along the platforms, but it wasn't dark yet. It was not until later, when they were crossing the open fields, that they noticed that night was falling, the windows of the scattered farm-houses starting to gleam like stars.

Then suddenly, a few miles outside La Rochelle, a light mist, which came not from the country but from the sea, began to mingle with the darkness, and the spark of a distant lighthouse shone for a moment.

There were two other people in the carriage, a man and a woman, who had been reading throughout the journey, looking up occasionally to exchange a few words. Most of the time, especially towards the end, Joseph Gastin had kept his weary eyes fixed on the chief-inspector.

The train crossed some points. Small houses slid past. The lines became more numerous, and at last they reached the platforms, the doors with their familiar notices, the people waiting, looking just like the people in previous stations. The moment the carriage door opened one felt a strong, cool breath from the empty blackness into which the rails seemed to vanish; and looking more attentively, one saw ships' masts and gently-rocking funnels, heard gulls screaming, recognized the smell of salt water and tar.

The three uniformed men standing near the entrance did not move. Lieutenant Daniélou was still young, with a little black moustache and thick eyebrows. Not until Maigret and his companion were within a few paces did he step forward, holding out his hand with a military gesture.

'Delighted, Chief-Inspector,' he said.

Maigret, noticing that one of the policemen was producing a pair of handcuffs from his pocket, murmured to the lieutenant:

'I don't think that's necessary.'

The lieutenant made a sign to his subordinate. A few heads had turned in their direction, not many. The passengers were trooping out, weighed down by their suitcases, now walking diagonally across the entrance hall.

'I have no intention of interfering in your inquiry in any way, Lieutenant. I hope you understood that. I'm not here in any official capacity.'

'I know. I discussed it with the examining magistrate.'

'I hope he isn't annoyed!'

'On the contrary, he's delighted that we'll be able to have your help. As things stand at present we can't do otherwise than put him under arrest.'

Joseph Gastin, three feet away, was pretending not to listen, could not help overhearing.

'Anyway, it's in his own interest. He'll be safer in prison than anywhere else. You know how people react in small towns and villages.'

All this was rather stilted. Maigret himself didn't feel too comfortable.

'Have you had dinner?'

'Yes, on the train.'

'Do you mean to spend the night at La Rochelle?'

'I'm told there's an inn at Saint-André.'

'May I offer you a drink?'

As Maigret neither accepted nor refused, the lieutenant turned to give orders to his men, who moved towards the schoolmaster. There was nothing the chief-inspector could say to Gastin, so he merely gave him a serious look.

'You heard. You'll have to go through with it,' he seemed to be saying apologetically. 'I'll do my best.'

Gastin gazed back at him, turned his head shortly afterwards for another glance, finally went out of the door, walking between the two constables.

'We'll do best to go to the buffet,' murmured Danièlou. 'Unless you'd like to come to my place?'

'Not tonight.'

A few travellers were eating in the ill-lit refreshment-room.

'What will you have?'

'I don't know. A brandy.'

They sat down in a corner, at a table which was still laid for dinner.

'You're not having anything to eat?' asked the waitress.

They shook their heads. Not until the drinks came did the lieutenant inquire, with an air of embarrassment:

'You think he's innocent?'

'I don't know.'

'Until the boy gave his evidence we were able to leave him at liberty. Unfortunately for him that evidence is conclusive, and the boy seems sincere, he has no reason to be lying.'

'When did he tell his story?'

'This morning, when I questioned the whole class for the second time.'

'He hadn't said anything yesterday?'

'He was scared. You'll see him. If you like I'll give you the file tomorrow morning, when I'm down there. I spend most of my time at the *mairie*.'

There was still a certain awkwardness. The lieutenant seemed overawed by the chief-inspector's massive bulk and by his reputation.

'You're accustomed to the things and people of Paris. I don't know if you're used to the atmosphere of our small villages.'

'I was born in a village. What about you?'

'At Toulouse.'

He managed to smile.

'Would you like me to drive you out there?'

'I think I'll find a taxi.'

'If you'd rather. There's a rank outside the station.'

They parted at the door of the taxi, which drove off along the sea-front, and Maigret leant forward to make out the fishing-boats in the darkness of the harbour.

He was disappointcd to have arrived at night. When they turned away from the sea and left the town, they drove through a stretch of country that looked like any other stretch, and soon, at the third village, the car stopped outside a lighted window.

'Is this it?'

'You said the *Bon Coin*, didn't you?'

A very stout man came to look out through the glass panelled door, and, without opening it, watched while Maigret went to and fro, took out his suitcase, put it on the ground, paid the driver, finally walked towards the inn.

Men were playing cards in a corner. The inn smelt of wine and stew, and smoke hovered round the two lamps.

'Have you a room?'

Everyone was staring at him. A woman came to the kitchen door to look at him.

'For the night?'

'For two or three days, perhaps.'

They looked him up and down.

'Have you your identity card? The constables come here every morning and we have to keep the register up to date.'

The four men had stopped playing, were listening. Maigret, now standing at the counter, which was loaded with bottles, held out his card and the landlord put on his glasses to read it. When he looked up again, he gave a sly wink.

'So you're the famous inspector? My name's Paumelle, Louis Paumelle.'

He turned towards the kitchen and called:

'Thérèse! Take the inspector's suitcase up to the front room.'

Without paying special attention to the woman, who looked about thirty years old, Maigret had the impression that he'd seen her before somewhere. It only struck him later on, as with the people he used to see when he went past 'Purgatory'. He thought she had given a slight start, too.

'What will you take?'

'Whatever you have. A brandy, if you like.'

The others, for the sake of appearances, had returned to their game of *belote*.

'You've come because of Léonie?'

'Not officially.'

'Is it true the schoolmaster has been found in Paris?'

'He's in the prison at La Rochelle by now.'

It was hard to guess what Paumelle thought of the business. Although he was an innkeeper, he looked more like a peasant in his own farm.

'You don't think he did it?'

'I don't know.'

'I imagine that if you reckoned he was guilty you wouldn't have come all this way. Am I right?'

'Maybe.'

'Your very good health! There's a man here who heard the shot. Théo! It's true you heard the shot, isn't it?'

One of the card-players, sixty-five years old or perhaps more, his reddish hair going white here and there, cheeks unshaven, and his eyes shifty and spiteful, turned towards them.

'Why shouldn't I have heard it?'

'This is Inspector Maigret, who's come from Paris to...'

'The lieutenant told me about it.'

He did not get up nor give any greeting; he was holding his grimy cards between black-nailed fingers. Paumelle explained in an undertone:

'That's the deputy mayor.'

And Maigret, in his turn, answered just as laconically:

'I know.'

'You mustn't take any notice. By this time of night...'

He made the gesture of emptying a glass.

'What about you, Ferdinand, what did you see?'

The man he called Ferdinand had only one arm. His complexion was ruddy-brown, that of a man who spent all his time out of doors.

'The postman,' explained Louis. 'Ferdinand Cornu. What did you see, Ferdinand?'

'Nothing at all.'

'You saw Théo in his garden.'

'I even brought him a letter.'

'What was he doing?'

'Planting out onions.'

'What time was it?'

'Just ten by the church clock. I could see the clock-face, above the houses. *Belote! Rebelote!* My nine beats it... Ace of spades, King of diamonds, takes all...'

He flung down his cards on the table where the glasses had left a wet circle, and glared defiantly at the other players.

'And to hell with people who come here to make trouble for us!' he added, getting to his feet. 'Pay up, Théo.'

His movements were clumsy, his gait unsteady. He took down his postman's cap from a peg and made for the door, growling out something indistinguishable.

'Is he like that every evening?'

'Pretty much.'

Louis Paumelle was about to fill the two glasses, and Maigret put out a hand to stop him.

'Not for the moment.... You won't be closing just yet, I suppose, and I've time for a stroll before going to bed?'

'I'll wait for you.'

He went out, amid dead silence. He found himself in a small open space, neither round nor square, with the dark mass of the church to his right, opposite him an unlighted shop, above whose window he could just decipher the words: *'Coopérative Charentaise'*.

There was a light in the house at the corner, a grey stone-built place. The light came from the first floor. Going up to the door, with its three steps, Maigret noticed a brass plate, lit a match, and read:

Xavier Bresselles: M.D.

For lack of something to do, and puzzled as to how to make a beginning, he was on the point of ringing the bell; then he shrugged his shoulders and reflected that the doctor was probably getting ready for bed.

Most of the houses were in darkness. He recognized the *mairie*, a one-storey building, by its flagstaff. It was a very small *mairie*, and above its courtyard a lamp was burning in a first-floor room of a building, probably the Gastins' house.

He went down the road, turned to the right, strolled past some houses and gardens, not long afterwards met the deputy mayor, who was coming up from the opposite direction and gave a grunt by way of good-night.

He could neither hear the sea nor get any glimpse of it. The slumbering village looked like any small country place and did not fit in with his expectation of oysters with white wine on a café terrace overlooking the ocean.

He was disappointed, for no definite reason. The lieutenant's greeting at the station had chilled him, to begin with. He could not blame the man. Daniélou knew the district, where he had most likely been stationed for some years. A crime had been committed, he had done his best to clear it up, and now Maigret had arrived from Paris, without warning, and appeared to think he was mistaken.

The examining magistrate must be annoyed too. Neither of them would dare to show their irritation, they would be polite, would put their files at his disposal. Maigret would still be a nuisance, interfering in what wasn't his business, and he began to wonder what had suddenly decided him to come on this trip.

He heard footsteps and voices, probably the other two *belote* players on their way home. Then, further on, a yellowish dog brushed against his leg and he gave a startled jump.

When he opened the door of the *Bon Coin* only one of the lamps was still burning, and the landlord, behind the counter, was putting away the glasses and bottles. He was wearing neither waistcoat nor jacket. His dark-coloured trousers were hanging very low on his bulging stomach, and his sleeves were rolled up, revealing fat, hairy arms.

'Made any discoveries?'

He was trying to be clever, doubtless thought himself the most important person in the village.

'A nightcap?'

'If you'll let this be my round.'

Ever since morning Maigret had been thirsting for some

local white wine, but he asked for brandy again, feeling that this was not an hour to drink wine.

'Here's how!'

'I thought,' remarked the chief-inspector quietly, wiping his mouth, 'that Léonie Birard wasn't very popular.'

'She was the nastiest shrew on earth. She's dead. May the Lord have her soul, or more likely the devil, but she was undoubtedly the most unpleasant woman I've ever known. And I knew her when she still had pigtails down her back, and we went to school together. She was... wait a minute... three years older than me. That's right. I'm sixty-four. So she must have been sixty-seven. Even at twelve she was poisonous.'

'What I don't understand...' began Maigret.

'There are lots of things you won't understand, although you're such a smart chap, let me warn you.'

'I don't understand,' he began again, as though talking to himself, 'that although she was so much hated, everybody is so down on the schoolmaster. Because after all, even if he did kill her, one would rather expect...'

'That people would say, *Good riddance!* That's what you're thinking, isn't it?'

'More or less.'

'Yes, but you're forgetting that Léonie was a local woman.'

He refilled the glasses without being asked.

'It's like in a family, don't you see. Relations have the right to hate one another, and they certainly do. But if an outsider gets mixed up in it, things change. People loathed Léonie. They loathe Gastin and his wife still more.'

'His wife as well?'

'His wife particularly.'

'Why? What has she done?'

'Nothing — here.'

'Why: "here"?'

'Everything gets known in the end, even in a godforsaken village like ours. And we don't like to be landed with people who aren't wanted anywhere else. This isn't the first time the Gastins have been mixed up in some funny business.'

He was interesting to watch, as he stood leaning on his

bar. He obviously wanted to talk, but after each sentence he was peering at Maigret to see what effect he was producing, ready to retreat, or even to contradict himself, like a peasant bargaining for a yoke of oxen in the market.

'Looks as though you'd come here without knowing anything?'

'Except that Léonie Birard was killed by a bullet through her left eye.'

'And you came all this way!'

He was laughing at Maigret, after his own fashion.

'You hadn't the curiosity to break the journey at Courbevoie?'

'Ought I to have?'

'You'd have heard a fine tale. It took a long time to get here. It's only about two years since we heard it, at Saint-André.'

'What tale?'

'Madame Gastin was a schoolteacher, together with her husband. They taught in the same school, she on the girls' side, he on the boys'.'

'I know.'

'Have you heard about Chevassou?'

'Who's Chevassou?'

'One of the municipal councillors there, a handsome fellow, tall and strong, with black hair and a southern accent. There was a Madame Chevassou too. One fine day when the children were going home from school, Madame Chevassou turned up in the street and shot at the schoolmistress, hitting her in the shoulder. Guess why? Because she'd discovered that her husband and Gastin's wife were having fun and games together. It seems she was acquitted. After which, the best thing the Gastins could do was to leave Courbevoie, and they suddenly developed a hankering for country air.'

'I don't see the connection with the murder of Léonie Birard.'

'There may be no connection.'

'From what you tell me, Joseph Gastin did nothing wrong.'

'He's a cuckold.'

Louis was grinning, thoroughly pleased with himself.

'He's not the only one, of course. This village is full of them. I wish you joy. One more drop?'

'No thank you.'

'Thérèse will show you to your room. Tell her what time you'd like your hot water brought up.'

'Thank you. Good night.'

'Thérèse!'

She went ahead of him up a staircase with uneven steps, turned into a corridor with flower-patterned wallpaper, opened a door.

'Call me about eight,' he said.

She didn't move, but stood watching him as though she wanted to tell him something. He looked more closely at her.

'Haven't I met you before?'

'You remember?'

He didn't admit that it was a rather vague recollection.

'You won't talk about it here, will you?'

'Aren't you from the village?'

'Yes. But I went away when I was fifteen, to work in Paris.'

'Did you really work there?'

'For four years.'

'And then?'

'You saw me, so you know. Inspector Priollet will tell you I didn't take the pocket-book. It was my friend Lucille, and I didn't even know about it.'

A picture came back to his mind and he remembered where he had seen her. One morning he had called in, as he often did, at the office of his colleague Priollet, head of the *'mondaine'* section, the Vice Squad. On a chair sat a dark, tousled-haired girl, dabbing at her eyes and snivelling. There was something about her pale, sickly face which had appealed to him.

What's she done?' he had asked Priollet.

'The old story. A skivvy who's started picking up men along the Boulevard Sébastopol. Two days ago a shopkeeper from Béziers came to complain that his pocket had been picked, and was able, for once, to give us a fairly accurate description. Last night we caught her in a dance-hall in the Rue de Lappe.'

'It wasn't me!' stammered the girl between sobs. 'I swear to you on my mother's head that it wasn't me that took the pocket-book.'

The two men had exchanged winks.

'What do you think, Maigret?'

'Has she never been arrested before?'

'Not so far.'

'Where does she come from?'

'Somewhere in the Charentes.'

They often put on a little act of this kind.

'Have you found her girl friend?'

'Not yet.'

'Why not send this one home to her village?'

Priollet had turned solemnly to the girl.

'Would you like to go back to your village?'

'As long as they don't know about it there.'

It was strange to find her here now, five or six years older, still pale-faced, with big dark eyes that looked pleadingly at the chief-inspector.

'Is Louis Paumelle married?' he asked in a low voice.

'A widower.'

Do you sleep with him?'

She nodded.

'Does he know what you were doing in Paris?'

'No. He musn't find out. He's always promising to marry me. He's been promising for years, and sooner or later he's sure to make up his mind.'

'Thérèse!' called the landlord from the foot of the stairs.

'Just coming!'

And, to Maigret:

'You won't tell him?'

He shook his head, with an encouraging smile.

'Don't forget my hot water at eight o'clock.'

He was glad to have come across her again, because really with her he felt he was on familiar ground, and it was rather like meeting an old acquaintance.

He felt as though he knew the rest of them too, although he had only had a glimpse of them, because in his own village there had been a deputy mayor who drank, there had been card-players — it wasn't *belote* in those days, it was piquet — a postman who thought himself somebody, and an innkeeper who knew everyone's secrets.

Their faces were still graven in his memory. But he had seen them with a child's eyes, and he realized, now, that he hadn't really known them.

While he was undressing he heard Paumelle coming upstairs, and then some thuds in the next room. Thérèse joined the innkeeper a little later and began undressing in her turn. Both were talking in low voices, like a married couple getting to bed, and the last sound was the creaking springs.

He had some difficulty in hollowing out a place for himself in the two huge feather mattresses. He recognized the country smell of hay and damp and, either because of the feathers or because of the brandies in tumblers which he had drunk with the landlord, he began to sweat profusely.

Before daylight, sounds began to reach him through his sleep, including those of a herd of cows which went past the inn, with an occasional moo. The forge began work soon afterwards. Downstairs, someone was taking down the shutters. He opened his eyes, found the sun shining even more brilliantly than the day before in Paris, sat up and pulled on his trousers.

With slippers on his bare feet he went downstairs, found Thérèse in the kitchen, busy making coffee. She had put on a kind of dressing-gown with a sprigged pattern over her nightdress, and her legs were bare; she smelt of bed.

'It isn't eight yet. Only half past six. Would you like a cup of coffee? It'll be ready in five minutes.'

Paumelle came down in his turn, unwashed and unshaven, wearing bedroom slippers like the chief-inspector.

'I thought you didn't want to get up before eight o'clock.'

They drank their first cup of coffee in thick china bowls, standing up near the stove.

Outside the house there was a group of women dressed

in black, carrying baskets and shopping-bags.

'What are they waiting for?' inquired Maigret.

'The bus. It's market day at La Rochelle.'

Hens could be heard cackling in crates.

'Who's taking school now?'

'Yesterday there was nobody. This morning they're expecting a substitute from La Rochelle. He's to come on the bus. He'll sleep here, in the back room, as you've got the front one.'

He was up in his room again when the bus stopped in the square and he saw a timid-looking young man get out, carrying a big gladstone-bag; this must be the schoolmaster.

The crates were piled on the roof of the bus. The women packed themselves into it. Thérèse knocked on his door.

'Your hot water!'

Casually, without looking at her, he asked:

'Are you another who thinks Gastin killed Léonie?'

Before replying she glanced towards the half-open door.

'I don't know,' she said in a very low tone.

'You don't think so?'

'It doesn't seem like him. But they all want it to be him, you understand?'

The chief thing he was beginning to understand was that, for no reason, he had taken a difficult, if not impossible, job.

'Who stood to benefit by the old woman's death?'

'I don't know. They say she disinherited her niece for getting married.'

'Who'll get her money?'

'Some charity, perhaps. She changed her mind so often! ...Or it might be Maria, the Polish woman....'

'Is it true she's had one or two children by the deputy mayor?'

'Maria? So they say. He often goes to see her, and sometimes stays for the night.'

'In spite of the children?'

'That doesn't worry Maria. Everybody goes there.'

'Paumelle too?'

'I expect he did when she was younger. She's not very

tempting nowadays.'

'How old is she?'

'About thirty. She takes no trouble about herself, and her house is worse than a pigsty.'

'Thérèse!' came the landlord's voice, as on the previous evening.

Better not detain her. Paumelle didn't seem to like it. Was he perhaps jealous? Or merely anxious that she shouldn't tell too much?

When Maigret went downstairs, the young schoolmaster was having breakfast and looked inquisitively at him.

'What will you have, Inspector?'

'Have you any oysters?'

'Not at neap-tide.'

'Will that last much longer?'

'Another five or six days.'

Ever since Paris he'd been wanting to eat oysters washed down with white wine, and it looked as though he wouldn't get any all the time he was here.

'There's soup. Or we can do you some ham and eggs.'

He ate nothing at all, drank another cup of coffee, standing at the open door and looking at the sunlit square and at two dark figures moving about in the *'Coopérative Charentaise'*.

He was wondering whether to ask for a glass of white wine all the same, to take away the taste of the abominable coffee, when a cheerful voice exclaimed, close beside him:

'Inspector Maigret?'

It was a small, thin, lively man, whose expression was youthful although he must be over forty. He held out his hand with a cordial gesture.

'Dr. Bresselles!' he introduced himself. 'The lieutenant told me yesterday that you were expected. I came along before surgery, to know if I could help you. An hour from now my waiting-room will be packed.'

'Will you have something to drink?'

'In my house, if you'll come, it's next door.'

'I know.'

Maigret followed him to the grey stone house. All the other houses in the village were colour-washed, some in harsh white, others in a creamier shade, and the pink roofs gave the whole place a very gay appearance.

'Come in! What would you like to drink?'

'Ever since I left Paris I've been longing for oysters and local white wine,' confessed Maigret. 'But I've already discovered that I shall have to do without the oysters.'

'Armande!' he called, crossing to the door. 'Bring up a bottle of white wine. From the red bin.'

He explained:

'That's my sister. She's been keeping house for me since my wife died. I have two boys, one at Niort, at the *Lycée*, the other's doing his military service. What do you think of Saint-André?'

Everything seemed to amuse him.

'I'm forgetting you've not seen much of it yet. Just wait! By way of a sample, you have that scoundrel Paumelle, who was a farm-hand and married the owner of the *Bon Coin* when her husband died. She was twenty years older than Louis. She liked her little drop to drink. So as she was fiendishly jealous and the money was hers, he killed her by encouraging her weakness. See what I mean! He did his best to fill her up with drink, and by the time lunch was over she often had to go upstairs to bed. She held out for seven years with a liver as hard as stone, and in the end he was able to give her a handsome funeral. Since then, he's been going to bed with his servants. One after another they left, till it came to Thérèse, who seems to be sticking it out.'

The sister came in, timid and colourless, carrying a tray with a bottle and two glasses, and Maigret thought she looked like a priest's housekeeper.

'My sister. Inspector Maigret.'

She went out backwards, and this, too, seemed to amuse the doctor.

'Armande has never married. I'm inclined to think she's been waiting all her life for me to be a widower. Now she has her own house at last, and can spoil me as she would have spoilt a husband.'

'What do you think of Gastin?'

'He's pathetic.'

'Why?'

'Because he does his best, despairingly, and people who do their best are pathetic. He gets no thanks from anyone. He struggles away to teach something to a bunch of snotty little boys whom their parents would rather keep at home on the farm. He even tried to get them to wash. I remember the day he sent one of them home because his head was lousy. A quarter of an hour later the father turned up, furious, and they nearly came to blows.'

'His wife is an invalid?'

'Your very good health! She isn't really an invalid, but she isn't very well either. I've learnt not to put too much confidence in medicine, you know. Madame Gastin pines. She's ashamed. She blames herself, day in and day out, for ruining her husband's career.'

'Because of Chevassou?'

'You know about that? Yes, because of Chevassou. She must have been really in love with him. What's called a devouring passion. You'd never think it to look at her, for she's an insignificant little woman; she and her husband are as like as two peas. Maybe that's the real trouble. They're too much alike. Chevassou, who's a big brute full of vitality, a kind of satisfied bull, did what he liked with her. Her right arm still hurts her now and then, it's remained a bit stiff.'

'How did she get on with Léonie Birard?'

'They never saw each other except through their windows, across the courtyard and the gardens, and Léonie put out her tongue at her now and then, as she did at everyone. What strikes me as most extraordinary in this business is that Léonie, whom one would have imagined to be indestructible, was killed by a little bullet fired from a child's rifle. And that isn't all. There are some incredible coincidences. The left eye, the one that was hit, was her bad eye; she'd always been slightly wall-eyed, and she hadn't been able to see with it for years. What do you say to that?'

The doctor raised his glass. The wine had greenish lights in it, it was dry and light, with a strong local flavour.

'Your good health! They'll all try to put spokes in your

wheel. Don't believe a word they say, whether it's the parents or the children. Come and see me whenever you like, and I'll do my utmost to help.'

'You don't like them?'

The doctor's eyes began to sparkle with laughter, and he retorted emphatically:

'I adore them! They're quite crazy!'

CHAPTER THREE

The door of the *mairie* stood open into a corridor on whose recently whitewashed walls various official notices were fixed with drawing-pins. Some of the smaller ones, such as the announcement of a special meeting of the Council, were written in pen and ink, with the headings in round-hand, probably by the schoolmaster, The floor was grey-tiled, the woodwork painted in grey also. The door on the left presumably led into the council-room, with its bust of Marianne and its flag, while the right-hand door, which stood ajar, gave into the secretary's office.

The room was empty; it smelt of stale cigar-smoke; Lieutenant Daniélou, who had made the office his head-quarters for the past two days, had not yet arrived.

Opposite the street entrance, at the far end of the passage, a double door stood open onto the courtyard, in the middle of which grew a lime-tree. To the right of this yard, the low building, of which three windows were visible, was the school, with rows of boys' and girls' heads and, standing up, the outline of the substitute teacher whom Maigret had seen at the inn.

There was a monastic hush over all this, and only the clang of the blacksmith's hammer could be heard. Beyond, there were hedges and gardens, with the tender green of budding leaves on lilac bushes, white and yellow houses, an open window here and there.

Maigret turned left, towards the Gastins' two-storey

house. As he was about to knock on the door it opened, and he found himself on the threshold of a kitchen where a small spectacled boy was seated at the oilcloth-covered table, bending over an exercise book.

It was Madame Gastin who had opened the door to him. Looking out of the window, she had seen him in the yard, glance around, come slowly forward.

'I heard yesterday that you were coming,' she said, standing aside to let him pass. 'Come in, Inspector. If you only knew how relieved I feel!'

She wiped her wet hands on her apron, turned towards her son, who had not looked up and seemed to be ignoring the visitor.

'Aren't you going to say how do you do to Inspector Maigret, Jean-Paul?'

'How do you do.'

'Run along up to your room now.'

The kitchen was small but, even at this early hour, meticulously clean, without a trace of untidiness. Young Gastin picked up his book without protest, went out into the corridor and up the stairs to the floor above.

'Come this way, Inspector.'

They crossed the passage in their turn, went into a room which served as a parlour and was doubtless never used. There was an upright piano against one wall, a round, massive oak table, armchairs with lace antimacassars, photographs on the walls, ornaments all over the place.

'Please sit down.'

The house had four rooms, all tiny, and it made Maigret feel too tall and too broad, in addition to which he had had, ever since he came in, the impression of having suddenly entered an unreal world.

He had been warned that Madame Gastin was the same type as her husband, but he had never imagined that she was so much like him that they might practically have been taken for brother and sister. Her hair was of the same indeterminate colour, already thinning too, the middle of her face was, as it were, thrust forward, and she had pale, short-sighted eyes. And the child, too, was like a caricature of both his parents combined.

Was he trying, from upstairs, to overhear the conversation, or had he gone back to his exercise-book? He was only about twelve and already he looked like a little old man, or, to be more exact, like a being with no definite age.

'I kept him away from school,' explained Madame Gastin as she closed the door. 'I thought it was better. You know how cruel children are.'

If Maigret had remained standing he would almost have filled the room, and he now sat motionless in an armchair, signed to his hostess to sit down too, because it made him feel tired to see her standing.

She was as ageless as her son. He knew she was only thirty-four, but he had seldom seen a woman who had so completely discarded every feminine touch. Under her dress, whose colour was undefinable, her body was thin, tired; there was a hint of breasts that hung down like empty pockets, and her shoulders were already slightly rounded, her face, instead of being tanned by the country sunshine, had turned grey. Even her voice sounded washed-out!

But she was doing her best to smile, put forward a timid hand to touch Maigret's arm as she said:

'I'm so grateful to you for having confidence in him!'

He couldn't reply that he didn't know yet, couldn't confess to her that it was because of the first spring sunshine in Paris, of a memory of oysters and white wine, that he had suddenly decided to come.

'If you knew how much I blame myself, Inspector! Because what is happening is all my fault. I've ruined his life and the boy's. I'm doing my best to make up for it. I try so hard, you know....'

He felt as uncomfortable as if he had come unawares into a house where someone he didn't know had died, and was at a loss for words. All of a sudden he was in a world apart, which didn't belong to the village in the centre of which he was now ensconced.

These three, Gastin, his wife and their son, belonged to a race so different that the chief-inspector could understand the peasants' mistrust.

'I don't know how it will all end,' she was continuing

after a sigh, 'but I can't believe that the law will condemn an innocent man. He's such an exceptional character! You've met him, but you don't know him. Tell me, how was he, last night?'

'Very well. Very calm.'

'Is it true they handcuffed him, on the station platform?'

'No. He went freely between the two constables.'

'Were there any people there to see him?'

'It was all done discreetly.'

'Do you think there's anything he needs? His health isn't good. He's never been very strong.'

She was not crying. She must have wept so much in her life that there were no more tears left in her. Just above her head, to the right of the window, hung the photograph of a young woman who was almost plump, and Maigret could not tear his eyes away from this, wondering if she had really looked like that, with laughing eyes and dimpled cheeks even.

'You're looking at my picture when I was young?'

There was another, of Gastin, to match it. He had scarcely changed at all, except that in those days he had longish hair, like an artist, as people used to say, and no doubt he used to write poems.

'Have you been told?' she asked softy, after glancing at the door.

And he could feel that that was what she chiefly wanted to talk about, it had been in her mind ever since she had been told he was coming, it was the only thing that mattered to her.

'You mean about what happened at Courbevoie?'

'Yes, about Charles...'

She stopped short and blushed, as though the name were taboo.

'Chevassou?'

She nodded.

'I'm still wondering how it could ever have happened. I've been so miserable, Inspector! And I do wish someone would explain to me! I'm not a bad woman, you know. I met Joseph when I was only fifteen, and I knew at once that he was the man I should marry. We planned our lives together. We both decided to take up teaching.'

'Was it he who gave you the idea?'

'I think so. He's cleverer than I am. He's a very exceptional man. People don't always realize that, because he's too modest. We took our degrees the same year and got married; thanks to a cousin who had influence, we managed to get appointments at Courbevoie together.'

'Do you think that has any connection with what happened here on Tuesday?'

She looked at him in surprise. He would have done better not to interrupt her, for she lost the thread of what she was saying.

'It's all my fault.'

She frowned, anxious to explain.

'If it hadn't been for what happened at Courbevoie, we shouldn't have come here. People thought well of Joseph there. Their ideas are more modern, you know. He was getting on. He had good prospects.'

'And you?'

'I had, too. He used to help me, give me advice. And then, from one day to the next, it was as though I'd gone mad. I still can't understand what took possession of me. I didn't want it. I fought against it. I told myself I'd never do such a thing. And then, when Charles was there...'

She blushed again, stammered, as though it were an offence to Maigret himself to refer to the man:

'I beg your pardon.... When he was there I couldn't resist. I don't think it was love, because I love Joseph, I always have loved him. It was like a sort of fever, and I lost all thought of anything else, even of our boy, who was quite a baby. I was ready to leave him, Inspector. I really thought of leaving them both, going off somewhere, anywhere.... Can you understand it?'

He hadn't the courage to tell her that she had doubtless never had any sexual enjoyment with her husband and that her story was a commonplace one. She needed to believe that her adventure had been exceptional, she needed to lament, to be filled with remorse, to regard herself as the lowest of women.

'You are a Catholic, Madame Gastin?'

He was touching on another sensitive point.

'I was, like my parents, until I met Joseph. He only believes in science and progress. He loathes priests.'

'You stopped being a practising Catholic?'

'Yes.'

'Since those things happened, you haven't been back to church?'

'I couldn't. I feel as though I should be betraying him again. Besides, what would be the good! During our first few years here I did hope we were beginning a new life. The people looked at us suspiciously, as country people always do. But I felt sure that one day they would learn to appreciate my husband's qualities. Then, I don't know how, they found out about Courbevoie, and after that even the children didn't respect him any more. I told you it is all my fault...'

'Did your husband have arguments with Léonie Birard?'

'Now and then. As secretary of the *mairie*. She was a woman who always made difficulties. There were questions of pensions to be settled. Joseph is strict. He refuses to go beyond his duty, he'll never sign a false certificate to please anybody.'

'Did she know your story?'

'Yes, everyone did.'

'She used to put out her tongue at you too?'

'And make filthy remarks when I went past her house. I used to avoid going that way. Not only did she put her tongue out, but sometimes, when she saw me at the window, she'd turn round and pull up her skirts. I beg your pardon. One would hardly believe it, of such an old woman. She was like that. But it would never have occurred to Joseph to kill her, all the same. He'd never kill anyone. You've seen him. He's a gentle creature, who'd like everyone to be happy.'

'Tell me about your son.'

'What is there to tell you? He takes after his father. He's a quiet, studious boy, very advanced for his age. The only reason he isn't head of the class is that then my husband would be accused of favouritism. Joseph gives him lower marks than he deserves, on purpose.'

'Doesn't the boy object to that?'

'He understands. We've explained to him why it has to be that way.'

'Does he know about the Courbevoie business?'

'We've never mentioned it to him. But the other boys do. He pretends to know nothing about it.'

'Does he ever go to play with the others?'

'He used to at first. The last two years, since the village became openly hostile to us, he's preferred to stay at home. He reads a great deal. I'm teaching him the piano. He already plays very well for his age.'

The window was shut, and Maigret was beginning to feel stifled, to wonder whether he hadn't suddenly been caught fast in an old photograph-album.

'Your husband came into the house on Tuesday morning, soon after ten o'clock?'

'Yes. I think so. I've been asked that so often, in all kinds of ways, as though they were determined to make me contradict myself, that I'm no longer positive about anything. He usually comes to the kitchen for a moment during the break, and helps himself to a cup of coffee. I'm generally upstairs at that time.'

'He doesn't drink wine?'

'Never. He doesn't smoke either.'

'On Tuesday, didn't he come in during the break?'

'He says he didn't. So I said the same, because he always tells the truth. Then they maintained he'd come in later.'

'You denied that?'

'I was speaking in good faith, Monsieur Maigret. Sometime afterwards, I remembered finding his empty coffee-bowl on the kitchen table. I don't know whether it was during break or later, that he came.'

'He could have gone to the tool-shed without your seeing him?'

'The room I was in upstairs doesn't overlook the kitchen-garden.'

'You could see Léonie Birard's house?'

'If I'd looked that way, yes.'

'You didn't hear the shot?'

'I didn't hear anything. The window was shut. I feel the

cold a great deal. I always have. And even in summer I shut the windows during the break, because of the noise.'

'You tell me the local people don't like your husband. I'd like to get that clearer. Is there anyone in the village who particularly dislikes him?'

'Indeed there is. The deputy mayor.'

'Théo?'

'Théo Coumart, yes, who lives just behind us. Our gardens are end to end. First thing in the morning he begins to drink white wine in his cellar, where there's always a barrel on tap. By ten or eleven o'clock he's at Louis', and he goes on drinking till evening.'

'Hasn't he any work?'

'His parents owned a big farm. He's never done a stroke of work in his life. One afternoon last winter, when Joseph had gone to La Rochelle with Jean-Paul, he came into the house, at about half-past four. I was upstairs, changing. I heard heavy footsteps on the stairs. It was he. He was drunk. He pushed the door open and began to laugh. Then, all of a sudden, as though this were a brothel, he tried to push me over onto the bed. I grabbed at his face, giving him a long scratch down his nose. It bled. He began to swear, shouting that a woman like me had no business to put on airs. I opened the window and threatened to call for help. I was in my underclothes. At last he went away, chiefly because of his bleeding face, I think. He's never spoken to me since.

'He's the village leader. The mayor, Monsieur Rateau, owns a mussel-bed; he's occupied all the time with his business, and only comes to the *mairie* for Council meetings.

'Théo arranges the elections just as he likes, does good turns to people, is always ready to sign any paper they want...'

'You don't know whether he was in his garden on Tuesday morning, as he makes out?'

'If he says so it's probably true, because other people must have seen him. Though of course if he asked them to oblige him by telling a lie, they wouldn't hesitate to do it.'

'Would you mind if I had a little chat with your son?'

She stood up, resignedly, and opened the door.

'Jean-Paul, come down, will you?'

'Why?' asked the voice from upstairs.

'Inspector Maigret wants a word with you.'

Hesitant steps were heard. The little boy appeared, carrying a book, and stood waiting in the doorway, with a suspicious expression on his face.

'Come in, my boy. You're not afraid of me, I take it?'

'I'm not afraid of anyone.'

He spoke in almost the same toneless voice as his mother.

'You were at school on Tuesday morning?'

He glanced from the chief-inspector to his mother, as though uncertain whether he should answer even such a harmless question.

'Go on, Jean-Paul. The inspector's on our side.'

She looked at Maigret as though silently apologizing for this statement. But she could elicit no more than a nod from the boy.

'What happened after break?'

The same silence. Maigret was becoming a monument of patience.

'You want your father to come out of prison, don't you, and the real murderer to be arrested?'

It was hard to read the expression in his eyes, through the thick lenses of his spectacles. He did not look aside, but stared his questioner straight in the face, without the slightest flicker of his pinched features.

'Just now,' the chief-inspector went on, 'I don't know what people are saying. Some little thing, that seems quite unimportant, may give me a clue. How many of you are there in the school?'

'Answer, Jean-Paul.'

Reluctantly, he said:

'Thirty-two altogether.'

'What do you mean by "altogether"?'

'Seniors and juniors. The whole lot whose names are on the list.'

His mother explained:

'There are always some who are away. At times,

especially in the summer, only about fifteen come, and we can't always be sending constables to their homes.'

'Have you any school-friends?'

He replied shortly: 'No.'

'Not one friend, among the village children?'

The answer came with an air of defiance:

'I'm the schoolmaster's son.'

'Is that why they don't like you?'

He didn't reply.

'What do you do in the breaks?'

'Nothing.'

'You don't come to see your mother?'

'No.'

'Why not?'

'Father doesn't let me.'

Madame Gastin explained again:

'He doesn't want to make any difference between his boy and the others. If Jean-Paul came here during break there would be no reason why the forester's boy, or the butcher's, for instance, shouldn't cross the road to their own homes.'

'I see. Do you remember what your father was doing on Tuesday during the break?'

'No.'

'Doesn't he keep an eye on the boys?'

'Yes.'

'Standing in the middle of the playground?'

'Sometimes.'

'He didn't come in here?'

'I don't know.'

He had seldom questioned anyone so recalcitrant. If he had been dealing with a grown-up person he would probably have lost his temper, and Madame Gastin, feeling this, stood protectively beside her son, laid a conciliatory hand on his shoulder.

'Answer the Inspector politely, Jean-Paul.'

'I'm not being rude.'

'At ten o'clock you all went back into the classroom. Did your father go to the blackboard?'

Through the window-curtains he could see a section of

the board, with words written on it in chalk, in the opposite building.

'Perhaps.'

'What lesson was it?'

'Grammar.'

'Did someone knock at the door?'

'Perhaps.'

'Aren't you sure! Didn't you see your father go out?'

'I don't know.

'Now listen. When the teacher leaves the class, the boys generally begin jumping up, chattering, playing the fool.'

Jean-Paul said nothing.

'Is that what happened on Tuesday?'

'I don't remember.'

'You didn't leave the room?'

'What for?'

'You might have gone to the lavatory, for instance. I see it's in the yard.'

'I didn't go there.'

'Who went to look out of the window?'

'I don't know.'

By this time Maigret was standing up, and his fists, in his pockets, were tightly clenched.

'Now listen...'

'I don't know anything. I didn't see anything. I've nothing to tell you.'

And the boy suddenly rushed out of the room and up the stairs; they heard him, up above, shutting his door.

'You mustn't be cross with him, Inspector. Put yourself in his place. Yesterday the lieutenant questioned him for over an hour, and when he got home he didn't say a word to me, went and lay down on his bed and stayed there till it was dark, with his eyes wide open.'

'Is he fond of his father?'

She didn't quite understand the question.

'I mean, has he a particular affection or admiration for his father? Or does he prefer you, for instance? Is it in you that he confides, or in his father?'

'He doesn't confide in anyone. He's undoubtedly fonder of me than of his father.'

'How did he behave when your husband was accused?'

'Just as you've seen him now.'

'He didn't cry?'

'I've never seen him cry since he was a baby.'

'How long has he had that gun?'

'We gave it to him for Christmas.'

'Does he often use it?'

'He goes off alone now and then, with his gun on his arm, like a sportsman, but I don't think he often fires it. Two or three times he pinned a paper target to the lime-tree in the yard, but my husband explained that he was wounding the tree.'

'If he'd left the classroom on Tuesday while your husband was away, I suppose the other boys would have noticed it?'

'Certainly.'

'And they would have said so.'

'You can't have thought that Jean-Paul...?'

'I have to think of every possibility. Who is the boy who claims to have seen your husband come out of the tool-shed?'

'Marcel Sellier.'

'Whose son is he?'

'His father is the village policeman, who's also the ironmonger, the electrician and the plumber. He mends roofs too, when it's needed.'

'How old is Marcel Sellier?'

'The same age as Jean-Paul, to within two or three months.'

'Does he work well?'

'The best of them all, with my son. So as not to seem to favour Jean-Paul, my husband always puts Marcel at the head of the class. His father is intelligent too, and hardworking. They're a good kind of people, I think. Are you very cross with him?'

'With whom?'

'Jean-Paul. He was almost rude to you. And here am I, not even offering you anything to drink. Won't you have something?'

'Thank you, but the lieutenant must have arrived by

now, and I promised to go and see him.'

'You'll keep on helping us?'

'Why do you ask me that?'

'Because if I were you, I think I should have lost heart. You've come so far, and what you find here is so uninspiring....'

'I'll do my best.'

He went towards the door, to prevent her from seizing his hands in a gesture he could feel she was on the point of making, and kissing them, perhaps. He was eager to get out, to feel the fresh air on his face, to hear sounds other than the tired voice of the schoolmaster's wife.

'I shall be coming to see you again, I expect.'

'You don't think there's anything he needs?'

'If there is, I'll let you know.'

'Oughtn't he to choose a lawyer?'

'There's no need to do that yet.'

While he was crossing the yard without looking back, the double, glass-paned doors of the school were thrown open and a pack of children rushed out, yelling. Some of them stopped dead on seeing him, knowing doubtless from their parents who he was, and stared.

They were of all ages, from shrimps of six to big lads of fourteen or fifteen, who looked almost grown-up already. There were girls, too, who collected in one corner of the yard, as though taking refuge from the boys.

At the far end of the corridor, where both doors were open, Maigret saw the car from the constabulary. He stopped at the secretary's office and knocked. Daniélou's voice said:

'Come in!'

The lieutenant, who had taken off his belt and unbuttoned his tunic, stood up to shake hands. He was sitting in Gastin's chair, papers spread in front of him, *mairie* stamps lying all round. Because she was seated in a dark corner, Maigret did not immediately notice a stout girl with a baby in her arms.

'Sit down, Chief-Inspector. I'll be with you in a moment. I thought it would be a good thing to send for all the witnesses again and go right through the interrogations a second time.'

Doubtless because the chief-inspector had come to Saint-André.

'A cigar?'

'No, thank you. I only smoke a pipe.'

'I was forgetting.'

The lieutenant himself smoked very black cigars, which he chewed as he talked.

'Excuse me.'

And, turning to the girl:

'You say she promised to leave you all she had, including the house?'

'Yes. She promised.'

'Before witnesses?'

She didn't seem to understand what this meant. In fact she didn't seem to understand anything much; she looked as though she might be the village idiot.

She was a big, stolid, manly girl, wearing a black dress that someone must have given her, and there were wisps of hay in her untidy hair. She stank. The baby, too, smelt dirty and unkempt.

'When did she give this promise?'

'A long time ago.'

Her large eyes were of an almost transparent blue and she was frowning with the effort to understand what was wanted of her.

'What do you call a long time? A year?'

'Maybe a year.'

'Two years?'

'Maybe.'

'How long have you been working for Léonie Birard?'

'Wait a minute.... After I had my second baby.... No, the third....'

'How old is he now?'

Her lips moved, as though in church, while she made a mental calculation.

'Five.'

'Where is he now?'

'At home.'

'How many of them are there at home?'

'Three. I've got one here, and the eldest is at school.'

'Who's looking after them?'

'Nobody.'

The two men exchanged glances.

'So you've been working for Léonie Birard for about five years. Did she promise at once that she'd leave you her money?'

'No.'

'After two years, or three?'

'Yes.'

'Was it two, or three?'

'I don't know.'

'Didn't she sign a paper?'

'I don't know.'

'You don't know either why she made you that promise?'

'To annoy her niece. She told me so.'

'Used her niece to come and visit her?'

'Never.'

'She's Madame Sellier, the village policeman's wife, isn't she?'

'That's right.'

'Didn't the policeman ever come to see her either?'

'Yes.'

'They hadn't quarrelled?'

'Yes.'

'Why did he come to see her?'

'To threaten to summons her for throwing her rubbish out of the window.'

'Did they get angry?'

'They shouted insults at each other.'

'Were you fond of your employer?'

She gazed at him with her round eyes, as though the notion of being fond of anyone, or the contrary, had never occurred to her.

'I don't know.'

'Was she kind to you?'

'She used to give me left-overs.'

'Left-overs from what?'

'Food. And her old dresses too.'

'Did she pay you regularly?'

'Not much.'

'What do you mean by not much?'

'Half what other women give me to work for them. But she took me every afternoon. So that...'

'Have you heard her quarrelling with other people?'

'With near everyone.'

'In her own home?'

'She never left home lately; she used to shout things at people through the window.'

'What things?'

'Things they'd done and didn't want known about.'

'So everyone hated her?'

'I think so.'

'Did anyone hate her especially, enough to want to kill her?'

'Must have, seeing she was killed.'

'But you haven't the faintest idea who can have done it.'

'I thought you knew.'

'What do you mean?'

'Well, you've arrested the schoolmaster.'

'You think he did it?'

'I don't know.'

'Do you mind if I ask a question?' intervened Maigret, turning to the lieutenant.'

'By all means.'

'Is Théo, the deputy mayor, the father of one or more of your children?'

She was not offended, seemed to be pondering.

'He may be. I'm not sure.'

'Did he get along well with Léonie Birard?'

She thought again.

'Same as the rest.'

'He knew she'd promised to remember you in her will?'

'I told him.'

'What was his reaction?'

She didn't understand the word. He tried again:

'What did he say to that?'

'He told me to ask her for a paper.'

'You did so?'

'Yes.'

'When?'

'A long time ago.'

'Did she refuse?'

'She said everything was arranged.'

'When you found her dead, what did you do?'

'I called out.'

'Straight away?'

'As soon as I saw there was blood. At first I thought she'd fainted.'

'You didn't hunt through her drawers?'

'What drawers?'

Maigret signed to the lieutenant that he had finished. The latter stood up.

'Thank you, Maria. If I need you again, I'll send for you.'

'Didn't she sign any paper?' inquired the woman, pausing near the door, with her baby in her arms.

'We've found nothing so far.'

Turning her back on them, she grumbled:

'I might have known she'd cheat me.'

They saw her going past the window, talking to herself with a discontented air.

CHAPTER FOUR

The lieutenant sighed, as though apologizing:

'You see? I do my best.'

And that was undoubtedly true. He was all the more conscientious now that there was a witness to his investigation, someone from the famous Police Headquarters, who must seem very impressive to him.

His was a curious story. He came of a well-known family at Toulouse, and on the insistence of his parents he had gone to the Polytechnique, where he acquitted himself more than creditably. And then, instead of choosing between the army and a business career, he had opted for the constabulary and decided to read law for two years.

He had a pretty wife, who also came of a good family, and they were one of the most popular couples at La Rochelle.

He was doing his best to appear at ease in the greyish room in the *mairie*, into which the sun was not yet shining, so that, in contrast with the brightness outside, it was almost dark.

'It's not easy to discover what they think!' he remarked, lighting another cigar.

Six .22 rifles were leaning against the wall in a corner of the room; four of them were exactly alike, and one was of an older type, with a carved butt.

'I think I've got them all. If there are any more around, my men will find them this morning.'

From the mantelpiece he picked up what looked like a cardboard pill-box, and took out a flattened scrap of lead.

'I've inspected this carefully. I studied ballistics at one time, and we've no expert at La Rochelle. It's a lead bullet, of the type sometimes called "soft", which squashes flat as soon as it hits anything, even a pinewood plank. So it's no use looking it over for the kind of marks one finds on other bullets, which often help to identify the actual weapon used.'

Maigret nodded his understanding.

'You're familiar with the .22 rifle, Chief-Inspector?'

'More or less.'

Less rather than more, for he could not recall any crime committed in Paris with such a weapon.

'Two types of cartridge can be used in it, short or long. The short ones have a small range, but the long ·22 can hit its target at over a hundred and fifty yards.'

On the veined marble mantelpiece other scraps of lead, some twenty in all, lay in a little heap.

'Yesterday we made some tests with these different rifles. The bullet which hit Léonie Birard is a long .22, of the same weight as those we fired.'

'The cartridge-case hasn't been found?'

'My men have been over the gardens, behind the house, with a fine-tooth comb. They'll make another search this afternoon. It's not impossible that whoever fired the shot picked up the case. What I'm trying to explain is that we have very few definite clues.'

'Have all these guns been used recently?'

'Fairly recently. It's difficult to be quite sure, because the boys don't bother to clean and oil them after use. The medical report, which I've got here, doesn't help much, either, because the doctor couldn't say, even approximately, from what distance the shot was fired. It might be fifty yards or it might be over a hundred.'

Maigret, standing near the window, was filling his pipe and listening with only half an ear. In the opposite building, next to the church, he could see a man with tangled black hair, shoeing a horse whose hoof was being held by a younger lad.

'I've been over all the different possibilities with the examining magistrates. The first thing we thought of, strange as it may seem, was that it might have been an accident. There's something so incredible about the crime, there was so little chance of killing the old woman with a .22 bullet, that we wondered whether she hadn't been shot by pure chance. Somebody in one of the gardens might have been taking pot-shots at sparrows, as the kids often do. One hears of stranger coincidences. You see what I mean?'

Maigret nodded. The lieutenant had an almost childish desire for his approval, and his good intentions were touching.

'That's what we called the pure and simple accident theory. If Léonie Birard had been killed at any other time of day, or on a holiday, or in another part of the village, we should probably have been satisfied with that, for it's the most plausible. But when she was killed the children were at school.'

'All of them?'

'Practically all. The three or four absentees, one of them a girl, live a good way off, on farms, and weren't seen in the village that morning. Another, the butcher's son, has been in bed for nearly a month.

'Then we turned to a second possibility, that of mischief-making.

'Someone, any one of the neighbours, who'd quarrelled with old Léonie as nearly all of them had, someone she'd made fun of once too often, might, in a fit of anger, have fired from a distance, meaning to frighten her or break one of her windows, without even dreaming that she might be killed.

'I haven't quite rejected that theory yet, because the third possibility, that of deliberate murder, implies a crack shot to begin with. If she'd been hit anywhere except in the eye she'd have been only slightly wounded. And to shoot her deliberately in the eye from some distance, an exceptionally fine shot would be needed.

'Don't forget that this happened in broad daylight, in this group of buildings, at a time of day when most women are at home doing their housework. There's a maze of yards and gardens all around. It was a fine day, and most windows were open.'

'Have you tried to discover where everybody was at about a quarter past ten?'

'You heard Maria Smelker. The other statements aren't much clearer than hers. People are reluctant to answer questions. When they go into details they get so confused that it only complicates things.'

'The deputy-mayor was in his garden?'

'Apparently. It depends whether we're to go by wireless time or by the church clock, because the clock is fifteen or twenty minutes fast. Someone who was listening to the wireless claims to have seen Théo on his way to the *Bon Coin*, at about a quarter past ten. The people at the *Bon Coin* declare that he didn't arrive there till after half past ten. The butcher's wife, who was hanging out her washing, says she saw him go into his cellar for a drink, as he usually does.'

'Has he a rifle?'

'No. Only a double-barrelled sporting gun. That shows you how difficult it is to get hold of reliable evidence. The boy's the only one whose statement holds together.'

'That's the policeman's boy?'

'Yes.'

'Why didn't he say anything the first day?'

'I asked him that. His reply is plausible. I expect you know that his father, Julien Sellier, is married to the old woman's niece?'

'Yes, and Léonie Birard had said she was disinheriting her.'

'Marcel Sellier felt it would look as though he were trying to shelter his father. He didn't mention it at home till the following evening. And Julien Sellier brought him along to us on Thursday morning. You'll be seeing them. They're pleasant people and seem to be sincere.'

'Marcel saw the schoolmaster coming out of his tool-shed?'

'So he says. The children were left to themselves in the classroom. Most of them were fooling around; Marcel

Sellier, who's rather a serious, quiet boy, went across to the window and saw Joseph Gastin coming out of the shed.'

'He didn't see him go in?'

'Only coming out. The shot must have been fired then. The schoolmaster, however, stubbornly denies setting foot in the tool-shed that morning. Either he's lying, or the boy made up the story. But why?'

'Yes, why?' muttered Maigret in a detached tone.

He felt like a glass of wine. It was, he felt, the right time of day. The break was over, in the playground. Two old women went past with shopping-bags, on their way to the Co-operative.

'Might I have a look at Léonie Birard's house?' he asked.

'I'll take you there. I've got the key.'

That, too, was on the mantelpiece. He put it into his pocket, buttoned up his tunic and put his cap on. The air outside had a smell of the sea, but not enough to satisfy Maigret. They walked along to the corner of the street, and as they reached Louis Paumelle's inn, the chief-inspector asked casually:

'What about a drink?'

'Do you think so?' said the lieutenant, awkwardly.

He wasn't the type of man to go for drinks to a *bistro* or an inn. The invitation embarrassed him, and he didn't know how to refuse.

'I wonder whether...'

'Just a quick glass of white wine.'

Théo was there, seated in a corner, his long legs outstretched, a jug of wine and a glass at his elbow. The postman, who had an iron hook where his left arm should have been, was standing in front of him. They both stopped talking as the other men came in.

'What will you take, gentlemen?' inquired Louis, who stood behind his bar, shirt-sleeves rolled up high.

'A *chopine*.'

Daniélou was uncomfortable, but trying to carry it off. Perhaps that was why the deputy-mayor stared mockingly at the two of them. He was tall and must once have been stout. Now that he had lost weight, his skin seemed to hang in folds, like a garment that was too loose.

The expression on his face combined the cunning self-assurance of the peasant with that of the politician, skilled in juggling with the village elections.

'Well, what's become of that scoundrel Gastin?' he inquired, as though speaking to nobody in particular.

And Maigret, without quite knowing why, retorted in the same tone:

'He's waiting for someone to go and take his place.'

The lieutenant was shocked at this. The postman turned his head sharply.

'You've discovered something?' he demanded.

'You must know the district better than anyone, you make the round of it every day.'

'And what a round! At one time, not so long ago, there were still people who practically never had any letters. I remember some farms where I only used to set foot once a year, to take the almanac. Nowadays they not only all get newspapers, which have to be delivered to them, but there isn't one who doesn't claim some allowance or pension. If you knew what a lot of papers that means!...'

He repeated, with an air of profound dejection: 'Papers! Papers!'

To hear him, one might have supposed that he had to fill them in himself.

'To begin with, there are the ex-servicemen. That I can understand. Then there are the widows' pensions. Then the health insurance, the large family allowances. And the allowances for...'

He turned to the deputy-mayor.

'Can you sort them all out? I sometimes wonder whether there's a soul in the village who doesn't draw something or other from the government. And I'm certain some of them have kids just for the sake of the children's allowance.'

His glass misted over in his hand, Maigret enquired jokingly:

'Do you think the allowances have something to do with Léonie Birard's death?'

'One never knows.'

It seemed to be an obsession. He must draw a pension

himself, for his arm. He was paid by the government. And it infuriated him that other people benefited as well. In fact, he was jealous.

'Give me a *chopine*, Louis.'

Théo's eyes were still twinkling. Maigret drank his wine in sips, and this was almost like what he had expected of his trip to the seaside. The air was the same colour as the white wine, tasted the same. Out in the square, two hens were pecking at the hard ground; they could hardly be finding worms there. Thérèse was in the kitchen, peeling onions, wiping her eyes from time to time with the corner of her apron.

'Shall we be going?'

Daniélou, who had scarcely touched his wine, followed him with relief.

'Don't you think those peasants seemed to be laughing at us?' he murmured, when they were outside.

'And how!'

'You seem to find it funny!'

Maigret made to reply. He was beginning to find his feet in the village, and no longer regretted the Quai des Orfèvres. He hadn't telephohed to his wife that morning, as he had promised to do. He hadn't even noticed the post office. He'd have to take a look at that, presently.

They went past a haberdashery, and the chief-inspector saw, through the window, a woman so old and so emaciated that he felt she might snap in two at any moment.

'Who's that?'

'There are a couple of them, about the same age, the Demoiselles Thévenard.'

Two old maids had kept a shop in his native village, too. One would really think French villagers were interchangeable. Years had gone by. The roads had become crowded with fast cars. Buses and vans had replaced the former carts. Cinemas had sprung up all over the place. Wireless and numbers of other things had been invented. And yet Maigret was finding, in this village, the characters of his childhood, unchanged as figures in a holy picture.

'Here is the house.'

It was an old one, and the only one in the street which had not been whitewashed for years. The lieutenant put the big key into the lock of the green-painted door, pushed it open, and they were met by a sickly smell, doubtless also to be found next door, where the two old maids lived, a smell that clings to places where very old people live with the windows shut.

The first room was not unlike the one where Madame Gastin had received him, except that the oak furniture was not so well polished, the upholstery was shabbier, and there was a set of huge copper fire-irons. There was also, in one corner, a bed which must have been brought in from another room, and which was still unmade.

'The bedrooms are upstairs,' explained the lieutenant. 'For the last few years Léonie Birard had refused to go up. She lived on the ground floor, slept in this room. Nothing has been touched.'

A half-open door led into a fair-sized kitchen, with a stone fireplace beside which a coal-burning kitchen range had been installed. Everything was dirty. Saucepans had left rusty circles on the stove. Splashes starred the walls. The leather armchair near the window must be the one in which the old woman had spent the greater part of her time.

Maigret understood why she preferred this room to the front one. There were hardly any passers-by on the road, which led to the sea, whereas from the back, just as from the schoolmaster's house, one could see the liveliest part of the houses, the yards and gardens, including the school playground.

It was almost homely. From her armchair, Léonie Birard could share the daily life of nine or ten families, and if she had sharp eyes she could see what they all had for their meals.

'The chalk line shows where she was found, of course. That stain you can see...'

'I understand.'

'She hadn't bled much.'

'Where is she now?'

'They took her to the morgue at La Rochelle, for the

post-mortem. The funeral's tomorrow morning.'

'You still don't know who gets her property?'

'I've looked everywhere for a will. I telephoned to a solicitor at La Rochelle. She'd often talked to him about making a will, but she'd never done it with him. He has some securities she deposited with him, some bonds, the title-deeds of this house and of another one she owns, a mile from here.'

'So that if nothing is found, her niece will get the lot?'

'I imagine so.'

'What does she say about it?'

'She doesn't seem to count on it. The Selliers aren't hard up. They're not rich, but they have a flourishing little business. You'll be seeing them. I haven't your experience with people. These seemed frank, honest, hard-working.'

Maigret was opening and closing drawers, discovering half-rusted kitchen utensils, odds and ends of all kinds, old buttons, nails, bills, jumbled up with threadless cotton-reels, stockings, hairpins.

He went back to the front room, where there stood an old chest of drawers which was not without value, and there too he opened the drawers.

'You've been through these papers?'

The lieutenant blushed slightly, as though he had been caught out or brought face to face with some disagreeable fact.

He had had the same expression at Louis' bar, when he had been obliged to take the glass of white wine held out to him by Maigret.

'They're letters.'

'So I see.'

'They go back more than ten years, to the time when she was still postmistress.'

'So far as I can see, they aren't addressed to her.'

'That's true. I shall put the whole lot in the file, of course. I've already mentioned them to the examining magistrate. I can't do everything at once.'

The letters were still in their envelopes, each of which bore a different name: Évariste Cornu, Augustin Cornu, Jules Marchandon, Célestin Marchandon, Théodore

Coumar, and so on; women's names too, including those of the Thévenard sisters, who kept the haberdashery.

'It looks to me as though Léonie Birard, in the days when she was postmistress, didn't give *all* the letters to the people they were addressed to.'

He glanced over a few of them:

'Dear Mamma,

'This comes to tell you that I am well, as I hope you are. I like my new place, except that the grandfather, who lives with the family, coughs all day and spits on the floor....'

Another said:

'I met cousin Jules in the street and he looked ashamed when he saw me. He was dead drunk and for a moment I thought he didn't recognize me.'

Léonie Birard had evidently not opened all the letters. She seemed to be more interested in some families than in others — especially the Cornus and Rateaus, who were numerous in the district.

Several envelopes bore the Senate postmark. They were signed by a well-known politician who had now been dead for two years.

'My dear Sir,

'I have received your letter about the storm that wrecked your mussel-beds and washed away more than two hundred posts. I am prepared to arrange for the funds earmarked for victims of national calamities....'

'I asked about that,' explained the lieutenant. 'The mussel-beds consist of pinewood piles driven into the sea-bed, with bundles of twigs hung between them. The bunches of young mussels are slung there and left to grow. Whenever the tide comes in a bit violently, some of the piles are washed out to sea. They're expensive, because they have to be brought from a distance.'

'So the clever chaps get them paid for by the Government under the heading of "national calamity"!'

'That Senator was very popular,' said Daniélou with a wry smile. 'He never had any difficulty in getting re-elected.'

'You've read all these letters!'

'I've glanced through them.'

'They don't provide any clues?'

'They explain why the Birard woman was detested by everyone in the village. She knew too much about them all. She was probably pretty outspoken with them. But I found nothing really serious, anyhow nothing serious enough to induce anyone, especially after ten years had gone by, to finish her off with a bullet through the head. Most of the people those letters were meant for are dead now, and their children don't bother much about what went on in the old days.'

'Are you taking these letters away with you?'

'I needn't take them this evening. I can leave you the key of the house. You don't want to go upstairs?'

Maigret went up, to satisfy his conscience. He learnt nothing from the two upper rooms, which were full of odds and ends and pieces of dilapidated furniture.

Outside, he accepted the key the lieutenant proferred.

'What are you going to do now?'

'When is school over?'

'Morning class ends at half past eleven. Some of the children, those who live fairly near, go home for lunch. The rest, those who come from the farms and the seaside, bring sandwiches and eat them at school. Lessons begin again at half past one and finish at four o'clock.'

Maigret pulled out his watch. It was ten past eleven.

'Are you staying in the village?'

'I must go and see the examining magistrate, who's been questioning the schoolmaster this morning, but I'll be back sometime in the afternoon.'

'See you later, then.'

Maigret shook his hand. He felt inclined for another glass of white wine before the end of morning school. He stood for a moment in the sunshine, watching the lieutenant move away with a light step, as though a weight had fallen from his shoulders.

Théo was still at Louis'. In the opposite corner there now sat an old man dressed almost in rags, looking like a tramp, with a bushy white beard. Filling his glass with an unsteady hand, he had only an indifferent glance to spare for Maigret.

'A *chopine*?' inquired Louis.

'The same as before.'

'It's the only one I've got. I suppose you'll be eating here? Thérèse is cooking a rabbit that'll make your mouth water.'

The maid appeared.

'You like rabbit with white wine sauce, Monsieur Maigret?'

It was only to get a glimpse of him, to shoot him a conspiratorial, grateful glance. He hadn't given her away. In her relief she looked almost pretty.

'You get along back to your kitchen.'

A van drew up, and a man in butcher's overalls came into the taproom. Unlike most butchers he was thin and sickly-looking, with a crooked nose and bad teeth.

'A *pernod*, Louis.'

He turned towards Théo, who was smiling seraphically.

'Hello, you old scoundrel!'

The deputy-mayor's sole response was a vague movement of the hand.

'Not too tired? I can't think how lazy hounds like you get by!'

He switched his attention to Maigret.

'So it's you who're going to dig out the secret, is it?'

'I'm trying to!'

'Try hard. If you find anything you'll deserve a medal.'

He dipped his drooping moustache in his glass.

'How's your boy getting on?' asked Théo, still lazily sprawling in his corner.

'Doctor says it's time he began to walk. Easier said than done. As soon as he's put on his feet, he falls down. Doctors don't know their job. No more than deputy-mayors!'

He spoke jokingly, but with a bitter undercurrent in his voice.

'Have you finished your round?'

'I've still to go to Bourrages.'

He asked for a second glass, swallowed it at one gulp, wiped his moustache, and called to Louis:

'Chalk that up with the rest.'

Then, turning to the chief-inspector:

'Enjoy yourself!'

Finally, on his way out, he deliberately knocked against Théo's legs.

'So long, you dirty dog!'

They watched him start up the van and turn it in the square.

'His father and mother died of TB,' explained Louis. 'His sister is in a sanatorium. He's got a brother shut up in a lunatic asylum.'

'And he himself?'

'He does his best, sells his meat in the villages round here. He opened a butcher's shop at La Rochelle once, and it swallowed up every penny he'd got.'

'Has he several children?'

'A boy and a girl. The two others died at birth. The boy was knocked down by a motorbike a month ago, and he's still in plaster. The girl, who's seven, is at school, I suppose. By the time he's finished his round he'll have swallowed at least half a bottle of *pernod*.'

'Amuses you, does it?' Théo asked in his mocking voice.

'What amuses me?'

'Telling all that.'

'I'm not saying harm of anyone.'

'Would you like me to tell about your little affairs?'

This seemed to frighten Louis, who seized a *chopine* of wine from under the counter and went across to put it on the table.

'You know there's nothing to tell. One has to make conversation, doesn't one?'

Théo seemed somehow jubilant. His mouth was unsmiling, but there was a strange glint in his eyes. Maigret couldn't help thinking the man was like an old faun who'd retired from active life. There he was, in the midst of the village, like a mischievous god who knew everything that went on behind people's walls, inside people's heads, and who was watching with solitary relish the spectacle the world presented.

He regarded Maigret as an equal rather than an enemy.

'You're a very smart chap,' he seemed to be saying. 'You're supposed to be the star performer in your game. In Paris, you unearth everything people try to hide from you.

'But I'm a smart chap too. And down here, I'm the one who knows.

'Go ahead! Play your game. Ask people questions. Drag out their secret thoughts.

'We'll see whether you tumble to it in the end!'

He slept with Maria, an unlovely slattern. He had tried to sleep with Madame Gastin, who had nothing feminine left about her. He drank from morning to night, never entirely fuddled, floating in a private world which must be comic, since it brought a grin to his face.

The old woman Birard, too, had known the little village secrets, but they had infuriated her, acting on her like a poison that she had to work out of her system in one way or another.

His way was to watch the people, mock them, and when any of them wanted a fake certificate in order to draw one of those allowances that made the postman so angry, he supplied it, endorsing the paper with one of the *mairie* stamps which he always carried in the pockets of his shapeless trousers.

He didn't take them seriously.

'Another glass, Inspector?'

'Not just now.'

Maigret could hear children's voices from the direction of the school. Those who went home for lunch were coming out. He saw two or three going across the square.

'I'll be back in half an hour.'

'The rabbit will be ready.'

'Still no oysters?'

'No oysters.'

Hands in pockets, he strolled over to the Selliers' shop. A little boy had gone in just ahead of him, making his way among the buckets, hose-pipes, spraying apparatus that cluttered the floor and hung from the ceiling. There were other tools to be seen everywhere, in the dusty light.

A woman's voice asked:

'What can I do for you?'

He had to peer through the dimness to make out a youngish face, the light patch of a blue-and-white checked apron.

'Is your husband here?'

'At the back, in the workshop.'

The little boy had gone into the kitchen and was washing his hands at the pump.

'If you'll come this way, I'll call him.'

She knew who he was, and did not seem to be alarmed. In the kitchen, which was the centre of life in the house, she pushed forward a rush-bottomed chair for him, then opened a door into the yard.

'Julien!... Someone to see you....'

The little boy was drying his hands and gazing inquisitively at Maigret. And he, too, brought childhood memories back to the chief-inspector. In his form at school, in every form he had been in, there had always been one boy who was fatter than the others and had this same innocent, intent expression, this same clear skin, this same air of having been well brought-up.

His mother was not a big woman, but his father, who came in a moment later, must have weighed well over fourteen stone; he was very tall, very broad, with an almost babyish face and guileless eyes.

He wiped his feet on the doormat before coming in. Three places were laid on the round table.

'Excuse me,' he murmured, going in his turn to the pump.

One could feel that in this house there was a ritual, each person doing certain things at certain times of day.

'Were you just going to have your meal?'

It was the woman who answered:

'Not at once. Dinner's not ready yet.'

'As a matter of fact, what I really wanted was to have a word with your little boy.'

Both parents looked at the child, with no sign of surprise or uneasiness.

'You hear that, Marcel?' asked his father.

'Yes, Papa.'

'Answer the inspector's questions.'

'Yes, Papa.'

Turning squarely to face Maigret, the boy settled into the attitude of a pupil preparing to answer his schoolmaster.

CHAPTER FIVE

While Maigret was lighting his pipe there took place a kind of silent ceremony which reminded him, more vividly than anything else he had seen at Saint-André since the previous evening, of the village of his childhood. For a moment, in fact, Madame Sellier seemed to have been transformed into one of his own aunts, in a blue-and-white checked apron, her hair screwed into a knot on top of her head.

The woman had merely looked at her husband, with the very slightest widening of her eyes, and Julien had understood the message, gone over to the back door, through which his tall figure had vanished for a moment. His wife, without waiting for him to come back, had opened the cupboard and taken out two glasses belonging to the best service, those that were kept for when visitors came, and she was now wiping them with a clean cloth.

When the ironmonger reappeared, he was carrying a corked-up bottle of wine. He said nothing. Nobody needed to say anything. Anyone who had come from a great distance, or from some other planet, might have imagined that these actions formed part of a rite. They heard the sound of the cork being drawn from the bottle, the splash of the golden wine into the two glasses.

Obviously a little shy, Julien Sellier picked up one glass, looked through it sideways, and finally said:

'Your very good health.'

'Your very good health,' responded Maigret.

After which the man withdrew to a shadowy corner of the room, while his wife went across to the stove.

'Tell me, Marcel,' began the chief-inspector, turning back to the boy, who had not moved, 'I suppose you've never told a lie?'

The hesitation, if any, was brief, accompanied by a quick sidelong glance towards his mother.

'Yes, sir, I have.'

He added hastily:

'But I've always confessed.'

'You mean you've gone to confession afterwards?'

'Yes, sir.'

'At once?'

'As soon as I could, because I didn't want to die in sin.'

'But they can't have been very important lies?'

'Pretty important.'

'Would you very much mind telling me one of them, as an example?'

'There was the time I tore my trousers, climbing a tree. When I got home I said I'd caught them on a nail in Joseph's yard.'

'And you went to confession that same day?'

'The next day.'

'And when did you own up to your father and mother?'

'Not till a week later. Another time I fell into the pond when I was catching frogs. Papa and Mamma don't let me play round the pond, because I catch cold easily. My clothes were all wet. I said another boy had pushed me when I was crossing the little bridge over the stream.'

'And did you wait a week that time, before telling them the truth?'

'Only two days.'

'Do you often tell lies like that?'

'No, sir.'

'About every how often?'

Marcel paused for reflection, just as though this were an oral examination.

'Less than once a month.'

'Do your friends do it more often?'

'Not all of them. Some do.'

'Do they go to confession afterwards, like you?'

'I don't know. I expect so.'

'Is the schoolmaster's son a friend of yours?'

'No, sir.'

'Don't you play with him?'

'He doesn't play with anybody.'

'Why not?'

'Perhaps because he doesn't like playing. Or perhaps because his father's the teacher. I did try to be friends with him.'

'You don't like Monsieur Gastin?'

'He's unfair.'

'In what way unfair?'

'He always gives me top marks, even when it's his son who ought to have them. I like to be top of the class when I've deserved it, but not when I haven't.'

'Why do you suppose he does that?'

'I don't know. Perhaps because he's afraid.'

'Afraid of what?'

The boy struggled to find a reply. He undoubtedly knew what he wanted to say, but realized that it was too complicated, that he wouldn't find the words. He merely repeated:

'I don't know.'

'You remember Tuesday morning?'

'Yes, sir.'

'What did you do during break?'

'I played with the others.'

'What happened a little time after you'd gone back to the classroom?'

'Old Piedbœuf, from Gros-chêne, knocked on the door, and Monsieur Gastin went over to the *mairie* with him, after telling us to keep quiet.'

'Does that often happen?'

'Yes, sir. Fairly often.'

'Do you keep quiet?'

'Not all of us.'

'You yourself keep quiet?'

'Most of the time.'

'When had this happened last?'

'The day before, on Monday, when there was a funeral. Someone came to have a paper signed.'

'What did you do on Tuesday?'

'At first I stayed in my place.'

'Had the other boys begun to fool about?'

'Yes, sir. Most of them.'

'What exactly were they doing?'

'They were fighting for fun, throwing things at each other, india-rubbers and pencils.'

'And then?'

The boy occasionally hesitated before replying, but not from embarrassment, merely like someone searching for the exact answer.

'I went to the window.'

'Which window?'

'The one overlooking the yards and kitchen gardens. That's the one I always go to.'

'Why?'

'I don't know. It's the one nearest to my desk.'

'It wasn't the sound of a shot that made you go to the window?'

'No, sir.'

'If a shot had been fired outside, would you have heard it?'

'I mightn't have. The others were making a lot of noise. And a horse was being shod at the forge.'

'Have you a .22 gun?'

'Yes, sir. I took it to the *mairie* yesterday, like the others. Everybody who had a gun was asked to take it to the *mairie*.'

'You didn't leave the classroom while the master was away?'

'No, sir.

Maigret was speaking in a quiet, encouraging tone. Madame Sellier had tactfully departed to tidy the shop, while her husband, glass in hand, was watching Marcel with an air of pride.

'You saw the schoolmaster crossing the yard?'

'Yes, sir.'

'You saw him when he was on his way to the tool-shed?'

'No, sir. He was coming back from it.'

'You saw him come out of the shed?'

'I saw him shutting the door behind him. Then he came across the yard and I said to the others:

' "Look out!"

'Then they all went back to their places. Me too.'

'Do you play a great deal with the other boys?'

'Not much, no.'

'Don't you like playing?'

'I'm too fat.'

He blushed as he said this, glanced at his father, as though apologizing.

'Haven't you any friends?'

'Joseph's my best friend.'

'Who's Joseph?'

'Monsieur Rateau's son.'

'The mayor's son?'

Julien Sellier broke in to explain.

'There are a lot of Rateaus at Saint-André and in the neighbourhood,' he said, 'nearly all cousins. Joseph's father is Marcellin Rateau, the butcher.'

Maigret took a sip of wine and relit his pipe, which he had allowed to go out.

'Was Joseph with you at the window?'

'He wasn't at school. He's been at home for a month, because of his accident.'

'Is he the boy who was knocked down by a motor bicycle?'

'Yes, sir.'

'Were you with him when it happened?'

'Yes, sir.'

'Do you often go to see him?'

'Nearly every day.'

'Did you go yesterday?'

'No.'

'The day before yesterday?'

'Not then either.'

'Why not?'

'Because of what had happened. Nobody was thinking

of anything except the crime.'

'You wouldn't have dared to tell a lie to the constabulary lieutenant, I suppose?'

'No, sir.'

'Are you glad the schoolmaster's in prison?'

'No, sir.'

'Do you realize it's your evidence that sent him there?'

'I don't understand what you mean.'

'If you hadn't said you'd seen him coming out of the tool-shed, they probably wouldn't have arrested him.'

He made no reply to this, embarrassed, shifting from one foot to the other, glancing again at his father.

'If you really did see him, you were quite right to tell the truth.'

'I did tell the truth.'

'You didn't like Léonie Birard?'

'No, sir.'

'Why not?'

'Because she used to shout rude things at me when I went past.'

'More at you than at the others?'

'Yes, sir.'

'Do you know why?'

'Because she was cross with Mamma for marrying my father.'

Maigret half closed his eyes, trying to think of another question, failed to find one and emptied his glass instead. He rose to his feet, rather heavily, for he had already that morning drunk quite a few glasses of white wine.

'Thank you, Marcel. If you had anything to say to me — for instance, if you remembered any little thing you'd forgotten, I'd like you to come and see me at once. You're not scared of me?'

'No, sir.'

'Another glass?' asked the boy's father, reaching out for the bottle.

'No, thank you. I don't want to delay your lunch any longer. Your son's an intelligent boy, Monsieur Sellier.'

The ironmonger flushed with pleasure.

'We're doing our best to bring him up properly. I don't

think he often tells lies.'

'That reminds me: when did he tell you about the schoolmaster going to the tool-shed?'

'On Wednesday evening.'

'He hadn't said anything about it on Tuesday, when the whole village was talking about Léonie Birard's death?'

'No. I think he was a bit overcome. On Wednesday, while we were at dinner, he looked rather strange, and suddenly he said to me:

' "Papa, I think I saw something." '

'He told me the story, and I went and reported it to the police lieutenant.'

'Thank you.'

Something was bothering him, he didn't know exactly what. Once outside, he made first for the *Bon Coin*, where he saw the substitute schoolmaster seated near the window, eating his lunch and reading a book. He remembered he had meant to telephone to his wife, walked to the post office, which was one of another group of houses, and was received there by a girl of about twenty-five, who wore a black overall.

'Would it take very long to get Paris?'

'Not at this time of day, Monsieur Maigret.'

While he waited for his call he watched her doing her accounts, wondered whether she was married, whether she would get married one day, or if she would turn out like the old Birard woman.

He stayed in the telephone booth for about five minutes, and the only words the girl at the switchboard could hear through the door were:

'No, no oysters.... Because there aren't any.... No.... The weather's lovely.... Not in the least cold....'

He decided to go to lunch. The schoolmaster was still there, and Maigret was shown to a seat at the opposite table. The whole village knew who he was by this time. They didn't speak to him, but they watched him go along the street, and no sooner had he gone by, than they began to talk about him. The schoolmaster looked up from his book three or four times. Just as he went away he seemed to hesitate for a moment. Perhaps he had something he wanted to say? One couldn't be sure. In any case, as he went past he gave him a nod which might have been interpreted as an unintentional jerk of the head.

Thérèse had a spotless white apron over her black dress. Louis was eating in the kitchen, where he could be heard calling to the girl from time to time. When he had finished he came over to Maigret, his mouth still greasy.

'Well, what did you think of the rabbit?'

'It was first-class!'

'A drop of *marc* to wash it down? This is on me.'

His manner towards the chief-inspector was protective, as though without him he would have been lost in the jungle of Saint-André.

'Queer chap, that!' he growled as he sat down, legs wide apart because of his fat stomach.

'Who?'

'Théo. Cleverest fellow I know. All his life he's managed to take things easy, without doing a stroke of work.'

'Do you really think nobody else heard that shot?'

'Well, in the country, people don't pay much attention to a rifle-shot. If it had been a sporting gun, everybody would have noticed. But those little things don't make much noise, and we've got so used to them since all the kids began to have them....'

'Théo was in his garden and is supposed not to have seen anything?'

'In his garden or in his wine-cellar, since what he calls gardening usually means going to tap the barrel. But if he did see anything he probably wouldn't say so.'

'Even if he saw someone fire the shot?'

'All the more reason to keep quiet.'

Louis was pleased with himself, refilled the little glasses.

'I warned you you wouldn't understand a thing.'

'Do you believe the schoolmaster wanted to kill the old woman?'

'Do you?'

Maigret replied positively:

'No.'

Louis looked at him, smiling as though to say:

'Neither do I.'

But he did not say it. The two of them were probably in the same torpid condition, because of what they had had to eat and drink. They sat in silence for a moment, looking out at the square which was cut in two by the sun, at the greenish glass windows of the co-operative stores, the stone porch of the church.

'What's the priest like?' asked Maigret, for the sake of something to say.

'He's a priest.'

'Is he on the schoolmaster's side?'

'No.'

At last Maigret got up, stood hesitating for a moment in the middle of the room, then decided on laziness and moved towards the staircase.

'You can call me in an hour,' he said to Thérèse.

He had been wrong to use the familiar '*tu*'. Officials at Police Headquarters usually speak like that to women of her type, and it had not been lost on Louis, who frowned. In the bedroom the green shutters were closed, with only thin shafts of sunlight stealing through. He did not undress, only took off his jacket and shoes, lay on the bed without turning it down.

A little later, while he was still only dozing, he seemed to hear the regular sound of the sea — could it be that? Then he went right off to sleep and did not wake until there was a knock on the door.

'It's more than an hour, Monsieur Maigret. Would you like a cup of coffee?'

He still felt heavy, sluggish, uncertain as to what he really wanted to do. Downstairs, going through the front room, he saw four men playing cards; one was Théo and another Marcellin, the butcher, still in his working clothes.

He still felt there was a detail jarring somewhere, though he couldn't think what it was. He had had that impression during his talk with little Sellier. At what moment exactly?

He began walking, first to Léonie Birard's house, the key of which was in his pocket. He went in, sat down in the front room, where he read all the letters he had glanced over that morning. They did not tell him anything important, merely familiarized him with certain names, the Dubards, the Cornus, the Gillets, Rateaus and Boncœurs.

On leaving the house he meant to go down the path to the sea, but a little way along he found the cemetery and went in, spelt out the names on the tombs, much the same as those he had found in the letters.

He could have pieced together the family histories, telling how the Rateaus had been related by marriage to the Dubards for two generations back, and that a Cornu daughter had married a Piedbœuf who had died at the age of twenty-six.

He went on for another two or three hundred yards, and the sea was still not in sight, the meadows were sloping gently upwards on either side; all he could see, far ahead, was a shimmering mist that he gave up hope of reaching.

The villagers kept meeting him in their streets and alleys, hands in pockets, stopping now and then, aimlessly, to stare at a house-front or a passer-by.

He couldn't resist another glass of white wine before going to the *mairie*. The four men were still playing cards and Louis sat astride a chair, watching the game.

The sun was shining full on the *mairie* steps, and looking down the corridor he could see the caps of the two *gendarmes*, in the kitchen-garden at the back. They must be still hunting for the cartridge-case.

The windows of the schoolmaster's house were shut. Rows of children's heads could be seen through the schoolroom window.

He found the lieutenant making notes, in red pencil, on a witness's statement.

'Come in, Chief-Inspector. I've seen the examining magistrate. He questioned Gastin this morning.'

'How is he?'

'Like a man who's just spent his first night in prison. He was anxious to know whether you were still here.'

'He sticks to his denial, I suppose?'

'Closer than ever.'

'Has he any theory of his own?'

'He doesn't believe anyone meant to kill the old woman. He thinks it was more likely a practical joke that proved fatal. People often played tricks of that kind.'

'On Léonie Birard?'

'Yes. Not only the children, but grown-ups as well. You know what it is when a whole village takes a dislike to someone. Whenever a cat died it would be tossed into her garden, if it wasn't thrown through the window into the house. A couple of weeks ago she found her door all plastered with dung. The schoolmaster thinks someone fired a shot to frighten her or make her angry.'

'What about the tool-shed?'

'He still makes out that he never set foot in it on Tuesday.'

'He didn't do any gardening on Tuesday morning, before school?'

'Not on Tuesday, but on Monday he did. He gets up at six o'clock every morning, it's only then that he has a little time to himself. Did you see the Sellier boy? What do you think about him?'

'He answered my questions without hesitation.'

'Mine, too, without once contradicting himself. I questioned the other boys, who all declare he didn't leave the classroom after break. If that had been a lie, I imagine one of them would certainly have slipped up on it.'

'I imagine so. Do they know who inherits?'

'They still haven't found a will. Madame Sellier's chances look good.'

'Did you check on how her husband spent his time on Tuesday morning?'

'He was busy in his workshop.'

'Any witnesses to that?'

'His wife, for one. And for another, Marchandon, the blacksmith, who went across to speak to him.'

'What time was that?'

'He doesn't know exactly. Before eleven o'clock, he says. According to him, they chatted for at least a quarter of an hour. Not that that proves anything, of course.'

He leafed through his papers.

'Especially as young Sellier says the forge was working when the schoolmaster left the classroom.'

'So his father could have gone away?'

'Yes, but don't forget that everybody knows him. He'd have had to go across the square and into the gardens. If he'd been carrying a rifle they'd have noticed him all the more.'

'But they mightn't say so.'

In fact there was nothing reliable, no firm foundation, except two contradictory statements: one from Marcel Sellier, who said that from the schoolroom window he had seen Gastin coming out of the tool-shed; and the other from Gastin himself, who would swear that he had never set foot in the shed that day.

All these happenings were recent. The villagers had been questioned on the evening of the very day, Tuesday, and the questioning had gone on during Wednesday. They had had no time to forget things.

If the schoolmaster had not fired the shot, why should he tell a lie? And, above all, what motive had he for killing Léonie Birard?

Neither had Marcel Sellier any motive for making up the tool-shed story.

As for Théo, he maintained, in his bantering style, that he had heard a shot, but seen nothing at all.

Had he been in his kitchen-garden? Had he been in his wine-cellar? Impossible to rely on the times given by any of them, for time doesn't count much in the country, except when it comes to meals. Neither was Maigret very convinced by assurances that such and such a person had or had not gone past along the street at a particular moment. When you're accustomed to seeing people a dozen times a day in the same familiar places, you don't pay attention any longer, and you may quite sincerely mix up one meeting with another, say that a particular incident took place on Tuesday whereas really it happened on Monday.

The wine was making him feel hot.

'What time is the funeral?'

'Nine o'clock. Everybody will be there. It isn't every day that they have the pleasure of burying the local bugbear. Have you got an idea?'

Maigret shook his head, went on pottering about the

office, fingered the rifles, the lead pellets.

'I believe you told me the doctor wasn't certain what time she was killed?'

'He puts it at between ten and eleven in the morning.'

'So that if it weren't for young Sellier's evidence...'

They always came up against that. And each time, Maigret had the same impression that the truth had given him the slip again, that he had been on the verge, at one moment, of discovering it.

He wasn't interested in Léonie Birard. What did it matter to him whether someone had meant to kill her or only to frighten her, or whether it was by accident that the bullet had gone through her left eye?

It was the Gastin business that excited him, and consequently, little Sellier's evidence.

He walked into the courtyard, and was half-way across it when the children began emerging from the schoolhouse, less hurriedly than at break, and making their way in small groups to the gate. Brothers and sisters could be distinguished among them. The big girls were leading smaller children by the hand, and some of them would have nearly two miles to walk home.

Only one boy greeted him, except Marcel Sellier, who raised his cap politely. The others went past, staring inquisitively. The schoolmaster was standing in the doorway. Maigret went up to him and the young man stepped aside to let him in, stammering:

'Did you want to speak to me?'

'Not particularly. Had you been to Saint-André before this?'

'No. This is the first time. I've taught in schools at La Rochelle and at Fourras.'

'Did you know Joseph Gastin?'

'No.'

The desks and forms were black, cut about with penknives and splashed with patches of purple ink, which had a bronze sheen here and there against the varnish. Maigret went to the first window on the left, through which he saw part of the courtyard, the gardens, the tool-shed. Then, from the right-hand window, he could see the back of Léonie Birard's house.

'Did you notice anything special about the children's behaviour today?'

'They're quieter than town children. Perhaps they're shy.'

'They've not been holding discussions in groups, or passing notes in class?'

The deputy teacher was less than twenty-two years old. He was obviously in awe of Maigret, rather because he was a celebrity than because he belonged to the police. He would no doubt have behaved in the same way if confronted with a famous politician or a film star.

'I'm afraid I didn't pay attention to that. Should I have done?'

'What do you think of young Sellier?'

'Just a moment… which one is that?… I don't know their names yet….'

'A taller, fatter boy than the others, who's very good at his lessons….'

The young man's eyes turned towards the seat at the end of the front row, which was evidently Marcel's place, and Maigret went and sat down there, though the desk was too low for him to get his knees under it. Sitting here and looking out of the second window, it was not the kitchen gardens he saw, but the lime-tree in the courtyard and the Gastins' house.

'He didn't strike you as uneasy or worried?'

'No. I remember asking him some questions in arithmetic and noticing that he was very intelligent.'

To the right of the schoolmaster's house, further off, one could see the first-floor windows of two other houses.

'Tomorrow I may perhaps ask you to let me come and see them for a moment during school.'

'Whenever you like. We're both staying at the inn, I believe. It'll be easier for me to prepare my lessons over here.'

Maigret left him, and was about to go to the schoolmaster's house. It was not Madame Gastin he wanted to see, but Jean-Paul. He walked more than half the distance, saw a curtain move at one of the windows, stopped, depressed at the thought of finding himself once again in a stuffy little room, confronted with the tragic faces of the woman and her little boy.

He felt cowardly. Overcome by laziness which must be due to the leisurely village life, the white wine, the sun which was now beginning to sink behind the roofs.

What, in fact, was he doing here? Scores of times before, during an investigation, he had had this same feeling of helplessness, or rather of futility. He was suddenly pitchforked into the life of a group of people he had never set eyes on before, and his job was to worm out their deepest secrets. This time it wasn't even his job. He had come of his own accord, because a schoolmaster had waited for him for hours in the Purgatory at Police Headquarters.

The air was taking on a bluish tint, becoming cooler, damper. Windows were lighting up here and there, and Marchandon's forge stood out, red; one could see the flames dancing every time the bellows blew them.

In the shop opposite were two women, as motionless as the picture on an advertisement calendar, with only their lips moving slightly. They seemed to be speaking in turns, and at the end of every sentence the shopwoman shook her head disconsolately. Were they talking about Léonie Birard? Very likely. And about tomorrow's funeral, which would be a memorable event in the history of Saint-André.

The men were still playing cards. They must spend hours this way, every afternoon, exchanging the same phrases, now and again putting out a hand to pick up a glass, then wipe their lips.

He was about to go in, order a *chopine* for himself, sit down in a corner to wait for dinner-time, when a car pulled up close beside him, making him jump.

'Did I frighten you?' called the cheery voice of the doctor. 'You haven't fathomed the mystery yet?'

He got out of the car, lit a cigarette.

'Makes a change from the Grands Boulevards,' he remarked, with a wave of the hand at the village around them, the dimly-lit shop-windows, the forge, the church door, which was half open, letting out a faint glow of light. 'You should just see it in the middle of the winter. Have you begun to get used to our local life?'

'Léonie Birard used to keep letters addressed to different people.'

'She was an old scoundrel. Some people called her the louse. You can't imagine how scared she was of dying!'

'Was she ill?'

'Ill enough to have died long ago. But she didn't die. Like Théo, who ought to have been in his grave these ten years or more, and yet goes on drinking his two quarts of white wine a day, not to mention *apéritifs*.'

'What do you think of the Selliers?'

'They're doing their best to join the middle class. Julien came here as an apprentice from the Waifs and Strays, and worked hard to establish himself. They've only one child, a boy.'

'I know. He's intelligent.'

'Yes.'

It seemed to Maigret that there was a certain reserve in the doctor's tone.

'What do you mean?'

'Nothing. He's a well brought up lad. He's one of the choirboys. The priest's pet.'

It looked as though the doctor didn't like priests, either.

'You believe he's been lying?'

'I didn't say that. I don't believe anything. If you'd been a country doctor for twenty-two years, you'd be like me. The only thing that interests them is making money, turning it into gold, putting the gold into bottles and burying the bottles in their gardens. Even when they're ill or injured, they have to make something out of it.'

'I don't understand.'

'There's always the insurance, or the allowances, one way or another of turning everything into money.'

He was talking almost like the postman.

'A bunch of scoundrels!' he concluded, in a tone which seemed to contradict his words. 'They're a scream. I'm quite fond of them.'

'Léonie Birard too?'

'She was phenomenal!'

'And Germaine Gastin?'

'She'll spend the rest of her life tormenting herself and everybody else because she went to bed with Chevassou. I'll bet it didn't happen often, perhaps only once. And just because she enjoyed herself once in her life... If you're still here tomorrow, come and have lunch with me. This evening I have to go to La Rochelle.'

It was dark already. Maigret hung about a little longer in the square, emptied his pipe, knocking the bowl against his heel, and, with a sigh, went into Louis' inn, walked over to a table which was already his table, and Thérèse, without being asked, put a *chopine* of white wine and a glass in front of him.

Théo, sitting opposite with his pack of cards, glanced at him from time to time with eyes that sparkled with malice, as though to say:

'You're coming on: You're coming on: A few years of that, and you'll be like the rest of them.'

CHAPTER SIX

It was not because of the postmistress's funeral, which was to take place that day, that Maigret woke up with a weight on his mind. The death of Léonie Birard, in the sunshine, had not upset anyone, there had been nothing tragic about it, and the people of Saint-André, in the houses and farms, were doubtless dressing for her burial as cheerfully as for a wedding. So much so that Louis Paumelle, out in the yard very early, already wearing his starched white shirt and black cloth trousers, but with no collar or tie, was pouring wine into an impressive number of *chopines*, which he was lining up not only behind the bar, but on the kitchen table as well, as though this were a fair-day.

The men were shaving themselves. Everybody would be wearing black, as though the whole village were in mourning. Maigret remembered how once, when he was little, his father had asked one of his aunts why she had bought yet another black dress.

'Well, you know, my sister-in-law has cancer of the breast and may be dead in a few months or even in a few weeks. It is so bad for clothes, to dye them!'

In any village people have so many relations who may die any moment, that they spend all their time dressed in black.

Maigret shaved himself, too.

He saw the La Rochelle bus go off almost empty, although this was a Saturday. Thérèse had brought him up a cup of coffee and his hot water, because she had seen him sitting for hours in his corner, the previous evening, drinking wine and then, after dinner, glass upon glass of brandy.

But it wasn't, either, because of the amount he had drunk, that he now had a feeling of tragedy. Perhaps, after all, it was simply because he had slept badly. All night he had been seeing children's faces, in close-up, as though at the cinema, faces which all resembled little Gastin and little Sellier, but were not exactly either of theirs.

He tried, without success, to recall those dreams. Someone had a grudge against him, one of the boys; he couldn't say which, they were indistinguishable. He kept telling himself that it was easy to recognize them apart, because the schoolmaster's son wore glasses. But immediately afterwards he saw Marcel Sellier wearing glasses too and saying, when he expressed surprise:

'I only put them on when I go to confession.'

Gastin's being in prison was not so very tragic, for the police lieutenant did not really believe he was guilty; neither, in all probability, did the examining magistrate. He was better off there for a few days than going about the village or shut up in his own house. And he couldn't be found guilty on the evidence of a single witness, especially when that witness was a child.

It seemed to Maigret to be more complicated than that. This often happened to him. One could even say that during each case that came along, his mood followed more or less the same curve.

At the beginning you see people from the outside. Their little traits are what show most clearly, and that's amusing. Then, gradually, you begin to put yourself in their shoes, to wonder why they behave in this or that fashion; you catch yourself thinking like them, and that's much less amusing.

Later on, perhaps, when you've seen so much of them that nothing surprises you any longer, you may be able to laugh at them, like Dr. Bresselles.

Maigret had not reached that stage. He was worried about the little boys. At least one of them, somewhere, he felt must be living in a kind of nightmare, in spite of the bright sunlight that was still shining over the village.

By the time he went downstairs to his corner for breakfast, farmers from the outlying districts were already arriving in the square in carts. They did not come straight into the café, but stood in dark-clad groups in the street and outside the church, and their tanned skin made their shirts look dazzling white by contrast.

He did not know who had made the arrangements for the funeral, it had not occurred to him to ask. In any case the coffin had been brought from La Rochelle and taken straight to the church.

The black figures were rapidly increasing in number. Maigret noticed faces he had not seen before. The police lieutenant came up and shook hands.

'Anything fresh?'

'Not a thing. I saw him last night in his cell. He sticks to his denial, can't understand why Marcel Sellier persists in accusing him.'

Maigret went into the school playground; there were to be no lessons today, and the windows of the schoolmaster's house were closed, no one to be seen: the boy and his mother would certainly not go to the funeral, they would stay at home, silent, terrified, waiting for something to happen.

But the crowd did not seem to be angry. The men were calling to one another, some were going into Louis' for a quick glass, and coming out again, wiping their lips. As the chief-inspector went past they all fell silent, then began to talk in low voices, following him with their eyes.

A young man who, despite the cloudless sky, was wearing a tightly-belted raincoat, came up to him, an outsized pipe in his mouth.

'Albert Raymond, reporter on *La Charente*,' he announced cockily. He was not more than twenty-two. He was thin, long-haired, kept his mouth twisted into a sardonic smile.

Maigret merely nodded.

'I tried to get along to see you yesterday, but I hadn't the time.'

His way of speaking and general manner implied that he felt himself to be on equal terms with the chief-inspector. Or rather, that they were both outside this crowd. They could both look down on it with condescension, as men who knew, who had penetrated to the most hidden springs of human nature.

'Is it true,' he asked, grasping his pencil and notebook, 'that the schoolmaster came and offered you all his savings if you'd get him out of the mess?'

Maigret turned towards him, looked him up and down, was about to say something, then, with a shrug of the shoulders, turned his back on him.

The idiot would probably think he'd guessed right. It didn't matter. The bells were ringing. The women were pouring into the church, with a few men as well. Then came the soft notes of the organ, the tinkle of a choirboy's bell.

'Is it to be a mass, or only an intercession?' the chief-inspector inquired of a man he did not know.

'A mass and an intercession. We've got plenty of time.'

Time to go to Louis' for a drink. Most of the men had gradually gathered in front of the inn or went inside in groups to drink a *chopine* or two of wine without sitting down, and then emerge again. There was a perpetual coming and going: there were people in the kitchen and even in the yard. Louis Paumelle, who had already been into the church for a moment, was now in his shirt-sleeves again and bustling about, helped by Thérèse and by a young man who seemed to be accustomed to lending him a hand.

Sellier was in church, with his wife. Maigret had not seen Marcel go past, but a little later, when he too went to the church, he understood why. Marcel was there, in his choirboy's surplice, serving mass. He could apparently get straight into the vestry by going through his parents' backyard.

'Dies irae, dies illa...'

The women really seemed to be praying, their lips were moving. Were they praying for Léonie Birard's soul, or for themselves? A few old men were standing, hat in hand, at the back of the nave, and others peeped in from time to time, half opening the door, to see how the service was getting along.

Maigret went out again, caught sight of Théo, who acknowledged his presence with his usual juicy, sarcastic grin.

Somebody obviously must know. There might even be several who knew and were keeping quiet. The voices in Louis' bar-parlour were growing louder now, and one thin farmer, with a drooping moustache, was already more than half drunk.

The butcher, too, seemed to Maigret to have brighter eyes and a more unsteady gait than usual, and the chief-inspector saw him drain three large glasses within a few minutes, invited by one man or another.

The lieutenant, either less inquisitive than he or more sensitive to the curiosity of the crowd, had taken refuge in the office at the *mairie,* where the courtyard was empty around its lime-tree.

A cart went by, which was to serve as a hearse, drawn by a chestnut horse with a black rug draped over its back. It pulled up outside the porch and the driver came across for a drink.

A light breeze was stirring the air. Far up in the sky, a few clouds were gleaming like mother-of-pearl.

At length the church doors opened. The drinkers rushed outside. The coffin appeared, carried by four men among whom Maigret recognized Julien Sellier and the deputy-mayor.

It was hoisted, not without difficulty, onto the cart. It was then covered with a black, silver-fringed pall. Young Sellier appeared next, bearing a silver cross on a black wooden shaft, and his surplice blew out round him two or three times, like a balloon.

The priest followed, repeating prayers, finding the time to glance at each person in turn; his eyes lingered for a moment on Maigret's face.

Julien Sellier and his wife led the procession; both were in black and she had a veil over her face. Next came the mayor, a tall, powerful man with a placid face and grey hair, surrounded by the members of the local council, then the general public, men in front and women behind; some of the latter, especially those at the tail end of the procession, were dragging children by the hand.

The young journalist was hurrying to and fro, making notes, talking to people whom Maigret did not know. Slowly the procession moved on, passing Louis' inn where Thérèse stood alone in the doorway, for Paumelle was with the local councillors' group.

For the second time that morning, Maigret was tempted to go and knock on the Gastins front door and talk to Jean-Paul. Now that all the inhabitants were off to the cemetery, the mother and son must surely be feeling lonelier than ever in the deserted village.

He followed the others, however, for no definite reason. They went past Léonie Birard's house, then past a farm; a calf in the farmyard began to bellow.

As they turned into the cemetery there was a certain amount of tramping and confusion. The priest and the choirboy were already at the grave-side before the rest had all come through the gate.

It was then that Maigret noticed someone looking over the wall. He recognized Jean-Paul. One of his glasses was reflecting the sun like a mirror.

Instead of following the crowd, the chief-inspector remained outside and began to walk round the cemetery, meaning to join the boy. The latter was, he thought, probably too concentrated on what was happening beside the grave, to notice this manœuvre.

He was walking along a strip of waste ground. He had got to within about thirty yards of the boy, when he trod on a dead branch.

Jean-Paul looked round quickly, jumped down from the stone he had been standing on, and bolted for the road.

Maigret was about to call to him, refrained because the others would have heard him, merely walked on more quickly, hoping to catch up with the boy on the road.

The situation was, he realized, ridiculous. He could not venture to run. Neither could Jean-Paul. The child was afraid even to glance behind him. He was probably the only one in the village who was wearing his school clothes, not dressed in his best.

To make his way home, as he probably wanted to do, he would have had to pass the cemetery gate, outside which stood a group of farmers.

He turned left, towards the sea, hoping, perhaps, that the chief-inspector would not follow him.

Maigret followed. There were no more farms or houses to be seen, only fields and meadows where a few cows were grazing. The sea was still invisible, behind a low hill. The road sloped gently upwards.

The boy was walking as fast as he could do without breaking into a run, and Maigret, too, had lengthened his stride. He did not even know exactly why he was pursuing him like this, began to realize it was cruel.

To Jean-Paul it must seem as though a terrifying power were on his tracks. But the chief-inspector could not very well begin to shout:

'Jean-Paul!... Stop!... I only want to talk to you...'

The cemetery had vanished behind them, and the village. Little Gastin had now reached the top of the hill and began to go down the other side; and Maigret could only see his head and shoulders, then only his head. There came a moment when he saw nothing at all, until he, in his turn, reached the top of the hill; and then, at last, the sparkling expanse of sea lay before him, with what he took to be an island in the distance, or perhaps the Pointe de l'Aiguillon, and a few brown-sailed fishing-boats, looking as though they were floating in space.

Jean-Paul was still walking. There was no path, either to right or left. Down beside the sea stood five or six red-roofed huts, where the mussel-breeders kept their tackle.

'Jean-Paul!' he made up his mind and called.

His voice sounded so strange that he hardly recognized it, and he turned his head to make sure nobody was watching. He noticed a momentary change in the rhythm of the boy's step. Surprise at hearing his name called had made him hesitate, almost pause, but now the surprise was over he was walking as fast as ever, practically running, panic-stricken.

The chief-inspector was ashamed of his persistence, he felt like a hulking brute bearing down on a defenceless creature.

'Wait for me boy...'

What made the position even sillier was that he was out of breath and his voice didn't carry. The distance between them remained about the same. To reduce it, he would have had to run.

What was Jean-Paul hoping? That Maigret would be disheartened and turn back?

It was more likely that he wasn't thinking at all, that he was just plunging on as though it were the only hope of escaping a danger. All that lay ahead of him was the sea, its shining fringe of foam washing over the pebbles.

'Jean-Paul...'

At the point he had reached, it would be as silly to give up as to go on.

The boy came to the beach, halted as though uncertain whether to take the path which no doubt led to the next village, finally stopped, still with his back turned, and only when he heard the chief-inspector's footsteps quite close by, did he swing round to face him.

He was not red but pale, his nostrils pinched. His chest was visibly heaving fast, his lips were parted, it seemed as though his heart-beats must be audible, like those of a bird held in the hand.

Maigret said nothing. For the moment he could think of nothing to say, and he, too, was out of breath.

Jean-Paul had turned away from him and was looking at the sea. They both stared in that direction, and the silence lasted a long time, as long as was needed for their hearts to return to a calm, regular rhythm.

Then Maigret walked a few steps and sat down on a stack of posts which smelt of fresh pinewood. He took off his hat, unashamedly mopped his forehead, and began, very slowly, to fill his pipe.

'You're a fast walker,' he muttered at last.

The boy, who was standing with his legs braced like a young cock, made no reply.

'Won't you come and sit by me?'

'I don't want to sit down.'

'Are you angry?'

Jean-Paul threw him a quick glance and asked:

'Why?'

'I wanted to talk to you without your mother being present. At your home it can't be done. When I saw you over the cemetery wall, I thought that was my chance.'

So as not to startle the child, he paused for a long time between sentences.

'What were you looking at?'

'The people.'

'You couldn't have been watching them all at the same time. I'm sure you were watching one particular person. Am I right?'

Jean-Paul neither admitted this nor denied it.

'Do you usually go to church?'

'No.'

'Why not?'

'Because my father and mother don't go.'

Conversation would have been easier with a grown-up. It was so long since Maigret's childhood. He had no son or daughter of his own. But he had to try to see things from this boy's standpoint.

'Did you tell your mother you were going out this morning?'

'No.'

'You didn't want her to know?'

'She'd have stopped me.'

'So you waited till she was upstairs, so as to slip out quietly? And you went round by the back lanes?'

'I wanted to see.'

'What?'

It wasn't the crowd, nor the coffin being lowered into the grave. Maigret felt certain of that.

He remembered the surplice puffed out by the wind, and the cross Marcel had been carrying; he recalled the time when, hardly seven years old, he himself had yearned to be a choirboy. He had had to wait two years. Then it had been his turn to carry the silver cross and trot towards the cemetery, with a rustic hearse following behind.

'You wanted to see Marcel?'

He saw the boy give a start, the astonishment of a child on suddenly realizing that a grown-up is capable of guessing his thoughts.

'Why aren't you friends with Marcel?'

'I'm not friends with anyone.'

'Is there no one you like?'

'I'm the schoolmaster's son, I told you that already.'

'You'd rather be the ironmonger's son, or the mayor's, or the son of one of the local farmers?'

'I didn't say that.'

It was important not to frighten him, for he would have been capable of taking to his heels again. Yet it was not only fear of being caught up by Maigret that kept him where he was. He could move faster than the chief-inspector. Could it be that now they were face to face he felt a kind of relief? Could it be that at the bottom of his heart he had a secret longing to talk to somebody?

'Won't you sit down now?'

'I'd rather stand.'

'Are you very sorry your father's in prison?'

Instead of replying at once in the negative, he said nothing.

'You aren't sorry?'

Maigret was feeling like a stalker, creeping forward only with infinite caution. He must not go too quickly. The slightest word would be enough to startle the child, and then there would be nothing to be got out of him.

'Does it make you unhappy to be different from the others?'

'Why am I different from the others? Who said I was?'

'Suppose I had a little boy and he went to school, and played in the street near our home. The other boys would say,

' "His father's the chief-inspector!"

'And because of that, they wouldn't treat him quite like one of themselves. You understand?

'Well, your father is the schoolmaster.'

The little boy looked at him again, longer and more intently than before.

'Would you have liked to be in the choir?'

He could feel he was on the wrong track. It was hard to say how he knew it. Some of the things he had said caused an almost imperceptible reaction. Others seemed to make Jean-Paul close up in himself.

'Marcel has friends?'

'Yes.'

'When they're together, they talk in whispers? They tell one another secrets, begin to laugh when they look at the rest of you?'

This was all coming back to him from so long ago that it astonished him. Never before, he thought, had he recalled such vivid memories of his own childhood; he could even smell the scent of the lilacs that flowered in the school play-ground in spring-time.

'Have you tried to be friends with them?'

'No.'

'Why not?'

'No reason.'

You thought they wouldn't want you?'

'Why are you asking me all these questions?'

'Because your father's in prison. He didn't shoot Léonie Birard.'

He was staring hard at the boy, who did not blink.

'You know quite well he didn't. So someone else must have done it. Would you like your father to be found guilty?'

'No.'

There had been an almost imperceptible hesitation, and Maigret decided to let this point drop. It had occurred to him already, sitting in his corner the evening before, that Jean-Paul might feel some concealed resentment against his father and mother for being different from other people.

Not only because his father was the schoolmaster. They didn't go to church. They didn't dress him the same way as the other boys. Their house wasn't like the other houses either, nor was their way of life. His mother never laughed, she glided about like a shadow, humble and contrite. She had done something very wrong, and a woman had shot at her, to punish her.

The woman hadn't been sent to prison, which proved that she must have been right.

But perhaps Jean-Paul was fond of them all the same. Whether he liked it or not, he belonged to their clan, their race.

It was difficult to express all this. There were shades of meaning that vanished when one tried to put them into words.

'Suppose you knew something that would get your father out of prison...'

He himself didn't know what he was making for, and was surprised when Jean-Paul suddenly raised his head, stared at him with a mixture of terror and admiration. The boy opened his mouth, was about to say something, but bit it back, clenching his fists in the effort to restrain himself.

'Look, I'm only trying to understand. I don't know your father very well, but I feel sure he's not a man to tell lies. He says he didn't set foot in the tool-shed on Tuesday morning, and I believe him.'

The boy, still on the defensive, continued to watch him closely.

'On the other hand, Marcel Sellier seems like a good boy. When he does tell a lie, he goes to confession at once, so as not to remain in a state of sin. He has no reason to make trouble for your father. He's never unfair to him, in fact always puts him at the top of the class when you're the one who should be there.

'But Marcel says he saw your father coming out of the shed.'

It was like a bubble bursting suddenly at the surface of a pool. Jean-Paul, hanging his head, without looking at Maigret, declared:

'He's telling a lie.'

'You're quite sure of that, aren't you? It isn't just your own impression. You aren't saying it out of jealousy.'

'I'm not jealous of Marcel.'

'Why didn't you say so before?'

'What?'

'That Marcel was telling a lie.'

'Because!'

'You're quite certain he didn't see your father?'

'Yes.'

'What makes you so certain?'

Maigret had expected tears, perhaps even screams, but Jean-Paul's eyes, behind his spectacles, were dry. Only, his body had relaxed. There was nothing aggressive in his attitude now. He was not even on the defensive any longer.

The only visible sign of his surrender was that, feeling unsteady on his feet, he now sat down, at a little distance from the chief-inspector.

'I saw him.'

'Who did you see?'

'Marcel.'

'Where? When?'

'In class, standing by the window.'

'Tell me exactly what happened.'

'Nothing happened. Monsieur Piedbœuf came to fetch Father. They went together to the *mairie* office.'

'You saw them go?'

'Yes. I could see them from where I sat. They went in at the front door, and all the other boys began to fool about, as usual.'

'You stayed at your desk?'

'Yes.'

'Don't you ever fool about?'

'No.'

'Where was Marcel?'

'Standing by the first window on the left, the one that looks on to the playground and the gardens.'

'What was he doing?'

'Nothing. He was just looking out.'

'Doesn't he fool around either?'

'Not often.

'Sometimes?'

'When Joseph's there.'

'The butcher's son?'

'Yes.'

'You were sitting at your desk. Marcel was standing at the left-hand window. Your father and Monsieur Piedbœuf were in the office. That's right, is it?'

'Yes.'

'Were the windows open?'

'They were shut.'

'You could hear the noise of the forge all the same?'

'I think so. I'm almost certain.'

'What happened?'

'Marcel left the window and walked across the room.'

'Where was he going?'

'To one of the two windows on the right.'

'The one that overlooks the back of Madame Birard's house?'

'Yes.'

'Your father was still at the *mairie* then?'

'Yes.'

'Marcel didn't say anything?'

'No. He looked out of the window.'

'You don't know what he was looking at?'

'From where I was sitting I couldn't see.'

'Do you often watch Marcel?'

He admitted awkwardly:

'Yes.'

This time, Maigret did not ask him why. The two boys were both good at their lessons, but because Jean-Paul was the schoolmaster's son, Marcel was put at the head of the class. Marcel was a choirboy and wore a surplice on Sundays. Marcel had friends, he had Joseph, the butcher's son, with whom he talked in whispers at break and to whose house he went to play when school was over.

'You saw your father come out of the *mairie* after that?'

'He walked over to our house, and went in for a cup of coffee.'

'Was the kitchen window open?'

'No. I know he had a cup of coffee. He always does.'

'Was your mother downstairs?'

'Upstairs in my room. I could see her through the open window.'

'After that your father didn't go into the tool-shed?'

'No. He came across the playground, back to the classroom.'

'Marcel was still standing at the window, the one on the right?'

'Yes.'

'Why didn't you say so at once?'

'When?'

Maigret paused for a moment to sort out his recollections.

'Wait a minute. Léonie Birard's body was found at the beginning of the afternoon. They didn't question you children at once?'

'They didn't question us at all that day. We didn't know exactly what had happened. We just noticed people coming and going. Then we saw the *gendarmes*.'

In fact, on Tuesday no one had openly accused the schoolmaster. Marcel Sellier had said nothing, either to his parents or to anyone else. So Jean-Paul had had no reason to contradict him and no chance of doing so.

'Were you there next day, when they questioned Marcel?'

'No. They sent for us one by one, in the office.'

'And when he came back on Thursday morning? When did you first hear that he was maintaining he had seen your father?'

'I can't remember now.'

'Did your parents talk about Léonie Birard on Tuesday evening?'

'Not till I was in bed. I heard part of what they were saying. Mother said it was her fault. Father said no, it was only rumours, people would soon realize he'd had nothing to do with it.'

'Why didn't you protest when you discovered that Marcel was accusing him?'

'Nobody would have believed me.'

Again Maigret seemed to catch a flicker, a mere nothing, something too subtle to be put into words. The little boy had not been pleased when his father was accused. He had probably been rather ashamed to think that he was in prison. But hadn't he been rather cowardly? Hadn't he been tempted, however slightly, without admitting it even to himself, to desert his parents' cause?

He already bore them a grudge for not being like other people. Now they were even less like other people, and the village, instead of simply cold-shouldering them, had turned against them.

Jean-Paul envied Marcel.

Was he to accuse him in his turn?

When one came to think of it, he had not been carried away by bad feelings. It hadn't been a question of cowardice, at any rate not only of cowardice.

Couldn't it even be said to be a kind of loyalty to the others?

He had had a chance of contradicting Marcel, showing him up as a liar. It would have been easy. Had it seemed to him to be too easy, too cheap a triumph?

Besides, it was a fact that people wouldn't have believed him. Who indeed in the village would have believed him, if he had gone to them and said:

'Sellier is a liar. My father didn't come out of the tool-shed. I saw him go into our house, come out again, cross the playground. And at that time Marcel was standing at the opposite window, where he couldn't see him.'

'You haven't told this to your mother?'

'No.'

'Is she crying a lot?'

'She doesn't cry.'

That was even worse. Maigret could imagine the atmosphere in the house during the last few days.

'Why did you come out this morning?'

'To see.'

'To see Marcel?'

'Perhaps.'

Perhaps also, without realizing it, from an urge to share, even at a distance, in the village life? He must surely feel smothered in that little house at the far end of the yard, where his mother was afraid to open the windows.

'Are you going to tell the lieutenant?'

'I must have a word with Marcel first.'

'Will you tell him you heard about it from me?'

'Would you rather he didn't know that?'

'Yes.'

It looked as though he hadn't entirely given up hope of one day being admitted to the alluring company of Marcel, Joseph and the rest.

'I think he'll tell me the truth without my needing to bring you into it. Some of the others must have seen which window he was standing by.'

'They were fooling about.'

'All of them?'

'All except one of the girls, Louise Boncœur.'

'How old is she?'

'Fifteen.'

'Doesn't she fool about with the rest of them?'

'No.'

'You think she was watching Marcel?'

For the first time the boy's face was red, especially his ears.

'She watches him all the time,' he mumbled.

Was it because she was in love with Marcel that she hadn't contradicted him, or simply because she hadn't distinguished between one window and another? Marcel had said he was standing by the window. The other children probably hadn't thought twice about which one it had been.

'It's time we went back to the village.'

'I'd rather not go back with you.'

'Would you like to go ahead?'

'Yes. You're sure you won't say anything to Marcel?'

Maigret nodded, and the boy hesitated, touched his cap, set out in the direction of the fields, soon breaking from a walk into a run.

The chief-inspector, who was at last by the sea, forgot to look at it, was gazing after the small figure departing along the lane.

Then he set out in his turn, stopped to fill his pipe, blew his nose, muttered something unintelligible, and anyone seeing him advancing slowly along the road would doubtless have wondered why he shook his head every now and then.

When he went past the cemetery the grave-diggers had finished heaping yellowish earth on Léonie Birard's coffin; her tomb could be recognized from a long way off, because of the bunches of flowers and fresh wreaths.

CHAPTER SEVEN

The women had gone home and, except for a few who came from distant farms, had probably taken off their black dresses and best shoes by this time. The men were still there, as though this were fair-day, and were overflowing from Louis' inn on to the pavement and into the yard, where they stood, putting down their bottles on the windowsills or on an old iron table that had been left outside all winter.

The pitch of their voices, their laughter, their slow, fuddled gestures made it clear that they had drunk a lot, and one, whose face Maigret did not see, was relieving himself behind the hedge.

Thérèse, busy as she was, had found time to pass him a *chopine* and a glass. He had gone only a few paces into the room, and could hear snatches of several conversations at once; he had had a glimpse of the doctor in the kitchen, but there were so many people in the way that he could not join him for the moment.

'I'd never have thought we'd have had the burying of her,' one old man was saying, shaking his head.

There were three of them, all much of an age. All three were certainly over seventy-five, and behind them, as they stood in a corner, against the white wall, was a copy of the law on establishments for the sale of alcoholic beverages and on public intoxication. They held themselves more stiffly than usual, because of their black Sunday suits and starched shirts, and this lent them a certain solemnity.

It was strange to see that though their faces were wrinkled with deep furrows, their eyes, when they looked at one another, had an innocent, childish expression. Each of them had a glass in his hand. The tallest of the three, who had a magnificent crop of white hair and a silky moustache, was swaying slightly, and whenever he was disposed to speak he laid a finger on the shoulder of one of his companions.

Why did Maigret suddenly imagine them in the school playground? They were just like schoolboys in their laughter and in the glances they exchanged. They had been to school together. Later in life they had pulled the same girls into ditches and had seen one another married, attended the funerals of their respective parents, their children's weddings and the christenings of their grand-children.

'She might almost have been my sister; my father used to tell me he didn't know how often he'd pushed her mother down under the haystack. It seems she was a hot bitch and her husband was a cuckold from start to finish.'

Didn't that go far to explain the village? Behind Maigret, in another group, someone was saying:

'When he sold me that cow, I said to him:

' "Look here, Victor, I know you're a thief. But don't forget we did our military service together at Montpellier, and there was that evening..." '

Louis hadn't had time to change, he had only taken off his jacket. Maigret was edging slowly forward, remembering that the doctor had invited him to lunch at his house that day. Could Bresselles have forgotten about it?

He had a glass in his hand, like everyone else, but he had not lost his head, and was trying to quieten Marcellin, the butcher, who was the most drunk of them all and seemed very excited. It was difficult, from a distance, to make out exactly what was going on. Marcellin appeared to be angry with somebody, was trying to thrust the little doctor aside and push his way into the front room.

'I tell you I'm going to tell him!' the chief-inspector heard him say.

'Be quiet, Marcellin. You're drunk.'

'I've a right to be drunk, haven't I?'

'What did I tell you the last time you came to me for a check-up?'

'Be damned to what you told me!'

'If you go on like this, the next funeral will be yours.'

'I won't be spied on. I'm a free man.'

Wine did not suit him. He was white-faced, with an unhealthy flush on his cheekbones and eyelids. He was losing control of his movements. His voice was becoming thick.

'You hear that, Doc? I never could stand spies. And what's he doing here, except...'

It was Maigret he was looking at, from a distance, struggling to rush at him and vent his feelings. Two or three of the others were watching him and laughing. Someone held out a glass, which the doctor intercepted, emptying its contents on the ground.

'Don't you see he's had a skinful, Firmin?'

So far there had been no quarrelling, no scuffle. Indeed, they all knew one another too well to start fighting, and everyone knew exactly who was strongest among them.

Maigret went no closer; to avoid irritating the butcher he pretended not to notice what was going on. But he kept an eye on the group, and witnessed a little scene which distinctly surprised him.

The tall figure of Théo, the deputy-mayor, came lounging up, with the usual glint of mockery in his eyes, and joined the others; he was brandishing a glass which contained not wine but *pernod*, a strong dose, to judge by the colour.

He made some remark to the doctor in an undertone and passed the glass to the butcher, laying a hand on his shoulder. He said something to him too, and Marcellin at first seemed inclined to struggle, to push him away.

Finally he grabbed the glass, swallowed its contents at one gulp, and almost at once his eyes glazed over, losing all expression. He made one more attempt to point a threatening finger at the chief-inspector, but his arm had grown too heavy to lift.

Whereupon, as though he had just felled him with a blow, Théo pushed him towards and up the stairs; after the first few steps he had to hoist him on to his shoulder.

'You haven't forgotten my invitation?'

The doctor, who had walked across to Maigret, gave a sigh of relief as he remarked, in almost the same words as the old man in the corner:

'They've put her underground! Shall we go now?'

They both slipped through the crowd and out onto the pavement, where they strolled a few steps.

'Before three months are up it'll be Marcellin's turn. I'm telling him regularly:

' "Marcellin, if you don't stop drinking you won't last long!"

'He's reached a stage where he eats practically nothing.'

'He's a sick man?'

'They're all sick, in his family. He's a pathetic case.'

'Théo's putting him to bed upstairs?'

'He had to be got rid of somehow.'

He opened the door. There was a good smell of cooking in the house.

'Will you have an *apéritif*?'

'Thank you, I'd rather not.'

The smell of wine had been so strong at Louis' inn that one could have got drunk just by breathing it in.

'Did you see the funeral?'

'From a distance.'

'I looked for you as I left the cemetery, but I didn't see you. Is lunch ready, Armande?'

'In five minutes.'

Only two places were laid. The doctor's sister, just like a priest's housekeeper, preferred not to sit down at table. She no doubt took her meals standing up in the kitchen, between two courses.

'Sit down. What do you think about it?'

'About what?'

'About nothing. About everything. She had a terrific funeral!'

Maigret grunted: 'The schoolmaster's still in prison.'

'Somebody had to go there.'

'I'd like to ask you a question, Doctor. Do you think that among all that crowd at the funeral there were many people who believed that Gastin killed Léonie Birard?'

'There must have been a few. Some people will believe anything.'

'And what about the rest?'

At first the doctor did not see the point of the question. Maigret explained:

'Let's suppose that one person in ten believes that Gastin fired that shot.'

'That's about the proportion.'

'Then the other nine-tenths have their own idea.'

'Undoubtedly.'

'Whom do they suspect?'

'That depends. In my opinion each of them suspects, more or less sincerely, the person he himself would prefer to be found guilty.'

'And nobody says anything about it?'

'Among themselves, I expect they do.'

'Have you heard any such suspicions expressed?'

The doctor looked at him with something of Théo's irony.

'They don't say that kind of thing to me.'

'But although they know or believe that the schoolmaster is innocent, it doesn't worry them that he's in prison.'

'It assuredly doesn't worry them. Gastin isn't a local man. They consider that if the constabulary lieutenant and the examining magistrate have thought fit to arrest him, that's their affair. That's what those two are paid for.'

'Would they let him be condemned?'

'Without batting an eyelid. Of course, if it had been one of their own folk, it'd be a different story. Are you beginning to understand? If there has to be a guilty party, they'd rather it was an outsider.'

'Do they think the Sellier boy is telling the truth?'

'Marcel's a good boy.'

'He's told a lie.'

'Perhaps so.'

'I wonder why.'

'He may have thought his father would be accused.

Don't forget that his mother is old Léonie's niece and will get all she's left.'

'I thought the old post-woman had always said her niece wouldn't get a penny.'

The doctor looked slighdy embarrassed. His sister brought in the hors-d'œuvre.

'Did you go to the funeral?' Maigret asked her.

'Armande never goes to funerals.'

They began to eat in silence. Maigret was the first to break it, by saying, as though to himself:

'It wasn't on Tuesday that Marcel Sellier saw Gastin coming out of the tool-shed, it was on Monday.'

'He's admitted that?'

'I haven't asked him yet, but I'm practically certain of it. On Monday, before school, Gastin worked in his garden. Going across the playground during the morning, he noticed a hoe lying around and went to put it away. On Tuesday evening, after the body had been found, Marcel said nothing, and it didn't occur to him to accuse his teacher then.

'The idea came to him later, or some conversation he overheard made him decide to do it.

'He didn't tell an outright lie. Women and children specialize in such half-lies. He didn't make anything up, he simply changed a real event to another day.'

'That's rather comic!'

'I'll bet he's trying now to convince himself that it really was on Tuesday that he saw the schoolteacher coming out of the shed. He can't manage it, of course, and he must have been to confession.'

'Why don't you ask the priest?'

'Because if he told me, he'd be indirectly betraying the secrets of the confessional. The priest won't do that. I was thinking of asking the neighbours, the people at the cooperative stores, for instance, whether they'd seen Marcel going into the church at a time when there was no service, but now I know he goes in from the courtyard.'

The mutton was done to a turn and the beans melted in the mouth. The doctor had produced a bottle of old wine. A dull humming sound could be heard from outside, the noise of people talking in the inn yard and on the square.

Did the doctor realize that Maigret was simply talking in order to try out his ideas on a listener? He was going round and round the same subject, lazily, never coming right to the point.

'Actually, I don't think it was to save his father from suspicion that Marcel told that lie.'

At that moment he had the impression that Bresselles knew more about the matter than he would admit.

'Really?'

'You see, I'm trying to look at things from a child's point of view. From the very begining I've had the impression that this is some children's business in which grown-ups have become mixed up just by accident.'

Looking the doctor straight in the face he added placidly, weightily:

'And I'm more and more convinced that other people know it too.'

'In that case perhaps you'll be able to persuade them to talk?'

'Perhaps. It's difficult, isn't it?'

'Very difficult.'

Bresselles was laughing at him, just as the deputy-mayor did, again.

'I had a long talk with the little Gastin boy this morning.'

'You went to their house?'

'No. I saw him watching the funeral, over the cemetery wall, and I followed him down to the sea-shore.'

'Why did he go down to the sea?'

'He was running away from me. At the same time he wanted me to catch up with him.'

'What did he tell you?'

'That Marcel Sellier was standing at the right-hand window, not the left. Marcel might, at a pinch, have seen Léonie Birard fall when the bullet hit her in the eye, but he couldn't possibly have seen the schoolmaster coming out of the shed.'

'What conclusion do you draw from that?'

'That it was in order to protect somebody that little Sellier decided to tell his lie. Not at once. He took his time.

The idea probably didn't enter his head straight away.'

'Why did he choose the schoolmaster?'

'For one thing because he was the most likely person. And for another because it just so happened that he'd seen him the day before, almost at the same time, coming out of the shed. And perhaps because of Jean-Paul, too.'

'You think he hates him?'

'I'm not saying anything positive, Doctor. I'm simply groping in the dark. I've questioned both boys. This morning I was watching some old men who were children themselves once, in this very village. If the village people are so liable to be hostile to strangers, isn't it because, without realizing it, they're envious of them! They themselves spend the whole of their lives at Saint-André, except for a trip to La Rochelle now and then, with only an occasional wedding or funeral by way of distraction.'

'I see what you're getting at.'

'The schoolmaster comes from Paris. In their eyes, he's an educated man who pokes into their little affairs and takes upon himself to give them advice. Among the children, the schoolmaster's boy has much the same status.'

'So Marcel told his lie because he hates Jean-Paul?'

'Partly because he envies him. The funny thing is that Jean-Paul, on his side, envies Marcel and his friends. He feels lonely, different from the others, rejected by them.'

'All the same, somebody shot the old Birard woman, and it can't have been either of the boys.'

'That's true.'

A home-made apple-tart was brought in, and the smell of coffee came in from the kitchen.

'I feel more and more convinced that Théo knows the truth.'

'Because he was in his garden?'

'Because of that and for other reasons. Last night, Doctor, you informed me cheerfully that they were all scoundrels.'

'I was joking.'

'Only half-joking, isn't that it? They all cheat, to some extent, they all go in for what you would call little mean tricks. You're an outspoken man. You haul them over the coals now and then. But you'd never actually give them away. Or am I wrong?'

'You say the *curé* would refuse to answer any questions you might put to him about Marcel, and I think you're right. Well, I'm their doctor. It's the same thing, in a way. Doesn't it strike you, Inspector, that this lunch is beginning to be rather like an interrogation? What will you have with your coffee? Brandy or *calvados*?'

'*Calvados.*'

Bresselles got up to fetch the bottle from an antique sideboard, and filled the glasses, still gay and playful, but his eyes rather more serious now.

'Your good health.'

'I'd like to talk to you about the accident,' said Maigret, almost timidly.

'What accident?'

It was only to gain time for thought that the doctor asked this question, for accidents in the village were few and far between.

'The motor-bicycle accident.'

'You've heard about that?'

'All I've heard is that Marcellin's son was knocked down by a motor-bike. When did it happen?'

'One Saturday, just over a month ago.'

'Near old mother Birard's house?'

'Not far away. A hundred yards, perhaps.'

'In the evening?'

'Not long before dinner-time. It was dark. The two boys...'

'What boys?'

'Joseph, Marcellin's lad, and Marcel.'

'Were they by themselves?'

'Yes. They were going home. A motor-bike came up from the direction of the beach. Nobody knows exactly how it happened.'

'Who was on the bike?'

'Hervé Jusseau, a man of about thirty, who owns some mussel-beds, and got married last year.'

'Was he drunk?'

'He doesn't drink. He was brought up by his aunts, who are very strict and who still live in his house.'

'Was his headlamp lit?'

'Yes, that was established by the inquiry. The boys must have been playing about. Joseph tried to cross the road, and got knocked down.'

'Was his leg broken?'

'In two places.'

'Will he be lame?'

'No. In a week or two he'll be as good as new.'

'He can't walk yet?'

'No.'

'Will Marcellin get anything out of the accident?'

'The insurance will pay a fair amount, because Jusseau admitted that it was probably his fault.'

'Do you think it was?'

The doctor was obviously ill at ease, and took refuge in a burst of laughter.

'I'm beginning to understand what you chaps at Police Headquarters mean by "third degree" questioning. I'd rather come clean. That's what you call it, isn't it?'

He refilled the glasses.

'Marcellin's a pathetic chap. Everyone knows he won't last much longer. He can't be blamed for drinking, because he's been unlucky all his life. There's always been illness somewhere in his family, and everything he's undertaken has gone wrong. Three years ago he rented some pasture-land to fatten bullocks, and there was such a drought that he lost every penny. He can hardly make both ends meet. His van is more often broken down by the roadside than on its way delivering meat.'

'So Jusseau, who, being insured, has nothing to lose, took the blame on himself?'

'That's about it.'

'Everyone knows this?'

'Pretty well everyone. An insurance company is a vague, far-away set-up, like the government, and people feel quite justified in taking money off it.'

'You made out the certificates?'

'Of course.'

'And worded them in such a way that Marcellin would get the highest possible sum?'

'Let's say I stressed the possibility of complications.'

'Were there any complications?'

'There might have been. As often as not, when a cow dies of some sudden illness, the vet certifies that it was an accident.'

It was Maigret's turn to laugh.

'Unless I'm mistaken, Marcellin's boy might have been up and about for the last week or two.'

'For the last week.'

'By keeping the plaster on his leg, you're enabling his father to demand more money from the insurance?'

'Even the doctor has to be a bit of a scoundrel, you see. If I refused that kind of thing, I'd have been gone from here long ago. And it's because the schoolmaster won't oblige with certificates, that he's in prison today. If he'd been more adaptable, if he hadn't been constandy scolding Théo for being too generous with Government money, they might have ended by adopting him.'

'In spite of what happened to his wife?'

'All the men here are cuckolds themselves.'

'So Marcel Sellier was the only witness of the accident?'

'I told you it was after dark. There was nobody else on the road.'

'Somebody might have seen them from a window.'

'You're thinking of old Léonie?'

'Well, I suppose she wasn't *always* in her kitchen; she must have gone into the front room now and then.'

'There was no mention of her during the inquiry. She didn't come forward.'

The doctor scratched his head, perfectly serious now.

'I have the impression you're beginning to see your way. Not that I can follow you yet.'

'Are you sure of that?'

'Of what?'

'Why did Marcellin try to throw himself on me this morning?'

'He was drunk.'

'Why pick on me particularly?'

'You were the only stranger in the inn. When he's tight he gets persecution mania. So he began to imagine you'd come here simply to spy on him...'

'You were trying hard to calm him down.'

'Would you have preferred a fight?'

'Théo finished him off by making him drink a double or triple *pernod*, and carted him upstairs. It's the first time I've seen the deputy-mayor do a good turn.'

'Marcellin's his cousin.'

'I'd rather he'd been allowed to come out with what he wanted to say to me.'

The others had obviously wanted to stop him talking, they'd whisked him away, so to speak, and at present he must be sleeping off his drink in one of the first-floor bedrooms.

'I must getting back to my surgery,' said Bresselles. 'There'll be at least a dozen people in the waiting-room by now.'

The consulting surgery was a low-roofed, two-roomed building in the yard. People could be seen sitting in a row against the wall; among them a child with a bandaged head and an old man with crutches.

'I think you'll end by getting somewhere!' sighed the little doctor, referring, of course, not to Maigret's career, but to the present investigation.

His attitude now betokened some respect, but a certain embarrassment as well.

'You'd rather I didn't find out anything at all?'

'I'm wondering. It might have been better if you hadn't come.'

'That depends on how it's all going to end. Have you no idea about that?'

'I know about as much as you do on the subject.'

'And you'd have left Gastin in prison?'

'They can't keep him there for long, in any case.'

Bresselles wasn't a local man. He was a townsman like the schoolmaster. But he had been living with the village for over twenty years, and couldn't help feeling himself a part of it.

'Come and see me whenever you like. Please believe I do

what I can. It's just that I'd rather live here and spend most of my day on the road, than be shut up in a surgery in a town or in some suburb or other.'

'Thank you for the lunch.'

'Are you going to question young Marcel again?'

'I haven't decided yet.'

'If you want him to talk, you'd better see him when his father isn't there.'

'Is he afraid of his father?'

'I don't think it's that. It's more that he admires him. If he's told a lie he must be in a state of terror.'

When Maigret emerged from the house, there were only a few people clustered at Louis' and on the square. Théo was sitting in a corner, playing cards, as on any other day, with the postman, the blacksmith and a farmer. His eyes met Maigret's, and though they were still mocking they held a dawning respect as well.

'Is Marcellin still upstairs?' the chief-inspector asked Thérèse.

'Snoring! He's messed up the whole room. He can't carry drink any longer. The same thing happens every time.'

'Nobody been asking for me?'

'The lieutenant came past just now. He didn't come in, he only gave a glance round as though looking for somebody, it may have been you. Will you have something to drink?'

'No, thank you.'

The very smell of wine was making him feel sick. He strolled over to the *mairie*. One of the gendarmes was talking to Lieutenant Daniélou.

'Were you wanting to see me?'

'Not specially. I went across the square a little time ago and took a look in case you were at the inn.'

'Nothing fresh?'

'It may be of no importance. Nouli, here, has found a seventh rifle.'

'A .22?'

'Yes. Here it is. It's the same type as the others.'

'Where was it?'

'In the stable behind the butcher's house.'

'Hidden?'

It was the gendarme himself who replied:

'I was still hunting for the cartridge-case, with one of the other men. We were going through the gardens. I noticed that one of the stable doors was open, and there were bloodstains all over the place. Then I saw the rifle in a corner.

'Did you question the butcher's wife?'

'Yes. She said that when Sellier went round with his drum to announce that all rifles must be taken to the *mairie*, she forgot all about her little boy's gun, because he was in bed. He had an accident about a month ago, and...'

'I know.'

Maigret stood holding the weapon, puffing at his pipe. Finally he put down the rifle, propping it in a different corner from the others.

'Will you come with me for a moment, Lieutenant?'

They went across the courtyard and opened the door of the schoolroom, which smelt of ink and chalk.

'Now I don't know yet where this is going to lead us. On Tuesday morning, when the schoolmaster left this room with Piedbœuf, the farmer, Marcel Sellier came over to this window.'

'That's what he told us.'

'To the right of that lime-tree, one can see the tool-shed. One can also see certain windows, including those on the first floor of the butcher's house.'

The lieutenant was listening, with a slight frown.

'The boy didn't remain here long. Before the schoolmaster left the office, he went to the other side of the classroom.'

Maigret was doing the same, walking past the blackboard and the teacher's desk to the window right opposite the first one.

'From here, as you can see for yourself, there's a view of Léonie Birard's house. If, as the investigation seems to have established, she was standing at her window when she was shot, Marcel may have seen her fall.'

'You think he had some reason for crossing from one

window to the other? He might have seen something, and...'

'Not necessarily.'

'Why did he tell a lie?'

Maigret preferred not to answer this.

'You have suspicions?'

'I think so.'

'What are you going to do?'

'What has to be done,' replied Maigret without enthusiasm.

He sighed, emptied his pipe on the greyish floorboards, looked down at the ashes with an air of embarrassment and added, as though regretfully:

'It isn't going to be pleasant.'

From a first-floor window in the opposite house, Jean-Paul was watching them across the courtyard.

CHAPTER EIGHT

Before he left the classroom, Maigret noticed another figure, at a window, an open one this time, in a more distant house, beyond the gardens. Someone was sitting on the windowsill, with his back turned, but from the shape of the head and the plump body, he recognized Marcel Sellier.

'That's the butcher's house, I suppose?'

The lieutenant followed the direction of his glance.

'Yes... Joseph, the son, and Marcel are great friends.'

The boy at the window turned round and looked down at a woman who was hanging out washing in a garden. Automatically, his eyes swept round in a half-circle just as Maigret and the lieutenant were coming out of the school and facing his way.

In spite of the distance it was clear, from his movements, that he was saying something to somebody in the room; then he slid off the windowsill and disappeared.

Daniélou turned to the chief-inspector and said quietly, pensively:

'Good luck!'

'Are you going back to La Rochelle?'

'Would you rather I waited for you?'

'If you did I might perhaps be able to take the evening train.'

He had not more than a hundred and fifty yards to go. He covered the distance at a swinging stride. The butcher's was a low, squat house. There was no proper shop. The left-hand ground-floor room had been fitted up for the purpose with a quaint-looking counter, a pair of scales, an old-fashioned refrigerator and a table on which the meat was cut up.

The front door opened into a passage at the far end of which, to the left of the stairs, one saw through to the backyard.

Before knocking, Maigret had gone past the right-hand window, the kitchen window, which was open; inside, at a round table, sat three women, one of whom was old and wore a white cap; they were eating slices of tart. One of them must be Marcellin's wife and the others her mother and sister, who lived in the neighbouring village and had come over for the funeral.

They had seen him go by. The windows were so small that for a moment his bulk had blocked this one. They listened while he paused at the open door, looked for a bell and, not finding one, took two steps forward, purposely making a noise.

The butcher's wife got up, half-opened the kitchen door, began by asking:

'What is it?'

Then, recognizing him, probably from having seen him about the village, she went on:

'You're the policeman from Paris, aren't you?'

If she had been to the funeral, she had already changed her clothes. She could not be very old, but she was round-shouldered, hollow-cheeked, with feverish eyes. Avoiding his eye, she added:

'My husband's out. I don't know when he'll be back. Did you want to see him?'

She did not ask him into the kitchen, where the other two women sat silent.

'I'd like a word with your little boy.'

She was frightened, but that didn't mean anything; she was the kind of woman who would always be frightened, always expecting some disaster.

'He's in bed.'

'I know.'

'He's been up there for over a month.'

'You don't mind if I go up?'

What could she do? She let him pass without daring to protest, as she crumpled a corner of her apron with tense fingers. He had only gone up four or five steps when he saw Marcel coming down towards him, and it was he, Maigret, who stood back against the wall.

'Excuse me...' stammered the boy, avoiding Maigret's eye in his turn.

He was in a hurry to get outside, must have expected Maigret to stop him or call him back, but the chief-inspector did neither and continued on his way upstairs.

'The door on the right,' said the mother when he reached the landing.

He knocked. A child's voice said:

'Come in.'

The mother was still standing below, looking up at him while he opened the door and closed it behind him.

'Don't trouble to move.'

Joseph had made as if to get up from the bed where he was sitting with several pillows at his back and one leg in plaster to well above the knee.

'I passed your friend on the stairs.'

'I know.'

'Why didn't he wait for me?'

The room was low-ceilinged, and Maigret's head nearly came up to the central rafter. It was a small room. The bed took up the greater part of it. It was untidy, scattered with illustrated magazines and pieces of wood hacked with a penknife.

'Are you bored?'

There was in fact a chair, but it was heaped with a variety of objects, a jacket, a catapult, two or three books, and some more bits of wood.

'You can take off all that stuff,' said the boy.

Jean-Paul Gastin took after his father and mother. Marcel took after his father.

Joseph resembled neither the butcher nor his wife. He was undoubtedly the handsomest of the three boys, and seemed to be the healthiest and most well-balanced.

Maigret sat down on the windowsill, with his back to the view of yards and gardens, in the place where Marcel had been sitting a few minutes ago, and he seemed to be in no hurry to talk. This was not because he wanted to puzzle the other person present, as sometimes happened at the Quai des Orfèvres, but because he didn't know where to begin.

Joseph opened the conversation by inquiring:

'Where's my father?'

'At Louis'.'

The boy hesitated, then asked:

'How is he?'

Why try to conceal what he must know perfectly well?

'Théo's put him to bed.'

He seemed to be relieved rather than worried by this.

'Mother's downstairs with my grandmother?'

'Yes.'

The sun, now low although the sky was still bright, was gently warming Maigret's back, and the song of birds came up from the gardens; some unseen child was blowing a tin trumpet.

'Wouldn't you like me to take off that plaster?'

It seemed almost as though Joseph was expecting this, he understood the hint. He was not uneasy, like his mother. He didn't seem scared. He was gazing at the heavy figure of his visitor and at his apparently inscrutable face, and considering what line to take.

'You know about that?'

'Yes.'

'Did the doctor tell you?'

'I'd already guessed. What were you up to, you and Marcel, when the motor-bike knocked you down?'

Joseph showed genuine relief.

'You haven't found the horse-shoe?' he asked.

And these words brought a picture into Maigret's mind. He had seen a horse-shoe somewhere. It was while he'd been going round Léonie Birard's house. There had been a rusty horse-shoe lying on the floor, in the corner to the right of the window, not far from the chalk marks which showed where the body had been found.

He had noticed it at the time. He had been on the point of asking about it. Then, as he straightened up, he had caught sight of a nail and reflected that the horse-shoe had probably been hung on that. Many country people will pick up a horse-shoe on the road and keep it, for luck.

Daniélou and his men, who had searched the house before him, must have thought the same.

'Yes, there was a horse-shoe in Léonie Birard's house,' he replied.

'It was me that found it, the evening I had the accident. I was coming along the sea lane with Marcel when I stumbled over it. It was in the dark. I picked it up. We got to the old woman's house and I was carrying the horse-shoe. The window that looks onto the road was open. We crept close up to it without making a noise.'

'Was the postmistress in the front room?'

'In the kitchen. The door was half-open.'

He couldn't prevent himself from grinning.

'First of all I thought of throwing the horse-shoe into the house, to frighten her.'

'Just as you used to throw in dead cats and other filth?'

'I wasn't the only one who did that.'

'You changed your mind?'

'Yes. I thought it would be more fun to put it in her bed. I climbed over the windowsill, without any noise, and went two or three steps inside: then, by bad luck, I knocked into something, I don't know what. She heard. I dropped the horse-shoe and jumped out of the window.'

'Where was Marcel?'

'He was waiting for me, a bit further on. I began to run. I heard the old woman yelling threats out of her window, and that's when the motor-bike ran over me.'

'Why didn't you say so?'

'To begin with, they took me to the doctor, and it hurt a lot. They gave me some medicine to put me to sleep. When I woke up, Father was there, and he began at once to talk to me about the insurance. I understood that if I told the truth, they'd say it had been my own fault and the insurance wouldn't pay up, Father needs money.'

'Did Marcel come to see you?'

'Yes. I made him promise not to say anything either.'

'And since then he's been to see you every day?'

'Nearly every day. We're friends.'

'Isn't Jean-Paul friends with you?'

'He isn't friends with anybody.'

'Why not?'

'I don't know. He doesn't want to be, I suppose. He's like his mother. His mother never talks to the other women in the village.'

'Aren't you bored, staying up in this room all alone for a month?'

'Yes.'

'What do you do all day?'

'Nothing. I read. I carve little boats and people out of bits of wood.'

There were dozens scattered around him, some of them quite skilfully made.

'Don't you ever go to the window?'

'I oughtn't to.'

'For fear people may find out you can walk?'

He answered frankly:

'Yes.'

Then he asked:

'Are you going to tell the insurance people?'

'It's no business of mine.'

There was a silence, during which Maigret turned to look out at the backs of the houses opposite, and the school playground.

'I suppose it's mostly during playtime that you look out of the window?'

'Often.'

Just opposite on the far side of the little gardens, he could see Léonie Birard's windows.

'Did the postwoman ever notice you?'

'Yes.'

The boy's face clouded at this; he hesitated for a moment, but already knew he would have to tell.

'Even before, whenever she saw me, she used to pull faces.'

'Used she to put out her tongue at you?'

'Yes. After the accident she used to tease me by holding up the horse-shoe.'

'Why?'

'It must have been to make me understand that she might go and tell the whole story.'

'She didn't do so.'

'No.'

The ex-postmistress had behaved rather as though she were the same age as the little boys she used to curse, who made a set against her. She would shout, threaten, put out her tongue at them. She had been reminding Joseph, from a distance, that she could make trouble for him if she chose.

'Did she frighten you?'

'Yes. Father and Mother needed the money.'

'Do they know about the horse-shoe business?'

'Father does.'

'Did you tell him?'

'He guessed I'd done something I hadn't told him about, and he made me own up.'

'Was he cross with you?'

'He said I'd better keep quiet about it.'

'How many times did Léonie Birard show you the horseshoe through the window?'

'Twenty times, perhaps. She did it every time she saw me.'

Just as he had done in the morning with Jean-Paul, Maigret slowly lit his pipe; his manner was as reassuring as possible. He seemed to be listening absent-mindedly to some trivial story, and his relaxed attitude and innocent face might have led the boy to forget that he was not talking to one of his own school friends.

'What did Marcel come to tell you just now?'

'That if he was questioned again he'd have to own up.'

'Why? Is he scared?'

'He's been to confession. Besides, I think the funeral made him feel a bit funny.'

'He'll say he saw you at this window before he went across to the opposite window of the schoolroom?'

'How did you know that? You see! Everything goes

wrong, in this house. Other people do worse things and nothing happens to them. In our family it's the other way round.'

'What were you doing at the window?'

'I was looking out.'

'The old woman was showing you the horse-shoe?'

'Yes.'

'Tell me exactly what happened.'

'There's nothing else I can do, is there?'

'Not at the point we've reached.'

'I took my rifle.'

'Where was your rifle?'

'In that corner, by the cupboard.'

'Was it loaded?'

An almost imperceptible hesitation.

'Yes.'

'With long or short .22 cartridges?'

'Long ones.'

'Do you generally keep the rifle in your bedroom?'

'Often.'

'Have you ever shot at sparrows through the window, lately?'

He hesitated again, thinking as rapidly as possible, as though he could not afford to make the slightest slip.

'No. I don't think so.'

'You wanted to scare the old woman?'

'I suppose so. I'm not quite sure what I wanted. She was teasing me. I thought she'd end by telling everything to the insurance people, and then Father wouldn't be able to buy a new van.'

'That's what he's decided to do with the money?'

'Yes. He feels sure that if he had a good van and could make a longer round, he'd earn money.'

'Doesn't he earn any as it is?'

'Some months he makes a loss, and it's Grandma who...'

'She helps you?'

'When there's no other way. She makes a scene every time.'

'Did you fire the gun?'

He nodded, with a kind of apologetic smile.

'Did you aim it?'

'I was aiming at the window.'

'In other words, you meant to break a pane of glass?'

He nodded again, eagerly.

'Will they send me to prison?'

'Boys of your age aren't sent to prison.'

He seemed disappointed at this.

'Then what will they do?'

'The judge will lecture you.'

'And then?'

'He'll talk severely to your father. The final responsibility is his.'

'Why, when he didn't do anything?'

'Where was he when you fired?'

'I don't know.'

'Was he on his round?'

'I don't suppose so. He never goes off as early as that.'

'Was he in the shop?'

'Perhaps.'

'He didn't hear anything? Nor your mother?'

'No. They didn't say anything to me.'

'Don't they know it was you who fired the shot?'

'I haven't said anything to them about it.'

'Who took the rifle down to the stable?'

This time he blushed, looked around him in evident embarrassment, avoided meeting Maigret's eyes.

'You can hardly have gone downstairs and across the yard with that plaster on your leg,' insisted the chief-inspector. 'So what?'

'I asked Marcel...'

He stopped short.

'No. That's not true,' he admitted. 'It was father. You'd find out sooner or later, anyway.'

'You asked him to take down the gun?'

'Yes. I didn't explain why.'

'When?'

'On Wednesday morning.'

'He didn't ask you any questions?'

'He only looked at me, kind of worried.'

'Didn't he tell your mother about it?'

'If he had done, she'd have been up here at once to drag the whole story out of me.'

'Does she usually drag stories out of you?'

'She always guesses when I try to tell lies.'

'Was it you who asked Marcel to say he'd seen the schoolmaster coming out of the tool-shed?'

'No. I didn't even know he'd be questioned.'

'Why did he do that?'

'I expect it was because he'd seen me at the window.'

'With the gun. You were holding the gun?'

Joseph was getting hot, but he went on valiantly, doing his best not to contradict himself and not to be seen hesitating.

Although Maigret was still speaking in a colourless voice, without emphasis, as though his words had no importance, the boy was intelligent enough to realize that he was slowly and steadily nearing the truth.

'I don't remember exactly. Perhaps I hadn't picked up the rifle yet.'

'But when he looked through the other window and saw the postwoman fall down, he guessed it was you who'd shot her?'

'He's never said so to me.'

'Haven't you talked it over together?'

'Not until today.'

'And then he simply announced that if he was questioned he'd have to own up?'

'Yes.'

'Was he upset?'

'Yes.'

'And you?'

'I'd like to get it over.'

'But you'd rather go to prison?'

'Perhaps.'

'Why?'

'No special reason. Just to see.'

He refrained from adding that prison would probably be more fun than his home.

Maigret stood up with a sigh.

'Would you have let the schoolmaster be found guilty?'

'I don't think so.'

'You're not sure?'

The answer to this was no. Joseph was not sure. It didn't seem to have occurred to him that he was doing any harm to Gastin. Had it occurred to the rest of the village?

'Are you going away?' he asked in surprise, as he saw the chief-inspector turn towards the door.

Maigret paused on the threshold.

'What else can I do?'

'You're going to tell everything to the lieutenant?'

'Except about your accident, perhaps.'

'Thank you.'

He did not seem overjoyed at being left.

'You've nothing more to tell me, I suppose?'

He shook his head.

'You're sure you've told me the truth?'

He nodded again, and then, instead of opening the door, Maigret sat down on the edge of the bed.

'Now suppose you tell me *exactly* what you saw in the yard.'

'In what yard?'

The little boy had blushed hotly and his ears were scarlet.

Before replying, Maigret, without having to get up, half-opened the door and said to Marcellin's wife, who was standing at the top of the stairs:

'Please be good enough to go down.'

He waited till she was down below, then shut the door again.

'In this yard.'

'Our yard?'

'Yes.'

'What could I have seen there?'

'That's for you to say, not for me.'

The boy had withdrawn to the far side of his bed close to the wall and was staring aghast at Maigret.

'What do you mean?'

'You were at the window and the old woman was showing you the horse-shoe.'

'That's what I told you already.'

'Only, the gun wasn't in your room.

'How do you know?'

'Your father was down there, in the yard, with the stable door open. What was he doing?'

'He was quartering a lamb.'

'From where he was he could see you at your window, and he could see Léonie Birard too.'

'Nobody can have told you all that,' murmured the little boy, more astonished than distressed. 'Did you just guess it?'

'He was quite as much at loggerheads with the old woman as you were. She used to shout at him whenever he went past her house.'

'She used to call him a good-for-nothing and a beggar.'

'Used she to put out her tongue at him?'

'She had a craze for doing it.'

'Then your father went into the stable?'

'Yes.'

'When he came out, he was carrying your gun?'

'What will they do to him?'

'That depends. Have you decided to stop telling me lies?'

'I'll tell you the truth.'

'Could your father still see you then?'

'I don't think so. I'd stepped back.'

'So he shouldn't know you were watching?'

'Perhaps. I don't remember. It happened very quickly.'

'What happened very quickly?'

'He looked round him and then fired. I heard him growl: ' "There's one for you, you louse!" '

'Did he aim carefully?'

'No. He just lifted the gun to his shoulder and fired.'

'Is he a good shot?'

'He can't hit a sparrow at ten yards.'

'Did he see Léonie Birard fall down?'

'Yes. He stood quite still for a moment, as though he was thunderstruck. Then he rushed into the stable to put away the gun.'

'And after that?'

'He looked up at my window, then went indoors. Later

on I heard him go out.'

'Where was he going?'

'To Louis', to drink.'

'How do you know?'

'Because he came home tight.'

'Was Théo in his garden?'

'He'd just come out of his wine-cellar.'

'Did he see your father fire the shot?'

'He couldn't have, from where he was standing.'

'But he saw you at the window?'

'I think so.'

'He heard the shot?'

'He must have heard it.'

'Your father hasn't said anything to you about it since?'

'No.'

'Nor you to him?'

'I didn't dare.'

'Marcel thought it was you who'd fired?'

'Surely.'

'And that's why he told a lie?'

'We're friends.'

Maigret patted the boy's head with a mechanical gesture.

'That's all, my lad!' he said, standing up.

He was on the verge of adding:

'Some people have to grow up quicker than others.'

What would be the point? Joseph wasn't taking the thing over-tragically. He was so accustomed to little everyday dramas that this one hardly struck him as exceptionally serious.

'Will he go to prison?'

'Not for long. Unless they prove that he was aiming at Léonie Birard and meant to hit her.'

'He only wanted to give her a fright.'

'I know.

'The whole village will stand up for him.'

After a moment's thought, the boy nodded.

'Yes, I think they will. They're fond of him, in spite of everything. It isn't his fault.'

'What isn't his fault?'

'Everything.'

Maigret was half-way downstairs when the little boy called him back.

'Won't you take the plaster off my leg?'

'It'll be better for me to send the doctor along.'

'Will you send him at once?'

'If he's at home.'

'Don't forget.'

As Maigret reached the bottom of the stairs, he heard a soft:

'Thank you.'

He did not go into the kitchen. The sun was sinking behind the houses, and mist was rising from the ground. The three women were still there, motionless, and watched him in silence as he went past the window.

Outside the church, the *curé* was talking to an elderly woman, and it looked to Maigret as though he felt an impulse to come across the road and speak to him. He, too, must know the truth. He knew about Marcel's lie, from his confession. But he was the only person who had the right to say nothing.

Maigret raised his hat, and the priest seemed rather surprised. Then the chief-inspector went into the *mairie*, where he found Daniélou waiting, smoking a cigar; the lieutenant looked inquiringly at him.

'You can release the schoolmaster,' said Maigret.

'Was it Joseph?'

Maigret shook his head.

'Who?'

'His father, Marcellin.'

'So all I have to do is arrest him?'

'I'd like a word with him first.'

'Hasn't he confessed?'

'He's in no condition to confess anything whatever. If you'll come with me...'

The two men walked over to the inn, but as they were about to enter, Maigret remembered a promise he had made, and went along to ring Bresselles' door-bell.

The sister opened the door.

'The doctor isn't here?'

'He's just gone off to deliver a baby.'

'When he gets back, will you ask him to go and take the plaster off Joseph's leg?'

She, too, would be imagining that Joseph was the criminal. The lieutenant was waiting at Louis' door. There was no one standing about outside, now. Ten or a dozen drinkers were still lolling in the taproom, one of them asleep with his head on a table.

'Where did they put Marcellin?' Maigret asked Thérèse. He had spoken loud enough for Théo to hear. And now it was the chief-inspector's turn to throw the deputy-mayor a sparkling, mischievous glance. Théo, however, proved himself a good loser. Instead of scowling, he merely shrugged, as though saying:

'Well, that's that! It's not my fault...'

'The room to the left of the stairs, Monsieur Maigret.'

He went alone; as he opened the door, the butcher, startled by the sound, sat and stared at him, wide-eyed.

'Whaddye want, you?' he queried thickly. 'What's time?'

'Five o'clock.'

He swung his feet to the ground, rubbed his eyes, looked round for something to drink. His breath smelt so strongly of alcohol that the chief-inspector felt slightly sick, and the floor was spattered with vomit.

'The lieutenant's waiting for you downstairs, Marcellin.'

'Me? Why? What have I done?'

'He'll tell you that.'

'Have you been to my house?'

Maigret made no reply.

'You've been pestering the kid?' the butcher persisted, in a toneless voice.

'Get up, Marcellin.'

'I'll do as I please.'

His hair was tousled, his eyes glassy.

'Clever chap, aren't you! Must be proud of yourself! Pestering children! That's what you came here for!... And the government pays you to do it!'

'Come down.'

'Don't you touch me.'

He stood up, swaying, and growled:

'All this because the other fellow's a schoolmaster, an educated man, who takes the taxpayers' money too...'

He emphasized his contempt by spitting on the floor, staggered out, nearly fell downstairs.

'A *pernod*, Louis!' he ordered, holding tight to the bar.

He wanted to make a handsome exit, was staring round at the others, a forced sneer on his face.

Louis glanced at Maigret as though asking whether he should serve the requested drink, and the chief-inspector made a gesture of indifference.

Marcellin emptied the glass at one gulp, wiped his mouth, turned to face Théo and declared:

'I got her all the same, the louse!'

'Don't brag about!' the deputy-mayor muttered, looking at the cards in his hand.

'Well, didn't I get her?'

'Not on purpose. You couldn't hit a bullock at thirty yards.'

'Did I get her or did I not?'

'You got her, all right! Now shut up.'

The lieutenant intervened, saying:

'Please come with me quietly, so I don't have to handcuff you.'

'And suppose I want to be handcuffed?'

He was defiant to the last.

'As you like.'

There was a glint of metal, the sound of the handcuffs snapping round the butcher's wrists.

'See that, you chaps?'

He bumped against the doorpost as he went out, and a few seconds afterwards, they heard the slamming of a car door.

Silence fell. The air was saturated with the smell of wine and spirits; thick smoke hovered round the lamp which had just been lit, though it was still daylight outside. In half an hour it would be quite dark and the village would have vanished except for a few spots of light, two or three ill-lit shop windows, an occasional shadowy figure gliding past the house-fronts.

'I'd like my bill, please,' said Maigret, who was the first to speak.

'Are you leaving at once?'

'I'm catching the evening train.'

The others still remained silent, as though in suspense.

'How can I send for a taxi?'

'Just ask Marchandeau. He'll take you in his van. He always takes people to the station.'

Théo spoke suddenly:

'Are we playing or are we not? I said spades were trumps. And I'm declaring a *tierce*.'

'With what?'

'The queen.'

'Good.'

'I'm playing the knave.'

Maigret seemed slightly depressed, or tired, as he nearly always did at the end of a case. He had come here to eat oysters, washed down with the local white wine.

'What will you have on me, Inspector?'

He hesitated. The smell of wine-dregs was sickening him. But because of what he had intended before leaving Paris, he said:

'A *chopine* of white wine.'

The light was on in the ironmonger's. One could see past the hanging buckets and pans in the shop to the kitchen at the back, where Marcel Sellier was sitting with a book in front of him, his head between his hands.

'Your health!'

'Yours!'

'You must have a queer opinion of this place?'

He made no reply, and a little later Thérèse brought down his suitcase, which she had packed for him.

'I hope your wife will find everything tidy,' she said.

Actually, it was pleasant to be suddenly reminded of Madame Maigret, of their flat in the Boulevard Richard-Lenoir, and of the brightly lit Grands Boulevards, where he would take her to their usual cinema, the very first evening.

When, sitting in the front of the van, he was driven past the *mairie*, he saw a light in the Gastins' house. In an hour or two the schoolmaster would be home, and the three of them would be together again, as like as three peas, trying to hide away, as it were, on a lost island.

Further on he failed to notice the masts swaying in the darkness to his right, and at the station he bought a whole sheaf of Paris newspapers.

Shadow Rock Farm,
Lakeville (Connecticut),
8 December 1953.

MAIGRET
Sets a Trap

CHAPTER ONE

Commotion at the Quai des Orfèvres

From half-past three onwards, Maigret began raising his head every now and then to look at the time. At ten minutes to four he initialled the last page on which he had been making notes, pushed back his chair, mopped his forehead, and threw a hesitant glance at the five pipes lying in the ashtray, which he had smoked without bothering to knock them out afterwards. His foot pressed a button on the floor under his desk, and there came a knock at the door. Mopping himself again with an outspread handkerchief, he growled:

'Come in!'

It was Inspector Janvier; like the superintendent he was in his shirt-sleeves, but he still wore his tie, whereas Maigret had taken his off.

'Give this to be typed. Tell them to bring it me to sign as soon as it's finished. Coméliau has to have it this evening.'

This was August 4. All the windows were open, but that made the room no cooler, for they let in hot air which seemed to rise up out of the softened tarmac, the scorching stones and the Seine itself, which one half expected to be steaming like water on a stove.

The taxis and buses on the Pont Saint-Michel were going more slowly than usual, as though dragging along, and it was not only at Police Headquarters that people were in their shirt-sleeves; outside on the pavements the men were carrying their jackets, and just now Maigret had noticed a few in shorts, as though at the seaside.

There couldn't be more than a quarter of the population left in Paris, and they must all be thinking with equal envy of those who, at this very moment, were lucky enough to be dipping in the little wavelets or fishing on the shady bank of some peaceful stream.

'Have they arrived, over there?'

'I've not seen them yet. Lapointe's looking out for them.'

Maigret rose to his feet, as though with an effort, and selected a pipe which he emptied and proceeded to refill; after which he strolled over to a window and stood there, looking across the river at a certain café-restaurant on the Quai des Grands-Augustins. It had a yellow-painted front. The door was two steps down, and inside there it must be almost as cool as a cellar. The bar was a real, old-fashioned, pewter-topped affair, there was a slate hanging on the wall with the menu written on it in chalk, and the place always smelt of calvados.

Even some of the booksellers' boxes along the riverside were shut and padlocked!

He stood motionless for four or five minutes, puffing at his pipe, saw a taxi pull up not far from the little restaurant, and three men get out and make for the steps. The most familiar of the three figures was Lognon, the inspector from the 18th *arrondissement*, who at this distance looked even smaller and thinner than usual; it was the first time Maigret had seen him wearing a straw hat.

What would the three men drink? Beer, no doubt.

Maigret pushed open the door of the inspectors' room, where the atmosphere was as lazy as in the rest of the town.

'The Baron's in the corridor?'

'Been there half an hour, Chief.'

'No other journalists?'

'Young Rougin's just arrived.'

'Photographers?'

'Only one.'

The long corridor of the Judicial Police Headquarters was almost empty too, except for two or three people waiting outside doors to see one or other of Maigret's colleagues. It was at Maigret's request that Bodard, of the Financial Section, had summoned, for four o'clock, the man of whom the papers were talking every day — a certain Max Bernat, unknown a fortnight ago, but now the central figure in the latest financial scandal, in which thousands of millions of francs were at stake.

Maigret had nothing to do with Bernat, and at the present stage of the investigation Bodard had nothing to ask of Maigret. But because Bodard had casually announced that he would be seeing the crook at four o'clock that afternoon, there were at least two gossip-column journalists and a photographer in the corridor. They would stay there until the end of the interview. If it got about that Max Bemat was at the Quai des Orfèvres, other journalists might even turn up.

At precisely four o'clock, sounds of a slight commotion reached the inspectors' office, denoting the arrival of the crook, who had been brought from the Santé prison.

Maigret waited for about ten minutes, pacing round the room, smoking his pipe, mopping his forehead from time to time and throwing a glance at the little restaurant on the other side of the Seine. Then he snapped his fingers and said tersely to Janvier:

'Go ahead!'

Janvier went to the telephone and called the restaurant. Lognon must be near the telephone-box, on the look out, and would say to the proprietor:

'That's surely for me. I'm expecting a call.'

Everything went as expected. Maigret, moving a little heavily, feeling rather uneasy, went back to his office. Before sitting down he fetched himself a glass of water from the enamel wash-basin.

Ten minutes later a familiar scene was taking place in the corridor. Lognon and another inspector from the 18th, a Corsican called Alfonsi, came slowly up the stairs; between them walked a man who seemed embarrassed and held his hat in front of his face.

The Baron and his fellow-journalist Jean Rougin, who were standing outside Superintendent Bodard's door, understood the situation at a glance and sprang forward, while the photographer brought his camera into action.

'Who's that?'

They knew Lognon. They knew the police almost as well as the staff of their own newspapers. If two inspectors belonging, not to Judicial Police Headquarters but to the Montmartre police-station, brought a man to the Quai des Orfèvres and the fellow was hiding his face even before he'd caught sight of the journalists, that could only mean one thing.

'Is it for Maigret?'

Lognon made no reply, but went to Maigret's door and knocked softly. The three men disappeared inside and the door closed again.

The Baron and Jean Rougin exchanged glances, like men who had just surprised a State secret; but knowing they were both thinking the same thing they felt no need for comment.

'Got a good one?' Rougin asked the photographer.

'Except that the hat was hiding his face.'

'That'll do to be going on with. Send it off to the paper quickly and come back here. We can't tell when they'll be out.'

Alfonsi came out almost at once.

'Who is it?' they asked him.

He looked embarrassed.

'I can't say anything.'

'Why not?'

'Orders.'

'Where does he come from? Where did you pick him up?'

'Ask Superintendent Maigret.'

'A witness?'

'Don't know.'

'A fresh suspect?'

'I promise you I don't know.'

'Thanks for being co-operative.'

'I suppose if it was the killer you'd have put handcuffs on him?'

Alfonsi went away with the regretful expression of one who would have liked to say more; silence returned to the corridor, and there were no comings or goings for more than half an hour.

Max Bernat, the crook, came out of the Financial Section office, but he had already declined to second place in the interest of the two journalists. As a matter of conscience they put a few questions to Superintendent Bodard.

'Did he give any names?'

'Not yet.'

'Does he deny that he was helped by some political flgures?'

'He neither denies it nor admits it, he leaves it in doubt.'

'When will you be interrogating him again?'

'As soon as certain points have been checked.'

Maigret emerged from his office, still in his shirt-sleeves and with his collar unbuttoned, and made for the Director's office; he looked preoccupied.

This was another sign: in spite of the holidays, in spite of the heat, Judicial Police Headquarters was preparing for one of those important evenings, and the two reporters remembered how an interrogation had sometimes lasted all night, even gone on for twenty-four hours and more, without anyone being able to discover what was happening behind the closed doors.

The photographer had come back.

'You didn't tell them anything at the office?'

'Only that they were to develop the film and keep the prints handy.'

Maigret stayed with the Director for half an hour; then he came back to his office, waving the reporters aside with a weary gesture.

'Do at least tell us whether this has any connection with…'

'I have nothing to say for the moment.'

At six o'clock the waiter from the Brasserie Dauphine brought a trayful of mugs of beer. Lucas had been seen to leave his office and go into Maigret's, from where he had not yet emerged. Janvier, with his hat on, had been seen to rush out and jump into a police car.

Something more unusual was that Lognon appeared and went to the Director's office, as Maigret had done.

True, he was only there for ten minutes, after which, instead of leaving the building, he went into the inspectors' office.

'Did you notice something?' the Baron asked his colleague.

'His straw hat, when he first arrived?'

It was difficult to imagine the Gloomy Inspector, as everyone in the police and the Press used to call him, wearing an almost jaunty straw hat.

'More than that.'

'He didn't smile, did he?'

'No. But he's wearing a red tie.'

He had always worn dark ones, fixed to some kind of celluloid collar.

'What does that mean?'

The Baron knew everything, and would tell everybody's secrets with a thin-lipped smile.

'His wife's away on holiday.'

'I thought she was a cripple.'

'She was.'

'She's cured?'

For years poor Lognon had been obliged, between his spells of duty, to do the shopping and cooking, clean the flat in the Place Constantin-Pecqueur, and as well as all that, to nurse his wife, who had decided to be a permanent invalid.

'She got to know a new tenant who came to live in the house, a woman who talked to her about Pougues-les-Eaux and put it into her head to go and take the cure there. Strange as it may seem, she's gone, without her husband, who can't leave Paris just now, but with the neighbour in question. They're the same age and the neighbour's a widow...'

The coming and goings between offices were getting more and more numerous. Nearly all the members of Maigret's squad had left. Janvier had come back. Lucas was bustling to and fro, his forehead gleaming with sweat. Lapointe appeared from time to time; so did Torrence, Mauvoisin — a new member of the Force — and others. The reporters tried to catch them in passing, but not a word could be got out of them.

Young Mademoiselle Maguy, a reporter for one of the morning papers, arrived before long, looking as cool as though it hadn't been 102° in the shade all day.

'What have you come here for?'

'The same thing as you.'

'Meaning?'

'To wait.'

'How did you find out that something was happening?' She shrugged and applied lipstick.

'How many of them are there in there?' she inquired, pointing at Maigret's door.

'Five or six. You can't count 'em. They go in and out as though they were taking turns.'

'Turning on the heat?'

'Anyhow the chap must be beginning to feel warm.'

'Any beer come up?'

'Yes.'

That was a sign. When Maigret sent for a tray of beer it meant he expected to be there for some time.

'Lognon still with them?'

'Yes.'

'Pleased with himself?'

'It's hard to tell, with him. He's wearing a red tie.'

'Why?'

'His wife's away for a cure.'

She knew what that meant. They belonged to the same crowd.

'Did you see him?'

'Who?'

'The man they're grilling.'

'All of him except his face. He was hiding behind his hat.'

'Young?'

'Neither young nor old. Over thirty, so far as one could judge.'

'How was he dressed?'

'Like anyone else. What colour was his suit, Rougin?'

'Dark grey.'

'I'd have said beige.'

'What did he look like?'

'Anyone you might pass in the street.'

Steps were heard on the stairs, and Maguy murmured, as the others looked round, 'That must be my photographer.'

By half-past seven there were five Press representatives in the corridor, and they watched the waiter from the Brasserie Dauphine coming upstairs with more beer and some sandwiches.

This time it was big stuff. One by one the reporters went to a little office at the far end of the corridor to telephone to their respective newspapers.

'Shall we go and have some dinner?'

'Suppose he comes out while we're away?'

'But suppose this goes on all night?'

'Shall we send for sandwiches too?'

'Good idea!'

'And some beer?'

The sun was sinking behind the roof-tops, but it was still daylight, and though the air was no longer sizzling the heat was just as oppressive.

At half-past eight Maigret opened his door; he looked exhausted, his hair was sticking to his forehead. He glanced down the corridor, seemed about to come over to the journalists, but changed his mind, and the door closed again behind him.

'Looks as if things are humming!'

'I told you we were in for a night of it. Were you there when they interrogated Mestorino?'

'I was still in the cradle.'

'Twenty-seven hours.'

'In August?'

'I don't remember what month it was, but...'

Little Maguy's printed cotton dress was clinging to her body; there were big dark circles under the arms, and one could see the outline of her bra and panties through the material.

'What about a game of cards?'

The lamps along the ceiling lit up. Darkness fell. The office-boy on the night shift took up his position at the far end of the corridor.

'Couldn't you raise a draught somehow?'

He went and opened the door and window of an office, and then of another office, and after a few moments, by paying great attention, they managed to make out something like a faint breeze.

'That's all I can do for you, gentlemen.'

At last, at eleven o'clock, there were sounds of movement from Maigret's office. Lucas came out first and then motioned out the unknown man, who was still holding his hat in front of his face. Lognon brought up the rear. All three walked towards the stairs connecting the Judicial Police with the Palais de Justice and thence with the cells.

The photographers jostled one another. Rapid flashes lit up the corridor. Less than a minute later the glass door closed again and everyone rushed into Maigret's office, which looked like a battlefield. Glasses, cigarette-ends, ash and torn paper were lying about, and the air smelt of tobacco that was already cold. Maigret himself, still in his shirt-sleeves, was hidden down to the waist in his cupboard, washing his hands in the enamel basin.

'You'll give us a few tips, Superintendent?'

He looked at them with the round eyes he always had on such occasions, not seeming to recognize anyone.

'Tips?' he repeated.

'Who was it?'

'Who?'

'The man who's just left here.'

'Somebody with whom I've been having a fairly long talk.'

'A witness?'

'I have nothing to tell you.'

'You have put him under arrest?'

He seemed to come to life a little and apologized good-naturedly.

'Gentlemen, I'm really sorry not to be able to give you an answer, but frankly, I have no announcement to make.'

'You expect to make one soon?'

'I don't know.'

'Are you going to see the examining magistrate, Coméliau?'

'Not tonight.'

'Has this some connection with the killer?'

'Once again, forgive me if I can't tell you anything.'

'Are you going home?'

'What time is it?'

'Half-past eleven.'

'In that case the Brasserie Dauphine will still be open; I'll go there and have a bite.'

They watched them go — Maigret, Janvier and Lapointe. Two or three journalists followed them to the *brasserie*, where they had a drink at the bar while the three men sat down at a table in the inner room and gave their order to the waiter; they looked tired and worried.

A few minutes later Lognon joined them, but not Lucas.

The four were talking in low tones, and it was impossible to hear what they were saying, or to read anything from their lips.

'Shall we be off? Want a lift home, Maguy?'

'No — to the office.'

Not until the door closed behind them did Maigret stretch himself. A very cheerful, very youthful smile spread over his face.

'There we are!' he sighed.

Janvier said, 'I think they fell for it.'

'And how!'

'What will they write about?'

'I've no idea, but they'll manage to get something sensational out of it. Especially little Rougin.'

Rougin was a newcomer to journalism, young and combative.

'Suppose they realize we've fooled them?'

'They mustn't realize.'

This was almost a new Lognon they had with them, a Lognon who had drunk three pints of beer since four o'clock that afternoon and who didn't refuse the brandy the proprietor invited them to take.

'How's your wife, old man?'

'She writes that the cure's doing her good. She's only

anxious about me.'

They didn't laugh at this, or even grin. Some subjects are sacred. All the same he was relaxed, almost optimistic.

'You played your part very well. I'm most grateful. I hope no one except Alfonsi is in the know, at your station?'

'No one.'

It was half-past twelve when they parted. There were still people sitting outside the cafés, and more people in the street, enjoying the comparative coolness of the night, than there had been during the day.

'Are you taking the bus?'

Maigret shook his head. He preferred to walk home, alone; and as he went along his excitement diminished and his face took on a graver expression, a look almost of distress.

Several times he passed solitary women who were walking along close to the house-fronts, and they always started, as though at his least gesture they would begin running or cry out for help.

In the last six months, five women who, like these, were on their way home or to visit a woman friend, five women walking along the Paris streets, had been murdered by the same man.

The strange thing was that all five crimes had been committed in a single one of the twenty *arrondissements* of Paris, the 18th, in Montmartre; and not only in the same *arrondissement* but in the same district, the small sector that lay between the four Métro stations *Lamarck, Abbesses, Place Blanche* and *Place Clichy*.

The names of the victims and of the streets where they had been attacked, and the hours of the different murders had become familiar to all newspaper readers, and for Maigret they were a veritable obsession.

He knew the list by heart and could repeat it without thinking, like some fable learnt at school.

February 2. Avenue Rachel, quite close to the Place Clichy and just off the brightly-lit Boulevard de Clichy: Arlette Dutour, aged 28, prostitute, who lived in a cheap hotel in the Rue d'Amsterdam.

Two stabs in the back, one of which had caused almost

instantaneous death. Clothes methodically torn, and a few superficial lacerations on the body.

No trace of sexual violence. Her jewels had not been taken, they were of little value, but neither had her handbag, which contained a fairly substantial sum of money.

March 3. Rue Lepic, a little above the Moulin de la Galette. Eight-fifteen in the evening. Joséphine Simmer, born at Mulhouse, midwife, aged 43. She lived in the Rue Lamarck, and had just delivered a woman at the top of the Butte.

A single stab in the back, right to the heart. Clothes torn and superficial lacerations on the body. Her midwife's bag lay beside her on the pavement.

April 17. (In view of the similarity of dates between February 2 and March 3 they had expected another crime on April 4, but nothing had happened.) Rue Etex, running beside the Montmartre cemetery, nearly opposite the Hôpital Bretonneau. Three minutes past nine, again at night. Monique Juteaux, dressmaker, aged 24, living with her mother in the Boulevard de Batignolles. She had been to see a friend who lived in the Avenue de Saint-Ouen. It was raining and she had an umbrella.

Stabbed three times. Lacerations. Nothing stolen.

June 15. Between twenty-past and half-past nine. Rue Durantin this time, still in the same sector. Marie Bernard, widow, aged 52, Post Office clerk, living with her daughter and son-in-law in a flat in the Boulevard Rochechouart.

Stabbed twice. Lacerations. The second blow had severed her carotid artery. Nothing stolen.

July 21. The most recent of the crimes. Georgette Lecoin, a married woman with two children, aged 31, who lived in the Rue Lepic, not far from the scene of the second murder.

Her husband was a night worker in a garage. One of her children was ill. She was going down the Rue Tholozé, looking for an open chemist's, and had been killed at about nine forty-five, nearly opposite a dance-hall.

Stabbed once. Lacerations.

It was horrible and monotonous. They had sent extra

police to the Grandes-Carrières district. Lognon and his colleagues had postponed their holidays. Would they ever be able to take them?

The streets were patrolled. Policemen stood at all the strategic points. They had been there already when the second, third, fourth and fifth murders were committed.

'Tired?' asked Madame Maigret, opening the door of the flat at the very moment when her husband arrived on the landing.

'It's been a hot day.'

'Still nothing?'

'Nothing.'

'I heard on the wireless just now that there'd been a great commotion at the Quai des Orfèvres.'

'Already?'

'It's thought to have some connection with the crimes in the 18th. Is that true?'

'More or less.'

'You're on a trail?'

'I just don't know.'

'Have you had dinner?'

'Yes, and even supper, half an hour ago.'

She said no more about it, and before long they were both asleep, with the window wide open.

He got to his office at nine the next morning without having had time to read the newspapers. They were lying on his desk and he was about to glance through them when the telephone rang. At the first syllable he recognized the voice.

'Maigret?'

'Yes, sir.'

It was Coméliau, of course, the examining Magistrate in charge of the five Montmartre crimes.

'Is all this true?'

'To what are you referring?'

'To what this morning's papers say.'

'I haven't seen them yet.'

'You've made an arrest?'

'Not that I know of.'

'It would perhaps be best if you came round to my office

at once.'

'Very good, sir.'

Lucas had come in and had been listening to the conversation. He understood the grimace with which the Superintendent said:

'Tell the Chief I've gone to the Palais de Justice and don't expect to be back in time for the report.'

He look the route that had been followed the night before by Lognon, Lucas and the mysterious visitor to the Judicial Police, the man who held his hat in front of his face. In the examining magistrates' corridor the gendarmes saluted him; some of the accused persons and witnesses who were waiting there recognized him, and a few of them made a slight gesture of greeting.

'Come in. Read that.'

He had been expecting all this, naturally, expecting to find Coméliau irritable and aggressive, controlling with difficulty the indignation that made his little moustache quiver.

One of the papers said:

Killer caught at last?

Another was headed:

Commotion at the Quai des Orfèvres
Is this the Montmartre maniac?

'I would like to point out, Superintendent, that yesterday at four o'clock I was here, in my office, less than two hundred yards from your own office and within reach of a telephone. I was still here at five o'clock, at six o'clock, and I did not leave to fulfil other obligations until ten minutes to seven. Even then I could have been reached, first of all at home, where you have frequently telephoned me before now, and afterwards at the house of friends whose address I had made a point of leaving with my man.'

Maigret stood listening without a twitch of the eyelid.

'When an event as important as...'

The superintendent raised his head and said quietly,

'There has been no event.'

Coméliau was too excited to calm down immediately; he hit the papers with the flat of his hand.

'What about this? Are you going to tell me the journalists have made it up?'

'They have been making assumptions.'

'In other words nothing whatsoever took place, and these journalists just imagined that you had an unknown man brought to your office, questioned him for more than six hours and then sent him to the cells, and that...'

'I didn't question anybody, sir.'

This time Coméliau was shaken; he stared at Maigret with a baffled expression.

'You would do well to explain matters, so that I, in my turn, may be able to explain them to the Public Prosecutor, whose first idea this morning was to ring me up.'

'Someone did, it's true, come to see me yesterday afternoon, accompanied by two inspectors.'

'Someone these inspectors had arrested?'

'It was more in the nature of a friendly visit.'

'Is that why the man hid his face with his hat?'

Coméliau pointed to a photograph spread across two columns on the front page of the various newspapers.

'That may have been just an accident, a mechanical gesture. We chatted...'

'For six hours?'

'Time passes so quickly.'

'And you sent for beer and sandwiches?'

'That is so, sir.'

Coméliau again brought his hand down on the newspaper.

'This gives a detailed account of all your movements.'

'I'm sure it does.'

'Who was this man?'

'A delightful fellow called Mazet, Pierre Mazet, who worked under me for a time about ten years ago, when he had just passed his examinations. After that, hoping for more rapid promotion — and partly, I think, as a result of some kind of unhappy love-affair — he applied for a transfer to Central Africa, where he stayed for five years.'

Comméliau, now completely baffled, stood frowning at Maigret, wondering if the superintendent was making fun of him.

'He went down with fever and had to leave Africa, and the doctors won't let him go back there. Once he's in good shape again he will probably ask for re-admission to the Judicial Police.'

'And it was in order to receive him that you put the place into fighting trim, as the newspapers don't hesitate to declare?'

Maigret went over to the door and made sure no one was listening outside.

'Yes, sir,' he confessed at last. 'I needed a man whose description would be as unimpressive as possible and whose face would not be known to the public or to the Press. Poor Mazet has altered a great deal while he's been in Africa. You understand?'

'Not very well.'

'I made no announcement to the reporters. I didn't utter a single word to suggest that the visit had any connection with the Montmartre crimes.'

'But you did not deny it.'

'I kept saying I had nothing to say, which was true.'

'And the result...' the little magistrate exclaimed, again pointing to the newspapers.

'The result I hoped for.'

'Without consulting me, of course. Without even keeping me informed.'

'Simply in order not to make you share my responsibility, sir.'

'What are you hoping for?'

Maigret's pipe had gone out a few minutes before; he relit it with a reflective expression on his face, and then said slowly:

'I don't know yet, sir. I just thought it was worth trying something.'

Comméliau was no longer quite sure where he stood, and sat staring at Maigret's pipe, to which he had never become accustomed. The superintendent was the only man who ventured to smoke in this office, and

Coméliau regarded it as a form of defiance.

'Sit down,' he said at last, reluctantly.

And before sitting down himself, he went and opened the window.

CHAPTER TWO

Professor Tissot's Theories

It was on the previous Friday that Maigret and his wife had made their tranquil way, in the evening, to a neighbourly visit in the Rue Picpus, and all the local streets had been lined with people sitting in their doorways or even on chairs they had put out on the pavement. The traditional monthly dinners with Doctor Pardon still continued, but for the last year or so there had been a slight variation in the system.

Pardon had formed the habit of inviting some other member of his profession at the same time as the Maigrets; he nearly always chose someone who was interesting either for his own sake or for his line of work and quite often the superintendent would find himself seated opposite some great specialist or famous surgeon.

He had not realized at first that it was these people who had asked to meet him, and who were studying him as they put endless questions to him. They had all heard about him, and were curious to make his acquaintance. Before long they always found some common ground for discussion, and with the help of an old liqueur the after-dinner conversation in the Pardons' quiet drawing-room, where the windows overlooking the busy street were nearly always open, had often continued until quite late at night.

A dozen times the other party to one of these conversations had suddenly looked gravely at Maigret and asked him, 'Did you never feel tempted to go in for medicine?'

Maigret, almost shamefaced, would reply that that had been his first intention, but that his father's death had made it necessary for him to give up his studies.

Wasn't it a strange thing that they should feel this, after so many years? Their way of being interested in people, their attitude towards people's troubles and failings, were almost the same as his.

And the policeman did not try to hide the fact that he felt flattered when medical men with world-famous names ended by discussing their work with him just as though he were one of them.

Had Pardon made his choice deliberately that evening because of the Montmartre killer who had been worrying everybody for months? Possibily he had. He was a very simple man, but at the same time he had very delicate and subtle perceptions. He had had to take his holidays early in the season this year, in June, because that was the only time when he could find a locum.

When Maigret and his wife arrived there were two people already sitting in the drawing-room beside the tray of drinks — a broad-shouldered man, built like a peasant, with short, wiry grey hair and a ruddy face, and a dark-complexioned woman of exceptional vivacity.

'My friends the Maigrets... Madame Tissot... Professor Tissot...' said Pardon, making the introductions.

This was the celebrated Tissot, director of Sainte-Anne, the mental hospital in the Rue Cabanis. Although he often came into court to give expert evidence, Maigret had never actually met him, and found him to be a sturdy, human, jovial type of psychiatrist such as he had not come across before.

Before long they sat down to dinner. It was a hot evening, but towards the end of the meal a fine, gentle rain began to fall, and its whispering sound outside the open windows formed an accompaniment to the rest of their talk.

Professor Tissot was not taking a holiday, for though he had a flat in Paris he used to go out nearly every evening to his country house at Ville-d'Avray.

Like previous guests, while keeping up a random conversation he began scrutinizing the superintendent, with short, rapid glances, each of which seemed to add a touch to the picture of Maigret that he was forming. It was not until they were back in the drawing-room and the women had settled down in a corner of their own accord, that he made a point-blank attack:

'Doesn't your responsibility frighten you a bit?'

Maigret understood at once.

'I suppose you're referring to the murders in the 18th *arrondissement?*'

The other man merely blinked. And it was true that for Maigret this was one of the most disturbing cases of his whole career. It wasn't simply a matter of tracking down a criminal. The question, from the standpoint of the community, was not the usual one, of punishing a murderer.

It was a question of defence. Five women were dead, and there was no reason to suppose that things would stop at that.

And the customary methods of defence were not working. This was proved by the fact that the whole police mechanism had been brought into action after the first crime, without preventing the subsequent murders.

Maigret thought he understood what Tissot meant by referring to his responsibility. It was upon him, or to be more precise, *upon his method of approach to the problem*, that the fate of an unknown number of women would depend.

Had Pardon felt this too, and was that why he had arranged this meeting?

'Although in a way it's my own line,' Tissot had gone on, 'I wouldn't like to be in your place, with the public getting panic-stricken, the newspapers doing nothing to reassure them, and highly-placed people all clamouring for contradictory measures. That's the correct picture, I take it?'

'That's it, all right.'

'I imagine you've noted the features of the different crimes?'

He was going straight to the heart of the matter, and Maigret might have been talking to one of his colleagues of the Judicial Police.

'Between ourselves, Superintendent, may I ask what you've found most striking?'

This was a bit of a poser, and Maigret, who seldom found himself in such a situation, felt that he was blushing. But he replied without hesitation: 'The type of victim. You asked me for the chief feature, didn't you? I'm not talking about the others, of which there are quite a number.

'When there's a series of crimes, as on this occasion, the first thing we do at the Quai des Orfèvres is to look for what they have in common.'

Tissot nodded approvingly; he was holding a glass of armagnac, and dinner had considerably heightened his colour.

'Such as the time?' he inquired.

One could feel he wanted to show that he knew the case, that he too, through the newspapers, had studied it from every angle, including the strictly police angle.

It was Maigret's turn to smile now, for this was rather touching.

'Yes, the time. The first attack took place at eight o'clock in the evening, and it was February. So it was dark by then. The crime on March 3 was committed a quarter of an hour later, and so on and so forth, the last, in July, having taken place a few minutes before ten o'clock. Obviously the murderer waits for darkness.'

'What about the dates?'

'I've gone over them twenty times, till they ended by getting mixed up in my head. On my office desk you'd see a calendar covered with notes in black, blue and red. I've tried every system, every code, as though I were deciphering a secret language. First of all people talked about the full moon.'

'People always think the moon plays an important part in actions they can't account for.'

'Do you believe it does?'

'As a doctor, no.'

'As a man?'

'I don't know.'

'In any case that explanation won't work, because only

two of the five attacks took place on nights when the moon was full. So I looked for something else. The day of the week, for example. Some people get drunk every Saturday. Only one of the crimes was committed on a Saturday. Then there are occupations where the weekly holiday doesn't fall on Sunday but on some other day.'

He had the impression that Tissot, too, had considered these different hypotheses.

'The first constant, if I may so call it, that we hit upon,' he continued, 'was the district. The murderer obviously knows that marvellously well, in every nook and corner. In fact it is thanks to his familiarity with the streets, the places that are brightly lit and those that are not, the distance between two given points, that he has not only never been caught, but never been seen.'

'The papers have mentioned witnesses who declared they had caught sight of him.'

'We've taken statements from them all. The first-floor tenant in the Avenue Rachel, for example, who's the most positive of the lot. She declares he's tall and thin and was wearing a yellowish raincoat and a felt hat pulled down over his eyes. In the first place that's a standard description which turns up too often in cases like this, and we're always suspicious of it at the Quai. In the second place it has been proved that from the window where this woman says she was standing, the spot in question can't be seen.

'The evidence of the little boy is more dependable, but too vague to be any use. That relates to the business in the Rue Durantin. You remember?'

Tissot nodded.

'In short, the man knows the district wonderfully well, and that's why everybody thinks he lives there — which is creating a particularly distressing local atmosphere. They're all looking at their neighbours with suspicion. We've received hundreds of letters describing the strange behaviour of perfectly normal people.

'We've considered the hypothesis that the man doesn't live in the district, but works there.'

'That's a considerable job.'

'It represents thousands of hours. Not to mention the

hunting through our files, or the lists of all the criminals and maniacs we've brought up to date and checked. Like all hospitals, yours must have received a questionnaire about the patients you've discharged over the last few years.'

'It was answered by my staff.'

'The same questionnaire was sent to asylums in the provinces and in foreign countries, and to general practitioners.'

'You said something about another constant.'

'You'll have seen the photographs of the victims in the newspapers. They were all printed on different dates. I don't know if you've had the curiosity to put them side by side.'

Again Tissot nodded.

'The women were all of different origin, geographically to begin with. One was born at Mulhouse, another in the South of France, another in Britanny, and two in Paris or the suburbs.

'From the occupational point of view there was no resemblance between them either: a prostitute, a midwife, a dressmaker, a Post Office clerk and a housewife.

'They didn't all live in the district.

'We have made certain that they didn't know one another and more than probably had never met.'

'I had no idea you made inquiries from so many different angles.'

'We went further. We made sure they didn't all attend the same church, for instance, or go to the same butcher, that they didn't have the same doctor or dentist, that they didn't go, on more or less definite dates, to the same cinema or dance-hall. When I say it took thousands of hours...'

'With no result?'

'None. In any case I wasn't expecting results, but I had to check up. We have no right to leave even the smallest possibility unexplored.'

'You thought about holidays?'

'I see what you mean. They might have taken their holidays at the same place every year, in the country or by the sea; but they didn't.'

'So the murderer chose them at haphazard, as the opportunity occurred?'

Maigret felt sure Professor Tissot didn't believe this, that he had noticed the same thing as he himself had done.

'No. Not altogether. Looking carefully at their photographs one discovers, as I said, that these women did have one point of resemblance — their figures. If you don't look at their faces, only at their figures, you'll notice that all five were shortish and rather plump, almost fat, with thick waists and broad hips, even Monique Juteaux, the youngest of the lot.'

Pardon and the Professor exchanged glances, and Pardon's expression said: 'I told you so! He'd noticed it too!'

Tissot smiled.

'Congratulations, my dear Superintendent. I see there's nothing I can teach you.'

He hesitated for a second then added:

'I'd mentioned it to Pardon, wondering whether the police would have noticed that point. It was partly for that reason, and partly because I've been wanting to meet you for a long time, that he invited me and my wife this evening.'

All this time they had been standing up. At Doctor Pardon's suggestion they now went and sat down in a corner near the window, from where they could hear sounds of a wireless. The rain was still falling, so softly that the tiny drops seemed to be alighting gently one on top of another, to form a kind of dark varnish on the surface of the road.

It was Maigret who resumed the conversation.

'Do you know, Professor, what question it is that worries me the most — the answer to which, if we could find it, would in my opinion lead us to the killer?'

'Go on.'

'The man is no longer a child. So he must have lived for quite a number of years — twenty, thirty or more — without ever committing a crime. Yet in the course of the last six monlhs he has killed five people in succession. The question I'm asking myself is, how did it all begin? Why, on February 2, did he suddenly change from a harmless citizen into a dangerous maniac? You're a scientist, do you see any explanation?'

Tissot smiled and threw another glance at his colleague.

'People are very apt to credit us scientists, as you call us, with knowledge and powers we don't possess. But I'll try to answer your question, not only as regards the initial impulse but as regards the case itself.

'I shall not, incidentally, use any scientific or technical terms, for more often than not they merely serve to disguise our ignorance. Isn't that so, Pardon?'

He must be alluding to certain medical men against whom he had a grudge, for Pardon seemed to understand what he meant.

'Confronted with a series of crimes such as we are considering, everybody's first reaction is to declare that a maniac or a lunatic must be responsible for them. By and large, that is correct. To kill five women in the circumstances in which those five murders were committed, for no apparent reason, and then to tear their clothes, is conduct that has nothing in common with that of a sane man, as we understand the term.

'As for why and how it all began, that is a very complicated question, and hard to answer.

'Nearly every week I am called into court to give evidence as an expert. In the course of my career I have seen the concept of the criminal's responsibility changing so rapidly that in my opinion all our ideas about justice have been altered by it, if not actually unsettled.

'In the old days we used to be asked: "At the time he committed the crime, was the accused responsible for his actions?"

'And the word "responsibility" had a fairly precise meaning.

'Nowadays we are asked to assess the responsibility of Man, with a capital M; so much so that I often have the impression that the fate of a criminal is no longer determined by the judge and jury, but by us, the psychiatrists.

'Yet in most cases we know no more about it than the layman.

'Psychiatry is a science as long as there is a traumatism, a tumour, or an abnormal development in a particular gland or function.

'In such cases, it's true, we can say with a clear conscience whether a man is healthy or sick, whether he is or is not responsible for his actions.

'But those are the rarest cases, and such people are for the most part in an asylum.'

'Why do others, probably including the man we are discussing, behave differently from their fellow creatures?

'In my opinion, Superintendent, you know as much about that as we do, if not more.'

Madame Pardon had come over to them with the bottle of armagnac.

'Carry on, gentlemen. On our side of the room we're exchanging cooking recipes. A little armagnac, Professor?'

'Just half a glass.'

They had gone on chatting like this, in a light as soft as the rain that was falling outside, until past one o'clock. Maigret didn't recall the whole of their long conversation, which had often moved over to related subjects.

He remembered that Tissot had said, for example, in the ironical tone of a man with an old score to settle:

'If I were a blind believer in the theories of Freud, Adler, or even of the present-day psychoanalysts, I wouldn't hesitate to declare that our man has sexual obsessions, although none of the victims was interfered with sexually.

'I might also talk about complexes and work back to early childhood impressions...'

'You rule out that explanation?'

'I don't rule out any explanation, but I distrust the ones that are too easy.'

'You have no theory of your own?'

'Not a theory, no. An idea, perhaps, but I admit I'm rather afraid to mention it to you, for I'm not forgetting that the responsibility for the investigation rests on your shoulders. It's true that your shoulders are as broad as mine. Son of a peasant, eh?'

'In the Allier.'

'I'm from Cantal. My father's eighty-eight and still living on his farm.'

One felt he was prouder of this than of his own scientific accomplishments.

'A lot of lunatics, or semi-lunatics — to use an unscientific term — have passed through my hands after they had committed crimes, and in the matter of constants, as you said a while back, there is one I've found in nearly all of them: a conscious or unconscious need to assert themselves. You understand what I mean by that?'

Maigret nodded.

'Nearly all of them, rightly or wrongly, had for a long time been regarded in their own circle as unstable, second-rate or mentally retarded, and had felt humiliation as a result. By what process does such humiliation, battened down for a long time, suddenly break out in the form of a crime, an attack, some gesture of defiance or bravado? Neither I nor, so far as I know, any of my fellow doctors can say for certain.

'What I'm saying is perhaps not orthodox, especially when compressed into a few words, but I am convinced that the majority of crimes which are said to have no motive, and repeated crimes in particular, are a manifestation of wounded pride.'

Maigret had become pensive.

'That fits in with something I'd noticed,' he muttered.

'What's that?'

'That's if criminals didn't sooner or later feel the need to boast of what they'd done, there wouldn't be nearly so many of them in prison. Do you know where we go first of all to look for a man who's committed what's known as a sexual crime? In the old days we went to the brothels; now that they've ceased to exist we look for him in the arms of some form of prostitute. And they talk, those men! They feel confident that with such women it doesn't matter, that they run no risk; and in most cases that's true. They tell their whole story. Often they embroider it.'

'You've tried this time?'

'There isn't a tart in Paris, especially in the Clichy and

Montmartre district, who hasn't been questioned in the last few months.'

'With no result?'

'None.'

'Then that makes it worse.'

'You mean that since he hasn't relieved his mind, he's bound to begin again?'

'Practically bound to.'

Maigret had recently been studying all the historical cases which bore some resemblance to the business in the 18th *arrondissement*, from Jack the Ripper to the Düsseldorf Vampire, by way of the Viennese lamp-lighter and the Pole who operated among the farms in the Aisne Department.

'You think they never stop of their own accord?' he asked. 'But there's the precedent of Jack the Ripper, who was never heard of again from one day to the next.'

'How do we know he wasn't killed in an accident, or that he didn't die of illness? I'll go further than that, Superintendent, and now I'm not speaking as the medical director of Sainte-Anne, because this takes me too far away from the official theories.

'People like your man are driven, without knowing it, by a need to get themselves caught, and that, again, is a form of vanity. They can't bear the idea that those around them are still taking them for ordinary people. They have to be able to proclaim from the house-tops what they've done, what they have been capable of doing.

'I don't mean to say they give themselves away on purpose; but nearly always, as one crime follows another, they take fewer precautions, as though they were defying the police, defying fate.

'Some of them have admitted to me that it came as a relief to them when they were arrested at last.'

'I've been told the same thing.'

'You see!'

Whose idea had it been? The evening had gone on so long, they had considered and reconsidered the subject from so many angles, that afterwards it was difficult to be certain what had come from one of them and what from the other.

Perhaps the suggestion had been put forward by

Professor Tissot, but so tactfully that even Pardon had not noticed.

It had been past midnight already when Maigret muttered, as though to himself:

'Suppose someone else were arrested and took the place of our killer, as it were, usurping what he regards as his fame...'

They had got there now.

'Yes,' replied Tissot, 'I think your man would have a feeling of frustration.'

'It remains to be seen how he would react. And *when* he would react.'

Maigret was already ahead of the others, leaving theory behind and considering practical possibilities.

They knew nothing about the killer. They had no description of him. Up to now he had operated in only one district, in one particular sector, but there was no guarantee that he would not break out tomorrow in some other part of Paris or elsewhere.

What made the threat so disturbing was that it remained vague, indefinite.

Would a month go by before his next crime? Or only three days?

All the streets of Paris could not be kept indefinitely in a state of siege. Even the women, who scuttled to their homes after every murder, would soon resume a more normal life, venturing out in the evening, telling themselves the danger was past.

'I have known two cases,' Maigret began again after a silence, 'of criminals writing to the newspapers to protest because innocent people had been arrested.'

'People like that often write to the papers, driven by what I call their exhibitionism.'

'That would help us.'

Even a letter composed of words cut out of a newspaper might be a starting-point, in an investigation where there was nothing to take hold of.

'Of course he would be faced with another solution...'

'I'd just thought of that.'

An extremely simple solution: immediately after the

arrest of an alleged criminal, the real one might commit another murder, similar to the previous ones! Perhaps two, or three...

They said goodbye outside the house, standing beside the Professor's car. He and his wife were going back to Ville-d'Avray.

'Can we give you a lift home?'

'We live near here, and we're used to walking.'

'I have an idea this case will have me back in the criminal courts as an expert.'

'Provided I lay hands on the criminal.'

'Trust you for that!'

They shook hands, and Maigret had the impression that this was the beginning of a friendship.

'You didn't have a chance to talk to her,' said Madame Maigret a little later, while they were on their way home side by side. 'A pity, because she's the most intelligent woman I've ever met. What's her husband like?'

'A very nice fellow.'

She pretended not to notice what Maigret was doing, furtively, like when he was a small boy. The rain was so cool and refreshing that from time to time he would put out his tongue and catch a few drops; they had a taste of their own.

'You seemed to be having a serious discussion.'

'Yes...'

That was all they said on the subject. They got back to their house and up to their flat, where the windows had been left open; the rain had come in a little, and Madame Maigret mopped the floor.

It may have been in his sleep, or it may have been when he woke up next morning, that Maigret reached his decision. And as luck would have it, Pierre Mazet, his ex-inspector whom he hadn't seen for eight years, came to his office that very morning.

'What are you doing in Paris?'

'Nothing, Chief. I'm getting myself fit again. The mosquitos in Africa did me a bit of no good, and the doctors insist that I must rest for another few months. After that, I'm wondering whether there'd still be a corner for me at the Quai.'

'I should certainly think so!'

Why not Mazet? He was intelligent, and there was little danger of his being recognized.

'Like to do me a good turn?'

'Do you need to ask me, of all people?'

'Come and pick me up about half-past twelve, and we'll have lunch together.'

Not at the Brasserie Dauphine, they'd certainly be noticed there.

'Or rather, don't come back here, and don't go round the other offices now. Meet me at the Châtelet Métro station instead.'

They had lunched at a restaurant in the Rue Saint-Antoine, and the superintendent had explained to Mazet what he wanted him to do.

It would be better, more convincing, if he were not brought to Judicial Police Headquarters by a man belonging to the Quai des Orfèvres, but by inspectors from the 18th *arrondissement*; and Maigret thought at once of Lognon. Who could tell? It might give the man a chance. Instead of patrolling the streets of Montmartre he would be more closely involved in the investigation.

'Choose one of your colleagues who'll keep his mouth shut.'

Lognon had chosen Alfonsi.

And the comedy had been acted — with complete success as far as the Press was concerned, for all the papers were already talking about a sensational arrest.

Maigret told Coméliau, the examining magistrate, once more:

'They watched certain comings and goings, and drew their own conclusions. Neither I nor my staff told them anything. On the contrary, we denied their suggestions.'

It was unusual to see Coméliau smile, even sardonically.

'And suppose that, tonight or tomorrow, because this arrest — or this false arrest — has caused people to neglect their precautions, another crime is committed?'

'I've thought of that. In the first place, for the next few evenings every available man from our own staff and from the station in the 18th *arrondissement* will keep a close watch on the district.'

'That has been done already, without result, if I'm not mistaken?'

That was true. But was nothing new to be attemped?

'I've taken another precaution. I went to see the Prefect of Police.'

'Without telling me?'

'As I said before, I wish to take the sole responsibility for whatever may happen. I'm only a policeman. You are a magistrate.'

The word pleased Coméliau, who struck a more dignified attitude.

'What did you ask the Prefect?'

'For permission to use a certain number of volunteers from the women's section of the municipal police.'

This was an auxiliary corps, whose members usually dealt only with matters concerning children and prostitutes.

'He sent for a number of them who satisfied certain conditions.'

'Such as?'

'Height and plump figure. From among the volunteers, I selected those with the closest physical resemblance to the five victims. Like them, they will be unassumingly dressed. They will appear to be local women, going about their business, and some of them will carry parcels or baskets.'

'In fact you're setting a trap.'

'All those I selected have taken P.T. courses and judo training.'

Coméliau was rather nervous all the same.

'Am I to tell the Public Prosecutor about this?'

'Better not.'

'You know, Superintendent, I don't like this at all.'

To which Maigret replied, with disarming candour: 'No more do I, sir!'

Which was true. But surely they must try anything that might put an end to the slaughter?

'Officially I know nothing about it, do I?' said Coméliau as he walked to the door with his visitor.

'You know absolutely nothing.'

And Maigret wished this had been true.

CHAPTER THREE

A District in a State of Siege

The Baron, who as a reporter had been frequenting Judicial Police Headquarters for almost as many years as Maigret, little Rougin, still a youngster but already knowing the ropes better than most journalists, and four or five others of less eminence — including Maguy, who was the most dangerous because for all her air of innocence she never hesitated to open any door one had not taken the precaution of locking, or to pick up a stray paper — together with one or two photographers, more of them for a time, spent the greater part of the day in the corridor at the Quai des Orfèvres, where they had established their main base.

Sometimes the bulk of them went off to the Brasserie Dauphine in search of refreshments, or to make a telephone call, but they aways left somebody behind, so that the door of Maigret's office was continually under observation.

Rougin had had the additional idea of sending a man from his paper to follow Lognon, who found himself being trailed from the moment he left his flat in the Place Constantin-Pecqueur in the morning.

These people knew the racket, as they put it, they were almost as experienced in police business as an inspector with years of seniority.

Yet not one of them suspected what was going on almost before their eyes, the kind of gigantic deployment of forces which had begun in the early hours of the morning, long before Maigret's visit to Coméliau.

For example, inspectors from distant *arrondissements* such as the 12th, 14th and 15th had left home wearing clothes that were not their usual ones, some of them taking a suitcase or even a trunk; and acting on instructions, they had been careful to begin by making their way to one of the railway stations.

The heat was almost as oppressive as the day before, and life was proceeding in slow-motion except in the districts popular with tourists. Coaches full of foreigners were to be seen all over the place, with the voices of guides proceeding from them.

In the 18th, particularly in the sector where the five crimes had been committed, taxis were stopping outside hotels and lodging-houses and people were getting out, with luggage that indicated they had come from the provinces, and asking for rooms; most of them insisted on overlooking the street.

All this was in accordance with a careful plan, and some of the inspectors had been told to bring their wives with them.

It wasn't often that such precautions had to be taken. But this time, could they trust anybody whatsoever? They knew nothing about the killer. This was another aspect of the question which had been discussed by Maigret and Professor Tissot that evening at the Pardons'.

'In fact, in between these impulses he must necessarily behave like an ordinary man, otherwise his peculiarities would already have attracted attention.'

'Necessarily, as you say,' the psychiatrist had agreed. 'Indeed it's probable that in appearance, behaviour and occupation he's the least suspicious of people.'

He was not one of the sex-obsessed characters who were known to the police, for ever since February 2 those had been kept under surveillance, with no result. Nor was he one of those human wrecks or disturbing creatures who attract attention in the streets.

What had he done until his first crime? And what was he doing between one crime and the next?

Was he a man who lived alone in a flat or in lodgings?

Maigret would have sworn he wasn't, that he was a married man leading a well-ordered life; and Tissot was inclined to think the same.

'Anything's possible,' he had said with a sigh. 'If I were told it was one of my own colleagues I wouldn't protest. It may be anybody — a workman, a clerk, a small shopkeeper or a prominent businessman.'

He might also be the manager of one of the hotels the inspectors were invading, and that was why they couldn't go in in the usual way and say:

'Police! Give me a room overlooking the street, and don't say a word to a soul.'

It was safer not to rely on the concierges either. Nor on the informers who lived in the district.

When Maigret returned to his office after leaving Coméliau, he was assailed by the journalists, just like the evening before.

'You've been in conference with the examining magistrate?'

'I have been to see him, as I do every morning.'

'You told him about yesterday's interrogation?'

'We had a chat.'

'You still won't say anything?'

'I have nothing to say.'

He went to see the Director. The report had been finished some time ago. The big boss, too, was worried.

'Coméliau didn't insist on your giving it up?'

'No. Of course if there's any hitch he'll drop me.'

'You still feel confident?'

'I have to.'

Maigret was not embarking on this experiment lightheartedly, and he realized what a responsibility he was shouldering.

'You think the reporters will go on swallowing it?'

'I'm doing my best to make sure they will.'

He usually worked on friendly terms with the Press, which can be very helpful at times. But now he must not risk an unintentional give-away. Even the inspectors who were pouring into the Grandes-Carrières district did not yet know exactly what was being planned. They had been ordered to do so-and-so, go to such-and-such a place, and wait for instructions. Naturally they suspected this had something to do with the killer, but they knew nothing of the operation as a whole.

'Do yo think he's a clever man?' Maigret had asked Professor Tissot the other evening.

He had his own idea about that, but hoped for confirmation of it.

'Clever in the same way as most people of that kind. For example, he must instinctively be an excellent actor. Supposing he's a married man, for instance, he has to be able to resume his usual manner, not to mention recovering his self-control, when he arrives home after one of his crimes. Even if he's a bachelor he must meet other people, if only his landlady, his concierge, his charwoman and so on. Next morning he goes to his office or workshop, and people will inevitably talk to him about the Montmartre killer. Yet in six months nobody has suspected him.

'What's more, in six months he has never made a mistake about time or place. No reliable witness claims to have seen him in action, or even running away from the scene of one of his crimes.'

This had led Maigret to ask about something that was worrying him.

'I'd like to have your opinion about a particular point. You just said that he behaves most of the time like an ordinary man; and that presumably means that he thinks more or less like an ordinary man as well?'

'I understand. Very likely.'

'Five times he has had what I may call a crisis, five times he has departed from his ordinariness and killed somebody. When does the impulse occur? Do you see what I mean? At what moment does he stop behaving like you or me and begin to behave like a killer? Does it come over him just at any time during the day, and does he wait for darkness while thinking out his course of action? Or does the impulse only come when the opportunity arises — at the moment when he's going along some deserted street and catches sight of a possible victim?'

The reply to this question was of the utmost importance

to him, for it might either restrict or extend the field of investigation.

If the impulse came at the moment of the murder, the man must necessarily live in or near the Grandes-Carrières district, or at any rate be obliged to go there in the evening, either owing to his work or for some other commonplace reason.

In the contrary case, the man might come from anywhere, and have chosen the streets leading from the Place Clichy to the Rue Lamarck and the Rue des Abbesses for reasons of convenience or for some reason personal to himself.

Tissot had thought for quite a time before answering.

'I can't, of course, make a diagnosis as though I had the patient in front of me...'

He had said 'patient' as though referring to one of his people at Sainte-Anne; this did not escape the superintendent, and it pleased him. It confirmed his impression that they both looked at the tragedy in the same light.

'But in my opinion, if I may make the comparison, there comes a moment when he sets out on the hunt, like a wild animal, a lion or tiger, or simply like a cat. You've watched cats?'

'Often, when I was a boy.'

'His movements are no longer the same. He's gathered up in himself and all his senses are on the alert. He becomes capable of perceiving the faintest sound, the most imperceptible movement, the slightest smell, from a considerable distance. From that time on, he senses dangers and avoids them.'

'I see.'

'It's rather as though, when he's in that state, our man had second sight.'

'I suppose you have no grounds for a hypothesis as to what starts up the mechanism?'

'None. It might be a random memory, the sight of a woman passing in the crowd, a whiff of a particular scent, or a few words overheard. It might be no matter what, such as the sight of a knife, or of a dress of a particular colour. Was any attention paid to the colour of the victims' clothes? The papers haven't mentioned that.'

'The colours were different, but almost all so neutral that they wouldn't have shown in the dark.'

'When he got back to his office he took off his jacket and tie, like the day before, unbuttoned his shirt-collar and, because the sun was shining straight onto his chair, lowered the pale-coloured blind. After which he opened the door of the inspectors' office.

'You there, Janvier?'

'Yes, Chief.'

'Nothing new? No anonymous letters?'

'Only letters from people denouncing their neighbours.'

'Get those checked. And have Mazet brought to me.'

Mazet had not slept in the lock-up; he had left the Palais de Justice by a side door and gone home. But he must have been back in the cells since eight o'clock that morning.

'Shall I go down myself?'

'That would be best.'

'Still no handcuffs?'

'No.'

He didn't want to cheat to that extent in his game with the journalists. Let them draw whatever conclusions they chose from what they saw. Maigret wouldn't go so far as to load the dice.

'Hello! Give me the Grandes-Carrières police-station, please... Inspector Lognon... Hello — Lognon?... Nothing new at your end?'

'Someone was waiting for me outside my door this morning, and followed me. He's across the road from here now.'

'He's not concealing himself?'

'No. I think he's a journalist.'

'Have his papers checked. Everything going according to plan?'

'I've found three rooms, with friends. They don't know what it's about. Do you want the addresses?'

'No. Come here in about forty-five minutes.'

The previous day's scene in the corridor was repeated when Pierre Mazet made his appearance, flanked by two inspectors and with his hat in front of his face again. The photographers got to work. The journalists called out questions that remained unanswered. Maguy managed to knock down the hat, and while she was picking it up from the floor the unknown man hid his face with both hands.

The door was shut again, and Maigret's office promptly took on the aspect of a control-room.

The deployment was silently continuing, up the hill, in the quiet streets of Montmartre, where many shops were closed for a fortnight or a month because of the holidays.

More than four hundred people had a part to play, not only those who were watching from the hotels and the few flats that could be made use of with no danger of giving away the secret, but others who were taking up pre-arranged positions in the Métro stations, at the bus-stops, and in even the most insignificant of the cafés and restaurants that stayed open in the evening.

So that it should not have the air of an invasion, the plan was carried out in stages.

The women police, too, were given detailed instructions by telephone; and Maigret's office was like an army headquarters, with maps spread out on which every individual's position was marked.

Twenty inspectors, from among those not usually seen in public, had hired — not only in Paris, but in the suburbs and as far afield as Versailles — cars with non-committal registration numbers, which would be parked at the right moment at strategic points, where they would not be noticed among the other cars.

'Send for some beer, Lucas.'

'And sandwiches?'

'Yes, just as well.'

Not only because of the journalists, to make them think another interrogation was going on, but because everyone was busy and there would be no time to go out for lunch.

Lognon arrived in due course, still wearing his red tie and his straw hat. At the first glance one wondered what was different about him, and it was surprising to see how the colour of a tie can change a man's appearance. He looked almost gay.

'Your chap followed you?'

'Yes. He's in the corridor. He's a reporter, sure enough.'

'Any of them stay around the station?'

'There's one right inside.'

The next newspaper came out about noon. It repeated what had been said in the morning papers, adding that the excitement characteristic of great occasions still prevailed at the Quai des Orfèvres, but that the deepest secrecy was being maintained about the arrested man.

If the police had been able, said the article, among other things, *they would no doubt have provided their prisoner with an iron mask.*

That amused Mazet. He was helping the others, making telephone calls himself, making red and blue crosses on the street-plan — delighted to be back in the atmosphere of the building where he felt at home already.

The atmosphere changed when the waiter from the Brasserie Dauphine knocked on the door, for they had to play-act even for him. Once he had gone they flung themselves on the beer and sandwiches.

The afternoon papers published no message from the murderer, who did not seem to intend to communicate with the Press.

'I'm going to take a short rest, boys. I shall need to be fresh this evening.'

Maigret went through the inspectors' office to a small, unoccupied room, where he sat down in an arm-chair: a few minutes later he was dozing.

About three o'clock he sent Mazet back to the cells and told Janvier and Lucas to take turns for a rest. Lapointe, wearing blue overalls, was steering a carrier-tricycle round the streets of the Grandes-Carrières district. With his cap over one ear and a cigarette clinging to his lower lip he looked about eighteen years old. From time to time he stopped at some bistro for a white-wine-and-Vichy, and telephoned from there to headquarters.

As time went by everybody began to get fidgety, and even Maigret lost a little of his confident manner.

There was nothing to show that anything would happen that evening. Even if the man decided to assert himself by committing another murder it might not happen until the following evening, or the one after that, or in a week or ten days, and it would not be possible to keep such a large force on the alert for very long.

Nor would it be possible for a secret shared by so many people to be kept for a whole week.

And if the man decided to act right away?

Maigret's conversation with Professor Tissot was always at the back of his mind, and snatches of it were constantly coming to memory.

At what moment would the impulse seize the man? Just now, while the trap was being prepared, he was appearing to all those around him as just an ordinary man. People were talking to him, serving him a meal, no doubt, shaking him by the hand. He was talking too, smiling, perhaps laughing.

Had the spark already been struck? Had it happened this morning, when he saw the papers?

Wouldn't he be rather inclined to say to himself that since the police thought they had caught the criminal they would drop the search, so that he was safe?

What proof was there that Tissot and the superintendent had not been mistaken, that they had not been wrong in their estimate of how the 'patient,' as the professor had called him, would react?

Until now he had never killed anyone before evening, he had waited for darkness. But at this very hour, because of the holidays and the heat, there were plenty of streets in Paris where several minutes might go by without a soul being seen.

Maigret remembered the streets in the South of France in the summertime, at the hour of the siesta — their closed shutters, the way in which a whole village or town would sink into torpor every day beneath the torrid sun.

On this very day there were streets in Montmartre which were almost similar.

Moreover, the police had reconstructed the crimes.

At each point where one of them had been committed, the lie of the land was such that the murderer had been able to vanish in the briefest imaginable time. The time would be shorter at night than during the day, of course.

But even in broad daylight, given favourable circumstances, he would be able to kill his victim, slash her clothes, and get away in less than two minutes.

Besides, why should it necessarily happen in the street? What would prevent him from knocking at the door of a flat where he knew he would find a woman alone, and then behaving as he used to do in the streets? Nothing, except that maniacs — like most criminals, and even thieves — *nearly always* use the same technique and repeat themselves down to the smallest detail.

It would be light until about nine o'clock; darkness would not really have fallen until about half-past nine. The moon, now in its third quarter, would not be too bright, and there was a chance that, as on the previous night, it would be veiled by heat-clouds.

All these details had their importance.

'Are they still in the corridor?'

'Only the Baron.'

They sometimes arranged among themselves for one to stay on guard and let the others know if anything happened.

'At six o'clock everyone will leave here as usual, except for Lucas, who will stay on and be joined by Torrence about eight.'

Maigret left with Janvier, Lognon and Mauvoisin, and they all went to the Brasserie Dauphine for a drink.

He got home at seven and had dinner, with the window open on to the Boulevard Richard-Lenoir, which was quieter than at any other time of year.

'You've been hot!' remarked Madame Maigret, looking at his shirt. 'If you're going out you'd better change.'

'I am going out.'

'He hasn't confessed?'

He preferred not to answer, for he didn't like lying to her.

'Will you be back late?'

'More than likely.'

'Do you still think there's a chance that we can holiday once this case is over?'

During the winter they had talked of going to Britanny,

to Beuzek-Conq, near Concarneau; but as happened nearly every year, his holidays were postponed from month to month.

'Perhaps!' sighed Maigret.

If not, it would mean he had missed his stroke, that the killer had found a loophole in the net, or hadn't reacted as Tissot and himself had anticipated. It would also mean fresh victims, impatience among the public and in the Press, sarcasm or rage from Coméliau and even, perhaps, as happened only too often, questions in the Chamber and a demand for explanations from high places.

Worst of all, it would mean the deaths of women, of small, plump women looking like good housewives, who had been out on an errand or visiting friends in the evening in their own district.

'You look tired.'

He was not in a hurry to leave. Dinner over, he pottered about the flat, smoking his pipe, hesitantly pouring himself a little glass of sloe-gin, sometimes halting in front of the window and finally sitting down with his elbows propped on the sill.

Madame Maigret did not disturb him. Only when he looked round for his jacket she brought him a clean shirt and helped him to put it on. He tried to act as unobtrusively as possible, but all the same she saw him open a drawer, take out his revolver and slip it into his pocket.

He didn't often do that. He had no desire to kill anyone, not even a creature so dangerous as this one. All the same he had ordered all his men to be armed and to protect the women *at all costs*.

He did not go back to the Quai. It was nine o'clock when he got to the corner of the Boulevard Voltaire, where a car — not a police car — was waiting for him with a man at the wheel. The man, who belonged to the police-station in the 18th *arrondissement*, wore a chauffeur's uniform.

'Do we start, Chief?'

Maigret, already half concealed by the dusk, got into the back of the car, which now looked like one of those that tourists hire by the day from a garage near the Madeleine or the Opera.

'Place Clichy?'

'Yes.'

On the way he didn't say a word, merely grunting, when they reached the Place Clichy, 'Go up the Rue Caulain-court, not too quickly, as though you were trying to read the numbers of the houses.'

The streets in the neighbourhood of the boulevards were fairly lively, with people at many of the windows, enjoying the cool of the evening. There were people in various stages of dishevelment on the terraces of all the cafés down to the very smallest, and at most of the restaurants people were eating out of doors.

It seemed impossible for a crime to be committed in such circumstances; and yet the circumstances had been almost identical when Georgette Lecoin, the most recent of the victims, was killed in the Rue Tholozé, less than fifty yards from a dance-hall whose red neon sign lit up the pavement.

Anyone who really knew the district could think of a hundred deserted alleys close to the wide, busy streets, a hundred corners where a crime could be committed with practically no risk.

Two minutes. They had calculated that the killer would need only two minutes, and if he were spry enough he might need even less.

What was it that impelled him, his crime once committed, to slash his victim's clothing?

He didn't touch her. He never attempted to uncover her privy parts, as had been known in certain cases. He tore the material with great knife-slashes, seized by a kind of fury, like a child tearing a doll to pieces or stamping on a toy.

Tissot had spoken of this too, but guardedly. One could feel he was tempted to adopt some of the theories of Freud and his disciples, but it seemed as if he thought that would be too easy.

'One would need to know his past, right back to his childhood, to discover the first shock, which he may not remember himself...'

Every time he thought about the murderer like this,

Maigret fell into a fever of impatience. He was in a hurry to be able to conjure up a face, with definite features, a human figure instead of the sort of vague entity that some people called the killer, or the lunatic, or the monster, and that Tissot, involuntarily, as though by a slip of the tongue, had referred to as the patient.

His own helplessness enraged him. This thing was like a challenge flung at him personally.

He would have liked to find himself face to face with the man, no matter where, to look him full in the face, straight in the eye, and to order:

'Now, start talking...'

He had to know. The suspense was harrowing him, preventing him from devoting his full attention to practical details.

Mechanically, he checked the presence of his men at the different points where he had posted them. He didn't know them all personally. Many of them were not on his own staff. But he knew that the figure glimpsed through the curtain of a particular window went by such and such a name, and that a certain woman walking past, out of breath, going heaven knew where and moving jerkily because of her absurdly high heels, was one of the police auxiliaries.

Since February, since his first crime, the man had been later on each occasion, ranging from eight in the evening to nine forty-five. But now the days were drawing in instead of getting longer, now that darkness was falling earlier...?

At any moment they might hear a cry from some passerby who had stumbled in the darkness over a body lying on the pavement. That was how most of the victims had been found, nearly always within a few minutes — only once, according to the official pathologist, after about a quarter of an hour.

The car had crossed the Rue Lamarck and entered a sector where nothing had happened up to now.

'What shall I do, Chief?'

'Carry on, and come back by the Rue des Abbesses.'

He could have kept in touch with some of his assistants if he had taken a radio car, but it would have been too conspicuous.

Who could say whether, before each crime, the man didn't spend hours watching the local traffic?

One nearly always knows that a murderer belongs to such and such a category; even if one hasn't got a description of him, one has some idea of his general appearance and of the class he comes from.

'Don't let there be a victim this evening!'

It was a prayer like those he used to say as a child, before going to sleep. He wasn't even conscious of uttering it.

'Did you notice?'

'What?'

'The drunkard, by the gas-lamp.'

'Who was it?'

'A pal of mine, Dutilleux. He loves dressing up, especially as a drunk.'

A quarter to ten, and nothing had happened.

'Stop outside the Brasserie Pigalle.'

Maigret ordered a beer on his way through, shut himself up in the telephone-box and called the Judicial Police. It was Lucas who answered.

'Nothing?'

'Nothing so far. Only a prostitute, complaining that a foreign sailor had knocked her about.'

'Torrence is with you?'

'Yes.'

'What about the Baron?'

'He must have gone to bed.'

It was past the time at which the last crime had been committed. Did that mean the man was less interested in darkness than in the actual time? Or that the sham arrest had had no effect on him?

Maigret was smiling ironically as he returned to the car, and the irony was addressed to himself. Who could tell? The man he was hunting through the Montmartre streets like this might perhaps be holidaying by the seaside in Normandy, or in a country boarding-house.

Discouragement swept over him, suddenly, from one second to the next, as it were. His own efforts and those of his assistants struck him as futile, almost ridiculous.

What was the foundation for all this set-up, which had

taken so long to arrange? Nothing. Less than nothing. A sort of intuition he'd had after a good dinner, while he was chatting with Professor Tissot in a quiet drawing-room in the Rue Picpus.

But wouldn't Tissot himself be dismayed if he knew how much the superintendent had made out of their casual conversation?

And suppose the man simply was not impelled by vanity, by the need to assert himself?

Even those words, which he had uttered as though he'd made a discovery, rather sickened him now.

He'd been thinking too much about it. He'd worked too hard at the problem. He was ceasing to believe in it, almost beginning to doubt whether the killer really existed.

'Where do we go now, Chief?'

'Wherever you like.'

The astonishment he read in the face the man turned towards him made him conscious of his own discouragement, and he was ashamed. He had no right to lose confidence in front of his assistants.

'Go up to the top of the Rue Lepic.'

They went past the Moulin de la Galette, and he looked at the exact spot on the pavement where the body of Joséphine Simmer, the midwife, had been found.

So the facts were there. Five crimes had been committed. And the killer was still at liberty, perhaps ready to strike again.

That woman, aged about forty, hatless, who was coming down the hill with short steps and leading a poodle on a leash — wasn't she one of the auxiliaries?

There were others in the surrounding streets, risking their lives at this very moment. They were volunteers, but the fact remained that it was he who had given them their jobs. It was up to him to protect them.

Had all possible precautions been taken?

On paper this afternoon, the plan had seemed perfect. Each of the sectors regarded as dangerous was under surveillance. The women volunteers were on their guard. Invisible watchers stood ready to intervene.

But had no corner been forgotten? Might not someone

relax his attention, if only for a moment?

His discouragement was giving way to fright, and had it still been possible he would perhaps have ordered the whole thing to be stopped.

Hadn't the experiment gone on long enough? It was ten o'clock. Nothing had happened. Nothing would happen now, and it was better so.

The Place du Tertre looked like a fair-ground, there were crowds round the little tables where people were drinking vin rosé; music blared from every corner, a man was eating fire and another, amid all the clamour, was patiently playing some tune of 1900 on his violin. Yet at less than a hundred yards aways the alleys were deserted and the killer could take action with no risk.

'Go down again.'

'The same way?'

It would have been better to stick to the usual methods, even if they were slow, even if they had yielded no results in six months.

'Go towards the Place Constantin-Pecqueur.'

'By the Avenue Junot?'

'If you like.'

A few couples were strolling along the pavements, arm in arm, and Maigret noticed another, mouth to mouth and with their eyes shut, in a corner just under a gas-lamp.

In the Place Constantin-Pecqueur two cafés were still open and there was no light in Lognon's window. It was he who knew the district best; he would be prowling round the streets like a game-dog nosing its way through the undergrowth, and for a moment the superintendent imagined him with the dangling tongue and hot breath of a spaniel.

'What time is it?'

'Ten past ten. Nine minutes past, to be precise.'

'Hush...'

They stretched their ears and had the impression that running footsteps could be heard higher up, towards the Avenue Junot which they had just left behind them.

Before the footsteps there had been another sound — a whistle-blast, perhaps two of them.

'Where is it?'

'I don't know.'

It was hard to tell the exact direction of the sounds. While they were still motionless a small black car, one of the Judicial Police cars, rushed close past them, making for the Avenue Junot at top speed.

'Follow that.'

Other cars, parked ones which had seemed empty a few moments before, had now started up and were all tearing in the same direction: two more whistles shrilled through the air, closer this time, for Maigret's car had already covered five hundred yards.

Men's and women's voices could be heard. Somebody was running along the pavement, while another figure came hurtling down the stone steps.

Something had happened at last.

CHAPTER FOUR

The Policewomen's Date

At first there was such a confusion in the badly-lit streets that it was impossible to make out what was going on, and it was not until much later, by comparing statements which varied in accuracy, that a general idea could be formed.

Maigret, whose driver was rushing at top speed up narrow streets which at night took on the aspect of scenes in a theatre, no longer knew exactly where he had got to, except that they were approaching the Place du Tertre; he seemed to hear faint echoes of its bands.

What added to the confusion was that there was movement in both directions. Cars and running figures — most of them police, no doubt — were converging towards a point that seemed to lie somewhere in the Rue Norvins, whereas other figures, a bicycle without a lamp, and two, then three cars, were tearing along in the opposite direction.

'That way!' someone shouted. 'I saw him go...'

They were chasing a man, perhaps one of those the superintendent had seen. He also thought he recognized the Gloomy Inspector — a small figure who was running very fast and had lost his hat — but he couldn't be certain.

What mattered to him at the moment was to find out whether the killer had succeeded, whether a woman had died; and when at last he saw a group of some ten people on a shadowy pavement, his first anxious glance was directed towards the ground.

He didn't get the impression that the people were bending down. He could see them gesticulating, and at the corner of an alley a uniformed policeman, who had sprung from heaven only knew where, was already trying to stop the inquisitive crowd that was pouring down from the Place du Tertre.

Someone emerged from the darkness and came up to him as he got out of the car.

'Is that you, Chief?'

The ray, of an electric torch picked out his face, as though everyone mistrusted everyone.

'She's not hurt.'

It took him a moment to recognize the speaker, though the man was one of his own inspectors.

'What's happened?'

'I don't know exactly. The man got away. They're chasing him. I'd be surprised if he escapes, with the whole district in a state of siege.'

At last he reached the focal point of the excitement, a woman in a fairly light blue dress who reminded him of something. She was still breathing fast, but managed to summon a smile, the tremulous smile of one who had had a narrow escape.

She recognized Maigret.

'I'm sorry I didn't manage to get the better of him,' she said. 'I still can't think how he slipped through my fingers.'

She wasn't sure which of them had already heard the beginning of her adventure.

'Hello! One of his jacket buttons came off in my hand.'

She held it out to the superintendent — a little smooth, dark object with the thread still in it, and what might be a scrap of cloth clinging to it as well.

'He attacked you?'

'As I was going past that alley.'

A kind of corridor, in complete darkness and with no gate, led out of the street.

'I was on the alert. When I saw the alley I had a kind of intuition, and I had to make an effort to keep on walking at the same pace.'

Maigret thought he recognized her now; at any rate he recognized the blue shade of her dress. Wasn't she the girl he'd seen just now in a corner, leaning against a man, their mouths pressed hard against each other?

'He let me get past the opening, and at that very second I sensed a movement, the air stirring behind me. A hand grabbed at my throat and then, I don't know how, I managed a judo hold.'

A rumour of what had happened must have gone round the Place du Tertre, and most of the people were leaving the tables with their red-checked cloths, the Venetian lanterns and the pitchers of vin rosé and streaming in one direction. The uniformed policeman was being overwhelmed. A coachload of police was coming up the Rue Caulaincourt. They would try to make the crowd move on.

How many inspectors were hunting the fugitive through the neighbouring streets, with their unexpected bends and innumerable corners?

Maigret had the impression that from that point of view at least the game was already lost. Once again the killer had had a stroke of genius — that of operating less than a hundred yards away from a kind of fairground, knowing perfectly well that if the alarm were given the crowd would clutter up the whole place.

As far as he could remember — he didn't pause to look at his plan of battle — it was Mauvoisin who was to be at the head of the sector, so he would be directing operations. Maigret looked round for him, but couldn't see him.

The superintendent's presence was of no use. The rest, now, was mostly a matter of luck.

'Get into my car,' he said to the girl.

He had recognized her as one of the auxiliaries, and it still vexed him to have seen her in a man's arms a little while before.

'What is your name?'

'Marthe Jusserand.'

'You are twenty-two years old?'

'Twenty-five.'

She was of much the same build as the killer's five victims, but very muscular.

'To Police Headquarters!' said Maigret to the driver.

It would be better for him to go to the place where all information was bound to arrive, than to remain in the middle of what seemed like a confused bustle.

A little further on he saw Mauvoisin, giving instructions to his men.

'I'm going back to the Quai,' he called to him. 'Keep me informed.'

A radio car arrived now. Two others, which must be cruising in the neighbourhood, would soon come up as reinforcements.

'Were you frightened?' he asked his companion, after they came to streets where the atmosphere was normal.

In the Place Clichy people were crowding out of a cinema. The cafés and bars were brightly-lit, reassuring, with people still sitting on their terraces.

'Not so much at the time, but directly afterwards. I thought my legs would give way.'

'Did you see him?'

'For a second his face was close to mine, and yet I'm not sure whether I'd know him again. I was a P.T. instructress for three years before taking the police exam. I'm very strong, you know. I've learnt judo, like the other girls.'

'You didn't call out?'

'I can't remember.'

They were to learn afterwards, from an inspector who had been posted at the window of a lodging-house not far off, that she had not called for help until her aggressor had run away.

'He was wearing a dark suit. He had light brown hair and looked fairly young.'

'What age, would you say?'

'I don't know. I was in too much of a state. I knew perfectly well in my mind what I was to do if I were attacked, but when it happened I forgot everything. I was thinking of the knife he had in his hand.'

'You saw it?'

She was silent for a few seconds.

'I wonder now whether I saw it, or if I only thought I saw it because I knew it was there. On the other hand I'd swear his eyes were blue or grey. He seemed to be in pain. I'd managed to get a grip on his forearm, and I must have been hurting him badly. It was a matter of seconds before he would have to bend over and fall flat on the pavement.'

'And he managed to free himself?'

'I suppose so. He slipped out of my hands, I'm still wondering how. I caught hold of something — his jacket button — and a second later there I was with the button in my hand, while a dim figure was running away. It all happened very quickly, though to me, of course, it seemed to take a long time.'

'Would you like a drink to pick you up?'

'I never drink. But I'd be glad of a cigarette.'

'Then please smoke.'

'I haven't any cigarettes. A month ago I decided to give up smoking.'

Maigret stopped the car at the nearest tobacconist's.

'What kind?'

'American, please.'

It must have been the first time the superintendent had ever bought American cigarettes.

At the Quai des Orfèvres, where he made her walk upstairs ahead of him, they found Lucas and Torrence each at a telephone. Maigret looked at them questioningly, and they replied, one after another, with a rueful grimace.

The man had not been caught yet.

'Sit down, Mademoiselle.'

'I feel quite all right now. So much for the cigarette. It's going to be hard to go without smoking in the next few days.'

Lucas had finished his telephone call, and Maigret gave him the description he had just received himself.

'Pass that on to everyone, including the railway stations.'

'What height was he?' he asked the girl.

'No taller than I am.'

So the fellow was on the short side.

'Thin?'

'Not fat, at any rate.'

'Aged twenty? Thirty? Forty?'

She had said 'young,' but that word can have very

different meanings.

'I should say more like thirty.'

'You don't remember any other details?'

'No.'

'Was he wearing a tie?'

'I suppose so.'

'Did he look like a prowling tramp, like a workman, or like a clerk?'

She was doing her best to help, but her recollections were scrappy.

'It seems to me that in any other circumstances I shouldn't have noticed him in the street. He looked like a gentleman, one might say.'

Suddenly she put up her hand, like a girl in the schoolroom — and it was not so very long since she had been a schoolgirl.

'He had a ring on his finger.'

'A wedding ring, or a signet-ring?'

'Wait a minute...'

She shut her eyes and seemed to be getting into the same position as during the struggle.

'First of all I felt it between my fingers, and then, when I put the judo hold on him, his hand came close to my face... A signet-ring would have been thicker... There'd have been a flat place on it... It was certainly a wedding-ring...'

'You heard that, Lucas?'

'Yes, Chief.'

'Hair long, or short?'

'Not short. I can see it hanging over one of his ears while his head was bent, nearly parallel to the pavement.'

'You're taking all this down?'

'Yes, Chief.'

'Come into my office.'

He automatically took off his jacket, although the night was fairly cool, at least compared with the daytime.

'Sit down. You're sure you won't have a drink?'

'Sure.'

'Before the man attacked you, didn't you meet someone else?'

A flood of crimson rose to her cheeks and ears. In spite

of her athlete's muscles she had a very thin, soft skin.

'Yes.'

'Tell me all about it.'

'If I did wrong it can't be helped. I'm engaged.'

'What does your fiancé do?'

'He's in his last year of Law. He means to go into the police force too…'

Not the way Maigret had done, from the bottom beginning on the beat, but through a series of competitive examinations.

'You saw him this evening?'

'Yes.'

'You told him what was going to happen?'

'No. I asked him to spend the evening in the Place du Tertre.'

'You were frightened?'

'No. But I liked to feel he wasn't too far away.'

'And you arranged another meeting with him?'

She was ill at ease, shifting from one foot to the other, trying to discover, by little glances, whether Maigret was angry or not.

'I'll tell you the whole truth, Superintendent. So much the worse if I made a mistake. We'd been given instructions, you know, to behave as naturally as possible, like any girl or any woman who happens to be out of doors in the evening. And in the evening one often sees a couple kissing and then separating, each going a different way.'

'And that's why you arranged for your fiancé to come?'

'Yes, honestly it was. I'd arranged to meet him at ten o'clock. Something was expected to happen before that. So by ten o'clock I wouldn't be risking anything if I tried another way.'

Maigret looked closely at her.

'It didn't occur to you that if the murderer saw you leaving a man's arms and going off by yourself, that would probably bring on a crisis?'

'I don't know. I suppose it was just chance. Did I do wrong?'

He thought it wiser not to reply. This was the old dilemma, discipline versus initiative. Hadn't he himself made some serious deviations from discipline, tonight and in the last few days?

'Take your time. Sit down at my desk. And write down, as though you were at school, exactly what happened this evening, trying to remember the smallest details, even those that don't seem important.'

He knew from experience that this often produced results.

'May I use your pen?'

'If you like. When you've finished, call me.'

He went back to the office where Lucas and Torrence were still sharing the incoming calls. In a tiny room at the end of the corridor a wireless operator was writing down the messages from the radio cars on scraps of paper and sending them along by the office-boy.

Up in Montmartre they had gradually got rid of most of the crowd, but as was to be expected, the reporters had been warned and had hastened to the scene.

They had begun by surrounding three blocks of houses, then four, and then a whole district, as time went by and the man had had the chance to get further away.

Hotels and lodging-houses were being searched and their occupants woken up, asked for their identity-cards, and made to answer a short interrogation.

There was every prospect that the murderer had already slipped away, probably in the first few minutes, when the whistles were blown, people began running, and the inquisitive crowd came pouring out of the Place du Tertre.

There was one other possibility — that the killer lived in the district, close to the scene of this latest attempt, and had simply gone home.

Maigret was fidgeting absently with the button Marthe Jusserand had given him, an ordinary button, dark grey lightly veined with blue. It bore no distinguishing mark. A strand of thick tailor's cotton hung from it, and some tiny scraps of cloth from the suit still clung to the cotton.

'Ring Moers and tell him to come at once.'

'Here, or to the laboratory?'

'Here.'

He had learnt from experience that an hour lost at a

certain point in an inquiry might give the criminal a lead of several weeks.

'Lognon would like to speak to you, Chief.'

'Where is he?'

'In a café somewhere in Montmartre.'

'Hello — Lognon?'

'Yes, Chief. The chase is still going on. They've surrounded a good part of the district. But I'm practically certain I saw the fellow running down the steps leading out of the Place Constantin-Pecqueur, just opposite my house.'

'You weren't able to catch up with him?'

'No. I ran as fast as I could, but he's quicker than I am.'

'You didn't shoot?'

For that had been the order — to shoot at sight, preferably at the legs, on the one condition that it involved no danger to any passer-by.

'I didn't dare, because there was a drunken old woman asleep on the bottom steps and I might have hit her. Afterwards it was too late. He melted into the darkness, almost as though he'd vanished into the wall. I searched all round, yard by yard. All the time I had the impression he wasn't far off, that he was watching every movement I made.'

'And that's all?'

'Yes. Some of the other fellows arrived then, and we organized a round-up.'

'Without discovering anything?'

'Only that about that time a man came into a bar in the Rue Caulaincourt where some customers were playing cards. He didn't stop at the bar, but went straight to the telephone-box. So he must have had some counters in his pocket. He made a call and went out just as he'd come in, without a word, without even looking at the proprietor or the card-players. That's what made them notice him. They hadn't a clue about what was happening.'

'Nothing else?'

'He's fair-haired, youngish, slender, and had no hat.'

'His suit?'

'Dark. My idea is that he rang up somebody who came

with a car to pick him up at an agreed spot. We never thought of stopping cars with several people in them.'

It would indeed have been the first time in the annals of crime that a maniac of this kind was not acting entirely on his own.

'Thanks, old man.'

'I'm staying here. We shall carry on.'

'It's the only thing to do.'

It might have been only a coincidence. Anybody might go into a bar to make a telephone call and not want a drink, or have time for one.

All the same it worried Maigret. He was remembering the wedding-ring the young policewoman had told him about.

Had the man had the nerve to send for his wife to get him out of the police cordon? If so, what explanation had he given her? First thing in the morning she would see the papers, with the story of what had happened in Montmartre.

'Is Moers coming?'

'Right away, Chief. He was reading in bed. I told him to take a taxi.'

Marthe Jusserand brought in her essay, that is to say her report on the events she had been through.

'I haven't bothered about style, of course. I've tried to put everything down, as objectively as possible.'

He glanced over the two pages, finding nothing new in them, and only when the girl turned away to pick up her handbag did he notice that her dress was torn at the back. This detail suddenly brought home to him the danger to which he had exposed her and the other women volunteers.

'You can go to bed now. I'll tell them to drive you home.'

'There's no need, Superintendent. Jean is sure to be down below, and he has his little Renault.'

He stared at her, quizzical and amused.

'But you can't have told him to meet you at the Quai des Orfèvres — you couldn't have known you would be coming here?'

'No. But he was one of the first to come running from

the Place du Tertre. I saw him among the people watching, with the inspectors. He saw me too, while I was talking to you and when I got into your car. He'll certainly have guessed that you'd be bringing me here.'

Maigret was flabbergasted; he held out his hand and muttered: Well, my child, I wish you good luck with Jean. And thank you. I'm sorry to have given you such a scare. The Press must still be kept in the dark about the trap we'd prepared, of course. We shan't give them your name.'

'I'd rather you didn't.'

'Goodnight...'

He escorted her politely to the head of the stairs and returned to his inspectors, shaking his head.

'Strange girl,' he grunted.

Torrence, who did not think much of the younger generation, murmured:

'They're all like that nowadays.'

Moers came in a few minutes later, as fresh as though he'd had a good night's sleep. He didn't know a thing. The plans for hunting down the killer had not been communicated to the laboratory staff.

'A job, Chief?'

Maigret handed him the button, and Moers pulled a face.

'Is that all?'

'Yes.'

'Moers turned it first on one side, then on the other.

'Want me to go upstairs and look at it?'

'I'll come with you.'

This was almost out of superstition. The telephone calls were still coming in uninterrupted succession. Maigret's confidence had not returned. And yet every time the phone rang he gave an involuntary start, hoping the miracle had happened. Perhaps if he were not there it would happen at last, and they would come to the laboratory to tell him the killer had been caught!

Moers turned on the lights and began by using a magnifying-glass, tweezers and a number of delicate instruments, before putting the thread and the scraps of cloth under the microscope.

'I suppose you want to know where the garment from which this button was torn off was made?'

'I want to know everything it's possible to find out.'

'Well, to begin with, although it's an ordinary-looking button, it's of very good quality. It's not the kind used for mass-produced suits. I don't think it will be difficult to find out tomorrow morning where it was made, for there aren't very many button manufacturers. Nearly all of them have their offices in the Rue des Petits-Champs, side by side with the wholesale drapers.'

'And the thread?'

'The same that practically every tailor must use. The cloth interests me more. As you see, it's basically a quite ordinary grey; but there's a light blue thread woven in that gives it a special character. I'd swear the stuff wasn't made in France, but imported from England. And imports of cloth pass through the hands of a limited number of dealers, of whom I can give you a list.'

Moers had all kinds of lists, yearbooks and catalogues, thanks to which he could quickly discover where any object came from, whether it was a weapon, a pair of shoes or a handkerchief.

'There! As you see, half of the importers have their offices in the Rue des Petits-Champs too...'

In Paris, fortunately, wholesale firms are still more or less assembled in particular districts.

'None of the offices opens before eight o'clock, most of them not till nine.'

'I'll have a start made with those that open at eight.'

'Is that all for tonight?'

'Unless you can think of anything else that might be done.'

'I'll try, on the off-chance.'

He would no doubt try to find, on the thread or in the scraps of cloth, some kind of revealing dust or other substance. Three years previously one criminal had been identified by traces of sawdust on a handkerchief, and another by a spot of printer's ink.

Maigret suddenly felt tired. The tension of the last few days, the last few hours, had left him, and he felt no energy, no interest in anything, no optimism.

Tomorrow morning he would have to face Coméliau, and the journalists, who would pester him with awkward questions. What was he going to say to them? He couldn't tell them the truth. Nor could he tell lies all along the line.

When he got down to Judicial Police Headquarters again, he found his ordeal with the reporters was not to take place tomorrow, but at once. The Baron wasn't there, but there were three others, including young Rougin, his eyes sparkling with excitement.

'May we see you in your office, Superintendent?'

He shrugged his shoulders, admitted them, and stared at the three of them, all grasping their notebooks and with pencils at the ready.

'Your prisoner has escaped?'

They were bound to ask him about that business, which was becoming a distinct embarrassment now that things had begun to move so quickly.

'Nobody's escaped.'

'You released him?'

'Nobody has been released.'

'But the killer has attacked again tonight, hasn't he?'

'A young woman was attacked in the street, not far from the Place du Tertre, but she got off with a fright.'

'She wasn't hurt?'

'No.'

'Did her aggressor pull out a knife?'

'She isn't sure.'

'Isn't she here any longer?'

They looked round them, suspiciously. They must have been told in Montmartre that the young woman had got into the superintendent's car.

'What's her name?'

'Her name is of no importance.'

'You're keeping it a secret?'

'Let's say there is no point in publishing it.'

'Why? Is she married? Had she no business to be where she was?'

'That's one explanation.'

'The right one?'

'I don't know.'

'Don't you think this makes a lot of mystery?'

'The mystery that worries me most is the identity of the killer.'

'You've discovered that?'

'Not yet.'

'Have you some new factors thanks to which you hope to discover it?'

'Perhaps.'

'Naturally you won't tell us what they are?'

'Naturally not.'

'Did the young woman whose name is such a secret actually see her assailant?'

'Indistinctly, but well enough for me to give you a description of him.'

Maigret gave the description, incomplete though it was, but said nothing about the button torn off the man's jacket.

'Vague, isn't it?'

'Yesterday it was even vaguer, considering we knew nothing whatsoever about him.'

He was in a bad mood, and felt vexed with himself for treating them like this. They were doing their job, just as he was. He knew he was annoying them by his answers, and even more by his silences; but he couldn't manage to be his usual friendly self.

'I'm tired, gentlemen.'

'Are you going home?'

'As soon as you give me a chance.'

'The hunt is still going on, up there?'

'Yes.'

'Are you going to release the man Inspector Lognon brought to you yesterday, and whom you've questioned twice?'

He had to think of a reply.

'That man was never held in custody. He wasn't a suspect, he was a witness whose identity, for certain reasons, cannot be revealed.'

'As a matter of precaution?'

'Perhaps?'

'He's still being guarded by the police?'

'Yes.'

'It wouldn't have been possible for him to get to Montmartre this evening?'

'No. You have no more questions?'

'When we got here you were in the laboratory.'

They knew the building almost as well as he did.

'Up there they work on objects, not on suppositions.'

He looked at them unblinkingly.

'May we conclude that the man in the Rue Norvins left something behind him, perhaps in the hands of his victim?'

'It would be preferable, in the interests of the investigation, for no conclusions to be drawn from my comings and goings. Gentlemen, I'm worn out, and with your permission I will leave. In twenty-four hours, or in forty-eight, I shall perhaps have something to tell you. For the moment you will have to rest content with the description I've given you.'

It was half-past one by this time. There were pauses now between the telephone-calls in the neighbouring office, where he went to say goodnight to Lucas and Torrence.

'Still nothing?'

He only had to look at them to realize that the question was superflous. The police would continue to surround the district and to search it alley by alley and house by house, until dawn broke, revealing the dustbins lined up along the pavements.

'Goodnight, boys.'

To be on the safe side he had kept the car, and the driver was pacing up and down in the courtyard. To get a glass of cold beer he would have had to go a long way, to Montparnasse or somewhere near the Place Pigalle, and he hadn't the heart for it.

Madame Maigret, in her nightdress, opened the front door before he had time to get the key out of his pocket; he went in, with a grunt and a stubborn face, and made for the sideboard where the bottle of sloe-gin stood. It wasn't that he wanted, it was beer; but as he emptied his glass at a gulp he had a kind of impression that he was getting his own back.

CHAPTER FIVE

The Cigarette-burn

It might have taken weeks. At the Quai des Orfèvres that morning everybody was exhausted, with a bad taste in the mouth. Some of them, like Maigret, had had three or four hours' sleep. Others, who lived in the suburbs, hadn't slept at all.

Some of them were still up there, searching the Grandes-Carrières district, guarding the Métro stations, watching the men who came out of the houses.

'Did you sleep well, Superintendent?'

It was young Rougin, full of beans, even more vivacious than usual, who had hailed Maigret in the corridor in his high-pitched, slightly metallic voice. He seemed particularly cheerful this morning, and it was only when he saw the paper the lad worked for, that the superintendent understood why. He too had taken a risk. The day before, already, and again during the evening, and finally while the three or four of them had been harrying Maigret at the Quai des Orfèvres, he had suspected the truth.

He had no doubt spent the remainder of the night in questioning various people, particularly hotel-keepers.

In any case his paper carried a big headline:

Killer Escapes from Police Trap

Out in the corridor, Rougin must be waiting for Maigret's reaction.

Our good friend Superintendent Maigret, he had written, *will probably not contradict us if we say that the arrest made the day before yesterday, and deliberately kept a great mystery, was only a feint, intended to lure the Montmartre killer into a trap...*

Rougin had gone even further. In the middle of the night he had woken up a well-known psychiatrist and asked him questions not unlike those the superintendent had put to Professor Tissot.

Was it thought that the murderer would come and hang about the Judicial Police Headquarters to get a glimpse of the man who was being accused in his place? That is possible. But it is more likely that they hoped, by wounding his vanity, to drive him into making a fresh attack, in a district previously occupied by a force of police...

Only Rougin's paper took this line. The other reporters were at a loss.

'Still here, are you?' growled Maigret when he saw Lucas. 'Aren't you going to bed?'

'I slept for a bit in a chair, and then went for a swim at the Deligny Baths and shaved in my changing-room.'

'Who's on hand?'

'Nearly everyone.'

'No news, of course?'

Lucas replied with a slight shrug.

'Get me Janvier, Lapointe, and two or three of the others.'

He had drunk nothing all night except one pint of beer and a glass of sloe-gin, and yet he had a kind of hangover. The sky was covered this morning, but not with real clouds that would have cooled the air a bit. A greyish veil had gradually spread above the city, glutinous vapour was slowly drifting down into the streets, heavy with dust, and with a smell of petrol that took one by the throat.

Maigret opened his window, but shut it again almost at once, for the air outside was more stifling than that in the office.

'Get along to the Rue des Petits-Champs, boys. Here are some addresses. If you don't find anything there, hunt up some others in the telephone directory. Some of you had better deal with the button and the others with the cloth.'

He explained what Moers had told him about the wholesalers and the importers.

'It's possible we may be lucky this time. Keep me informed.'

He was still glum, and it wasn't, as they all supposed, because he had had a setback, because the man they were pursuing had managed to slip through the net.

He had expected that. In point of fact it was not a setback, because his expectations had been proved correct and because they at last had a clue, a starting-point, however insignificant it might seem.

His thoughts were on the killer, who was beginning to take definite shape in his mind, now that at least one person had had a glimpse of him. He thought of him, still young, fair-haired, probably melancholy or embittered. Why was it that Maigret would have wagered, at this moment, that he came of a good family and was accustomed to a comfortable life?

He wore a wedding-ring. So he had a wife. He had had a father and a mother. He had been a schoolboy, perhaps a student.

This morning he was alone against the Paris police force, against the entire population of Paris; and he too, no doubt, had read young Rougin's article in the newspaper.

Had he gone to sleep, once he had escaped the ambush in which he had almost been caught?

Assuming that his crimes brought him appeasement, or even a certain sense of well-being, what effect would an unsuccessful attack produce on him?

Without waiting for Coméliau to ring him up, Maigret went to the magistrate's office, where he found him reading the newspapers.

'I warned you, Superintendent. You can't say I was enthusiastic about your scheme, or even that I approved of it.'

'My men are following a trail.'

'Something serious?'

'They have a piece of material evidence in their hands. It's bound to lead somewhere. It may take weeks, or it may take two hours.'

It didn't even take two hours. Lapointe's first visit in the Rue des Petits-Champs had been to an office where the walls were covered with buttons of all kinds. *Established 1782,* was the announcement inscribed on the door, beneath the names of the firm's two partners. And the collection on the walls included every type of button manufactured from the beginning.

After showing his police badge, Lapointe asked:

'Is it possible to discover where this button comes from?'

For him, for Maigret, or for anyone else, it was just a button like any other; but the clerk looked at it carefully and replied without hesitation:

'It comes from Mullerbach's, at Colmar.'

'Do Mullerbach's have a Paris office?'

'In this building, two floors up.'

For as Lapointe and his companion noticed, the whole house was occupied by button-merchants.

There was no Monsieur Mullerbach nowadays; the firm was run by the son of a son-in-law of the last Mullerbach. He received the police officers very courteously in his office, looked the button over carefully, and asked:

'What exactly did you want to know?'

'Did your firm make that button?'

'Yes.'

'Have you a list of the tailors to whom you sold buttons of that kind?'

The manufacturer pressed a bell as he explained:

'As you perhaps know, cloth-manufacturers change the colours, and even the weave, of most of their goods every year. Before they put their new lines on sale they send us samples, so that we can make buttons to match. The buttons are sold direct to the tailors...'

A young man who seemed prostrated by the heat came in.

'Monsieur Jeanfils, will you look up the reference for this button and bring me the list of the tailors to whom we sold that type?'

Monsieur Jeanfils went out noiselessly without having opened his mouth. While he was away his employer went on describing the workings of the button business to the two police officers. Less than ten minutes later there was a knock on the glass-panelled door. Jeanfils reappeared, and laid the button and a sheet of typewritten paper on the desk.

It was a list of about forty tailors, four at Lyons, two at Bordeaux, one at Lille, a few in other French towns, and the remainder in Paris.

'There you are, gentlemen. And good luck.'

They were back again in the street, where the noise and bustle came almost as a shock after the cloistered calm that reigned in the offices upstairs.

'What do we do now?' asked Broncard, Lapointe's companion. 'Shall we get down to it at once? I counted. There are twenty-eight in Paris. If we took a taxi...'

'Do you know where Janvier went?'

Yes. Into that big building, or rather into the offices at the far end of the courtyard.'

'Wait for him.'

He himself went into a little bar with a sawdust-scattered floor, ordered a *blanc-vichy*, and shut himself into the telephone-box. Maigret was still with Coméliau and Lapointe got on to him there.

'Forty tailors in all,' he explained. 'Twenty-eight of them in Paris. Shall I start a round?'

'Just keep four or five names and dictate the rest to Lucas; he'll send out men.'

Before he had finished dictating, Janvier, Broncard and a fourth inspector came into the bistro, where they waited for him at the bar. All three were looking pleased. After a moment Janvier came and half-opened the glass door.

'Don't ring off,' he said, 'I have to talk to him too.'

'It's not the chief. It's Lucas.'

'Put me on to him all the same.'

Lack of sleep had made them all slightly feverish, with hot breath and eyes that were tired but bright.

'That you, old man? Tell the chief everything's going well. Yes, this is Janvier. We've hit the bull's-eye. A bit of luck, the fellow's suit being made of English cloth. I'll explain; I know the whole routine by now. To cut it short, only about ten tailors, so far, have ordered that cloth. A lot more have been sent books of samples. It's those they show their customers, and when a suit is ordered they send for the length. In other words there's every hope things will move quickly, unless the suit was actually made in England, which isn't likely.'

Outside the bistro they split up, each with two or three names on a scrap of paper, and it was like drawing a lottery. One of the four would probably — perhaps that very morning — get hold of the name they had been trying to find for the last six months.

It was young Lapointe who won the big prize. He had reserved the part of the Left Bank round the Boulevard Saint-Germain for himself; he knew it well because he lived there.

The first tailor, in the Boulevard Saint-Michel, had indeed ordered a length of the cloth. He was even able to show the inspector the suit he had made from it, for it hadn't been delivered yet; in fact it wasn't finished, but with one sleeve in place and the collar not sewn on yet, it was waiting for the customer to come for a fitting.

The second address was that of a little Polish tailor, on the third floor of a house in the Rue Vaneau. He had only one workman. Lapointe found him sitting on his table; he wore steel-rimmed spectacles.

'Do you recognize this cloth?'

Janvier had asked for several samples for his colleagues.

'Certainly. Why? You want a suit?'

'I want the name of the customer for whom you made one.'

'It was some time ago.'

'How long?'

'It was last autumn.'

'You don't remember the customer?'

'I remember him.'

'Who was it?'

'Monsieur Moncin, Marcel Moncin.'

'Who is Monsieur Moncin?'

'A very nice gentleman, who has bought his clothes from me for several years.'

Lapointe was trembling, he hardly dared to believe his

ears. The miracle was happening. The man they'd been looking for so long, who had caused so much ink to flow, the man the entire police force had spent so many hours in hunting, had suddenly acquired a name. He was about to have an address, a status, and soon, no doubt, a visible shape.

'Does he live in the district?'

'Not far from here, in the Boulevard Saint-Germain, next door to the Solférino Métro station.'

'You know him well?'

'As I know all my customers. He's a well-bred, charming man.'

'Is it long since he came to see you?'

'The last time was last November, for an overcoat, not long after I'd made him this suit.'

'You have his exact address?'

The little tailor turned the pages of an exercise-book where names and addresses were written in pencil, with figures, no doubt the prices of the suits, which he crossed through in red when they were paid for.

'Do you know if he's married?'

'His wife has been here with him several times. She always comes to help him choose.'

'Is she young?'

'About thirty, I suppose. She's very distinguished, a real lady.'

Lapointe couldn't stop trembling from head to foot. Panic was creeping over him. So close to the goal, he was afraid of some sudden hitch that would send them right back to the beginning.

'Thank you. I may come to see you again.'

Forgetting to ask what Marcel Moncin's profession was, he rushed downstairs and hurried to the Boulevard Saint-Germain, where No. 228 *bis* attracted his fascinated gaze. It was a block of flats just like the others along the Boulevard, with wrought-iron balconies. The door was open, showing a corridor with beige-painted walls, at the far end of which the lift-cage was just visible. The concierge's lodge was on the right.

Lapointe almost ached with longing to go in, ask for

Moncin's flat, go up and deal with the killer by himself; but he knew he mustn't.

A uniformed policeman was on duty just opposite the entrance to the Metro; Lapointe hailed him and disclosed his identity.

'Will you watch that house during the few minutes it will take me to ring up the Quai des Orfèvres?'

'What do I have to do?'

'Nothing. Or rather, if a man of about thirty, lightly-built and fairish, should happen to come out, manage to delay him somehow — ask to see his papers, do whatever you like.'

'Who is he?'

'His name's Marcel Moncin.'

'What's he done?'

Lapointe preferred not to explain that in all probability the man was the Montmartre killer.

A few moments later he was again in a telephone-box.

'The Quai? Give me Superintendent Maigret at once. Lapointe here.'

He was actually stammering with excitement.

'That you, Chief? Lapointe. Yes. I've found... What?... Yes... His name and his address... I'm just opposite his house...'

It suddenly occurred to him that other suits had been made of the same cloth and that this might not be the right one.

'Janvier hasn't phoned? Yes? What did he say?'

Three of the suits had been found, but the descriptions did not correspond to what Marthe Jusserand had said.

'I'm speaking from the Boulevard Saint-Germain... I've put a police officer outside the house-door... Yes... Yes... I'll wait for you... just a second while I look for the name of this bistro.'

He went out of the telephone-box and read, back to front, the name written in enamel lettering on the window of the café.

'Café Solférino...'

Maigret had told him to stay there without showing himself. Less than fifteen minutes later, as he stood at the bar with another *blanc-vichy* in front of him, he saw some little police cars stopping at different points.

Maigret himself got out of one of them; Lapointe thought he looked even bulkier and heavier than usual.

'It was so easy that I'm afraid to believe it, Chief...'

Was Maigret as nervous as himself? If so it didn't show. Or rather, for anyone who knew him well, it was revealed by a surly, or stubborn, manner.

'What's that you're drinking?'

'A *blanc-vichy*.'

Maigret pulled a face.

'Have you any draught beer?'

'Certainly, Monsieur Maigret.'

'You know me?'

'I've seen your photo in the papers quite often. And last year, when you were dealing with what was going on opposite, at the Ministry, you came here several times for a drink.'

He swallowed his beer.

'Come along.'

Meantime there had been a deployment of forces which, though on a smaller scale than that of the night before, was no less thorough. Two inspectors had gone up to the top floor of the house. There were others on the pavement outside, and yet others across the Boulevard and at the corner of the street, not to mention a radio car close by.

It would no doubt prove superfluous. Killers of that type seldom defend themselves, at any rate with weapons.

'Do I come with you?'

Maigret nodded, and both men went into the concierge's lodge. It was a cosy place, with a little sitting-room divided from the kitchen by a red velvet curtain. The concierge was a woman of about fifty, placid and amiable.

'Can I help you, gentlemen?'

'Monsieur Moncin, please?'

'The second floor, on the left.'

'Do you know if he's at home?'

'Very likely. I haven't seen him go out.'

'Is Madame Moncin there too?'

'She got back from shopping about half an hour ago.'

Maigret could not help thinking of his conversation with Professor Tissot at Pardon's. The house was quiet and comfortable, and its old-fashioned style, dating from the middle of the nineteenth century, had something reassuring about it. The lift stood waiting for them, well-oiled and with its brass handle shining; but they preferred to walk up. There was a thick, dark-red carpet on the stairs.

Most of the mats outside the doors — which were of dark wood — bore one or more initials in red, and all the bell-pushes were well polished. No sound came from the flats, and no smell of cooking drifted out to the stairs.

Beside one of the first-floor doors was the brass plate of a lung specialist.

Beside the left-hand door on the second floor there was a brass plate of the same size, but with more stylized, modern lettering, which read:

Marcel Moncin
Architect—decorator

The two men paused and exchanged glances, and Lapointe had the impression that Maigret was as agitated as himself. It was the superintendent who put out his hand and pressed the electric button. They didn't hear the bell ring, it must be somewhere in the depths of the flat. After what seemed a long time the door was opened by a white-aproned maid, less than twenty years old, who looked at them in surprise and asked:

'What is it?'

'Is Monsieur Moncin at home?'

She seemed embarrassed, and faltered:

'I don't know.'

So he was.

'If you'll wait a minute I'll go and ask Madame...'

She had no need to go. A woman appeared at the far end of the corridor — a woman who was still young and who was wearing a dressing-gown she must have slipped on for coolness after getting back from the shopping.

'What is it, Odile?'

'Two gentlemen who want speak to Monsieur, Madame.'

She came forward, wrapping the dressing-gown round her staring at Maigret as though he reminded her of someone.

'You want...?' she inquired, trying to understand.

'Is your husband here?'

'That's to say...'

'That means he is.'

She reddened slightly.

'Yes. But he's asleep.'

'I must ask you to wake him.'

She hesitated, and then murmured:

'May I ask who...?'

'Judicial Police.'

'You're Superintendent Maigret, aren't you? I thought I recognized you...'

Maigret, who had advanced unobtrusively, was now in the hall.

'Please wake your husband. I suppose he got home late, last night?'

'What do you mean?'

'Does he usually sleep in the morning until after eleven?'

She smiled.

'Often. He likes to work in the evening, sometimes late into the night. He's an intellectual, an artist.'

'He didn't go out last night?'

'Not that I know of. If you will wait in the drawing-room I'll go and tell him.'

She had opened the glass-panelled door of a drawing-room done up in a modern style which was unexpected in this old house, but which had nothing aggressive about it; Maigret told himself he wouldn't mind living in a setting like this. Only the paintings on the walls displeased him, he couldn't make head or tail of them.

Lapointe stood looking down towards the front door. An unnecessary precaution, however, for by now all the entrances would be closely guarded.

The young woman departed with a rustle of silk; she was away only two or three minutes, but by the time she returned she had tidied her hair.

'He'll be here in a moment. Marcel is curiously shy in

one way — I sometimes tease him about it: he hates to be seen when he's just out of bed.'

'You have separate rooms?'

This gave her a slight shock, but she replied quite simply:

'So do a lot of married couples, don't they?'

And indeed, wasn't it almost the general rule among people belonging to their kind of circle? It meant nothing. What he was trying to decide was whether she was playing a part, whether she knew something, or whether on the contrary she was really wondering what connection there could be between Superintendent Maigret and her husband.

'Your husband works here?'

'Yes.'

She crossed the room and opened a door leading into a spacious office with two windows overlooking the Boulevard Saint-Germain. One could see drawing-boards in there, and rolls of paper, and some curious models made of plywood or wire, which resembled stage scenery.

'He works a lot?'

'Too much for his health. He's never been strong. We should have been in the mountains now, we always go at this time of year; but he's accepted a commission which will prevent us from taking a holiday at all.'

He had seldom seen a woman so composed, with such self-control. Surely she ought to have been panic-stricken at seeing Maigret arrive like this, considering that the papers were full of the killer and everyone knew he was in charge of the investigation? But she was simply watching him, as though interested to see such a famous man at close quarters.

'I'll go and see if he's nearly ready.'

Maigret sat down in an arm-chair, slowly filling his pipe and lit it; there was another exchange of glances between him and Lapointe, who could hardly keep still.

When the door through which Madame Moncin had vanished opened again it was not she who came in, but a man who looked so young that one was tempted to think there must be some mistake.

He was wearing a pyjama suit in a light shade of beige which emphasized his fair hair, delicate skin and bright blue eyes.

'I'm sorry to have kept you waiting, gentlemen...'

A smile which had something fragile and childish about it hovered over his lips.

'My wife woke me up just now, to tell me...'

Had his wife no curiosity about the purpose of this visit? She did not seem to be coming back. Perhaps she was listening at the door her husband had closed behind him?

'I've been working very hard just lately on the interior decoration of a huge house one of my friends is building on the Normandy coast...'

Taking a lawn handkerchief from his pocket, he wiped his forehead and upper lip, which were beaded with sweat.

'It's even hotter than yesterday, isn't it?'

He looked out of the window and saw that the sky was a purplish colour.

'It's no use opening the windows. I hope we shall have a storm.'

'I must apologize,' Maigret began, 'for being obliged to ask you some personal questions. To begin with, I would like to see the suit you were wearing yesterday.'

This appeared to take him by surprise, but without alarming him. His eyes widened slightly. His lips curled. He seemed to be thinking: What a weird idea!

Then he turned towards the door, saying:

'Excuse me a moment.'

After not more than half a minute, if that, he came back with a well-pressed grey suit over his arm. Maigret inspected it and found inside a pocket the name of the little tailor in the Rue Vaneau.

'You were wearing this yesterday?'

'I was.'

'In the evening?'

'Until just after dinner. Then I changed into the suit I'm wearing now, before starting work. I work mostly at night.'

'You didn't go out after eight o'clock in the evening?'

'I stayed in my office until about two o'clock, or half-past two, which explains why I was still asleep when you arrived. I need a lot of sleep, like all highly-strung people.'

He seemed anxious for their approval; he still seemed more like a student than a man of over thirty.

From close to, however, his face had a worn look which contrasted with its youthful appearance. His complexion had something sickly or faded about it, which was not unattractive, as sometimes happens with women who are past their first youth.

'Might I ask you to show me your whole wardrobe?'

At this he stiffened slightly, as though on the point of protesting, or refusing.

'If you wish. Come this way…'

If his wife had been listening at the door she had time to get away, for they saw her at the other end of the corridor, talking to the servant in a bright, modern kitchen.

Moncin opened another door, leading to a bedroom decorated in light brown, with an unmade divan-bed in the middle. He went over and drew back the curtains, for the room was in semi-darkness, and then opened the sliding doors of a cupboard which filled the whole of one wall.

There were six suits hanging at the right-hand end, all of them immaculately pressed, as though they had never been worn or were fresh from the cleaner's. There were also three overcoats, one a light-weight one, a dinner-jacket and a tail-coat.

None of the suits was in the same material as the sample Lapointe had in his pocket.

'Will you give it to me?' the superintendent asked him.

He held it out to Moncin.

'Last autumn your tailor made you a suit in this material. Do you remember it?'

Moncin looked at it.

'I remember.'

'What has become of it?'

He seemed to reflect. After a moment he said, 'I know. Someone standing on a bus platform burnt the lapel with a cigarette.'

'You gave it to be mended?'

'No. I hate anything, no matter what, which has been damaged. It's a fad, but I've always been like that. Even when I was a child I'd throw away a toy that had a scratch on it.'

'You threw the suit away? You mean you put it in the dustbin?'

'No. I gave it away.'

'Yourself?'

'Yes. I took it out with me one evening when I was going for a walk by the Seine, as I do now and then, and I gave it to a tramp.'

'Was this long ago?'

'Two or three days.'

'Be precise, please.'

'The evening before last.'

In the left-hand section of the cupboard there were at least a dozen pairs of shoes, lined up on shelves, while in the middle were drawers full of shirts, pants, pyjamas and handkerchiefs, all in perfect order.

'Where are the shoes you were wearing yesterday evening?'

He didn't contradict himself, or falter.

'I wasn't wearing shoes, I was wearing the slippers I have on now, since I was in my office.'

'Will you call the maid? We can go back to the drawing-room.'

'Odile!' he called in the direction of the kitchen, 'Come here a minute.'

The girl must have arrived only recently from her native village, she still had a country freshness about her.

'Superintendent Maigret wants to ask you a few questions. Please answer them.'

'Very well, sir.'

She was not alarmed either, only flustered at finding herself face to face with a public figure who was talked about in the papers.

'Do you sleep in the flat?'

'No, sir. I have my room on the sixth floor, like the other servants in the house.'

'Was it late when you went up last night?'

'About nine o'clock as it almost always is — as soon as I'd finished the washing-up.'

'Where was Monsieur Moncin then?'

'In his office.'

'How was he dressed?'

'Like he is now.'

'You're sure of that?'

'Certain.'

'How long is it since you saw his grey suit with the little blue line in it?'

She reflected.

'The fact is, I don't look after Monsieur's clothes. He's very... very particular about them.'

She had almost said 'fussy'.

'You mean he presses them himself?'

'Yes.'

'And you're not allowed to open the cupboards?'

'Only to put the linen away when it comes back from the laundry.'

'You don't know when he last wore his grey suit with the blue thread in it?'

'It seems to me it was two or three days ago.'

'You never heard anything said — when you were waiting at table, for example — about a burn on the lapel?'

She looked at her employer as though asking for guidance, and faltered:

'I don't know... No... I don't listen to what they say at meals... They're nearly always talking about things I don't understand...'

'You can go now.'

Marcel Moncin was waiting, smiling calmly, only with beads of sweat along his upper lip.

'I must ask you to get dressed and come with me to the Quai des Orfèvres. My inspector will go with you to your room.'

'And into my bathroom as well?'

'Into your bathroom as well — I'm sorry. Meantime I will have a chat with your wife. I regret all this, Monsieur Moncin, but I cannot do otherwise.'

The architect made a vague gesture, as if to say: 'As you wish.'

It was only at the door that he looked round and asked: 'May I inquire for what reason...'

'No, not now. Presently, in my office.'

And Maigret, from the door in the passage, called to Madame Moncin, who was still in the kitchen:

'Do you mind coming here, Madame?'

CHAPTER SIX

The Division of the Grey-blue Suit

'Got the right one this time?' young Rougin had jeered while the superintendent and Lapointe were going along the corridor at the Quai des Orfèvres with their prisoner.

Maigret had merely paused, turned his head slowly, and let his eyes rest on the reporter. The young man had coughed slightly, and even the photographers had slacked off a little in their activity.

'Sit down, Monsieur Moncin. If you are too hot you may take your jacket off.'

'Thank you. I always keep it on.'

True, it was hard to imagine him untidy. Maigret had taken off his own jacket, and now went into the inspectors' office to give some instructions. He looked rather sunk into himself, his neck drawn down between his shoulders, and his eyes sometimes had a blank gaze.

Back in his own office he arranged his pipes and filled two of them with precise movements, after signing to Lapointe to stay where he was and take down what was said. Certain great pianists take their seat like this, hesitating, altering the height of the stool, touching the piano here and there as though to put it in a good humour.

'Have you been married long, Monsieur Moncin?'

'Twelve years.'

'May I ask your age?'

'I am thirty-two. I got married when I was twenty.'

There was a longish silence during which the superintendent stared at his hands, spread out flat on the desk in front of him.

'You are an architect?'

Moncin corrected him, 'Architect-decorator.'

'That means, I suppose, that you are an architect who specializes in interior decoration?'

He had noticed a slight flush on Moncin's face.

'Not exactly.'

'You don't mind explaining to me?'

'I am not allowed to draw up the plans of a building, because I haven't actually a degree in architecture.'

'What degree have you?'

'I began as a painter.'

'At what age?'

'Seventeen.'

'You had your secondary-school leaving certificate?'

'No. Ever since I was a kid I had wanted to be an artist. The pictures you saw in our drawing-room are by me.'

Maigret had been unable at the time to guess what they were supposed to represent, but there was something gloomy and morbid about them that had made him uncomfortable. Neither the lines nor the colours were definite. The dominant colour was a purplish red which mingled with strange greens that made one think of light filtering down through water; and the paint seemed to have spread of itself, like a drop of ink on a piece of blotting-paper.

'In short, you are not a qualified architect, and if I understand you correctly, anybody can call himself a decorator?'

'I appreciate your amiable way of making things clear. I suppose you are trying to imply that I am a failure?'

He was smiling sourly.

'You're entitled to do so. I have heard it before,' he went on.

'You have a great many clients?'

'I prefer having a few clients, who trust me and give me a free hand, rather than a great many, who would demand concessions.'

Maigret knocked out his pipe and lit another. Seldom had an interrogation opened on such a muted note.

'You were born in Paris?'

'Yes.'

'Whereabouts?'

Moncin hesitated for a second.

'At the corner of the Rue Caulaincourt and the Rue de Maistre.'

In other words, in the very middle of the sector where the five crimes and the unsuccessful attack had taken place.

'Did you live there long?'

'Until I got married.'

'Are your parents still alive?'

'Only my mother.'

'Who lives...?'

'Still in the same house, the one where I was born.'

'You are on good terms with her?'

'My mother and I have always got on well.'

'What was your father's occupation, Monsieur Moncin?'

This time, again, there was a pause, whereas Maigret had not noticed one when Moncin's mother was referred to.

'He was a butcher.'

'In Montmartre?'

'At the address I have given you.'

'He died...?'

'When I was fourteen.'

'Your mother sold the business?'

'She put in a manager for a time, and then sold the shop but kept the house, where she has a flat on the fourth floor.'

There came a gentle knock on the door. Maigret went into the inspectors' office and returned with four men, all resembling Moncin in age, height and general appearance.

They were clerks at the Prefecture, hastily collected by Torrence.

'Will you get up, Monsieur Moncin, and stand with these gentlemen against the wall?'

There was a few minutes' wait, during which no one spoke, and then another knock on the door.

'Come in!' called the superintendent.

Marthe Jusserand appeared, looked surprised to find so many people in the office, glanced first at Maigret and then at the row of men, and frowned when her eye fell on Moncin.

Everyone held his breath. She had turned pale, for she had suddenly understood, and realized the responsibility that rested on her shoulders. She realized it so clearly that she was visibly on the point of weeping from sheer nerves.

'Take your time,' said the superintendent encouragingly.

'That's he, isn't it?' she murmured.

'You should know best, since you're the only person to have seen him.'

'I have the impression it's he. I feel convinced it is. And yet...'

'And yet?'

'I'd like to see him in profile.'

'Turn sideways, Monsieur Moncin.'

He obeyed, not a muscle of his face moving.

'I'm practically sure. He wasn't wearing the same clothes. And his eyes didn't have the same expression...'

'This evening, Mademoiselle Jusserand, we shall take both of you to the spot where you saw your assailant, with the same lighting, and perhaps with him in the same clothes.'

Inspectors were hastening along the banks of the Seine, going round the Place Maubert, searching all the tramps' haunts in Paris, in a hunt for the suit with the missing button.

'You don't need me any longer?'

'No, thank you. As for you, Monsieur Moncin, you can sit down again. Cigarette?'

'No thank you, I don't smoke.'

Maigret left him in Lapointe's care, having instructed the latter not to ask him any questions or speak to him at all, and to reply evasively if Moncin asked him anything.

In the inspectors' office the superintendent met Lognon, who had come to ask for instructions.

'Would you put your head into my office and take a look, on the off-chance at the fellow who's in there with Lapointe?'

Meanwhile he himself rang up Coméliau, the examining magistrate, and paid a short visit to the Director's office to put him in the picture. He got back to find the Gloomy Inspector frowning like a man trying in vain to remember something.

'You know him?'

Lognon had been working at the Grandes-Carrières police-station for the last twenty-two years. He lived only five hundred yards from the house where Moncin was born.

'I'm sure I've seen him before. But where? In what circumstances?'

'His father was a butcher in the Rue Caulaincourt. He's dead, but the mother is still living in the same house. Come with me.'

They took one of the little police cars, and an inspector drove them up to Montmartre.

'I'm still racking my brains. It's exasperating. I'm certain I know him. I could even swear there had been something between us...?'

'Perhaps you've given him a parking ticket?'

'It wasn't that... It'll come back to me.'

The butcher's shop was a fairly large one, with three or four assistants and a fat woman at the cash-desk.

'Am I to go up with you?'

'Yes.'

The lift was a tight fit. The concierge came hurrying when she saw them get in.

'Who's it for?'

'Madame Moncin.'

'Fourth floor.'

'I know.'

The house was clean and well-kept, but it was a cut or two below the one in the Boulevard Saint-Germain. The lift-shaft was narrower, so were the doors on the landings; the stairs were polished or varnished, without a carpet, and in most cases there were visiting-cards on the doors instead of brass plates.

The woman who opened the door was much younger than Maigret had expected, very thin, and so nervous that her face kept twitching.

'What do you want?'

'Superintendent Maigret, of the Judicial Police.'

'You're sure it's me you want to speak to?'

She was as dark as her son was fair, with small, bright eyes and a few stray hairs on her upper lip.

'Come in. I was just doing the housework.'

The flat was perfectly tidy all the same. The rooms were small. The furniture dated from the time of the owner's marriage.

'You saw your son yesterday evening?'

This was enough to make her stiffen up.

'What have the police got to do with my son?'

'Please be good enough to answer my question.'

'Why should I have seen him?'

'I imagine he comes to see you now and then?'

'Often.'

'With his wife?'

'I don't see what that has to do with you.'

She did not ask them to sit down, and remained standing herself, as though hoping the conversation would be brief. On the walls there were photographs of Marcel Moncin at all ages, some of them taken in the country, and also some drawings and childish paintings, which he must have done when he was small.

'Did your son come here yesterday evening?'

'Who told you so?'

'He did come?'

'No.'

'Nor during the night?'

'He's not in the habit of coming to see me at night. Are you or are you not going to explain the meaning of these questions? I warn you I shall answer no more of them. I am in my own home and I can keep quiet if I choose.'

'Madame Moncin, I regret to inform you that your son is suspected of having committed five murders in the last few months.'

She faced him, ready to tear his eyes out.

'What did you say?'

'We have good reason to believe that he is the man who has been attacking women on street corners in Montmartre, and who missed his stroke last night.'

She began to tremble, and he had the impression, for no definite reason, that she was acting. He felt her reaction was not the natural reaction of a mother who wasn't expecting anything of this kind.

'You dare to accuse my Marcel!... But if I tell you it's not true, that he's innocent, as innocent as...'

She turned to look at the photographs of her son as a child, and then said, clenching her hands:

'Look at him! Take a good look at him, and you won't dare to say such abominable things again...'

'Your son has not been here within the last twenty-four hours, has he?'

'No, no, no!' she repeated vehemently.

'When did you last see him?'

'I don't know.'

'You don't remember his visits?'

'No.'

'Tell me, Madame Moncin, did he have any serious illness as a child?'

'Nothing more serious than measles and an attack of bronchitis. What are you trying to get me to admit? That he's mad? That he's always been mad?'

'When he got married, it was with your approval?'

'Yes. I was fool enough. It was even I who...'

She left the sentence unfinished, as though catching it back in mid-flight.

'It was you who arranged the marriage?'

'What does it matter, now?'

'And now you are no longer on good terms with your daughter-in-law?'

'What's it got to do with you? That concerns my son's private life, which is nobody else's business, do you hear, neither mine nor yours. If that woman...'

'If that woman...?'

'Nothing! You've arrested Marcel?'

'He is in my office at the Quai des Orfèvres.'

'Handcuffed?'

'No.'

'You're going to put him in prison?'

'Possibly. In fact probably. The girl he attacked last night has recognized him.'

'She's lying. I want to see him. I want to see her too, and tell her...'

It was the fourth or fifth sentence she had cut short like that. Her eyes were dry, though glittering with fever or rage.

'Wait a minute. I'm coming with you.'

Maigret and Lognon looked at each other. She had not been asked to come. It was she who was suddenly taking the decisions, and she could be heard in the next room, the door of which she had left ajar, changing her dress and taking a hat out of its box.

'If you feel awkward about having me with you, I'll take the Métro.'

'I warn you the inspector is going to stay here and search the flat.'

She looked at Lognon's skinny form as though about to take him by the scruff of the neck and push him downstairs.

'He is?'

'Yes, Madame. If you want things to be done according to regulations, I am prepared to sign a search-warrant.'

With no reply, but muttering something they could not make out, she walked to the door.

'Come along!' she ordered Maigret, adding to Lognon as she stood on the landing:

'As for you, I've a feeling I've seen you before. If you are unlucky enough to break something, or to untidy my cupboards...'

All the way along in the car, seated beside Maigret, she was talking to herself in an undertone.

'Ah, no, it's not going to be like that! I'll go as high up as need be... I'll see the Minister, I'll see the President of the Republic if necessary... As for the newspapers, they'll just have to print what I tell them, and...'

In the corridor of the Judicial Police Headquarters she noticed the photographers, and when they turned their cameras on her she walked straight up to them with the obvious intention of wrenching them away. The men had to beat a retreat.

'This way.'

When she suddenly found herself in Maigret's office, where apart from Lapointe, who appeared to be dozing, there was nobody except her son, she stopped, looked at him with relief and said — not rushing over to him, but enfolding him in a protective gaze:

'Don't be frightened, Marcel. I'm here.'

Moncin had got up, and was looking reproachfully at Maigret.

'What are they doing to you? At least they haven't beaten you up?'

'No, Mama.'

'They're mad! I tell you they're mad. But I'm going off to find the best lawyer in Paris. I don't care how much he wants. I'll spend my last penny if necessary. I'll sell the house. I'll go and beg in the streets.'

'Hush, Mama, hush.'

He was almost afraid to look her in the face, and seemed to be apologizing to the police for her behaviour.

'Yvonne knows you're here?'

She looked round for her daughter-in-law. How could she possibly not be at her husband's side at such a moment?

'She knows, Mama.'

'What did she say?'

'If you will sit down, Madame...'

'I don't need to sit down. What I want is to have my son back. Come along, Marcel. We'll soon see if they dare to keep you.'

'I am sorry to have to tell you we shall.'

'So, you're arresting him?'

'At any rate I'm keeping him at the disposal of the law.'

'It's the same thing. Have you thought it over properly? Do you realize your responsibilities? I warn you I won't be pushed about, I'm going to move heaven and earth...'

'Be good enough to sit down and answer a few questions.'

'I'm answering nothing whatsoever!'

This time she stalked over to her son and kissed him on both cheeks.

'Don't be afraid, Marcel. Don't let them intimidate you. Mother's here. I'm taking care of you. You'll soon be hearing from me.'

She glared at Maigret, and walked to the door with an air of determination. Lapointe had the attitude of one waiting for orders. Maigret signed to him to let her go, and she could be heard in the corridor, shouting heaven knew what at the journalists.

'Your mother seems to be very fond of you.'

'I'm all she has left.'

'She was very much attached to your father?'

He opened his mouth to reply, but thought better of it. The superintendent guessed his meaning.

'What kind of man was your father?'

Moncin still hesitated.

'Your mother was not happy with him?'

At this he brought out, in a voice full of repressed anger:

'He was a butcher.'

'You were ashamed of that?'

'I beg you not to ask me such questions, Superintendent. I know perfectly well what you are getting at, and I may tell you you are mistaken all along the line. You see what a state you've put my mother into.'

'She put herself into it.'

'I suppose that somewhere or other, in the Boulevard Saint-Germain or elsewhere, your men are now putting my wife through the same treatment.'

It was Maigret's turn to keep silent.

'There is nothing she can tell you. Any more than my mother. Any more than I can myself. Question me as much as you like, but leave them in peace.'

'Sit down.'

'Again? Will it be long?'

'Probably.'

'I suppose I shall get nothing to eat or drink?'

'What would you like?'

'Some water.'

'You wouldn't rather have beer?'

'I don't drink beer, or wine, or spirits.'

'And you don't smoke,' said Maigret pensively.

He drew Lapointe over to the half-open door.

'Begin questioning him, little by little, without pushing things too far. Talk to him again about that suit; ask him what he was doing on February 2 and March 3 — on all the dates when crimes were committed in Montmartre. Try to find out whether he goes to see his mother on any particular day, whether it's during the day or in the evening, and why she and his wife have quarrelled...'

He himself went off to lunch alone at the Brasserie Dauphine, where he had a table to himself and ordered stewed veal because it smelt good, like home cooking.

He rang up his wife to tell her he wouldn't be home for lunch, and very nearly rang Professor Tissot as well. He would have liked to see him, to chat with him again the way they had in the Pardon's drawing-room. But Tissot was a busy man, like himself. Besides, Maigret had no specific questions to put to him.

He was tired and depressed, for no definite reason. He felt he was close to the goal. Things had moved faster than he would have dared to hope. Marthe Jusserand's attitude spoke for itself, and if she hadn't been more positive it was because she had scruples. The story of the suit given to a tramp didn't hold water. In any case they would no doubt soon hear more about that, for there are not so very many tramps in Paris and practically all of them are known to the police.

'You don't need me any longer, Chief?'

This was Mazet, who had taken the role of the supposed criminal, and now had nothing left to do.

'I went round to the Quai. They let me take a look at the fellow. You think it's he?'

Maigret shrugged his shoulders. More than anything

else, he felt the need to understand. It is easy to understand a man who has robbed his victim, or who has killed someone to escape being caught, or out of jealousy, or in a fit of rage, or even to make sure of an inheritance.

That kind of crime, the common-or-garden crime, as one might say, sometimes gave him a lot of bother, but didn't upset him.

'Imbeciles!' he would growl on such occasions.

For like some of his illustrious predecessors, he maintained that if a criminal were intelligent he would not need to kill anyone.

Nevertheless, he was able to put himself in their place, to reconstruct their arguments or the sequence of their emotions.

Faced with a man like Marcel Moncin he felt like a tyro; so much so that he hadn't yet dared to push the interrogation to its limit.

This was not just a man like other men, who had broken the laws of society and put himself more or less consciously beyond the pale.

He was a man unlike others, a man who killed without any of the reasons other people can understand, in an almost childish way, afterwards tearing his victims' clothing as though by whim.

Yet in a certain sense Moncin was intelligent. There had been nothing particularly abnormal about his early years. He had got married and seemed to be on good terms with his wife. And though his mother was a bit much, there was certainly an affinity between them.

Did he realize he was lost? Had he realized it this morning, when his wife had gone to wake him up and had told him the police were waiting for him in the drawing-room?

What were the reactions of a man like that? Was he unhappy? In between his crimes, did he feel shame or hatred of himself and his instincts? Or did it give him a kind of satisfaction to feel that he was different from other people, different in a way he might think of as superior?

'Coffee, Maigret?'

'Yes.'

'Brandy?'

No! If he drank he might get drowsy, and he felt heavy enough as it was, as he nearly always did at a certain point of a case, when he was trying to identify himself with the people he had to deal with.

'It seems you've got him?'

He stared at the proprietor, round-eyed.

'It's in the mid-day papers. They seem to think it's the right man this time. He's certainly given you trouble, that fellow! Some people were saying he'd never be found, like Jack the Ripper.'

He drank his coffee, lit a pipe and went out into the hot, motionless air imprisoned between the paving-stones and the lowering sky, which was slowly turning slate-colour.

Some sort of tramp was sitting, cap in hand, in the inspectors' office, and he was wearing a jacket that did not go with the rest of his outfit.

It was Marcel Moncin's notorious jacket.

'Where did you find this chap?' Maigret asked his men.

'Down by the river, near the Pont d'Austerlitz.'

Maigret put his questions not to the tramp, but to his own inspectors.

'What does he say?'

'That he found the jacket on the river-bank.'

'When?'

'This morning at six o'clock.'

'And the trousers?'

'They were there too. He was with a pal. They divided the suit between them. We've not laid hands on the one with the trousers yet, but it won't take long.'

Maigret went up to the poor devil, bent down and saw that there was indeed a hole in the lapel, made by a cigarette burn.

'Take that off.'

He had no shirt underneath, only a torn vest.

'You're sure it was this morning?'

'My friend will tell you the same. He's Big Paul. All these gentlemen know him.'

So did Maigret. He handed the garment to Torrence.

'Take it up to Moers. I don't know whether it's possible,

but it seems to me they should be able to discover, by testing, whether a burn in cloth is recent or old. Tell him that in the present case it's a question of forty-eight hours. You undersand?'

'I understand, Chief.'

'If the lapel was burnt last night or this morning...'

He waved a hand towards his own office.

'Where have they got to, in there?'

'Lapointe has had beer and sandwiches sent up.'

'For both of them?'

'The sandwiches, yes. The other fellow drank Vichy water.'

Maigret opened the door. Lapointe was sitting in his chair, bending over some papers on which he was making notes, and trying to think of another question to ask.

'You shouldn't have opened the window. It only lets in hot air.'

He went and shut it. Moncin's eyes followed him with a reproachful expression, like some defenceless animal being tormented by children.

'Let's see.'

He glanced over the notes, questions and answers, which taught him nothing.

'No fresh developments?'

'Maître Rivière telephoned to say he was to be the defending counsel. He wanted to come right away. I asked him to speak to the examining magistrate.'

'That's right. And then?'

'Janvier rang up from the Boulevard Saint-Germain. In the office there are erasing-knives of all types, which might have been used for the different crimes. He also found, in the bedroom, a flick-knife of a well-known type, which has a blade only about three inches long.'

Doctor Paul, the official pathologist who had carried out the post-mortems, had had a lot to say about the weapon which intrigued him. Crimes of this type are usually committed with a fairly large knife, such as a butcher's knife or a carving-knife, or else with a dagger or a stiletto.

'To judge by the shape and depth of the wounds,' he had said, 'I am tempted to think the criminal used an ordinary pen-knife. An ordinary pen-knife would have closed up, of course. This one must at least have had a safety-catch. In my opinion the weapon is not dangerous in itself. What makes it fatal is the skill with which it is used.'

'We have found your jacket, Monsieur Moncin.'

'Down by the river?'

'Yes.'

He opened his mouth, but no words came out. What had he been about to ask?

'Have you had enough to eat?'

The tray was still there and there was half a ham sandwich left. The Vichy water bottle was empty.

'Tired?'

He responded with a half-smile of resignation. Everything about him, including his clothes, was in half-tones. He had retained from his boyhood something timid and charming which was hard to define. Did it come from his fair hair, his complexion, his blue eyes, or from delicate health?

By tomorrow he would no doubt be in the hands of doctors and psychiatrists. But one must not go too fast. Afterwards it would be too late.

'I'll take your place,' Maigret said to Lapointe.

'Can I go?'

'Wait in the other room. Let me know if Moers finds anything new.'

When the door had shut again he took off his jacket, dropped into his arm-chair, and put his elbows on the desk.

For perhaps five minutes he let his gaze weigh on Marcel Moncin, who had turned his head aside and was staring at the window.

'Are you very unhappy?' he said softly at last, as though in spite of himself.

'The other man started, avoided his eyes, and paused for a second before replying:

'Why should I be unhappy?'

'When did you discover you were not like other people?'

The man's face quivered, but he managed to say with a

derisive titter:

'You find I'm not like other people?'

'When you were a young man...'

'Well, what?'

'Did you know already?'

Maigret had a feeling, at that moment, that if he could find exactly the right words the barrier between himself and the man sitting stiffly in his chair on the other side of the desk would be broken down. He had not imagined that quiver. For a few seconds the tension had been reduced, and very little would have been needed, no doubt, to bring tears into Moncin's eyes.

'You realize, do you not, that you are in no danger either of execution or of a prison sentence?'

Had Maigret chosen the wrong tactics — the wrong words?

Moncin had drawn himself up again, recovered his self-control, his appearance of absolute calm.

'I am in no danger of anything, since I am innocent.'

'Innocent of what?'

'Of what you are accusing me of. I have nothing more to say to you. I shall answer no more questions.'

These were not light words. One could feel he had made a decision and would stick to it.

'As you like,' sighed the superintendent, pressing a bell.

CHAPTER SEVEN

Trusting in Providence!

Maigret made a mistake. Would another man, in his situation, have avoided it? That was a question he was often to ask himself afterwards, and of course he never found a satisfactory answer to it.

It must have been about half-past three when he went up to the laboratory and Moers asked:

'You got my note?'

'No.'

'I just sent you one; I expect you passed my man on your way up. The burn on the jacket is not more than twelve hours old. If you'd like me to explain...'

'No. You're sure of what you're saying?'

'Certain. All the same, I'm going to make some experiments. I suppose there's no reason why I shouldn't burn the jacket in two other places, in the back, for example? Those burns might be useful as controls if the case comes up for trial.'

Maigret nodded and went downstairs again. At that moment Marcel Moncin must already have been in the Judicial Identity office, where he would strip for a preliminary medical examination and for the usual measurements to be taken, and then, dressed again but without a tie, be photographed full face and in profile.

The newspapers were already publishing photographs their reporters had taken when he had arrived at the Quai, and several inspectors, likewise armed with photographs, were going over the Grandes-Carrières district yet again, endlessly putting the same questions to the staff of the Métro, to shopkeepers, to anyone who might have noticed Moncin the evening before or on the evening of one of the earlier crimes.

In the courtyard of the Judicial Police Headquarters the superintendent got into one of the waiting cars and had himself driven to the Boulevard Saint-Germain. The maid he had seen in the morning answered the bell.

'The other gentleman's in the drawing-room,' she informed him.

She meant Janvier, who was there by himself, making clean copies of the notes he had made during his search.

Both men were equally tired.

'Where's his wife?'

'About half an hour ago she asked me if she might go and lie down.'

'How did she behave until then?'

'I didn't see much of her. Now and then she came and put her head into whatever room I was in, to see what I was up to.'

'You didn't ask her any questions?'

'You didn't tell me to.'

'I suppose you haven't found anything interesting?'

'I had a chat with the maid. She's only been here six months. The Moncins entertain very little and seldom go out. They don't seem to have any close friends. From time to time they go for the week-end to her parents, who it seems have a house out at Triel where they live all the year round.'

'What sort of people?'

'The father had a chemist's shop in the Place Clichy; he retired a few years ago.'

Janvier showed Maigret a photograph of a group in a garden. Moncin was there in a light suit, his wife in a thin dress, a man with a pepper-and-salt beard, and a fattish woman who stood smiling broadly, with her hand resting on the bonnet of a large car.

'And here's another. The young woman with the two children is Madame Moncin's sister, who is married to a garage-proprietor at Levallois. They have a brother too, he lives in Africa.'

There was a box full of photographs, chiefly of Madame Moncin, including one in her First Communion dress, and the inevitable portrait of the couple on their wedding-day.

'A few business letters, not many. He seems to have only about a dozen clients. Bills. From what I can see, they don't pay them until they've been sent in three or four times.'

Madame Moncin, who had perhaps heard the superintendent arrive, or had been warned by the maid, now appeared in the doorway. Her face looked more strained than in the morning, and she had visibly been tidying her hair and repowdering.

'Haven't you brought him back?' she asked.

'Not until he gives us a satisfactory explanation of certain coincidences.'

'You really believe it was he?'

He made no reply, and she did not begin to protest vigorously, but merely shrugged her shoulders.

'One day you will see you were mistaken, and then you'll be sorry for the harm you're doing him.'

'You love him?'

The moment he had asked the question it struck him as foolish.

'He's my husband,' she replied.

Did that mean she did love him or simply that, as his wife, it was her duty to stand by him?

'You've put him in prison?'

'Not yet. He's at the Quai des Orfèvres. We're going to question him again.'

'What does he say?'

'He refuses to answer. You really have nothing to tell me, Madame Moncin?'

'Nothing.'

'You realize, don't you, that even if your husband is guilty, as I have every reason to suppose, he will neither go to the guillotine nor to hard labour? I told him that just now. I have no doubt the doctors will say he is not responsible for his actions. The man who kills five women in the street and then slashes their clothes is a sick man. When he is not in a moment of crisis, he may deceive people. He certainly does, for no one has found his behaviour strange until now. Are you listening?'

'I'm listening.'

She was listening, perhaps, but one might have supposed that this digression did not concern her and in no way related to her husband. At moments her eyes were even following the movements of a fly as it climbed up a muslin curtain.

'Five women have died so far, and as long as the killer, or the maniac, or the lunatic, call him what you like, remains at liberty, other lives will be in danger. Do you realize that? And do you realize that although up to now he has only attacked women going along the street, the process may change, and perhaps tomorrow he may begin to attack the people around him? Aren't you afraid?'

'No.'

'You don't have the impression that for months, perhaps for years, you yourself have been in mortal danger?'

'No.'

It was disheartening. Her attitude was not even defiant. She remained calm, almost serene.

'You have seen my mother-in-law? What did she say?'

'She protested. May I ask why the two of you are on bad terms?'

'I don't care to speak about it. It is of no importance.'

What more could he do?

'You can come now, Janvier.'

'You're not going to send my husband back to me?'

'No.'

She went with them to the door and shut it behind them. That was about all for that afternoon. Maigret had dinner with Lapointe and Janvier, while Lucas took his turn at remaining alone with Marcel Moncin in the superintendent's office. Afterwards they had to resort to a stratagem to get the suspect out of the Judicial Police building, for the corridors and waiting-rooms were full of journalists and photographers.

A few big drops of rain had splashed on to the

pavements about eight o'clock, and everyone had hoped for a thunderstorm; but if there had been one at all it must have broken somewhere towards the east, where the sky was still a poisonous-looking black.

They did not wait until the exact time at which the previous evening's unsuccessful attack had taken place, for by nine o'clock the streets were dark as they had been then, and the lighting precisely the same.

Maigret went out alone, down the main staircase, chatting with the reporters. Lucas and Janvier pretended to take Moncin away to the cells — he was handcuffed now — but once downstairs they went to the central police-station and put him into a car there.

They all met at the corner of the Rue Norvins, where Marthe Jusserand was already waiting, accompanied by her fiancé.

It only took a few minutes. Moncin was led to the exact spot where the girl had been attacked. He was wearing the burnt jacket again.

'There were no other lights?'

The girl looked round and then shook her head.

'No. It was just the same.'

'Now try to look at him from the angle at which you saw him.'

She bent in various ways, had the man moved to two or three places.

'You recognize him?'

Very agitated, her breast heaving, she cast a rapid glance at her fiancé, who was standing at a tactful distance, and murmured:

'It's my duty to tell the truth, isn't it?'

'It is your duty.'

She looked again at Moncin, as though to ask his pardon; he was waiting with no sign of interest.

'I am certain it was he.'

'You formally identify him?'

She nodded and then her courage left her and she burst into tears.

'I shan't need you any more this evening. Thank you very much,' said Maigret, pushing her towards her fiancé.

'You heard that, Monsieur Moncin?'

'I heard.'

'You have nothing to say?'

'Nothing.'

'Take him back, you two.'

'Goodnight, Chief.'

'Goodnight, boys.'

Maigret got into one of the cars.

'Drive me home, Boulevard Richard-Lenoir.'

But this time he stopped the car just off the Square d'Anvers and went into a *brasserie* to have a beer. His own role was almost finished. Tomorrow morning Coméliau would no doubt want to interrogate Moncin, and would then send him to the specialists for a mental examination.

The Judicial Police would be left with the rountine work of looking for witnesses, questioning them, and compiling the fullest possible record.

Why Maigret did not feel satisfied, was another story. From the professional standpoint he had done all he had to do. Only, he didn't understand, even yet. There had been no 'shock'. He had never, at any moment, had the impression of a human contact between himself and Moncin.

Madame Moncin's attitude worried him too. He would have another go at her.

'You look done in,' remarked Madame Maigret. 'Is it really over?'

'Who says so?'

'The papers. And the radio.'

He shrugged his shoulders. After all these years she still believed what she read in the papers!

'In a certain sense, yes, it's over.'

He went into the bedroom and began to undress.

'I hope you'll be able to sleep on a bit, tomorrow morning?'

He hoped so too. He was not so much tired as disgusted, though he couldn't have said exactly why.

'Are you cross?'

'No. Don't worry. You know I often get like this in cases of this kind.'

The excitement of the investigation, the search, having come to an end, one suddenly found oneself in a kind of vacuum.

'You shouldn't take any notice. Pour me a tot of sloe gin, and let me sleep like a log for ten hours.'

He didn't look at the time before he fell asleep; he tossed and turned for a while between sheets that were already damp; a dog was howling persistently somewhere not far off.

He had lost all idea of time and of everything else, even of where he was, when the telephone rang. After it had rung for a good bit, he put out his hand, so clumsily that he upset the glass of water that stood on the night table.

'Hello...'

His voice was hoarse.

'Is that you, Superintendent?'

'Who's speaking?'

'Lognon here... I'm sorry to disturb you...'

The Gloomy Inspector's voice sounded somehow melancholy.

'Yes. I'm listening. Where are you?'

'In the Rue de Maistre...'

And lowering his voice, Lognon went on, as though reluctantly:

'There's just been another crime... A woman... Stabbed several times... Her dress has been slashed...'

Madame Maigret had put the light on. She watched her husband, who had been lying down until then, sitting up and rubbing his eyes.

'You're sure?... Hello — Lognon?'

'Yes. I'm still here.'

'When? And to begin with, what time is it?'

'Ten-past twelve.'

'When did it happen?'

'About three-quarters of an hour ago. I tried to get you at the Quai. I was all alone at my station.'

'I'll be right along...'

'Another?' his wife asked.

He nodded.

'I thought the murderer was locked up?'

'Moncin is in the cells. Get the Judicial Police on the line for me while I'm dressing.'

'Hello... Judicial Police?... Superintendent Maigret wants to speak to you...'

'Hello — who's that?' Maigret growled. 'That you, Mauvoisin? You've already heard, from Lognon? I suppose our man hasn't budged?... What?... You've just checked up on that?... I'm dealing with it... Will you send me a car at once?... Yes, to my house...'

Madame Maigret realized that the best she could do in the circumstances was to keep quiet, and it was she who opened the sideboard and poured out a glass of sloe-gin, which she handed to her husband. He drank it mechanically and she followed him out to the landing and listened as the sound of his footsteps receded down the stairs.

On the way to Montmartre he never opened his mouth, but sat staring ahead of him; and when he got out of the car, close to a group of some twenty people standing at a dimly-lit spot in the Rue de Maistre, he banged the car door behind him.

Lognon came to meet him with the face of one announcing a family bereavement.

'I was on night duty when the news came through by telephone. I came here at once.'

There was an ambulance standing by the kerb, with the attendants waiting for orders; they could be seen as paler forms in the darkness. There were also a few idlers, standing in timid silence.

A female figure lay on the pavement, almost touching the wall, and a trickle of blood zigzagged away from it, dark and already coagulating.

'Dead?'

A man approached Maigret — a local doctor, he learnt afterwards.

'I counted at least six knife-strokes,' he said. 'I was only able to make a superficial examination.'

'In the back, as usual?'

'No. At least four in the chest. Another in the throat, which seems to have been delivered after the others, probably when the victim had already fallen to the ground.'

'The *coup de grâce,*' laughed Maigret bitterly.

Didn't it mean that for him too, this crime was a sort of *coup de grâce*?

'There are other wounds, more superficial, on the forearms and hands.'

At this Maigret frowned.

'Do we know who she is?' he asked, pointing to the body.

'I found her identity card in her handbag. Jeanine Laurent, a general servant working for Monsieur and Madame Durandeau in the Rue de Clignancourt.'

'Her age?'

'Nineteen.'

Maigret preferred not to look at her. The poor child was wearing what must have been her best dress; it was made of sky-blue tulle, almost a ball-dress. She had doubtless been out dancing. She was wearing very high-heeled shoes, one of which had fallen off.

'Who gave the alarm?'

'I did, Superintendent.'

The speaker was a cycle patrolman who had been waiting patiently for his turn.

'I was making my round with a fellow-officer, here present, when I observed, on the left-hand pavement...'

He had seen nothing of what happened. When he found the body it had still been warm and the wounds had still been bleeding. Because of that, he had thought for an instant that the girl was not dead.

'Take her to the Medico-Legal Institute and inform Doctor Paul,' said Maigret. He added, turning to Lognon:

'Have you given any orders?'

'I've sent all the men I could find to search the district.'

What was the good? Hadn't that been done before, to no purpose?

A car drove up at full speed and stopped with a squeal of brakes. Young Rougin got out of it, his hair bristling.

'Well, my dear Superintendent?'

'Who told you?'

Maigret was gruff, aggressive.

'Someone in the street... There are still some people who

think the Press has its uses... So it still wasn't the right chap?'

Withdrawing his attention from the superintendent, he hurried across to the pavement, followed by his photographer, who got down to work while Rougin questioned the bystanders.

'You see to the rest of it,' Maigret muttered to Lognon.

'You don't need anyone?'

Maigret shook his head and went back to his car, his eyes on the ground, with the expression of one brooding over unpalatable thoughts.

'Where do we go, Chief?' asked his driver.

He looked at the man, not knowing what to reply.

'Go downhill, anyway, towards the Place Clichy or the Place Blanche.'

There was nothing for him to do at the Quai des Orfèvres. What was there that hadn't been tried already?

And he hadn't the heart to go back to bed.

'Wait here for me.'

They had reached the bright lights of the Place Blanche, where some of the café terraces were still lit up.

'What can I give you?'

'Whatever you like.'

'Beer? Brandy?'

'A beer.'

At a nearby table a woman with platinum-blonde hair, her breasts half emerging from a skin-tight dress, was talking in a low voice to the man she was with, trying to persuade him to take her to a night-club the neon sign of which could be seen across the street.

'I promise you you won't regret it. It's expensive, perhaps, but...'

Did the man understand? He was an American or an Englishman; he kept shaking his head and saying:

'*No!... No!*'

'Is that all you know how to say — *No!... No!...?* And suppose I say *No* too, and leave you?...'

He smiled placidly at her, and she called impatiently to the waiter to bring another round of drinks.

'You can give me a sandwich as well, if he won't go

opposite and have supper...'

At another table people were discussing the different scenes of a revue they had just seen at a neighbouring cabaret. An Arab was selling peanuts. An old flower-seller recognized Maigret and thought it wiser to take herself off.

He smoked at least three pipes without moving, while be watched the people going by and the taxis, and listened to snatches of conversation, as though he felt the need to steep himself in an everyday atmosphere again.

A woman of about forty, fat but still appetizing, who was sitting alone at a table with a *menthe à l'eau* in front of her, was sending winning smiles in his direction, with no idea who he was.

Maigtet signed to the waiter.

'The same again,' he ordered.

He must give himself time to calm down. Just now, in the Rue de Maistre, his first impulse had been to rush back to headquarters, go to Marcel Moncin's cell, and shake him until he decided to talk.

'Admit that it was you, you filthy swine.'

He felt a certainty that was almost physically painful. It was not possible that he'd been mistaken all along the line. And what he felt now for the sham arehitect was not pity or even curiosity. It was anger, almost rage.

This evaporated little by little, in the relative cool of the night, as he watched the scene in the street.

He had made a mistake, he knew that; and now he knew what it had been.

It was too late to put things right now, when a little girl was dead, a country girl who, like thousands of others every year, had come to try her luck in Paris, and who had gone dancing after a day spent in the kitchen.

It was too late even to get confirmation of the idea that had occurred to him. By this time he would find nothing. And if any clues did exist, if there were any chance of finding some witnesses, it could wait till morning.

His men were as worn-out as he was. The thing had been going on too long. In the morning, when they read their newspapers in the Métro or the bus, on their way to the Quai des Orfèvres, they would all feel the same stupefaction, the same despondency that had descended upon the superintendent just now. Might not some of them begin to lose confidence in him?

Lognon had been embarrassed when he rang up; and in the Rue de Maistre he had almost seemed to be commiserating with him.

Maigret could imagine Coméliau's reaction, his imperious telephone call the moment he opened his newspaper.

He went inside the *brasserie* with a heavy step and asked at the bar for a telephone counter. He wanted to telephone his wife.

'Is that you?' she exclaimed, in surprise.

'I only wanted to tell you I shan't be back tonight.'

For no definite reason. He had nothing to do for the time being, except to stew in his juice. He felt a need to get back to the familiar atmosphere of the Quai des Orfèvres, to his own office, with a few of his men.

He did not want to sleep. There would be time for that once the thing was really over; then, perhaps, he might even decide to put in for leave.

It was always like that. He promised himself a holiday and then, when the moment arrived, found some excuse to stay in Paris.

'Waiter, what do I owe you?'

He paid and walked out to the little car.

'To the Quai!'

There he found Mauvoisin with two or three of the others, one of whom was eating sausage and washing it down with red wine.

'Don't bother about me, boys. Nothing fresh come in?'

'Always the same thing. They're questioning the passers-by. They've arrested two foreigners whose papers weren't in order.'

'Ring Janvier and Lapointe. Ask them both to be here at five-thirty this morning.'

For about an hour, alone in his office, he read and re-read the minutes of the interrogations, paying particular attention to those of Moncin's mother and wife.

After that he slumped back in his chair, unbuttoned his

shirt to the waist, and seemed to doze off, facing the window. Perhaps he did actually fall asleep? He didn't realize it, but in any case he didn't hear Mauvoisin, who came into his office once and withdrew again on tiptoe.

The window-panes turned from dark to pale, the sky became grey, then blue, and at last the sun broke through. When Mauvoisin came in for the second time he was carrying a cup of coffee; he had just made some on an electric ring. Janvier had arrived, and Lapointe would be there any minute.

'What time is it?'

'Twenty-five past five.'

'Are they there?'

'Janvier is. As for Lapointe...'

'Here I am, Chief,' came the voice of the last-named.

Both of them were freshly shaved, whereas those who had been up all night had bristly cheeks and muddy complexions.

'Come in, both of you.'

Was he making another mistake in not contacting the examining magistrate? If so, he would accept full responsibility, as in the other instances.

'Janvier, you get along to the Rue Caulaincourt. Take one of the other fellows with you, it doesn't matter which, whoever's the freshest.'

'To the old woman's flat?'

'Yes. Bring her here to me. She'll protest, she'll most likely refuse to come.'

'Sure to.'

Maigret held out a paper he had just signed as though trying to break the nib on it.

'Give her this subpoena. And you, Lapointe, go to the Boulevard Saint-Germain and get Madame Moncin.'

'Are you giving me a subpoena too?'

'Yes. Though in her case I doubt whether it's absolutely necessary. Then put them both together in an office, lock them up safely, and come and tell me.'

'The Baron and Rougin are in the corridor.'

'You bet!'

'It doesn't matter?'

'They can see them.'

The two men departed to the inspectors' office, where the lights were still burning, and Maigret opened his cupboard. He always kept shaving-tackle there. While he was about the business he cut his upper lip slightly.

'Any coffee left, Mauvoisin?' he called out.

'In just a moment, Chief. I'm making a second lot.'

Outside, the first tugs had come to life and were off to collect from the river banks the strings of barges they were to haul up or down stream. A few buses were crossing the almost deserted Pont Saint-Michel, and just beside the bridge a fisherman had settled down with rod and line, his legs dangling above the dark water.

Maigret began going to and fro, avoiding the corridor and the reporters, while the inspectors were careful not to ask him any questions, or even to meet his eye.

'Lognon didn't ring up?'

'Yes, about four o'clock, to say there were no fresh developments, except that the little girl definitely had been to a dancehall somewhere near the Place du Tertre. She used to go there once a week, she had no steady boyfriend.'

'She left by herself?'

'The boys think so, though they're not sure. They have the impression she was a good girl.'

Sounds could be heard in the corridor, a woman was talking in a high-pitched voice, though the words were indistinguishable.

A few seconds later Janvier came into the office, looking like a man who has just carried out a disagreeable job.

'Done it! It wasn't altogether easy.'

'She was in bed?'

'Yes. To begin with she talked to me through the door, she wouldn't open it. I had to threaten to fetch a locksmith. In the end she got into a dressing-gown.'

'You waited while she got dressed?'

'Out on the landing. She still wouldn't let me into the flat.'

'She's by herself now?'

'Yes. Here's the key.'

'Go and wait for Lapointe in the corridor.'

After about ten minutes both inspectors came into Maigret's office.

'They're there?'

'Yes.'

'Did the sparks begin to fly?'

'After one glance they pretended not to know each other.'

Janvier hesitated and then ventured on a question.

'What are we to do now?'

'For the moment, nothing. You go and sit in the next-door office, near the communicating door. If they decide to talk, try to hear what they say.'

'And if they don't?'

Maigret made a vague gesture which seemed to say, 'We must trust in providence!'

CHAPTER EIGHT

Moncin Gets Cross

Nine o'clock came, and the two women, confined in a very small office, had still not uttered a word. Each of them sat motionless on her straight-backed chair — for the room had no easy-chairs — as though in some doctor's or dentist's waiting-room which did not offer the resource of magazines to look at.

'One of them got up and opened the window,' Janvier told Maigret, who had gone in search of news. Then she went back to her place and I've heard nothing since.'

Maigret had overlooked the fact that at least one of them knew nothing of last night's crime.

'Have some newspapers taken in. Have them put on the desk as though that were the usual thing, but making sure that from where they're sitting they can both see the headlines.'

Coméliau had already telephoned twice, first from home, where he had read the paper over breakfast, and again from the Palais de Justice.

'Tell him I'm somewhere about the building and that they've gone to look for me.'

One important question had already been cleared up by a couple of inspectors Maigret had sent out early that morning. So far as Moncin's mother was concerned, the reply was straightforward. She could go in or out of the house in the Rue Caulaincourt at any hour of the night, for she had kept a key from the time when she owned the whole place. And the concierge put her light out and went to bed at ten o'clock, or half-past at the latest.

The Moncins had no key to the front door in the Boulevard Saint-Germain, and there the concierge went to bed later, about eleven o'clock. Was that why all the crimes, except last night's, had taken place fairly early? As long as she was still up and the front door was open, the concierge paid little attention to any tenants who might be coming back from the cinema, from the theatre, or from an evening with friends.

In the morning she opened the door about half-past five, dragged the dustbins out on to the pavement, and went indoors again to get dressed. Occasionally she went back to bed for an hour.

That explained how Marcel Moncin could have slipped out without being seen, after the unsuccessful attack, so as to get rid of the suit by leaving it on the river bank.

Could his wife have gone out on the previous evening and got back fairly late, probably after midnight, without the concierge recollecting that she had pulled the cord to open the door for her?

The inspector who had been sent to the Boulevard Saint-Germain said yes.

'The concierge denies it, of course,' he explained to Maigret. 'But the tenants don't agree. Since her husband died she has got into the habit, every evening, of taking two or three little glasses of some kind of liqueur that comes from the Pyrenees. Sometimes they have to ring two or three times before she opens the door, and when she does she's half asleep, and doesn't hear the name they mutter as they go past the lodge.'

'Other information was coming in pell-mell, some of it by telephone. They learnt, for example, that Marcel Moncin and his wife had known each other since childhood, and had gone to the same primary school. One summer, when Marcel was nine years old, the wife of the chemist on the Boulevard de Clichy had taken him away on holiday with her own children, to a house they had rented at Etretat.

It was also discovered that after their marriage, the

young couple had lived for several months in a flat that old Madame Moncin had let them have in the Rue Caulaincourt house, on the same floor as her own.

At half-past nine Maigret made up his mind.

'Tell someone to bring Moncin up here from the cells. Unless, of course, he's already in Coméliau's office.'

Janvier, from his observation-post, had heard one of the two women get up, and then the rustle of a newspaper. He didn't know which of them it had been. No voice had been raised.

The weather was bright again, and the sunshine dazzling; but the heat was not so oppressive as on the last few days, for a breeze was stirring the leaves of the trees, and sometimes the papers on Maigret's desk.

Moncin came in without a word, looked at the superintendent with an imperceptible nod of greeting, and waited to be told to sit down. He had had no chance to shave, and his fair beard was softening the firm lines of his face slightly, making it look weaker, the features somehow blurred — from fatigue too, no doubt.

'You have been informed of what happened last night?'

He answered, as though reproachfully:

'No one has told me a word.'

'Read that.'

Maigret held out the paper which gave the fullest report on what had happened in the Rue de Maistre. While the prisoner was reading, the superintendent never took his eyes off him, and he felt certain he was not mistaken in thinking that *Moncin's first reaction was annoyance*. He had frowned, as though surprised and displeased.

In spite of Decorator's Arrest,
Another Victim in Montmartre.

For a second Moncin seemed to think it was a trap, perhaps that a special copy of the newspaper had been printed to make him give himself away. He read with concentration, checked the date at the top of the page, finally recognized that the report was true.

Wasn't he feeling a kind of suppressed anger, as though

something were being spoilt for him?

At the same time he was reflecting, trying to understand; and finally he seemed to have hit on the solution of the problem.

'As you see', said Maigret, 'someone is doing the utmost to save you. So much the worse if it costs the life of a poor girl who's only just come to Paris!'

Didn't Moncin's lips twitch in a furtive smile? He tried to repress it, but all the same it betrayed a childish satisfaction, quickly concealed.

'The two women are here,' Maigret went on casually, pretending not to look at the other man.

It was a curious struggle, he didn't remember one like it before. Neither of them was sure of his ground. The slightest shade of expression was important, a glance, a quiver of the lips, a blinking eyelid.

If Moncin was tired, the superintendent was even more so; and he, in addition, was disgusted. He had once again felt tempted to hand the whole thing over, as it stood, to the examining magistrate and leave him to make what he could out of it.

'They'll be brought in presently, and you can have it out among yourselves.'

What were Moncin's feelings at that moment? Was he furious? Perhaps. His blue eyes went blank, he clenched his teeth and threw the superintendent a reproachful glance. But he might be frightened, too, for at the same time sweat broke out on his forehead and upper lip, as it had on the previous day.

'You are still determined to keep silent?'

'I have nothing to say.'

'Aren't you beginning to feel it's time to finish with all this? Don't you think, Moncin, that this makes at least *one crime* too many? If you had talked yesterday, this one wouldn't have been committed.'

'It has nothing to do with me.'

'You know, don't you, which of them foolishly made up her mind to save you?'

Moncin was no longer smiling. On the contrary his face hardened again, as though he were angry with the woman who had done that.

'Well, I'll tell you what I think about you. You are probably a sick man, for I prefer to believe that no man whose brain was normal would do what you have done, in any circumstances. But that is a question for the psychiatrists. So much the worse if they say you are responsible for your actions.'

He was watching Moncin closely all the time.

'You'd be vexed, wouldn't you, if they decided you were irresponsible?'

For the man's pale eyes had gleamed for a second.

'Never mind. You were just an ordinary child, at least in appearance. A butcher's son. Did you feel humiliated at being a butcher's son?'

He did not need a reply.

'It made your mother feel humiliated too; she saw you as a kind of aristocrat who had strayed into the Rue Caulaincourt. I don't know what your father looked like, poor chap. Among all the photographs your mother has piously preserved, I didn't find one of him. She's ashamed of him, I suppose. Whereas you, from the time you were a baby, were photographed from every angle, and at the age of six you went to a fancy-dress party as an eighteenth-century *marquis*, in an expensive suit that had been made for you. You love your mother, Monsieur Moncin?'

The man still said nothing.

'Didn't you find it irksome in the long run, to be fussed over like that, treated like a delicate creature in need of continual care?

'You might have rebelled, as so many boys do in such circumstances, you might have broken away. Listen to me. Other people will take you in hand later on, and they may not be too gentle about it.

'For me, you're still a human being. Don't you understand that that's precisely what I'm trying to do — to strike a little human spark out of you?

'You didn't rebel, because you're lazy and your vanity is without bounds.

'Some people are born with a title, with money, with servants and a whole system of comfort and luxury around them.

'You were born with a mother who took the place of all that for you.

'Whatever might happen to you, your mother was there. You knew it. You could do whatever you chose.

'Only you had to pay for it — by submissiveness.

'You belonged to your mother. You were her property. You were not allowed to grow up into an ordinary man.

'Was it she who married you off at the age of twenty, for fear you'd begin to have love affairs?'

Moncin was staring at him intently, but it was impossible to guess what was at the back of his mind. One thing was certain: he was flattered at receiving so much attention, at the idea that an important man like Maigret should be studying his behaviour and trying to read his thoughts.

If the superintendent suddenly made a slip, wouldn't he react, protest?

'I don't think you were in love, because you're too self-centred for that. You married Yvonne for the sake of peace, and perhaps in the hope of escaping from your mother's influence.

'When she was still a little girl, Yvonne was lost in admiration for you, such a fair-haired, elegant boy. You seemed to be made of different clay from your little schoolfriends, even if you were a butcher's son.

'Your mother was taken in. She thought Yvonne was just a little goose with whom she could do as she liked; and she set you both up in the flat across the landing from hers, so that she could keep a firm hold over you.

'But all that put together doesn't explain the killings, does it?

'The real explanation won't come from the doctors, who will only be able, like me, to shed light on one aspect of the problem.

'You're the only one who knows the whole story.

'And I'm convinced that you would never be capable of explaining yourself.'

This time he extorted a smile with a touch of defiance in it. Did that mean that if he chose, Moncin, could make his behaviour comprehensible to everybody?

'I've nearly finished. The little goose turned out to be not only a real wife, but a female as possessive as your mother. A battle began beween the two of them, with you as the stake, while you, no doubt, were dragged in both directions.

'Your wife won the first round, for she got you away from the Rue Caulaincourt and transplanted you to a flat in the Boulevard Saint-Germain.

'She gave you a new outlook, new surroundings, new friends; and from time to time you slipped away and went back to Montmartre.

'Didn't you begin to feel rebellious towards Yvonne, just as you used towards your mother?

'Both of them, Moncin, were preventing you from being a man!'

The prisoner threw him a glance charged with resentment, and then looked down at the carpet.

'That's what you imagined, what you tried hard to believe. But at the bottom of your heart you knew quite well it wasn't true.

'You hadn't the courage to be a man. You weren't one. You needed them, the atmosphere they created round you, their attention, their admiration, their indulgence.

'And that was precisely what humiliated you.'

Maigret went and stood at the window to recover his breath. He took out his handkerchief and mopped his forehead; his nerves were on edge, like those of an actor at the climax of his role.

'You won't answer — all right, and I know why you can't manage to answer: it would be too painful to your vanity. You suffer too acutely from your own cowardice, from the perpetual compromise in which your life has been passed.

'How many times have you wanted to kill them? I don't mean the poor unknown girls you've been attacking in the street. I mean your mother and your wife.

'I'd bet that when you were still a kid, or in your teens, the idea of gaining your freedom by killing your mother sometimes passed through your mind.

'Not as a real plan, no! Just one of those stray thoughts

one forgets immediately, or ascribes to a moment of rage.

'And it was the same later, with Yvonne.

'You were the prisoner of them both. They fed you, looked after you, spoilt you, but at the same time they owned you. You were their creature, their property, something they fought over.

'And you, tossed to and fro between the Rue Caulaincourt and the Boulevard Saint-Germain, you went about like a ghost, so as to get peace.

'When, why, under the stress of what emotion, of what humiliation, worse than the others, did the thing trigger off? I have no idea. Only you could answer that question, and I'm not even sure that you could.

'Anyhow, a plan for asserting yourself came into your mind, vaguely at first, then more and more definitely.

'How could you assert yourself?

'Not in your profession, for you know you have always been a failure, or what's worse, an amateur. No one takes you seriously.

'So how are you to assert yourself? By what outstanding action?

'To satisfy your vanity it would have to be outstanding, it must be something everybody would talk about, something that would make you feel far superior to the common herd.

'Did you then have the idea of killing the two women?

'That would be dangerous. The search would automatically lead in your direction, and there would be no one left to back you up, flatter you, encourage you.

'But it was they, the domineering females, that you resented.

'And it was females you turned upon, in the street, haphazard.

'Did it come as a relief, Moncin, to discover that you were capable of killing someone? Did it give you the impression that you were superior to other men, or simply that you were a man?'

He stared Moncin straight in the face, sternly, and the man nearly fell backwards, taking his chair with him.

'Because, ever since there have been men in the world,

murder has always been regarded as the greatest of all crimes, and there are people who consider that it must take exceptional courage.

'I suppose the first time, on February 2, it brought you relief, a momentary intoxication.

'You'd taken your precautions, for you didn't wish to pay the price, to go to the scaffold, to prison, or to some lunatic asylum.

'You are a middle-class criminal, Monsieur Moncin, a mollycoddle of a criminal, a criminal who must have his comforts and his little attentions.

'That is why, ever since I set eyes on you, I have been tempted to employ the methods for which the police are so often blamed. You are afraid of being hit, afraid of physical pain.

'If I hit you across the face with the back of my hand you would collapse; and who knows whether you wouldn't choose to confess, for fear of being hit again.'

Maigret, unintentionally must have been terrible in the anger that had gradually taken possession of him; for Moncin had shrunk into himself and his face was ashen.

'Don't be afraid. I'm not going to hit you. In fact I'm even wondering whether it's you I'm really angry with.

'You proved yourself to be clever. You chose a district where you knew every hole and corner, as only those brought up in a place can know it.

'You chose a weapon which was silent and which at the same time gave you a feeling of physical satisfaction as you used it. It wouldn't have been the same to pull the trigger of a revolver, or to pour out poison.

'You had to have some furious, violent gesture. You needed to destroy and to feel that you were destroying.

'Just to strike the blow was not enough; you had to go on and on afterwards, like an angry little boy.

'You tore your victim's dress and underclothes, and the psychiatrists will no doubt see something symbolic in that.

'You didn't rape your victims because you're not capable of that, because you've never been a real man.'

Moncin suddenly raised his head and glared at Maigret clenching his teeth; he looked ready to tear his eyes out.

'Those dresses, slips, bras and panties were just so much womanliness that you were tearing to pieces.

'What I'm wondering now is whether one of those two women suspected you, not necessarily the first time, but later.

'When you went to Montmartre, usen't you to tell your wife you were going to see your mother?

'Didn't she make the connection between the crimes and those visits of yours?

'You know, Monsieur Moncin, I shall remember you all my life, because never before in my career has a case bothered me so much, taken so much out of me.

'When you were arrested, yesterday, neither of those women thought you were innocent.

'And one of them decided to save you.

'If it was your mother, she had only a few steps to go, to get to the Rue de Maistre.

'If it was your wife, that implies that, on the assumption we should release you, she was prepared to spend her life married to a killer.

'I do not reject either hypothesis. The two women have been here since the early hours of this morning, face to face in an office, and neither of them has uttered a word.

'The one who has committed murder knows what she did.

'The one who is innocent knows that the other is not, and I wonder if she doesn't feel a secret jealousy.

'For years they've been competing to prove which of them loved you the most, which of them possessed you most completely.

'And how could either possess you more completely than by saving your neck?'

The telephone interrupted him as he was about to continue.

'Hello!... Yes, it's me... Yes, sir... He's here... I beg your pardon, but I need him for an hour longer... No, the papers were telling the truth... An hour!... They're both at the Quai...'

He rang off impatiently, and went and opened the door of the inspectors' office.

'Bring me those two women.'

He felt an urge to get it over. If the attack he had just launched did not bring him to the goal, he realized he wouldn't be able to settle the case.

He had asked only for an hour, not because he was sure of himself, but as a kind of petition. In an hour's time he would throw in his hand and Coméliau could do as he chose.

'Come in, ladies.'

His rage was betrayed only by a kind of vibration in his voice, by the exaggerated calm of some of his movements, such as when he pulled a chair forward for each of them.

'I will not try to deceive you. Shut the door, Janvier. No, don't go away. Stay here and take notes. As I said, I will not try to deceive you, to make you think Moncin has confessed. I might have questioned you separately. As you see, I have decided not to resort to the usual police stratagems.'

Moncin's mother, who had refused to sit down, strode over to him, her moth open, and he said sharply:

'Be quiet! Not now...'

Yvonne Moncin was sitting quietly on the edge of her chair, like a young lady paying a call. She had glanced at her husband, without lingering, and was now staring at the superintendent as though, not content with listening to him, she was trying to read his lips.

'Whether he confesses or not, he has committed five murders, and you know it, both of you, for you know his weaknesses better than anyone. Sooner or later it will be proved. Sooner or later he will end up in prison or in an asylum.

'One of you took it into her head that by committing another murder she could avert suspicion from him.

'All that remains is for us to find out which of you, last night, killed a certain Jeanine Laurent at the corner of the Rue de Maistre.'

Moncin's mother at last had a chance to speak.

'You had no right to question us with no lawyer present. I forbid them to speak, either of them. It is our right to have legal advice.'

'Kindly sit down, Madame, unless you have a confession to make.'

'That's the last straw — to suggest I should make a

confession! You are behaving like… like a boor, which is what you are, and you… you…'

During the hours she had spent alone with her daughter-in-law she had been silently assembling so many resentful thoughts that she had now lost the power to express them.

'I tell you once again to sit down. If you continue to make a scene I shall have you taken away by an inspector who will question you while I deal with your son and daughter-in-law.'

This prospect suddenly calmed her down. The change took place from one second to the next. She stood for an instant with her mouth open in stupefaction, and then she seemed to be retorting:

'I'd like to see you do that!'

Wasn't she his mother? Weren't her rights more long-standing, more self-evident, than those of a chit her son just happened to have married?

It wasn't Yvonne who had put him into the world, it was she.

'Not only,' Maigret resumed, 'did one of you hope to save Moncin by committing a crime similar to his while he was locked up, but that one, I am convinced, had known for a long time what was going on. So she had the courage to remain alone with him day after day, in the same room, with no protection, with no chance of escape if he should suddenly have the idea of killing her too.

'That one loved him enough, in her own way, to…'

The glance Madame Moncin threw at her daughter-in-law did not escape him. Never, perhaps, had he read such hatred in a human eye.

As for Yvonne, she had not flickered an eyelash. Holding her red morocco bag with both hands, she continued to stare at Maigret as though hypnotized, not losing one expression that passed over his face.

'It only remains for me to tell you that Moncin will almost certainly save his head. The psychiatrists, as usual, will not agree about him, they will argue in front of a jury who will not understand what it is all about, and there is every chance that he will get the benefit of the doubt, in which case he will be sent to spend the rest of his days in an asylum.'

The man's lips quivered. What was he thinking of at that precise moment? He must be horribly afraid of the guillotine, and afraid of prison as well. But wasn't he now conjuring up the picture of a lunatic asylum as the popular imagination sees such places?

Maigret felt convinced that if he could be promised a room to himself, a nurse, the latest thing in treatment and the attention of some distinguished specialist, he would not hesitate to talk.

'For the woman, it isn't the same thing. For six months, Paris has been living in terror, and people never forgive those who have frightened them. The members of the jury will be Parisians, the fathers or husbands of women who might have been stabbed to death by Moncin at some street corner.

'There will be no question of madness.

'In my opinion it is the woman who will pay.

'She knows that.

'It is one or the other of you.

'One or the other of you, to save a man, or more precisely, in order to preserve what she regards as her property, has risked her neck.'

'I am perfectly willing to die for my son,' said Madame Moncin, suddenly and distinctly. 'He is my child. It does not matter to me what he has done. It doesn't matter to me what becomes of the little tarts who walk the streets of Montmartre at night.'

'You killed Jeanine Laurent?'

'I do not know her name.'

'You are responsible for the murder committed in the Rue de Maistre last night?'

She hesitated, looked at Moncin, and finally said 'Yes.'

'In that case, can you tell me the colour of the victim's dress?'

This was a detail Maigret had asked the Press not to make public.

'I... It was too dark to...'

'Excuse me! You are aware that she was set upon less than five yards away from a street-lamp...'

'I didn't pay attention.'

'But when you slashed the material...'

The crime had been committed more than fifty yards away from the nearest street-lamp.

In the ensuing silence Yvonne Moncin's voice was heard to say calmly, like a schoolgirl in class:

'The dress was blue.'

She was smiling, she had not moved; now she turned to stare defiantly at her mother-in-law.

In her own mind, didn't she consider she had won the match?

'Yes, it was blue,' sighed Maigret, at last allowing his nerves to relax.

And the relief was too sudden, so violent, that tears came into his eyes — tears of weariness, perhaps.

'You finish it, Janvier,' he muttered, getting to his feet and picking a pipe at random from the row on his desk.

Moncin's mother had sunk into herself, she suddenly looked ten years older, as though her only reason for existence had been snatched from her.

Maigret did not look at Marcel Moncin, whose head had fallen forward on his chest.

The superintendent pushed through the crowd of reporters and photographers who assailed him in the corridor.

'Who was it? You know now?'

He nodded, stammering: 'Presently... In a few minutes...'

And he hurried to the little glass-panelled door that communicated with the Palais de Justice.

He was only with the examining magistrate for about fifteen minutes. When he came back, it was to give out his orders.

'Let the mother go, of course. Coméliau wants to see the other two as soon as possible.'

'Together?'

'Yes, to begin with. It's he who'll make an announcement to the Press...'

There was someone he would have liked to see, though not in an office and not in the corridors or the wards of an asylum: Professor Tissot, with whom he would have enjoyed a long chat such as they had had that evening in Pardon's drawing-room.

He couldn't ask Pardon to arrange another dinner. And he was too tired to go to Sainte-Anne and wait till the professor could see him.

He opened the door of the inspectors' office, where all eyes turned towards him.

'It's over, boys...'

He hesitated, looked round at them all, gave a weary smile, and admitted:

'Personally, I'm going to bed.'

And it was true. It had seldom happened before, even when he'd been up all night.

'Tell the Director...'

'Then in the corridor, to the journalists:

'In the examining magistrate's office... Monsieur Coméliau will give you the particulars...'

They saw him going downstairs all alone, with bowed shoulders; he stopped on the first landing and slowly lit the pipe he had just filled.

One of the drivers asked him if he wanted the car, but he shook his head.

The first thing he wanted was to go and sit on the terrace of the Brasserie Dauphine, the way he had sat for a long time on another café terrace last night.

'A pint, Superintendent?'

He looked up and replied as though ironically, with an irony intended for himself:

'Two!'

He slept till six o'clock that evening, in the damp sheets, with the window open on the Paris street-noises; and when at last he appeared in the dining-room, his eyes still swollen with sleep, it was in order to inform his wife:

'We're going to the cinema this evening...'

Arm-in-arm, as was their custom.

Madame Maigret asked him no questions. She felt, confusedly, that he had been a long way away, that he needed to get used to everyday life again, to rub shoulders with men who would restore his confidence.

July 12, 1955

The Patience of MAIGRET

CHAPTER ONE

The day had started like a memory of childhood, dazzling and delectable. For no reason, because life was wonderful, Maigret's eyes laughed as he had his breakfast, and the eyes of Madame Maigret sitting opposite him were just as merry.

The windows of the flat were wide open, letting in the smells from outside, the familiar noises from the Boulevard Richard-Lenoir, and the air, already warm, was quivering; a fine vapour filtered the sun rays and made them almost tangible.

'You're not tired?'

He replied in surprise, sipping his coffee which seemed better than on other days:

'Why should I be tired?'

'All that work you did yesterday in the garden... You hadn't touched a spade or a rake for months....'

It was Monday. Monday, July 7. On Saturday night they had taken the train to Meung-sur-Loire, to the little house they had been preparing for several years, for the day when Maigret would be obliged to retire.

In two years and a few months. At the age of fifty-five! As if a man of fifty-five, who had never really been ill and was not handicapped by any infirmity, would suddenly be unable to run the crime squad!

What Maigret found most difficult to conceive was that he had lived fifty-three years.

'Yesterday,' he corrected her, 'I slept most of the time.'

'In the sun!'

'With my handkerchief over my face....'

What a pleasant Sunday! A stew simmering in the low kitchen with its blue stone tiles, the scent of the St. John's wort which spread through the house. Madame Maigret going from one room to the other, a scarf on her head because of the dust, Maigret in his shirt sleeves, his collar open, wearing a straw hat, weeding, digging, hoeing, raking, and finally dropping off to sleep after lunch and the local white wine, in a red-and-yellow striped hammock-chair where the sun soon reached him but could not rouse him.

In the train back they both felt heavy and sluggish, their eyelids stinging, and with them they carried a smell that reminded Maigret of his youth in the country, a mixture of hay, dry earth and sweat: the smell of summer.

'More coffee?'

'I'd love some.'

Even his wife's checked apron delighted him by its freshness, by a sort of simplicity, just as he was delighted by the glint of the sun on one of the panes of the sideboard.

'It's going to be hot!'

'Very.'

He would open his windows overlooking the Seine and work in his shirt sleeves.

'What would you say to lobster mayonnaise for lunch?'

It was pleasant, too, to walk along the street where the awnings of the shops formed dark rectangles, pleasant to wait for the bus next to a girl in a light dress on the corner of the Boulevard Voltaire.

Luck was on his side. An old bus with a platform drew up by the pavement and he could go on smoking his pipe as he watched the scenery and the figures of the passers-by glide past.

Why did that remind him of a brightly coloured procession which had drawn the whole of Paris when he had just got married and was only a shy young secretary in the Saint-Lazare police station? Some foreign sovereign and his plumed court were riding in landaus while the helmets of the Republican Guard glimmered in the sun.

Paris had the same smell as today, the same light, the same languor.

He had not thought of retirement then. The end of his career, the end of his life seemed very distant, so distant that he did not worry about it. And here he was preparing the home for his old age!

No melancholy. A rather sweet smile, really. The Châtelet. The Seine. An angler — there was always at least one — near the Pont au Change. Then some lawyers in black robes gesticulating in the courtyard of the Palais de Justice.

Finally the Quai des Orfèvres whose every stone he knew and from where he had almost been banished.

Less than ten days earlier a martinet of a Chief Commissioner, who did not approve of detectives of the old school, had asked him to resign — to retire before his time, as he more elegantly put it — on the pretext of some rash act the Superintendent was supposed to have committed.

Everything, or almost everything, in the file he had leafed through with a negligent finger, was false, and, for three days and three nights, without even being allowed to make use of his colleagues, Maigret had endeavoured to prove it.

Not only had he succeeded, but he had extracted a confession from the perpetrator of the deed, a dentist in the Rue des Acacias, who had several crimes on his conscience.

That was all over. After greeting the two constables on duty he climbed the wide staircase, entered his office, opened the window, took off his hat and jacket, and stood contemplating the Seine and its boats as he slowly filled a pipe.

Despite the unforeseen events there were almost ritual movements which he made automatically, like, once his pipe was alight, pushing open the door of the detectives' office.

There were gaps in front of the typewriters and

telephones because the holidays had started.

'Hello, boys... Can you come in for a second, Janvier?'

Janvier was leading the investigation on the burglaries in the jewellers' shops, or rather in the jewellers' windows. The last one had been on Thursday, in the Boulevard du Montparnasse, and the criminals had employed methods which had proved effective for over two years.

'Anything new?'

'Hardly anything. Young boys, again: aged from twenty to twenty-five according to the witnesses. Two of them did it, as usual. One broke the window with a tyre-lever. The other, who had a black sack in his hand, swept up the jewels with the help of his friends. It was carefully timed. A cream-coloured car stopped just long enough to pick up the two men and disappeared in the traffic.'

'Handkerchiefs round their faces?'

Janvier nodded.

'The driver?'

'The witnesses don't all agree, but it seems he's young too, very dark hair, and sunburnt. There's only one new clue, and that's pretty vague: just before the burglary a vegetable seller noticed a man, not tall, tough, with a face like a boxer's, standing a few yards away from the jeweller's as though he were waiting for someone, often looking up at the clock over the window and then checking his wrist-watch. According to the woman he didn't once take his hand out of his right pocket. During the burglary he didn't budge, and, after the cream-coloured car had moved off, he got into a taxi.'

'Did you show your vegetable seller the photographs of the suspects?'

'She spent three hours with me in the files office. In the end she didn't give a formal recognition of anybody.'

'What does the jeweller say?'

'He's tearing the little hair he's got left. Three days earlier, he claims, the burglary wouldn't have mattered much because he doesn't usually like having valuable jewels on show. Last week he was able to buy a batch of emeralds and on Saturday morning he decided to put them in the window.'

Maigret did not yet realize that what was building up in his office that morning was the beginning of the end of a case which was henceforth to be known at the Quai des Orfèvres as 'Maigret's longest investigation'.

And so certain facts gradually become legendary. 'Maigret's longest interrogation' was still being discussed, for example, and new-comers were told about the interrogation which had lasted twenty-seven hours during which the waiter from the 'Brasserie Dauphine' had never really stopped bringing up beer and sandwiches.

Maigret was not the only one to question the suspect. Lucas and Janvier took over, perpetually starting from scratch an interrogation which seemed tedious but nevertheless ended in a full confession.

And the recollections all included 'Maigret's most dangerous arrest' — the arrest of the gang of Poles in broad daylight, in the Rue du Faubourg Saint-Antoine, without a shot being fired although the men were armed to the teeth and determined to save their skins.

It might in fact be said that the jewel case started twenty years earlier for the Superintendent, when he took an interest in a certain Manuel Palmari, a vagrant from Corsica who had started humbly as a pimp.

It was the time of relief. The old gang leaders, brothel owners before the war, keepers of secret gambling dens and organizers of spectacular burglaries, had gone into retirement one after the other, on the banks of the Marne, in the South, and, the less lucky ones or the less clever ones, to the prison of Fontevrault.

Young lads, thinking they were going to smash everything to smithereens, took over, bolder than their predecessors, and, for a long time, the police force was baffled and kept at bay.

It was the beginning of attacks on cashiers and jewel burglaries, in broad daylight, in the middle of the crowd.

A few culprits were eventually arrested. The crimes ceased for a while, resumed and decreased again, to continue with renewed vigour two years later.

'The kids we arrest are only carrying out orders,' Maigret had stated ever since the raids began.

Not only were new faces reported each time, but most of those who were arrested had no police record. They were not from Paris either, and appeared to have come up from the provinces, mainly from Marseilles, Toulon and Nice, for a specific operation.

Only on a couple of occasions had they chosen the big jewellers', in the Place Vendôme and the Rue de la Paix, with alarm systems that discouraged criminals.

Their technique had soon changed. They now aimed at unimportant jewellers', no longer in the heart of Paris, but on the outskirts and even in the suburbs.

'Well, Manuel?'

Ten times, a hundred times. Maigret had upbraided Palmari, first at the 'Clou Doré', the bar he had bought in the Rue Fontaine and turned into a luxurious restaurant, and then in the flat he shared with Aline in the Rue des Acacias.[1]

Manuel never let himself be put out and their meetings could have passed as meetings between two old friends.

'Sit down, Superintendent. What do you want now?'

Manuel was now nearly sixty and, ever since he had been hit by several machine-gun bullets as he was lowering the blind of the 'Clou Doré', he had never left his little wheel-chair.

'Do you know a young man, a real little pest, called Mariani, who was born in your island?'

Maigret filled his pipe, because this always lasted a long time. He finally knew every nook of the flat in the Rue des Acacias, above all the little corner room, full of cheap novels and gramophone records, where Manuel spent his days.

'What's this Mariani done? And why pester me again, Superintendent?'

'I've always been straight with you, haven't I?'

'That's true.'

'I've even done you little favours....'

That was true too. Without Maigret's intervention Manuel would have had a number of difficulties.

[1]See *Maigret on the Defensive*

'If you want it to continue, tell me...'

Manuel occasionally told, or in other words, gave up an operator.

'You know, it's only a theory. I've never been in trouble and my record's clear. I don't know Mariani personally. I've just heard....'

'Who from?'

'I don't know. A rumour...'

Since he lost a leg Palmari hardly saw a soul. He knew his telephone was tapped and he made sure he only made innocent calls.

Moreover, for the last few months, since the revival of the jewel robberies, two detectives had been permanently posted in the Rue des Acacias.

If there were two of them it was because one had to trail Aline while his colleague watched the building.

'Very well... To do you a favour... There's an inn near Lagny — I've forgotten its name — which is kept by an old man who's half deaf and his daughter... I believe Mariani is keen on the girl and likes staying there....'

Every time, over the last twenty years, that Manuel had shown signs of increased prosperity, this prosperity had coincided with a revival of the jewel robberies.

*

'Was the car found?' Maigret asked Janvier.

'In a side street in the Halles.'

'Any clues?'

'Nothing. Moers virtually went over it with a microscope.'

It was time for the report in the Chief's office and Maigret joined the other Superintendents.

They each summarized the current cases.

'And you, Maigret? These jewellers?'

'Do you know how many jewellers there are in Paris, sir, not to mention the suburban ones? Just over three thousand. Some of them only display jewels and watches of no great value, but on the whole we can say that a good thousand of these shops have something on show to tempt an organized gang.'

'What are your conclusions?'

'Let's take the jeweller's in the Boulevard du Montparnasse. For months it only displayed mediocre objects. By chance, the other week, the dealer got hold of some valuable emeralds. On Saturday morning he decided to put them on show. On Thursday the window was smashed to bits and the jewels were stolen.'

'You think...'

'I'm almost certain that a man in the trade does the rounds of the jewellers, periodically changing the districts. Someone is alerted the minute the best pieces are displayed in a good place. Some lads who have been taught the technique and who aren't suspected by the police are brought up from Marseilles or elsewhere. Two or three times I set a trap, asking the jewellers to show some rare pieces.'

'Did the gang fall into it?'

Maigret shook his head and relit his pipe.

'I'm patient,' was all he muttered.

The Chief, less patient than he was, did not conceal his displeasure.

'And it's been going on for...' he began.

'Twenty years, sir.'

A few minutes later Maigret was back in his office, happy to have remained serene and good-humoured. Once again he opened the detectives' door because he hated calling them on the house telephone.

'Janvier!'

'I was waiting for you, chief. I've just received a call...'

He came into Maigret's office and shut the door.

'Something unexpected... Manuel Palmari...'

'Don't say he's disappeared?'

'He's been killed. He was shot in his wheel-chair. The Superintendent from the 17th *arrondissement* is on the spot and he's informed the Public Prosecutor.'

'Aline?'

'Apparently she called the police.'

'Come on.'

At the door Maigret retraced his steps to take a spare pipe from his desk.

*

As Janvier drove the little black car up the Champs-Elysées in a halo of light Maigret retained the slight smile on his lips, the twinkle in his eyes, which he had had since he woke up and which he had seen on the lips and in the eyes of his wife.

And yet, deep within himself, if there was not a feeling of sadness there was at least a certain nostalgia. The death of Manuel Palmari would not send the world into mourning. Apart, perhaps — and that was not certain — from Aline who had lived with him for several years and whom he had picked up in the street; apart, too, from certain vagrants who owed him everything, his only funeral eulogy would be a vague:

'He had it coming to him....'

One day Manuel had disclosed to Maigret that he too had been a choirboy in his home village, a village so poor, he added, that the boys left it at the age of fifteen to get away from the misery. He had wandered round the docks at Toulon where he was later to be found as a barman and where he soon realized that women constituted a capital which could provide a large income.

Had he one or several crimes on his conscience? Some people made insinuations, but it had never been proved and one fine day Palmari had become proprietor of the 'Clou Doré'.

He thought he was cunning and it was true that until the age of sixty he had moved so adroitly that he had never run the risk of being convicted.

Admittedly he had not escaped the machine-gun bullets, but in his wheel-chair, among his books and his records, between the radio and the television, he continued to love life and Maigret suspected him of loving even more passionately, even more tenderly, this Aline who called him Daddy.

'You shouldn't see the Superintendent, Daddy. I know the cops and I'm fed up with them. This one's no better than the rest of them. One day, you'll see, he'll use what he pumps out of you against you.'

The girl sometimes used to spit on the floor, at Maigret's feet, and walk away with dignity, waggling her hard little behind.

Maigret had left the Rue des Acacias less than ten days ago and here he was again, in the same building, in the same flat where, standing by the open window, he had suddenly had an intuition which had enabled him to reconstruct the crimes of the dentist living across the street.

Two cars were parked in front of the building. A constable in uniform was standing by the door and, recognizing Maigret, he saluted.

'The fourth floor on the left,' he murmured.

'I know.'

The Police Superintendent, called Clerdent, stood in the sitting-room talking to a small, plump man with very fair, tousled hair, white, baby-like skin, and ingenuous blue eyes.

'Good morning, Maigret.'

Seeing Maigret look at his companion, not knowing whether to shake hands, he added:

'Don't you know each other?... Superintendent Maigret ...Monsieur Ancelin, the examining magistrate....'

'Pleased to meet you, Superintendent.'

'It's my pleasure, Monsieur Ancelin. I've heard a lot about you but I haven't yet worked with you.'

'I was only appointed to Paris five months ago. I spent a long time in Lille.'

He had a high-pitched voice and, despite his plumpness, seemed far younger than he was. He looked more like one of those students who stay on at university, in no hurry to leave the Latin Quarter and the easy life. Easy, of course, for those who have a rich daddy.

He was sloppily dressed, his jacket too narrow, his trousers too wide, baggy round the knees, and his shoes needed a brush.

It was said at the Palais de Justice that he had six children, that he had no control over his family, that his old car was about to fall to pieces at any moment, and that to make ends meet he lived in a cheap suburban flat.

'Immediately after calling the Judicial Police I informed the Public Prosecutor,' the Police Superintendent explained.

'Has the Deputy arrived?'

'He'll be here in a minute.'

'Where's Aline?'

'The girl who lived with the victim? She's crying, laid out on her bed. The maid's with her.'

'What does she say?'

'I didn't find out much, and in the state she's in I didn't persevere. According to her she got up at half past seven. The maid only comes in at ten. At eight o'clock Aline brought Palmari his breakfast in bed and then washed him.'

Maigret knew the house routine. Ever since he was disabled Manuel no longer dared get into a bathtub. He stood under the shower on one leg and Aline helped him dress.

'What time did she go out?'

'How do you know she went out?'

Maigret would be sure after he had asked his two men on guard in the street. They had not telephoned him. They must have been surprised to see the Police Superintendent arrive, then the examining magistrate, and finally Maigret himself, because they did not know what might have happened inside the building. There was something quite ironical about it.

'Excuse me, gentlemen.'

A tall young man with an equine face burst in, shook hands and asked:

'Where's the body?'

'In the next room.'

'Any clues?'

'I was telling Superintendent Maigret what I know. Aline, the young woman living with Palmari, claims to have left the building around nine, without a hat, and holding a string bag.'

One of the detectives on duty must have followed her.

'She went to several local tradesmen. I haven't yet had a written statement because all I could get out of her were disjointed phrases.'

'It was when she was out that...'

'So she says, of course. She came back at five to ten.'

Maigret looked at his watch, which said ten past eleven.

'In the next room she found Palmari who had slipped from his wheel-chair on to the carpet. He died after losing a great deal of blood, as you will see.'

'What time did she ring you? Because I was told she was the one who rang the police station.'

'Yes. It was a quarter past ten.'

The Deputy Public Prosecutor, Alain Druet, asked the questions while the plump magistrate listened with a vague smile. He too, despite the difficulty of feeding his brood, seemed to enjoy life. From time to time he glanced furtively at Maigret, as if to establish a certain complicity.

The two others, the Deputy Public Prosecutor and the Police Superintendent, spoke and behaved like conscientious officials.

'Has the doctor examined the body?'

'He just came in and out. He claims that it's impossible to tell before the post-mortem how many bullets Palmari received, that it's also impossible to see the bullet holes without undressing him. The bullet through his neck, however, seems to have been fired from behind.'

So, thought Maigret, Palmari didn't suspect a thing.

'Let's have a look, gentlemen, before someone from the Records Office gets here.'

Manuel's little room had not changed and the sun flooded in. On the ground was a twisted, almost ridiculous body, and handsome white hair smeared with blood around the neck.

Maigret was surprised to see Aline Bauche standing by the curtain of one of the windows. She was wearing a light blue linen dress which he knew, and her black hair framed a pale face covered with red blotches as though she had been hit.

She looked at the three men with such hatred or such defiance that it seemed as though she were going to pounce on them with her claws out.

'Well, Monsieur Maigret, so I suppose you're satisfied?'

Then, to all of them:

'Can't you leave me alone with him, like any woman who's just lost the man of her life? You're probably going to arrest me, aren't you?'

'Do you know her?' the examining magistrate asked Maigret in a whisper.

'Pretty well.'

'Do you think she did it?'

'You must have been told I never think anything, Monsieur Ancelin. I can hear the men from the Records Office with their equipment. May I question Aline on my own?'

'Are you taking her away?'

'I'd rather do it here. I'll tell you what I find out afterwards.'

'When the body's been removed it may be necessary to seal the doors of this room.'

'The Police Superintendent will see to that, if you don't mind.'

The magistrate still looked at Maigret, his eyes full of mischief. Was that how he had imagined the famous Superintendent? Was he disappointed?

'You can have a free hand, but let me know what happens.'

'Come along, Aline.'

'Where are you taking me? The Quai des Orfèvres?'

'Not so far. To your room. Janvier, go and get our men outside and wait for me in the sitting-room.'

With hard eyes Aline watched the experts invade the room with their equipment.

'What are they going to do to him?'

'The usual. Photographs, fingerprints, etc. By the way, has the weapon been found?'

She pointed to the table near the sofa where she would lie for days on end, as she kept her lover company.

'Did you pick it up?'

'I haven't touched it.'

'Have you seen this gun before?'

'As far as I know it belonged to Manuel.'

'Where did he keep it?'

'In the daytime he hid it behind the radio, within reach; in the evening he put it on his night table.'

A Smith and Wesson 38, the weapon of a professional, which knows no mercy.

'Come along, Aline.'

'What for? I don't know anything.'

She followed him unwillingly into the sitting-room, opened the door of a very feminine bedroom with a huge low bed such as one sees more frequently in the cinema than in Parisian houses.

The curtains and hangings were of buttercup silk; a large white goatskin rug covered almost the whole of the floor, while tulle curtains transformed the light from the window into golden dust.

'I'm listening,' she said peevishly.

'So am I.'

'It can last some time.'

She sank into an armchair covered in ivory silk. Maigret did not dare sit on the fragile chairs and did not know whether to light his pipe.

'I know you didn't kill him, Aline.'

'No kidding?'

'Don't be unpleasant. You helped me last week.'

'That can't be the most intelligent thing I've ever done. The proof is that your two men are always standing across the street and that the tallest one trailed me again this morning.'

'I'm doing my job.'

'Doesn't it ever disgust you?'

'Let's stop playing at war. Let's say I'm doing my job just as you're doing yours and it doesn't much matter if we're on different sides of the fence.'

'I've never hurt a soul.'

'That's possible. On the other hand Manuel has just been hurt irreparably.'

He saw the tears well up behind the young woman's eyelids and they seemed genuine. Aline blew her nose clumsily, like a little girl trying to stop sobbing.

'Why must...'

'Why must what?'

'Nothing. I don't know. Why must he be dead? Why did they pick on him? As though he wasn't unhappy enough with one leg and living between four walls.'

'He had you.'

'That made him suffer too, because he was jealous and God knows he had no reason to be.'

Maigret grabbed a gold cigarette-case on the dressing-table and offered it open to Aline. She took a cigarette automatically.

'You came back from your shopping at five to ten?'

'The detective can confirm that.'

'Unless you gave him the slip, as you have done now and again.'

'Not today.'

'So you didn't have to contact anyone for Manuel, no instructions to give, no 'phone calls.'

She shrugged her shoulders, automatically brushing away the smoke.

'Did you go up by the main stairs?'

'Why should I have gone up the back stairs? I'm not a servant, am I?'

'You went first to the kitchen?'

'As I always do after shopping.'

'Can I see?'

'Open the door. It's opposite, in the corridor.'

He just glanced in. The maid was making some coffee. Vegetables were piled on the table.

'Did you empty your string bag?'

'I don't think so.'

'You're not sure?'

'There are some things one does automatically. After what happened I can hardly remember.'

'Knowing you, you then went into the little room to kiss Manuel.'

'You know as well as I do what I found.'

'What I don't know is what you did.'

'First, I think I screamed. I instinctively rushed towards him. Then, I admit, when I saw all that blood I drew back in horror. I couldn't even give him a last kiss. Poor Daddy!'

Tears ran down her face and she did not think of drying them.

'You picked up the gun?'

'I've already said I didn't. You see! You pretend to believe me and the moment we're alone together you set me traps.'

'You didn't touch it, even to wipe it?'

'I didn't touch a thing.'

'When did the maid arrive?'

'I don't know. She goes up the back stairs and never bothers us when we're in that room.'

'You didn't hear her come in?'

'One can't hear from the little room.'

'Is she ever late?'

'Frequently. She has a sick son she has to look after before she comes.'

'You only rang the police station at a quarter past ten. Why? And why wasn't the first thing you did to call a doctor?'

'You've seen him, haven't you? Are many people alive in that condition?'

'What did you do in the twenty minutes between finding the body and telephoning? Here's a piece of good advice, Aline: don't answer too quickly. I know you. You've often lied to me and I haven't minded. I'm not sure whether the examining magistrate feels as I do. And he's going to decide about your liberty!'

She resumed her derisive, common sneer and said:

'That would cap it all! Have them arrest me! And people still believe in justice! Do you still believe in it after what happened to you? Do you believe in it?'

Maigret preferred not to answer.

'You see, Aline, these twenty minutes could be of primary importance. Manuel was a careful man. I don't think he kept compromising documents or objects in this flat, and even less jewels or large sums of money.'

'What are you driving at?'

'Didn't you guess as much? One's first reaction on finding a corpse is to call a doctor or the police.'

'I suppose I don't have the same reactions as the average mortal.'

'You didn't stand immobile in front of the body for twenty minutes.'

'For a while, at any rate.'

'Doing nothing?'

'If you want to know, I started by praying. I know it's idiotic since I don't believe in their wretched God. And yet there are times when it gets you in spite of yourself. Whether it did any good or not I said a prayer for the rest of his soul.'

'And then?'

'I started walking.'

'Where?'

'From the little room to this room and from this room to the door of the little room. I talked to myself. I felt like an animal in a cage, like a lioness robbed of her male and her cubs. Because he was everything for me, both my man and my child.'

She spoke passionately as she paced the room as if to reconstruct what she had done that morning.

'It lasted twenty minutes?'

'Perhaps.'

'Didn't it occur to you to tell the maid?'

'I didn't even think of her and I was never at any point aware of her presence in the kitchen.'

'You didn't leave the flat?'

'To go where? Ask your men.'

'Very well. Let's assume you've told the truth.'

'That's all I do.'

She could be kind. She may have had a kind heart and her love for Manuel may have been sincere. Only, like many others, her past experiences had left her peevish and aggressive.

How could one believe in goodness, in justice, how could one trust men after the life she had led until she met Palmari?

'We're going to make a little experiment,' muttered Maigret, opening the door.

He called:

'Moers! Can you come in with the paraffin?'

It now looked as though the flat had been taken over by the removal men and Janvier, who had brought in Inspectors Baron and Vachet, did not know where to stand.

'Wait a moment, Janvier. Come in, Moers.'

The expert had understood and was preparing his instruments.

'Your hand, please.'

'What for?'

The Superintendent explained:

'To prove that you haven't used a fire-arm this morning.'

Without blinking she held out her right hand. Then, just in case, the experiment was repeated on the left hand.

'When can you let me know, Moers?'

'In about ten minutes. I've got all I need down in the van.'

'Is it true you don't suspect me and that you do that as routine?'

'I'm almost sure you didn't kill Manuel.'

'Then what do you suspect me of?'

'You know better than I do, my dear. I'm in no hurry. It'll come in its own time.'

He called Janvier and the two Inspectors who looked ill at ease in this white-and-yellow bedroom.

'It's all yours, boys.'

As if she were preparing for battle Aline lit a cigarette and puffed out the smoke with a disdainful pout.

CHAPTER TWO

When he left his house Maigret certainly did not expect to return to the Rue des Acacias where he had spent so many anxious hours a week earlier. It was nothing but a radiant day which he began at the same time as several million other Parisians. Still less did he expect to be sitting at table at about one o'clock in the afternoon together with the magistrate, Ancelin, in a bistro called 'Chez l'Auvergnat'.

Opposite Palmari's, it was an old-fashioned bar with its traditional counter, its apéritifs which hardly anybody, except for old men, ever drank, its owner in his blue apron, his shirt sleeves rolled up, his face barred by a fine black moustache.

Sausages, chitterlings, gourd-shaped cheeses, hams with greyish rinds as though they had been kept under ashes, hung from the ceiling and in the window could be seen enormous flat loaves straight from the Massif Central.

Beyond the glazed door of the kitchen the owner's wife worked away in front of her oven, thin and gaunt.

'Is it for lunch? A table for two?'

There was no tablecloth, but over the oilcloth was some crinkled paper on which the owner wrote out the bills. One could read, chalked up on a slate:

Rillettes du Morvan
Fillet of veal with lentils
Cheese
Tarte Maison

The plump magistrate perked up in this atmosphere, greedily sniffing the thick scent of food. There were only two or three silent clients left, regular customers whom the owner called by name.

For months this had been the headquarters of the detectives who took it in turns to watch Manuel Palmari and Aline, one of them always ready to follow the young woman the minute she left the building.

For the moment their task seemed over.

'What do you think of it, Maigret? Do you mind if I call you that, although we've only met once? A meeting, as I just said, which I have long wished for. You know, you fascinate me.'

Maigret simply muttered:

'Do you like fillet of veal?'

'I like all country food. I'm the son of peasants, too, and my younger brother runs the family farm.'

Half an hour earlier, when Maigret left Aline's bedroom, he had been surprised to find the magistrate waiting for him in Palmari's little room.

At that time Moers had already made his first report to the Superintendent. The paraffin test was negative. In other words it was not Aline who had fired the shots.

'No fingerprints on the gun, which has been wiped with care. So have the handles on all the doors, including the front door.'

Maigret frowned.

'You meant to say the door handle hasn't even got Aline's fingerprints?'

'That's right.'

She interrupted:

'I always wear my gloves when I go out, even in the summer, because I hate having damp hands.'

'What gloves were you wearing this morning when you did your shopping?'

'White cotton gloves. Look! Here they are.'

She took them out of a handbag shaped like a holdall. Some green marks proved that she had handled the vegetables.

'Baron!' called Maigret.

'Yes, chief.'

'Was it you who followed Aline this morning?'

'Yes. She went out shortly before nine, carrying a red string bag as well as the handbag on the table.'

'Was she wearing gloves?'

'White gloves, as usual.'

'You didn't let her out of your sight?'

'I didn't go into the shops but she didn't give me the slip for a second.'

'No telephone calls?'

'No. At the butcher's she waited for her turn quite a long time, without talking to the women queuing with her.'

'Did you make a note of the time she got back?'

'To the minute. Six minutes to ten.'

'Did she seem in a hurry?'

'On the contrary, she seemed to be dawdling and smiling, like someone making the most of a fine day. It was already hot and I noticed patches of sweat under her arms.'

Maigret, too, was sweating and he felt his shirt damp under his light jacket.

'Call Vacher. Good. Tell me, Vacher, while your colleague was following Aline Bauche, did you stay on guard outside the building? Where were you?'

'By the dentist's house, right opposite, except for the five minutes I took to drink a glass of white wine at "Chez l'Auvergnat". You can see the front door of the building very well from the bar.'

'Do you know who came in and out?'

'First I saw the concierge who came to shake out a mat on the doorstep. She recognized me and muttered something because she hates us and thinks we're insulting her personally by watching the building.'

'Then?'

'At about ten past nine a girl came out with a portfolio under her arm. That was Mademoiselle Lavancher, from the family on the first floor on the right. Her father is a métro inspector. Every morning she goes to an art school in the Boulevard des Batignolles.'

'And then? Didn't anyone go in?'

'The butcher's boy delivered the meat, I don't know to whom. I know him because I always see him at the butcher's shop farther up the street.'

'Who else?'

'The Italian woman on the third floor beat her rugs out of the window. Then, a few minutes before ten, Aline came back, loaded with shopping, and Baron joined me. We were surprised to see the Police Superintendent arrive a little later, then the examining magistrate, and then you. We didn't know what to do. We thought that since we had no orders the best thing to do was to wait in the street.'

'By the early afternoon I would like to have a complete list, floor by floor, of the tenants of the building, with every member of their families, occupation, habits, etc. Do it together.'

'Must we question them?'

'I'll do that.'

Manuel's body had been taken away and the medical expert was probably performing the post-mortem.

'I must ask you not to leave the flat, Aline. Inspector Janvier will stay here. Have your men left, Moers?'

'They've finished their job on the spot. We'll have the photographs and an enlargement of the fingerprints around three o'clock.'

'Are there some fingerprints in spite of everything?'

'Everywhere, as usual, on the ashtrays, for example, on the radio, the television set, the records, on masses of objects the murderer probably didn't touch and didn't think worth wiping.'

Maigret frowned and it was then that he noticed that the magistrate was watching intently his slightest change of expression.

'Shall I send some sandwiches up, boys?'

'No, we'll go and have lunch after you.'

On the landing the magistrate asked:

'Are you having lunch at home?'

'I'm afraid not, despite the lobster awaiting me.'

'May I invite you?'

'You don't know the neighbourhood as well as I do. I'll

invite you, if you don't mind eating Auvergnat food in a bistro.'

So they were sitting at table in front of the paper tablecloth and the Superintendent occasionally pulled out his handkerchief to mop his brow.

'I suppose you consider the paraffin test conclusive, Maigret? I once studied the scientific methods of investigation but I must admit I haven't remembered much.'

'Unless the murderer wore rubber gloves his hands certainly carry minute traces of powder which last for two or three days and which the paraffin test always reveals.'

'Don't you think that Aline, whose maid only comes for a few hours a day, wears rubber gloves, if only to do the washing up?'

'Probably. We'll soon see.'

He started to look at the little magistrate with curiosity.

'These *rillettes* are fabulous. They remind me of the ones we made on the farm when we killed the pig. I believe you usually carry out your investigations alone, Maigret — I mean alone with your colleagues — and wait for more or less definite results before sending your report to the Public Prosecutor and the examining magistrate?'

'It's no longer really possible. After the first interrogation the suspects have the right to have a lawyer present, and the lawyers, who don't much care for the atmosphere at the Quai des Orfèvres, feel more at ease before a magistrate.'

'If I stayed behind this morning and wanted to lunch with you, it isn't to check your initiative, believe me, and even less to curb you. As I said, I'm curious about your methods and from seeing you at work I'll learn an excellent lesson.'

Maigret merely answered the compliment with a vague gesture.

'Is it true you've got six children?' he asked in his turn.

'I'll have seven in three months.'

The magistrate's eyes were laughing, as though he were cracking a good joke at the expense of society.

'You know, it's very instructive. From their extreme youth children have the qualities and defects of adults, so that one gets to know men from watching them live.'

'Does your wife...'

He was going to say:

'Does your wife agree with you?'

But the magistrate went on:

'My wife's dream is to be a mother rabbit in a hutch. She's never so gay and carefree as when she's pregnant. She grows enormous, and puts on up to sixty pounds which she bears light-heartedly.'

A gay, optimistic examining magistrate, eating a fillet of veal and lentils in an Auvergnat bistro as though he had frequented it all his life.

'You knew Manuel well, didn't you?'

'For over twenty years.'

'A tough?'

'Tough and tender, it's hard to say which. When he arrived in Paris after wandering round Marseilles and the Riviera he was a wild animal. Most of his sort soon get to know the police, the courts, the assizes, prison.

'But although Palmari lived in that circle he made sure he was never noticed and when he bought the "Clou Doré", which was only a bistro at the time, he didn't need much coaxing to give us some information about his customers.'

'Was he one of your informers?'

'Yes and no. He kept his distance, and said just enough to keep on the right side of us. So he always pretended not to have seen the two men who fired at him when he was about to lower the blinds. As if by chance two killers from Marseilles were bumped off in the South a few months later.'

'Did he get on well with Aline?'

'He lived for her. Make no mistake about it, Monsieur Ancelin: despite her origins that girl is somebody. She's far more intelligent than Palmari and if she'd been well managed she could have made a name for herself on the stage or the screen: she could have undertaken anything.'

'You think she loved him in spite of the difference of age?'

'I know from experience that for women, for some at any

rate, age is of no importance.'

'So you do not suspect her of this morning's murder?'

'I suspect nobody and I suspect everybody.'

There was only one customer left sitting at table, and two others at the bar, some workmen working in the neighbourhood. The fillet of veal was delicious and Maigret did not remember ever having eaten such succulent lentils. He promised himself he would return one day with his wife.

'Knowing Palmari, the gun was in its usual place behind the radio this morning. If it wasn't Aline who killed him the murderer was somebody whom Manuel trusted implicity, somebody who probably had the key of the flat. Well, for all the months that the house has been watched Palmari hasn't had any visitors.

'It was necessary to cross the sitting-room with its door which is always open, to go into the little room and round the wheel-chair to get hold of the weapon. If it's a vagrant he knows about the paraffin test. But I can't see Palmari welcoming a visitor in rubber gloves. And finally, my detectives didn't see any suspect go in. The concierge has been questioned and didn't notice anyone. The butcher's boy, who makes his deliveries every day at the same time, is out of the question.'

'Could someone have entered the building yesterday evening or last night and hidden on the staircase?'

'It's one of the things I'm going to check this afternoon.'

'You just said you had no idea. Would you resent it if I suspected you nevertheless of having an idea at the back of your mind?'

'It's quite true. But it might not lead anywhere. The building has five floors, not counting the ground floor and the attics. Each floor has two flats. That constitutes a certain number of tenants.

'For months Palmari's telephone conversations were always recorded and they were always perfectly innocent.

'I never could believe that that man had entirely withdrawn from circulation. I had Aline followed every time she went out.

'That was how I discovered that she sometimes telephoned from the back-shop of a tradesman from whom she did her shopping.

'She also periodically managed to give us the slip for a few hours by the old trick of the double exit — from a big store or on the métro.

'I have the dates of those telephone calls and the escapes. I compared them with the jewel robberies.'

'Do they tally?'

'Yes and no. Not all of them. The telephone calls were frequently five or six days before a jewel robbery. The mysterious escapes, on the other hand, sometimes took place several hours after the robberies. Draw your own conclusions, keeping in mind that these raids have nearly all been committed by young boys with no record come up on purpose from the South or the provinces. Do you want some more tart?'

It was a juicy plum tart, scented with cinnamon.

'If you have some yourself.'

They ended their meal with a marc-brandy with no label which must have been at least sixty-five per cent proof, and which set their cheeks on fire.

'I'm beginning to see...' sighed the magistrate mopping his brow in his turn. 'What a pity my work keeps me in the Palais de Justice and that I can't follow your investigation step by step. Do you already know how you're going to set about it?'

'I haven't the slightest idea. If I had a plan I'd have to change it in a few hours. For the time being I'll deal with the tenants of the building. I'll go from door to door, like a vacuum-cleaner salesman. Then I'll see Aline again. She hasn't said everything and she'll have had time to think, but that doesn't mean she'll be any more talkative than this morning.'

They got up after a short argument about the bill.

'I invited myself,' protested the magistrate.

'I'm almost at home here,' claimed Maigret. 'The next time, somewhere else, it'll be your turn.'

From behind his bar the owner asked them:

'Have you had a good lunch, gentlemen?'

'Very good.'

So good that they both felt a little heavy, particularly once they were in the sun.

'Thanks for the meal, Maigret. Get in touch with me soon.'

'I promise.'

And as the florid magistrate slipped behind the wheel of his dilapidated motor car, the Superintendent went once more into the building which was becoming more and more familiar to him.

He had had a good lunch. He could still taste the marc-brandy. The heat, even if it did make one drowsy, was pleasant, the sun full of gaiety.

Manuel too liked good meals, marc-brandy and this drowsiness on fine summer days.

He must now be under a rough sheet in one of the metal drawers of the medico-legal institute.

*

Baron paced the sitting-room whistling. He had taken off his jacket, opened the window and Maigret guessed that he was in a hurry to have his lunch after a large glass of beer.

'You can go. Put your report on my desk.'

The Superintendent saw Janvier, in his shirt sleeves too, in the little room where he had lowered the Venetian blinds. When Maigret came in he got up, put back on its shelf the novel he was busy reading, and grabbed his jacket.

'Has the maid left?'

'I questioned her first. She isn't very talkative. She's new, she was taken on at the beginning of the week. Apparently the other one went back to the country, to Brittany, I believe, to look after her sick mother.'

'What time did she arrive today?'

'At ten o'clock, according to her.'

In Paris, as elsewhere, there are several types of maid. This one, called Madame Martin, belonged to the most disagreeable category — of women who have had misfortunes and continue to attract disasters so that they hold it against the world in general.

She wore a black, almost shapeless dress, down-at-heel shoes, and she looked at people furtively and fiercely, as though she were always expecting to be attacked.

'I don't know anything,' she told Janvier before he had even opened his mouth. 'You have no right to pester me. I've only been working here for four days.'

One could tell she was in the habit of muttering vengeful phrases between her teeth during her solitary work.

'I'm leaving and nobody's going to stop me. I'm never going to put another foot in this house. I suspected they weren't married and that there'd be trouble one day.'

'What makes you think that Monsieur Palmari's death has anything to do with his not being married?'

'It's always like that, isn't it?'

'Which stairs did you use?'

'The back ones,' she replied bitterly. 'Once, when I was young, people would have been pleased to have me come up the main stairs.'

'Did you see Mademoiselle Bauche?'

'No.'

'Did you go straight into the kitchen?'

'I always start there.'

'How many hours a day did you come?'

'Two hours, from ten to twelve. All morning on Monday and Saturday, but, thank God, I won't be doing a Saturday.'

'What did you hear?'

'Nothing.'

'Where was the young lady?'

'I don't know.'

'Didn't you have to ask for instructions?'

'I'm old enough to know what to do after I've been told once.'

'And what did you have to do?'

'Put away the things she had just bought, which were on the table. Then wash the vegetables. Then pass the vacuum-cleaner round the sitting-room.'

'Did you have time to do it?'

'No.'

'What came after the sitting-room on other days?'

'The bedroom and the bathroom.'

'Not the little room?'

'The gentleman's study? The young lady looked after that herself.'

'Did you hear a shot?'

'I didn't hear anything.'

'You didn't even hear the young lady's voice on the telephone?'

'The door was closed.'

'What time did you see Mademoiselle Bauche this morning?'

'I don't know exactly. Ten minutes or a quarter of an hour after I came in.'

'How did she look?'

'She'd been crying.'

'She wasn't crying any more?'

'No. She said:

' "Don't leave me alone. I'm frightened I'm going to faint. Daddy's been killed." '

'Then?'

'She went towards the room where I followed her. It was only once she'd fallen on to the bed that she started crying again. Then she said:

' "Open the door when the bell rings. I've called the police." '

'You weren't curious enough to ask for details?'

'What people do is none of my business. The less one knows the better.'

'You didn't even go and have a look at Monsieur Palmari?'

'Why should I?'

'What did you think of him?'

'Nothing.'

'And of the young lady?'

'Nothing either.'

'You've been here since Monday. Have you seen any visitors?'

'No.'

'Nobody asked to talk to Monsieur Palmari?'

'No. Is that all? Can I go?'

'Provided you leave me your address.'

'It's not far. I live in a garret in the shabbiest house in the Rue de l'Etoile, 27 B. You'll only find me in in the evening because I work all day. And remember I don't like the police.'

Janvier had just read the Superintendent this statement which he had taken down in shorthand.

'Did Moers leave a long time ago?'

'About three-quarters of an hour. He searched everything in this room, examined the books one by one, and the record sleeves. He told me to tell you he didn't find anything. No hiding place in the walls either, and no double drawers in the furniture.

'He passed the vacuum-cleaner round just in case and took away the dust to analyse it.'

'Go and have lunch. I recommend the fillet of veal at "Chez l'Auvergnat" if you can still get some at this hour. Then come back and fetch me. Did you tell the Police Superintendent not to say anything to the Press?'

'Yes. See you later. Incidentally, was the magistrate a bore?'

'On the contrary. I'm beginning to like him.'

Once he was alone Maigret took off his jacket, slowly filled a pipe and started to look round as if he were taking the place over.

Palmari's wheel-chair, which he saw empty for the first time, suddenly became impressive, particularly since the leather of the seat and the back bore the imprint of the body and the hole of one of the bullets which had got lodged in the padding.

He automatically fingered the books, the records, turned on the radio for a moment and heard it advertise a make of baby food.

He pulled up the blinds on the windows, one of which overlooked the Rue des Acacias and the other the Rue de l'Arc-de-Triomphe.

For three years Palmari had lived in this room from morning to night, only leaving it to go to bed after Aline had undressed him like a child.

According to what he had maintained ten days earlier and what the detectives had confirmed, he did not have any visitors and, apart from the radio and television, his companion was his only link with the outside world.

Finally Maigret crosssd the sitting-room and knocked at the door of the bedroom. Receiving no answer he opened it and found Aline lying on her back on the enormous bed, staring at the ceiling.

'I hope I didn't wake you up?'

'I wasn't asleep.'

'Have you had lunch?'

'I'm not hungry.'

'Your maid has said she isn't coming back.'

'What do I care? If only you wouldn't come back.'

'What would you do?'

'Nothing. If you were killed too, would your wife appreciate having her flat invaded and being asked question after question?'

'I'm afraid it's essential.'

'I can't think of anything more inhuman.'

'Yes: murder.'

'And you think I committed it? In spite of the test your expert performed this morning?'

'You do your own cooking, I suppose?'

'Like all women who haven't got a cook.'

'Do you wear rubber gloves?'

'Not for the cooking, but to clean the vegetables and do the washing up.'

'Where are they?'

'In the kitchen.'

'Can you show them to me?'

She got up unwillingly, her eyes dark with spite.

'Come along.'

She had to open two drawers before she found them.

'There you are! You can send them to your artists. I didn't wear them this morning.'

Maigret put them in his pocket without a word.

'Contrary to what you may think, Aline, I like you very much and even admire you.'

'Should I be moved?'

'No. I'd like to have a word with you in Manuel's little room.'

'Or else?...'

'What do you mean?'

'If I refuse? I suppose you'll take me to your office in the Quai des Orfèvres?'

'I'd rather it happened here.'

She shrugged her shoulders, went ahead of him and sank on to the narrow sofa.

'You think it's going to upset me to see the scene of the crime.'

'No. It would be better if you stopped being so stubborn, if you gave up being on the defensive and hiding what you'll have to tell me one day.'

She lit a cigarette and looked at Maigret indifferently.

Pointing to the wheel-chair the Superintendent murmured:

'You want whoever did that to be punished, don't you?'

'I'm not counting on the police.'

'Would you rather do it yourself? How old are you, Aline?'

'You know. Twenty-five.'

'So you've got your entire life ahead of you. Did Manuel leave a will?'

'I never asked.'

'Did he have a solicitor?'

'He didn't mention one.'

'Where did he put his money?'

'What money?'

'What he got from the "Clou Doré", to start with. I know it was you who picked up the money due to Manuel from the manager each week. What did you do with it?'

She looked like a chess player imagining all the possible consequences of his next move.

'I put the money in the bank, keeping only what I needed for the household.'

'Which bank?'

'The branch of the Crédit Lyonnais in the Avenue de la Grande-Armée.'

'Is the account in your name?'

'Yes.'

'Is there another account in Palmari's name?'

'I don't know.'

'Look, Aline. You're an intelligent girl. Up to now, together with Manuel, you have been leading a special sort of life more or less on the fringe of society. Palmari was a gang leader, a tough, who made himself respected for years.'

She pointed ironically at the wheel-chair, and then at the half-erased patch of blood on the carpet.

'If a man like him, who knew all the ropes, got done in, what do you think will happen to a young woman who is from now on defenceless?

'Do you want my opinion? I can only see two alternatives. Either whoever had it in for him will soon take care of you and they won't miss you any more than they missed him. Or else they'll leave you alone and as far as I'm concerned that will mean that you're in league with them.

'You see, you know too much, and in that set only the dead keep quiet.'

'Are you trying to scare me?'

'I'm trying to make you think. We've been trying to get the better of each other for too long.'

'Which proves, according to your theory, that I can keep quiet.'

'Do you mind if I open the window?'

He opened the one in the shade, but the air outside was hardly cooler than the air in the room and Maigret went on sweating. He could not make up his mind whether to sit down.

'For three years you've been living here with Manuel who, according to him and according to you, had no contact with the outside world. In fact he had contacts through you.

'Officially you only went once a week, rarely twice, to check the accounts of the "Clou Doré", to pick up Palmari's share and put the money in the bank, in an account in your name.

'But you frequently found it necessary to give my detectives the slip either to make some mysterious telephone calls or to have a few hours on your own.'

'I might have a lover, for instance?'

'Doesn't it upset you to say something like that today?'

'It's just to show you that there are masses of possibilities.'

'No, my dear.'

'I'm not your dear.'

'I know! You've told me time and again. But even so there are moments when you behave like a child and one wants to slap you.

'A minute ago I mentioned your intelligence. But you don't seem to be aware of the hornets' nest you've got yourself into.

'That you should have behaved like that as long as Palmari was there to give you advice and protect you is all very well. But from now on you're alone, you hear? Is there another weapon in the house apart from the one in the hands of the experts?'

'Some kitchen knives.'

'You want me to go away and stop having you watched...'

'That's just what I want.'

He shrugged his shoulders, discouraged. Nothing worked with her in spite of her obvious dejection and a certain anxiety which she did not quite manage to conceal.

'Let's start from another end. Palmari was sixty. For about fifteen years he was proprietor of the "Clou Doré" which he ran himself until his infirmity prevented him. With his restaurant alone he earned a lot of money and he had other sources of income.

'Now, apart from buying this flat, the furniture and current expenses he never spent a great deal. Where is the fortune he amassed?'

'It's too late to ask him.'

'Did he have any family you knew of?'

'No.'

'Don't you think that loving you as he did he arranged for the money to go to you?'

'You're the one who's said it.'

'His sort usually dislike entrusting their money to a

bank, because it's too easy to check the date of payments.'

'I'm still listening.'

'Manuel didn't work alone.'

'At the "Clou Doré"?'

'You know I don't mean that, but the jewels.'

'You came to see him about it at least twenty times. Did you get anything out of him? Why do you think that now Daddy's dead you'll succeed with me?'

'Because you're in danger.'

'Is that any of your business?'

'I wouldn't like to have to repeat this morning's little ceremony for you.'

She seemed to Maigret to be thinking, but nevertheless, as she put out her cigarette in the ashtray, she sighed:

'I've got nothing to say.'

'In that case you'll allow me to leave one of my men in this flat night and day. Another one will continue to trail you when you go out. Finally, I must ask you officially not to leave Paris before the end of the investigation.'

'I see. Where will your detective sleep?'

'He won't sleep. If you ever have anything to say to me ring me at my office or my home. Here's my number.'

She did not touch the card he held out and finally put on the table.

'Now that our talk is over I can tell you how sorry I am. Palmari had chosen to live on the fringe but I must admit I rather admired him.

'Good-bye, Aline. The door bell rang and it must be Janvier who's finished his lunch. He'll stay here until I send a detective to replace him.'

He was about to give her his hand. He felt she was upset. But knowing she would not respond to his gesture he put on his jacket and went to the door to open it for Janvier.

'Anything new, Chief?'

He shook his head.

'Stay here until I send someone to replace you. Watch her and mind the back stairs.'

'Are you going to the Quai?'

After a vague gesture Maigret sighed:

'I don't know.'

A few minutes later he was drinking a large beer in a brasserie in the Avenue de Wagram. He would have preferred the atmosphere at 'Chez l'Auvergnat' but there was no call-box in the bistro. The telephone hung near the counter and the customers could hear the conversations.

'Another beer, waiter, and some coins for the telephone. Make it five.'

A bloated prostitute, her face smeared with multi-coloured make-up, smiled at him ingenuously without guessing who he was. He felt sorry for her and signalled to her not to waste her time on him.

CHAPTER THREE

Gazing vaguely through the windows of the call-box at the customers sitting round the tables Maigret first rang the magistrate, Ancelin, to ask him to postpone the affixing of seals in the Rue des Acacias.

'I left one of my detectives in the flat and I'm going to send another to spend the night there.'

'Have you questioned the young woman again?'

'I've just had a long talk with her, with no result.'

'Where are you right now?'

'In a brasserie in the Avenue de Wagram where I still have a few more calls to make.'

He thought he heard a sigh. Did the plump little magistrate envy him for being deep in the bustle of the city while he himself was in a dusty office dealing with abstract files and monotonous formulae?

At school young Maigret used to look nostalgically out of the window of his classroom at the men and women coming and going in the street while he was shut in.

The brasserie was almost full and he was still astonished, after so many years, to see so many people coming and going at times when others were slaving away in offices, shops or factories.

When he first arrived in Paris he could spend an entire afternoon outside a café in the Grands Boulevards, or the Boulevard Saint-Michel, gazing after the moving crowd, watching the faces, trying to guess what everyone was thinking about.

'Thank you, Monsieur Ancelin. The minute there's anything new I'll let you know.'

Now for the medical expert, whom he reached in his surgery. It was no longer Doctor Paul but his young successor, less picturesque but who nevertheless did his job conscientiously.

'As you know, your men found a bullet in the back of the wheel-chair. It was fired from the front, when the victim was already dead.'

'From about how far away?'

'Less than a yard and over two feet. I can't be more specific without being theoretical. The bullet which killed Palmari was shot from behind, in the neck, almost point-blank, sloping slightly upwards, and was lodged in the brain-pan.'

'Are the three bullets of the same calibre?'

'As far as I can see. The gunnery expert has them. You'll be getting my official report tomorrow morning.'

'A last question: the time?'

'Between half past nine and ten.'

Now for Gastinne-Renette.

'Did you have time to examine the weapon I sent you and the three bullets?'

'I've got a few more tests to do but so far it's almost certain that the three bullets were fired from the Smith and Wesson.'

'Thank you.'

A shy young man in the brasserie walked round in a circle and finally sat next to the prostitute with the thick hips and over-made-up face. Without daring to look at her he ordered a beer and his fingers which tapped the table revealed his embarrassment.

'Hello! The financial department? Maigret here. Let me talk to Superintendent Belhomme, will you?'

Maigret still seemed more interested in what was going on in the room than in what he was saying.

'Belhomme? Maigret here. I need you, old boy. It's about a certain Manuel Palmari who lives, or rather who lived, in the Rue des Acacias. He's dead. Some of his little pals reckoned he'd lived long enough. Palmari owned a restaurant in the Rue Fontaine, the "Clou Doré", which he gave over to a management about three years ago.

'Have you got it? He lived with a certain Aline Bauche. She has an account in her name at the branch of the Crédit Lyonnais in the Avenue de la Grande-Armée. Apparently she deposited each week part of the returns from the "Clou Doré".

'I have reason to believe that Palmari had larger sources of income. Nothing was found in his flat except for a few notes of a thousand and a hundred francs in his wallet and about two thousand francs in his mistress's handbag.

'I don't need to be more specific. The hoard must be somewhere, maybe with a solicitor, maybe invested in some firm or house property. Either I'm wrong, or there's a great deal of it.

'Yes, urgent as always. Thanks, old boy. See you tomorrow.'

A telephone call to Madame Maigret, like the one he gave that morning.

'I doubt if I'll be back for dinner and I may only come home very late... Now?... In the Avenue de Wagram, in a brasserie... What are you having to eat?... A savoury omelet?...'

Finally the Judicial Police.

'Let me speak to Lucas, will you?... Hello, Lucas?... Can you come immediately to the Rue des Acacias?... Yes... And get someone to take over from you at about eight... Who's there?... Janin... Perfect... Tell him he'll have to spend a sleepless night... No, not outside... He'll have a good armchair....'

The young man got up, his cheeks crimson, followed between the rows of tables and chairs by the woman who could have been his mother. Was it the first time?

'A beer, waiter.'

Outside the air was sizzling and the women looked naked under their light dresses.

If that martinet of a Chief Commissioner could see Maigret now he would probably have accused him of doing a job unworthy of a Superintendent.

And yet that was how the Superintendent had succeeded with most of his investigations: climbing stairs, sniffing in the corners, having a chat here and there, asking apparently futile questions, often spending hours in rather shady bistros.

The little magistrate had understood and envied him.

A few minutes later Maigret went into the lodge of the building where Aline lived. Concierges are like maids: all good or all bad. He had known charming ones, neat and gay, whose lodges were models of tidiness and cleanliness.

This one, who must have been about fifty-five, belonged to the other category, the cross-patches, the grumblers always ready to complain about the wickedness of the world and their sad lot.

'You again?'

She was shelling peas, with a cup of coffee in front of her, on the oilcloth covering the round table.

'What do you want now? I told you I didn't see anyone except for the butcher's boy who's been delivering for several years.'

'I suppose you've got a list of the tenants?'

'How else would I get the rent? If only everyone paid on quarter day! When I think that I have to climb four or five floors to get to people who don't stint themselves!...'

'Will you give me the list?'

'I don't know if I can. Maybe I ought to ask the landlady.'

'Has she got a telephone?'

'Even if she hadn't I wouldn't have far to go.'

'Does she live in the building?'

'Well! Are you pretending you don't know her? It's too bad if I'm putting my foot in it. This isn't the day to bother her, she's got enough worries as it is.'

'You mean?...'

'You didn't know? Too bad! You'd have found out sooner or later. When the police start sticking their nose into things... Yes, it's Mademoiselle Bauche....'

'Are the receipts signed by her?'

'Who else would have signed them since the house is hers?'

Without being asked Maigret had sat down in a wicker-work armchair out of which he had driven the cat.

'Let's have a look at the list....'

'So much the worse for you. You'll have to settle it with Mademoiselle Bauche, who isn't always easy.'

'Is she tight-fisted?'

'She doesn't care for people who don't pay. And besides, she has her moods.'

'I see that the flat next to yours is occupied by someone called Jean Chabaud. Who is he?'

'A young man in his early twenties who works on television. He's nearly always travelling because he specializes in sport — football, motor racing, the Tour de France....'

'Married?'

'No.'

'Does he know Aline Bauche?'

'I shouldn't think so. I made him sign the lease.'

'And the flat on the right?'

'Can't you read? There's a plate on the door: Mademoiselle Jeanine Hérel, chiropodist.'

'Has she been living here long?'

'Fifteen years. She's older than I am. She's got a fine practice.'

'The first floor on the left, François Vignon...'

'Can't one be called Vignon?'

'Who is he?'

'He's in an insurance company, married with two children. The second is only a few months old.'

'What time does he leave the building?'

'At about half past eight.'

'In the flat on the right, Justin Levancher.'

'Métro inspector. He starts work at six in the morning and wakes me up as he goes by at half past five. An old cross-patch with a liver complaint. His wife's a disagreeable woman and they'd both do better to watch their daughter who's only just sixteen.'

The second floor on the left: Mabel Tuppler, an American woman of about thirty, living alone and writing articles for American newspapers and magazines.

'No. She doesn't see any men. Men leave her cold. I wouldn't say as much about women.'

On the same floor on the right a retired couple over sixty, the Maupois, who had been in the shoe business, and their maid Yolande living in the garret. Three or four times a year the Maupois took a trip to Venice, Barcelona, Florence, Naples, Greece or somewhere else.

'How do they spend their days?'

'Monsieur Maupois goes out at about eleven to have his apéritif, always dressed up to the nines. In the afternoon, after his siesta, he goes for a walk or shopping with his wife. If only they weren't so mean...'

The third floor. On one side a certain Jean Destouches, physical training instructor at a gymnasium at the Porte Maillot. Goes out at eight in the morning, often leaving in his bed his companion of an evening's or a week's standing.

'I've never seen such a procession. How can one do P.T. if one goes to bed at two nearly every night?'

'Do Destouches and Aline Bauche know each other?'

'I've never seen them together.'

'Was he here before she owned the building?'

'He only moved in last year.'

'You've never seen Mademoiselle Bauche stop on his floor, go in or out of his flat?'

'No.'

'On the right Gino Massoletti, representative for France of a make of Italian motor cars. Married to a very pretty woman.'

'Butter wouldn't melt in her mouth,' added the sour concierge. 'As for their maid who lives in the garret like the Lavanchers' maid, she's a hot little piece and I have to open the door for her in the small hours at least three times a week.'

The fourth floor: Palmari, or rather, the late Palmari, on the left, and Aline.

On the same landing, the Barillards.

'What does Fernand Barillard do?'

'Commercial traveller. He represents a de luxe packing firm, chocolate boxes, almond bags, boxes for scent bottles. For the new year he tips me with a bottle of scent and some *marrons glacés* which don't cost him a penny.'

'How old is he? Married?'

'Forty or forty-five. Quite a pretty wife, nice and plump, who's always laughing, Belgian, with very fair hair. She sings all day.'

'Have they got a maid?'

'No. She does her own house-work and shopping, and every afternoon she goes to a tea-room.'

'A friend of Aline Bauche?'

'I've never seen them together.'

On the fifth floor Tony Pasquier, second barman at Claridges, his wife and two children of eight and eleven. A Spanish maid living in the garret like the two other maids of the building.

In the flat on the right an Englishman, James Stuart, a bachelor, never going out before five in the afternoon, and coming back at dawn. No profession. A daily maid in the late afternoon. Frequent visits to Cannes, Monte Carlo, Deauville, Biarritz and the Swiss resorts in the winter.

'No dealings with Aline Bauche?'

'Why should the whole building have dealings with her? And anyhow, what do you mean by dealings? Do you think they go to bed together? Not one of the tenants even knows she's the landlady.'

Just in case, Maigret put a cross against the name of the Englishman, not because he thought he had any connection with the present case, but because he might be an eventual client of the Judicial Police. Of the gambling squad, for instance.

That left the seventh floor, in other words the garrets. From right to left the four maids were: Yolande, the maid of the Maupois, the retired couple on the second floor; the Spanish maid of the Massolettis; the Levanchers' maid and finally the maid of Tony the barman.

'Has Stuart been living here long?'

'Two years. He succeeded an Armenian carpet dealer whose furniture and fittings he bought.'

Another tenant of the garret: Mademoiselle Fay, known as Mademoiselle Josette, an old maid who was the oldest tenant of the building. She was eighty-two and still did her own shopping and house-work.

'Her room's full of bird-cages which she puts on the window-sill in turn. She's got at least ten canaries.'

An empty room, and then Jef Claes' room.

'Who is he?'

'A deaf and dumb old man who lives on his own. In 1940 he fled from Belgium with his two married daughters and his grand-children. In the North, in Douai, I think, while they were waiting for a refugee train, the station was bombed and there were over a hundred killed.

'Hardly anything was left of the daughters and grand-children. The old man was wounded in the head and face.

'One of his sons-in-law died in Germany; the other remarried in America.

'He lives alone, only going out to get something to eat.'

The peas had been shelled long ago.

'Now I hope you're going to leave me in peace. I'd just like to know when the body's being brought back and when the funeral's taking place. I have to make a collection for the tenants' wreath.'

'We can't settle anything yet.'

'Somebody's looking for you...'

It was Lucas who had come into the building and had stopped by the lodge.

'I can smell the police ten yards away!'

Maigret smiled.

'Thank you!'

'If I answered your questions it's just because I had to. But I'm no police-spy, and if everyone minded their own business...'

As if to purify the lodge of the fumes Maigret might have left she went to open the window overlooking the courtyard.

'What shall we do, chief?' asked Lucas.

'We're going up. Fourth floor on the left. Janvier must be dreaming of a glass of cold beer. Unless Aline's been humanized and has offered him one of the bottles I saw this morning in the refrigerator.'

*

When Maigret rang at the door of the flat the Janvier who opened it had an odd expression. The Superintendent realized why when he entered the sitting-room. Aline went out through the other door, into the bedroom; instead of the light blue dress she had been wearing in the morning, she wore an orange silk négligé. On a table were two glasses, one half full, some beer bottles and some playing cards which had just been dealt.

'You know, chief, it isn't what you think it is,' said the Inspector awkwardly.

Maigret's eyes laughed. He casually counted the hands.

'Belote?'

'Yes. Let me explain. When you left I insisted on her having something to eat. She wouldn't hear of it and shut herself in her room.'

'Did she try to telephone?'

'No. She stayed in bed for about three quarters of an hour and then re-appeared in a dressing-gown, looking nervous, like someone who had tried to sleep and couldn't.

' "Well, Inspector, it's all very well my being at home but I'm a prisoner all the same," she said. "What would happen if I decided to go out?"

'I thought I was right in replying:

' "I wouldn't stop you, but a detective would follow you."

' "Are you going to stay all night?"

' "Not me. One of my colleagues."

' "Do you play cards?"

' "Sometimes."

' "Let's play a game of belote to pass the time? It'll help me not to think." '

'By the way,' said Maigret to Lucas, 'you ought to ring the Quai for one of our men to post himself outside the building. Someone who's not going to be given the slip.'

'Bonfils is there. He's the best for this sort of job.'

'Tell him to warn his wife he won't be back tonight. Where's Lapointe?'

'In the office.'

'Tell him to wait for me here, to come up and stay with you until I come back. Can you play belote, Lucas?'

'Not too badly.'

'Aline will probably put you through it too.'

He knocked at the bedroom door, which was opened at once. Aline must have been listening.

'Excuse me.'

'You're at home, aren't you? No point in telling you!'

'I'd just like to put myself at your service in case there is anyone you want to inform. The papers won't mention anything before tomorrow, at the earliest. Would you like me to tell the manager of the "Clou Doré" what happened, for example? Or maybe the solicitor, or some member of the family?'

'Manuel didn't have a family.'

'And you?'

'They don't care any more about me than I do about them.'

'If they knew you owned a building like this they'd soon come to Paris, don't you think?'

She registered the blow but did not protest, did not ask any questions.

'Tomorrow there'll be time to call the undertaker because we can't yet tell when the body will be returned. Do you want it brought back here?'

'He lived here, didn't he?'

'I advise you to eat something. I'm leaving you with Inspector Lucas, whom you know. If you've got anything to say to me I'll be in the building for a while.'

This time the young woman's expression sharpened.

'In the building?'

'I wanted to meet the tenants.'

She watched him as he sent Janvier home.

'I'll have you replaced at about eight or nine this evening, Lucas.'

'I'd asked Janin to come, but I'd rather stay, chief. If only some sandwiches could be sent up.'

'And some beer...'

Lucas pointed at the empty bottles.

'Unless there's some left in the refrigerator.'

For almost two hours Maigret scoured the building from top to bottom, from one end to the other, agreeable and patient, with the obstinacy of an expert salesman.

The names he had made a note of in the concierge's flat progressively ceased to be abstractions, became shapes, faces, eyes, voices, attitudes, human beings.

The chiropodist on the ground floor could just as easily have been a fortune-teller, with her very pale face devoured by almost hypnotic black eyes.

'Why the police? I've never done anything wrong in my life. Ask my clients who've been coming to me for nine years.'

'Somebody died in the building.'

'I saw a body being carried out, but I was busy. Who is it?'

'Monsieur Palmari.'

'I don't know him. On what floor?'

'The fourth.'

'I've heard of him. He's got a very pretty wife, a little affected. I never saw him. Was he young?'

Chabaud, the one who worked on television, was away. The métro inspector was not back but his wife was in the flat with a friend, sitting in front of some cakes and cups of chocolate.

'What can I say? I don't even know who lives above us. If this man never left his flat it's not surprising I never met him on the stairs. As for my husband he never went farther than our floor. Why should he have gone up there?'

Another woman opposite, a baby in its cradle, a little girl with a bare behind, on the ground, some feeding-bottles in a sterilizer.

On the next floor Miss Tuppler was typing. She was tall, broad, and because of the heat she was only wearing a pair of pyjamas with the jacket open on her breasts. She felt no need to button it up.

'A murder in the building? Gee! how exciting! Have you arrested the murderer?... And your name's Maigret?... The Maigret of the Quai des Orfèvres?...'

She went towards the bottle of Bourbon on the table.

'Do you drink?'

He drank, listened to her gibberish for about ten minutes, wondering if she would eventually cover her breasts.

'The "Clou Doré"?... No... Never been... But in the States nearly all the night-clubs belong to gangsters... Was Palmari a gangster?...'

The Superintendent was scouring a sort of condensed Paris, with, from one floor to the other, the same contrasts one finds between the districts and the streets.

In the American girl's flat reigned an untidy Bohemian atmosphere. In the flat of the retired couple opposite everything was padded, with the softness of jam, and it smelt of sweets and jam. A man with white hair was asleep in an armchair, a newspaper on his knees.

'Don't talk too loudly. He hates waking up with a start. Have you come for charitable works?'

'No. I'm from the police.'

This seemed to surprise the old lady.

'Really! From the police! In such a quiet house! Don't tell me a tenant's been burgled?'

She smiled, her face gentle and kind, like a nun under a coif.

'A crime? Is that why there's been so much coming and going this morning? No, I don't know anyone except for the concierge.'

The physical training instructor, on the third floor, was out too, but a young woman, her eyes blurred with sleep, came to open the door, her body wrapped up in a blanket.

'What? No. I don't know when he'll be back. It's the first time I've been here.'

'When did you meet him?'

'Last night, or rather this morning since it was past twelve. In a bar in the Rue de Presbourg. What's he done? He looked so nice.'

No point in persevering. She spoke with difficulty because she had a bad hang-over.

At the Massolettis' flat there was only the maid who explained in bad French that her mistress had gone to join her husband at Fouquet's and that they were both dining in town.

The furniture was modern, lighter and gayer than in the other flats. A guitar lay on a sofa.

On Palmari's floor Fernand Barillard was not back. It was a woman of about thirty, with very fair hair, nice and plump, who opened the door, humming.

'Well! I've already passed you on the stairs. What are you selling?'

'The Judicial Police.'

'Are you investigating what happened this morning?'

'How do you know something happened?'

'Your colleagues made enough din! I just had to open the door ajar to hear what they said. Incidentally, that's a funny way to talk about a dead man, especially the ones who were joking as they carried the body down.'

'Did you know Manuel Palmari?'

'I never saw him, but I sometimes heard him howl.'

'Howl? What do you mean?'

'He can't have been easy. I understand it because the concierge said he was an invalid. He used to get so angry!...'

'With Aline?'

'Is she called Aline? She's pretty odd, anyhow. To begin with, when I met her on the stairs, I used to nod good-morning to her, but she looked right through me. What sort of a woman is she? Were they married? Did she kill him?'

'What time does your husband start work?'

'It depends. He hasn't got a set timetable like an office worker.'

'Does he come home for lunch?'

'Rarely, because he's usually far away or in the suburbs. He's a commercial traveller.'

'I know. What time did he leave this morning?'

'I don't know, because I went out very early to do the shopping.'

'What do you call early?'

'About eight. When I came back at half past nine he was no longer here.'

'Did you meet your neighbour in the shops?'

'No. We probably don't go to the same ones.'

'Have you been married long?'

'Eight years.'

Dozens and dozens of questions and as many answers were recorded in Maigret's mind. In the heap, a few, or maybe only one, might suddenly have a meaning.

The barman was in because he only started work at six. The maid and the two children were in the first room which had been turned into a nursery. A child fired at the Superintendent shouting:

'Bang! bang! You're dead!'

Tony Pasquier, whose hair was thick and coarse, was shaving for the second time in the day. His wife was sewing a button on to a pair of children's trousers.

'What name did you say? Palmari? Should I know him?'

'He's your downstairs neighbour, or rather he was your downstairs neighbour until this morning.'

'Didn't something happen to him? I came across some policemen on the stairs and when I came back at half past two my wife told me a body was carried out.'

'Have you ever been to the "Clou Doré"?'

'Not personally, but I've occasionally sent customers there.'

'Why?'

'Some of them ask us where to eat in such and such a district. The "Clou Doré" has a good reputation. I used to know the head waiter, Pernelle, who worked, in Claridges. He knows his job.'

'You don't know the name of the owner?'

'I never asked.'

'And the woman, Aline Bauche, have you ever met her?'

'The girl with black hair and tight dresses whom I've passed on the stairs?'

'She's your landlady.'

'That's the first I've heard of it. I've never said a word to her. Have you, Lulu?'

'I hate that type.'

'You see, Monsieur Maigret. Not much for you. Maybe you'll be luckier next time.'

The Englishman was away. On the seventh floor the Superintendent found a long passage lit by a skylight. On the side of the courtyard was a huge attic where the tenants stored old suitcases, dressmakers' dummies, chests, a whole lot of junk.

On the side facing the street the doors were in a row, as in a barracks. He started with the one at the end, belonging to Yolande, the maid of the pensioners on the second floor. It was open and he saw a transparent nightgown on an unmade bed, some sandals on the rug.

The next door, that of Amelia, according to the plan Maigret had drawn in his notebook, was shut. So was the next one.

When he knocked at the fourth door a weak voice asked him in and, through the bird-cages cluttering up the room, he saw, near the window, in a Voltaire chair, a moon-faced old woman.

He almost went out, leaving her to her reverie. She was practically ageless, was just connected to the world by a slender thread and watched the intruder with smiling serenity.

'Come in, my dear sir. Don't be frightened of my birds.'

He had not been told that besides the canaries an enormous parrot was at liberty, perched on a see-saw in the middle of the room. The bird started shrieking:

'Polly... Pretty Polly!... are you hungry, Polly?...'

He explained that he was from the police, that a crime had been committed in the building.

'I know. The concierge told me when I went to do my shopping. It's so unfortunate to kill each other when life is so short! It's like war. My father fought in 1870 and in 1914. I too have lived through two of them.'

'Did you know Monsieur Palmari?'

'Neither him nor anyone else apart from the concierge who's not as bad as one might think. She's had so many misfortunes, poor woman. Her husband was a philanderer and, to make matters worse, he drank.'

'Did you hear any tenant come up to this floor?'

'From time to time people come to fetch or put away something in the attic. But with my window open and my birds singing, you know...'

'Do you see your neighbour?'

'Monsieur Jef? You might think we were the same age. In fact he's far younger than I am. He can't be much over seventy. It's because of his wounds that he looks older. Do you know him too? He's deaf and dumb and I wonder if it isn't worse than being blind.

'Blind people are supposed to be gayer than the deaf. I'll soon know because my sight gets worse every day and I can't even tell what your face is like. I can only make out a light patch and some shadows. Won't you sit down?'

Finally the old man, who, when Maigret came in, was reading a children's comic. His face was scarred and one of the scars drew up the corner of his mouth so he always looked as if he were smiling.

He wore blue glasses. In the middle of the room a large table of white wood was covered with odds and ends, unexpected objects, a little boy's Meccano set, pieces of carved wood, old magazines, clay out of which the old man had modelled an animal difficult to identify.

The iron bed looked as though it were out of a barracks, as did the coarse blanket, and on the whitewashed walls hung coloured prints representing sunny towns: Nice, Naples, Istanbul... On the ground were more piles of magazines.

With his hands, which did not shake in spite of his age, the old man tried to explain that he was deaf and dumb, that he could say nothing, and in his turn Maigret gave a sign of helplessness. Then he explained that he could read the words on Maigret's lips.

'I'm sorry to disturb you. I'm from the police. Would you happen to know a tenant called Palmari?'

Maigret pointed to the floor to show that Palmari lived downstairs, held up two fingers to specify the number of floors. Old Jef shook his head and the Superintendent spoke about Aline.

As far as he could gather the old man had met her on the stairs. He described her comically, carving in space her narrow face, her slim, curving figure.

Back on the fourth floor Maigret felt he had visited a

whole universe. He felt heavier, rather sad. Manuel's death in his wheel-chair had only caused a very slight stir and people who had for years only been separated from him by a partition, a floor or a ceiling did not even know who had been carried away under a sheet.

Lucas was no longer playing cards. Aline was not in the sitting-room.

'I think she's asleep.'

Young Lapointe was there, thrilled to be working with the chief.

'I took a car. Was that all right?'

'Is there any beer left, Lucas?'

'Two bottles.'

'Open one for me and I'll have half a dozen delivered to you.'

It was six o'clock. The traffic jams were beginning to form in Paris and despite the regulations an impatient driver was hooting under the windows of the building.

CHAPTER FOUR

The 'Clou Doré' in the Rue Fontaine was flanked on one side by a third-rate striptease joint and on the other by a lingerie shop specializing in highly fanciful female underclothes which foreigners took home with them as a souvenir of 'Gay Paree'.

Maigret and Lapointe, who had left the Judicial Police car in the Rue Chaptal, slowly wandered up the street where the daytime workers began to mingle with the very different figures of night life.

It was seven o'clock. The bouncer, whom everyone called Big Armed Jo, was not yet at his post, in his blue uniform with gold braid, on the doorstep of the restaurant.

Maigret, who was looking round for him, knew him well. He looked like a former side-show boxer although he had never worn six- or eight-ounce gloves, and, at the age of forty, he had spent half his life in the shade, first as a minor in an approved school, then in prison, serving six months to two years at a time, for petty theft or assault and battery.

He had the intelligence of a child of ten and in an unexpected situation his eyes became blurred, almost pleading, like those of a schoolboy being asked about a subject he has not studied.

He was indoors, in his uniform, busy passing a rag over the fawn leather seats and when he recognized the

Superintendent his face had about as much expression as a block of wood.

The two waiters were busy laying the tables, putting on to the tablecloths the plates with the crest of the house, glasses and silver, and, in the middle of each table, two flowers in a crystal vase.

The lamps with pink shades were not lit because the sun still gilded the pavement opposite.

The barman Justin, in a white shirt and black tie, gave a last wipe to his glasses and the only customer, a large man with a red face, sitting on a high stool, was drinking a *menthe verte*.

Maigret had seen him before somewhere. It was a familiar face but he could not place it immediately. Had he met him at the races, or even here, or in his officc in the Quai des Orfèvres?

Montmartre was full of people who had had dealings with him, sometimes years earlier, and who vanished for a longer or shorter period of time, either to do a cure at Fontevrault or Melun, or to sink into the background waiting to be forgotten.

'Good evening, sir. Good evening, Inspector,' said Justin airily. 'If it's for dinner you're rather early. What can I give you?'

'A beer.'

'Dutch, Danish, German?'

The manager came out of the back room silently, his hair scanty, his face pale and rather puffy and mauve rings under his eyes.

With no surprise or apparent emotion he went up to the detectives, gave Maigret a soft hand, and then shook Lapointe's hand before leaning against the bar, but not sitting down. He had only to put on his dinner jacket before being ready for his customers.

'I expected you today. I was even surprised you didn't come sooner. What do you think of it?'

He seemed worried or gloomy.

'What do I think of what?'

'Somebody finally managed to do him in. Have you any idea who it could have been?'

So although the papers had not mentioned Manuel's death, although Aline had been watched all day and had not made a single telephone call, they knew the news at the 'Clou Doré'.

If a policeman from the Ternes district had talked it would have been to a reporter. As for the tenants of the building, they did not seem to have any connection with the Montmartre set.

'Since when have you known about it, Jean-Loup?'

The manager, who was also the head waiter, was called Jean-Loup Pernelle. The police did not have anything against him. Born in the Allier, he had started as a waiter at Vichy. Married young, he was the father of a family; his son studied at the Medical College and one of his daughters had married the owner of a restaurant in the Champs-Elysées. He led a bourgeois life in the villa he had had built at Choisey-le-Roi.

'I don't know,' he answered in surprise. 'Why do you ask? I suppose everyone knows?'

'The papers haven't mentioned the crime. Try to remember. Did you know anything at lunch-time?'

'I think so, yes. The customers tell us so many things! Can you remember, Justin?'

'No. It was mentioned at the bar, too.'

'Who by?'

Maigret was up against the law of silence. Even if Pernelle, the manager, did not belong to the set, and led the most orderly of lives, he was no less bound to secrecy by some of his customers.

The 'Clou Doré' was no longer the bar it used to be, where one only encountered vagrants. And Manuel, who had then owned the place, had not needed much coaxing to tip the Superintendent off about them.

The restaurant had acquired some wealthy customers. There was a large number of foreigners, some pretty girls, too, at about ten or eleven at night, because dinner was served until midnight. A few of the gang leaders still stuck to their habits but they were no longer young and ready for anything. They had houses of their own and most of them had wives and children.

'I'd like to know the first person to tell you both about it.'

And Maigret went fishing, as he put it.

'It wasn't a certain Massoletti?'

He had had time to memorize the names of all the tenants of the building in the Rue des Acacias.

'What does he do?'

'He deals in cars... Italian cars...'

'I don't know him. Do you, Justin?'

'It's the first I've heard of him.'

They both seemed sincere.

'Vignon?'

Not a glimmer in their eyes. They shook their heads.

'A physical training instructor called Destouches?'

'Don't know him here.'

'Tony Pasquier?'

'I know him,' broke in Justin.

'So do I,' continued Pernelle. 'He sends me customers sometimes. He's the second barman at Claridges, isn't he? I haven't seen him for months.'

'He hasn't telephoned today?'

'He only telephones to give a customer a special recommendation.'

'Your bouncer wouldn't have heard the news, would he?'

The bouncer, who had overheard, spat on the ground in feigned disgust and muttered between his teeth:

'Well, if that's not the limit!'

'James Stuart, an Englishman? No? Fernand Barillard?'

At each name the two men looked as though they were thinking and shook their heads once more.

'Who do you think would want to get rid of Palmari?'

'It isn't the first time someone's had a go at him.'

'Except that the men who sprayed him with the machine-gun were bumped off. And Palmari never left his flat. Tell me, Pernelle, when did the "Clou Doré" change hands?'

A slight blush on the manager's pale face.

'Five days ago.'

'Who's the present owner?'

He hesitated for a second. He realized Maigret knew and

that there was no point in lying.

'I am.'

'Who did you buy the place from?'

'From Aline, of course.'

'How long has Aline been the real owner?'

'I can't remember the date. It's over two years.'

'Was the bill of sale authenticated by a solicitor?'

'Quite legally.'

'Which solicitor.'

'Maître Desgrières, in the Boulevard Pereire.'

'How much was it?'

'Two hundred thousand.'

'New francs, I suppose?'

'Of course.'

'Paid in cash?'

'Yes. So it even took some time to count the notes.'

'Did Aline take them away in a portfolio or a case?'

'I don't know. I left first.'

'Did you know that Manuel's mistress also owns the building in the Rue des Acacias?'

The two men were more and more ill at ease.

'There are always rumours. You see, Superintendent, I'm an honest man, like Justin. We've both got a family. Because the restaurant is in Montmartre we get all sorts of customers. And besides, the law forbids us to throw them out unless they're blind drunk, and that's very rare.

'One hears stories, but one likes to forget them. Isn't that so, Justin?'

'Precisely.'

'I wonder,' murmured the Superintendent, 'whether Aline had a lover.'

Neither of them flinched, said either yes or no, which rather surprised Maigret.

'Did she ever meet men here?'

'She didn't even stop at the bar. She came straight up to my office on the mezzanine and checked the accounts like a businesswoman before going off with the amount due to her.'

'Aren't you surprised that a man like Palmari apparently transferred to her name all or a good part of what he possessed?'

'Many tradesmen and businessmen put all their property in their wife's name for fear of confiscation.'

'Palmari wasn't married,' objected Maigret. 'And there were thirty-five years between them.'

'I thought of that too. You see, I think Manuel was really gone on Aline. He trusted her implicitly. He loved her. I could swear he'd never been in love before he met her. He felt belittled in his invalid's chair. She became his life more than ever before, his only contact with the outside world.'

'And she?'

'As far as I can see she loved him too. It happens to girls like her as well. Before meeting him she had only met men who had their fun without considering her as a human being, you see? Girls like Aline are far more susceptible than honest women to attention, affection, the prospect of security.'

The large, red-faced man at the end of the bar ordered another *menthe*.

'Right away, Monsieur Louis.'

And Maigret whispered:

'Who is Monsieur Louis?'

'A customer. I don't know his name but he comes quite frequently to drink one or two *menthes* with water. I suppose he's from the neighbourhood.'

'Was he here at midday?'

'Was he here, Justin?' Pernelle repeated in a whisper.

'Just a minute. I think so. He asked me for a tip on some race.'

Monsieur Louis mopped his brow and watched his glass gloomily.

Maigret pulled out his notebook and wrote a few words which he showed Lapointe.

'Follow him if he goes out. Meet you here. If I've left ring me at home.'

'I say, Pernelle, while you're not too busy do you mind if we go up to the mezzanine for a minute?'

It was an invitation a restaurant owner can hardly refuse.

'This way...'

He had flat feet and waddled along like most elderly

head-waiters. The staircase was narrow and dark. There was none of the luxury and comfort of the restaurant. Pernelle pulled a bunch of keys out of his pocket, opened a brown door, and they both found themselves in a little room looking on to the courtyard.

The cylindrical desk was covered with bills, pamphlets, two telephones, pens, pencils and headed documents. On some white wooden shelves was a row of green filing cases and on the wall opposite hung framed photographs of Madame Pernelle, twenty or thirty years younger, a boy of about twenty, and a girl leaning her head forward pensively, her chin in her hand.

'Sit down, Pernelle, and listen to me. Let's play straight.'

'I've always played straight.'

'You know that you haven't and that you can't or you wouldn't be the owner of the "Clou Doré". To put you at your ease I'm going to tell you something that no longer matters for the person concerned.

'When Manuel bought what was only a bistro twenty years ago I sometimes came here for a drink in the morning when I was almost sure of finding him alone.

'He also sometimes gave me a ring or made a discreet visit to the Quai des Orfèvres.'

'An informer?' murmured the manager without much surprise.

'Did you suspect it?'

'I don't know. Maybe. I suppose that's why they fired at him three years ago.'

'Possibly. Only, Manuel was clever and if he occasionally tipped me off about some small fry he looked after the big jobs himself and hushed them up.'

'Don't you want a bottle of champagne sent up?'

'It's about the only drink that doesn't tempt me.'

'Some beer?'

'Not for the moment.'

Pernelle was obviously suffering.

'Manuel was very clever,' Maigret went on, still looking his companion in the eyes. 'So clever that I could never get any evidence against him. He knew I knew a great deal of the truth, at least. He didn't bother to deny it. He used to look at me calmly, with a touch of irony, and whenever it was necessary he handed over one of his confederates.'

'I don't understand.'

'Yes, you do.'

'What do you mean? I never worked for Manuel except here, doing my job as head-waiter and then as manager.'

'And yet from twelve o'clock on you knew what had happened to him. As you said, one hears a lot at the bar or in the restaurant. What do you think of the jewel burglaries, Pernelle?'

'What I read in the papers: some boys trying their hand and who end up by being caught.'

'No.'

'They mention an older man who's always near by in case of emergency.'

'Then?'

'Nothing. I swear I know nothing else.'

'Well, I'll tell you something else, although I'm sure it's not new to you. What is the main risk the jewel burglars run?'

'Being nabbed.'

'How?'

'When they sell.'

'Good! You're getting there. All stones of a certain value have a sort of civil status and the people in the business know them. The minute a burglary is committed a description of the jewels is circulated not only in France but abroad.

'A receiver, if the burglars know one, will only give ten to fifteen per cent of the value of the goods. Nearly always, a couple of years later, when he puts the stones in circulation, the police will identify them and trace them back. Are you with me?'

'I presume that's what happens. You know more about it than I do.'

'Well, for years jewels have been disappearing periodically as a result of hold-ups or window breakages, without ever being found again. What does that mean?'

'How should I know?'

'Come along, Pernelle. One doesn't do your job for

thirty or forty years without knowing the tricks of the trade even if one doesn't take a hand in it.'

'I haven't been in Montmartre for so long.'

'The first problem is not only to unset the stones, but to transform them, which entails the complicity of a diamond cutter. Do you know one?'

'No.'

'Not many people do, for the simple reason that there aren't many of them around, not only in France but in the world. There aren't more than about fifty in Paris, nearly all living in the Marais, near the Rue des Francs-Bourgeois, and they form a very closed little set. Besides, the brokers, the diamond dealers and the big jewellers who give them work have got their eye on them.'

'I hadn't thought of that.'

'You don't say!'

There was a knock on the door. It was the barman who handed Maigret a slip of paper.

'That's just been dropped for you.'

'Who by?'

'The waiter from the café on the corner.'

Lapointe had written in pencil on a page from a notebook:

'He went into the call-box. Through the window I saw him dial Etoile 42.39. Not sure of the last number. He's sitting in a corner reading a newspaper. I'm staying here.'

'Do you mind if I use one of your telephones? By the way, why have you got two lines?'

'I've only got one. The second telephone connects with the restaurant.'

'Hello! Directory inquiries? Superintendent Maigret from the Judicial Police here. I'd like to know urgently the name of the subscriber to Etoile 42.39. I'm not sure about the last number. Could you ring me back here?'

'Now,' he said to Pernelle, 'I wouldn't mind a glass of beer.

'Are you sure you don't know any more than what you said about Monsieur Louis?'

Pernelle hesitated, realizing the matter was becoming serious.

'I don't know him personally. I see him at the bar. I've served him sometimes when Justin was away and we've said a few words about the weather.'

'Is he ever with anyone?'

'Hardly ever. I've occasionally seen him with some boys and I even wondered if he was queer.'

'You don't know either his surname or his address?'

'I've always heard him called Monsieur Louis with a certain respect. He must live in the neighbourhood because he never comes by car...'

The telephone rang. Maigret answered.

'Superintendent Maigret? I think I've got the information you wanted,' said the girl on the directory inquiries. 'Etoile 42.39 has been temporarily discontinued because the subscriber has gone abroad. The subscriber to Etoile 42.38 is called Fernand Barillard and lives...'

The Superintendent knew the rest. The traveller in de luxe packings who lived on the same landing as Palmari!

'Thank you, miss.'

'Don't you want the preceding numbers?'

'Just in case...'

He did not know the names or the addresses. Maigret got up heavily, dazed by the heat and an exhausting day.

'Think about what I said, Pernelle. You're your own boss, now, and you've got a place that's doing well. It would be too bad to be in trouble, wouldn't it? I feel I'll be seeing you soon. Here's a piece of advice: don't talk too much, on the telephone or anywhere else, about the conversation we've just had. Incidentally, do de luxe packings mean anything to you?'

The new owner of the 'Clou Doré' looked at him with genuine surprise.

'I don't understand.'

'Certain cardboard makers specialize in chocolate boxes, almond bags, etc. Now, this 'etc.' could include the boxes used by jewellers instead of cases.'

He went down the dark and dirty staircase, crossed the restaurant where by now a couple sat in a corner, and four rather tipsy diners were sitting round a table.

He went up the street to the café and saw Lapointe

sitting soberly before an apéritif and Monsieur Louis reading an evening paper in a corner. Neither of them saw him and a few minutes later the Superintendent got into a taxi.

'The Rue des Acacias on the corner of the Rue de l'Arc-de-Triomphe.'

The sky turned a flaming red, colouring the faces of the passers-by. There was not a breath of air and Maigret felt his shirt sticking to his body. He seemed to be sleeping during the ride and maybe he really was asleep since he started when the driver said:

'We're there, chief.'

He raised his head to look from top to bottom at the light brick building, with the white stone window frames, which must have been built around 1910. The lift took him to the fourth floor and out of habit he almost rang at the door on the left.

At the door on the right he was kept waiting for some time and it was the fair-haired woman he had questioned that afternoon who finally opened it, her mouth full, holding a table-napkin.

'You again!' she said without ill-humour but with surprise. 'My husband and I are having dinner.'

'I'd like to have a few words with him.'

'Come in.'

The sitting-room looked like the one opposite, only less luxurious, with a plainer carpet. It did not open on to the sort of little room Palmari lived in but a bourgeois dining-room with rustic furniture.

'It's Superintendent Maigret, Fernand.'

A man of about forty, his face cut by a dark moustache, got up, also holding his table-napkin. He had removed his jacket, undone his tie, and opened his shirt collar.'

'Pleased to meet you,' he murmured looking in turn at his wife and the visitor.

'The Superintendent came once this afternoon. I didn't have time to tell you. Because of the tenant who died he went all round the building ringing at every door.'

'Go on eating,' said Maigret. 'I'm in no hurry.'

On the table was some roast veal and noodles with

tomato sauce. The couple resumed their meal awkwardly as the Superintendent sat at the end of the table.

'Will you have a glass of wine?'

The decanter of white wine, which had just come out of the refrigerator, was misty and Maigret could not resist. He was right, because it was a wine from Sancerre, both dry and fruity, which had certainly not been bought at a grocer's.

There was an embarrassed silence when the Barillards started eating again before the inscrutable gaze of their guest.

'All I could tell him was that we don't know this Palmari. Personally, I've never set eyes on him and I didn't even know his name this morning. As for the woman...'

Her husband was a handsome man, slim and muscular, who must have been successful with women, and his moustache emphasized greedy lips and impeccable teeth which showed at the slightest smile.

'Do you know them?'

'No. But let the Superintendent talk. I'm listening, Monsieur Maigret.'

He gave the impression of irony, of aggression close to the surface. He was the handsome male, sure of himself, ready for a fight, who doubted neither his charm nor his strength.

'Finish your meal first. Did you have a long round today?'

'In the Lilas district.'

'By car?'

'In my car, of course. I've got a Peugeot 404. I'm very pleased with it and it looks respectable. That's the main thing in my job.'

'I suppose you carry a case of samples.'

'Naturally, like all my colleagues.'

'When you've had your fruit I'd like you to show it to me.'

'Your curiosity is rather unexpected, isn't it?'

'That depends on the point of view.'

'May I ask you whether you have made similar requests on the other floors of this building?'

'Not yet, Monsieur Barillard. I must add that you have the right not to agree to my demand, in which case I will call up a very agreeable examining magistrate who will send an orderly round with a search warrant or, if necessary, a warrant for detention. Maybe you'd rather we continued our talk in my office in the Quai des Orfèvres?'

Maigret did not fail to notice a fairly striking contrast in the two people's attitudes. The woman opened her eyes wide, astonished by the turn the conversation had taken, by the quite unexpected aggression of the two men. Putting her hand on her husband's she asked:

'What's going on, Fernand?'

'Nothing, dear. Don't worry. Superintendent Maigret will soon be apologizing. When the police are faced with a crime they can't understand they're apt to get excited.'

'Did you have a telephone call a little less than an hour ago, Madame Barillard?'

She turned to her husband as though she wanted to know what to say, but, without looking at her, he seemed to size up the Superintendent, to guess what he was driving at.

'I had a telephone call.'

'From a friend?'

'From a client.'

'A chocolate maker? A confectioner? A perfumer? Those are your clients, aren't they?'

'You're pretty well informed.'

'Unless it was a jeweller. May I ask you his name, Monsieur Barillard?'

'I must admit I can't remember it since the matter didn't interest me.'

'Really! A client who calls you after work. What did he want?'

'A price-list.'

'Have you known Monsieur Louis long?'

The blow struck home. Handsome Fernand frowned and even his wife noticed he was suddenly less at ease.

'I don't know Monsieur Louis. Now if you think we ought to continue our talk let's go into my study. I'm against bringing women into business on principle.'

'Women?'

'My wife, if you'd rather. Do you mind, darling?'

He led him into an adjoining room, about the same size as Manuel's little room, quite comfortably furnished. Since the windows looked on to the courtyard it was darker than the other rooms and Barillard put on the light.

'Sit down if you want to, and as I have no alternative, I'm listening.'

'You've just said something rather amusing.'

'I can assure you my intention is not to amuse you. My wife and I planned to go to the cinema tonight and you're going to make us miss the opening of the film. What did I say that was funny?'

'That you were against bringing women into business on principle.'

'I'm not the only one.'

'We'll come to that later. With regard to Madame Barillard, at any rate, I'm prepared to believe you. Have you been married long?'

'For eight years.'

'Were you doing the same sort of work as you are now?'

'Just about.'

'What was the difference?'

'I worked in a cardboard factory in Fontenay-sous-Bois.'

'Were you living in this building?'

'I lived in a house in Fontenay.'

'Let's see the case of samples.'

It was on the floor, to the left of the door, and Barillard hoisted it unwillingly on to the desk.

'The key?'

'It isn't locked.'

Maigret opened it and, as he expected, among the de luxe boxes, nearly all tastefully decorated, he found the boxes in which jewellers pack the watches and jewels sold without a case.

'How many jewellers' have you visited today?'

'I don't know. Three or four. Watchmakers aad jewellers aren't our only clients.'

'Do you make a note of the firms you go to?'

For the second time Fernand Barillard winced.

'I haven't got the mentality of an accountant or a statistician. I'm content to write down the orders.'

'And of course you keep a copy of these orders made to your firm?'

'Maybe that's what other people do. I trust my employers and like to carry around as little paper as possible.'

'So that it's impossible for you to give me a list of your clients?'

'Yes, it's impossible.'

'What firm do you work for?'

'Gelot and Sons, in the Avenue des Gobelins.'

'Their accounts must be in a better state than yours and I'll pay them a visit tomorrow morning.'

'Can you tell me what you're driving at?'

'First, a question. You claim that you never bring women into your business matters, don't you?'

Barillard, who was lighting a cigarette, shrugged his shoulders.

'Even if this woman is called Aline and lives on your doorstep?'

'I didn't know she was called Aline.'

'But you knew at once whom I meant.'

'There's only one flat opposite ours, or on our doorstep, and only one woman, as far as I know, in that flat.

'I've sometimes passed her on the stairs, been in the lift with her, raised my hat to her, but I don't remember ever having spoken to her.

'Maybe, occasionally, to murmur as I held the door of the lift open:

' "After you..." '

'Does your wife know?'

'About what?'

'About everything. About your job. About your various activities. About your relationship with Monsieur Louis?'

'I've told you I don't know a Monsieur Louis.'

'And yet an hour ago he told you on the telephone that I was investigating in the Rue Fontaine and he reported part of my conversation with the manager of the "Clou Doré" and the barman.'

'What can I say?'

'Nothing. As you see, I'm doing the talking. There are times when it's better to play straight, to show your opponent the cards.

'I could have waited to meet your employers and question the accountant in the Avenue des Gobelins. Between now and tomorrow they won't be able to fake their books to help you out. And you know perfectly well what I'm going to find.'

'Names, addresses and figures. So many Pompadour boxes at a hundred and fifty francs the dozen. So many...'

'So many jewel boxes at so much the dozen or the hundred.'

'So what?'

'Imagine, Monsieur Barillard, that I happen to have a list of the jewellers in Paris and the suburbs which have been, for a certain number of years, the objects of major burglaries, whether it be a hold-up or, more recently, windows broken with the aid of a tyre-lever.

'Are you beginning to understand? I am practically sure that, on the list of your clients which I will receive from the firm Gelot and Sons, I will find almost all the names on my own list.'

'And then what? Since I visit most of the jewellers in the district, except the large firms which only use fancy leather cases, it's normal...'

'I doubt if that will be the opinion of the examining magistrate in charge of the Palmari case.'

'Did my next-door neighbour deal in jewels too?'

'In his own way. And for the three years he's been an invalid he's been doing it through a woman.'

'That's why you just asked me if...'

'Exactly. Now I'm asking you if you're Aline Bauche's lover and since when.'

It was instinctive. The man could not help glancing at the door, and then crept up to open it a little in order to make sure his wife was not listening.

'If you'd said that in the dining-room I think I'd have knocked your face in. You have no more right than anyone else to spread suspicion in a family.'

'You haven't answered.'

'The answer is no.'

'And you still don't know a Monsieur Louis?'

'And I don't know a Monsieur Louis.'

Maigret reached for the telephone, dialled the number of the flat opposite, and recognized Lucas' voice.

'What's your client doing?'

'She slept for some time and then she decided to eat a slice of ham and an egg. She gets nervous, paces the rooms, and looks at me murderously every time she goes past.'

'She hasn't tried to telephone?'

'No. I'm keeping my eyes open.'

'Has anyone been there?'

'No one.'

'Thank you. I'll be round in a few minutes. Can you ring the Quai in the meantime and tell them to send an extra man? Here, yes. I know Bonfils is downstairs.

'I'd like a second man, and give him the following orders: first, to get a car. Then, to park it by the door and not let the door out of his sight.

'Because I want him to trail a certain Fernand Barillard if he decides to go out alone or with his wife. He's a commercial traveller who lives in the flat opposite the one you're in.

'I'm there, yes. Have his telephone tapped.

'Barillard's description: about forty years old, five foot seven, thick dark hair, narrow dark moustache, fairly elegant, the sort of man who appeals to women. His wife, if she's with him, is about ten years younger, fair-haired, attractive, rather plump.

'I'll wait here until the detective arrives downstairs. See you later, old boy.'

As he spoke the commercial traveller looked at him with hatred.

'I suppose,' said Maigret almost suavely, 'that you still have nothing to say to me?'

'Absolutely nothing.'

'My detective will take about ten minutes to get here. I intend to keep you company in the meantime.'

'Just as you like.'

Barillard sat in a leather armchair and pretended to be deep in a magazine he had grabbed off a table. Maigret stood up and started to examine the room in detail, reading the titles of the books in the library, lifting up a paper-weight, half opening the drawers of the desk.

They were long minutes for the commercial traveller. Over his magazine he occasionally glanced at this thick-set, placid man who seemed to fill the whole study with his bulk, crush it under his weight, and on whose face not a thought could be read.

From time to time the Superintendent pulled his watch out of his pocket, because he had never got used to wrist-watches and he treasured the gold hunter he had inherited from his father.

'Four more minutes, Monsieur Barillard.'

Barillard tried not to flinch, but his hands began to betray his impatience.

'Three minutes.'

He controlled himself with more and more difficulty.

'There! I hope you have a good night until our next meeting which will, I trust, be as cordial as this one.'

Maigret left the study and found the young woman in the dining-room with red eyes.

'My husband hasn't done anything wrong, has he, Superintendent?'

'You must ask him, my dear. I hope not, for your sake.'

'Despite his appearance he's a very gentle, very affectionate man. He occasionally flares up but he's always the first to be sorry.'

'Good night, Madame Barillard.'

She accompanied him to the door with anxious eyes and saw him go not to the lift but to the door opposite.

CHAPTER FIVE

It was a strained Aline, with a sharp, set expression emphasized by heavy rings under her eyes, who opened the door for Maigret, more placid than ever. In the time it took to cross the landing he had adopted the good-natured look which his detectives knew well and which did not deceive them.

'I didn't want to leave the building without wishing you as good a night as possible.'

Lucas, sitting in an armchair, put the magazine he was reading on the carpet and got up lazily. It was not difficult to realize that the relationship was by no means cordial between the two people who had just spent several hours shut up in the flat and were going to stay there until the morning.

'Don't you think you ought to go to bed, Aline? You've had quite an emotional day. I'm afraid tomorrow is going to be just as arduous, if not more so. Haven't you got a sleeping-pill or some sort of tranquillizer in your medicine-chest?'

She watched him intently, trying to tell what was at the back of his mind, furious to see that the Superintendent was not giving in.

'Personally I've found out a great deal since this morning, but I have to check a number of points before discussing my discoveries with you. As a matter of fact this very evening I met a rather interesting man who lives on your landing.

'At first I was wrong about him: I thought he was just a commercial traveller in boxes for sweets and chocolates.

'It appears that his activity is far broader and includes the world of jewellers, in particular.'

He took his time, filled his pipe pensively.

'What with all that I haven't had dinner yet. I hope Monsieur Louis will have been patient enough to wait for me at the "Clou Doré" and that we'll be able to dine together.'

Another silence. He piled the tobacco into his pipe with a familiar movement of the index finger, removed the strand that protruded and finally struck a match while Aline followed his excessively scrupulous movements with growing impatience.

'A handsome fellow, Fernand Barillard. I'd be surprised if he were satisfied with one woman, especially since his wife seems a little too colourless for him. What do you think?'

'I don't know him.'

'Of course, the landlady of a building can't know all her tenants intimately. Particularly since I wonder whether this house is the only one you own.

'I'll know tomorrow from the solicitor, Desgrières, with whom I've made an appointment. This case is so complicated, Aline, that I sometimes think I'm losing my footing.

'Anyhow, I've posted a man downstairs in case Barillard wants to go out. And from now on his telephone is tapped, just like yours.'

'You see how kind of me it is to warn you? You've probably got nothing to tell me?'

Pursing her lips, she walked with sharp, mechanical steps to the bedroom and slammed the door behind her.

'Is all you've said true, chief?'

'Just about. Good night. Try to keep awake. Make as much strong coffee as you need and if anything happens ring me at the Boulevard Richard-Lenoir. I don't know what time I'll be there but I'm determined to get some sleep.'

Instead of taking the lift he slowly went down the stairs, imagining the life of the tenants as he passed their doors.

Some of them were watching the television and the same voices and music could be heard in several flats. Stamping feet in Mabel Tuppler's flat suggested that one or two couples were dancing.

Inspector Lagrume was dozing at the wheel of a Judicial Police car and Maigret vaguely shook his hand.

'Haven't you got a car, chief?'

'I'll get a taxi in the Avenue de la Grande-Armée. Have you got your orders?'

'To follow the chap, Fernand Barillard.'

Maigret did not feel as light as when he had woken up that morning in the flat quivering with the sun or when, on the platform of the bus, he had gorged himself on images of a Paris coloured like a children's book.

People had a mania for asking him about his methods. Some of them even thought they could analyse them and he would look at them with bantering curiosity because they knew more about it than he, who usually improvised at the whim of his instinct.

The Chief Commissioner certainly would not have appreciated what the Superintendent's instinct suggested to him that day and the little examining magistrate, in spite of his admiration, would undoubtedly have frowned.

For example, before questioning Fernand Barillard, Maigret should have assembled as much information as possible about him, compiled a file, have all the dates he was sure of getting from Gelot and Sons, the details that would eventually be supplied by Maitre Desgrières.

He preferred to arouse the anxiety of the commercial traveller, put him voluntarily on his guard, without being watched.

For a moment he had thought he should not say anything to Aline, so as to surprise her the next day by confronting her with her neighbour, and watch her reactions.

He had finally decided to do just the opposite and from now on she knew that he had established a link between her and the traveller in cardboard boxes.

They were both watched. They could neither meet nor telephone each other. It was impossible for them to leave the building without being followed.

Were they, in these circumstances, going to have a good night's sleep? Maigret had done the same thing with Monsieur Louis, letting him know that whatever he said and did was from now on recorded by the police.

It was still impossible to establish a link between these three different characters. All they had in common was anxiety, which Maigret did his best to make as acute as possible for each one.

'To the "Clou Doré" in the Rue Fontaine.'

There too he had put his cards on the table, or almost. And since he had to dine somewhere he might as well choose the restaurant which Palmari had owned for such a long time before putting it in Aline's name and then leaving it to Pernelle.

When he went in he was surprised to find such a lively atmosphere. Nearly all the tables were taken and there was a noise of conversation interrupted by women's laughs, while the smoke of cigars and cigarettes formed an almost opaque cloud a yard from the ceiling.

In the pink light of the lamps he saw Monsieur Louis sitting at a table opposite a pretty girl while Lapointe was moping at the bar with a lemon squash.

Pernelle went from customer to customer with a professional smile, shaking hands, leaning over to tell a good story or to take an order which he handed to one of the waiters.

Two women perched on bar stools were showing off for the benefit of Lapointe, who tried to look elsewhere in embarrassment.

When Maigret arrived one of them leant over to her friend, probably to whisper:

'He's a cop!'

So that when the Superintendent reached Lapointe the latter lost all interest in the eyes of the young ladies.

'Have you had dinner?'

'I had a sandwich in the café where he stayed over an hour. Then he came back here and waited to dine with that young woman.'

'Not too tired?'

'No.'

'I'd like you to go on following him. When he goes home call the Quai and ask someone to relieve you. Do the same thing if he goes to the girl's place, which is possible, or if he takes her to a hotel. You'd better have something to eat with me.'

'A beer, Monsieur Maigret?'

'It's a little late, Justin. I've had as much beer as I can carry for today.'

He signalled to Pernelle who got them a little table lit by a golden lamp with a silk shade.

'I recommend the *paëlla* this evening. You could start with *ramequins à la niçoise*. To go with it, a dry Tavel, unless you prefer a Pouilly Fumé.'

'We'll take the *paëlla* and the Tavel.'

'For two?'

He nodded and during the meal he only seemed to be concerned with the food and the deliciously fruity wine. As for Monsieur Louis, he pretended to have eyes only for his companion who nevertheless turned round two or three times towards the detectives and must have been asking him about them.

'The longer I look at him,' sighed the Superintendent, 'the surer I am that I know him. That was a long time ago, perhaps ten years or more. He might have had dealings with me when he was young and slim, and his present plumpness may be baffling me.'

When it came to the bill Pernelle bent over very professionally and found time to whisper in Maigret's ear:

'I remembered something when you left. Some time ago it was rumoured that Palmari owned a hotel in the Rue de l'Etoile. It was a house of call then, the Hôtel Bussière, or Bessière.'

Maigret paid as though he attached no importance to it.

'I'm going there, Lapointe,' he whispered a little later. 'I don't expect I'll stay long. Good luck!'

Monsieur Louis watched him go to the door. A taxi was cruising. Ten minutes later Maigret got out opposite the Hôtel Bussière, about a hundred yards from the police station, which did not prevent two or three girls from standing in the street with very obvious intentions.

'Coming?'

He shook his head, found a night porter behind the counter which separated the corridor from a little room with a cylindrical desk, a key board, and a camp bed.

'Is it for the night? Are you alone? No luggage? In that case I must ask you to pay in advance. Thirty francs plus twenty per cent service charge.'

He pushed a book in front of the Superintendent.

'Name, address, number of passport or identity card.'

If Maigret had gone up with a girl he would have avoided these formalities. After the trap he had been set two weeks earlier and which had almost made him retire before his time he preferred not to compromise himself.

He wrote his name, his address, the number of his identity card, and left out his occupation. He was handed a key and the ill-shaven night porter pressed an electric bell which rang on the next floor.

It was not a maid but a man in shirt sleeves and a white apron who met him on the first floor, took the key and looked at the number sulkily.

'Number forty-two? Follow me.'

The hotel had no lift, which accounted for the ill humour of the valet. In second- and third-class establishments the night staff is frequently composed of grubby specimens of humanity and it would be quite easy to populate an entire chamber of horrors with them.

Here the valet had a limp and his face with its crooked nose was an ugly yellow which suggested a ruined liver.

'These stairs! These stairs again!' he muttered to himself. 'Bloody hell!'

On the fourth floor he went down a narrow passage and stopped by room forty-two.

'There you are. I'll get some towels.'

Because there were no towels in the rooms, the old trick for getting a tip in addition to the twenty per cent service charge.

The valet then pretended to make sure nothing was missing and his eyes finally fell on the fifty-franc note that Maigret was holding ostentatiously between two fingers.

'You mean it's for me?'

He became suspicious, but could not stop his eyes sparkling.

'Do you want a pretty girl? You couldn't find what you wanted downstairs?'

'Close the door a minute.'

'Hey, you haven't got any ideas, I hope? That's odd, you look familiar.'

'Maybe I look like somebody? Are you always on night duty?'

'Not me. If I'm on night duty every other week it's because I go to the hospital for treatment.'

'If you sometimes work during the day I suppose you know the regular clients?'

'I know some of them, others just pass through.'

His little red-rimmed eyes went from the banknote to the Superintendent's face and a furrow crossed his brow, showing an arduous attempt at thought.

'Do you know this woman?' Maigret pulled out of his pocket a photograph of Aline Bauche which he had had taken without her knowing it seven months earlier.

'I wonder if she ever comes here with a man.'

The valet barely glanced at the photograph and his brow darkened still more.

'Are you having me on?'

'Why?'

'Because it's a picture of the proprietress. At least, as far as I know.'

'Do you see her frequently?'

'Never at night, anyhow. I sometimes see her in the daytime.'

'Has she got a room in the hotel?'

'A room and a sitting-room on the first floor.'

'But she doesn't use them regularly?'

'I tell you I don't know. We see her. We don't see her. It's none of our business and we aren't paid to watch her.'

'Do you know where she lives?'

'How should I know?'

'And her name?'

'I heard the manageress call her Madame Bauche.'

'Does she stay long when she comes to the hotel?'

'It's impossible to tell because of the spiral staircase which connects the manageress's office on the ground floor to the suite on the first.'

'Can one get to this suite by the main stairs?'

'Of course.'

'Take this. It's yours.'

'Are you from the police?'

'Perhaps.'

'I say, you aren't Superintendent Maigret by any chance, are you? I thought I knew you. I hope you aren't going to get the proprietress into any trouble because I'll be in trouble too.'

'I promise you you won't be mentioned.'

A second note had appeared as if by magic in the hand of the Superintendent.

'For the right answer to one question.'

'Let's hear the question.'

'When Madame Bauche, as you call her, comes to the hotel, does she meet anyone apart from the manageress?'

'She doesn't have anything to do with the staff, if that's what you mean.'

'That isn't what I mean. In her suite she could see people from outside who don't necessarily go up the spiral staircase but who use the main stairs...'

The note was as tempting as the first one. And Maigret cut the man's hesitations short by the straight question:

'What's he like?'

'I've only seen him occasionally, nearly always in the afternoon. He's younger and slimmer than you.'

'Dark hair? A narrow black moustache? Good-looking?'

The valet nodded.

'Did he have a case?'

'Usually, yes. He takes a room on the first floor, always the same one, number seven, the one nearest the suite, and he never stays the night.'

The note changed hands. The valet rapidly slipped it into his pocket but he did not leave immediately, maybe wondering if there were a third question which would earn him another fifty francs.

'Thank you. I promise you I won't get you into any trouble. I'm leaving in a few minutes.'

A bell rang and the waiter rushed out of the room shouting:

'Coming!'

*

'You weren't too hot?' asked Madame Maigret anxiously. 'I hope you had time for lunch and dinner and didn't just have sandwiches?'

'I had an excellent *paëlla* at the "Clou Doré". As for lunch, I've forgotten. Oh yes, I was with a funny little magistrate in an Auvergnat bistro.'

He had difficulty in getting to sleep because the characters who had populated his day returned to haunt him, one by one, and in the foreground was the almost grotesque, curiously twisted bulk of Palmari at the foot of the wheel-chair.

For the magistrate he was only a victim at the beginning of an investigation which would occupy him for a few weeks. But Maigret had known Manuel at different stages of his career, and although they were both on different sides of the fence, subtle, almost indefinable bonds had formed between the two men.

Could it be said that the Superintendent respected the former proprietor of the 'Clou Doré'? The word respect was too strong. Judging the man impartially the experienced detective could not help holding him in some esteem.

In the same way he had, from the beginning, been curious about Aline who had a sort of fascination for him. He tried to understand her, sometimes thought he had succeeded, only to have to defer his judgement immediately.

He finally reached the floating state between sleep and waking, and the figures of his characters got blurred, his thoughts became more hazy and imprecise.

Basically there was fear. He had often discussed it late at night with Doctor Pardon who also had an experience of men and was not far from sharing his conclusions.

Everybody is afraid. People try to erase children's fear by reading fairy stories and the minute the child goes to school he is afraid to show his parents a copy-book with bad marks.

Fear of water. Fear of fire. Fear of animals. Fear of the dark.

Fear at fifteen or sixteen of choosing the wrong career, of failing one's life.

In his semi-consciousness all these fears became like the notes of a muted, tragic symphony: the latent fears which we drag behind us to the end, acute fear which makes us scream, fear we laugh about when it's over, fear of accidents, disease, policemen, fear of people, of what they say, of what they think, of the looks they give us when we go by.

A short time ago, as he gazed at the tempting note in the Superintendent's fingers, the sickly valet in the Hotel Bussière had been divided between the fear of losing his job and temptation. Subsequently, as each note appeared, the same mechanism had been at work.

Was he afraid now, afraid that Maigret would talk, that he would bring him into a matter he suspected was serious and which would lead him into God knows what complications?

Was it from fear, too, that Pernelle, the very recent proprietor of the 'Clou Doré', had whispered into the Superintendent's ear the address in the Rue de l'Etoile? Fear of being pestered by the police, fear of having to close his establishment because of some obscure law.

Wasn't Monsieur Louis frightened too? Until now he had kept in the background, with no apparent link with Manuel and Aline. Now here he was with the Judicial Police on his heels and one can't live to his age in Montmartre without knowing what that means.

Who was more frightened at the moment, Aline or Fernand Barillard?

As late as that morning no one suspected any connection between the two flats on the fourth floor. Madame Barillard gaily enjoyed her life, without asking any questions, as a housewife looking after the household as well as she could.

Had Aline decided to go to bed? Lucas had virtually dug himself into her flat, calm and determined. Nothing would make him budge. She could neither go out nor telephone. She suddenly found herself on her own, cut off from the rest of the world.

Would she not rather have been taken to the Quai des Orfèvres where she could have protested, insisted on having a lawyer of her choice present?

Officially the police were only with her to protect her.

Two doors, a landing, separated her from the man she had met several times in her secret suite at the Hôtel Bussière.

Did Palmari know? He too lived for months with the police opposite his house, his telephone tapped, and, what was more, he was an invalid.

He had nevertheless continued his activities, directing his men through Aline.

It was Maigret's last thought before dropping off completely: Aline... Manuel... Aline called him Daddy... She who was sarcastic and aggressive with everybody, became tender with the old gang leader and defended him like a tigress.

Aline... Manuel...

Aline... Fernand...

Someone was missing. Maigret was no longer lucid enough to remember who was not at the roll call. One of the cogs. He had mentioned it to somebody, maybe to the magistrate? An important cog, because of the diamonds.

Aline... Manuel... Fernand... Count Manuel out, since he was dead... Aline... Fernand.

Each one revolving in his cage, waiting for an initiative from Maigret.

When he woke up Madame Maigret opened the window wide and then handed him a cup of coffee.

'Have you slept well?'

'I don't know. I dreamt a great deal, but I can't remember about what.'

The same sun as the day before, the same gaiety in the air, in the sky, in the chirping of the birds, in the noises and smells of the street.

It was Maigret who was different, who no longer took part in the joyful song of the day which begins.

'You seem tired.'

'I've got a big day ahead of me and responsibilities to assume.'

She had guessed that the evening before when he came in, but she had taken care not to ask him any questions.

'Wear your grey pin-striped suit. It's lighter than the other one.'

Did he hear? He ate his breakfast automatically, swallowed two cups of black coffee without tasting them. He did not hum in the shower and dressed with a vague expression, forgetting to ask what there was for lunch. His only question was:

'Incidentally, was the lobster good yesterday?'

'There's enough left for a salad.'

'Call me a taxi, will you?'

No bus this morning, even with a platform. No landscape, no coloured images which glided voluptuously over his retina.

'The Quai des Orfèvres!'

First his office.

'Get me Fernand Barillard... Etoile 42.38... Hello. Madame Barillard?... Superintendent Maigret here... Can I speak to your husband, please... I'll wait, yes...'

His hand automatically leafed through the reports piled on his desk.

'Hello!... Barillard?... It's me again... Yesterday I forgot to ask you to stay at home this morning and probably most of the day... I know!... I know! Too bad! Your clients will wait... No, I have no idea when I'll see you....'

Lucas' account was only a confidential note for the Superintendent and his official report would be made later.

'Nothing important to report. She walked round the flat until two in the morning and on several occasions, when she passed near me, I thought she was going to scratch my face. She ended up by shutting herself into her room and after about half an hour I no longer heard any sound. At eight, when Jarvis relieved me, she seemed to be asleep.

I'll ring the Quai around eleven to know if you need me.'

Lapointe's report was hardly more interesting. It had been telephoned at three in the morning.

'For Superintendent Maigret. Monsieur Louis and his companion stayed at the "Clou Doré" until half past eleven. The girl is called Louise Pégasse, nicknamed Lulu the Torpedo, the name under which she appears at the end of the programme in a striptease club, the "Boule Verte" in the Rue Pigalle.

'Monsieur Louis accompanied her there. I followed him and sat at a table next to him. After using the stage door Lulu reappeared on the stage and when her act was over she sat at the bar where she and her colleagues have to encourage the customers.

'Monsieur Louis did not move, did not telephone, never left the room.

'Shortly before three Lulu whispered a few words in his ear. He fetched his hat and, one behind the other, we waited in the street. Lulu soon came out. The couple went on foot to a residential hotel in the Place Saint-Georges: the Hôtel du Square.

'I questioned the night porter. Louise Pégasse has been living in the hotel for several months. She often comes back with a man, rarely the same one. It's the second or third time Monsieur Louis has followed her to her room. I'm calling from a bistro which is about to close. I'll stay on guard."

'Janvier! Where's Janvier? Hasn't he arrived?'

'He's in the lavatory, sir.'

Janvier came in.

'Send a man opposite the Hôtel du Square in the Place Saint-Georges to relieve Lapointe who must be all in. If he's got nothing new to report he can go home to bed and ring in the late afternoon. I may need him then.'

He only just had time to rush to the conference where he arrived last by a long chalk. There were conspiratorial glances in his direction, because he had the expression he adopted on big days, his set look, his pipe at an angle, squeezed so tightly between his teeth that he had been known to snap the ebonite tip.

'I'm sorry, sir.'

He did not listen to any of the things that were said. When his turn came he just mumbled:

'I'm continuing the investigation on Palmari's death. If all goes well I might conceivably break up the jewel robbery organization at the same time.'

'Your same old theory! How many years have you suspected Palmari?'

'Quite a number, I admit.'

Other reports were awaiting him, in particular those of Gastinne-Renette and the medical expert. The three bullets which had hit Manuel and one of which had lodged in the back of the wheel-chair had indeed been fired from Palmari's Smith and Wesson.

'Janvier! Come in for a minute.'

He gave him instructions to organize the guard duty in the Rue des Acacias.

A little later he went past the glass door leading from the Judicial Police to the Palais de Justice. He went up two floors before finding the office of the magistrate, Ancelin, right at the top of the building.

It was one of the premises which had not been modernized, reserved for the new-comers, and the magistrate had to pile his papers on the bare floor and keep the lights on all day.

On seeing Maigret the plump magistrate rubbed his hands.

'You can take a few minutes off,' he told his clerk. 'Sit down, my dear Superintendent. I'm eager to know how far you've got.'

Maigret summed up his activities of the day before, and the reports received that morning.

'Do you expect all these scattered elements will fit into something conclusive?'

'Every character implicated in this case is afraid. Everyone, at the moment, is isolated from the others, with no means of communication....'

'I see! I see! Very cunning! Not very regular, on the other hand. I couldn't do anything like that but I'm beginning to understand your tactics. Now what are you going to do?'

'First a little round of the Rue La Fayette where they have the diamond market every morning, in a brasserie and in the street. I know a certain number of diamond-dealers. It's a place I've often had occasion to visit. Then, for the reasons you can guess, I'll be going to the Gélot cardboard factory.'

'So, if I understand correctly, the case is as follows...'

And with a mischievous expression the magistrate analysed the mechanism of the case, which proved that he had spent part of the night studying the file.

'I suppose you think Palmari is at the head of the business. For years in his bar in Montmartre he came across vagrants of all ages who used to meet there. The older generation had gradually dispersed all over France, but it had nevertheless retained its contacts.

'In other words, with a well-placed telephone call, Palmari could produce the two or three men he needed for such and such a job. Right?'

Maigret agreed, amused by the magistrate's excitement.

'Although he was isolated from the world as a result of his accident nothing stopped him directing his organization through Aline Bauche. In rapid succession he bought the building where he lived with her and I now wonder whether he had a definite aim when he did that.'

'Amongst other things it enabled him to give certain tenants notice to quit when he needed a vacant flat.'

'Barillard, for example. Very convenient to have an accomplice on your landing when you're being watched by the police. Do you think Barillard is capable of recutting precious stones and putting them into circulation?'

'Putting them into circulation, yes. Cutting them, no, because it's one of the most expert jobs in the world. Barillard reported on the jewellery displays worth having a crack at. In view of his profession, this was easy.

'Through Aline who periodically gave us the slip and went to the Hôtel Bussière...'

'Hence the purchase of the hotel, which was also a good investment.

'Some accomplices used to come up from the provinces for a couple of days. Aline, or maybe Barillard, would wait for them in an appointed place, to take possession of the jewels.

'On the whole the perpetrators of the smash-and-grab raids could leave without any difficulty, without even knowing who they had been working for, which is why the few vagrants we arrested couldn't tell us a thing.'

'So someone is missing.'

'Precisely. The diamond cutter.'

'Good luck, Maigret. Do you mind if I call you that? Call me Ancelin.'

And the Superintendent replied with a smile:

'I'll try. In view of my past dealings with examining magistrates, particularly with a certain Coméliau, I doubt if I'll succeed at once. In the meantime, good day, sir. I'll keep in touch.'

It was Gélot the son who answered the telephone when he rang the cardboard factory in the Avenue des Gobelins from his office.

'No, no, Monsieur Gélot. There's nothing to worry about. It's simply a matter of checking something which has nothing to do with the reputation of your firm. You say Fernand Barillard is an excellent traveller and I'm prepared to believe you.

'I would just like to know, for our information, which jewellers have given him orders over the last two years, for example. I suppose your accounts department will have no difficulty in making out this list which I'll come and collect at the end of the morning. Don't worry. We know how to be discreet.'

In the detectives' office he gazed slowly at the faces round him and ended up, as usual, by picking on Janvier.

'Doing anything important?'

'No, chief. I was finishing a report which can wait. All this paper work!'

'Take your hat and follow me.'

Maigret belonged to the generation which included many men who did not want to drive. He personally feared his absent-mindedness, the brown studies he would fall into during an investigation.

'To the corner of the Rue La Fayette and the Rue Cadet.'

In the police force one of the principles when taking an important step is always to be accompanied. If he had not had Lapointe with him the night before at the 'Clou Doré' he would not have been able to have Monsieur Louis trailed and he would probably have taken several days before getting interested in Barillard.

'I'll park the car and join you.'

Like him Janvier knew the precious stone market. Most Parisians, on the other hand, even those who pass the Rue La Fayette every morning, do not suspect that those unassuming-looking men dressed like office clerks, who chat in groups in the street and round the tables of the brasserie, have fortunes' worth of precious stones in their pockets.

These stones, in little cases, pass from hand to hand without the deals being accompanied by any immediate receipt.

In this closed set, where everyone knows everyone else, trust reigns supreme.

'Hello, Bérenstein!'

Maigret shook hands with a tall thin chap who had just left his two companions after pocketing a packet of diamonds like an ordinary letter.

'Hello, Superintendent. Another jewel robbery?'

'Not since last week.'

'You haven't found your man yet? I've discussed it for at least the twentieth time with my colleagues. Like me they know all the diamond cutters operating in Paris. As I told you, there aren't many of them and I'm prepared to answer for them. Not one of them would risk recutting stolen or even suspect stones. Those people have a good nose, believe me! Will you have a beer with me?'

'With pleasure. The moment my Inspector has crossed the street.'

'Well! Janvier. You've arrived in force, I see!'

They sat round a table and some brokers stood talking between the rows. Occasionally one of them pulled a magnifying glass out of his pocket to examine a stone.

'Before the war the two main stone-cutting centres were Antwerp and Amsterdam. Curiously enough, for reasons I haven't yet discovered, most of the stone cutters were, or still are, from the Baltic, Latvia or Estonia.

'In Antwerp they had foreign identity cards and when they retreated from the German advance they were all directed to Royan and then to the United States.

'After the war the Americans did what they could to keep them. They hardly managed to keep a tenth of them because they were all homesick.

'And yet some of them, when they came back, were seduced by Paris. You'll find them in the Marais and Saint-Antoine. Each of them is known, has a sort of pedigree because it's a trade which is handed down from father to son and which has its secrets.'

Maigret suddenly looked at him vaguely, as though he were no longer listening.

'Wait. You said...'

A word Bérenstein had said struck him in retrospect.

'What did I say that worried you?'

'Just a minute! The German advance... The stone cutters from Antwerp... The United States... Some of them staying there... And why couldn't some have stayed in France at the time of the exodus?'

'It's possible. Since they're almost all Jews they might well have ended up in concentration camps or ovens.'

'Unless...'

The Superintendent suddenly got up.

'Off we go, Janvier! Where's your car? 'Bye, Bérenstein. I'm sorry. I should have thought of it earlier....'

And Maigret slipped as fast as he could past the groups crowding the pavement.

CHAPTER SIX

Janvier looked straight ahead, squeezing the steering wheel of the little black car slightly tighter than usual, and he had to resist his desire to watch the face of Maigret, sitting next to him. At a certain moment he opened his mouth to ask a question that was scalding his lips, but he had enough self-control to say nothing.

Although he had been working for the Superintendent ever since he joined the Judicial Police and had collaborated with him in hundreds of investigations he was nevertheless impressed each time the phenomenon, which had just been set in motion, was produced.

The day before, Maigret had plunged into the case in a light-hearted frenzy, producing characters out of the dark, turning them this way and that in his large paws like a cat with a mouse, and then putting them back in their corners. He sent detectives left and right, as though he had no definite scheme, telling himself something would always emerge.

Suddenly he was no longer playing. Janvier was sitting next to another person, a human bulk which nothing could affect, an almost terrifying monolith.

At the end of the morning the avenues, the streets of Paris, were a real firework in the July heat. There were splashes of light everywhere. They burst from the slate and red-tiled roofs, from the window-panes where a red geranium sang; they ran off the multicoloured bodywork of motor cars, off blue, green, yellow, horns, voices, a squeal of brakes, the ring of a bell, the shrill whistle of a policeman.

It was as though the black car were as resistant in this symphony as an island of silence and immobility, as though Maigret himself were an impassive block, and he certainly saw nothing, heard nothing, did not even notice that they had arrived at the Rue des Acacias.

'We're there, chief.'

He stepped heavily out of the car which had become too narrow for him, gazed blankly at the familiar street, then raised his head, looking as though he were going to take over the whole building, its floors and its occupants.

He still took the time to empty his pipe on the pavement by tapping it on his heel, and to fill another and light it.

Janvier did not ask if he should go with him, nor did he say anything to Janin who was watching the building and wondered why the chief did not seem to recognize him.

Maigret made for the lift, and the Inspector followed him. Instead of going up to the fourth floor the Superintendent went on to the fifth, and strode up to the garrets.

Turning to the left he stopped at the door of the deaf and dumb man, and, knowing he would receive no answer, he turned the knob. The door opened. The Fleming's garret was empty.

The Superintendent almost ripped off the curtain on the wardrobe and made a short inventory of the few clothes he found in more or less poor condition.

His eyes photographed every corner of the room, after which he went down a floor, hesitated, and plunged once again into the lift which took him to the ground floor.

The concierge was in her lodge, a shoe on her right foot, a slipper on her left foot.

'Do you know if Claes has gone out this morning?'

Seeing him so tense impressed her deeply.

'No. He hasn't come down yet.'

'You haven't left your lodge?'

'Not even to do the stairs. My neighbour did them for me because I've got my pains again.'

'He didn't go out last night?'

'Nobody went out. I only opened the door to tenants coming home. Anyhow, you've got a detective in the street and he can tell you.'

Maigret was thinking hard, thinking tough, according to the expressions Janvier had invented for his personal usage.

'Tell me... Each tenant has a part of the attic at his disposal, as far as I can see....'

'Precisely. And as a rule they can each rent an additional maid's room.'

'That's not what I'm asking. And the cellars?'

'Before the war there were only two large cellars and everyone put his own coal in a corner. During the war, when stone coal got as expensive as caviare, quarrels broke out and all the tenants claimed their heaps were getting smaller. Anyhow, the landlord at that time had partitions built with doors and padlocks.'

'So every tenant has his own cellar.'

'Yes.'

'Claes too?'

'No. He's not a proper tenant since he lives in a maid's room.'

'And the Barillards?'

'Of course.'

'Have you got the keys of the cellars?'

'No. I've just said they've got padlocks. Each tenant has his own.'

'Can you see who goes down to the basement?'

'Not from here. The cellar stairs are opposite the back stairs, down there. You just have to push the door with nothing written on it, with no door mat.'

Maigret went back to the lift and looked Janvier in the eye without saying anything. He did not have the patience to ring at Barillard's door but rapped violently with his fist. Madame Barillard, in a cretonne dress, opened it with a frightened face.

'Your husband?'

'He's in his study. He says you won't let him go to work.'

'Call him in.'

Barillard's silhouette could be seen still in pyjamas and a dressing-gown. Despite his efforts he did not look as well or as self-confident as the day before.

'Get the key of the cellar.'

'But...'

'Do as I say.'

It was all happening in unreality, in a dream, or rather a nightmare. Suddenly the relationship between the protagonists was no longer the same. It seemed as though everyone was in a state of shock and that the words changed value, as did the movements and looks.

'Go ahead.'

He pushed him into the lift and on the ground floor ordered shortly:

'To the basement.'

Barillard became increasingly irresolute, Maigret firmer and firmer.

'Is this the door?'

'Yes.'

A single, very weak electric bulb lit up the white wall, the doors with their faded numbers, and obscene graffiti could barely be distinguished on the peeling paint.

'How many keys open this padlock?'

'I've only got one.'

'Who might have the other?'

'How should I know?'

'You haven't given the key to anyone?'

'No.'

'Are you and your wife the only people who use this cellar?'

'We haven't used it for years.'

'Open it.'

The hands of the commercial traveller were shaking and down here he looked more grotesque than in the bourgeois surroundings of his flat.

'Well? Open it!'

The door had moved about a foot and got stuck.

'There's something behind it.'

'Push harder. Use your shoulder.'

It was Maigret whom Janvier gazed at in bewilderment, suddenly realizing that the Superintendent expected — but since when? — the present turn of events.

'It's giving way.'

Suddenly a leg could be seen hanging. The door, as it opened, released another leg. A body was suspended in mid-air, the bare feet about half a yard above the mud floor.

It was old Claes, wearing a shirt and an old pair of trousers.

'Handcuff him, Janvier.'

The Inspector stared at the hanged man and Barillard in turn. When the latter saw the handcuffs he protested.

'Just a minute, please.'

But Maigret's inscrutable eyes weighed on him and he surrendered.

'Go and get Janin. He's no longer necessary outside.'

As he had done upstairs Maigret inspected the long narrow room and one felt that every detail was being eternally lodged in his memory. With his finger he touched several tools which he pulled out of a bag, and then he seemed to caress, thoughtfully, a heavy steel table fastened to the ground.

'Stay here, Janin, until those gentlemen arrive. Don't let anyone in. Not even your colleagues. And don't touch anything yourself either. Understood?'

'Understood, chief.'

'Let's go.'

He looked at Barillard, his silhouette different now his hands were tied behind his back and he walked like a puppet.

They did not take the lift but went up the back stairs to the fourth floor without meeting anybody. Madame Barillard, in her kitchen, screamed when she saw her husband in handcuffs.

'Monsieur Maigret!'

'I'll see you in a minute, Madame Barillard. I've got some telephone calls to make first.'

And, taking no notice of the others, he went into Barillard's study which smelt of stale cigarette smoke, and dialled the magistrate's number.

'Hello!... Yes, it's Maigret. I'm a fool, my dear Monsieur Ancelin. And I feel responsible for the death of a man. Yes, another corpse. Where? In the Rue des Acacias, of course. I should have realized from the start. I was beating about the bush instead of sticking to the only important clue. The worst of it all is that this third element, if I can call it that, has been worrying me for years.

'Forgive me if I don't give you any details right now. There's a hanged man in the cellar. The doctor will undoubtedly discover that he didn't hang himself, that he was dead or wounded when the noose was put round his neck. It's an old man.

'May I ask you to make sure that the Public Prosecutor doesn't come in too much of a hurry? I'm very busy on the fourth floor and I'd just as soon not be disturbed before getting some results. I don't know how long that will take. See you later. Oh no, we won't be having lunch in that nice "Chez l'Auvergnat" today.'

A little later he had his old friend Moers on the line, the expert from the Criminal Records Office.

'I need a very intricate job done and I don't want it done in a rush. There's no point in the Public Prosecutor and the examining magistrate fiddling with everything in the cellar. You'll find some objects which will surprise you. You might have to examine the walls and search the floor.'

He got up from Barillard's armchair with a sigh, crossed the sitting-room where Barillard sat in a chair opposite Janvier who was smoking a cigarette. Maigret went into the kitchen, opened the refrigerator.

'May I?' he asked Madame Barillard.

'Tell me, Superintendent...'

'Just a minute, if you don't mind. I'm dying of thirst.'

As he opened a beer bottle she handed him a glass, both submissive and frightened.

'You don't think my husband...'

'I don't think anything. Come with me.'

She followed him in bewilderment into the study where he automatically sat in Barillard's chair again.

'Sit down. Make yourself comfortable. Your name is

Claes, isn't it?'

'Yes.'

She hesitated, blushing.

'Look, Superintendent. I suppose it's important?'

'From now on, Madame Barillard, everything is important. I admit that every word counts.'

'I am called Claes. It's my maiden name written on my identity card.'

'But?'

'I don't know if it's my real name.'

'Was the old man who lived in the garret a relation?'

'I don't think so. I don't know. It all happened so long ago! And I was only a little girl.'

'When do you mean?'

'When Douai was bombed, at the time of the exodus. Trains and more trains which we got out of to sleep on the ballast. Women carrying wounded babies. Men with arm bands running in every direction and the train leaving again. Finally the explosion which seemed like the end of the world.'

'How old were you?'

'Four? A little over or a little under?'

'Where does the name Claes come from?'

'I suppose it belonged to my family. Apparently that's what I said.'

'And the Christian name?'

'Mina.'

'Did you speak French?'

'No. Only Flemish. I'd never seen a town.'

'Can you remember the name of your village?'

'No. But why aren't you talking about my husband?'

'I will in time. Where did you meet the old man?'

'I'm not sure. What happened just before and just after the explosion is very vague. I think I was walking along with someone holding my hand.'

Maigret took the receiver off the telephone and asked for the Town Hall in Douai. He was connected immediately.

'The Mayor is away,' said the town clerk.

He was very surprised to hear Maigret ask:

'How old are you?'

'Thirty-two.'

'And the Mayor?'

'Forty-three.'

'Who was Mayor when the Germans arrived in 1940?'

'Doctor Nobel. He remained Mayor for ten years after the War.'

'Is he dead?'

'No. In spite of his age he still practises in his old house in the Grand-Place.'

Three minutes later Maigret had Doctor Nobel on the line and Madame Barillard listened in amazement.

'Excuse me, Doctor. This is Superintendent Maigret from the Judicial Police. It's not about one of your patients but an old story which might cast a light on some recent events. It was the station of Douai, wasn't it, which was bombed in broad daylight in 1940 while several refugee trains were there and hundreds of other refugees were waiting?'

Nobel had not forgotten what had been the event of his life.

'I was there, Superintendent. It's the most appalling recollection a man can have. All was quiet. The reception committee was giving food to the Belgian and French refugees whose trains were going south.

'The women with babies were gathered in the first-class waiting room where feeding bottles and clean swaddling clothes were distributed. About ten nurses were at work.

'As a rule nobody was allowed to leave the train, but the refreshments proved too tempting. Anyhow, there were people everywhere.

'And suddenly, just as the sirens started hooting, the station shook, the glass roof broke, people screamed and it was impossible to realize what was going on.

'It is still not known how many raids there were.

'The scene was as ghastly outside as in, by the station and on the platforms: mutilated bodies, arms, legs, wounded with crazed eyes rushing round gripping their chests or their stomachs.

'I was lucky enough not to be hit and I tried to turn the waiting-rooms into first-aid stations. We didn't have enough ambulances or beds in the hospitals for all the wounded.

'I performed emergency operations on the spot, in worse than precarious conditions.'

'You probably don't remember a tall, thin man, a Fleming, who must have had his face cut right open and remained deaf and dumb?'

'Why do you ask about him?'

'Because he's the one who interests me.'

'On the contrary, it so happens that I remember him very well and that I've often thought about him.

'I was there as Mayor, as President of the local Red Cross and the Reception Committee, and finally as a doctor.

'In my capacity as Mayor I tried to regroup the families, identify the most seriously wounded and the dead, which wasn't always easy.

'Between ourselves, we buried several bodies which have never been identified, and in particular half a dozen old men who looked as though they were out of a home. We later tried vainly to find out where they came from.

'In the midst of the confusion and the crowd I clearly remember one group: an entire family, an elderly man, two women, three or four children whom the bombs had literally torn to pieces.

'It was near this group that I saw a man whose head was nothing but a bleeding mass. I had him carried to a table and was surprised to find that he was neither blind nor wounded in any vital organ.

'I have no idea how many stitches I gave him. A little girl stood unharmed a few yards away, following my movements with no apparent emotion.

'I asked her if he was a member of her family, her father or her grandfather, and I don't know what she answered in Flemish.

'Half an hour later, as I was operating on a wounded woman, I saw the man walking away, followed by the little girl.

'It was a pretty flabbergasting sight in the confusion. I had wrapped the wounded man's head in an enormous bandage with which he wandered around heedlessly in the middle of the crowd and he seemed not to notice the girl who trotted along at his heels.

' "Go and fetch him," I told one of my assistants, "he's in no condition to leave without further attention."

'That's about all I can tell you, Superintendent. When I had time to think about him again I inquired in vain. He had been seen wandering among the ruins and the ambulances. The stream of every sort of vehicle continued to flow from the North, carrying furniture, families, mattresses, sometimes pigs and cows.

'One of my scouts thought he saw a tall, elderly man, slightly bent, get on to a military truck together with a little girl whom the soldiers helped to climb in.

'During and after the war, when we tried to tidy the whole thing up, there were a certain number of queries. In the villages of Holland, Flanders and the Pas-de-Calais a good many Town Halls had been destroyed or plundered, and the registers had been burnt.

'Do you think you have found this man?'

'I'm almost sure.'

'What's happened to him?'

'He's just been found hanged, and at the moment I'm sitting in front of that little girl.'

'Will you let me know what happens?'

'As soon as it becomes clear. Thank you, Doctor.'

Maigret mopped his brow, emptied his pipe, filled another one and said gently to his companion:

'And now tell me your story.'

*

She had been watching him with large anxious eyes as she bit her nails, curled up in the armchair like a little girl.

Instead of replying, she asked him bitterly:

'Why do you treat Fernand like a criminal and why have you handcuffed him?'

'We'll come to that later if you don't mind. For the moment it's by giving me frank answers that you are most likely to assist your husband.'

Another question came to the young woman's lips, a

question which she seemed to have been asking herself for a long time, if not for ever:

'Was Jef mad? Jef Claes?'

'Did he behave as though he were mad?'

'I don't know. I can't compare my childhood to any other or him to any other man.'

'Start with Douai.'

'Lorries, refugee camps, trains, policemen who questioned the old man — because he seemed old to me — and who, unable to get anything out of him, questioned me. Who were we? Which village did we come from? I didn't know.

'We went farther and farther and I'm sure that one day I saw the Mediterranean. I remembered it later and I thought we'd been as far as Perpignan.'

'Did Claes try to get into Spain? To get from there to the United States?'

'How could I know? He couldn't hear, couldn't speak. To understand me he stared at my lips and I had to repeat the same question several times.'

'Why did he take you with him?'

'It was I. I've thought about it since. I suppose that seeing all my family dead around me I hung on to the nearest man, who may have looked like my grandfather.'

'Why did he take your name, assuming your name really was Claes?'

'I found out later. He always kept some slips of paper in his pocket and he sometimes wrote a few words in Flemish because he couldn't understand French yet. Nor could I. After weeks or months we ended up in Paris and he rented a room and a kitchen in a district which I have never found since.

'He wasn't poor. When he needed money he pulled out one or two gold pieces sewn in a large canvas belt under his shirt. They were his savings. We used to go a long way round to choose a jeweller's or a pawnbroker's, which he would enter furtively, afraid of being caught.

'I knew why the day the Jews had to wear a yellow star on their clothes. He wrote his real name for me on a piece of paper which he subsequently burnt: Victor Krulak. He was a Jew from Latvia, born in Antwerp where, like his father and his grandfather, he worked in the diamond business.'

'Did you go to school?'

'Yes. The schoolchildren made fun of me.'

'Did Jef cook the meals?'

'Yes, and he was very good at grilling meat. He didn't wear a star. He was always frightened. In the police stations he was teased mercilessly because he couldn't provide the papers necessary for an identity card.

'Once he was sent to some asylum because they thought he was mad, but he escaped the next day.'

'Was he fond of you?'

'I think he behaved like that because he didn't want to lose me. He had never been married. He didn't have any children. I'm sure he imagined God had put me in his path.

'We were twice driven back to the frontier, but he always returned to Paris, found a furnished room with a kitchenette, either near the Sacré-Cœur or in the Faubourg Saint-Antoine.'

'Did he work?'

'Not at this period.'

'How did he spend his time?'

'He wandered round, watched people, learnt to lip read, to understand their language. One day, towards the end of the war, he came home with a false identity card which he had been trying to obtain for four years.

'He had officially become Jef Claes and I was his granddaughter.

'We moved to slightly bigger lodgings, not far from the Hôtel de Ville, and people came to give him work. I wouldn't be able to recognize them now.

'I went to school. I grew up and worked as a salesgirl in a jeweller's in the Boulevard Beaumarchais.'

'Did old Jef get you that job?'

'Yes. He did odd jobs for various jewellers: repairs, restoration of old jewels.'

'Is that how you met Barillard?'

'A year later. As a commercial traveller he should only

have come to see us every three months, but he came more often and finally waited for me at the shop door. He was handsome, very gay and lively. He loved life. It was with him, at the "Quatre Sergents de La Rochelle", that I drank my first apéritif.'

'Did he know you were Jef's grand-daughter?'

'I told him I was. I told him about our adventure. Since he was going to marry me he naturally asked to meet him. We got married and we went to live in a little house in Fontenay-sous-Bois, taking Jef with us.'

'Did you ever see Palmari there?'

'Our former neighbour? I don't know because I've never met him since we've been here. Fernand sometimes brought home a few friends, charming men who liked laughing and drinking.'

'And the old man?'

'He spent most of his time in a tool-shed at the bottom of the garden, where Fernand had set up a workshop for him.'

'You never suspected anything?'

'What should I have suspected?'

'Tell me, Madame Barillard, does your husband usually get up during the night?'

'Never really.'

'He doesn't leave the flat?'

'Why?'

'Before going to bed do you have some sort of tea?'

'Verbena, sometimes camomile.'

'Did you wake up last night?'

'No.'

'Could you show me your bathroom?'

It was not large, but quite smart and gay, with yellow tiles. A medicine cabinet was fitted over the washbasin. Maigret opened it, examined a few bottles, and kept one in his hand.

'Do you take these pills?'

'I don't even know what they are. They've been there for ages. I remember! Fernand couldn't sleep and a friend recommended these pills.'

But the label was new.

'What's going on, Superintendent?'

'Last night, as on many other nights, you took a certain amount of this dope with your tea, without knowing it, and you slept heavily. Your husband went to fetch Jef in his garret and went down with him to the cellar.'

'To the cellar?'

'Where a workshop had been installed. He hit him with a piece of lead piping or some other similar object and then hanged him from the ceiling.'

She screamed but did not faint, instead she started running, went into the sitting-room and said in a shrill voice to her husband:

'It isn't true, is it, Fernand? It isn't true you did that to old Jef?'

Curiously enough she had her former Flemish accent.

*

Without giving them time to become emotional Maigret took Barillard into the study and signalled to Janvier to watch the young woman. The evening before the two men had been in the same study, but they were now in different places. Today it was the Superintendent who sat enthroned in the traveller's revolving chair and the traveller who sat in front of him, less caustic than at the previous interview.

'It's cowardly!' he muttered.

'What's cowardly, Barillard?'

'To pick on a woman. If you had any questions to ask you could have asked me, couldn't you?'

'I haven't any questions to ask you because I already know the answers. You suspected that after our talk yesterday, which was why you thought it necessary to silence the man you considered the weak point in your organization.

'After Palmari, Victor Krulak, known as Jef Claes. A poor old man with a feeble mind who would have done anything to be near the little girl who had put her hand in his on a day of doom. You're a swine, Barillard.'

'Thank you.'

'You see, there are swine and swine. With some of them, like Palmari, for instance, I can shake hands. You yourself are the worst kind, the kind one can't look at without wanting to punch or to spit at.'

And the Superintendent really had to control himself.

'Go ahead! I'm sure my lawyer will be delighted.'

'In a few minutes you'll be taken to the Central Police Station and this afternoon probably, or this evening, or tomorrow, we'll resume our conversation.'

'In front of my lawyer.'

'At the moment there's someone to whom I owe a visit which might take a fairly long time. You know who I mean. Well, it's largely from this visit that your future will depend.

'Because now that Palmari's liquidated, there are only two of you left at the top of the pyramid: Aline and you.

'I now know you were both going to leave at the first chance after having discreetly removed Manuel's hoard.

'Aline... Fernand... Aline... Fernand... When I next see you I'll know which of you is, I won't say guilty, because you both are, but the real instigator of the double deed. See?'

Maigret called:

'Janvier! Will you take the gentleman to the Central Police Station? He's got the right to dress decently, but don't let him out of your sight for a second. Have you got a gun?'

'Yes, chief.'

'There must be swarms of detectives downstairs, and you'll find a man to go with you. See you later.'

On his way out he stopped in front of Madame Barillard.

'Don't blame me, Mina, for the pain you have and will be caused.'

'Did Fernand kill him?'

'I'm afraid so.'

'But why?'

'You'll have to get this idea into your head sooner or later: because your husband's a swine, you poor little thing. And because in the flat opposite he found his mate.'

He left her in tears and a few minutes later he went into

the cellar where searchlights had replaced the yellow bulb. It was as though they were shooting a film.

Everyone was talking at once. The photographers were at work. The bald doctor was demanding silence and Moers could not get to the Superintendent.

The little magistrate found himself next to Maigret who dragged him into the open air.

'How about a glass of beer, sir?'

'I wouldn't say no if I could get by.'

They slipped by as best they could. The death of old Jef, who was almost unknown, had not gone as undetected as that of Manuel Palmari, and in front of the building a crowd had gathered which two constables could hardly keep back. Reporters pursued the Superintendent.

'Nothing this morning, boys. After three at the Quai.'

He took his stout companion to 'Chez l'Auvergnat' where some regular customers were already lunching and it was cool.

'Two beers.'

'What are you going to do about this, Maigret?' asked the magistrate, mopping his brow.

'Apparently they're discovering a modern apparatus for cutting diamonds in that cellar. Were you expecting it?'

'I've been searching for it for twenty years.'

'Are you serious?'

'Very serious. I knew how all the other pawns worked. Cheers!'

He slowly emptied his glass and put it on the bar, murmuring:

'The same again.'

Then, his face still set:

'I should have understood yesterday. Why didn't I remember that story about Douai? I sent my men in every direction except the right one, and when it finally occurred to me it was too late.'

He watched the owner pour him a second beer. He breathed heavily, like a man restraining himself.

'What are you going to do now?'

'I've sent Barillard to the Central Police Station.'

'Have you questioned him?'

'No. It's too soon. I have someone to question before him, right now.'

He looked out of the restaurant at the building across the street, in particular at a certain window on the fourth floor.

'Aline Bauche?'

'Yes.'

'At her flat?'

'Yes.'

'Wouldn't she be more impressed in your office?'

'She isn't impressed anywhere.'

'Do you think she'll confess?'

Maigret shrugged his shoulders, was about to order a third beer, decided not to and held out his hand to the nice little magistrate who looked at him both with admiration and a certain anxiety.

'See you later. I'll let you know.'

'I may be lunching here, and, as soon as they've finished across the street, I'll go back to the Palais de Justice.'

He didn't dare add:

'Good luck!'

His shoulders hunched, Maigret crossed the street and looked once more at the window on the fourth floor. The crowd made way for him and only one photographer had the presence of mind to take a picture of the Superintendent charging in.

CHAPTER SEVEN

When Maigret knocked noisily at the door of what used to be Manuel Palmari's flat he heard irregular steps within, and it was Inspector Janin who opened the door, looking, as usual, as though he had been caught out. Janin was a skinny fellow and when he walked he flung out his left leg. Like certain dogs he always seemed to expect to be beaten.

Was he afraid the Superintendent would upbraid him for not having his jacket on, a grimy shirt open on his thin and hairy chest?

Maigret hardly looked at him.

'Anyone used the telephone?'

'I did, chief, to tell my wife...'

'Have you had lunch?'

'Not yet.'

'Where is she?'

'In the kitchen.'

Maigret charged on. The flat was in a mess. In the kitchen Aline was smoking a cigarette in front of a plate where some fried eggs had left unappetizing traces. That woman bore no resemblance to the spruce and fresh Aline, the 'little lady', who dressed carefully in the morning to do her shopping in the neighbourhood.

She must have been naked under the old blue dressing gown with its silk sticking to the sweat on her body. Her black hair had not been combed, her face not made up. She had not had a bath and she gave off a spicy smell.

It was not the first time that Maigret had noticed this phenomenon. He had known masses of women as coquettish and elegant as Aline who, from one day to the next, left to themselves by the death of their husband or lover, had gone to seed in that way.

Their tastes, their attitudes suddenly changed. Their clothes became gaudier, their voices more vulgar, they used a language they had long tried to forget, as though their natural instincts were getting the upper hand.

'Come along.'

She knew the Superintendent well enough to realize that this time he was in earnest. Nevertheless, she got up slowly, extinguished her cigarette in the greasy plate, put the packet in her dressing-gown pocket and went towards the refrigerator.

'Are you thirsty?' she asked after a second.

'No.'

She did not insist, grabbed a bottle of brandy and a glass out of the cupboard.

'Where are you taking me?'

'I told you to come along, with or without the brandy.'

He made her cross the sitting-room, pushed her roughly into Palmari's little room where the wheelchair still evoked the presence of the old gang leader.

'Sit down, lie down or stay standing...' muttered the Superintendent taking off his jacket and searching for his pipe in his pocket.

'What's happened?'

'It's all over, that's what's happened. The moment of reckoning has come. Do you understand that?'

She was sitting on the edge of the yellow sofa, her legs crossed, and her shaky hand tried to light the cigarette she held between her lips.

She didn't care if she exposed a part of her thigh. Maigret didn't care either. Whether she was dressed or naked the time was gone when she could appeal to a man.

The Superintendent was witnessing a sort of collapse. He had known her sure of herself, frequently arrogant, teasing him in an acid tone or insulting him in such terms that Manuel had to intervene.

He had known her when she was naturally beautiful, and her slight smell of the streets had made her exciting.

He had known her in tears, as a grief-stricken woman or as an actress feigning grief so well that he was taken in by it.

Now all that was left was a sort of hunted animal, crouching, smelling of fear and wondering what would happen to it.

Maigret fiddled with the wheel-chair, turned it this way and that, finally sat down on it in the position in which he had often seen Palmari.

'He lived here three years, imprisoned by this instrument.'

He was speaking as if to himself, his hands groping for the controls of the chair which he turned to right and left.

'You were his only link with the outside world.'

She turned her head away, upset by seeing a man of Manuel's build in his chair. Maigret went on, as though she were not there.

'He was a criminal of the old school, a criminal of leisure. And those old men were suspicious in a different way to the lads of today. Above all, they never let women interfere in their business, except to exploit them. Manuel had got beyond that stage. Are you listening?'

'I'm listening,' she stammered like a little girl.

'The truth is that late in life the old crocodile started to love you like a schoolboy, to love a girl he'd picked up in the Rue Fontaine, by a shady hotel.

'He'd put aside a hoard with which he could have retired to the banks of the Marne or somewhere in the South.

'The poor fool thought he was going to make a real lady out of you. He dressed you up like a housewife. He taught you how to behave. He didn't have to teach you how to count because you learnt that at birth.

'How tender you were with him! Daddy this. Daddy that.

'How do you feel, Daddy? Don't you want me to open the window? Aren't you thirsty, Daddy? A little kiss from Aline?'

Suddenly getting up, he growled:

'Bitch!'

She did not flinch, did not budge. She knew that in his anger he could have slapped her, or even punched her.

'Did you get him to put the buildings in your name? And the bank accounts? It doesn't matter! As long as he was here, stuck between four walls, you met his accomplices, you gave them instructions, you collected the diamonds. You still have nothing to say?'

The cigarette fell from her fingers and, with the toe of her slipper, she crushed it on the carpet.

'How long have you been the mistress of that peacock Fernand? One year, three years, a few months? The hotel in the Rue de l'Etoile was very convenient for your appointments.

'And one day, somebody, one of you two, Fernand or you, got impatient. However disabled he was Manuel was still strong and he could have lived another ten or fifteen years.

'His hoard was big enough for him to want to end his days elsewhere, in some place where he could be wheeled round the garden, where he could feel in the country.

'Was it you or Fernand who couldn't stand the idea? Speak up, but be quick.'

He walked heavily from one window to the other, occasionally looking into the street.

'I'm listening.'

'I haven't got anything to say.'

'Was it you?'

'I've got nothing to do with it.'

And, as if with an effort:

'What have you done with Fernand?'

'He's at the Central Police Station where he's cooling his heels waiting for me to question him.'

'Did he say anything?'

'It doesn't matter what he said. I'll put it another way. You didn't kill Manuel with your own hands, of course. Fernand did it while you were shopping. As for the second crime…'

'What second crime?'

'You really don't know there's been another death in the building?'

'Who?'

'Come along! Use your head, if you aren't acting. Palmari was out of the way. But Barillard, whom no one had ever suspected, was suddenly implicated by the police.

'Before being taken to the Quai des Orfèvres and faced with each other you were both left in your traps, you here, the man opposite with his wife, with no communication with the outside, no communication between yourselves.

'And what happened? You went from your bed to a chair, from the chair to the kitchen where you nibbled something without even bothering to wash.

'He wondered how much we knew. And above all he wondered who could provide evidence and give him away. For one reason or another he wasn't frightened about you. Only, upstairs in the garret, there was a confederate who may have been slightly mad, or cleverer than he seemed, who might have squealed.'

'Is old Jef dead?' she stammered.

'You didn't have any doubts about his heading the list, did you?'

She stared at him, baffled, not knowing what to hang on to.

'How do you mean?'

'He was found hanged this morning in Barillard's cellar, which had long been turned into a workshop where Jef Claes, or rather Victor Krulak, recut stolen jewels.

'He didn't hang himself. Somebody went to fetch him upstairs. He was taken down to the cellar where he was killed before having a noose slipped round his neck.'

He took his time, never looking the young woman in the eyes.

'At the moment it's no longer a matter of burglaries, precious stones or who slept with whom in the Hôtel Bussière. It's a matter of two murders, or rather two killings both committed in cold blood, with premeditation. At least one head is at stake.'

Unable to stay seated any longer she got up and started walking up and down in her turn, taking care not to go too near the Superintendent.

'What do you think?' he heard her murmur.

'That Fernand is a wild beast and you're his mate. That you've lived here for months and years with the man you called Daddy and who trusted you while you were waiting for the chance to get into bed with that rat.

'That you must each have been as impatient as the other. It doesn't much matter who held the gun that killed Manuel.'

'It wasn't me.'

'Sit here.'

He pointed to the wheel-chair and she tautened, her eyes opened wide.

'Sit here!'

He suddenly grabbed her arm to make her sit where he wanted her.

'Don't move. I'm going to put you exactly where Manuel spent most of the day. Here! That's it! So as to have the radio within reach of one hand and the magazines within reach of the other. Is that right?'

'Yes.'

'And where was the gun without which Manuel never moved?'

'I don't know.'

'You're lying, because you said Palmari put it there every morning after having taken it into his room at night. Is that true?'

'Maybe.'

'It's not maybe, damn it! It's the truth! You're forgetting I came here twenty or thirty times to talk to him.'

She sat rooted to the chair where Manuel died, her face colourless.

'Now listen to me carefully. You went out to do your shopping, all spruced up, after kissing Daddy on the forehead and a last smile from the sitting-room door.

'Suppose that at that moment the weapon was still in its place behind the radio. Fernand came in with his key, because he had a key which enabled him to contact the boss when it was necessary.

'Look at the furniture well. Can you imagine Fernand going round the chair and sliding his hand behind the radio to seize the gun and fire a bullet into Manuel's neck?

'No, my dear. Palmari was no choirboy and he'd have had his suspicions after the first movement.

'You see, the truth is that when you kissed Daddy, when you smiled at him, when you tripped out with the step of a smart and pretty young woman, waggling your little behind, the gun was in your handbag.

'It was all timed. On the landing you simply had to pass it to Fernand who was coming out of his flat as if by chance.

'While you got into the lift and went to do your shopping — nice red meat, vegetables smelling of the kitchen garden — he stayed at home waiting for the right time.

'It wasn't necessary to go round the old man's chair and slip an arm between him and the radio.

'A quick movement after a few words. I know how carefully Manuel kept his weapons. The gun was well oiled and I'm sure we'll find traces of that oil in your handbag.'

'It isn't true!' she shouted, rushing at Maigret, beating his shoulders and face with her fists. 'I didn't kill him! It was Fernand! He did everything! It was all his idea!'

Without bothering to ward off the blows the Superintendent merely called:

'Janin! Will you look after her?'

'Shall I handcuff her?'

'Until she calms down. Ah! Let's put her on this sofa. I'll send you up some food and I'll try to get some lunch. She'll soon have to dress or we'll have to dress her.'

CHAPTER EIGHT

'A beer to start with.'

The little restaurant still smelt of the luncheon cooking, but the paper tablecloths had vanished from the tables and only one customer was reading a newspaper in the corner.

'Could your waiter take two or three sandwiches and a bottle of red wine across the street, to the flat on the left of the fourth floor.'

'How about you? Have you had lunch? Is it all over?'

'Would you like some sandwiches too? Cantal ham?'

Maigret felt damp under his clothes. His massive body was empty, his limbs limp, rather like someone who has just been fighting a high fever and has suddenly recovered.

For hours he had been charging ahead, unaware of the familiar scenery surrounding him, and he would hardly have been able to tell what day it was. He was surprised to see that the clock said half past two.

What had he forgotten? He vaguely realized he had missed an appointment, but which one? Oh yes! Gélot in the Avenue des Gobelins who must have made out the list of jewellers visited by Fernand Barillard.

All that was over. The list would come into use later, and the Superintendent thought of the little magistrate, for weeks to come, summoning witness after witness to his untidy office, gradually compiling a thicker and thicker file.

The world returned to life around Maigret. He heard the noises of the street again, found the shimmer of the sun again, and slowly relished his sandwich.

'Is the wine good?'

'A bit hard for some, but that's because it hasn't been fiddled around with. It's straight from my brother-in-law who only produces about twenty bottles a year.'

He had some of the same wine sent to Janin and when he left 'Chez l'Auvergnat' he no longer looked like a menacing bull.

'When will my house return to normal?' complained the concierge as he went by.

'Very soon, very soon, my dear lady.'

'And do I still have to pay the rent to the young lady?'

'I doubt it. The examining magistrate will decide.'

The lift took him up to the fourth floor. First he rang at the door on the right which Madame Barillard opened, her eyes red, still wearing her flower-patterned dress of the morning.

'I've come to say good-bye, Mina. Forgive me for calling you that but I can't help thinking of the little girl who, in the hell of Douai, put her hand into the hand of a man with a bleeding face walking away and not knowing where he was going. You didn't know where he was taking you either.'

'Is it true, Superintendent, that my husband is a...' She did not dare say the word: murderer.

He nodded.

'You're young, Mina. Cheer up!'

Madame Barillard's lips quivered and she managed to murmur:

'Why didn't I notice anything?'

She suddenly fell on to Maigret's chest and he let her weep her fill. One day, no doubt, she would find a new support, another hand to hold.

'I promise I'll come back and see you. Look after yourself. Life goes on.'

Opposite, Aline was sitting on the edge of the sofa.

'We're leaving,' said Maigret. 'Would you like to get dressed, or would you rather come as you are?'

She looked at him like someone who has thought a great deal and has taken a decision.

'Shall I see him?'

'Yes.'

'Today?'

'Yes.'

'Can I talk to him?'

'Yes.'

'As much as I like?'

'As much as you like.'

'Can I have a shower?'

'Provided you leave the bathroom door open.'

She shrugged her shoulders. She didn't much care who saw her. For almost an hour she did her toilet, undoubtedly one of the most meticulous ever.

She took the trouble to wash her hair and dry it with an electric drier, and took some time to select a simple black satin dress.

All the while she continued to look firm and determined.

'Janin! Go and see if there's a car downstairs from the Quai.'

'Going, chief.'

For a moment Maigret and the young woman were alone in the sitting-room. She put on her gloves. The sun flooded in through the two windows opened onto the street.

'Admit you had a soft spot for Manuel,' she murmured.

'In a way, yes.'

After hesitating she added, without looking at him:

'For me too, didn't you?'

And he repeated:

'In a way.'

After which he opened the door, shut it after them and put the key in his pocket. They took the lift down. There was an Inspector at the wheel of the black car. Janin, standing on the pavement, did not know what to do.

'Go home and sleep ten hours on end.'

'If you think my wife and children will let me sleep! Thanks all the same, chief.'

Vacher was at the wheel and the Superintendent

whispered a few words to him. He then got into the back seat next to Aline. After about a hundred yards the young woman, who was looking out, turned to her companion:

'Where are we going?'

Instead of going straight to the Judicial Police they were actually going down the Avenue de la Grande-Armée and round the Place de l'Etoile to go along the Champs-Elysées.

She looked as intently as she could, knowing she might well never see this sight again. And if she ever saw it again she would be a very old woman.

'Did you do it on purpose?'

Maigret sighed without replying. Twenty minutes later she followed him into his office, which the Superintendent reoccupied with evident pleasure.

He automatically put his pipes in order, went to the window, and finally opened the door of the detectives' office.

'Janvier!'

'Yes, chief.'

'Will you go down to the Central Police Station and bring back Barillard? Sit down, Aline.'

He now treated her as though nothing had happened. One would have thought he had nothing more to do with the business, that the whole case had just been an interval in his existence.

'Hello! Let me speak to the examining magistrate, Monsieur Ancelin, please. Hello!... Hello!... Monsieur Ancelin? Maigret here... I'm at my office, yes... I've just arrived together with a young woman whom you know... No, but it soon will... I wonder if you'd like to witness the encounter... Yes... Right now. I'm expecting him at any moment.'

He was about to take off his jacket, but he did not do it on account of the magistrate.

'Nervous?'

'What do you think?'

'That we're going to see a fight of wild beasts.'

The woman's eyes glinted.

'If you were armed I wouldn't stake much on his life.'

The sprightly little magistrate was the first to arrive and he looked with interest at the young woman in black who had just sat down.

'Sit in my chair, sir.'

'I don't want...'

'Please do. My part is almost over. I've only got a few things to check, some witnesses to question, some reports to make out and give over to you. A week of paper work.'

Steps were heard in the passage and Janvier knocked at the door and pushed Fernand, in handcuffs, into the office.

'As for these two, they're yours from now on.'

'Shall I take his handcuffs off, chief?'

'I don't think that's wise. You stay here. I'll make sure there are some tough chaps next door.'

Aline had got up with a start, as though she had scented the man who had long been her lover.

Not her lover: her mate. Just as she had been his.

They were two animals looking at each other, in this peaceful office, just as they would have looked at each other in an arena or in the jungle.

Their lips quivered, their nostrils contracted, Fernand began to hiss:

'What have you...'

Standing in front of him, her chest thrown out, her muscles strained, she thrust forward a face filled with hate and spat at him.

Without wiping the spit off he too stepped forward, his hands in front of him, threateningly, while the little magistrate fidgeted, ill at ease in Maigret's chair.

'You bitch, you...'

'Swine!... Rat!... Murderer!...'

She managed to scratch his face but in spite of his handcuffs he seized her arm in mid-air and twisted it, leaning over her, his eyes full of all the hatred in the world.

Maigret, standing between his office and the detectives', gave a sign and two men rushed in to separate the couple rolling on the floor.

For a few seconds there was a scuffle and finally Barillard, his face bleeding, was pulled up while Aline, in handcuffs, was pushed over to a chair.

'I think it'll be all right to interrogate them separately, Monsieur Ancelin. The most difficult thing of all won't be to make them talk but to stop them talking.'

Louis Ancelin got up, led the Superintendent to the window and, leaning towards him, murmured, still shaken by what he had just seen:

'I've never seen such a display of hatred, such an explosion of brutality!'

Over his shoulder Maigret said to Janvier:

'You can lock them up!'

And he added ironically:

'Separately, of course.'

He did not watch them leave, turned as he was to the peaceful face of the Seine. On the banks he looked for a familiar figure, the figure of an angler. He had called him 'his' angler for years, although it was probably not always the same one. What mattered was that there was always a man to fish near the Pont Saint-Michel.

A tug pulling four barges sailed upstream and lowered its funnel to pass under the stone arch.

'Tell me, Maigret, which of the two, in your opinion...'

The Superintendent lit his pipe before he said, still looking out:

'You're the magistrate, aren't you? I can only let you have them as they are.'

'It wasn't a pretty sight.'

'No, it wasn't a pretty sight. It wasn't a pretty sight in Douai, either.'

Epalinges, March 9, 1965

MAIGRET and the Madwoman

CHAPTER ONE

Flanking the main gate of Police Headquarters, Constable Picot stood guard on the left, and his old friend Latuile on the right. It was about ten o'clock on a fine morning in May. The sunlight was dazzling and Paris was aglow with colour, like a pastel drawing.

Picot could not have said exactly when he first noticed her. It did not seem important at the time. She was a tiny little old woman in a white hat, white cotton gloves and a dress of gun metal grey. Her legs were very thin, and slightly bowed with age.

Had she been carrying a shopping basket or a handbag? He could not remember. He had not been aware of her approach. She was only a few feet away from him, standing on the pavement, peering at the rows of little cars parked in the forecourt of Police Headquarters.

Not that sightseers were uncommon at the Quai des Orfèvres, but mostly they were tourists. She drew nearer, went right up to the gate, inspected the policeman from top to toe, then turned and made off in the direction of the Pont-Neuf.

Picot was on duty again the following morning, and at about the same time as on the previous day he saw her once more. This time, after some considerable hesitation, she came up and spoke to him.

'This is the place where Chief Superintendent Maigret has his office, isn't it?'

'Yes, madame. On the first floor.'

She raised her head and gazed up at the windows. She had very delicate, finely modelled features, and her clear grey eyes were full of wonderment.

'Thank you, officer.'

She went on her way with little mincing steps. This time he noticed that she was carrying a string shopping bag, which would seem to indicate that she lived some where nearby.

On the third day Picot was off duty. His replacement paid no attention to the little old woman, who sidled through into the forecourt. She wandered around for a minute or two, and then went in through the door on the left and began climbing the stairs. On the first floor she stopped and peered down the long corridor, apparently feeling a little lost.

Old Joseph, the messenger, went up to her and asked, in his friendly way, if he could be of any assistance.

'I'm looking for Chief Superintendent Maigret's office.'

'Do you wish to see the Chief Superintendent?'

'Yes. That's what I'm here for.'

'Have you an appointment?'

Looking very downcast, she shook her head.

'Can't I see him without an appointment?'

'Would you care to leave a message?'

'I must speak to him personally. It's terribly important.'

'If you'll fill in one of these forms, I'll see if the Chief Superintendent can see you.'

She sat down at a table covered with a green baize cloth. They had just had the decorators in, and the whole building smelt strongly of paint. Unaware of this, she was struck by the cheerful look of things, not at all what one would have expected of a Government Department.

Having filled in one form, she then proceeded to tear it up. She wrote slowly, composing her sentences with great care, and underlining a word here and there. A second form followed the first into the waste-paper basket, and then a third. It was not until after her fourth attempt that she appeared satisfied. She went over to Joseph with the form.

'You'll see that it's handed to him personally, won't you?'

'Yes, madame.'

'He's very busy, I daresay.'

'Very.'

'Do you think he'll see me?'

'I couldn't say, madame.'

She was at least eighty-five, eighty-six or seven perhaps, and as light and slender as a little girl. Age had fined her down, and her delicate skin was translucent. She looked up at Joseph, good-hearted fellow that he was, and gave him a shy smile, anxious to win him over.

'You will do your best, won't you? It's so terribly important to me!'

'Take a seat, madame.'

He went up to one of the doors, and knocked. Maigret was in conference with Janvier and Lapointe, who were both standing by the window, which was wide open, letting in all the hubbub of the street outside.

Maigret took the form from Joseph, glanced at it, and frowned. 'What's she like?'

'A very respectable old lady. A little shy. She was most insistent that I should beg you to see her.'

On the dotted line at the head of the form, she had written her name in a surprisingly firm, neat hand:

Madame Antoine de Caramé.

And below, the address:

8b Quai de la Mégisserie.

She stated as the object of her visit:

The caller has something of the utmost importance to communicate to Chief Superintendent Maigret. It is a matter of life and death.

Here the handwriting was more shaky, and the words irregularly spaced. 'Chief Superintendent' and 'utmost importance' were underlined. 'A matter of life and death' was underscored twice.

'Is she mad?' muttered Maigret, sucking at his pipe.

'That isn't how she strikes me. She's very quiet and composed.'

Everyone at the Quai des Orfèvres had at some time or other had to deal with letters from lunatics or cranks, and the underlining of words was a characteristic of most of them.

'You'd better see her, Lapointe. Unless someone does, we'll have her calling here every day.'

A few minutes later, the old woman was ushered into the little office at the back. Lapointe was waiting there alone, standing near the window.

'Please come in, madame. Take a seat.'

She looked him up and down in some bewilderment.

'Are you his son?'

'Whose son?'

'The Chief Superintendent's.'

'No, madame. My name is Inspector Lapointe.'

'But you're only a boy!'

'I'm twenty-seven.'

And so he was. All the same, he didn't look a day over twenty-two, and was more like most people's idea of a student than a police officer.

'It was Chief Superintendent Maigret I asked to see.'

'Unfortunately, he can't spare the time at the moment.'

She hesitated, standing in the doorway, fidgeting with her white handbag, uncertain whether to stay or go.

'What if I were to come back tomorrow?'

'He still couldn't see you.'

'Does Chief Superintendent Maigret never grant interviews?'

'Only in very special cases.'

'Mine is a very special case. Just that. It's a matter of life and death.'

'So you said on the form.'

'Well, then?'

'If you will tell me what it's all about, I'll report to the Chief, and let him be the judge.'

'You think he might agree to see me?'

'I can't promise, but he very well might.'

She remained standing for quite some time, pondering the pros and cons, and then, apparently having made up her mind, sat down on the very edge of a chair facing Lapointe, who was now seated at the desk.

'What's the trouble?'

'I should explain first of all that I've lived in the same flat on the Quai de la Mégisserie for the past forty-two years.

On the ground floor, there's a man who sells birds. In the summer, when he puts all the cages out on the pavement, I can hear them all day long. It's company for me.'

'You said you were in some sort of danger, I think.'

'I'm in danger all right, but I daresay you think I'm drivelling. The young always seem to imagine that old people aren't quite right in the head.'

'No such thought ever occurred to me.'

'I don't quite know how to put this. My second husband died twelve years ago, and since then I've been on my own in the flat, and no one other than myself ever has occasion to go into it. It's too big for me now really, but I've set my heart on living my time out there. I'm eighty-six, and I can still manage the cooking and housework without any help.'

'Do you keep a pet? A dog or a cat?'

'No. As I said, I can always hear the birds singing. My flat is on the first floor, just above the shop.'

'What is it that's worrying you?'

'It's hard to say. At least five times in the past fortnight, I've noticed that my things have been moved.'

'What do you mean? Are you saying that, when you've been out, you've come back to find your things disturbed?'

'That's right. A frame hanging slightly crooked, or a vase turned round. That sort of thing.'

'Are you quite sure?'

'There you are, you see! Because I'm an old woman, you think I'm wandering in my wits. I did tell you, don't forget, that I've lived forty-two years in that same flat. Naturally, if anything is out of place, I spot it at once.'

'Has anything been stolen? Have you missed anything?'

'No, Inspector.'

'Do you keep money in the flat?'

'Very little. Just enough to meet my monthly expenses. My first husband was in local government. I still draw a pension from the Hôtel de Ville. Besides that, I have a Post Office Savings account.'

'Do you have valuables, jewellery, ornaments, anything of that sort?'

'I have things that are of value to me, but I doubt if

they're worth much in terms of cash.'

'Were there any other signs of an intruder, such as a damp footprint, for instance?'

'There hasn't been a drop of rain for the past ten days.'

'Cigarette ash?'

'No.'

'Have you ever given anyone a key to your flat?'

'No. I have the only key, and I always keep it in my bag.'

He was hard put to it to conceal his embarrassment.

'In other words, all it amounts to is that, from time to time, you find some of your things not precisely as you left them?'

'That's right.'

'You've never caught any unauthorised person in the flat?'

'Never.'

'And you've no idea who the intruder might be?'

'None.'

'Have you any children?'

'Much to my sorrow, I never had a child.'

'Any other relations?'

'One niece. She's a masseuse. I don't see her very often, though she lives not far from me, just across the river.'

'What about friends? Men friends, women friends?'

'Most of the people I used to know are dead. And there's something else as well.'

She said it quite casually. There was no underlying note of hysteria, and her bright glance never wavered.

'I'm being followed.'

'In the street, do you mean?'

'Yes.'

'Have you actually seen the person who's following you?'

'Whenever I stop suddenly and look back there's someone there, but not always the same person. I don't know who it can be, really.'

'Do you go out much?'

'Every morning, for a start. I go out at about eight to do my shopping. I miss Les Halles very much, now that it's been moved. It was so convenient, just round the corner, and old habits die hard. Since then I've shopped around a bit locally, but it will never be quite the same again.'

'Is it a man who's following you?'

'I don't know.'

'I presume you get back at about ten?'

'Thereabouts. And then I sit by the window and shell peas, or whatever.'

'Do you stay in in the afternoon?'

'Only when the weather's bad. I like to get a bit of fresh air whenever I can. Usually, I sit on a park bench, preferably in the Tuileries Gardens. I have my own favourite bench. I'm not the only one. People of my age are like that, you know. I see the same old faces there, year in, year out.'

'Are you followed as far as the Tuileries?'

'Only part of the way. So as to make sure I won't be coming back immediately, I think.'

'Have you ever done that?'

'Three times. I pretended I'd forgotten something, and turned back.'

'And, needless to say, you found no one there?'

'That doesn't alter the fact that, on other occasions, my things have been moved. Someone has it in for me, though I can't think why. I've never done any harm to anyone. There may be more than one person involved.'

'You said your husband was in local government. What did he do?'

'He was Clerk to the Council. He had very heavy responsibilities. Unfortunately, he died young, of a heart attack. He was just forty-five.'

'And you married again?'

'Not till almost ten years later. My second husband was chief buyer at the Bazar de l'Hôtel de Ville. He was in charge of agricultural implements, and tools in general.'

'Is he dead too?'

'He'd been retired for some years when he died. If he'd lived, he'd have been ninety-two.'

'When did he die?'

'I thought I told you. Twelve years ago.'

'Had he any family? Was he a widower when you married him?'

'He only had one son. He lives in Venezuela.'

'I'll tell you what, madame, I'd best go and report all you've just told me to the Chief Superintendent.'

'Do you think he'll agree to see me?'

'If he does, he'll get in touch with you.'

'Have you got my address?'

'It's on the form you filled in, isn't it?'

'That's true, I'd forgotten. The thing is, you see, I think the world of him. It seems to me he's the only one who could possibly understand. I don't mean any disrespect to you, but you do seem a bit on the young side to me.'

He accompanied her to the door, and down the long corridor to the head of the main staircase.

When he got back to Maigret's office, Janvier was no longer there.

'Well?'

'I think you're right, sir. She must be a bit cracked. All the same, you wouldn't think it. She's very soft-spoken, very cool and self-possessed. She's eighty-six, and all I can say is I hope I'll be as bright as she is when I get to her age.'

'What about this threat or whatever it is that's hanging over her head?'

'She's lived in the same flat on the Quai de la Mégisserie for more than forty years. She's been married twice. She claims that, while she's out, some of her things get moved.'

Maigret re-lit his pipe.

'What sort of things?'

'Picture frames hanging crooked, vases turned back to front...'

'Has she a dog or a cat?'

'No. She makes do with birdsong. Apparently, there's a man who sells birds on the ground floor.'

'Anything else?'

'Yes. She's persuaded herself that she's being followed.'

'Has she actually seen anyone following her?'

'No, that's just it. But she seems to have an obsession about it.'

'Will she be coming back?'

'She's set her heart on seeing you personally. She talks about you as if you were the Good Lord Himself. You're the only one, it seems, who could possibly understand. What am I to do?'

'Nothing.'

'She's sure to be back!'

'We'll cross that bridge when we come to it. Meanwhile, you might go along and have a word with the concierge.'

Maigret turned his attention once more to the file which he had been reading, and young Lapointe went back to the Inspectors' Duty Room.

'A nut-case, was she?' Janvier asked.

'Probably, but a very unusual one.'

'Do you know many nut-cases?'

'One of my aunts is a patient in a mental hospital.'

'The old girl seems to have made quite an impression on you.'

'She did, in a way. To her, I'm just a kid, who couldn't possibly understand her problem. She's pinned all her hopes on Maigret.'

*

That same afternoon, Lapointe strolled along the Quai de la Mégisserie, where almost every shop window was filled with birds and other small pets. In response to the glorious weather, there were tables and chairs on the pavement outside every café. When he got to number 8, Lapointe looked up at the first floor windows, and saw that they were wide open. He had some difficulty in finding the lodge, which was across a courtyard at the back of the building. The concierge was sitting in a patch of sunlight, darning a pair of men's socks.

'Looking for anyone in particular?'

He showed her his official card.

'I'd be grateful for anything you could tell me about Madame Antoine de Caramé. That is her name, isn't it, the old lady who lives on the first floor?'

'I know, I know. Actually, Antoine was her second husband's surname, so, legally, her name is Madame Antoine. But she's very proud of her first husband, who was something quite high up in the Hôtel de Ville, so she likes to be known as Madame Antoine de Caramé.'

'What do you make of her?'

'How do you mean?'

'Is she at all peculiar?'

'What I want to know is why the police should be taking such an interest in her, all of a sudden?'

'She came asking for our help.'

'What seems to be the trouble?'

'Apparently things get moved about in her flat while she's out. Hasn't she said anything to you?'

'She just asked me if I'd ever seen any strangers going up to her flat. I said I hadn't. I wouldn't anyway, not from here. I can't see the front entrance or the staircase.'

'Does she get many visitors?'

'Only her niece, who comes once or twice a month. And even she sometimes doesn't show up for three months at a stretch.'

'Have you ever noticed anything odd about her behaviour?'

'She's very much like any other old woman living on her own. She's a real lady, you can see that, and she's always very polite to everyone.'

'Is she at home now?'

'No, she never misses a chance of sunning herself on her favourite bench in the Tuileries.'

'Does she talk to you at all?'

'Just a few words when we happen to meet. Most days she asks after my husband, who's ill in hospital.'

'I'm much obliged to you.'

'I take it you'd rather I didn't mention your visit?'

'It doesn't matter one way or the other.'

'At any rate, I don't think she's mad, if that's what you're getting at. She has her fads, all old people do, but no more than anyone else.'

'You may be seeing me again.'

*

Maigret was in high good humour. For ten days, there had not been a drop of rain, the pale blue sky was cloudless, and a gentle breeze was blowing. In this perfect spring weather, Paris was as gay and colourful as the backcloth of an operetta.

He stayed on rather late in his office to check through a report, which he had been working on for some time and was anxious to get rid of. He could hear the passing traffic, cars and buses, and occasionally a tug on the river sounding its siren.

It was nearly seven when he opened the communicating door to the inspectors' room, to tell Lucas and the two or three other inspectors on night duty that he was leaving.

He went downstairs, toying with the idea of dropping into the Brasserie Dauphine for an aperitif. As he went out through the main gate, he exchanged greetings with the two constables on guard.

After a moment or two of hesitation, he decided that he would rather go straight home. He had gone a few yards in the direction of the Boulevard du Palais, when the tiny figure of a woman stepped into his path. He had no difficulty in recognising her from Lapointe's description.

'It really is you, isn't it?' she said with great fervour.

She saw no need to address him by name. Whom could she mean but the great, the famous Chief Superintendent, every detail of whose cases she had read avidly in the newspapers? She even went so far as to paste into scrapbooks every word that was written about him.

'Please forgive me for accosting you in the street like this, but in there they wouldn't let me near you.'

Maigret felt a little foolish. He could just imagine the two constables exchanging amused glances behind his back.

'Mind you, I can see their point. I don't hold it against them. After all, it's their job to see that you're not disturbed when you're busy, isn't it?'

It was her eyes that made the deepest impression on the Chief Superintendent, clear, light grey eyes, very gentle and yet full of sparkle. She smiled at him. Clearly, she was in the seventh heaven. But there was something else about her too, an intense vitality, quite extraordinary in such a tiny little woman.

'Which way are you going?'

He pointed towards the Pont Saint-Michel.

'Would you mind very much if I walked with you?'

Trotting along at his side, she seemed tinier still.

'The main thing is, do you see, that you should realise that I'm not mad. I know how we old people look to the young, and I am a very old woman indeed.'

'You're eighty-six, are you not?'

'I see that the young man I spoke to has told you all about me. He seems very young for the job, but you can see he's been well brought up. He has beautiful manners.'

'Have you been waiting here long?'

'Since five to six. I thought you left your office at six. I saw a great many gentlemen come out, but you weren't among them.'

So she had stood there waiting a whole hour, ignored by the two incurious policemen on guard duty.

'I have this feeling that I'm in danger. Someone is sneaking into my flat and rummaging among my things. There must be some reason for it.'

'You say someone has been searching your flat. How do you know?'

'Because I find things not quite as I left them. I'm extremely tidy. It's almost an obsession. In my flat there is a place for everything, and, for more than forty years, everything has been in its place.'

'And this has happened more than once?'

'At least four times.'

'Do you have anything valuable?'

'No, Chief Superintendent. Nothing but the sort of odds and ends that one accumulates over the years and keeps for reasons of sentiment.'

She stopped suddenly, and looked back over her shoulder.

'Is anyone following you now?' he asked.

'Not at this moment, no. I beg you to come and see me. You'll understand it all much better when I've shown you over the place.'

'I'll do my very best to try and fit it in.'

'For an old woman like me, can't you do better than that? The Quai de la Mégisserie is just around the corner from here. Drop in and see me sometime in the next day or so. I promise I won't keep you long. And I promise I won't bother you at your office again.'

She was nothing if not artful.

'I'll come as soon as I can.'

'This week?'

'This week, if possible. Otherwise, at the beginning of next week.'

They had arrived at his bus stop.

'Please forgive me, I must be on my way home now.'

'I'm relying on you. I trust you.'

At that moment, he would have been hard put to it to say what he really felt about her. There was no denying that she might have made the whole thing up. That, at any rate, was what it sounded like. But when one was actually with her, looking into her face, it was almost impossible not to take her seriously.

He arrived home to find the table already laid for dinner. Kissing his wife on both cheeks, he said:

'It's been such a lovely day. I hope you managed to get out.'

'I went and did some shopping.'

And then he said something that surprised her.

'Tell me, have you ever sat on a bench in a public park?'

She was taken aback by the question. After a moment's reflection, she said:

'I suppose I must have done, when I was too early for a dental appointment, for instance.'

'I had a visitor this evening, who spends pretty well every afternoon sitting on a bench in the Tuileries.'

'There are lots of people like that.'

'Have you ever got into conversation with any of them?'

'On one occasion, at least. The mother of a little girl asked me to keep an eye on her while she got something from a shop just across the square.'

Here, too, the window was open. They had several kinds of cold meat, and a salad with mayonnaise. It might have been the height of summer.

'What would you say to a short walk?'

There was still a rosy glow in the sky from the setting

sun, and it was quiet in the Boulevard Richard-Lenoir. Here and there they could see people looking down into the street, their elbows resting on the window sills.

They enjoyed walking for its own sake. It was pleasant to be together, though they had nothing much to say to one another. Together, they watched the people crossing the roads, together they looked at the window displays in the shops, and occasionally one or other would make a remark. They went as far as the Bastille and came back along the Boulevard Beaumarchais.

'A very strange old lady came to see me this evening, though actually it was Lapointe who interviewed her. I didn't see her until later, when she accosted me in the street as I was leaving.

'From the story she tells, you'd think she was mad, or at least a bit touched.'

'What seems to be the trouble?'

'Nothing, really. It's just that she says that sometimes, when she's been out, she comes back to find some of her things slightly out of place.'

'Has she a cat?'

'That was the first thing Lapointe asked her. She doesn't keep pets. She lives above a shop which sells birds, and she can hear them singing all day long, which she says is company enough for her.'

'Do you think there's any truth in it?'

'When she was actually there, looking up at me, yes, I did. She's got wonderfully clear grey eyes, full of kindliness and honesty, utterly without guile, at any rate. She's been widowed twelve years. She lives alone. Except for a niece whom she hardly ever sees, she has no one in the world.

'Every morning she goes out to the local shops, in a white hat and gloves. She spends most of her afternoons sitting on a bench in the Tuileries. She doesn't complain, she's never bored, and loneliness doesn't seem to worry her.'

'That's true of a lot of old people, you know.'

'I daresay you're right, but there's something a little different about her, though I can't quite put my finger on it.'

It was dark by the time they got home, and much cooler. They went to bed early, and, next morning, seeing that it was another lovely day, Maigret decided to walk to work.

As usual, there was a formidable pile of letters for him. He just had time to glance through them, and have a word with his inspectors, before the Chief Commissioner's daily briefing. There was nothing very important on hand.

He spent the morning clearing up a few routine matters, and then decided, on the spur of the moment, to have lunch at the Brasserie Dauphine. He rang his wife to tell her he would not be lunching at home. He had intended, after he had eaten, to call on the old lady at the Quai de la Mégisserie, and was prevented from doing so only by the merest chance. He ran into an old colleague, whom he had not seen since his retirement, and they lingered for a quarter of an hour or more, chatting in the sunshine.

Twice that afternoon, he thought again of going to see the old lady, whom the inspectors had already nicknamed 'Maigret's old madwoman', but each time he found some excuse for putting it off, telling himself that tomorrow would do just as well.

If the newspapers were ever to get hold of the tale of the wandering ornaments, he would be the laughing stock of Paris.

That evening, they stayed in and watched television. Next morning he overslept, and had to go to work by bus. A few minutes before noon, the Divisional Superintendent of the *Ier Arrondissement* was on the phone to him.

'Something has happened here that I think may be of interest to your people. The concierge of the flats tells me that one of your inspectors, a young fellow, very handsome, called to see her the other day.'

He had a sudden foreboding.

'At the Quai de la Mégisserie?'

'Yes.'

'Is she dead?'

'Yes.'

'Are you ringing from the flat?'

'I'm downstairs in the bird shop. There's no telephone up there.'

'I'm on my way.'

He put his head round the door of the Inspectors' Duty Room, and said to Lapointe:

'Come with me.'

'Anything wrong, sir?'

'As far as you and I are concerned, yes, very wrong. It's the old lady.'

'The one with the grey eyes and the white hat?'

'Yes. She's dead.'

'Murdered?'

'I presume so. Why else should the Superintendent have thought fit to get in touch with me?'

They didn't bother with a car. It was quicker to walk. Superintendent Jenton, well-known to Maigret, was standing on the edge of the pavement, next to a parrot chained to its perch.

'Did you know her?'

'I only saw her once. I'd promised to come and see her as soon as I could. Yesterday, I very nearly did.'

Would it have made any difference if he had?

'Is there anyone up there?'

'One of my men, and Doctor Forniaux has just arrived.'

'How did she die?'

'I don't know yet. At about half-past ten this morning, one of the second-floor tenants noticed that her door was ajar. She didn't attach any importance to it, and went out to do her shopping. When she got back at eleven, and saw that it was still open, she called out:

' "Madame Antoine!... Madame Antoine!... Are you there?" '

'When there was no answer, she went into the flat and nearly tripped over the body.'

'Was it lying on the floor?'

'Yes. In the sitting room.'

'The neighbour had the good sense to ring through to us at once.'

Maigret went slowly up the stairs. His expression was grim.

'How was she dressed?'

'She must have been out earlier. She was still wearing

her white hat and gloves.'

'Any visible injuries?'

'None that I could see. The concierge told me that one of your men was round here three days ago, asking questions about the old lady, so of course I rang you at once.'

Doctor Forniaux, who was kneeling on the floor, stood up as the three men came into the room.

They shook hands.

'Can you tell us the cause of death?'

'Suffocation.'

'Do you mean she was strangled?'

'No. Some sort of cloth, a towel, perhaps, or even a handkerchief, was held over her nose and mouth until she stopped breathing.'

'Are you sure?'

'I'll be able to tell you for certain after the autopsy.'

The window was wide open, and they could hear the birds twittering in the shop below.

'When did she die?'

'Sometime yesterday. Late afternoon or early evening.'

In death, the old woman seemed even tinier than she had when she was alive. Lying there, so small, with one leg bent at an awkward angle, she looked like a disjointed puppet.

The doctor had closed her eyes. Her face and hands seemed carved in ivory.

'How long before the killer could be sure she was dead, would you say?'

'It's hard to tell, especially with a woman of her age. Five minutes perhaps, a little more, a little less....'

'Lapointe, ring Public Prosecutions and the Laboratory. Tell Moers to send his men along right away.'

'Unless there's anything further I can do for you,' said the police surgeon, 'I'll be on my way. I'll arrange for the mortuary van to collect her and take her to the Forensic Laboratory, as soon as you've done with her.'

A small crowd was beginning to collect outside the building. The Divisional Superintendent sent his man down to speak to them.

'Move them on. This isn't a public entertainment.'

Murder was scarcely a new experience to either of them, but they were none the less deeply affected on that account. She was so very old and — what made it seem worse — there was not even a mark on her.

Then there was the atmosphere of the place, recalling the Edwardian, if not the Victorian era. The furniture was of solid mahogany, massive pieces, all beautifully polished to a high gloss. The chairs, of the kind still to be found in provincial drawing rooms, were covered in crimson plush. There were a great many ornaments, and masses of photographs hanging on every wall, against a background of flowered paper.

'All we can do now is to wait for the D.P.P.'

'He won't be long. They'll send the first available Deputy. He'll arrive with his clerk in attendance, take a quick look round, and that will be that.'

This, indeed, was a fair description of what usually happened, as a prelude to the arrival of the forensic technicians, with all their cumbersome apparatus.

The door swung open without a sound. Maigret gave a start. A little girl sidled in, probably a neighbour's child, from one of the upper floors, curious to see what all the comings and goings were about.

'Do you often come here?'

'No. I've never been before.'

'Where do you live?'

'Just across the landing.'

'Did you know Madame Antoine?'

'I used to see her sometimes on the stairs.'

'Used she to talk to you?'

'She always smiled at me.'

'Did she ever give you anything, sweets or chocolates?'

'No.'

'Where's your mother?'

'In the kitchen.'

'Take me to her, will you?'

He turned to the Superintendent.

'Excuse me a moment. I'd be grateful if you'd let me know when the Deputy gets here.'

It was an old building. The walls were bulging in places,

and there were gaps between the floorboards.

'There's a gentleman to see you, Mummy.'

The woman came out of the kitchen, wiping her hands on her apron. Her arms, just below the elbow, were still spattered with soapsuds.

'I'm Chief Superintendent Maigret. I just happened to be in the flat across the landing when your daughter walked in. Was it you who found the body?'

'What body? Go to your room, Lucette.'

'Your neighbour, opposite.'

'So she's dead? I always said it was bound to happen sooner or later. A woman of her age ought not to live alone. I daresay she was taken bad, and hadn't the strength to call for help.'

'She was murdered.'

'I never heard a thing! But then, of course, with all the noise of the traffic...'

'There was no shooting, and it happened not this morning, but yesterday afternoon or evening.'

'Poor woman! She was a bit too high and mighty for my taste, but I had nothing against her.'

'Were you on friendly terms with her?'

'I doubt if we exchanged a dozen words in all the seven years I've lived here.'

'Do you know anything about her personal life?'

'I often used to see her go out in the morning. She wore a black hat in winter and a white one in summer, and she never went out without her gloves, even round the corner to the shops. Well, live and let live, I say.'

'Did she ever have visitors?'

'Not that I know of. No, wait, come to think of it, she did have one, a woman, rather on the heavy side, and a bit mannish. I saw her two or three times ringing the doorbell.'

'Was this during the day?'

'In the evening, as a rule. Soon after dinner.'

'Have you noticed any unusual comings and goings in the building recently?'

'There are always people milling about. The concierge hardly ever leaves the lodge there, across the yard. She takes no interest at all in the tenants.'

The little girl had sidled back noiselessly into the room. The woman turned to her.

'Didn't you hear what I said? Go straight back to your room.'

'You'll be seeing me again, I daresay. I shall have to have a word with all the tenants.'

'I suppose you've no idea who did it?'

'None.'

'Who found her?'

'Someone from the second floor. She noticed on her way out that the door was ajar, and when she came back and found it still open, she called out, and then went in.'

'I can guess who that was.'

'Why do you say that?'

'It must be old mother Rochin. She's the nosiest woman in the building.'

They could hear footsteps and voices outside on the landing. The men from the Department of Public Prosecutions had arrived. Maigret went across to join them.

'This way,' he said. 'Doctor Forniaux has been, but he has a great many calls this morning, so he couldn't wait.'

The Deputy was a tall young man, distinguished-looking and strikingly well-dressed. He looked about him in some surprise, as though he had never seen anything quite like it. Then he stood for a moment staring down at the crumpled little grey figure on the carpet.

'How did she die?'

'She was suffocated.'

'She can't have put up much of a fight, that's for sure.

Judge Libart arrived a few minutes later. He too looked round the flat with interest.

'It's just like an old film set,' he remarked.

Lapointe, by this time, had returned. He and Maigret exchanged glances. While neither of them actually shuddered, their feelings were plain enough.

CHAPTER TWO

'Maybe I'd better send along two or three men to keep the sightseers on the move,' suggested the District Superintendent.

Already the residents were pouring out of their flats and gathering on the landing and staircase. The Public Prosecutor's men would be arriving at any minute, not to mention the stretcher-bearers from the Forensic Laboratory.

Lapointe, glancing at Maigret, noted that he was looking unwontedly pale and grave. It was only three days since be had first set eyes on the dead woman. Up to that time, he had never even heard of her. Yet, in her distress — real or imagined — it was to him that she had turned for help. She had put her trust in him. She had sought a personal interview, and, failing that, had accosted him in the street. He could still see her looking up at him, her eyes glowing with hero-worship.

He had thought her mad, or at least not perfectly sane. And yet, all the while, there had been that little nagging doubt at the back of his mind. And so he had promised to go and see her. And probably would have done so, this very afternoon.

It was too late now. She had been well and truly done to death, just as she had feared.

'See that they go over every inch of every room for fingerprints. Make sure they don't miss anything out, not even the least likely surfaces.'

There was a sudden commotion on the landing. He opened the front door. At least a dozen reporters and cameramen were crowding round the door, with a solitary constable struggling to hold them back.

A camera clicked in his face.

'Can you give us a statement, Chief Superintendent?'

'Not at the moment, gentlemen, I'm afraid. You might say that the enquiry hasn't really started yet.'

'Who was she?'

'An old lady.'

'Madame Antoine de Caramé. That much we got from the concierge. What's more, she says that one of your men was here earlier in the week asking questions about her. What was that in aid of? Had you any reason to think she was in danger?'

'All I can say at present is that I'm as much in the dark as you are.'

'Is it true that she lived alone, and never had any visitors?'

'As far as we know, that's correct, except for a niece — I don't know her name — who used to come and see her from time to time. She's a masseuse, and lives quite near here, just across the river not far from the Pont-Neuf.'

A brief statement to this effect had already been broadcast, and would also feature in the afternoon editions of the newspapers. As a result, no doubt the niece would in due course come forward.

'May we go in and take pictures?'

'Not yet. The men from Criminal Records haven't finished. For the time being, I'd be obliged if you would leave the landing and staircase clear.'

'We'll wait downstairs in the courtyard.'

Maigret closed the door. He had not yet had time to look round the flat. Overlooking the street was the sitting room, where Madame Antoine had been attacked, no doubt on returning from her daily outing to the Tuileries.

Had she been right in suspecting that someone was in the habit of entering the flat while she was out? It seemed more than likely. If so, there was somthing here that the intruder very badly wanted. But what could it possibly be?

She must have got home earlier than usual, and caught the intruder red-handed. At any rate, he had not hesitated to put her out of the way. That seemed to suggest that he was someone she recognised. If not, he could easily have taken to his heels. It therefore looked as if he had had no choice but to murder her.

'Any fingerprints?'

'None but the old lady's so far. Oh, and the Police Surgeon's on the table in the sitting room. I'd know them anywhere.'

There were two windows in the sitting room, which was low-ceilinged like the rest of the flat. A communicating door led into the dining room. Both rooms were quaintly old-fashioned, as old-fashioned as Madame Antoine herself. On a pedestal table in the corner stood an enormous green plant in an earthenware pot, which was swathed in drapery.

It was all spotlessly clean, and there was not a thing out of place.

There was only one window in the dining room, and, facing it, a door which led into the kitchen. The loaf in the breadbin was still fresh. Maigret opened the refrigerator. It contained, neatly wrapped in pieces of grease-proof paper, a slice of ham and half a veal cutlet. There were also a lettuce and a half bottle of milk.

There was only one other room, the bedroom. Like the kitchen, it looked out on to the courtyard. The bedroom suite, which included a massive mirror-fronted wardrobe and an imposing bed, was of walnut. The floorboards were covered by a faded, threadbare carpet, vaguely oriental in design.

There was an indefinable air of dignity about the whole place. He would have to come back later, after lunch, probably, and examine the old lady's possessions one by one, including the contents of the cupboards and drawers.

'We're through now, Chief.'

The police photographers were dismantling and removing their cameras. No fingerprints had been found, other than those of the old lady herself.

Maigret instructed the constable at the door to admit no one except the Inspector, whom he would be sending up in a moment. He went slowly down the dark staircase, with its worn treads, and banister polished to a high gloss by two or three hundred years of use.

In the courtyard, the pressmen were bombarding the concierge with questions, and getting short shrift for their pains. Lapointe, unusually silent, followed Maigret downstairs. He, too, was much shaken. He had a mental picture of Madame Antoine as he had seen her in the little office where he had interviewed her, and formed the impression that she was not quite right in the head.

The owner of the birds — Monsieur Caille presumably, since that was the name painted over the pet shop — wearing a long grey denim overall, was standing on the pavement beside a row of cages.

'I wonder if I might use your telephone?'

'With pleasure, Chief Superintendent.'

He gave a knowing smile, very pleased with himself for having recognised Maigret. The telephone was at the back of the shop where, in addition to more birds in cages, there were several tanks full of goldfish. An old man, also in a grey overall, was engaged in feeding the fish.

'Hello! ... Lucas? ... I shall be needing another man here ... Quai de la Mégisserie ... 8b ... Janvier? ... Fine ... Tell him to go straight up to the flat, and not let anyone else in ... And I'd be obliged if you'd ring my wife and tell her I won't be home to lunch....'

He put down the receiver and turned to the pet-shop owner.

'Have you lived here long?'

'Ever since I was ten years old. My father owned the shop before me.'

'So you've known Madame Antoine ever since she moved in?'

'Yes, it must be forty years. That was in the time of her first husband, Monsieur de Caramé. A fine-looking man, he was. Impressive. He was very high up in local government, and whenever there was a do at the Hôtel de Ville, he always gave us complimentary tickets.'

'Did they do much entertaining in those early days?'

'There were two or three married couples who were close friends of theirs. They used to get together for a game of cards about once a week.'

'What was Madame Antoine like?'

'She was a dear little thing. Very pretty. It's strange how things turn out, though. She was so frail and delicate, you'd never have thought she'd make old bones. He, on the other hand, was strongly built, and, as far as I know, never had a day's illness. He enjoyed the good things of life. Yet he was the one who died suddenly in his office, when he was in the prime of life, while his wife lived on — until yesterday.'

'And she remarried soon after?'

'Oh, no! She was alone for the best part of ten years. Then she met Monsieur Antoine somewhere or other, and eventually married him. I have nothing to say against him. He was a thoroughly decent chap, but, compared with her first husband, he lacked distinction.

'He worked in the Bazar de l'Hôtel de Ville. He was head of one of the departments, I believe. He was a widower. I daresay you've seen his little workshop up in the flat. He loved nothing better than to be pottering about in there. He never said much beyond passing the time of day. They hardly ever went out.

'He had a car, and used to take his wife for a drive in the country on Sundays. In the summer, they always went on holiday to a place somewhere near Etretat.'

'Were any of the other tenants friends of theirs?'

'I fancy I must be the only one left. The others have all died off in the course of the years, and new people have moved in to take their place. I never see any of the old faces nowadays.'

'There's Monsieur Crispin, don't forget, father,' interpolated the son, who was still standing in the doorway.

'True enough, but as one never sees him about now, it's hard to remember that he's still alive. He's paralysed — has been for the past five years. He has a couple of rooms on the fifth floor, and the concierge takes him up his meals and cleans the place for him.'

'Was he friendly with the Antoines?'

'Let me think. At my age, you tend to lose track of time. He moved in a little while before Madame Antoine. So Monsieur de Caramé must still have been alive. But I don't think they were on visiting terms at that time. It was only later, when Madame de Caramé married Monsieur Antoine, that they became friends. He was in business too, you see, haberdashery, I think. He worked in a shop in the Rue du Sentier.'

'I'm much obliged to you, Monsieur Caille.'

Janvier was waiting for him in the front hall.

'Have you eaten?'

'A snack, but what about you?'

'Lapointe and I are just off to lunch. I want you to go up and wait for us in the flat. It's on the first floor. Don't touch anything, anything at all, however insignificant. You'll find out why later. Oh! there's just one person you'll have to let in if she turns up, and that's the niece.'

Ten minutes later, Maigret and Lapointe were seated at a table in the Brasserie Dauphine.

'A small aperitif?' suggested the proprietor.

'No, bring us a carafe of Beaujolais right away. What have you got on the menu today?'

'*Andouillettes*. They arrived fresh from Auvergne this morning.'

Maigret ordered fillets of herring as a first course, to be follwed by the *andouillettes*.

'What do you think, yourself?' asked Maigret, a little uncomfortably.

Lapointe scarcely knew what to say.

'It never entered my head that she was telling the truth. I could have sworn that she was just imagining things, the way old people so often do.'

'She's dead.

'And if the door hadn't been left ajar, it might have been days before anyone found her. The murderer must have been someone she knew, otherwise there'd have been no need to kill her.'

'I wonder what it was he was looking for.'

'When we know that — if we ever do — the case will be

virtually solved. Very shortly, we shall be going over the flat inch by inch. There must be something there that the murderer very much wanted to find. He searched the place several times without success, so it's probably well-hidden or not immediately recognisable as such.'

'What if he's already found what he was looking for?'

'In that case, there's not much hope of catching him. All the other tenants will have to be questioned. How many floors are there in the building?'

'Six, excluding the attics.'

'And there are at least two flats on every floor...'

The Beaujolais could not have been better, and the *andouillettes,* served with chips, were quite delicious.

'There's one thing that puzzles me. Madame Antoine was eighty-six. She'd been a widow for twelve years or more. Why wait until now to start searching her flat? Surely that must mean that whatever it is that the intruder was looking for had only recently come into the old lady's possession?'

'If that were so, she would have known what it was. Whereas, if I'm not mistaken, she told you that she hadn't the least idea what it was all about.'

'She seemed just as puzzled as we were.'

There was no mystery about either of her husbands. Quite the reverse. Both were typical middle-class Frenchmen, except that one was rather better-looking than the other.'

Maigret beckoned the proprietor:

'Two coffees, Léon.'

The sun was still shining in a cloudless blue sky. The Quais were crowded with tourists with cameras slung round their necks.

The two men made their way back to the Quai de la Mégisserie. All but one of the reporters had left, and he was pacing restlessly up and down the courtyard.

'I don't suppose there's anything you can tell me?' he muttered, somewhat sourly.

'Nothing for the present.'

'There's a woman up there. She arrived about ten minutes ago, but she wouldn't give her name.'

It was not long before Maigret and Lapointe were making her acquaintance. She was a heavily built woman of somewhat mannish appearance, aged about forty-five to fifty. She was seated in one of the armchairs in the sitting room.

Janvier, apparently, had not attempted to engage her in conversation.

'You are Chief Superintendent Maigret?'

'Yes, and these two gentlemen are Inspectors Janvier and Lapointe.'

'I am Angèle Louette.'

'Madame?'

'No, I'm not married, though I have a son of twenty-five. I'm not ashamed of it. Quite the reverse.'

'You are Madame Antoine's niece, I take it?'

'She and my mother were sisters. She was the elder, for all that my mother was the first to go. She's been dead more than ten years now.'

'Does your son live with you?'

'No. I'm on my own. I have a small flat in the Rue Saint-André-des-Arts.'

'And your son?'

'He moves around a good deal. At present, I believe he's on the Côte d'Azur. He's a musician.'

'When did you last see your aunt?'

'About three weeks ago.'

'Did you visit her often?'

'About once a month. Sometimes once in two months.'

'Did you get on well with her?'

'We didn't have rows.'

'Which means...?'

'We were never at all close. My aunt was a mistrustful old woman. I'm certain she believed I only came to see her so as to keep on good terms with her, in the hope of inheriting her money.'

'Had she anything to leave?'

'She must have had savings, but I shouldn't think they amounted to much.'

'Do you know if she had a bank account?'

'If so, she never told me. What she was always on about

was that I should see to it that she was buried beside her first husband in Montparnasse cemetery. She has a plot there.

'If you want my opinion, I believe she only remarried for the sake of company. She was still young. I don't know where she met my uncle Antoine. The first I heard of it was one day when she announced, out of the blue, that she was getting married again, and asked me to be a witness....'

Maigret was taking in every word, having indicated to Lapointe, who had got out his shorthand pad, that he did not wish him to take notes. She was the kind of woman who would probably shut up like a clam if subjected to an official interrogation.

'Tell me, Mademoiselle Louette, do you know of any reason why your aunt should have gone in fear of her life?'

'None at all.'

'Did she tell you that she had found traces of a mysterious intruder in the flat?'

'No, never.'

'Did she ever ring you up or call to see you?'

'No. I always came to see her. Just from time to time, you know, to make sure she was all right, and to find out if there was anything she needed. It worried me that she lived on her own. Anything might have happened to her, and not a soul would have known.'

'Did she never consider having a daily woman in to do the housework?'

'She could well have afforded it, on her two widow's pensions. I begged her to get someone to live in, but she wouldn't even entertain the idea of a daily. You can see how she kept the flat. Not a speck of dust anywhere.'

'You are a masseuse, I believe.'

'Yes, my time is fully occupied. I have nothing to complain of.'

'Tell me about your son's father.'

'He left me when my son was born. I wasn't sorry to see him go. He wasn't the man I thought him. I lost my head over him, as they say. I've no idea what's become of him, and I daresay I shouldn't recognise him now if I met him in the street.'

'I take it, then, that your son bears your name, and has a "father unknown" birth certificate?'

'Yes. His name is Emile Louette. But since he took up the guitar and became a night club entertainer, he's become known, for professional purposes, as Billy Louette.'

'Are you and he on good terms?'

'He comes to see me occasionally, usually when he's short of money. He's an out-and-out Bohemian, but he's a good lad, all the same.'

'Did he ever come and see his aunt?'

'I used to bring him with me when he was a child. The last time was when be was fifteen or sixteen, I think. As far as I know, he's never seen her since.'

'Might he not have come to her for money, as he did to you?'

'He wouldn't do a thing like that. I'm his mother, so that's different, but he would never ask anyone else. He's too proud.'

'Do you know your way around this flat?'

'Pretty well.'

'Where did your aunt spend most of her time?'

'Here, in this very armchair, drawn up close to the window.'

'How did she keep herself occupied?'

'First of all, she had the housework to do. Then she'd go out and do her shopping. When she got back, she cooked herself a meal. She wasn't the sort to make do with a slice of cold meat eaten off a corner of the kitchen table. In spite of the fact that she lived alone, she took her meals in the dining room, and the table was always properly laid, with a clean cloth.'

'Did she go out much?'

'On fine days, she liked to go and sit on a bench in the Tuileries.'

'Did she read a lot?'

'No. She had weak eyesight, and it tired her to read for any length of time. She enjoyed watching the people out for a stroll, and the children playing among the trees. She almost always wore a rather sad little smile. I daresay she lived in the past a good deal.'

'Did she never confide in you?'

'What could she possibly have had to tell me? Her life was an open book.'

'Hadn't she any friends?'

'All her old friends had died, and she didn't feel like making new ones; and that was why she moved away from the bench she had always sat on. I've just remembered.'

'How long ago was this?'

'Towards the end of last summer. For years she'd always sat on the same bench in the Tuileries Gardens. One day, she was approached by a woman of about her own age, who asked if she might share the bench with her. Presumably she said yes. Anyone is at liberty to sit down on a park bench. At any rate, this woman tried to strike up an acquaintance with her from the very first day. She told her that she was of Russian origin, and that she had been, in her day, a famous ballerina.

'Next day, she was there again, and spent an hour regaling my aunt with tales of her former glory. She had lived in Nice for years, and she went on and on about the awful Paris weather.

'My aunt wasn't given to idle chatter as a rule.

' "I had become so attached to that bench!" she said, with a sigh.

' "Not only was I forced to move away from it, but I had to go right to the other side of the Gardens, otherwise she'd have found me out, and I would never have got away from her." '

'Did this Russian woman ever visit her here?'

'Not that I know of. My aunt being what she was, I'm pretty sure she never got the chance.'

'You can't throw any light on the identity of the murderer, I suppose?'

'I'm afraid not, Chief Superintendent. What am I to do about the funeral arrangements?'

'You'd better let me have your telephone number. I'll be in touch. By the way, do you happen to have a recent photograph of your aunt?'

'Only one taken by my uncle Antoine about twelve years ago. I'd be grateful if you'd ring me in the evening, as I'm out at work most of the day.'

*

The police constable detailed to keep watch on the entrance was still there.

'What do you make of her, Chief?'

'She seems ready enough to talk. Rather a bossy woman, I'd say.'

Janvier looked about him in astonishment.

'Is it all like this?'

'Yes. The bedroom, if anything, is even more old-world. Lapointe, you know the layout of the building, more or less. I want you to call at all the flats. Find out which of the tenants knew the old lady by sight, and whether any of them were at all friendly with her. Also, of course, whether they ever saw anyone entering or leaving the flat.'

The only concession to the twentieth century was the television set in the sitting room. It stood in a corner, opposite an armchair upholstered in flowered chintz.

'Now,' said Maigret to Janvier, 'we're going to go over the flat inch by inch, recording the exact position of everything in it. It was the fact that she found some of her things very slightly displaced that first gave her cause for anxiety.'

The shrunken floorboards, with gaps between, were covered not with a carpet but with scattered rugs, on one of which stood a round tripod table covered in a lace cloth.

They moved the table and took up the rug, to satisfy themselves that nothing was hidden under it. Having done so, they returned the table to its original position and carefully put back the ornaments, a large seashell with *Dieppe* carved on it, an earthenware plant pot, and a fake bronze statuette of a schoolboy in a sailor suit with a satchel on his back.

The mantelpiece was covered in photographs, photographs of two men, the two husbands of the old lady, who, towards the end, it seemed, had almost forgotten which was which. One of them, round-faced, plumpish and clean-shaven, had struck a dignified attitude before the camera. He, no doubt, was the one who had been a senior official at the Hôtel de Ville.

The other, somewhat less impressive, had a greying moustache. Men like him were to be seen in their thousands every day on the buses and the underground. He looked more like a shop assistant or a cashier than the manager or buyer of a large store, which was what he had actually been. He was smiling in the photograph, a cheerful smile. He had been content with his lot.

'By the way, Janvier, how did the niece get in? Had she a key?'

'No, she rang the bell, and I let her in.'

'This drawer is locked. The key must be somewhere about.'

First he searched through the contents of the old lady's handbag, the white leather handbag which she must only recently have got out of her wardrobe, for use in the spring and summer. There was no lipstick, just a powder compact — the powder had a bluish tinge — and a handkerchief embroidered with the initial 'L'. Madame Antoine's Christian name, as the two men were soon to find out, had been Léontine.

No cigarettes. Obviously she didn't smoke. A small bag of violet-scented sweets from a shop in the Rue de Rivoli. The sweets must have been there for some time, as they were all stuck together.

'Here are the keys.'

He had been almost sure that he would find her keys in the handbag that went everywhere with her. There were three drawer keys, a key to one of the rooms and the front door key.

'She opened the door and put the keys back in her bag before coming in. Otherwise, they would have been left in the lock, or we should have found them on the floor. She must barely have had time to put her bag down on the chair before she was attacked.'

Maigret was not so much addressing Janvier as thinking aloud. He could not get rid of a nagging sense of uneasiness. Yet, even supposing he had been to see the old lady, would it have made that much difference? He would not have been able to find enough evidence to justify keeping a twenty-four hour watch on the flat. And the murderer, unaware of his visit, would still have acted as he did.

He tried the smaller keys, one after the other, and finally succeeded in opening the locked drawer of the chest.

It was full of papers and photographs. On the right-hand side lay a Post Office Savings book in the name of Léontine Antoine, Quai de la Mégisserie, recording deposits amounting to ten thousand francs; nothing but deposits, not a single withdrawal. She had been paying money into the account for twenty-five years, which was why the name Caramé could still be read, with a line through it, below the name Antoine.

Twenty-five years of thrift. Shopping in the morning. An hour or so on a park bench in the afternoon, perhaps an occasional visit to a cinema when the weather was bad. There was also a Savings Bank book, recording a total of twenty-three thousand two hundred francs. A few days before Christmas in the previous year, there had been a withdrawal of two thousand five hundred francs.

'What does that suggest to you?'

Janvier shook his head.

'The television set. I bet you anything you like that's where the two thousand five hundred francs went. In other words, she decided to give herself a treat for Christmas.'

The only other recorded withdrawal was twelve years old, and no doubt represented the cost of her second husband's funeral.

There were numerous postcards, most of them signed 'Jean'. They bore the postmarks of various towns and cities in France, Belgium and Switzerland. The sender, no doubt, had been attending conferences in these places. All the cards bore the same message: 'Much Love, Jean' in a distinguished, roundish hand. 'Jean' was Caramé. Antoine, apparently, had seldom been away on his own. There was not a single card from him. But there were innumerable photographs both of him alone and of him and his wife. The camera with which they had been taken, rather a sophisticated one, was also in the same drawer. Monsieur and Madame Antoine, it seemed, had gone to a different place each year for their holiday. Apparently, they had been great travellers. They had visited Quimper, La Baule, Arcachon and Biarritz. They had toured the Massif Central, and spent summers on the Riviera.

The photographs had been taken at different times, in some the couple appeared older than in others. It would have been a simple matter to arrange them in chronological order.

There were a few letters, mostly from Angèle Louette, the niece who was a masseuse. These, too, came from towns outside Paris.

'Emile and I are thoroughly enjoying our holiday. Emile is growing up fast. He spends all day rolling over and over in the sand....'

There was just one photograph of the boy, Emile, who was now calling himself Billy. It was taken when he was fifteen. He was looking straight in front of him, with an expression that spelt defiance of the whole world.

'No secrets. No surprises,' sighed Maigret.

In the drawer of a little occasional table they found nothing but some pencils, a pen, a rubber, and a few sheets of plain writing paper. Of late, Léontine had probably written few letters. Who was there left for her to write to?

She had outlived most of her contemporaries. Her niece and great-nephew were her only remaining relatives, and the boy scarcely counted. There was no trace of him among her effects, except for that one photograph, and the references in his mother's letter.

Sorting through the kitchen utensils, Maigret came upon several gadgets which were unfamiliar to him, and which did not look as though they were mass-produced. There was, for instance, a tin opener of highly sophisticated design, as well as a simple but ingenious potato-peeler.

It was not until he discovered the little cubby hole across the way that he understood the significance of these appliances. The key to the door was on Madame Antoine's keyring. It opened on to a tiny annexe, quite separate from the flat itself, which was lit by a skylight overlooking the courtyard. This annexe was furnished with a workbench and a wide selection of tools, hanging neatly from hooks all round the walls.

This, then, was where Monsieur Antoine had pursued his hobby. On a shelf in one corner stood a pile of technical journals, and there was a drawer full of exercise books filled with working drawings of all kinds, including a drawing of the potato-peeler.

There must be thousands of people like him all over Paris, thought Maigret, thousands of couples like the Antoines, living modest, tidy, well-organised lives. There was only one discordant note, the murder of the tiny little old woman with the marvellously clear grey eyes.

'There's still the bedroom and the cupboards.'

The entire contents of the wardrobe consisted of a Persian lamb coat, another of black wool, two winter dresses, one of which was mauve, and three or four summer dresses.

No men's clothes. After the death of her second husband she must have given away his things, unless she had stored them somewhere, possibly in the attics? He must find out from the concierge.

Everything was very clean and tidy, and all the drawers were lined with white paper.

But the lining paper of the bedside table drawer, which incidentally was empty, was discoloured by a large oil or grease stain.

Maigret, intrigued, took the paper out of the drawer and held it up to his nose. He called Janvier over to see what he would make of it.

'What do you think this is?'

'Grease.'

'Yes, but not just any sort of grease. It's gun-grease. The old lady must have kept a revolver or an automatic in this drawer.'

'Where is it now?'

'Not in the flat, that's for sure. We've searched every

inch, and we haven't found it. All the same, it looks quite fresh to me. Do you suppose the old woman's killer...'

It seemed highly unlikely that the murderer, whether man or woman, would have spent time looking for the revolver before making his or her getaway.

This grease-stain, which he had not discovered until the very end of his search, was a complication that he had not anticipated.

Had the old woman actually gone to the length of buying a gun to defend herself with? It seemed unlikely. From what Maigret had seen of her, she was hardly the sort to look upon firearms with anything but alarm. Moreover, he simply could not imagine her going into a gunsmith's, asking for a pistol, and trudging down to the basement for a few practice shots.

And yet, when all was said and done, why not? Hadn't he been struck by her extraordinary vitality? Frail she certainly had been, with her delicate wrists no thicker than a child's, yet her flat was as well cared for as any in the land, even better perhaps.

'It must have belonged to one of her husbands.'

'But where has it got to then? See that this paper is handed in to the lab for analysis. Though I'm quite sure in my own mind what the answer will be.'

A bell rang, and Maigret instinctively looked around for the telephone.

'It's the front door,' said Janvier.

He went to open it. It was Lapointe, looking absolutely worn out.

'Have you spoken to all the tenants?'

'All except those who were out. The worst of it is, I could hardly get a word in with any of them. It was nothing but questions, questions, questions! How did she die? What was the murder weapon? How come that no one had heard a shot?'

'Go on.'

'The flat immediately above is occupied by an elderly bachelor of about sixty. Apparently, he's quite a well-known historian. I saw some of his books on his library shelves. He seldom goes out. He lives alone with his little dog. He has a housekeeper who comes in daily to clean the flat and cook his meals. I say a housekeeper because that's how he described her. I saw her for myself. She's known as Mademoiselle Elise, and she's full of her own importance.

'It's almost as old-fashioned as this flat, except that it's furnished in better taste. In passing he said:

' "If only she hadn't bought that wretched television set! She had it on almost every night until eleven. And I'm up every morning at six, so as to get in my regular walk before breakfast." '

Lapointe went on:

'They never exchanged a word in all the twenty years he's been living here. When they met on the stairs, they merely nodded. He remembers the husband because he was noisy too. Apparently he had a workshop and a regular armoury of tools, and he would be sawing, hammering, filing, and heaven knows what else until all hours.'

'What about the flat opposite?'

'There was no one at home. I went down to the concierge to enquire about them. They're youngish people, apparently. He's a film technician, some sort of sound engineer, and his wife works in the cutting room. They usually dine out, and get home very late. They're late risers too, and they don't leave for work until midday.'

'And the third floor?'

Lapointe glanced at his notes.

'Some people called Lapin. There was no one in but the grandmother and the baby. The wife works in a men's wear shop in the Rue de Rivoli, and the husband is an insurance salesman. He's away a lot.'

'What about the flat opposite?'

'I'll come to them in a minute. I spoke to the grandmother, and she said:

' "No, young man, I did not know her. That woman was too clever by half, if you ask me. Look at the way she behaved with those two husbands of hers. I'm a widow myself, but did I go out looking for another husband? You wouldn't catch me setting up house with another man, in the same flat, with the same furniture." '

Once again, Lapointe consulted his notes.

'Father Raymond. I don't know which order he belongs to. He's very old, and scarcely ever sets foot outside his flat.

'He didn't even know of the existence of Léontine Antoine, formerly Léontine de Caramé....

'On the floor above, there's an empty flat, let to people who will be moving in in two weeks' time. The workmen are there now, redecorating. The new tenants are a couple of about forty, with two children at the lycée.

'I interviewed the old man the concierge does for. He's confined to a wheel chair, and you should just see how he gets around in it! I was expecting to see a querulous old dodderer, but not a bit of it, he's as chirpy as a cricket:

' "You don't say! " he exclaimed. "So she's actually gone and got herself murdered! I've been here fifty years or more, and nothing of any interest has ever happened before. And now we have a murder of our very own! Do you know who did it? I don't suppose it could possibly be a *crime passionel*, do you?" '

Lapointe went on:

'It was really comical. He was enjoying himself hugely. If it had been physically possible, he would have asked permission to visit the scene of the crime.

'The woman opposite is a Madame Blanche. She's about sixty, and works as a cashier in a brasserie. I didn't see her, as she doesn't get in before midnight.'

It was a tight little world that all these people lived in side by side, and yet the murder of the old lady on the first floor had caused scarcely a ripple.

'How was she killed?'

'Who did it?'

'Why didn't she call out?'

Most of these people knew one another by sight, and would nod in passing, without exchanging a word. A lot of little private cells, with the doors shut tight.

'I want you to stay here until I send someone to relieve you,' Maigret said to Janvier.

'It may seem far-fetched, but I have a notion that the

man or woman who searched this flat before may well be minded to do so again.'

'Send Torrence, if you can spare him. He's potty about television.'

Maigret took the grease-stained lining-paper with him. As soon as he got back to the Quai des Orfèvres he went straight up to Moers in his domain in the attics.

'I want this stain analysed.'

Moers sniffed at it, nodded to Maigret as if to assure him that this was no problem, and went over to one of the many technicians at work in the huge laboratory under the sloping roof of the building.

'It's as I thought, gun-grease.'

'I shall need an official report. It's the only clue we've got so far. Is it an old stain, would you say?'

'My man says that that will take a little time to establish.'

'Thanks. Send down the result when you have it.'

He returned to his office, calling into the Inspectors' Duty Room on the way. Lapointe was writing up his report, with his notebook open beside him. Torrence was also there.

'See here, Torrence, are you hungry?'

Fat Torrence stared at him in amazement.

'At five o'clock in the afternoon?'

'You probably won't get a chance to eat later on. Go and get a snack now, or if you'd rather, buy yourself some sandwiches. I want you to go to the Quai de la Mégisserie and relieve Janvier. It's the first floor flat. I'll send someone to relieve you first thing in the morning. You'll find the keys on the round table in the sitting room.

'Watch yourself, though, because the murderer must have a key to the front door. Otherwise there would have been signs of a forced entry.'

'Do you think he'll come back?'

'In this extraordinary case, anything might happen.'

Maigret rang through to Doctor Forniaux.

'Have you finished the autopsy yet?'

'I was just about to dictate my report. Would you believe it, that diminutive little old woman could well have lived to be a hundred? You wouldn't find many young girls with organs in a healthier condition.

'As I suspected from the first, she was suffocated; almost certainly with a scarf with scarlet threads in it. I found one lodged in a tooth. She tried to bite through it. She almost certainly put up a struggle, before she blacked out for want of air.'

'Thanks, doc. Let me have your report as soon as you can.'

'You'll get it tomorrow, by the first post.'

Léontine Antoine did not drink, at least she kept no wines or spirits in her flat. She ate a lot of cheese. The Chief Superintendent, standing by the window watching the traffic flow across the Pont Saint-Michel, pondered, trying to recreate the details of her life. A string of barges went under the bridge, drawn by a tug with an enormous white clover leaf painted on the funnel.

The sky was a delicate pink, faintly tinged with blue, the trees, not yet in full leaf, were pale green, and full of twittering birds.

It was at this moment that the constable who had first noticed the old lady arrived, asking to speak to the Chief Superintendent.

'I don't know if it's important — I've only just seen the photographs in the papers — but, you see, I recognised the old lady at once. What I mean to say is, that I saw her almost a week ago. I was on guard duty at the main gate. She wandered up and down outside for some time gazing up at the windows, and peering into the forecourt. I thought she was about to speak to me, but then she seemed to change her mind, and she went away without saying a word.

'She was back next day, and, this time, she plucked up the courage to go through into the forecourt. I didn't attempt to stop her. I thought she was just an ordinary tourist. We get so many of them...

'The following day, I was off duty. Lecoeur was on in my place, and he saw her go through the gate, and make straight for the Police Headquarters entrance. She looked so determined that he didn't even think to ask her if she had an appointment.'

'Thanks. Let me have a statement in writing, and one from Lecoeur too.'

So several days had gone by before she had been able to pluck up the courage to ask to see Chief Superintendent Maigret. And he had fobbed her off with Lapointe, whom she had at first taken to be his son.

But this had not prevented her from accosting the Chief Superintendent later, in the street.

Old Joseph was knocking at the door. There was no mistaking that distinctive knock. He opened it before Maigret had time to say 'Come in.'

He handed him a slip bearing the name *Billy Louette.*

Yet, only a few hours earlier, the masseuse had claimed that her son was away, somewhere on the Riviera.

'Bring him in, Joseph.'

CHAPTER THREE

'You've been trying to get in touch with me, I daresay?'

'Not yet. I understood from your mother that you were on the Côte d'Azur.'

'Oh, pay no attention to her! ... May I smoke?'

'Certainly, if you wish.'

The young man appeared by no means overawed. The precincts of Police Headquarters held no terrors for him, and, as far as he was concerned, Maigret was a policeman like any other.

But the impression he created was not that of a rebel or exhibitionist. His red hair was on the long side, but he was no hippy. He wore a check shirt, suede waistcoat, beige corduroy trousers, and moccasins.

'As soon as I read about my aunt in the paper, I felt sure you would want to see me.'

'I'm very glad you've come.'

He bore no resemblance to the masseuse. Whereas she was tall and heavily built, with shoulders like a man, he was small-boned and rather thin, with eyes as blue as periwinkles. Maigret, seated at his desk, motioned to the armchair facing him.

'Thank you. What was it exactly that happened yesterday? There's very little in the papers.'

'We know no more than they have reported, which is that she was murdered.'

'Was anything stolen?'

'Apparently not.'

'Anyway, she never kept much money in the flat.'

'How do you know that?'

'I used to go and see her occasionally.'

'When funds were low?'

'That goes without saying. There was nothing else for us to talk about. We had no interests in common.'

'Did she give you money?'

'As a rule, a hundred-franc note, but it wouldn't have done to ask too often.'

'You're a musician, I believe?'

'Of a sort, yes. I play the guitar. I work with a small group. We call ourselves the Bad Lads.'

'Do you make a living out of it?'

'We have our ups and downs. Sometimes we get a booking at a high-class night club, at other times we play in cafés. What did my mother say about me?'

'Nothing in particular.'

'Don't imagine she's overflowing with mother love. For one thing, we're so very different. She thinks of nothing but money, saving up for her old age, she calls it. If she could do without food, she would, so as to have more in the kitty.'

'Was she fond of your aunt?'

'She couldn't stand her. Many a time I've heard her say, with a sigh:

' "I do believe the old fool will live for ever! " '

'Why should she have wished her dead?'

'For the money, of course. The old woman, with her two widow's pensions, must have had a tidy bit put by.

'Mind you, I was fond of the old girl. And I think she liked me. She always insisted on making coffee, and serving it up to me with biscuits.

' "I'm sure there are days when you can't afford to eat. Why don't you take a training course of some sort, and get a decent job?"

'My mother felt the same way. She'd made up her mind before I was fifteen what she wanted me to be ... she had dreams of turning me into an osteopath:

' "They're in such demand that patients often have to

wait a month for an appointment. It's not uninteresting, and the pay is good." '

'When did you last go and see your great-aunt?'

'About three weeks ago. We'd been to London on spec. We were hoping to get a booking, but they've got all the groups they want over there, and most of them are a lot better than we are. So we had to give up and come home, and I went to see the old girl.'

'Did she give you your hundred francs?'

'Yes. And my biscuits.'

'Where do you live?'

'I move around a good deal. Sometimes I'm with a girl, sometimes on my own, as I am at the moment. I've got a furnished room in a small hotel in the Rue Mouffetard.'

'Are you in work?'

'In a manner of speaking. Do you know the Bongo?'

Maigret shook his head. The young man seemed surprised that there should be anyone who had not heard of the Bongo.

'It's a little café-restaurant in the Place Maubert. The proprietor comes from Auvergne. It didn't take him long to see what was happening in the Saint-Germain district. He sets up to run a hippy joint, and he sometimes lets them have free drinks. He's always glad to give a free dinner, and a few francs over, to any performer willing to put on a show. That's us. We do two or three shows a night. And then there's Line. She's a singer. She's got a fabulous voice.

'That's how he fetches in the customers. They come in droves to get a closer look at the notorious hippies, and when we tell them we don't smoke pot or hash, they won't believe us.'

'Do you intend to go on playing?'

'I should hope so. It's the only thing I care about. I've even started composing, though I haven't found my form yet. I can say this, at any rate, I didn't kill the old girl. First of all, killing people isn't my thing, and, secondly, I'd have known I'd be a prime suspect.'

'Did you have a key to the flat?'

'What on earth for?'

'Where were you round about six yesterday evening?'

'In bed.'

'Alone?'

'Alone at last, yes. We'd been at the Bongo nearly all night. I picked up a swell chick. She was Scandinavian, Danish or Swedish, I think. We'd had a lot to drink. In the small hours I took her back to my room. And it wasn't until three o'clock in the afternoon that I was able to get some sleep.

'Sometime later, I felt the bed creak, and heard noises. I was still half asleep. All I knew was that there was no longer anyone beside me in the bed.

'I felt battered, drained, and my mouth was like the bottom of a birdcage. I didn't get up until after nine.'

'In other words, no one saw you between, say, five and eight?'

'That's right.'

'Could you get in touch with the girl again?'

'If she's not at the Bongo tonight, she'll be in some other joint nearby.'

'Was she someone you already knew?'

'No.'

'She's a new one, then?'

'It's not like that at all. They drift in and they drift out. I told you we'd been to London. Well, we went to Copenhagen on spec as well. Wherever we go, we make friends right away.'

'Do you know her name?'

'Only her christian name. It's Hilda. I also happen to know that her father is something quite high up in the Civil Service.'

'How old is she?'

'Twenty-two, or so she said. I don't know who it was she had arranged to meet up with. If she hadn't, she'd probably have stayed with me for weeks. That's how it goes. Then, after a time, one drifts apart, without quite knowing why. No hard feelings, though.'

'Tell me about you and your mother.'

'As I said, we don't get on.'

'She brought you up, didn't she?'

'Not from choice. That was one of the things she had against the old girl. She hoped she'd offer to look after me. As she had to go out to work, she dumped me in a day nursery every morning, and fetched me on her way home at night. It was the same when I was at school.

'She didn't want a child about the place, especially when there was a man around. I was an embarrassment.'

'Were there many men?'

'They came and went. One lived with us for six months. He spent most of the day loafing around the house. I was made to call him "Daddy"....'

'Didn't he have a job?'

'He was supposed to be a commercial traveller, but he did precious little travelling. At other times, I'd hear noises in the night, but there was no one there in the morning. They were nearly all young men, especially of late.

'About a fortnight ago, I ran into her in the Boulevard Saint-Germain. She was with a bloke I've often seen around the night clubs. Everyone calls him Le Grand Marcel.'

'Do you know him?'

'Not personally, but he's reputed to be a pimp. And then, of course, she's fond of the bottle.'

He was cynical, yet at the same time refreshingly candid.

'Mind you, I'm not saying I suspect my mother of having killed the old girl. She is what she is, and I am what I am, and there's no changing either of us. Maybe I shall become a star, and maybe I'll be a flop, like so many others in Saint-Germain. Was there anything else you wanted to ask me?'

'A number of things, I daresay, but for the moment they escape me. Are you happy as you are?'

'Most of the time, yes.'

'Wouldn't you have been better off if you had done as your mother wished, and become an osteopath? You would probably have been married with children by this time.'

'It wouldn't suit me. Later, perhaps.'

'How did you feel when you heard of your great-aunt's death?'

'My heart missed a beat. I didn't know her well. To me she was just a very old woman, who, by rights, should have been put underground long ago. All the same, I was fond of her. It was those eyes of hers, and her smile.

' "Eat up," she used to say.

'And she used to watch me eat those biscuits of hers with a kind of loving concern. Apart from my mother, I was all she had in the way of a family.

' "Are you really quite set on wearing your hair so long?"

'That was the thing that upset her most.

' "It makes you look something different from what you really are. Because underneath it all, you're a good boy." '

'When is the funeral to be?'

'I can't say yet. Leave your address with me, and I'll let you know. It will probably be the day after tomorrow. It really depends on the Examining Magistrate.'

'Did she suffer, do you think?'

'She put up very little resistance. Do you, by any chance, own a red scarf, or at least one with red in it?'

'I never wear a scarf. Why do you ask?'

'No reason. I'm feeling my way, that's all.'

'Do you suspect anyone?'

'I wouldn't go as far as that.'

'Could it be some sort of perverted sex crime?'

'Why pick on Madame Antoine in particular, and why attack her at home, with the building swarming with people? No, the murderer was looking for something.'

'Money?'

'I'm not sure. If he was someone who knew her, he would have been aware that she never had more than a few francs in cash. Besides, he visited the flat several times while the old lady was out. Do you happen to know if she owned anything of value?'

'She had a few bits of jewellery, nothing of great value, just trinkets given her by her two husbands.'

Maigret had seen them, a garnet ring with ear-rings to match, a gold bracelet and a small gold watch.

There were, in the same box, a pearl tiepin and a pair of silver cufflinks, which must have belonged to Caramé. All old-fashioned stuff, worth virtually nothing on the open market.

'Had she any papers?'

'What do you mean by papers? She was just an ordinary old woman, who lived a quiet life with her first husband, and then later with her second. Caramé died before I was born, so I never met him, but I knew the other one, Joseph Antoine. He was a good sort....'

Maigret stood up with a sigh.

'Do you often visit your mother?'

'Hardly ever.'

'You don't happen to know, do you, whether she's living alone at the moment, or whether this Monsieur Marcel you mentioned is with her?'

'I don't, I'm afraid.'

'I'm very grateful to you for having come, Monsieur Louette. I'd like to see your show some night, if I can find the time.'

'About eleven is the best time to come.'

'I'm usually in bed by then.'

'Am I still a suspect?'

'Until I have evidence to the contrary, everyone is suspect, but you are no more suspect than anyone else.'

Maigret shut the door behind the young man, and went across to lean out of the window. It was already dusk. Everything looked a little blurred. He had learned a great many new facts, but none of them was of any use to him.

What could anybody possibly want from the old woman's home in the Quai de la Mégisserie?

She had lived in the same flat for over forty years. There was no mystery about her first husband, and after he died she had lived on there alone for nearly ten years.

As far as one could tell, there had been no mystery about her second husband either. He had been dead for years, and since his death she had led an uneventful existence, seeing no one except her niece and great-nephew.

Why had no one ever tried to break into her flat before? Was it because what the intruder was looking for had been there only a short time?

With a little grunt and a shrug, he opened the door to

the Inspectors' Duty Room.

'See you all tomorrow.'

Travelling home on the bus, he reflected that there was no other calling quite like his own. He did not know the names of his fellow passengers, yet he never knew from one moment to the next whether he might be having to shoulder his way into the life of any one of them.

He rather liked the young man with the long red hair, but his only interest in the mother was to find out the answers to several very personal questions.

As usual, Madame Maigret had the door open almost before he was across the landing.

'You look worried.'

'And with good reason. I'm caught up in something I simply don't understand.'

'The murder of the old woman?'

Naturally, she had read the paper and heard the news broadcast.

'Did you ever see her alive?'

'Yes.'

'What was she like?'

'I thought she was mad, or at least not quite right in the head. She was a tiny little thing, she looked as if a puff of wind would blow her away. She begged me to help her. The way she talked, you'd have thought that I was the only person in the world who could.'

'Didn't you do anything?'

'I couldn't very well detail an inspector to keep watch on her night and day.

'There was so little to go on. All she could say was that, once or twice, she had come home to her flat to find some of her things very slightly out of place.

'I confess I thought she was imagining things, or that her memory was playing her tricks. All the same, I had made up my mind to go and see her, if only to reassure her. Yesterday, she must have got home earlier than usual, and found the intruder still in her flat.

'It was all too easy to silence her. It needed no more than a scarf or a dishcloth held over her face for a minute or two....'

'Had she any family?'

'Just one niece, and a great-nephew. I've seen them both. The niece is a great hefty woman, more like a man. She's a masseuse. The young man, on the other hand, is small and thin and red-headed. He plays the guitar in a night club in the Place Maubert.'

'Has anything been stolen?'

'Impossible to say. There's just one thing, and it's not much to go on. She used to keep a revolver in her bedside table drawer, but it's not there now.'

'Surely no one would kill an old woman in cold blood just for the sake of a revolver? And it wouldn't need several visits to find it.'

'Let's eat!'

They dined facing one another across the table near the open window. Neither of them felt like watching television. It was a very mild evening. The air was still. As the night drew on, a pleasant light breeze blew up, creating a faint whisper among the leaves of the trees.

'As you weren't home for lunch, I've warmed up the lamb stew.'

'I'm delighted to hear it.'

He ate with relish, but his thoughts were elsewhere. He could not forget his meeting with the old lady in grey, on the pavement of the Quai des Orfèves. He could still see her looking up at him, her eyes bright with trust and admiration.

'Why don't you forget it, just for tonight?'

'I wish I could. I can't help myself. If there's one thing I hate, it's letting people down, and, as things turned out, it cost the poor old dear her life.'

'Let's go for a walk.'

He agreed. There was no point in moping around the flat all evening. Besides, it was his way — one might almost call it an obsession — when he was on a case, to establish a routine and adhere to it day after day.

They walked to the Bastille, and sat for a little while on a café terrace. A long-haired youth with a guitar strummed as he made his way among the tables, followed by a black-eyed girl holding out a saucer.

Needless to say, he was reminded of the redhead who, no doubt, when times were hard, had also done his stint as a café entertainer.

Maigret's contribution was more than generous, a fact which did not escape his wife. She said nothing, however, but merely smiled to herself. They sat on for some time, in silence, gazing out at the lights of the city.

He puffed gently at his pipe. At one point, he almost suggested going to the Bongo. But what was the use? What could he hope to find out beyond what he already knew?

The tenants of the building in the Quai de la Mégisserie were also suspects. Any of them might have known the old lady better than they were prepared to admit. It would have been easy enough for anyone to take a wax impression of the lock, and get a key cut to fit it.

But why? This was the question that haunted Maigret. Why? Why? What was the object of those repeated visits to the flat? Certainly not for the sake of the few francs the old lady kept there. There had been several hundred francs in the chest of drawers, just lying there for anyone to take. But they had not been taken. Maigret had found them inside the cover of the old lady's Post Office Savings book.

'Tomorrow, I'll start enquiring into the lives and backgrounds of the two husbands.'

It was absurd, really, especially taking into account how long the second husband had been dead.

Nevertheless, there was a secret somewhere, a secret important enough to warrant the taking of a human life.

'Shall we go?'

He had drunk a small glass of Calvados, and had just stopped himself in time from ordering another. His friend Pardon would have been displeased with him for even contemplating it. Maigret remembered his solemn warning just in time:

'One can drink wines and spirits for years without any ill effects, but a time comes when the system will no longer tolerate them.'

He shrugged, got up, and threaded his way between the tables. In the street, Madame Maigret took his arm. The Boulevard Beaumarchais. The Rue Servan. At last the

Boulevard Richard-Lenoir and their much-loved, shabby old flat.

Contrary to his expectations, he fell asleep almost at once.

*

The night passed without incident in the flat in the Quai de la Mégisserie, and fat Torrence was able to enjoy a full night's sleep in the old lady's armchair.

At eight in the morning, Loutrie arrived to relieve him, and found the concierge deep in conversation with a newspaper reporter.

At nine, Maigret, brooding and grumpy, pushed open the door of the Inspectors' room, and beckoned to Janvier and Lapointe.

'On second thoughts, Lucas, you'd better come too.'

He sat down at his desk, and proceeded to make a ceremony of choosing a pipe from his pipe-rack.

'Well, lads, we're no further forward than we were this time yesterday. As we don't seem to be able to find any lead in the present, we're going to do a little probing into the past. I want you to go to the Bazar de l'Hôtel de Ville, Lucas, the ironmongery department. There must still be people working there who knew old Antoine.

'Ask as many questions as you like. Find out all you can about the old boy, his personality, his interests, everything.'

'Will do, Chief. Mightn't it be better if I got the consent of the management first? They couldn't very well refuse, and the members of staff would probably feel freer to talk than if I approached them in an underhand way.'

'Agreed. As for you, Janvier, I want you to go to the Hôtel de Ville and do the same for Caramé. It will be more difficult, because he's been dead so much longer. If any of his contemporaries are still living in retirement, get their addresses and go and see them.'

All this was just routine, of course, but sometimes routine paid off.

'Lapointe, I want you with me.'

Downstairs in the forecourt, the young inspector asked:

'Shall we need a car?'

'No, we're just going across the bridge to the Rue Saint-André-des-Arts. A car would only slow us up.'

It was an old building, similar to that in the Quai de la Mégisserie and, indeed, all the other buildings in the neighbourhood. There was a picture-framer's shop to the right of it, and a confectioner's to the left. The glass door of the lodge was accessible from the entrance hall, which ran right through to a courtyard at the back.

Maigret went into the lodge, and introduced himself to the concierge. She was a plump little woman, with a high colour. As a child, she must have had dimples. Indeed, she still had when she smiled.

'I thought someone would be coming from the police.'

'Why?'

'When I read what had happened to that poor old lady, I had an idea that the niece they spoke of was one of my tenants.'

'Angèle Louette, you mean?'

'Yes.'

'Has she ever mentioned her aunt?'

'She's not very communicative, but, all the same, she does drop in for a chat occasionally. I remember once we were discussing people who don't pay their bills. She remarked that sometimes it was the high-ups who were the worst. Some of her own clients were in that class, she said, and she dared not press them too hard, they had too much influence.

' "It's a mercy that I've got my aunt's money to look forward to! "

'She brought it out just like that. She told me that the old lady had been twice widowed, and that she was drawing two pensions, and must have quite a bit put by.'

'Does she have many visitors?'

The concierge looked uncomfortable.

'How do you mean?'

'Does she often entertain women friends?'

'Not women friends, no.'

'Clients?'

'They don't come to her, she goes to them.'

'What about men?'

'Well, I don't suppose there's any harm in telling you. There are men from time to time. There was even one who stayed for nearly six months. He was ten years younger than she was, and he did all the housework and the shopping.'

'Is she in now?'

'She went out about an hour ago. She always starts on her rounds pretty early. But there is someone up there.'

'One of her regular visitors?'

'I don't know. She got in rather late last night. After I'd let her in, I heard two lots of footsteps. And if the person who was with her had left the building, I'd have known.'

'Does it happen often?'

'Not often. Just once in a while.'

'What about her son?'

'He hardly ever comes here. I haven't seen him for months. He looks like a hippy, but he's a good boy really.'

'Thank you. We'd better have a look round up there, I think.'

There was no lift. The flat was at the back, overlooking the courtyard. The door was not locked, and Maigret and Lapointe went in, to find themselves in a living room fitted out with fairly new, mass-produced furniture.

There was not a sound to be heard. There was a door, obviously leading to the bedroom. Maigret opened it, and saw a man asleep in the double bed. He opened his eyes, and stared in amazement at the Chief Superintendent.

'What is it? What do you want?'

'It's really Angèle Louette I came to see, but as you're here...'

'Aren't you...?'

'That's right. Chief Superintendent Maigret. We've met before, years ago. In those days, you worked in a bar in the Rue Fontaine. You were known as Le Grand Marcel, if I'm not mistaken?'

'I still am. Would you be so good as to leave me for a moment to get dressed? I haven't a stitch on.'

'Don't trouble yourself on my account.'

He was tall, thin and bony. Hastily he slipped on a pair of trousers, and searched about for his slippers, which he found eventually under the bed.

'You know it isn't the way you think between me and Angèle. We're just good friends. Yesterday, we spent the evening together and, by the end of it, I wasn't feeling too good. So, instead of trekking right across Paris to my own place in the Boulevard des Batignolles...'

Maigret opened the wardrobe. There were two men's suits in the hanging section, and, in the drawers, several shirts and two or three pairs of socks and underpants.

'I see! Well, what have you got to say for yourself?'

'Can I make myself a cup of coffee?'

Maigret followed Le Grand Marcel into the kitchen, and watched him make the coffee. It was obvious that he knew his way about.

'There's nothing to tell. I've had my ups and downs, as you very well know. I'm not a pimp, and never have been, in spite of what people say. You know yourself that the charges were dropped for lack of evidence.'

'How old are you?'

'Thirty-five.'

'How old is she?'

'I don't know exactly. Fiftyish, I suppose. Yes, she could be fifty.'

'The great love of your life, I daresay!'

'We understand one another. She can't do without me. I've kept away from her for as long as a week before now, and when that happens, she comes looking for me in all my old haunts.'

'Where were you in the late afternoon of the day before yesterday?'

'The day before yesterday? Let me think. I must have been somewhere in the neighbourhood, because I was due to meet Angèle at seven.'

'She didn't mention it.'

'It probably slipped her mind. We had a dinner date. I had an aperitif on the terrace of a café in the Boulevard Saint-Germain.'

'And did she meet you at seven, as arranged?'

'She may have been a bit late. Yes, come to think of it, she was very late. She was kept waiting by one of her clients. It must have been about half-past seven when she arrived.'

'Did you have dinner together, as arranged?'

'Yes, and afterwards we went to a cinema. You can check on it, if you don't believe me. The restaurant is Lucio's in the Quai de la Tournelle. They know me well there.'

'Where are you working at present?'

'To tell you the truth, I'm between jobs. It's not so easy to find work these days.'

'Does she keep you?'

'That's unkind. You've no call to go out of your way to wound me. For years, you people have been trying to pin something on me, and I'm not guilty. I tell you. It's true she lends me a little money now and then. It's the most she can do. She doesn't earn all that much herself.'

'Were you intending to sleep all morning?'

'I'm expecting her back any minute. She's got an hour free between two appointments. She went to see you yesterday, and told you all she knew.

'What I want to know is what you're doing here now.'

'Taking advantage of the opportunity to make your acquaintance!'

'Would you mind waiting in the other room while I take a shower?'

'You have my permission to shave as well,' retorted Maigret, a little unkindly.

Lapointe could not get over the presence of such a man in Angèle Louette's flat.

'He's been arrested four or five times for procuring. He was also suspected of being tied up with that Corsican gang that caused so much havoc in Paris a few years back. But he's as slippery as an eel, and nothing was ever proved.'

Someone was coming up the stairs. The door opened. Madame Antoine's niece stood transfixed in the doorway.

'Do come in! I was hoping for a word with you.'

She shot a furtive glance towards the bedroom door.

'Yes, he is in there. He's just having a shower and a shave.'

Defeated, she shut the door with a resigned shrug.

'After all, it's nobody's business but my own. Well, is it?'

'You may be right.'

'What do you mean?'

'He just happens to be an old acquaintance of mine, and in the past he's had one or two brushes with the law.'

'Are you telling me he's a thief?'

'No. At least, not to my knowledge. But in the days when he was a barman, there were always two or three women working for him, not to mention the lady in charge of the establishment.'

'I don't believe you. If what you say is true, he'd have been sent to prison.'

'The only reason he wasn't is that we didn't have enough evidence.'

'You still haven't told me why you're here.'

'First, let me ask you a question. Yesterday, when you mentioned your son to me, you told me he was on the Côte d'Azur...'

'I said I thought he was.'

'In fact he's still in Paris, and he's been good enough to tell me some very interesting things.'

'I'm well aware that he dislikes me.'

'But you didn't dislike your aunt, of course?'

'I can't imagine what he's been saying. He's full of crazy notions. Mark my words, he'll come to no good.'

'On the day your aunt died, you had an appointment with Le Grand Marcel for seven o'clock on the terrace of a café in the Boulevard Saint-Germain.'

'If that's what he says, it's the truth.'

'What time did you in fact get there?'

She was caught off her guard for a moment. She hesitated, then said:

'I was kept waiting by one of my clients. I must have arrived at about half-past seven.'

'Where did you have dinner?'

'At an Italian restaurant on the Quai de la Tournelle, Chez Lucio.'

'And then?'

'We went to the Saint Michel cinema.'

'Do you know what time your aunt was murdered?'

'No. I know nothing but what you told me.'

'It was between five and half-past seven.'

'What's that supposed to mean?'

'Do you possess a revolver?'

'Certainly not. I wouldn't know what to do with it.'

Le Grand Marcel emerged from the bedroom, nonchalantly tying a knot in his blue silk tie. He was freshly shaved, and wearing a white shirt.

'What do you know?' he said, making a jest of it. 'I woke up suddenly to find these gentlemen standing at the foot of the bed, towering over me. For a moment, I wondered if I was taking part in a gangster film.'

'Do you own a revolver?' barked Maigret.

'Not likely! Can you think of a surer way of getting nicked?'

'You live in the Boulevard des Batignolles, I believe. What number?'

'Twenty-seven.'

'I'm much obliged to you both for your co-operation. As to your aunt, Mademoiselle, the Forensic Laboratory have completed their work, so you are at liberty to send for the body, and make arrangements for the funeral at any time convenient to yourself.'

'Have I got to pay for it out of my own pocket?'

'That's entirely up to you. As her next-of-kin you will inherit enough and to spare to give her a decent burial.'

'What am I to do? Ought I to see a solicitor?'

'If I were you, I should see her bank manager. He'll tell you all you need to know. If you don't know the name of her bank, you'll find it on her bank book in the chest of drawers in the sitting-room.'

'Thank you.'

'Don't mention it.'

'Don't forget to let me know the date and time of the funeral.'

She was looking at him unblinkingly. He had seldom seen eyes colder or more steely than hers. As to Marcel, he was doing his best to look as though all this was no concern of his.

'I bid you good day, Monsieur Maigret,' he said with studied insolence.

Maigret and Lapointe left. The Chief Superintendent stopped at the bar on the corner.

'Those two have given me a thirst,' he said, and led the way in.

'A half of beer please. What will you have?'

'The same.'

'Two halves.'

Maigret got out his handkerchief and mopped his brow.

'What a way to conduct an investigation into the death by violence of an old lady with grey eyes! Calling on people, and asking them a lot of more or less pointless questions! Oh well, those two have got the laugh on us for the time being, but not for long, I hope!'

Lapointe wisely said nothing, but it troubled him to see the Chief so moody.

'Mind you, it's always like this at some stage. Things grind to a halt, and one doesn't know what to do next. Until something happens, often it's something quite trivial, and one doesn't realise its significance at the time....'

'Cheers!'

'Cheers!'

It was still quite early. Maigret was cheered by the sight of so many busy housewives bustling from shop to shop. They were not far from the Buci market, of which he was particularly fond.

'Come on.'

'Where are we going?'

'Back to the office. We'll see whether Lucas and Janvier have fared any better.'

Janvier was back, but not Lucas.

'No trouble at all, Chief. His successor is still there. He knew Caramé extremely well, right from the time when he joined the service.'

'Go on.'

'It's all perfectly open and above board, except that they

all called Caramé "His Majesty" behind his back. He had an air about him, and he was very fastidious in his dress. He was highly conscious of the dignity of his position. He had been promised the Légion d'Honneur, and was greatly looking forward to receiving it. He never missed an opportunity of appearing in a morning coat, in which he looked particularly well. His brother was a Colonel.

'He was killed in Indo-China. Caramé was always ready to talk about "my brother the Colonel." '

'Is that the lot?'

'More or less. Apparently he had no vices. His one great sorrow was that he had no children. One of the messengers, a very old man, told me something, though he couldn't guarantee that it was true....

'After they'd been married three or four years, he sent his wife to a gynaecologist, who subsequently asked to see him, the inference being that it was he, not she, who was sterile. From that time onwards, he never referred to the subject of children again.'

Maigret paced up and down his office, still wearing the same surly expression. From time to time, he would pause by the window and gaze at the Seine, as though calling the river to witness that, of all men, he was the most hard done by.

There was a knock at the door. It was Lucas. He was out of breath, having taken the stairs at a run.

'Take your time.'

'I found a chap in the ironmongery department, who had been Antoine's number two. He's sixty now and head of the department.'

'What did he say?'

'Apparently, Antoine was a bit of a nut-case. In the nicest way, of course. It seems he had a bee in his bonnet. When anyone asked him what he did for a living, he invariably replied that he was an inventor.

'And it is a fact that he patented a very ingenious design for a tin-opener, and sold it to a hardware manufacturer. He invented several other things as well....'

'Such as a potato peeler?'

'How did you know?'

'I saw one in the flat at the Quai de la Mégisserie.'

'He was always at work on some new invention or other. Apparently he had fitted up a workshop in the flat, and spent every spare minute pottering about in it.'

'I've seen the workshop, too. Were all his inventions household gadgets? Did he never try his hand at anything more ambitious?'

'Not as far as the man I spoke to knew. But, apparently, he had a way of wagging his head and dropping dark hints, such as:

' "One day I'll come up with something really big, something that will make me a household name." '

'Did he go into any detail?'

'No. Except when he was on his hobby-horse, he was rather reserved, although he was very conscientious in his work. He didn't drink. He never went out at night. He seemed very fond of his wife, fond of her rather than in love with her, which isn't surprising, considering that they were both well on in years. They got on well, and had a great respect for one another. The man I spoke to had been to dinner twice at the flat, and he was impressed by the pleasant, homely atmosphere.

' "She was a charming woman," he said. "Such distinction! There was just one thing I found a little embarrassing. When she talked of her husband, one couldn't be quite sure whether she meant her first or her second. I had the feeling that the two had become confused in her mind." '

'Anything else?'

'No, Chief, that's the lot.'

'There's only one thing we can be sure of. Until quite recently a pistol was kept in the old lady's bedside table drawer. And it isn't there now. It's vanished.

'I feel like paying a call at the Boulevard des Batignolles. Care to come with me, Lapointe? Whichever car you pick, make sure it isn't the one with the engine-rattle.'

Before leaving his office, he put his pipe in the rack, and selected another.

CHAPTER FOUR

The fake marble plaque beside the entrance to the little hotel bore the legend:

Furnished rooms to let by the day, the week or the month. All mod. cons.

Most of the rooms were let to monthly tenants, and the 'mod. cons.' consisted of a wash-basin in every room, and a bathroom shared between two floors.

Inside, on the right, was a desk, and behind it a row of pigeon holes and a board with a great many keys hanging from hooks.

'Is Le Grand Marcel in his room?'

'Monsieur Marcel? He's just gone up. That's his car at the door.'

It was a bright red convertible, several years old. Two teenage boys were inspecting it, if not with envy, at least with interest. No doubt they were wondering how fast it could go.

'Has he lived here long?'

'Over a year. He's a very pleasant gentleman.'

'I fancy he seldom sleeps in his room.'

'He usually gets home in the early hours of the morning, which isn't surprising, seeing that he's a barman in a nightclub.'

'Does he ever bring a girl?'

'Not often. And, anyway, it's no concern of mine.'

The landlord was fat, with two or three bristly chins. He

was wearing a pair of very old, misshapen bedroom slippers.

'What floor?'

'Second. Room number twenty-three. I hope you're not going to cause trouble. I know who you are. I don't much like having policemen tramping about the place.'

'You've nothing to hide, have you?'

'With you lot, one can never tell.'

Maigret went upstairs, followed by Lapointe. Dangling from the banister was a cardboard notice, which read: *Please wipe your feet.*

And underneath, written in by hand:

No cooking is permitted in the bedrooms.

Maigret knew what that meant. No doubt every single tenant had smuggled in his own spirit stove, on which to heat up the ready-cooked food that he regularly bought from the nearest delicatessen.

He knocked at the door of number twenty-three. There was a sound of approaching footsteps, and the door was flung open with some violence.

'Good heavens!' exclaimed Le Grand Marcel. 'You here already!'

'Were you expecting us?'

'Once the police start poking their noses into one's business, they're liable to turn up at any time.'

'Are you leaving here?'

There was a suitcase on the floor, and another on the bed, into which the ex-barman had been stuffing his clothes when they arrived.

'Yes. I'm quitting. I've had just about enough.'

'Enough of what?'

'Of that female sergeant-major.'

'Have you quarrelled with her?'

'You could say that. She called me every name under the sun, and all because I was still in bed when you arrived. She may be a masseuse, having to be up at crack of dawn to go poking and prodding people in their beds, but I'm not.'

'That doesn't explain why you're giving up your lodgings.'

'I'm not just giving up my lodgings. I'm giving up altogether. I'm off to Toulon. I've got friends there, real friends. They'll fix me up with something right away.'

Maigret recognised, folded on top of one of the cases, one of the suits he had seen earlier in the day, hanging in the wardrobe in the flat in the Rue Saint-André-des-Arts. Le Grand Marcel was wearing the other. His surname was Montrond, but no one ever called him by it. Even his landlord addressed him as Monsieur Marcel.

'Is that red car parked outside yours?'

'She's a bit past it. She's almost ten years old, but she can still rattle along.'

'I take it you intend to drive to Toulon?'

'As you say. Unless you lot take it into your heads to stop me.'

'Why should we want to do that?'

'You tell me. You're the cop.'

'Just one thing: have you ever been to the flat in the Rue de la Mégisserie?'

'Whatever for? To pay my respects to the old girl?

' "Greetings, dear lady. I'm your niece's boyfriend. As I'm in a bit of a spot at the moment, she's keeping me. She always has to have a man, you know. She's a right trollop, and it was a great mistake to get mixed up with her." '

He went on calmly packing his suitcases, looking through all the drawers to make sure he had not forgotten anything. He pressed down the contents of the cases to make room for a camera and a record-player.

'There! Unless I can be of any further use to you, I'm off.'

'Where can we get in touch with you in Toulon?'

'Write to me care of Bob, at the Bar de l'Amiral, Quai de Stalingrad. He's the barman, and a very old friend of mine. Do you think you'll be needing me again?'

'You never know.'

He had not yet closed the suitcases. Maigret felt about in them, but found nothing of interest.

'How much did you get out of her?'

'The sergeant-major? Five hundred francs. And that, mark you, was only on condition that I wouldn't stay away too long. You never can tell with her. One minute she's cursing you up hill and down dale, and telling you never to darken her doors again, and the next she's whimpering that she can't live without you.'

'Bon voyage!' murmured Maigret with a sigh, as he made for the door.

On his way out, he paused at the desk and said to the landlord:

'I fancy you're about to lose one of your tenants.'

'So he tells me. He's going to spend a few weeks in the South.'

'Is he keeping his room?'

'No. but I daresay I'll be able to fit him in somewhere.'

The two men drove back to the Quai des Orfèvres, and Maigret lost no time in putting a call through to Toulon.

'Would you get me Superintendent Marella? Maigret, Police Headquarters, Paris, speaking.'

It was pleasant to hear the familiar voice of his old colleague. They had joined the force at about the same time, and now Marella was the senior man in Toulon.

'How are things with you?'

'Mustn't grumble.'

'Do you know the Bar de l'Amiral?'

'Do I not! It's the favourite haunt of all the villains.'

'And a man of the name of Bob?'

'The barman. They all use him as an accommodation address.'

'Sometime tonight or tomorrow, a fellow called Marcel Montrond will show up in Toulon. I've an idea he'll make straight for l'Amiral. I'd be much obliged if you'd have him watched.'

'What's your interest in him?'

'It may be nothing. It may be something very serious indeed. I don't know. All I know is he's mixed up in some way in a case that's giving me a monumental headache.'

'The old lady at the Quai de la Mégisserie?'

'Yes.'

'Queer business, that. I only know what I've heard on the radio and read in the papers. All the same, it strikes me as damned odd. Have you caught up with the laddie who plays the guitar?'

'Yes, but I don't think he's our man. At the moment, I haven't a shred of evidence on any of them, and I can't for the life of me see any reason at all why the poor old dear should have been killed....'

'I'll be in touch. This Marcel fellow wouldn't by any chance be a character known as Le Grand Marcel?'

'That's the one.'

'He's a bit of a gigolo on the side, isn't he? He's quite well known around these parts, and he always seems to latch on to some woman or other.'

'Many thanks. I look forward to hearing from you.'

As soon as he had put down the receiver, the telephone rang.

'Chief Superintendent Maigret?'

'Yes.'

'Angèle Louette speaking. First of all, I thought you'd like to know that I've given that layabout his marching orders.'

'I know. He's on his way to Toulon.'

'Please believe me, he's not my type at all. I won't be taken in so easily another time.'

'What have you got against him?'

'He sponges on women, and loafs about in bed most of the day — and not even in his own bed! I had a job getting rid of him. He'd be here still if I hadn't paid him off.'

'I know.'

'He surely wouldn't boast about it?'

'He certainly did, and, incidentally, he called you "the Sergeant-Major".'

'The other thing was about the funeral. It's to be tomorrow morning. The body will be arriving at the Quai de la Mégisserie some time this afternoon. As my aunt had no friends, I won't be turning the place into a memorial chapel. The funeral will be tomorrow at ten.'

'Will there be a church service?'

'Just a memorial prayer at Notre-Dame-des-Blancs-Manteaux. Are you any further forward with your enquiries?'

'No.'

'Have you got my son's address?'

'He did leave it with me, yes.'

'I'd like to let him know. He may, in spite of everything, want to attend his great-aunt's funeral.'

'He's staying at the Hôtel des Iles et du Bon Pasteur, Rue Mouffetard.'

'I'm much obliged to you.'

Maigret, familiar with the ways of Examining Magistrates, knew that they did not like to be kept waiting, so, as soon as he could, he let himself through the communicating door between Police Headquarters and the Palais de Justice. The corridors of the Offices of the Examining Magistrates were lined with benches, on which sat witnesses waiting their turn and, here and there, handcuffed prisoners between two warders.

Judge Libart was alone in his room except for his clerk.

'What news, Chief Superintendent? How is that little matter of ours progressing?'

He rubbed his hands together, obviously in high good humour.

'As you know, it's my policy to leave you in peace to get on with the job. All the same, I trust you have made some progress?'

'None at all.'

'No likely suspects?'

'Not really, and nothing much to go on, except that the intruder was searching for something, when the old lady came back unexpectedly and found him.'

'Money?'

'I believe not.'

'Jewellery?'

'She had none worth stealing.'

'A lunatic?'

'Not very likely. Whoever it was had searched the flat several times before the afternoon of the crime. That doesn't look to me like the behaviour of a lunatic.'

'A family affair, perhaps? Someone in too much of a hurry to get whatever the old lady had to leave?'

'That's a possibility, but a somewhat remote one. The old lady's sole heir is her niece. She's a masseuse, and quite comfortably off.'

'Don't let it get you down.'

Maigret forced a smile.

'I'm sorry. It's just that I seem to have hit a bad patch. The funeral is tomorrow.'

'Will you be going?'

'Yes. I always make a point of it. I've been put on the right track before now by watching the mourners at a funeral.'

He went home for lunch, and Madame Maigret, noting his preoccupied expression, was careful to ask no questions.

She went about on tiptoe, and watched him anxiously as he ate the *fricandeau à l'oseille* which she had cooked for him, knowing it to be one of his favourite dishes.

Soon after he got back to the Quai des Orfèvres, there was a knock at his door.

'Come in.'

It was Lapointe.

'Sorry to bother you, sir, but you haven't given me any instructions.'

'I have none to give you. Do what you think best. If anything occurs to you...'

'I'd like another word with the man in the bird shop. Not many people would be able to enter or leave the building without his seeing them. Maybe, if I jog his memory a bit, he'll come up with something useful.'

'It's up to you.'

He hated himself for feeling as he did, bereft of inspiration and a prey to inertia. Thoughts buzzed in his head until he was sick of them, but none of them seemed to be leading anywhere.

Foremost in his mind was the thought that Madame Antoine had been as sane as he was himself.

Why had she hesitated so long, pacing up and down the Quai des Orfèvres, before plucking up the courage to speak to the constable at the gate? Had she known more than she was prepared to tell?

She must have realised that her complaint, namely, that she had found some of her ornaments almost imperceptibly displaced, was bound to be received with scepticism.

All the same, she had been right. The flat had indeed been subjected to a thorough search on several occasions.

But why? What had the intruder been looking for?

As he had explained to the Examining Magistrate, certainly not money or jewellery.

But one thing was certain: whatever it was, it was important enough to warrant the murder of the old lady, when she came back unexpectedly while the intruder was still there.

Had he or had he not in the end found what he was looking for?

Was he perhaps on his way out with his booty, when he heard Madame Antoine's key in the lock?

What could a very old woman, twice widowed, living quietly and modestly on her own, possibly possess that was worth committing murder for?

While these thoughts were going through his head, Maigret was doodling absent-mindedly on a large sheet of paper. Suddenly, he realised that what he had been doing was to make a rough sketch of an old lady, not unlike Madame Antoine.

By five o'clock he was beginning to feel stifled in his office. Taking with him a photograph of Le Grand Marcel, which be had got from the Vice Squad, he set off for the Quai de la Mégisserie.

It was a poor likeness — the man appeared more hard-featured than he was in real life — but it was still recognisable. He went first to the concierge.

'Have you ever seen this man?'

She went to fetch her spectacles, which were on the kitchen dresser.

'I wouldn't really like to say, though he does seem vaguely familiar. On the other hand, there are lots of people about who look a bit like him.'

'Take a closer look. If you saw him, it was probably quite recently.'

'Actually, it's the suit that rings a bell. I saw a check suit like that somewhere a week or two back, but I can't for the life of me think where.'

'Here, in the lodge?'

'No, I don't think so.'

'In the courtyard? On the stairs?'

'Honestly, I can't say. Your inspector was here again, asking questions, just a short while ago. You wouldn't want me to start inventing things, now, would you? You know they've brought her back?'

'Madame Antoine, you mean?'

'Yes. Her niece is up there with her. She's left the door open, and lit candles on either side of the bed. One or two of the tenants plucked up the courage to go in and say a little prayer. If I'd had anyone to look after things here. I'd have gone to the funeral tomorrow, but I'm all on my own. My husband is in a mental hospital. He's been there for three years.'

Maigret went out on to the pavement, where the birdcages were standing outside the petshop. Monsieur Caille's son recognised him immediately.

'Hello! One of your inspectors, the young one, has been here. He's only just left.'

'I know. I'd be obliged if you'd look carefully at this photograph.'

He did so, shook his head, held it up close, and then at arm's length.

'I can't exactly say I recognise him, but there is something...'

'Is it the suit?'

'No, not specially. It's his expression. That sort of devil-may-care look.'

'One of your customers, perhaps?'

'Oh no, I'm sure not.'

'Hadn't you better show it to your father?'

'I will, of course, but he's so terribly short-sighted.'

He came back shaking his head.

'He doesn't recognise him. Though you must remember that he spends most of his time in the shop, and really cares for nothing but his birds and his fish. In fact, he's so devoted to them that it wouldn't take much for him to refuse to sell them.'

Maigret went back into the building, and climbed the stairs to the first floor. The woman who lived opposite

Madame Antoine came out, with a string shopping bag over her arm.

'She's there,' she whispered, pointing to the half-open door.

'I know.'

'The funeral is tomorrow. It seems her first husband bought a plot in the Montparnasse cemetery, and she wanted to be buried beside him.'

'Who knew of her wishes?'

'Her niece, I daresay. And I know she told the concierge. She used to say that Ivry was too far out, and that she felt lost among all those thousands of graves.'

'There's something I'd like to show you. Could we go into your flat for a moment?'

It was very neat and tidy, somewhat darker than the old lady's, because the windows were almost entirely obscured by the overhanging branches of a tree.

'Have you ever seen this man before?'

Once again, he produced the little photograph taken by someone in Criminal Records.

'Is it someone I know?'

'I've no idea. You tell me.'

'You asked me if I'd ever seen him before. Well, I certainly have, not very long ago. He was smoking a cigarette. I knew there was something missing. That's it. The cigarette.'

'Take your time. Try to think back.'

'It isn't one of the tradesmen, nor anyone I've seen going in and out of the yard.'

She was obviously doing her best.

'I suppose it's important?'

'Yes.'

'Something to do with Madame Antoine?'

'I think it likely.'

'So if I identify him positively, it will mean trouble for him?'

'I'm afraid so.'

'You see my difficulty. I wouldn't want to get an innocent person into trouble.'

'If he's innocent, we shall soon know it.'

'That's not always the case. Even the police can make mistakes. Oh well, never mind! I was on my way out...'

'What day was this?'

'I don't remember. One day last week. I was going to fetch my daughter from school.'

There was a little girl of about twelve doing her homework in the next room.

'That would have been a little before four?'

'Or it might have been lunch-time. That's what I'm trying to remember. More likely it was four, because I had my shopping bag with me, and that's when I always buy the things I need for dinner. My husband doesn't come home for lunch, and my daughter and I just have something very light.

'I was on my way downstairs, not looking where I was going, when I bumped into someone. He was coming up the stairs four at a time. He nearly sent me flying. That's why I remember him.

'He turned round, and asked me if I was hurt. I said no, it was nothing.'

'Do you happen to know where he was going, which floor?'

'No. I was in a hurry. My daughter doesn't like to be kept hanging about outside the school gates, and, with all the traffic, I daren't let her come home alone.'

Maigret heaved a sigh. At last, a faint ray of hope!

A moment or two later he was in the bedroom gazing intently at the delicately modelled features of the old woman whom he had thought to be mad.

The curtains were three-quarters drawn, and the room was almost in darkness, except for a narrow strip of shimmering sunlight. Two wax tapers were burning, one on either side of the bed, making everything look strange and different.

Angèle Louette was there, sitting in an armchair, silent and motionless. At first Maigret thought she was asleep, until he looked again, and saw her sombre eyes fixed upon him.

He stood facing the dead woman for a minute or two, to give himself time to recover, then went into the sitting room. It was a relief to be back in daylight. As he had expected, she came out after him.

She looked even more hard-featured than usual.

'What have you come here for?'

'To pay my last respects to your aunt.'

'If you ask me, nothing was further from your mind. And the same goes for the neighbours. Only two of them bothered to put their heads round the door. Any more news of that scoundrel Marcel?'

'He got into his car and drove off to Toulon.'

This was a shock to her, he could see.

'Good riddance! I had trouble enough getting rid of him. Do you know, I had to give him five hundred francs to get him to leave?'

'That's demanding money with menaces. You could lay a charge.'

'Maybe I will. At any rate, if he makes any attempt to come back....'

'Did you know that he was here, in this building, one day last week?'

She started violently, and frowned.

'Do you know what day?'

'No.'

'What time of day?'

'Round about four.'

'Did he tell you himself?'

'No.'

'Have you asked him about it?'

'I haven't had a chance. How did he come to have your aunt's address?'

'One day, about a month ago, when we were crossing the Pont-Neuf, I pointed to the windows of the flat in the distance, and said:

' "My old aunt lives up there." '

'And I suspect you went on to say that you were hoping for a nice little legacy from that quarter in the not too distant future.'

'I can just hear him feeding you lies like that. All I said was that she had had two husbands, and was very comfortably-off. Where is he?'

'At this moment, unless he's changed his mind, he's on his way to Toulon.'

'He never stopped talking about Toulon, and all the friends he had there.'

'Do you know anything about his family?'

'No.'

'Did he never talk about his childhood?'

'No. All I know is that his mother is still alive, and that she lives in some little town in Central France.'

'Are you quite certain you never came here at any time during the past week or fortnight?'

'Not again, please!'

'Think before you say anything.'

'I'm quite sure.'

'Do you know what your aunt kept in her bedside table drawer?'

'I've never looked.'

'Not even this morning, when you were rearranging the furniture for the laying out of the body?'

'Not even then.'

'Did you know that your aunt had a gun?'

'Of course not! She wouldn't have dared even to pick it up.'

'Wasn't she nervous, living on her own as she did?'

'She was afraid of nothing and no one.'

'Did she ever talk about her second husband's inventions?'

'She showed me a little potato peeler once. She promised me one like it, actually, but I never got it. That was while Antoine was still alive. She showed me over his workshop as well, if you can call it that. It's hardly bigger than a cupboard, and there isn't room to swing a cat.'

'I'm much obliged to you.'

'Will you be at the funeral?'

'If I can possibly get there.'

'The hearse will be leaving here at a quarter to ten, arriving at the church at ten.'

'Till tomorrow, then.'

She was tough, all right, more like a man than a woman, but at times he could almost forgive her her brusque manner. Perhaps it was only the bluntness of plain speaking. She was no oil painting. She had never been attractive, and had coarsened with advancing years.

She behaved like a man, indulging in amorous adventures when the whim took her. Was that really so very reprehensible?

She was quite open about it. When she felt like it, she had a man in to stay for a night, or a week. The concierge had seen them come and go. The neighbours, too, must have realised what was going on.

On the other hand, she was very much on her guard, watching Maigret intently, always suspecting a trap.

On his way back to the Quai des Orfèvres, Maigret stopped at the Brasserie Dauphine for a glass of white wine from the Loire. He didn't feel like beer. The white wine in the frosted glass, with just a hint of a sparkle, seemed more appropriate on this lovely spring day.

It was the slackest time of the day. Except for a delivery man in a blue apron, there was no one in the café.

He decided to order another.

Doctor Pardon would never know. Besides, Pardon had done no more than warn him against excess.

Lapointe was waiting for him at the Quai des Orfèvres. He had once again combed the flats from top to bottom, showing the photograph of Le Grand Marcel to all the tenants.

'Any luck?'

'None at all.'

'I shall need you tomorrow morning to drive me to the funeral.'

He walked home, going over the old ground in his head. It was all very discouraging.

'The only thing we know for certain is that a revolver has disappeared.'

But were they really sure even of that? They had found gun grease on the lining-paper of a drawer. Might it not have got there in some other way?

Moers's men had stated positively that it had not been there for more than a month at most.

He was beginning to distrust everyone, himself included. If only he could find a new lead, however slender, he was ready to go back and start all over again, right from the beginning.

'You're early!'

For once, she had not been waiting for him in the doorway, and he had had to use his key, which he very seldom did.

'I shall probably be going out later.'

'Where to?'

'To a place where I think I'd better not take you, a little hippy bistro in the Place Maubert.'

He read slowly through the newspaper, and took a shower before dinner. As on the previous evening, they dined at the table drawn up under the open window.

'Tomorrow, I shall be going to the funeral.'

'Will there be many people?'

'Apart from the niece, I may well be the only one. Only two of her neighbours bothered to go and pay their last respects.'

'What about the press?'

'This case hasn't made the headlines. It only rates a small paragraph on page three of this evening's paper.'

He switched on the television. It would be ten at the earliest before he could hope to find Billy Louette at the Bongo.

On the corner of the Boulevard Voltaire, he hailed a taxi. The driver looked at him curiously when he gave the address, amazed that a thoroughly respectable-looking man from a district like this should lower himself by going to such a disreputable dive.

The place had been decorated with the minimum of expense. The walls were painted white, with a few meaningless squiggles of colour splashed on here and there.

This was the only attempt at originality. The bar was an ordinary zinc counter, with the proprietor, in shirt sleeves and a blue apron, serving behind it himself. An open door at the back led into a smoke-filled kitchen, from which came a stench of rancid fat.

There were ten or a dozen couples having dinner, which

consisted mainly of spaghetti, this apparently being the speciality of the house.

Some of the younger people were in jeans and flowered shirts, but it was not these whom the crowds came to see.

To see, and, above all, to hear, because the group, which consisted of three players, was making as much noise as a full orchestra. Besides Billy and his guitar there were a saxophone and drums.

All three of them had long hair, and were wearing black velvet trousers and pink shirts.

'Do you wish to order dinner?'

The proprietor had to shout to be heard at all.

Maigret shook his head, and ordered white wine. Billy, who had seen him come in, seemed to take his presence there quite as a matter of course.

The Chief Superintendent knew nothing whatever about pop music, but, as far as he could tell, the Bad Lads were no worse than many of the groups regularly to be heard on radio and television. The three young men went at it with great verve, building up to a positively frenetic climax.

They were loudly clapped. An interval followed, during which Billy joined Maigret at the bar.

'I take it it's me you've come to see?'

'Naturally. Have you heard from your mother?'

'Not today.'

'In that case, you won't know that the funeral is fixed for tomorrow morning. Leaving the Quai de la Mégisserie at a quarter to ten. The memorial service will be held at Notre-Dame-des-Blancs-Manteaux, and the burial at the Montparnasse cemetery.'

'Great-uncle Antoine was buried at Ivry, I seem to remember.'

'So he was, but your aunt expressed a wish to be buried beside her first husband.'

'We'll be playing again in a few minutes. How do we sound to you?'

'I'm sorry to say I'm no judge. There's just one thing I wanted to ask you. Do you happen to know if your aunt had a revolver?'

'Yes, she did.'

At last, a straight answer to a straight question!

'Did she tell you herself?'

'It was quite some time ago, at least a year or two. I hadn't a bean. I'd been to see her in the hope of making a touch, and I'd noticed that she kept several hundred-franc notes in the chest of drawers.

'A hundred francs is nothing to some people, but to others, including myself at times, it's a fortune.

'I remarked quite casually:

' "Don't you ever feel nervous?"

' "Who is there to be afraid of? You?"

' "No. But you live alone, and people know it. Someone might break in...." '

He broke off to mouth a message to his companions that he would not keep them waiting much longer.

'She said she had taken precautions against that, and she took me into her bedroom and opened her bedside table drawer.

' "And don't think for one moment I'd hesitate to use it." '

Now there was something more to go on than a grease-stain. Someone had actually seen the gun.

'Was it a revolver or an automatic?'

'What's the difference?'

'A revolver has a barrel. An automatic is flat.'

'In that case, as far as I can remember, it was a revolver.'

'How big?'

'I really couldn't say. I just had a glimpse of it. About the size of my hand, I should say.'

'Did you mention it to anyone?'

'No, not a soul.'

'Not even your mother?'

'I'm not in the habit of running to her with every bit of tittle-tattle. We're not that close.'

The young man returned to his companions, and the music started up again. He seemed genuinely carried away by the rhythm of his guitar, counterpointed by the beat of the drums.

'He's a good kid, that one,' remarked the proprietor, leaning across the bar counter. 'They're a decent lot altogether. Not one of them touches drugs, which is more than I can say for some of my customers.'

Maigret paid for his drink, and went out. He had some difficulty in finding a taxi to take him home.

Next morning he went upstairs to the Examining Magistrates' floor, and knocked on Judge Libart's door.

'I'd be grateful if you'd make out a search warrant for me, in the name of Angèle Louette, spinster, Occupation: Masseuse. Address: Rue Saint-André-des-Arts.'

The clerk duly wrote out the warrant.

'Does this mean that you'll be making an early arrest?'

'To tell you the truth, I haven't the least idea. I'm groping about in the dark.'

'Isn't she the old lady's niece?'

'Quite.'

'And her sole heir? I must say that does seem rather surprising.'

This Maigret had anticipated. One's first reaction was bound to be one of scepticism. Angèle Louette was secure in the knowledge that sooner or later — and in view of her aunt's great age, it would probably be sooner — she would inherit the old lady's money. Why then should she risk life imprisonment for the sake of a legacy which was as good as hers already?

'Oh well, never mind. You must do as you think fit, and the best of luck.'

At a quarter to ten, Maigret, driven by Lapointe, drew up in one of the little black cars at the entrance to the flats in the Quai de la Mégisserie. There were no black draperies over the door, and not a single interested spectator.

The hearse had only just arrived, and two hefty undertaker's men were on their way upstairs to fetch the coffin. There were no flowers, not even a wreath. At several of the windows, the curtains twitched. The concierge followed the coffin as far as the door, and crossed herself.

The old man with the birds ventured out of his dark shop for a moment, to join his son on the pavement.

That was all.

Angèle Louette, alone, stepped into the black car

provided by the undertaker. The church was deserted, except for two women waiting for the confessional. Everyone seemed in a hurry to get it over and done with, not only the undertaker's men, but the priest as well.

Maigret had sat at the back of the church, to be joined by Lapointe after he had parked the car.

'Somehow it wasn't even sad,' remarked the young inspector.

He was right. The aisle was bathed in sunlight. The door had been left open, and a babble of street noises was clearly to be heard.

Et ne nos inducat in tentationem...

Amen....

The coffin, probably lighter than most, was carried out. Less than a quarter of an hour later, they were in the Cemetery of Montparnasse. The small procession stopped at the end of a tree-lined avenue, and the coffin was lowered into a newly dug grave, beside a flat stone of pink marble.

'I told you no one would come,' whispered the masseuse, as the old woman was being laid to rest.

She went on:

'There wasn't time to have the stone engraved. She wanted her name put next to her first husband's. The stonemasons will be attending to it next week.'

She was wearing a very plain black outfit, which made her seem more forbidding than ever. She looked more like a governess or a headmistress than anything else.

'We'll go back to your flat now,' murmured Maigret.

'We?'

'We, yes, that's what I said.'

'What is it you want from me now?'

It was even more cheerful in the cemetery than in the church, with the sunlight dancing among the leaves of the trees, and the birds singing.

'One moment, I'll have to tip all these people, I suppose. I don't need to keep the car, do I?'

'There's room for you in ours.'

They forgathered at the gate. Angèle got into the back of the car. Maigret took his usual seat beside Lapointe.

'The Rue-Saint-André-des-Arts.'

Bitterly, the old lady's niece remarked:

'I was prepared for a certain amount of gossip. There are always people ready to talk behind one's back, and, if they have nothing to go on, to invent lies. But that the C.I.D., in the person of Chief Superintendent Maigret, should make my life a misery....'

'I'm truly sorry, but I'm only doing my job.'

'What possible reason could I have for sneaking into my aunt's flat?'

'What possible reason could anyone have had?'

'Do you really think me capable of murdering an old woman?'

'I don't think anything. I'm only trying to get at the truth. Join us upstairs, Lapointe, as soon as you've parked the car.'

Upstairs in the flat, she took off her hat and gloves, and the jacket of her suit, under which she was wearing a white shirt. For the first time. Maigret noticed that, in spite of her mannish appearance, she had quite a good figure, and was astonishingly well preserved for her age.

'Now will you kindly tell me, once and for all, what you want from me?'

He took the Examining Magistrate's warrant out of his pocket.

'Read it for yourself.'

'Does this mean that you're going to rummage among my things, and turn everything upside down?'

'There's no fear of that. We know our job. Two experts from Criminal Records will be here shortly, and they will see that everything is put back exactly as it was.'

'I still don't understand.'

'I noticed that your son wasn't at the funeral.'

'I must confess that, after everything that happened yesterday, I forgot to let him know. I haven't even got his exact address, I only know what you told me.'

'You didn't let him know, but I did, which is why I was surprised not to see him there. He struck me as a thoroughly good sort.'

'Provided he always gets his own way.'

'And provided no one tries to make an osteopath of him.'

'He told you about that, did he?'

'He was a great deal more forthcoming than you are, and I didn't have to ask him the same questions ten times before getting straight answers....'

'He hasn't had to go through what I've been through! I don't know about you, but I need a drink.'

It was not wine she needed, apparently, but whisky, which she got from a cupboard in the living room, crammed with bottles of various sorts.

'Will you join me? Or would you prefer a glass of wine? Red? White?'

'Nothing for the moment, thanks.'

The men from Criminal Records arrived before Lapointe, who, no doubt, had had to go miles to find a parking place.

'Right, lads, you'd better get started. Everything must be gone through with a fine toothcomb. You know what we're looking for, but you may find something else of interest as well. All I ask is that you should put everything back, exactly as you found it.'

She lit a cigarette, and went and sat in an armchair near the window, which commanded an extensive view of the rooftops of Paris, and from which a corner of the Eiffel Tower could also be seen.

When Lapointe finally arrived, Maigret said:

'You stay here with them. I have another call to make in the district.'

Once out in the street, he made off in the direction of the Rue Mouffetard, but not until he had gulped down a glass of white wine, in a little local bistro with a bowl of hard-boiled eggs on the bar counter.

CHAPTER FIVE

The hotel was tall and narrow, and permeated with a mixture of pungent smells. Maigret, having enquired at the desk and received a grudging answer, went up to the fourth floor, and knocked at the appropriate door.

A sleepy voice called out:

'Come in.'

The shutters were closed, and the room was in darkness.

'I thought it must be you.'

The redhead got out of bed, stark naked, and hastily tied a towel around his middle. In the bed, Maigret could just make out the contours of a girl. She was lying with her face to the wall, and all that could be seen distinctly was her dark hair spread out on the pillow.

'What time is it?'

'Much too late for you to attend the funeral.'

'I suppose you want to know why I wasn't there? Hang on a minute, while I swill out my mouth. It feels like the bottom of a birdcage.'

He filled the tooth mug under the running tap, and rinsed his mouth.

'It's a pity you left so early last night. You missed all the fun. It went like a bomb. Three guys from England turned up with their guitars, and we all got together and improvised for two hours or more. And they had a smashing girl with them. That's her over there.

'I just hadn't the courage to get up this morning, to go to

the old girl's funeral. I feel very badly about it, but, to tell you the truth, I wasn't madly keen to meet my mother.

'By the way, has she got hold of the loot yet?'

'What loot?'

'My great-aunt's savings. She must have had a tidy bit put by. She spent almost nothing on herself. And her second husband was a saver too. It looks as though my mother will soon get the little house she's always longed for.'

He opened the shutters a crack, letting a strip of sunlight into the room. The girl groaned and turned over, revealing a naked breast.

'Was your mother planning to buy a house?'

'A small house in the country, to use at weekends at first, and eventually to retire to. She's dreamt of nothing else for years. She tried to get the old girl to lend her the money, but it didn't work out. I'm sorry, I can't offer you anything.'

'I just happened to be passing.'

'Have you found the revolver yet?'

'No. By the way, Le Grand Marcel has taken himself off.'

'You don't say! My mother must be hopping mad!'

'She was the one who showed him the door. He's gone to Toulon, where he has friends.'

'She'll need to find someone else. I doubt if she could get along for three days without a man. Unless she takes to the bottle again — but that has its problems, and it's a lot more expensive.'

There was no malice in his cynicism. Indeed, there was a sort of wistfulness about him, perhaps because of the family life he had never known.

So he covered it up with a swagger.

'Don't leave Paris without letting me know. I'm nowhere near the end of this case, and I may still need your help.'

The young man jerked his chin towards the bed.

'As you see, I have plenty to keep me occupied here.'

Maigret returned to the Rue-Saint-André-des-Arts. The men from Criminal Records were still there, waiting for him.

'We're through here, Chief. There's nothing much to

report. Clothes, mostly in dark colours, underwear, stockings and shoes. She must have a thing about shoes, because we found no less than eight pairs.'

Angèle Louette was still sitting in the armchair by the window. She appeared completely unmoved.

'The refrigerator is well stocked. For a woman living on her own, she does herself very well. Photographs, mainly photographs of herself, when much younger, and a little boy. An account book recording the names of clients and payments received.'

'You've forgotten the most important thing,' broke in the second man.

The other man shrugged.

'For what it's worth! The top of the wardrobe is very dusty, and mixed in with the dust we found particles of oil or grease, almost certainly gun-grease.

Angèle interrupted:

'There's never been a gun in this flat.'

'Be that as it may, it's fresh grease. In the kitchen bin, I found some grease-stained paper which had been used as wrapping for a revolver.'

'If so, it must have been Marcel's, and no doubt he took it away with him.'

Maigret climbed on to a chair to see the stain for himself.

'I'd be obliged if you would attend at the Quai des Orfèvres at three o'clock this afternoon.'

'What about my appointments? I'm a professional woman, not a lady of leisure.'

'I'm afraid I shall have to make it an official summons.'

He took a yellow form from his pocket, and filled in the details.

'I said three o'clock, remember.'

Lapointe had been waiting patiently. They walked together to the little black car, which was parked some way off. Moers's men left at the same time.

'Is she on the telephone?'

'Yes.'

'She was probably only waiting to get rid of us before ringing Toulon. Among the photographs were there any of the old lady?'

'Three or four, taken a long time ago. There were also several of a man with a moustache, who she said was old Antoine.'

Maigret went home to lunch. His wife was still being tactful. She asked no questions, except about the funeral.

'Were there many people?'

'No one except the niece and ourselves, Lapointe and me. The memorial prayer was gabbled at top speed. You'd have thought they couldn't get rid of her fast enough.'

When he got back to his office, Janvier was waiting for him with a message.

'Superintendent Marella has been on from Toulon. He wants you to ring him back.'

'Get him for me, will you?'

A few minutes later, he was through to him.

'Marella?'

'Yes. I rang on the off-chance of finding you in. Your friend Marcel got here late last night, and made straight for the Bar de l'Amiral. He spotted me at once, and said, "Good evening", before taking a seat at the bar. He and Bob had their heads together for some time, but I couldn't hear a word they were saying, because the juke-box was going full blast.'

'Was there anyone else with them?'

'No. At one point, Bob went and shut himself up in the telephone box, and made a call. He seemed very pleased with himself when he came back, and gave Marcel the thumbs up sign.'

'Was that all?'

'No. Your friend Marcel has booked himself in at the Hôtel des Cinq Continents, in the Avenue de la République. He was up at nine this morning, and set off by car for Sanary. Does that ring a bell?'

'No.'

'It's where Pepito, the elder of the Giovanni brothers, lives.'

For years the Giovannis had been responsible for most of the crime on the Riviera. Marco, the younger of the two, lived near Paris. Pepito had built himself a luxury villa at Sanary, and now lived there quietly in retirement.

They had been arrested ten or a dozen times, but there had never been enough evidence to make the charges stick.

Now that they were getting on in years, they lived the life of rich, elderly, retired gentlemen.

'How long did Marcel stay at the villa?'

'Nearly an hour. Afterwards he went back to l'Amiral, and then he had lunch at an Italian restaurant in the old town.'

'Had he any previous connection with the Giovannis?'

'Not that I know of.'

'Better have Pepito watched. I'd like to know where, if anywhere, he goes in the next day or two, and also whether any of his old associates start turning up at the villa.'

'I'll see to it. I daresay you'll do as much for me some day. How's your case going?'

'I'm beginning to see a glimmer of light, but there's a long way to go yet. When it's over, I've half a mind to get away for a change of scene and a bit of sun. I might even look you up.'

'I should be delighted. How long is it since we last met?'

'Ten years? Twelve years? It was over that business at Porquerolles.'

'I remember. So long, Maigret.'

They had signed on together at the Quai des Orfèvres, and for more than two years had pounded the same beat until their promotion, after which they had first patrolled the railway stations, and then been assigned to detective work in the large department stores. They had both been young bachelors then.

Old Joseph came to the door, bearing the summons that Maigret had served on Angèle earlier in the day.

'Bring her in.'

She was paler and more tense than usual. Perhaps she was just overawed by the portentous atmosphere of Police Headquarters.

'Take a seat.'

He pointed to a straight-backed chair facing his desk, and opened the communicating door to the Inspectors'

Duty Room.

'Come in, will you, Lapointe, and bring your shorthand book.'

Young Lapointe often did duty as a shorthand writer. He sat down at one end of the desk, with pencil poised.

'As you see, you have been summoned here for an official interrogation. Everything you say will be taken down, and at the end you will be required to read and sign the transcript. I may have to repeat some questions that I have already put to you, but this time your answers will be on record.'

'In other words, I'm suspect number one, is that it?'

'You're a suspect, that's all. Numbers don't come into it. You had not the slightest affection for your aunt. Isn't that so?'

'When I told her I was pregnant, the best she could do for me was to hand me a hundred-franc note.'

'And you resented what you regarded as her meanness?'

'She was thoroughly selfish. She never gave a thought to others. And I'm quite sure in my own mind that the only reason she married again was because there was money there.'

'Was she a deprived child?'

'She didn't even have that excuse. Her father was a man of property, as they used to say. The family lived near the Luxembourg Gardens, and the two girls, my mother and my aunt, went to a very good school. It wasn't until my grandfather was well advanced in years that he began to speculate recklessly, and eventually lost all he possessed.'

'Was it then that she married Caramé?'

'Yes. He was a frequent visitor at my grandparents. Everyone thought at first that it was my mother he was interested in. I fancy she thought so, too. But it was my aunt who got him in the end.'

'And your mother?'

'She married a bank clerk. He was in poor health, and he died young. She went to work for a business firm in the Rue Paradis.'

'So life was none too easy for the two of you?'

'That's right.'

'Didn't your aunt offer to help?'

'No. I don't quite know what made me decide to become a masseuse. Unless it was that one of our neighbours was a masseuse, and I used to see her drive off in her car to visit her clients.'

'Have you a car?'

'A Mini.'

'To drive you down to your country house, when you get it?'

She frowned.

'Who told you that?'

'Never mind. I gather you've always had this dream of owning a little house, not too far out of town, where you could go for weekends.'

'Well, what's wrong with that? It's what lots of people want. It was my mother's dearest wish as well, only she died before it came true.'

'How much do you hope to get from your aunt's estate?'

'Forty to fifty thousand francs, perhaps. I don't know. I'm only going on what she told me. She may have had other investments that she didn't mention.'

'In other words, you went on seeing her because of what you were hoping to get?'

'You can put it that way if you like. At the same time, she was my only living relative. Have you ever had to live alone, Monsieur Maigret?'

'What about your son?'

'I hardly ever see him, except when he's short of money. I mean nothing to him.'

'Before I put my next question to you. I must remind you that everything you say is being taken down, and urge you to think carefully before you speak. Did you often go to your aunt's flat while she was out?'

It seemed to him that she had tumed a shade paler, but her self-possession was unshaken.

'Do you mind if I smoke?'

'Please do, but I'm afraid I haven't any cigarettes to offer you.'

On his desk there were pipes only, six pipes arranged in sizes, side by side in a rack.

'I asked you a question.'

'I'd be grateful if you would repeat it.'

He did so, slowly and clearly, and without hesitation.

'It depends what you mean by going to her flat. Sometimes I called at the Quai de la Mégisserie, and found her out. On those occasions, I waited until she got back.'

'In the flat?'

'No. Outside on the landing.'

'Did you often have to wait a long time?'

'When she was a long time coming, I used to go for a walk along the Quai, or more often just look at the birds.'

'Did it never occur to your aunt to give you a key to the flat?'

'No.'

'Supposing she had been taken ill suddenly?'

'She'd made up her mind that it couldn't happen to her. She never had so much as a fainting fit in the whole of her life.'

'Did she ever leave the door open?'

'No.'

'Not even when she was at home?'

'No. She always took good care to see that it was shut.'

'Was there someone in particular she didn't trust?'

'She didn't trust anyone.'

'Not even you?'

'I don't know.'

'Was her manner towards you affectionate?'

'It was completely matter-of-fact. She'd tell me to sit down. Then she'd make me coffee, and serve it up to me with some dry biscuits out of a tin.'

'Did she never ask after your son?'

'No. I imagine she saw him quite as often as I did, if not more.'

'Did she ever threaten to disinherit you?'

'Why ever should she do that?'

'To get back to the front door, I've had a look at the lock. There's nothing very special about it. Anyone could have taken a wax impression of it.'

'What for?'

'No matter. Allow me to put my question another way:

Were you never, on any occasion, alone in the flat?'

'Never.'

'Think carefully.'

'I have thought very carefully.'

'Did it never happen that, while you were there, your aunt had to slip out to get something from the shops, such as a fresh supply of biscuits, for instance?'

'No.'

'So you never got a chance to go through her drawers?'

'No.'

'And you never saw her Post Office Savings book?'

'I caught a glimpse of it once, when she was getting something out of the drawer, but I don't know what was in it.'

'What about her bank book?'

'I haven't the slightest idea how much she had in the bank. As a matter of fact. I didn't even know she had a bank account.'

'But you knew she had money?'

'I was pretty sure of it.'

'I don't mean just her savings.'

'I don't know what you're talking about. What do you mean?'

'Never mind. Did you ever try and borrow money from her?'

'Just the once, as I told you. That time when I was pregnant, and she gave me a hundred francs.'

'More recently than that, I mean. You wanted to buy a country cottage. Did you never ask her to help you towards that?'

'No. You don't know what she was like.'

'I did meet her.'

'And you were taken in, just like everyone else. You took her for a sweet old lady, with a gentle smile and a shy manner, whereas, in actual fact, she was as hard as nails.'

'Do you own a red striped or check scarf?'

'No.'

'Do you remember the red-striped cushion on the couch in your aunt's sitting room?'

'Vaguely, yes, I think I do.'

'You had a row with your friend Marcel yesterday morning. What was that about?'

'He was becoming impossible.'

'What do you mean by that?'

'Naturally, when I take up with a man, I don't ask for references. But Marcel went too far. He didn't even bother to look for work. He could have got a job as a barman ten times over.

'But he preferred to sponge on me.'

'Did he know your aunt?'

'I'd hardly be likely to introduce him to her, would I?'

'Did he know of her existence?'

'I may have mentioned her.'

'And told him, I daresay, that she had a nice little nest-egg tucked away?'

'I would hardly have put it quite like that.'

'Be that as it may, he knew where she lived and that, to say the least, she had a tidy bit put by.'

'Yes, I suppose he did.'

'Did you ever see him going into the flats at the Quai de la Mégisserie?'

'Never.'

'And yet there are at least two witnesses who saw him there.'

'Well, it's more than I ever did.'

'Did you ever consider marrying him?'

'Certainly not. Since my son was born, I've never once thought of marriage. I get what I want from a man when I want it, and that's all there is to it. Do I make myself clear?'

'Perfectly. Now, about the revolver.'

'What, again?'

'It must be somewhere, and I'm determined to find it. For some considerable time, your aunt kept it in the drawer of her bedside table. According to you, your aunt was terrified of firearms, and you find it hard to credit that she ever owned a gun.'

'That's right.'

'Nevertheless, she did own a gun, and she always kept it handy, which, incidentally, rather suggests that she was more concerned for her safety than you led me to suppose.'

'What's all this leading up to?'

Maigret, with great deliberation, refilled his pipe.

'This morning, at your flat, we found evidence that your aunt's gun had, at some time, been concealed on top of your wardrobe.'

'That's what you say.'

'I'm having tests done to confirm it. One of two people must have put the gun there, you or your lover.'

'I object to that term.'

'Does it embarrass you?'

'It's inaccurate. There was no love in our relationship.'

'Let's suppose, for the sake of argument, that he did go to the Quai de la Mégisserie.'

'To murder my aunt?'

'To look for her nice little nest-egg, to use the expression you objected to just now. The old lady came back, and found herself face-to-face with him. And he snatched up a cushion from the couch, and smothered her with it.'

'Where does the revolver come into it? Why should he have taken it? Why should he have hidden it on top of my wardrobe, and why, when he left for Toulon, should he have taken it with him?'

'So you think he took it with him?'

'If it really exists, it must, as you say yourself, be somewhere. For myself, I assure you that I was nowhere near my aunt's flat on the afternoon of her death. And I don't believe for a moment that Marcel was either. He may be a bad lot, as they say, but he's not a killer. Any more questions?'

'Have you done anything about claiming your inheritance?'

'Not yet. I have an appointment later today with a solicitor, the husband of one of my clients. If it hadn't been for him, I shouldn't have known where to turn.'

She stood up, with every appearance of relief.

'When will you want my signature?'

'On your statement, do you mean? How long will it take you to type it, Lapointe?'

'It'll be ready in half-an-hour.'

'In half-an-hour. I suggest you make yourself comfortable in the waiting room meanwhile.'

'Can't I come back some other time?'

'No. I want to get it over and done with. You can see your solicitor later, and by tonight you'll be some tens of thousands of francs the richer. Incidentally, do you intend to move into your aunt's flat?'

'No. My own suits me perfectly well.'

Holding herself stiffly erect, she went to the door and without another word left the room.

*

He caught the night train, and was fortunate enough to get a sleeping compartment to himself. He awoke at dawn, as he always did when travelling south, just as the train drew into Montélimar.

To him, Montélimar had always been the frontier town of Provence. From there on, he couldn't bear to miss an inch of the terrain. He loved everything about it, the trees and flowers, the countryside, the pale pink and lavender blue houses, with their sun-baked tiled roofs, the villages with their avenues of plane trees and their little bars, where people were already assembling.

At Marseilles, while the train was shunting in the Gare Saint-Charles, he listened with relish to the sing-song voices of the locals.

It was a long time since he and his wife had last been to the Riviera. Why should they not spend their next holiday there? But it would be the height of the season by then, and the whole area would be swarming with tourists.

A few more miles, and there was the sea, as blue as in any postcard, dotted with boats, with motionless fishermen aboard.

Superintendent Marella was waiting for him on the station platform and waving enthusiastically.

'Why don't you come more often? How many years is it since you were last in Toulon?'

'About ten, as I told you on the telephone. I hope you don't mind me trespassing on your territory like this?'

Maigret was outside his own territory. Here Marella was the boss. He was, needless to say, very dark. Though not above medium height, he was extremely ebullient. Since their last meeting, he had developed something of a paunch, which somehow lent him an air of respectability.

In the old days, he had looked more like a gangster than a police officer. Gangsters are no less prone to middle-aged spread than anyone else, but they usually retire before it overtakes them.

'Would you care for a coffee?'

'I'd love one. I had a cup on the train, but it tasted foul.'

'Right then, let's go. There's quite a decent little place across the square.'

The square was shimmering in the heat. They went into a café-restaurant and sat down at the bar.

'Come on then. Tell us all about it.'

'There's nothing to tell. It's a queer business. I can't make any sense of it. I'm just floundering. Where is Marcel at the moment?'

'In his bed. He spent half the night whooping it up with his buddies in the Restaurant Victor, opposite the Port-Marchand. A lot of layabouts, they are. Later, they were joined by some girls.'

'Did you ever come across him when he lived here?'

'He was never in Toulon for very long. His longest stay was two years. I should tell you that none of the villains hereabouts takes him very seriously. He's looked on as a bit of an amateur.'

'Who's this fellow Bob, that he uses as an accommodation address?'

'The barman at l'Amiral. He's up to every trick. At any rate, none of us here has ever been able to pin anything on him.'

'And the Giovanni brothers?'

'Only one of them lives here. Pepito, the older of the two. The other, I'm told, has a place just outside Paris. Pepito owns a magnificent villa, which he bought from a rich old American, who decided she wanted to go home and lay her bones in the old country. It's the finest property in Sanary, with its own private anchorage, in which he keeps his motor launch.

'He's practically a recluse, and scarcely ever sees any of his old cronies. Out of sight, out of mind, appears to be his motto. All the same, I've been keeping an eye on him. And, what's more, he knows it, and whenever we pass in the street, he greets me most cordially.'

'I wonder what on earth Marcel could possibly have had to say to him.'

'Me too. Especially as Marcel was never one of his boys.'

'Where is he staying?'

'At the Hôtel des Cinq Continents, in the Avenue de la République. It's almost next door to the Harbour-master's Office.'

It was still only eight o'clock.

'Would you mind coming with me? It will help put you in the picture. He'll be livid at being woken up at this time of the morning.'

Maigret did not book into a hotel, as he was hoping to be able to leave that same evening. Marella enquired at the desk for the number of Marcel's room, and they went up together and knocked loudly on his door. It was some time before a sleepy voice called out:

'Who's there?'

'Police.'

It was Marella who had spoken. Marcel, in crumpled pyjamas, and barefooted, stumbled to the door and opened it.

'Good Lord! Not you again!' he grumbled, catching sight of Maigret. 'Oh well, as you're with Superintendent Marella…'

He pulled back the curtains, lit a cigarette, and hastily removed a pair of trousers which were thrown on a chair.

'What have I done now?' he asked.

'Nothing new, as far as I know.'

'As a matter of fact,' broke in Marella, addressing Marcel, 'there was one thing. Yesterday afternoon you went to see La Belle Maria. Don't you know that, for months now, she's been Scarface's girl?'

'I also know that he's in the nick.'

'True enough. I brought him in last week, and this time

it's on a very serious charge, trafficking in drugs, no less. All the same, he's got friends on the outside, and you're on foreign soil here.'

'Thanks for the tip. But she's a very old friend. But what about you, Monsieur Maigret? What brings you all this way, only two days after our last meeting?'

'Maybe I've come to take you back to Paris.'

'What? You must be joking!'

'First of all, there's that little matter of the key.'

'What key?'

'The key to the old lady's flat. Who took the wax impression? Angèle couldn't have managed that on her own.'

Marcel didn't bat an eyelid.

'All right! Save your answers for your official statement, which will be taken down and which you will be required to sign.'

'Heavens above! Do you never listen? I know nothing whatever about that filthy business, I tell you! O.K., I was living with the Sergeant-Major, though only, I may say, until I found something better, and I was only too glad to be shot of her.'

'There are at least two witnesses who remember seeing you.'

'How did they identify me?'

'From a photograph on our files, or rather on the Vice Squad files.'

'And who, pray, are these two witnesses?'

'The owner of the pet-shop on the ground floor, and the tenant who lives in the flat across the landing from the old lady. You actually bumped into her on the stairs, because you weren't looking where you were going, and you apologised.'

'They must both be mad.'

'You were wearing the same check suit that you had on the day before yesterday.'

'I bought it in one of the big department stores. There must be thousands like it in Paris.'

'So, you had no key. Did you pick the lock?'

'How much longer is this going on?'

'I couldn't say. Why?'

'Because if you intend to stay, I'd like to order myself some breakfast.'

'Go ahead.'

He rang for the floor waiter, and ordered coffee and croissants.

'And if you were expecting me to order anything for you, you're in for a disappointment. I've never picked a lock in my life. I wouldn't know how.'

'When did she first tell you about the revolver?'

'Who?'

'You know very well who. Angèle. You're not suggesting, are you, that you guessed the old lady kept a revolver in her flat?'

'I didn't even know of the old girl's existence.'

'That's a lie. Angèle has admitted, in her signed statement, that she pointed to the windows of her aunt's flat, and told you that she was her heir.'

'And you believe her? She'd lie as soon as look at you, that one.'

'And you wouldn't, I suppose?'

'I'm telling you the truth. You won't trip me up, just because you've got your nasty, suspicious eye on me. Take that photograph you got from the Vice Squad. When was it taken, I'd like to know? I have no recollection of it.'

The waiter came in with the coffee and croissants, which filled the room with an appetising smell. He put the tray down on a small pedestal table. Marcel, still in his pyjamas and bare-footed, drew up a chair, and began to eat.

Marella glanced at Maigret with eyebrows raised, as though seeking permission to intervene.

'What were you talking to Bob about?'

'The night before last, soon after I got here? I told him all my news, and he told me his. We're old friends, and it's ages since we last met.'

'And what else?'

'I don't know what you mean.'

'Which of the two of you thought of Giovanni?'

'I think I did. I knew him too, back in the old days, when he lived in Montmartre. I was only a kid then.'

'Why, in that case, didn't you ring him yourself?'

'What on earth for?'

'To make an appointment to see him. As Bob did on your behalf. What was it you wanted to talk to him about?'

'I don't know what you mean.'

'Don't be an idiot. As you very well know, one can't just turn up on Giovanni's doorstep, especially if one happens to be nothing more than a miserable, down-and-out little pimp. But the fact remains that you did go and see him yesterday, and you were with him for nearly an hour.'

'I just went along for a chat, that's all.'

'And what, may I ask, did you chat about?'

Marcel was beginning to show signs of nervousness. He was not at all happy with this particular line of enquiry.

'Let's say I went along to ask him for a job. He has a great many irons in the fire, all on the level. I thought he could probably use a man he could trust.'

'Did he take you on?'

'He wanted time to think it over. He said he'd let me know in a day or two.'

Once more, Marella glanced at Maigret, to indicate that he had finished.

'You heard what my colleague, Marella, said just now. He will be giving the necessary instructions to his staff. You will therefore oblige us by calling at his office, and repeating all you have said to us. This will be taken down by a shorthand writer, and in due course you will be required to sign the transcript.

'Be sure you leave nothing out, especially where Bob and Giovanni are concerned.'

'Do I have to bring him in?'

'Have you told the truth?'

'Yes. But he wouldn't like it if he knew I'd been discussing him with the cops.'

'I'm afraid you have no choice. And don't attempt to leave Toulon until we give you the word.'

'Whatever you say, but if I don't manage to find a job, will you pay my hotel bill?'

'Maybe we can arrange to put you up somewhere else,' interposed Marella. 'It's nice and cool in there, at any rate.'

The two men went out into the avenue.

'I hope you didn't think I was taking too much on myself?' said Marella, a little anxiously.

'Far from it. You were most helpful. I'd be very grateful if you'd do the same for me with Bob.'

The Bar de l'Amiral was just on the other side of the avenue, on the corner of the quay and a narrow cul-de-sac. Out on the pavement, there were four tables, covered with cloths of a small check pattern. Outside, the sunshine, reflected on the shimmering expanse of water, was dazzling. In contrast, the interior of the bar was dark and pleasantly cool.

A barman, with the broken nose and cauliflower ears of a boxer, was busy washing glasses. It was too early in the day for customers, and the room was deserted, except for a waiter who was laying the tables.

'Good morning, Superintendent. What can I get you?'

He spoke to Marella, whom he knew. Maigret was a stranger to him.

'Have you a good local wine?' asked Maigret.

'A carafe of rosé?'

'Two glasses, or a carafe, as you wish.'

Both men were in high good humour. Only Bob appeared uneasy.

'You had a visitor last night, I noticed, Bob.'

'We're never short of visitors here. you know.'

'I don't mean a customer. I'm referring to someone who came all the way from Paris expressly to see you.'

'To see me, me in particular?'

'Well, let's say to ask you a favour.'

'I can't imagine what.'

'Have you known him long?'

'Seven or eight years.'

'Is he on the level?'

'He's never done time, if that's what you mean. He hasn't got a record.'

'And what about you?'

'You know the answer to that. I haven't got a perfectly clean sheet.'

'What was it he wanted?'

'He happened to be passing, and he just dropped in for a chat.'

'He asked you to make a telephone call for him.'

'Oh?'

'Don't play the fool with me. One of my men was in here at the time. You left your friend at the bar, and shut yourself up in the telephone box, and made a call. It was a long call. Your friend was very jumpy. When you got back, you talked to him at some length in an undertone, after which he looked a good deal relieved.'

'I dare say it was about his ex-girl friend, Maria. He'd been to see her.'

'Is she living at Sanary now?'

'You must be joking!'

'It's not in your interest to hold out on me, Bob. The person you spoke to on the telephone was Pepito Giovanni. You worked for him once upon a time, before he went straight. You persuaded him to see your mate Marcel. Quite a feat that, because Giovanni won't see any Tom, Dick or Harry, especially in his own house. How did you manage it?'

'I just told Giovanni that I had a friend with me, who was looking for a job.'

'No!'

'Why do you say no?'

'Because you know as well as I do that it's not true. Giovanni will laugh his head off when I tell him.'

'I told him that Marcel had an interesting proposition to put to him. And nothing illegal about it either.'

'Did he show you the prototype?'

'No.'

'Do you know what it is?'

'Marcel didn't tell me. All he would say was that it was something very, very big, with international potential, and likely to be of special interest to the Americans.'

'That's a bit more like it. Maybe we're getting to the truth at last. Was Giovanni interested?'

'He agreed to see Marcel yesterday afternoon at three.'

'Anything else?'

'He said to be sure and see that no one went with him,

and to tell him not to forget the protoype.'

The vin rosé was fruity in flavour and perfectly chilled. Maigret listened to the interchange, smiling a little to himself. He had always had a great affection for Marella, and it occurred to him that, had he stayed in Paris, he might well now be sitting in his, Maigret's, seat at the Quai des Orfèvres. But he was more in his element in Toulon. He had been born in Nice, and knew every delinquent and prostitute from Menton to Marseilles.

'Is there anything you want to ask him, Maigret?'

Bob frowned.

'Do you mean to say that's Chief Superintendent Maigret with you?'

'None other. And, if you don't watch out, he's the one you may find yourself up against.'

'Forgive me, I didn't recognise you.'

And, as Maigret was opening his wallet:

'No, no. It's on the house.'

'I'm sorry, I can't agree to that.'

He laid a ten-franc note on the table.

'I presume that, the minute we've left, you'll be on the phone to Giovanni?'

'Not if you don't want me to. I've no wish to get on the wrong side of you. Nor of Superintendent Marella, for that matter.'

They stood for a moment in the sunlit square, watching the sailors go by, with their navy blue collars and red pompoms.

'Do you want me to come with you to see Giovanni? Or would you rather go alone?'

'I wouldn't dream of going without you.'

'In that case, let's go back to Police Headquarters, and collect my car.'

They crossed the Seyne, where they saw a ship being broken up, and were soon in sight of Sanary Point, on the very end of which stood an imposing villa in its own grounds.

'That's the house. Even if Bob has kept his word. Marcel will have been in touch with him, so he'll be expecting us. It won't be quite such plain sailing with him.'

CHAPTER SIX

He came towards them, hand outstretched, across a huge drawing room which was bathed in sunlight. He was wearing a cream shantung suit.

'Good-day to you, Marella,' he said, then pretending to notice Maigret for the first time:

'Chief Superintendent Maigret, of all people! This is an unexpected honour.'

He was a fine-looking man, powerfully built, but without an ounce of surplus fat on him. Maigret knew that he must be over sixty, but, at first glance at least, he looked nearer fifty.

The drawing room was furnished with great taste, probably by an interior decorator, and there was a hint of the theatre about it, owing to its lofty proportions.

'Where would you prefer to sit, here or on the terrace?'

He led the way out, and installed them in comfortable lounging chairs under a beach umbrella.

The butler, in a white jacket, had followed them out and stood, a watchful figure, awaiting orders.

'What would you like to drink? May I suggest a Tom Collins? I know of nothing more refreshing at this time of day.'

Maigret and Marella indicated their approval.

'Two Tom Collinses, Georges, and the usual for me.'

He was close-shaven, with well-kept hands and manicured nails. His manner was easy and relaxed.

'Have you only just got here?' he asked Maigret, by way of making polite conversation.

The terrace looked out on to the sea, which seemed to extend to infinity. A motor-launch rocked gently in the little private anchorage.

'I came on the night train.'

'Don't tell me you came all this way just to see me!'

'I had no idea, when I arrived, that I should be coming to see you at all.'

'All the same, I'm flattered.'

Beneath his genial manner he was a hard man, however much he tried to conceal it by a display of affability.

'At any rate, you're not on home territory now, Chief Superintendent.'

'True enough, but my good friend Marella here is.'

'Marella and I understand one another perfectly. Don't we, Marella?'

'Just so long as you keep on the right side of the law.'

'I lead such a very quiet life, you know that. I hardly ever go out. You could almost say that my whole world is bounded by these four walls. I never see a soul, except for a friend occasionally, or a pretty girl from time to time.'

'Do you number Le Grand Marcel among your friends?'

He looked shocked.

That seedy little runt who came to see me yesterday morning?'

'Be that as it may, you did agree to see him.'

'It's a point of principle with me never to refuse a helping hand. There have been times in the past when I too was in need of help.'

'And did you help him?'

The butler reappeared with a tray, on which there were two tall frosted glasses and a smaller glass full of tomato juice.

'Please forgive me. I never touch wine or spirits. Cheers!

'But I interrupted you. What was it you were saying?'

'I asked you if you had been able to help him.'

'Unfortunately not. I couldn't see my way to fitting him in anywhere.

'You see, Monsieur Maigret, a lot of water has flowed

under the Pont-Neuf since last we met. Nowadays I'm a highly respected business tycoon, if I may say so.

'I own a dozen cinemas up and down the Côte d'Azur, two in Marseilles, one in Nice, one in Antibes, and three in Cannes, not to mention the one in Aix-en-Provence.

'I am also the proprietor of a night club in Marseilles, and of three hotels, one of them in Menton.

'And all perfectly respectable, I assure you. Isn't that so, Marella?'

'Quite correct.'

'I also own a restaurant in Paris, on the Avenue de la Grande-Armée. My brother manages it for me. It's an extremely smart place, and the food is superb. You'll be welcome there as my guest any time.'

Maigret was watching him closely, his expression inscrutable.

'You must see, Chief Superintendent, that in my kind of set-up, there's no room for a petty little pimp like Marcel.'

'Did he leave the protoype with you?'

Giovanni, for all his self-assurance, was visibly shaken.

'Prototype? What are you talking about? You must be making a mistake.'

'You agreed to see Marcel because Bob told you on the telephone that he was on to something big, something with almost unlimited potential.'

'I don't understand. It sounds like a fairy tale to me. Surely you didn't get it from Bob?'

'I understand that it was likely to be of particular interest to the Americans.'

'But I have no American business connections.'

'I'm going to tell you a little story, Giovanni, and I hope you may learn something from it. Once upon a time, there lived in Paris a dear little old lady who got it into her head that someone was sneaking into her flat while she was out and moving her things, so that, when she got back, everything was very slightly out of place.'

'I don't see what...'

'Let me finish. This same old lady came to Police Headquarters to ask for protection, but I'm sorry to say we all thought she was mad, to begin with at least. All the same, I had intended to go and see her, if only to reassure her.'

'I seem to remember reading something about it in the newspapers.'

'It was referred to briefly, but the press had no idea what it was really all about.'

'Would you care for a cigar?'

'Thanks all the same, but I prefer my pipe.'

'What about you, Marella?'

'With pleasure.'

There was a box of Havana cigars on the table. Giovanni and Marella each took one.

'Forgive me. I shouldn't have interrupted you. You went to call on the old lady....'

'There's a lot more before we get to that.'

'Please go on.'

'She had an elderly niece with a marked predilection for men much younger than herself. For the past six months, for instance, she's had Marcel living with her, that same Marcel who came to see you yesterday.'

Giovanni was now listening with interest.

'The old lady was murdered before I had a chance to go and see her as I had promised.'

'How was she killed?'

'She was suffocated with a cushion. She couldn't, at her age, put up very much of a fight.'

'I still don't understand what all this has to do with me.'

'As I told you, Le Grand Marcel and the old lady's niece were lovers. There are two witnesses who are prepared to swear that they saw him in the house where the old lady lived on at least one occasion.'

'Do you suspect him of the murder?'

'Either him or the niece. It comes to the same thing, more or less.'

'What were they after?'

'The prototype.'

'What do you mean?'

'Whatever it was that Marcel came to sell you.'

'And what might that be?'

'You should know better than I do, since, unless I'm

very much mistaken, it is now in your possession.'

'I still don't know what you're talking about.'

'I'm talking about a revolver. I may as well admit right away that I don't know what sort of revolver, or what there is about it that makes it so special.'

'I've never carried a gun in my life, as you very well know. Even in the very early days, when I was just a young delinquent, I was often stopped and searched by the police, but they were never once able to charge me with being in illegal possession of a firearm.'

'I know.'

'That being so, what possible inducement do you suppose there could be for me to take a revolver from a sleazy little pimp like Marcel?'

'Have no fear, I'm not going to ask my friend Marella to rummage through your house from cellar to attic. You're far too wily a customer to leave the article in question in any place where we could hope to find it.'

'You flatter me. How about another Tom Collins?'

'One is quite enough, thanks all the same.'

Marella had never seen Maigret so circumspect. He spoke very quietly, as though what he was saying mattered very little, and yet somehow every word struck home.

'It was more than I could expect, that you should admit the real purpose of Le Grand Marcel's visit. I came simply to warn you. You certainly won't have learnt from him that the revolver in question is a vital clue in a murder case.

'The murder itself was unpremeditated. The old lady, who used to spend the greater part of every afternoon sitting on a bench in the Tuileries must, for some reason, have returned home earlier than usual. The intruder, man or woman...'

'Do you mean the niece?'

'The niece, yes. He or she snatched up a cushion from the couch, and held it over the old lady's face for as long as was necessary.

'I'm sure I need not labour the point, but you must realise that any international deal you may have in mind could have unhealthy repercussions affecting your legitimate business interests, your hotels and restaurants and so forth.'

Maigret fell silent. His expression was bland. Giovanni was looking a little uneasy, and doing his best to conceal it.

'Thanks for the warning. I can assure you that if the fellow turns up here again, he won't get past the door.'

'He won't come back until you give him the word, and I know you won't do that.'

'Did you know about this, Marella?'

'Not until yesterday.'

'I trust you have put your colleague Maigret in the picture. Doesn't he know that I am now a highly respected business man, and that I'm on the very best of terms with all those in authority, from the Prefect downwards?'

'I did tell him, yes.'

'Then it only remains for me to repeat that I am in no way involved in this sordid little affair.'

Maigret stood up with a sigh.

'Thanks for the Tom Collins.'

Marella also got to his feet, and the two men, accompanied by Giovanni, crossed the vast drawing room, and stood for a moment in the doorway at the top of the broad flight of marble steps that led down to the garden.

'You'll always be welcome here at any time, gentlemen.'

They got into Marella's car.

When they were outside the main gates, Maigret said:

'There must be some little pub or other in the neighbourhood, from which we can see the villa. If you know of one, stop there.'

They found a little bistro, painted blue, in Sanary itself. Outside there were four men playing bowls.

'What will you have?'

'A glass of rosé. That Tom Collins left a nasty taste in my mouth.'

'I couldn't make out what you were up to,' murmured Marella. 'You didn't press home your advantage. I almost got the impression that you wanted him to think you believed him.'

'Well, for one thing, he's not the man to give anything away.'

'That's true.'

'And anyway, what have I got to go on? Following a telephone call from Bob the Barman, he agreed to see our shady little friend. I haven't even got an accurate description of the revolver.'

'So there really is a revolver?'

'There most certainly is. That was what the intruders were looking for when they disturbed the old lady's ornaments.

'And even if you were able to spare every man you've got for the search, what hope would we have of finding it in that great barracks of a place? You don't imagine, do you, that Giovanni just slipped it into his bedside table drawer?

'Anyway, we shall soon see whether I'm right.'

And a quarter of an hour later, they did see. A man in a yachting cap appeared, boarded the little motor launch, and started up the engine.

A few seconds later, Giovanni followed him down the steps to the landing stage, and climbed aboard.

'Don't you see, it's too hot for him to handle. He can't wait to get rid of it. At any rate, the deal is off.'

The launch nosed out of the anchorage, and headed for the open sea in a swathe of spray.

'In a few minutes, the revolver will be heaven knows how many fathoms deep on the ocean bed. It will never be found.'

'I see.'

'At any rate, there's nothing more for me to do here in Toulon.'

'I hope you'll stay and dine with us. We've got a spare room now.'

'I'm going back on the night train.'

'Must you?'

'I'm afraid so. I've got a very busy day ahead of me tomorrow.'

'The niece?'

'Among others. Le Grand Marcel will still need watching, and if you take my advice, you'll keep an eye on that fellow Bob. It strikes me he has a good deal too much influence for a mere barman. Do you really believe Giovanni is as straight as he makes out?'

'I've been trying to catch him for years. Men of his sort, even when they have bought their passport to respectability, like to keep discreetly in touch with their old chums in the underworld. You've just seen for yourself.'

The white launch, having described a wide arc in the sea, was now returning to the anchorage.

'I daresay he's feeling mighty relieved, now that he's got rid of his precious prototype.'

'What do you plan to do between now and catching your train?'

'I'd like another word with Le Grand Marcel. Do you think I might find him at Maria's?'

'I very much doubt it. After what I told him about her boy friend, he's sure to keep well away from her. He may act tough, but it's only an act. He's not the sort to stick his neck out.'

'What about l'Amiral?'

'He's sure to look in there sometime.'

It was five o'clock by the time they got to l'Amiral. The bar, once again, was deserted, and Bob was sitting at a table with Le Grand Marcel, who, on catching sight of the two police officers, burst out:

'What, again!'

'Yes, here we are again. Would you bring us a carafe of rosé, Bob?'

'How many times do I have to tell you that I didn't kill the old girl?'

'Be that as it may, you did go to her flat in the Quai de la Mégisserie.'

Maigret, looking very benign, had used the familiar *tu*.

'I'd like to see you prove it. I'd also be obliged if you'd tell me what I was supposed to be doing there.'

'Looking for the prototype.'

'I don't know what you're talking about.'

'I've just come from seeing someone else who said exactly the same thing, someone a lot tougher than you are. But, in spite of what he said, he knew well enough.'

'You've been to see Giovanni?'

Marcel had gone very white. Bob came up to the table with a carafe of wine and two glasses on a tray.

'What did he tell you?'

'A good prospect on the international market, did you say, and likely to be of particular interest to the Americans?'

'I still don't know what you're talking about.'

'No matter. Only I'm warning you that if you have it in mind to go back to the villa in Sanary in the hope of raking in a tidy sum, you'd better think again.'

Bob, resuming his seat at the table, asked:

'Have you seen Giovanni?'

'We've just come from there.'

'Did he tell you Marcel had been to see him?'

'And that you had rung to make the appointment.'

He savoured the local wine, sipping it with discernment. In two hours' time he would be in the train, on his way back to Paris.

Then he turned his attention once more to Marcel.

'If it really wasn't you who killed the old lady, you'd be well advised to tell me the whole truth, and come back with me to Paris.'

Nervously, the man clenched his long fingers.

'What have you to say about it, Bob?'

'It's no concern of mine. I'm ready to give a helping hand to a friend when I can, but that's as far as it goes. I know nothing about this business.'

'What should I go back to Paris for?' asked Marcel.

'To get yourself safely locked up in prison.'

'But I've already told you...'

'I know, I know. You didn't kill the old lady. It was her niece who did it. That won't prevent your being charged as an accessory.'

'And so you're advising me to leave Toulon, just so as you can arrest me?'

'I have a feeling you'd be safer there than here.'

A look of cunning spread over Marcel's features.

'Oh no, Chief Superintendent. I wasn't born yesterday. If you have a warrant for my arrest, show it to me and I'll come quietly. But, as you very well know, you can't arrest me without proof, and all you've got is a couple of lousy witnesses, who claim to have seen someone wearing a check suit like mine.'

'It's up to you.'

'So that's my reward for keeping my nose clean for years!'

'It's a pity you couldn't keep it up.'

This time, it was Marella who paid for the drinks. Then, glancing at his watch, he said:

'You'll just have time to come and say hello to my wife, and see over our new house.'

It was a little way out of the town, on a hill. It was quite a small villa, but pleasant and colourful, with a very attractive outlook.

A boy of fifteen was mowing the lawn. The motor buzzed like a gigantic blue-bottle.

'You know my son Alain.'

'He was a baby when I saw him last.'

'As you can see, the baby has grown somewhat.'

They went into the sitting room, which was really more of a spacious living room. Madame Marella emerged from the kitchen carrying a rolling pin.

'Oh sorry! I didn't realise we had a visitor.'

Maigret kissed her on both cheeks. Her name was Claudine, and he had never seen her without a smile.

'You'll stay for dinner, I hope. I'm just in the middle of making a strawberry tart.'

'He's got to catch the night train back to Paris.'

'Have you been here long, Maigret?'

'I arrived this morning.'

'Do you really have to go back so soon?'

'Thanks to your husband's invaluable help, I've done what I came to do.'

'What can I give you? You seem to like our local wines. I've got much better stuff in the cellar than anything they stock at l'Amiral.'

For nearly an hour they sat talking of this and that. Alain, the fifteen-year-old son, came in to shake the Chief Superintendent by the hand.

'Why aren't you at school?'

'It's Saturday. Had you forgotten?'

So it was. Maigret had forgotten. In the confusion of the past week he had lost all track of time.

'What form are you in?'

'Classical Third.'

'Will you be following in your father's footsteps?'

'Oh no! Just think of the hours! And even when one's in bed, there's no guarantee one won't be called out again. Father never knows when the telephone may ring.'

Maigret felt sad. He had always longed for a son of his own, even a son who didn't want to be a policeman.

'I must be on my way. It wouldn't do to miss my train.'

'I'll drive you to the station.'

A few minutes later they were in the car, and Claudine was waving goodbye from the top of the steps.

The Boulevard Richard-Lenoir, as always on a Sunday morning, was almost deserted. The sound of a taxi door slamming was enough to bring Madame Maigret running to the window.

She was waiting for him on the landing.

'I thought you'd be spending the night in Toulon. Why didn't you ring and let me know you were coming?'

'I thought I'd give you a surprise.'

She was doing the housework, with her head tied up in a scarf.

'You didn't overtire yourself, I hope?'

'Not in the least. I had a very good night's sleep.'

'Shall I run you a bath?'

'Yes, that would be lovely.'

He had shaved on the train, as he always did when returning to Paris.

'Everything work out all right?'

'More or less. Incidentally, Marella and Claudine sent you their kindest regards. They've built themselves a very pretty little house on the outskirts of the town.'

'Claudine was as cheerful as ever, I suppose?'

'She hasn't changed. The only one who has is their son. He's a hulking great lad now, with a very deep voice.'

'Are you free for the rest of the day?'

'Almost, though I shall have to go out for a little while

later.'

While his bath was running, he rang Police Headquarters. Once again it was dear old Lucas who was on duty.

'Anything been happening while I've been away?'

'Nothing special, chief.'

'Who have you got there with you?'

'Neveu, Janin, Loutrie....'

'Hold it! I don't need all that many. Tell them I want a twenty-four hour watch kept on the flat of the masseuse Angèle Louette in the Rue Saint-André-des-Arts. They can arrange a rota to suit themselves. There's no need for them to keep out of sight. Oh, and one other thing. Warn them that she's got a car.'

He lay soaking for a long time in the soapy water, while his wife made fresh coffee for him. At about half-past nine, he went down into the street, hailed a taxi, and asked the driver to take him to the corner of the Rue Saint-André-des-Arts. Janin was on duty at the door. The Chief Superintendent shook him by the hand.

'I'm going up to see her now, and it's possible that what I have to say to her may send her running for cover.'

'Don't worry. I'll keep my eyes skinned. Neveu and I have got it all worked out. Neither of us particularly wanted to do a long stint, so we're taking turn and turn about every three hours, and tomorrow night Loutrie will give us a hand.'

Maigret went upstairs and rang the bell. The door was opened almost at once.

Angèle Louette, still wearing her black suit, was just putting on a hat.

'You again!' she muttered sullenly. 'Can't you leave me alone even for one day?'

'Are you going out?'

'What do you think? I'm not in the habit of doing my housework with a hat on.'

'I've just got back from Toulon.'

'What's that got to do with me?'

'A great deal, I assure you. Your boy friend drove there in his car. I saw him there.'

'It's all over between us.'

'Oh no, it's not! He was the one who undertook to negotiate with Giovanni, remember?'

Involuntarily, she gave a start.

'I may as well tell you right away that he didn't pull it off. Your aunt died for nothing. Would you like to know where the revolver is now? It's at the bottom of the Mediterranean, buried heaven knows how many hundreds of fathoms deep.

'Didn't Marcel ring and tell you?'

'If he'd rung to tell me you were coming, I'd have made it my business not to be at home.'

'Where are you going now?'

'To Mass, if you must know. And if that surprises you, it's just too bad.'

'Kindly listen to me. You are required to attend for interrogation in my office at nine o'clock tomorrow morning. This is an official summons, so please don't be late. I advise you to bring a suitcase with such personal effects as you think you may need, including a change of underwear. In other words, we may be obliged to detain you for a time.'

'You mean I'm to be arrested?'

'It's a possibility you have to face, although the decision rests not with me but with the examining magistrate. Just one more thing, and then you can go. An hour ago, I gave instructions that you were to be kept under supervision for twenty-four hours a day, and this will continue until you arrive at my office tomorrow morning.'

'I hate you!'

'That doesn't surprise me.'

All the way down the stairs, Maigret could hear her pacing up and down the living room, swearing like a trooper.

'Do you know what she looks like?' he asked Janin.

'No.'

'She'll be down in a moment. I'll point her out to you.

Some ten minutes later, she appeared. As she came out and caught sight of the two men standing on the pavement opposite, she gave a violent start.

'You oughtn't to have any difficulty in keeping her in

sight. If she ever took up boxing, she'd be in the heavyweight class.'

He walked home, enjoying the sunshine in the quiet of a Sunday morning. How would they spend the afternoon, he wondered. Sometimes they went out in the car, with Madame Maigret at the wheel, but on the whole she preferred not to drive on a Sunday, especially on the busy roads out of Paris.

Not that it mattered what they did. Even if they only strolled side by side through the streets, they were never bored.

'Your friend Marella telephoned. You just missed him by five minutes. He wants you to ring him back at his house as soon as possible. He says he gave you his number.'

She looked enquiringly at her husband.

'You don't seem surprised that he should be ringing you on a Sunday morning, when you only saw him last night.'

'I was half expecting it.'

He put through a call to Toulon. Within a few minutes, Marella was on the line.

'Did you have a good journey?'

'Thanks to your local wine, I slept like a baby.'

'I daresay you can guess what I rang you about.'

'What's happened to him?'

'At seven o'clock this morning, he was fished out of the harbour.'

'Knifed?'

'No. A ·38 bullet right between the eyes.'

A silence followed, both men thinking their own thoughts.

'You did your best by advising him to go with you to Paris. But he was too clever by half. He thought you were lying, and that there was still something in it for him.'

'No hope of pinning it on Giovanni, I suppose?'

'You can bet your life he's covered his tracks. Probably the killer didn't even know who he was working for. No doubt he got his instructions from some intermediary, whom Giovanni knew he could trust.'

'Any ideas?'

'Too many. There are at least twenty men in this area

who could have done it. Very likely, he got someone from Nice or Cannes or Marseilles. And I bet you anything you like he isn't in Toulon now. He wouldn't be likely to hang around waiting to be recognised.'

Marella paused, apparently lost in thought.

'Mind you, we'll catch up with him eventually, but it will probably be in four or five years' time, and for something quite different.'

'You don't need to tell me. We have the same problems here. Thanks for letting me know, anyway. Were you there when they emptied his pockets?'

'Yes. Nothing of much interest. Two thousand francs in his wallet, along with his identity card and driving licence. His road-fund licence was in the glove compartment of his car, which was left all night outside the Hôtel des Cinq Continents.

'And there was also some small change and a key.'

'I'd be grateful if you'd let me have the key.'

'I'll post it to you as soon as I can. I'll take it to the railway station myself. Apart from the items I mentioned, there were a handkerchief, some cigarettes and a packet of chewing gum.'

'Have you been through his suitcase?'

'A black and white check suit. Some underwear. No papers. Nothing else, in fact, but a cheap paperback novel with a lurid cover.'

'Not even a notebook with telephone numbers?'

'No. But someone may have got to it before me. According to the Police Surgeon, he died somewhere around one in the morning. That's only a provisional estimate, of course. We won't know for sure until later today, after the autopsy.'

'I hope Claudine won't hold it against me?'

'Hold what against you?'

'Well, it's because of me that your Sunday morning has been ruined.'

'She's in the kitchen. Hold on! She's saying something. She wants to be remembered to you both. As far as I'm concerned, this is now no more than a routine enquiry, which I shall leave in the hands of my deputy.'

'Have you seen Bob again?'

'No. I hope he won't go the same way. I'd be sorry, because he's always played straight with me.'

'Surely he's too valuable to Giovanni?'

'So you've been thinking along the same lines as I have! There has to be a linkman between Giovanni and his chums in the underworld.'

'And who better than Bob, wouldn't you say?'

'Good day to you!'

'The same to you! And many thanks for all your help.'

Maigret replaced the receiver.

'Bad news?' asked Madame Maigret, noting his worried expression.

'From the professional angle, I suppose I should call it very good news. A petty crook has been murdered in Toulon, thus saving the state an expensive trial. He's been known to us for a long time as a pimp, and of late he's been living on a woman of fifty-five. If he wasn't a murderer himself, he was certainly an accomplice.'

'Are you talking about the old lady?'

The old lady in the white hat and gloves, yes. He could still see her, suddenly stepping into his path on the pavement of the Quai des Orfèvres, and looking up at him, her eyes glowing with admiration and hope.

She was dead. And now Le Grand Marcel was dead too, and the object for which the couple had searched so long, the precious revolver, which had been in the bedside table drawer all the time, was lost and gone forever.

'What are we having for lunch?'

'*Blanquette* of veal.'

They sat around until half-past twelve. Maigret even went so far as to turn on the radio for the news, though, as he had expected, there was no reference to the murder in Toulon.

'Don't think about her. It's such a lovely day.'

'Too lovely to stay shut up indoors, don't you think?'

'Have you anything particular in mind?'

'We can talk about that as we go.'

As always, she took his arm, and they walked towards the Quais. On the Quai de la Mégisserie they went past the bird shop, which today had the shutters up, and stopped for a moment outside the building where the old lady had lived.

'What floor?'

'First.'

'That's going to make someone very happy.'

'What do you mean?'

'The people who take her flat. They'll have one of the finest views in Paris.'

They walked on and, before very long, they were in the Tuileries Gardens.

'Let's sit down for a few minutes,' he suggested.

And thus he fulfilled a wish that had been growing on him ever since the previous night. As far as he could remember, this was the first time he had ever sat on a bench in a public park. He had always thought of park benches as serving no useful purpose, unless it were to provide resting places for tramps and lovers.

It took them some time to find an unoccupied bench. All the others were taken, and not only by elderly people. There were a great many young mothers watching their children at play. A man in his thirties was reading a book on biology.

'It's very pleasant here, isn't it?'

Little toy boats with white sails skimmed over the glassy surface of the pond.

'You'll get wet if you don't watch out, Hubert! If you lean over any further, you'll fall in!'

How restful it was. Seen from here, life seemed very simple and uneventful.

The old lady came here every day of her life, weather permitting. Perhaps, like that other old lady whom they could see over there, she scattered breadcrumbs for the birds, which flocked round her in ever growing numbers.

'Was it because of her that you brought me here?'

He admitted that it was.

'Besides, I wanted for once in my life to see what it felt like to sit on a park bench.'

With some warmth, he added:

'Especially with you.'

'You haven't got a very good memory!'

'Have we ever sat on a public bench together, then?'

'When we were engaged. It was in the gardens of the Place des Vosges. That was when you kissed me for the first time, as a matter of fact.'

'You're absolutely right. My memory must be going. I wouldn't mind kissing you now, but there are really too many people about.'

'We're a bit old for that sort of thing, don't you think?'

They decided not to go home for dinner. They went to a restaurant in the Place des Victoires. They liked the food and the atmosphere, and enjoyed going there from time to time.

'Shall we dine on the terrace?'

'I wouldn't advise it,' interposed the head waiter. 'The nights are still quite cold. It's really too early in the year to dine out of doors.'

They had sweetbreads, which were delicious, followed by tiny lamb cutlets and, to end with, strawberry shortcake.

'It's such a rare treat,' murmured Madame Maigret.

'What is?'

'Having you to myself for practically the whole day. I bet you anything you like that tomorrow I shall get a message to say you won't be in for lunch.'

'Very likely. Almost certainly, in fact. Tomorrow, I shall be having a battle of wits with the "Sergeant-Major".'

'Is that what you call that poor woman?'

'That poor woman, as you call her, in all probability murdered her aunt.'

'It wasn't premeditated, was it?'

'No.'

'I suppose, being discovered like that, she completely lost her head?'

'Are you trying to defend her?'

'No, but I can't help thinking about her. Didn't you say she was ugly?'

'A woman entirely devoid of charm, at any rate.'

'And presumably devoid of charm even as a young girl?'

'Almost certainly, I should think.'

'So, as no man would give her a second look, she had to go about things in a rather different way.'

'You would have made a good advocate.'

'Fifty-five! You did say she was fifty-five, didn't you? I daresay she thought she'd never get another after Marcel, so she clung on to him with all her might.'

'She's still clinging. She doesn't know yet what's happened to him.'

'Don't you think she'll try and make a run for it?'

'I'm having her watched twenty-four hours a day.'

'I shouldn't care to be in her place tomorrow morning.'

'I'm not exactly looking forward to it myself.'

But it was his job. And Angèle Louette was not the sort to inspire much compassion.

Madame Maigret had no difficulty in following her husband's train of thought, when he murmured:

'It's a fact that Marella's son has absolutely set his face against joining the force.'

If he himself had had a son, what advice would he have given him?

Arm in arm, they walked back to the Boulevard Richard-Lenoir, and for a long time neither spoke a word.

CHAPTER SEVEN

When, on the dot of nine, old Joseph ushered her in, Maigret found himself looking at her in rather a different light. He felt, in her presence, a degree of embarrassment that he had not felt hitherto. Perhaps it was because of what his wife had said the night before.

He even went so far as to get up to greet her, and as he did so it struck him that she looked a little pathetic, with her small overnight bag in her hand.

She was pale, but when had he ever seen her with colour in her cheeks? She was ugly. Would he have been equally hard on her if she had been an attractive woman?

'Put your case down over there, and take a seat.'

They were all set to begin. Lapointe, sitting at one end of the desk, was ready and waiting to take a shorthand note of the interview.

'It's just on nine, isn't it? I've already had to miss my eight o'clock appointment, and I had another at nine. You realise, don't you, that you're taking the bread out of my mouth?'

He had already had the reports of his inspectors on her movements the previous day. After returning from Mass, she had stayed in for the rest of the day. There had been lights burning in her flat until far into the night.

No one had been to see her. She had spent the long hours of waiting alone.

Was that why she was looking so very grave, why all the

fight seemed to have gone out of her?

He picked up the telephone.

'Would you see if Judge Libart is in yet?'

He heard the telephone ringing in an empty room.

'Not yet, Chief Superintendent, and his clerk isn't there either.'

'Thank you.'

He lit his pipe, and said to Angèle Louette:

'Do smoke if you want to.'

'You're very kind. Acceding to the last wish of the condemned woman.'

'The time has come, Mademoiselle, for us to get down to brass tacks. I may have to repeat some of the questions I have already asked you, but I sincerely hope this will be the last time.'

A mood of greyness and sullenness seemed to overhang this confrontation. It was reflected even in the weather. For the past two weeks, the sun had shone unremittingly, but now the sky was overcast, and a fine drizzle was spattering the streets of Paris.

'I take it you don't deny that your aunt was murdered?'

'The medical evidence seems conclusive.'

'Had she, as far as you know, any enemies?'

'No.'

She was calm, in a dull and heavy way, like the weather. Her expression was blank. She was looking composedly at the Chief Superintendent. Whatever her feelings, if any, she was concealing them admirably.

It was as though all those long hours of solitude on Sunday had drained the spirit out of her.

'Any friends?'

'I don't know of any friends either.'

'Were you the only person to visit her at the Quai de la Mégisserie?'

'As far as I know.'

'Used you to call by appointment?'

'My aunt hadn't a telephone. I tried to persuade her to have one installed, but she wouldn't hear of it.'

'Why did you go and see her?'

'Because I was her only relative.'

She was wearing the same black suit, as if to convey the impression that she was in mourning.

'You knew, I presume, when you were likely to find her at home?'

'Yes.'

'In other words, you were familiar with her routine.'

'She was a creature of habit.'

'Every morning she went out to do her shopping locally. Isn't that so?'

'That's right.'

'And after lunch, if I'm not mistaken, she took a nap in her armchair?'

She nodded.

'Later, weather permitting, she walked to the Tuileries Gardens, and stayed an hour or two sitting on a bench.'

'Surely we've been through all this before?'

'I have my reasons for going through it again. You were not fond of your aunt, were you?'

'No.'

'You never forgave her, did you, for palming you off with a hundred-franc note when you went to her for help because you were pregnant?'

'It's not the sort of thing one can easily forget.'

'Still, you went on going to see her. How many times a year, would you say?'

'I don't remember.'

'How many times in a month?'

'Once, sometimes twice.'

'Always at the same time of day?'

'Nearly always. I finish work at six. And she usually got in round about that time in the summer.'

'Used she to offer you a chair?'

'I didn't wait to be asked. After all, she was my aunt.'

'You were her sole heir?'

'Yes.'

'Did you often think about it?'

'I realised it would make things easier for me in my old age. It's harder work being a masseuse than most people realise. It takes a good deal of physical strength. In a few years' time I'll be too old for it.'

'In the meantime, did you ever ask her for money?'

'Occasionally. In my kind of work, there are bound to be slack periods. In the holiday season, for instance, when all my clients are away from Paris, some for two or three months.'

'Did you ever quarrel with your aunt?'

'Never.'

'Did you never reproach her for her meanness?'

'No.'

'Did she know how you felt about her?'

'I suppose so, yes.'

'Were you aware that she never kept much money in the flat?'

'I knew that, yes.'

'Who took the wax impression of the lock?'

'I didn't, at any rate.'

'Was it your lover?'

'If so, he never told me.'

'But he did show you the key he'd had cut?'

'I never saw any key.'

'Now you're lying again. Not only did you have a key to the flat, you also had a key to your Uncle Antoine's little cubby hole on the other side of the landing.'

She was sulkily silent, like a scolded child.

'I have some bad news for you, I'm afraid. When you've heard it, you may feel inclined to alter your statement. I was in Toulon the day before yesterday.'

She started violently. So she did know, as he had suspected, that Le Grand Marcel had gone to Toulon.

'First of all, you may as well admit that there was no quarrel between you, and that you did not, as you claim to have done, turn him out of doors.'

'Think what you like. I can't stop you.'

'All your indignation at his habit of spending half the day in bed was an act, put on for my benefit.'

No reaction.

'I saw him in Toulon. You, needless to say, knew perfectly well what he had gone there for.'

'No.'

'You're lying again. A few miles out of Toulon, there is a

villa belonging to a man by the name of Pepito Giovanni. He's a retired gangster. He's been going straight, more or less, for years, and is now the head of a substantial, and quite legitimate, business empire. Marcel, I imagine, must have worked for him at some time or other, though he can never have been more than a very small cog in a large machine.

'Marcel was never anything more than a petty crook. The most he ever had was a walk-on part.'

For an instant, the woman's eyes blazed with fury, but she did not speak.

'Do you go along with me so far?'

'I have nothing to say.'

'Excuse me a moment.'

He picked up the receiver again and, this time, was put through to the examining magistrate.

'Maigret speaking. May I come up and see you for a moment?'

'With pleasure, only make it as soon as you can. I have a witness to see in ten minutes' time.'

Leaving Lapointe in charge of his visitor, he let himself through the communicating door to the Palais de Justice.

'How is it going?'

'I don't want to sound over-optimistic, but I hope today will see the end of it. I went to Toulon on Saturday, as a result of which there have been several developments, but I won't bother you with them now.

'What I need at this moment is a warrant for the arrest of Angèle Louette.'

'Isn't that the niece?'

'Yes.'

'Do you really believe she killed the old lady?'

'I don't know yet, but I will very soon, I hope. Which is why I'm not sure whether or not I shall need to make use of the warrant.'

'You heard what the Chief Superintendent said, Gérard? Make out the warrant, will you?'

When Maigret got back to his office, he found the two occupants stiff and silent, like a couple of wax effigies.

He handed the warrant to Angèle.

'I take it you know what this means, and that you now understand why I asked you to bring a few personal things and a change of underwear with you?'

She neither stirred nor spoke.

'First, let's talk about Marcel. I found him in a bar in Toulon, the Bar de l'Amiral. It was an old haunt of his when he lived in the South. The barman, Bob, was a close friend of his. Did he ever speak of him?'

Dryly, she answered:

'No.'

But she was now very much on the alert, and waiting apprehensively for what was to follow.

'A man of Giovanni's standing wouldn't normally have any dealings with small fry like Marcel. An intermediary was required, and that was where Bob came in. I don't know what he said to Giovanni exactly, but it was to the effect that Marcel had something to sell, something very big. It had to be, since the former boss of the underworld agreed to see him the next morning. Do you follow me?'

'Yes.'

'You do understand that I'm talking about the revolver?'

'As I've said time and again, I've never seen the revolver to which you refer.'

'And each time you were lying. Giovanni was interested, so much so that he kept the prototype. I went to see him shortly afterwards, and we had a most interesting talk. Among other things. I told him where the revolver came from, and also how deeply Marcel was implicated in the murder of your aunt.

'Now if there's one person more touchy than another about getting mixed up in anything dirty, it's an underworld boss who has made a fortune and virtually retired from criminal activity.

'Giovanni had learnt from me that, as long as he was in possession of the gun, he was in grave danger, and I was scarcely through the gates of his house, when he boarded his motor launch and roared out to sea.

'And as a result, your uncle's precious revolver is now lying many fathoms deep on the ocean bed.'

Maigret tapped the ashes out of his pipe and filled

another.

'But that's not all that happened in Toulon. There were further developments after I left. A colleague of mine there rang me soon after I left you yesterday. But before I go into that, are you prepared to repeat your statement that everything was over between you and Marcel, and that you told him, once and for all, that you never wanted to see him again?'

'I'm waiting to hear the rest of your story.'

'Marcel himself had become something of a menace. As they say in the profession, dead men tell no tales.'

'Is he dead?'

She looked absolutely stricken. Even her voice was scarcely recognisable.

'It's no longer any concern of yours, is it?'

'What happened exactly?'

'He was shot between the eyes in the middle of the night. With a ·38 calibre gun, which no one but a professional would use. The body was found yesterday morning, floating in the old dock.'

'Is this a trap?'

'No.'

'Will you swear by everything you hold sacred?'

'I swear.'

And then the tears began to roll down her cheeks. She opened her handbag to get out a handkerchief.

CHAPTER EIGHT

He crossed over to the window, to give her time to recover. The light spring rain was still falling, and glistening umbrellas were to be seen all along the Quai.

He heard her blow her nose and, when he returned to his seat, she was dabbing a little rouge on to her cheeks.

'So you see, although your aunt paid with her life, it all came to nothing.'

She was still snuffling as she got a cigarette from her bag and lit it with a trembling hand.

'All that remains for me to discover is whether it was you or Marcel who smothered the old lady.'

Contrary to his expectations, she did not seize the opportunity of putting all the blame on her lover, who was no longer there to defend himself.

'As far as he is concerned, naturally, the case is closed. But that doesn't apply to you.'

'Why do you hate me so?'

'I don't hate you. I'm only doing my job, as humanely as possible, I hope, in the circumstances. You have persistently lied to me, right from the very first. That being so, how else could you expect me to react?'

'You know perfectly well that I loved him.'

'I'll go further than that. I believe you still love him, even now he's dead.'

'You're right, I do.'

'Why pretend you'd quarrelled and parted for ever?'

'That was his idea, to put you off the scent.'

'Did you know why he'd gone to Toulon?'

For the first time she looked him straight in the face, without attempting to lie or evade the question.

'Yes.'

'How long have you known of the existence of the revolver?'

'Thirteen or fourteen years. I got on very well with my Uncle Antoine. He was a thoroughly good sort, but rather a lonely man in a way. I don't think my aunt could give him the companionship he'd hoped for. So he spent most of his time shut up in his little cubby hole.'

'And you kept him company?'

'Quite often. He had this overriding passion for gadgets. Scarcely a year went by without his submitting an invention for the Lépine Prize.'

'Is that how you knew about the revolver?'

'I watched him at work on it for the best part of two years.

' "There's just one problem I don't seem to be able to overcome," he told me in confidence. "If I ever do manage it, it will go off with quite a bang."

'And then he burst out laughing.'

' "I don't mean that literally. Quite the reverse, in fact. Do you know what a silencer is?"

' "I've seen them on television and in films. It's a thing you fit on to the end of a gun, to prevent it from making a noise when it's fired."

' "That's it, more or less. Of course you can't just go into a shop and buy one. It's against the law. But suppose you could do away with the silencer as a separate piece of equipment, by incorporating it into the design of the gun itself?"

'He sounded tremendously excited.'

' "I'm very nearly there. There are just one or two small adjustments to be made. Then I'll register the patent, and in a few years all firearms, including those of the armed forces and the police, will be silent." '

She sat musing for a little while, and then said:

'A few days after that, he died. I know nothing about

firearms, and I forgot all about his precious revolver.'

'When did you mention it to Marcel?'

'About a month ago. No, less than that, three weeks ago. We were walking on the Pont-Neuf, and I pointed out my aunt's flat in the Quai de la Mégisserie. I mentioned that I would be inheriting some money from her one of these days.'

'What made you say that?'

She flushed and looked away.

'I didn't want to lose him.'

She cherished no illusions.

'A few minutes later, we stopped for a drink at an open air café, when I suddenly remembered about the revolver. I told him the story, and to my amazement he seemed terrifically excited about it.

' "Did you ever see the gun after your uncle died?"

' "No. I've never even been in his workshop since."

' "Did your aunt know about it?"

' "He may have mentioned it to her, but I doubt if she'll have given it a second thougbt, any more than I did. I'll ask her."

' "No, don't do that. Don't even mention it."

'This may surprise you, but we never used the familiar *tu* with one another. Except on very rare occasions,' she added, clearly embarrassed.

' "Have you a key to the flat?"

' "No."

' "And this room you call the cubby hole, does it have a separate key?"

' "Yes, but I don't know where my aunt keeps it. In her bag, I should think."

'It was several days before he mentioned the matter again. One evening, when I got home, he was standing there with two keys in his hand.

' "What are you going to do?"

' "Find the revolver."

' "What for?"

' "Don't you realise, it's worth a fortune. I want you to go to your aunt's sometime when you know she's out, and search every room in the flat, and the workshop."

' "What's the point? It will all come to me eventually in any case."

' "Women of that sort have a very strong grip on life. You may have to spend another ten years massaging women, all over Paris, before you see a penny." '

She looked at Maigret, and sighed.

'Now do you understand? At first, I refused to have anything to do with it, but he just wouldn't let it drop, and I was afraid of losing him. In the end, I agreed.

One aftenoon, I took the keys and went to the Quai de la Mégisserie. I saw my aunt set off for the Tuileries, and I knew she wouldn't be back before six.

'First, I searched the flat. I went through every drawer, and looked in every possible place where I thought it might be hidden. And then I put everything carefully back as it was before.'

'Not quite carefully enough, though. She knew someone had been there.'

'Two days later, I searched the workroom. In all, I went to the Quai de la Mégisserie four times.'

'And Marcel?'

'Just the once.'

'When was that?'

Once more, she turned her head away.

'On the afternoon of my aunt's death.'

'What did he say when he got back to your flat?'

'I wasn't there. I had an appointment with a client at half-past five. She kept me waiting. The client is someone I've been giving massage to for the best part of twenty years. She's Madame de la Roche, of 61 Boulevard Saint-Germain.'

'What time did you get home?'

'At seven. As usual, she kept me gossiping.'

'Why didn't you tell me you had an alibi?'

'That would have been as good as to accuse Marcel.'

'And you preferred to let me go on suspecting you?'

'As long as you didn't know which of us it was...'

'So the gun was hidden, for a time, on top of your wardrobe?'

'Yes.'

'And it was your lover who found it in the bedside table drawer?'

'Yes. It's the last place I'd have thought of looking for it. My aunt was scared stiff of firearms.'

'Have you got all that, Lapointe? Just ring and check with Madame de la Roche, of the Boulevard Saint-Germain, and then you can start typing.'

Left alone with her in his office, Maigret felt oppressed. He got up and went over to the window.

'As far as Marcel is concerned,' he mumbled, 'the case is closed. You can't prosecute a dead man. You, on the other hand, are very much alive. It's true that you had no hand in the death of the old lady, assuming your alibi is confirmed.'

She was no longer the same woman, sitting there at his desk facing his empty chair. All the stiffening had gone out of her. Her face was crumpled in misery, her shoulders drooping.

Five long minutes of silence passed before Lapointe came back into the room.

'The lady confirms her story,' was all he said.

'Thanks.

'Do you realise the position you're in at this moment?'

'You showed me the warrant. I realise what it means.'

'When I had the warrant drawn up. I didn't know whether it was you or Marcel who had smothered your aunt.'

'Well, you know now.'

'You were not present at the time. It was an unpremeditated crime, so you couldn't possibly have foreseen that it was going to happen. In other words, you are not implicated in the murder itself. Where you did wrong was in shielding your lover, and in concealing on your premises a stolen firearm.'

She looked at him blankly. It was as though she had lost all interest in life. She seemed to be miles away, in Toulon perhaps with Marcel?

Maigret went across and opened the door of the Inspectors' Duty Room. Fat Torrence happened to be the one nearest to him.

'Come into my office a minute, will you? Stay here till I get back, and don't let the lady go.'

'Right, Chief.'

Once more he climbed the stairs to the Examining Magistrates' floor. Judge Libart was interviewing a witness, but he sent him out for a few minutes, so that Maigret could have a word with him in private.

'Did she do it?'

'No. She's got an alibi as solid as a rock.'

Maigret told him the whole story as briefly as possible. All the same, it took him quite some time.

'There doesn't seem much point in going after Giovanni,' he murmured, in conclusion.

'It wouldn't do any good.'

'If you consider the matter carefully, she's no more guilty than he is.'

'You mean...?'

The judge scratched his head.

'That is what you have in mind, isn't it? To let her go scot-free?'

It would never do to admit that it was Madame Maigret who, indirectly at least, had put the idea into his head.

'First of all, we've got to prove that she was a party to the theft. And that won't be easy, especially now that the revolver has disappeared.'

'I see your point.'

It was another quarter of an hour before Maigret got back to his office, because, in the meantime, the Examining Magistrate had carted him off to see the Public Prosecutor.

The Chief Superintendent could not help being a little shocked at finding Torrence seated behind his desk in his own personal armchair.

'She hasn't moved a muscle, Chief.'

'Did she say anything?'

'She never opened her mouth. Can I go now?'

Angèle looked at Maigret without interest. She seemed to be resigned to her fate.

'How old are you exactly?'

'Fifty-six. I don't proclaim it to all and sundry, mind you, because some of my clients might begin to think I was past it.'

'Which of the two flats do you intend to live in, yours or your aunt's?'

She stared at him in amazement.

'Have I any choice in the matter?'

Deliberately, he picked up the warrant, and tore it across.

'You're free to go,' he said simply.

She did not get to her feet immediately. For a moment, it seemed as though she had not the strength. Tears rolled down her cheeks, but she made no attempt to wipe them away.

'I don't... I have no words...'

'There's nothing more to be said. I'd be obliged if you'd call back sometime this afternoon to sign your statement.'

She got up, hesitated for a moment, then went slowly towards the door.

He called after her:

'Your suitcase!'

'Yes, of course. I'd forgotten all about it.'

But there was so much that she would never forget.

Epalinges, May 7th, 1970